To: JERRY

Many Than.

Steve A. Arnts

A+H

Jan 11/10

G
2

ck

41/46

The Dark Side of the Mountain

S.A. CARTER

authorHOUSE®

AuthorHouse™
1663 Liberty Drive
Bloomington, IN 47403
www.authorhouse.com
Phone: 1-800-839-8640

First published by AuthorHouse 8/24/2009

ISBN: 978-1-4490-1934-1 (e)
ISBN: 978-1-4490-1912-9 (sc)

Library of Congress Control Number: 2009908613

Printed in the United States of America
Bloomington, Indiana

This book is printed on acid-free paper.

PROLOGUE

The American Civil War for many authors has been an ideal canvas upon which to portray a panorama of human emotions. In the story you are about to read, these emotions whole or in part caused a nation to split asunder, fight to a bloody conclusion and heal thereafter in the annealing fires of reconstruction. Regardless of where the reader stands on why the Civil War began, one thing is clear. Both sides, Confederate and Union, were determined to protect a way of life that took hundreds of years to perfect. Whereas slavery was an agrarian necessity south of the Mason-Dixon Line, to the industrialized North, it was not.

The sole purpose of "Lincoln's War" was the preservation of the Union. The abolition of slavery as a political expediency came much later when Republicans endorsed it out of necessity. Even as the war neared its conclusion, Lincoln made it a point to convince the slave states that he "had no intention of re-structuring race relations."

Long before the Civil War, many Americans were appalled by slavery and so in a variety of ways tried to abolish it. President Buchanan, William Lloyd Garrison of the American Anti-Slave Society, Harriet Beecher Stowe, author of Uncle Tom's Cabin, Harriet 'Minty' Tubman's underground railway, the fiery orator Abby Kelly Foster and the revolting John Brown are some of the more famous examples of how Americans dealt with slavery or at least tried to come to terms with it.

For many black Americans, inter-racial contacts were taboo. Frederick Douglas favored integrating the two solitudes through education and dialogue. Before the war, blacks could not vote or hold any local, state or federal office. For those two hundred thousand black Americans who fought for the Union, "It was better to live free in an imperfect democracy than live enslaved by a perfect dictatorship." For those hundred thousand blacks who fought for the Confederacy and their freedom; the South was 'home', despite all of its many failings.

After the "Great Schism" was concluded, the process of reconstruction commenced. To some, the defeat of the Confederacy was too much to bear. Vigilante veterans riding under the 'Southern Cross', terrorized anyone who supported the re-constructionists. 'Separate but equal' became the order of the day. For most black Southrons, the aftermath of the war was worse than the slavery that preceded it. Corrupt southern politicians and court officials manipulated local and state laws in order to deny blacks their constitutional rights. The oppressive legacy of segregation lasted nearly eighty years until Martin Luther King and other black leaders marched to end it. Their sacrifices bore fruit; for today, black Americans have been thrust into the mainstream of the nation, united under Barack Hussein Obama II, the first black President of the United States.

1

'REVELATION'

"Slavery can only be abolished by raising the character of the people who comprise the nation; and that can only be done by showing them a higher one."

Maria Weston Chapman, 1855.

BOOK ONE: CHAPTER 1
SLAUGHTER OF THE INNOCENTS

Bloody wisps of spindrift clung to either side of the Silver Ghost as its coppered hull sliced through a cobalt ocean. Barely clear of the clipper's stern, a horrific feeding frenzy marked the culmination of an event that would forever change the life of a young boy, and a nation at war with itself.

Heavily laden with twelve hundred tons of Indian tea and Chinese silk destined for Boston; the Silver Ghost sailed headlong before a stiff trade wind, somewhere over the Angola basin, an oceanic abyss due west of Africa. High above its black teak deck, ten thousand square feet of canvas cumulus strained to the very limits of its endurance. In the aftermath of a tempest, mountain ranges of white combers as far as the eye could see were shredded by a fierce wind into an arabesque of foam blowing about the clipper's bow sprite in wild abandon.

A few hours earlier, John Manly Saxton hung on desperately as he climbed tarred ratlines ever upward to a pendulous crows-nest high above him on the mainmast. He concentrated every fiber of his being into accomplishing the terrifying task at hand. Determined that he would prove to the crew below that he could earn their respect on his own terms, he thrust his calloused feet onto taut manila rungs, dragging himself ever upwards. Saxton, as the lad was called looked up, his long blonde hair tucked under a black cloth cap. After climbing for a few minutes, his thin legs and arms began to throb painfully. Rivers of sweat ran down his face but as he took off his cap to wipe the blinding moisture away, it was torn from his grasp. Thereafter, the warm trade wind that drove the sleek clipper forward far below him, threatened to tear his frail body from the rigging.

During his three years at sea, the ship's crew resented the owner's son being on board. An only child, Saxton at fourteen years was selfish, impudent and full of himself. Sent to sea by his father despite his mother's wishes, the boy rebelled. Over the intervening years on board the Silver Ghost, its crew grew tired of his insolence. In retaliation, they reciprocated with unwarranted slights, crude asides, jokes, and worst of all, a persistent shunning. Their rancor eventually took a terrible toll on the callow youth. Before the Silver Ghost set sail, Thomas Saxton charged Marcus Brown, the clipper's First Mate with the odious task of making his only child into a man. Marcus reluctantly agreed.

Yet, John Saxton's solution to the torment was an act of willful desperation. One morning he confronted the ships' crew as the Silver Ghost plied stolidly along before a quartering sea. The lad looked down the long gimbaled oak table that stretched the length of the narrow galley. It was eight bells and the starbolin crew was out and about trimming the sails. 'Cookie' had just finished washing the breakfast dishes. Saxton watched as the tough little Irishman put the last of the crockery away in the frogs. The ship rolled slightly. Saxton waited to regain his equilibrium.

John Saxton might have been born into a seafaring family, but for him the sea was an alien world fraught with sudden danger. To Saxton, time had run out to prove his manhood and gain the crew's respect. Again the ship yawed as the top-gallants caught a freshening wind. Long tree nails deep within the oaken timbers over Saxton's head squealed in protest.

Barely seventeen, John Saxton was ready to be a man but the crew thought otherwise, especially Billy Rolston, the clipper's Bosun. A brute of a man; his thick shoulders, bald head and a mean streak of major proportions put him in a class of his own amongst seafaring men. Marcus Brown came to blows many times with Rolston who crucified young Saxton for being the rich, spoiled son of the ship's owner, Thomas Saxton. As Rolston and a dozen crewmen finished their coffee, Saxton's pent up rage boiled up inside him, erupting like a dormant volcano coming to life. The full fury of the lad's venom was directed at Rolston sitting at the end of the table. While gripping an iron stanchion above his head, the boy screamed.

"Billy you bastard, I've something to say to you and I'm only going to say it once."

Rolston had been laughing and carousing with some of his cronies until a coffin-like silence permeated the galley. Only the occasional battle between wood and water could be heard as the clipper sliced through an ocean. Saxton had everyone's attention. He waited. Rolston stood up and barked,

"Well blow me down mates, the bog rat has spoken. What does he have on his little Irish mind?"

His cronies were tense as was everyone else. Saxton sensed their unease and continued unaware that Marcus Brown had slipped below decks and was watching the boy from deep shadows. Saxton's voice was hard, sharp as flint with an undertone of menace.

"I've taken enough of you Rolston and that goes for the rest of you too."

He proceeded to tell a bemused crew that he intended to be the ship's lookout. All of them laughed out loud until a stern look from Rolston told them to be quiet. He proclaimed,.

"Ok, boy, you can be the lookout if you've got the guts. Well boys, whadda ya say? Let's make it really interesting. Perhaps the next old fashioned storm will wet the lad's appetite for manhood cause his little Ming Lee in Shanghai sure couldn't."

Saxton withered under a barrage of ribald remarks. But, he persevered, determined to take control of his life from those who would throw it overboard. He stood straight, his face grim, agreeing that the challenge had been fairly set and he, John Saxton, was ready and willing to meet it.

A week later, as luck would have it, a vicious sou-wester swept in with a vengeance rarely seen before. At that moment, Saxton decided that the time was opportune for him to make good on his seemingly reckless promise. After trying mightily to dissuade the young lad from his foolhardy mission, Marcus offered to go up the rigging ahead of him. Young Saxton declined. Billy Rolston shouted over the roar of the gale that the lad would never do it, let alone survive. Bets were being made all around. A mob followed the boy to the quarter deck. Surging about below them, sea water was waist high in places as the clipper climbed up one cliff-like wave after another. The boy stood there paralyzed by fear until Captain Silas Wilkins tried to stop him. John Saxton was too quick. The barefoot lad sprinted upwards onto the portside backstay, just out of reach.

Now high above in the rigging with a stiff breeze tugging at every part of him, John Saxton wondered if he was premature in his decision. Far below him a loud deep voice cried out,

"Don't look down. For God's sake Sax, do not look down!"

But the warning was lost on the wind before it reached the young man struggling ever upward. Another rogue wave crashed aboard amidships. Shouts of alarm rose up from below. Saxton looked down onto a narrow main deck awash in a creamy torrent of foam boiling through starboard scuppers like a river in flood. The clipper's crew hung on desperately to manropes as they disappeared into the foaming maelstrom. Shortly thereafter, the wind died down, it's fury spent.

A thread of pearlescent light appeared over the eastern horizon as the sleek ship scudded across a ragged sea at over seventeen knots. A black and yellow burgee snapped and crackled high above the mainmast, pulsating like a living thing. Its anguish grew louder as Saxton climbed skyward one hundred feet above the clipper's deck. The ratlines upon which he clung to began to narrow but the lad continued, clawing his way ever upwards like an insect on a stem of waving grass. He heard his father's words ringing in his head,

"Saxton my son, I'm sending you to sea this year. You're fourteen years old and it's time you learned what it takes to be a man."

In typical fashion his father always concluded his speeches with, "I have spoken." There was no appeal, recourse, or compromise, but only complete and total surrender. No amount of pleading by his mother, Muriel, could change his father's mind. Thomas Saxton's Scottish brogue was as thick as the oak decking on one of his ships. Strong and uncompromising as his Episcopalian father was, the boy knew he was right. His only child, it was preordained that the young Saxton would take over his father's business. Thousands of people around the world depended on a seamless succession.

Generations of Saxtons had lived and died in the family's twenty-five room Georgian mansion. It was a close copy of the Shirley mansion in Boston's Roxbury district. Originally designed by Peter Harrison, the Saxton mansion included a large carriage house that lay behind it, similar in size and function to the Gardner carriage house nearby. Constructed of yellow bricks imported as ballast from England in 1768, the Saxton mansion stood at the corner of Sheafe and Snow Hill Streets in Boston's north end. It was set back astride two manicured acres of formal gardens and terraced copses atop Copps Hill. A tall clipped box-wood hedgerow bordered a long sloping pea gravel drive that morphed into a circular driveway fronting the mansion.

After buying the old Hunt and White's shipyard at the foot of Snow Street in 1848, Thomas Saxton demolished the yard then built three vast warehouses and a long shoreline wharf on the property. By the early 1850's, the Saxton Shipping Co.'s forty clipper ships sailed all over the world competing with the likes of Sampson & Tappan, Grinnell, Minturn & Co. and a growing Cunard Line. Competition was fierce for the tea and silk trade of Shanghai China, the mail and packet service from New York to Falmouth England and the highly lucrative trade in dry goods from New Orleans to the west coast of Africa. However, spurious tales of Saxton complicity in the slave trade began to surface.

Amongst the gin mills on Front Street in New York City, it was rumored that Saxton Shipping was involved in the slave trade even though slavery had been outlawed world-wide since 1823. To combat those determined to continue the heinous trade, American and British naval picket ships comprised what was called the 'Africa Patrol'. This 'thin blue line' plied treacherous waters off West Africa in a vain attempt to intercept a steady flow of human cargo to America. It was even said by some of the Saxton Shipping Co. competitors, that Saxton ships were leaving New Orleans with trade goods bound for Africa, and later return-ing with cargoes of human misery bound for St. Simon Island off Georgia. Furthermore, it was insinuated that Thomas Saxton had a black mistress in Africa and had fathered many children. Such accusations deeply troubled the young lad. But now these thoughts were swept away as Saxton lost his grip in a vain attempt to climb into the swaying crow's nest.

A large black hand reached down, grabbing him by the leather collar of his oil skin jacket. "I can't have the old man mad at me now, can I?"

With that pronouncement, Marcus, who finally caught up to and passed Saxton on the other side of the main mast, hauled the exhausted boy into a large wicker basket. Once out of the wind, Saxton was overwhelmed with a longing for the comforting caresses of his mother Muriel.

Muriel Saxton spoiled her only child, much to the dismay of his strict father. On many nights the boy would lay awake in his bedroom listening to his parents argue in the parlor over his future; their harsh and strident voices rising through an iron ventilation grate set into the parquet floor beside his bed. As always, Muriel was adamant, her voice rising, strident and anxious.

"Thomas Saxton, must you send him to sea? He's barely fourteen years old; not much older than a helpless child." Desperately she tried to reason with him.

"It's your duty to protect your son, not risk his life in a rising gale." She cried, "How could you? He's our only child Thomas, our only child!"

Finally spent, she sat primly on a green settee; a flounced taffeta dress spread out on either side of her. Thomas after much deliberation stopped his pacing. He put a knarled hand on a massive wooden mantle piece and demanded her attention. His sea blue eyes looked down upon a mother pining for her only child. This made no difference to Thomas, not one wit. It wasn't that he was insensitive to her wishes. He was not, but quite the opposite for Thomas Saxton belonged to a community of fellow seafaring businessmen that demanded conformity, rewarded propriety and shunned anyone who didn't abide by their unwritten rules. Saxton had to go to sea and that was that. Other sons had done so for eons and so would Thomas Saxton's.

Thomas stepped away from the warming fire and sat down beside his distraught wife. He put an arm around her. She stiffened, knowing full well what was coming.

"My dear Muriel, please listen to me. The boy has to go to sea. There's no one else to pass on the family business to, no one. Only at sea can anyone be taught how the business of ships, and the men that sail them, can be commanded with efficiency and respect. He must have respect, most importantly my respect. Every young man 'learns the ropes' from the keel up. Neither social rank nor privilege can change that. It is the unwritten law of the sea. Muriel please, no more remonstrating about this matter, for I have spoken."

These domestic disturbances festered in the lad's conscience, until one day he'd had enough of his parent's incessant squabbling. At dinner one evening, he solemnly announced,

"I'm going to sea father and I will return as a man ready to assist our family business in whatever capacity you so desire."

Thomas Saxton rose, walked over and shook his son's hand before the startled lad was barely clear of his chair. Never before had his father shown even the slightest sign of affection towards him. There were no affectionate hugs or pats on the backside. But now it seemed as if his father had arrived at some sort of pact within himself. An accord that clarified a future for both of them was in the offing. It meant that his mother was no longer a part of the young man's life as a full participant. Instead it would be that of a comforting mentor who offered help when help was asked for. Thomas Saxton looked down at his son, his Scottish brogue surprisingly tender,

"Ay laddie, tis time indeed as it is for every seafaring family with sons. The tradition must continue. I'm glad that as young as you are, you're loyal to your kith and kin, determined to go to sea as you should."

Boy and man parted. At that moment, Muriel rose stiffly from her chair, her dress crackling about her. She approached her son as if she was sleep-walking, completely unaware of her husband backing away from her or the arms of her son reaching out to her. A macabre dance of wills had been replaced by unspoken grief and visceral pain. For Muriel, it culminated in a blinding flash of reality. As she looked up into her son's blue eyes, she surrendered.

"Whatever makes you happy, dear, that's all I've ever cared about. I'll go to my room now. I'm extremely tired; please excuse me Thomas."

She turned to her husband; reached up caressed his face then kissed him on his bewhiskered cheeks. Muriel whispered softly,

"My dear Thomas, our boy has made up his mind. Perhaps it is best for all of us."

With that said, she turned, head bowed, and walked through the drawing room doors, closing them behind her. After she disappeared, boy and man stood listening to the trembling sounds of her dress fade away into the distance.

The giant black man looked into the crows-nest, reached down and pulled an ashen faced young man to his feet. Amidst the chaos going on around them, he exclaimed,

"There now Sax, I've got you stowed away safe and sound. Please don't ever do that again; not for me, Rolston or your father. Remember, a man is a man when he looks after his own. That's all I'm going to say. While we're here, let's have a look around! There's nothing like it to be sure!"

Marcus held the boy upright while the ship's wild gyrations rocked the pair back and forth. He exclaimed, "What a smashing sea it is this morning!"

The young lad peered somewhat tentatively over the leather rim of the crows nest. What he saw raised the hair on the nape of his neck. Before him a golden orb rose in the east over a ragged ocean crowned by millions of fiery crystals dancing above the ship's foaming wake.

At first, an overwhelming fear of heights within him refused to dissipate, but then Saxton's body began to become one with the motions of the ship. A glorious new day dawned within him as it was now dawning before him. He cried out in a long wondrous whoop of joy. Marcus clapped a large black hand upon the boy's backside. Drawing him close; Marcus with an echoing whoop, yelled out into a lashing wind,

"Hell yes Sax, doesn't it feel good to be really free?" The boy looked up at the scarred black face in wonderment.

"Is it really true?"

"What's true?"

"That a man is free when he does what doesn't make sense."

Moments later, the wind died and bowed down to a tropical sun resting on a throne of clouds in the east. The clipper's mainsails flapped in the slackening breeze. The helmsman flung the ship's great wheel about. On either side of the main deck, long lines of men, their calloused hands grasping a taut manila halyard, pulled in unison. Strong voices corralled by the lyrics of a sea shanty, rose upwards on the words, "What shall we do with a drunken sailor." Serried ranks of sails once properly trimmed, flung the clipper before the wind again. A symphony of wood, metal and canvas flew across a sparkling sea as if chased by King Neptune himself.

Built in 1851 by Donald McKay of Boston, the Silver Ghost originated from the same plans as The Flying Cloud. Although slower, the Silver Ghost could do well over four hundred nautical miles a day in ideal conditions. While her sister ship set all kinds of distance and speed records, the Silver Ghost's skippers were quite content to sail in a less reckless fashion.

During the next three years, Saxton marveled at the exotic harbor of Shanghai, the dusky dhows of Mombasa and the ancient Portuguese Fort at Goa. All of these smells, sights and experiences were wondrous to him. Marcus Brown, his appointed mentor and protector, encouraged him to go ashore at other ports of call, but after awhile Saxton was content to stay in his cabin away from the crew. Therein he studied books about navigation, semaphore and telegraphy. From Captain Wilkins, he learned to apply this knowledge in more practical terms. He tried learning Maa Swahili from Marcus but it was too much for the young lad. Apparently, he didn't have the mouth for it.

Marcus, an escaped slave, was barely thirty-five years old. A head higher than most men, his slim and powerful body was tempered by a calming personality. This trait made him a natural leader amongst his sea-going peers. Marcus or Matari, was from a Maasai tribe living a nomadic life on the Burrangat plain in the country of Kisongo. One night, he and others of his tribe were captured by Arab slavers. After many days shackled together they arrived at the Omani port of Dars es Salaam on the Indian Ocean. Months later, he escaped by stowing aboard on one of the Saxton ships anchored in the bay. Fortunately for Matari, Captain Wilkins knew enough Maa Swahili to understand that a very frightened young man, kneeling in front of him, would die a grisly death if put back ashore. 'Marcus the Maasai', as he became known to all, sailed away a free man. Over the next seven years at sea, he grew in stature until he stood well over seven feet. His cheerful nature endeared him to everyone aboard and so Thomas Saxton, promoted Marcus to First Mate on the Silver Ghost's maiden voyage.

Thomas Saxton was very pleased with the hard working black man with the mysterious facial scars. He named him Marcus Brown after a favorite First Mate swept overboard years before. Remaining devoted to Thomas Saxton as years went by, Marcus became like another son to him. For Matari, Thomas was the father he never had and for Thomas, Marcus was the obedient son he thought he never could have. Marcus was the 'civilized savage' as the elder man affectionately called him. Both men enjoyed each other's company; one a dour old Scot and the other an exuberant young man. It was said that the elder Saxton trusted Marcus more than anyone on the face of the planet other than his wife of twenty-six years, Muriel Stamford Saxton.

After a year abroad, the Silver Ghost was overdue. Its absence placed an unbearable strain on the Saxton household. Muriel blamed her truculent husband for sending their only child out to sea against her better judgment. Thomas remained silent knowing that any attempt to assuage his wife's fears would be useless. After two years, the Saxton's assumed that their son was probably lost at sea. The strain became unbearable to such an extent thereafter, that Muriel and Thomas began living apart, each in their own wing of the Saxton House. A third year passed. Muriel and her husband no longer took their chauffeured carriage to the Old North Church on Salem St. where the family pew in the front row provided a sanctuary for them. It seemed that the Saxton's had given up on receiving any help from the Almighty. Deeply religious for most of her life, Muriel came to a crossroads where faith alone could no longer erase the unbearable reality facing her.

Every morning, Muriel ate alone in the breakfast room while consulting the sailing news in the Boston Daily Mail. Once her inspection of every detail within it was complete, she'd ascend a spiral staircase to the roof of the Saxton House high up on Copps Hill. There, on the 'widows walk' she'd sit in a wicker rocking chair under the Saxton flag pole looking out over the inner and outer Boston harbors. Spread out before her at anchor, were ships from all over the world. Using a small brass telescope, she'd carefully peer out over the channel that ran south-east of the inner harbor towards President Roads. There, other ships were waiting their turn to enter Boston's inner harbor and unload at Long wharf, Central wharf and Rowe's wharf amongst many others. Thereto many waterfront warehouses lay beneath her for the Saxton Shipping Co. lay directly at the foot of Snow Hill Street at Hudson's Point.

Day after day Muriel followed the same routine and day after day she slowly descended the staircase, returning to her room despondent, in total despair. Every attempt by her husband to console her went unrewarded. Desperately, he tried everything to make her realize the futility of her actions but to no avail. After months of fruitlessly searching for an answer, Thomas gave up the struggle. He would let his wife deal with the demons deep within her mind. Besides, the financial panic of 1857 was another nightmare he had to contend with let alone the loss of his only child. But despite all his travails he did make one more attempt to soften his wife's inconsolable grief.

Thomas knew that as a child, Muriel once had a small dog. In this regard, he instructed one of his Captains enroute to Liverpool, to bring back a Jack Russell puppy. It was a new breed just being introduced there. Jack arrived none too soon. One day a small white dog, speckled with brown spots, sporting a docked tail that waved like a wand in a wind, chased his new red rubber ball into Muriel's bedroom. From that day forward they became inseparable. With Jack on her lap, Muriel would glass every ship that entered the inner harbor spread out far below them. The Harbor Master would hoist the Saxton burgee if one of their vessels were seen off Castle Island before entering the estuary of the Weymouth Fore river. Numerous sailing ships flew the Saxton colors, but none were the Silver Ghost.

Everyday Muriel consulted the Harbor Master's flag manual to see what ships were arriving. Over time she knew all the signals by heart. As time passed, she was quite unaware that one disaster after another kept the 'Ghost' as she called it from sailing home. Other ships that reached Boston reported seeing the Saxton clipper from time to time on the high seas fleeing Somali pirates or in some exotic port being careened. All these events were faithfully recorded in the Shipping News; a paper that became more important to Muriel than reading her family bible. She would sit intently reading the News for hours, hoping for any snippet of information, rumor or otherwise that might give her a clue as to her son's whereabouts.

Incessant conflicts between reality and fantasy began to take a toll on Muriel. Her body lost its once vibrant energy. As her melancholia worsened, she became frail, weak and delirious. Thomas pleaded with the leading medical minds of the day to save her. No sum of money was too much in his desperate search for a remedy. In the end, the doctors knew that the only cure for Muriel was to see her son Saxton alive and well. For now, Jack was her only comfort, as day after day the small dog lay beside her on her four poster bed.

In those years, Saxton was 'lost' at sea; Thomas used all his resources to find his son's ship. He posted a ten thousand dollar reward for anyone who could rescue his son and bring him home. By now, everyone including Thomas believed that the Silver Ghost had been lost at sea, captured by pirates in the Straits of Malacca or shipwrecked off the skeleton coast of West Africa. Thomas Saxton's considerable political influence induced British and American anti-slave picket ships patrolling the Atlantic shipping lanes to keep a sharp lookout for the sleek black ship or any of its bright yellow lifeboats. He blamed himself for the unfortunate events that were taking place. A melancholic ailment, symptomatic of inconsolable grief eventually reduced him to a mere shell of his former self. Over time, the two 'desperates' drowning apart in a sea of their own making, were not unlike two planets in parallel orbits contained within a common constellation of bitterness. No longer capable of loving each other as they had done so long ago, their marriage and the trust they once shared, vanished.

Saxton hung on grimly as the sleek ship below him pounded through high waves. Pushed aside by its slim bow, a golden wake streamed far astern eventually breaking into long rows of foaming wavelets. Saxton tasted sea salt in his mouth. He withdrew a linen handkerchief from his pants pocket to wipe his mouth then held the white cloth up into the brisk wind. Instantly it was ripped from his grasp, flying far out into the aqueous void. Carried down and down then up and up, as a capricious wind sprite played with it. It snagged on a deadeye where upon an alert seaman jumped up and plucked it away. Triumphantly he held his flapping trophy high, waving at his two shipmates far above him. The dark Maasai warrior and his blonde haired companion drank in the scene below but only for a moment as the sharp eyed Maasai spotted something far astern over the eastern horizon.

13

Marcus retrieved a large brass telescope from within an oilskin pouch. Carefully, he raised the heavy instrument to his eye, his tall frame braced against the main mast. After a few minutes he handed the telescope to Saxton who pointed it to where the First Mate indicated. Saxton grasped the tube while sliding its brass barrels in and out. Magically, a puff of white sail appeared in his eye far out to sea just over a heaving horizon. It would appear then disappear as rolling seas climaxed above it. Spin drift obliterated then distorted the fragile image each time it came into view. Minutes later, it became more distinct. A slim white hull appeared, crowned by pillowing sailcloth. Saxton's reluctantly relinquished the heavy telescope to his mentor who immediately refocused to view the mysterious ship again.

A hissing sound left his lips as Marcus swore. "Mavi, mavi." His face became contorted by rage as violent and as troubled as the seas below him. It startled the lad. Saxton backed away as the black giant pounded the leather rim inches from the lad's body. An odd look came over his face as he peered down at Saxton. The Maasai's facial scars became sharply outlined, making him even more terrifying. Gradually Marcus came to his senses. Over the howling wind, he cried out.

"So sorry Master Saxton, I'm so sorry! But I know that ship. I know that ship indeed."

Reassured, Saxton looked up and sputtered,

"Marcus, who is it?"

"Don't you worry none lad, we're safe up here. I'm going to relay the news to the skipper."

He reached down and pulled out a cork stopper on a long chain from within a brass tube, whereupon he bent down, spoke a few words into it then looked over the rim. Far below, Captain Silas Wilkins waved back up at him from behind the dodger. The Silver Ghost slewed to starboard as two helmsmen spun the wheel. Both boy and Maasai hung on as the cross trees around them swung about. Fairleads and jack blocks squealed as the sails began to gybe. Cliffs of canvas taut as drumheads, straining at the very limit of their endurance, sang in the wind. Gusts of sea spray flung high into the rigging, baptized them. The royals and skysail were released as the clipper swung leeward in an attempt to intersect the other ship at nearly twenty knots. Over the roar of the brails beating the canvas, Marcus screamed at the boy. Rivulets of sea spray coursed down over his scarred cheeks.

"It has no flag of origin or blue peter!" He shouted again,

"It's the Wanderlust out of Long Island, New York. Captain Josiah Garrow's aboard her, I'm sure of it! There's a reward out on her if she's found to be a slaver. I'm sure your father would want us to capture it." He grasped the brass speaking tube.

Once more he spoke into it. After a few moments the clipper's sails stiffened even more so, thrusting the Silver Ghost forward like a spear, ever and ever faster. The other ship hove into view, fully exposed, barely a league astern. All of its sails too were tight as drumheads. It was gaining speed. The crew of the Silver Ghost lined the starboard rail, straining to see the mystery ship angling towards them. Many in the backstays cheered as the gap narrowed. Saxton screamed,

"It must be caught, it has to be!"

The Wanderlust was unarmed, counting on speed alone to outrun any ship afloat. Marcus knew she was probably heading for Jekyll Island, Georgia, with a full load of nearly five hundred slaves. Built two years before as a pleasure craft, the Wanderlust was suspected at the time of becoming a slaver. Although they couldn't prove it, the port authorities allowed her to leave New York harbor on her maiden voyage. After that, no one knew where she was until now.

The crew of the clipper released even more sail. Her foresail and spankers were set out. The ship surged ahead again as it came athwart the other. The Ghost's crew manned their battle stations. Two, three inch deck howitzers, one for and one aft, were revealed as their canvas covers were untied and stowed. Canisters of grapeshot lay racked and ready in wooden crates beside them. The distance between the two ships was under a quarter mile. As they drew closer, a loud 'CRASH' was heard astern of the Silver Ghost. Marcus swung about and yelled,

"God all mighty look at that!"

Taking the telescope, Saxton raised it, adjusted it and focused it on a warship far astern. A puff of white smoke appeared from its bow cannon followed by a deafening whine. Ball and chain shot roared past them tearing through the mainsail of the slave ship. A terrible shrieking of ripped canvas and splintering wood was heard by all aboard the clipper ship. Once more a cannon roared. Two more heavy cannon balls connected by a short chain whirled by towards the luckless Wanderlust. This time one of its upper yardarms hit the deck with a horrendous crash. The stricken ship slewed to port, coming even closer.

Slavers crushed under tons of sail, rope, blocks and spars; screamed and wailed. Both Saxton and Marcus transfixed by the destruction, watched as men armed with axes desperately cleared away tangled debris, throwing it over board. A limp figure wearing a white panama hat lay bloodied on the black deck. Two slavers picked up the body and disappeared inside an aft cabin. The slaver's speed slackened. Marcus looked astern as the other ship began closing fast on the Wanderlust's starboard side. Raising the telescope to his eye one more time, he recognized it as the USS Constellation or 'Connie II' as sailors called affectionately it. His attention was diverted. Saxton screamed into his ear.

"Look! Look, Marcus! They're signaling to us to cut the slaver's wind."

Sure enough, yellow and red semaphore flags wigwagged at them from the USS Constellation II's quarter deck. Marcus patted the boy's shoulder.

"Good for you Saxton."

Again Marcus spoke into the brass speaking tube. Instantly, the clipper ship angled to starboard, pulling abreast of then sprinting close behind the Wanderlust cutting off its wind. The slaver's sails began to luff, flapping uselessly like a wounded bird. The Silver Ghost positioned itself fifty yards downwind. Marcus was pleased. He turned to congratulate the boy but stopped for Saxton's face was contorted into an unimaginable mask of shock and horror.

Marcus turned about and looked down in disbelief across violent seas at the slave ship. There in front of him, shackled slaves were being driven out of their odious prison up onto the slave ship's main deck. Screaming men, women and children chained together in one continuous line were being lashed unmercifully by their masters. Closer, ever closer they were forced to both sides of the prison ship. Once there, these unfortunates were hidden from the prying eyes of those chasing them. However, the atrocity the slavers were about to commit, was in full view of everyone aboard the Silver Ghost.

It seemed to young Saxton that everything was happening in slow motion. The slavers below him quickly removed long brass pins securing sections of railing in place on both sides of the ship. To his mounting horror they were swung wide over tumultuous seas then lashed to the ship. Left and right, lines of slaves were pushed overboard through the gaps. A terrible wail assaulted Saxton, as one after another, slaves in an ever quickening conga line of death were dragged to their death. Iron chains and leg-irons, rattled across the slaver's deck like dice in a tobacco tin. Saxton covered his ears as the screams, shrieks and piteous cries for help were born towards him on a slackening wind.

Into this canyon of chaos, line after line of slaves emerged from below decks, to be beaten on both sides towards the abyss. Many voided themselves in abject fear. Yet through this fecal slime, more slaves slithered ever forward. A trio grabbed three of their tormentors in a death grip. Despite countless blows upon them, they did not relinquish their prey. The irresistible weight of iron and flesh below bloody waters had become too much to resist. Gathering momentum, this writhing bundle of humanity slid towards the inevitable. For one moment Saxton thought he heard laughter as they and their screeching captives were swept over the edge causing all those slaves remaining on deck to be thrown down in a deafening thunderclap. The speed of their journey increased as they too were dragged forward in a writhing mass of arms and legs.

Great White sharks thrashed the water between the two ships into a bloody froth as they began feasting on those thrown into their enormous jaws. More human misery appeared from within the putrid bowels of the slaver. The process was repeated over and over but now the slavers were wary, for they stayed well away from the outstretched hands of the doomed.

One barefoot slaver in particular caught young Saxton's attention. Stripped to the waist, a large muscular man in bloody canvas trousers wielded an iron club to bludgeon those frozen by fear. Up and down it beat those too slow or too confused to move forward out of the hold. The slaver appeared as if he was enjoying the task of inflicting immense pain upon anyone who came within his domain. For whatever reason he stopped, looked up and pointed his bloody club at Saxton cowering high above him. Their eyes locked. Saxton knew instantly at that very moment that they would meet again.

The man turned away to continue his grisly work. Below decks more whips and clubs rained down quelling any shred of resistance. The macabre theater of the damned continued as the last lines of slaves were pulled across the bloody deck into a roiling cauldron of flesh and blood. Mercifully, the slaughter of the innocents ceased. The overpowering silence that followed was deafening in its sheer intensity. This sacred requiem was rudely interrupted as a resurgent wind began to flay the slave ship's flaccid sails. Below them, a red river of gore gurgled through the scuppers as the slave ship wallowed about in following seas. Marcus looked down weeping. He cried out in unrestrained anguish, "Goodbye, goodbye, Kwaheri! Kwaheri!"

Saxton could not breath, could not speak, could not cry out but remained in place, paralyzed by the horror that took place far below him. Marcus looked down as young Saxton fell unconscious to the wicker floor of the crows nest. He reached down and shook the boy but there was no response other than a horrific groaning. While foam lined the lad's open mouth, his eyes rolled up as he jerked spasmodically for a few moments then lay deathly still.

Down, down, down in his subconscious mind, the boy sank into the depths of a bloody ocean. Close by him were slaves, chained together, descending into a vortex of death. Their mouths and eyes remained open in disbelief as they were dragged ever deeper into a watery grave. The boy looked up at sinuous shadows streaking across a bloody sky just below the surface of a violent sea. As he did so, he spun into an ever widening circle of blackness wherein black hands reached out towards him as if in supplication. They grasped at him in a vain attempt at salvation. Saxton shrieked as he tried in vain to avoid their deadly embrace.

BOOK ONE: CHAPTER 2
THE HOMECOMING

"Wake up! Wake up Master Saxton, please wake up!" Millie shook her young master with ever increasing alarm. Saxton opened his eyes. The maid's black face peered down at him. Delirious, he shrieked when her hands reached out to comfort him.

"Away! Away! For God's sake! Don't touch me, I beg of you!"

He rolled away from her in the gloom of a dark and shrouded bedroom.

"I must be dying", he wailed, as he clenched a linen bed sheet tightly in his fists. A gentle voice rang in his ear.

"No Master Saxton, I'm Millie your maidservant. Do you remember me? I believe you are only dreaming. You have done so ever since you arrived two days ago. Please listen well as I'm about to give you word of your parents. They are anxiously awaiting you downstairs in the parlor. Please Master Saxton, it is time that you got up and dressed."

For a moment he remained quite still then rolled over and looked up at her distraught face.

"Millie, I guess you're right, although I'll never want to face these nightmares I've been having ever again."

He sat up overwhelmed by the immensity of his ordeal. The cherubic maid looked down upon him, willing him to go on. Shaking his head, the young man cried out,

"Is it really two days since I've arrived here?"

"Yes it is Master Saxton. You've been rambling the whole time until now. All of us have been powerless to help you. Cold sweats and hot fevers have taken their toll on you to be sure. A bath awaits you. Thank the Good Lord you've come back to us safe and sound."

She walked over to a tall bay window and drew back two curtains. Sunlight flooded the room. Saxton watched her glide through an aura of dust motes towards him. She smiled like an angel, opened the bedroom door and left. The heavy oak door closed behind her with a soft snick.

Saxton lay back. He wondered. 'What am I going to say to my parents?'

He'd gone to sea a boy and returned a man, albeit late but none the less intact. He thought pensively,

'God knows Captain Wilkins tried to get word to my parents that I was safe but one calamity after another over the past three years ---prevented it.'"

After tossing back a bed sheet and its white linen coverlet, Saxton's swung his tanned legs over the side of a large four poster bed. A white cotton robe lay across at the foot of it. He stumbled over to a claw-foot tub in a nearby bathroom. Therein lay water, scented and hot. After disrobing, Saxton slipped into it. Morning light illuminated his bathwater as if caressing it, reminding him of moonlight reflecting off the surface of unruffled tropical seas. Finished with his ablutions, Saxton dressed and prepared to meet his parents. His sea legs were still with him as he seemed to levitate towards the bedroom door; his mind at odds with his body. The rolling gait slowly dissipated as he made his way down a wide carpeted hallway to a curved federal staircase. Twice he fell descending it but staved off disaster by gripping its dark mahogany railing. His equilibrium returned shortly before he arrived at the formal parlor wherein his anxious parents awaited him.

To his surprise, Marcus was standing just outside, a knowing smile on his scarred face. Dressed in a gray frock suit, matching trousers, black patent shoes, frocked white shirt and black cravat; Marcus Brown was not the warrior from Africa that one might have surmised. Indeed he looked quite the country gentleman. Beside him sat a small white and brown dog with short fur and an even shorter tail. A red ball was stuck in its mouth. Instinctively Saxton bent down. The dog dropped the ball and stepped back. Saxton picked up the ball; throwing it down a hallway. The terrier barked as he ran after his favorite toy. Turning to Saxton, Marcus gave out a throaty laugh,

"So, John Saxton, you've met Jack, who's been keeping your mother company for the past two years. Don't worry, for I went through the same initiation a few days ago. It seems that everyone does." He slapped him on the back,

"Well, are you ready? You better be after all the trouble we had getting you out of that crow's nest in a bosun's chair two weeks ago."

Saxton reached out for his friend.

"You mean I've been delirious for that long. Why Marcus, I can't remember any part of it, none at all."

The giant of a man pulled him to his chest in a strong bear hug. He said,

"It's just as well you didn't." Saxton backed away, his voice tremulous.

"Marcus, I know I've been difficult at times…"

"You mean all the time, don't you Sax?" Saxton coughed nervous with anticipation.

"I guess I've been loose cannon from time to time haven't I? But now that we're home, I'm looking forward to seeing my parents once again. God only knows the distress my absence has put them through!" Marcus held him at arms length.

"Don't blame yourself Sax for something you had no control over. I know your parents have suffered a lot but yet their worst fears have not materialized."

Marcus led him forward. Sputtering gaslight soft and diffused greeted them. Saxton thought of the light from under the sea as being exactly the same. He shuddered but regained his composure as he paused before tall double doors. He looked up. Marcus smiled, nodded then whispered,

"The next few minutes will be some of the most important in your life. I'll wait for you outside. Now remember Sax, they each love you in their own way, so don't judge them but love them with all your heart, for in doing so you will earn the freedom and respect you desire. For you, the measure of a man is waiting on the other side of these doors."

Saxton did not reply, instead he steeled himself, gripped an ivory door knob firmly and stepped forward. He closed the door quietly behind him after Jack bounded past him. Within seconds the little dog was held firmly in place by his father sitting on a black horsehair settee under a stained glass window. His mother Muriel sat next to him in a wicker wheelchair, a blue mohair rug over her lap. Saxton was shocked by his parent's frail appearance. His mother noticed this immediately. She said,

"My dear Sax, do not be troubled, for we all grow older one way or another. Come now son, give me a kiss. I've missed you so very much."

Saxton knelt down, putting his head on his mother's lap. As she stroked his long blonde hair, he began weeping. His mother bent down to kiss the top of his head. A gentle crooning sound filled the room as they held onto each other. It seemed as if he'd never left her. A balm of love would heal any wounds caused by their long separation. They remained frozen in time until Saxton stood up and wiped tears from his face. He looked down at his mother. To his amazement, he could not believe the instant transformation taking place in her. No longer was she the fragile apparition that greeted him mere minutes ago. It seemed as if a wilted flower upon finding a new source of energy had miraculously burst forth into glorious color.

He faced his father who in turn was also transfixed by the sudden change in his wife. Tears flowed down his gaunt face. As he rose, he put Jack on his wife's lap then turned to hug his prodigal son. Both cried as one man. They clung to each other as the son had to his mother. Finally, Thomas backed away, saying with deep emotion,

"Dear Sax, oh how we've both longed for your return. It truly is a miracle that you're here at all. My God laddie, we've got so much to talk about."

Thomas turned to his wife for assurance. Young Saxton remembered what Marcus had told him. He asked his father to sit down. Standing erect in front of both of them, he said, "I have grown on the outside but I need more time to heal on the inside."

His father started to speak but Saxton asked him to be quiet. John Saxton recognized the importance of this moment by remaining mute. His father then realized his son needed time to come to terms with a new reality and a reoccurring nightmare. He brightened,

"Perhaps there's been enough said for now son. A good breakfast will get you off in the right direction. What do you say?"

A knock on the door interrupted him. Thomas rose and opened it. Packard, their black butler, presented a silver salver to his master. He left smiling as if he was concealing some raucous secret. Thomas closed the door, placed the salver on a side table then adjusted his pince-nez reading glasses carefully. He picked up a folded letter, opened it and after a few seconds of reading, exclaimed,

"This is very strange indeed. Here's a letter from a foreign emissary, requesting an audience with all of us at this very moment in the Grand Salon."

Muriel leaned forward in the shadows. Her movement got the attention of both men who turned in her direction, waiting for a voice to reveal her. Muriel emerged triumphant, her delicate hands gripping both wheels, propelling her forward into the light. While affected by waves of emotions raging deep within her, she spoke, her voice strong and vibrant.

"Thomas Dear, why don't we walk down and see who it is!" With that, she grasped the arms of her wicker wheel chair, rising up like a phoenix from its padded seat. Both men rushed forward to assist her but she waved them off. Exultant, she stood before him. Thomas cried out as she reached for his hand.

"May, the Lord be praised! May, the Lord be praised!"

Jack began barking as he bounded about the room. Muriel turned to her husband, her head held high.

"Shall we go my dear, to see who it is? Besides I'm sick of that damned chair anyway. In fact, I think I'll stand for the rest of the day if I so desire it. Don't you agree?"

Two men with Muriel between them, walked out of the parlor, strolled past an astonished Millie then walked together down the hallway to the Grand Salon. Packard was there to greet them. He bowed with a flourish, opened its French doors and announced,

"Your guest awaits you!"

The trio sauntered into a large Victorian Grand Salon with Jack scampering about in front of them. Scattered about were plush leather couches, velveteen settees, stuffed arm chairs and chaise lounges. A cavernous fieldstone fireplace graced the far end of the room. Above it a polished section of a ship's keel supported by two rudder-like corbels formed an impressive mantle piece. A crackling fire roared beneath it while overhead hung a large oil painting formerly entitled, 'The Flying Cloud off the Needles' by James E. Buttersworth. As a joke, Thomas had removed its brass plaque, replacing it with an identical one that read, 'The Silver Ghost off the Needles'. Thereafter in jest, Donald McKay who built both ships, referred to the Saxton clipper as the 'Slower Ghost'.

Florid silk drapes were drawn back from a row of floor to ceiling windows overlooking expansive ornamental gardens at the rear of the mansion. An intricate and colorful Herati motif woven into a Bidjar Persian rug lay upon the Grand Salon's polished parquet floor. Numerous gaslights in plaster wall sconces lined its walls. Above a cream chair rail, pale green damask wallpaper stretched upwards to a wide cream crown molding fourteen feet above. An ornamented plaster ceiling was centered by an immense Swarovski chandelier. Within it sprouted tiny gaslights that hissed and glowed below its lowest crystal ring. Packard reached over to pull down a brass wall lever. The gaslight surround dimmed, sputtered then flared out. Packard was barely able to contain himself. Turning to the trio, he drew his skinny frame upwards to announce grandly,

"May I present his Excellency, an Elder of the Kisongo Maasai, the Lion of the Serengeti; his Highness, Matari!"

With a flourish he pointed a white gloved hand at a high backed, red leather chair facing the fireplace. Curiously, everyone had overlooked a tawny lion's mane rising majestically over the back of the chair, except Jack. The dog began growling while stiffly advancing forward. The mane quivered slightly as it rose to reveal a Maasai Moran who strode around the chair and bowed low in front of them. This tall glorious creature was dressed in a black leather loin cloth covered by a bright red cloak or Shuka. Around his neck were strings of multi-colored glass beads. He gripped a deadly looking spear which peeked out behind a brightly painted elliptical cowhide shield. Thereon, a pair of bright yellow counter-poised chevrons sporting a large capital 'S' lay upon a black background trimmed in yellow. It was the Saxton Shipping Company flag on a Maasai battle shield.

This fearsome apparition in front of them was not only frightening but shocking in its effect as one was helplessly drawn to numerous facial scars that wriggled like worms down the Maasai's cheeks. Jack sprang forward, fangs bared. He attacked the fearsome warrior who in turn tried to defend itself from a frenzied canine. Dog and Maasai battled it out for a few moments before Muriel called off the assault. Sulking and growling, Jack retreated into Muriel's waiting arms whereupon he eyed the specter with great suspicion. The lion-maned giant laughed uproariously, rising again to his full majestic height. Saxton was stupefied, crying out,

"My God father it's Marcus! I don't believe it!"

As a group, they moved forward tentatively. Both men stood aside as Muriel stepped forward, saying with aplomb,

"Oh, mighty Lion of the Maasai, I salute you! What a brave warrior you are! So, you've come for breakfast, have you?"

They laughed until tears flowed down their cheeks. Packard beforehand had summoned his household staff. They crowded in behind him and joined in on the celebration. Muriel motioned for Packard to approach her. He bent down. She whispered in his ear. Packard dismissed his staff then backed out of the Grand Salon closing its stained glass doors quietly behind him. Only a faint shadow behind the door's intricate façade gave any indication that Stylus Packard was eavesdropping.

Marcus recovered his composure, motioning for Thomas and Muriel to sit down on a nearby couch. Standing fully erect, he pronounced gravely that young Sax was to come forward. Somewhat puzzled with a blush of amusement crossing his face, he obeyed the warrior's summons. Turning to Muriel and Thomas, Marcus in a rich baritone, proclaimed,

"We have here a man who was once a boy. In my homeland when a boy becomes a Moran, we celebrate with a ceremony called Emanyatta. There, a young man is given steel tipped Longo and a bull hide Isiphapha to signify his killing of a lion, an act known as 'Spear to Claw'. Saxton my dear friend, I have taught you all I know. Although you have never killed a lion, you have conquered your fears. Therefore, you face the world as a warrior who protects those he loves and the earth upon which they live."

Marcus gravely handed his shield and spear to Saxton. Muriel took out a lace hankie from her sleeve and began dabbing her eyes with it. Thomas himself was barely holding himself together for he realized this rite of passage, so important between a son and his parents was not to be his alone. It was happening between his son and a man from another world thousands of miles away. Thomas took his wife's hankie. He too dabbed his eyes. Both of them held hands and leaned close together as if two old trees embraced after weathering a storm. Before them, their son took the heavy shield and spear. Marcus turned Saxton around to face his parents.

"Thomas Sir, I have done as you asked of me. I have fulfilled my duty to you. To both of you may I present the man you prayed for all those lonely years. He left as a spoiled young lad and has returned home a mature man. May his life be long and fruitful; I have spoken!"

John Saxton turned and solemnly thanked his friend. He noticed that the metal spear point had a deeply incised engraving upon its polished surface. Emotion overcame him as he read the inscription.

"Welcome home son, safe from the sea. The Lord has given you back to me."

A long silence ensued. Saxton caressed the cold steel of the weapon, knowing intuitively that his mother had composed the couplet. As if an important question in his life was finally resolved, he turned and walked back towards his parents. They rose as one to greet him. His mother looked up into her son's sea blue eyes and said, "Welcome home son. Welcome home indeed."

Christmas of 1858, came to the Saxton family mansion that overlooked Boston's inner harbor high atop Copps Hill. It snowed heavily that Christmas day. The Saxton's were worried that no one would show up, but they did. Through the open black iron gates buttressed by granite supports, past the terraced gardens and around the circular drive; cutters and sleighs of every sort arrived with their merry guests. All were eager to participate in one of Muriel Saxton's legendary Christmas parties. The large carriage house at the rear of the mansion was soon filled to capacity with horses and their sleighs. Many tired, cold and hungry steeds were given feed then covered over by thick horse blankets. Their coachmen were taken to the large basement kitchen and staff quarters where they ate and drank merrily at a staff party arranged by Millie and Packard.

The wide Pompeii doorway was flanked by on either side by tall narrow windows. Four Corinthian pilasters on either side of these windows and door completed the Palladian effect. Once through this imposing edifice, the invited guests were greeted by Muriel and

Thomas who graciously ushered them into the Great Hall. Above it, a sixteen-light chandelier, imported from Oxford, England, hung down from the high ceiling.

Millie and Packard took everyone's fur coats, hats, scarves, gloves and muffs to be put aside in the library next door, all carefully tagged and numbered. On the large black and white marble tiles of the foyer beside the staircase, stood a twenty foot Nova Scotia spruce tree' It had been brought down especially for the occasion by Donald McKay's brother, John. Gilded baubles, bows, quilted snowflakes and stars were festooned everywhere upon it, intermingled with strings of bright silver and gold tinsel from Germany. Covering it in elaborate patterns, sparkling candles by the dozen graced its majestic bows, each one sitting inside small wooden hoops. Little red felt pouches containing secret gifts and tiny intricately made pine needle baskets filled with sugared almonds hung from every branch. As a final touch, a glorious silk Angel was firmly attached to the very top of the majestic tree.

After all the guests arrived and the small talk dispensed with, everyone made themselves comfortable in the Grand Salon. Saxton sat on a long couch between his parents. He remembered years before as a child waiting with gleeful anticipation for Santa Claus to appear. But now those years were behind him as only memories fondly remembered. He was a man now, but deep within himself he knew he was still a boy at heart. Thomas signaled Packard to open the French doors. Everyone turned about in anticipation. Led by a bewhiskered skirling piper playing 'Si Bheag Si Mhor', a strange procession entered the room. Behind the piper was Marcus dressed as a Maasai warrior. Gasps of delight issued from the spectators. This unseemly pairing was followed by Packard's uniformed household staff dressed as Santa's elves. Bringing up the rear was Donald McKay dressed as jolly old St. Nick himself, carrying a sack bulging with gifts. This menagerie approached the roaring fireplace then began arranging themselves on either side of it. Marcus moved forward and carefully installed Saxton's shield and spear onto iron hooks set into the field stones above the mantle. Nothing was said, as everyone there already knew the story of the shield and spear. Everyone applauded as Marcus, the household staff, and a choir, were led out by the piper playing a lively rendition of 'Scots Wha Ha'e'. Meanwhile Santa and his elves bestowed gifts to one and all. A hearty "HO, HO, HO!" was heard as he and his elves left the room. Amidst a rousing applause was Jack dashing about dressed up as a miniature reindeer.

The Christmas dinner was a resounding success for the Saxton's, especially the dessert. The Parker House Hotel in Boston was at the time famous for a cake called Parker House Chocolate Cream. Thomas stood up and declared that enough was enough. His Captains had taken this dessert all over the world. So in honor of its birth place, Thomas asked his guests to rise. As they did so, they each held up a silver dessert fork with a piece of cake impaled upon it. Thomas declared that from now on, it would be known as 'Boston Cream Pie'. And so it was thereafter.

BOOK ONE: CHAPTER 3
THE SLAVER

Harley Blackstone was covered in blood. It flowed in black rivulets down his broad chest and onto the deck about his bare feet. His thick woolen sea cap was matted with it too. Harley enjoyed killing, but not when it meant killing his profits that screamed and flowed by his feet over the side of the slave ship Wanderlust. His attention was diverted by something sparkling high up in the sails of that accursed interloper, the Silver Ghost. He stepped back, his feet sliding in fecal slime.

'Careful now.' he thought,' I don't want to go over the side!'

Blackstone looked up squinting into an equatorial sun as the Silver Ghost a hundred feet astern yawed to starboard. There were two people in its crows-nest as the sleek clipper careened past him. One was looking through a telescope. Harley scowled and raised his fearsome club at the Saxton burgee bristling in a stiff breeze high above him. Cursing again, he pointed at a tall black man looking down at him. He did not see the other person clearly but guessed that it was Thomas Saxton's son, John. The taller one was his sworn enemy, Marcus the Maasai.

Harley had collided with the 'Big Nigger' as everyone called him, on the Shanghai Bund years earlier. Two clipper crews squared off in a waterfront gin joint making a thorough shambles of it. Harley remembered the Maasai's scars jump out at him as both men wrestled on a bloody sawdust-covered floor. The police arrived and Marcus dived out a window, escaping into the night. He didn't like being beaten up and swore that it would be the first and last time. Many innocent men and woman thereafter suffered Harley's evil wrath. Blackstone's reverie was broken. He grimaced as he bludgeoned another slave, groping at him in desperation. He cursed,

"Goddamn it to hell, all my swag is goin' overboard!"

As First Mate of the Wanderlust, his share of the profits would have been substantial. It was supposed to have been his last run. Well, that much he was sure of as he looked aft. The Connie II was coming up fast astern. Blackstone took another look at the Silver Ghost as it swung once more in behind him. Sails above his head once taunt, began flapping in the wind. His mind screamed,

'Jesus Christ! They were cutting off our wind again, the bastards!'

Harley vowed that he'd even the score one day, but not now; for he was busy getting rid of incriminating evidence.

An hour later, it was all over. The storm in passing left the slaver ship's tattered sails luffing languidly in a pocket of calm airs. Blackstone barely managed to escape the carnage wrought upon the slavers as the balls and chains from the Connie II brought tons of spars and sails crashing down about his cauliflower ears.

Harley Blackstone, the body of Josiah Garrow and what was left of the slavers were taken aboard the Connie II and lined up on its quarter deck facing their ship. They watched as two carronades on its spar deck blasted the Wanderlust out of the water. Within seconds its square stern rose on high as errant gusts of wind racked its shredded sails back and forth. As it sank, a geyser of compressed air blew high above it like a harpooned whale about to sound. A thick mist from within its fetid bowels drifted back over the USS Constellation II. Many of its sailors began to throw up while the slavers never flinched for they were inured to the stench of rotting flesh. They laughed aloud at the sight. Harley raised his chained hands and danced in his chained feet, yelling,

"Hey boys, these here blue jackets want their mommas! Ain't that a sight for …"

He never finished. A lead sap came down on the back of his skull with a thud. Harley woke up hours later in leg irons, lying in the ship's brig along with his shipmates. He sat up with great effort. The back of his head as well as his whole body ached. He looked around at his sorry crew who seemed no different than when Josiah Garrow bribed their jailers to let them out after their brawl in Shanghai. Blackstone's skipper was dead. His captors had thrown him and seven other dead slavers overboard. To Harley, it didn't seem right not to give his dead mates a proper burial at sea. Harley rubbed his sore ankles. He mused,

'Fitting it was in a way, that that old bastard died the way he did. Josiah was the meanest old man there ever was to be sure; maybe even meaner than his son Horatio.'

Harley had never met Josiah's only son, but from what he'd heard, those who had, recognized evil when they saw it. A slaver sitting near him overheard Harley's cogitations. He said that Horatio was even meaner than Josiah and Harley put together. This surprised Harley who proceeded to beat the man for having the temerity to pass on that bit of information. 'Old Man' Garrow had been proud of his son working in the Customs House in New Orleans and bragged often enough to his crew about how his son stole whole cargoes or took substantial bribes to spare them. Despite his own illustrious reputation, to Blackstone, both Garrows were to be admired.

The 'Connie II' was on its last picket patrol, heading to the Gosport naval yard, in Norfolk, Virginia, its home port. At nearly two hundred feet long with a forty-one foot beam, its bronze howitzers had performed a remarkable job of throwing chain and ball at the Wanderlust. Later that day, Commodore Charles Bell stood on the afterdeck remembering how his thirty-two pounders blasted the slave ship into smithereens. He rubbed his white whiskers thinking,

'Thank God that clipper cut the slaver's wind or I never would have caught her.'

That year alone, Bell captured two slave ships, thereafter releasing hundreds of wretched slaves ashore on various beaches dotting the fog-bound skeleton coast of West Africa. The Bushman living there called it "The land that God made in Anger". Whether the freed slaves made it back to their homeland through the Namib Desert was not his concern. He mused again as he sucked on a long clay pipe.

'This, I've been told, is to be my last patrol with the African Squadron. Indeed, I'm quite pleased with myself. Christ, we chased that slaver for nigh on three hundred leagues. Only a speck she was from the top gallant let alone the foredeck. Reckon she was doing twenty knots fully loaded. I owe the Captain of the Silver Ghost a lot, at the very least a shandy in the Officer's mess in Norfolk. I wonder who he is, even though we'll probably never meet anyway.'

He turned about. His deck officer at that moment came up to him, saluted and said,

"Excuse me Sir, but the prisoners are stowed in the brig. Do we give 'em belly timber and dress their wounds?"

He waited patiently for a few moments. Barely out of his teens, the frail looking youngster was being groomed by his uncle Commodore Bell for a naval career. The portly Commodore looked out to sea where the slave ship had sunk in a cauldron of bloody water. He turned about sharply.

"No Shipton, only water for now; nothing more, nothing less. Let the bastards suffer until we get home. Make sure they remain chained up. They'll hang for sure, that scurvy lot."

Bell paused and turned back looking aft at the foaming wake of his beloved ship fanning out towards the eastern horizon.

"However, Shipton see to their wounds. 'Bones' will look after them. I want the bastards alive to see a rope. Double the guards! Shoot anyone that gets out of line, especially that big brute covered in blood. Throw some buckets of sea water over 'em! They stink to high heaven. Christ! What a filthy business this has been!"

His white gloved hand, gently patted the shoulder boards of the young man standing in front of him.

"I say Shipton; you'll go far in this man's navy. Remember son, its one hand for the ship and the other for your career."

Shipton grinned, saying with gusto, "Ay! Ay! Sir!"

He saluted, spun about, and then descended the companionway two stairs at a time. The ship rolled as an ominous looking squall line approached from the north-east. The Commodore staggered up against the taffrail, regained his balance and yelled at the Bosun standing below him.

"Look alive Carter, I betoken some weather!"

He pointed his long clay pipe at a sword of black clouds slicing through a distant horizon towards them. Carter brought a copper bullhorn to his lips. He barked. Deck crews in their blue jackets and red vests began frapping buntlines in a seamless choreography spanking out the topsails. The Connie II picked up speed, her oaken blocks and pulleys squealing in pain. She heeled about before the wind, exposing a coppered hull upon which a green patina reflected dark waters rushing past her. Below decks, Harley Blackstone felt the fourteen hundred ton ship heel to port then settle before the wind.

Thick oaken roof beams in the ship's brig barely reached his chest, hemming him in. Harley scowled, for as a child his brutal father, Silas Blackstone chained him periodically to a coal bin in their basement. Thereafter, Blackstone was claustrophobic in the extreme. Walls, decks and roofs closed in, growing into a sense of total oppression, Blackstone closed his eyes. Someone near him laughed. Harley smashed in the man's face. His former crew lying about him grew silent. Blackstone crawled away into a dark corner where no one could see tears flow down his face. Harley was alone once more.

Canvas hammocks near the ship's brig swung back and forth in concert with every motion of the ocean. Oak stemsons all about the prisoners squeaked and squealed in protest. A gun crew across from them was hard at work stowing gun barrel rams, cotton wads, sponges, leather water buckets, iron chain and shot. The two cannonades had to be swabbed, secured; their gun ports shut and dogged down. Young powder monkeys ran about with canvas haversacks. A multitude of bare feet slapped a tattoo on a wet oaken gun deck. As they headed for the powder rooms these youngsters ducked coal-oil lamps swinging about in brass gimbals. Not unlike ballet dancers, the lamps remained level every time the ship climbed over another ocean swell. Yellow streaks of lamp light whimpered across a glistening deck.

Harley felt miserable. Guards were everywhere. Some swore at the prisoners while prodding them with their bayonets. Over and over, cold steel clanged against black iron bars in concert with their oaths, saying,

"You're gonna' hang for sure you bloody bastards!"

Harley covered his ears while his fatalistic mind mused,

'Slaving has been dangerous, but damned profitable over the years. But now it is over, OVER! Christ almighty, those goddamned bible thumpin' Limeys have seen to that!'

He sank back, drawing two massive legs up to his chest like a night lion ready to kill.

As the USS Constellation II headed home, it sailed southward, well away from a becalmed Sargasso Sea or as sailors called it, "the sea of lost ships'. However, southern airs warmed a brooding cloak of blackness that spread like a pall over the ocean. Other ships appeared heading their way. Commodore Bell's deck officer was busy sending and receiving messages. Apparently, there was a hurricane ahead bearing down on Norfolk, Virginia. Standing in the shelter of the wheelhouse dodger, Commodore Bell decided to change course to a WNW direction. He directed his helmsmen accordingly.

"Watermain my lad, port steer WNW two hundred and ninety degrees. Be quick about it."

Watermain nodded, swung the ship's great helm to port then corrected it. He called out, "Steady on two nine zero."

Bell looked occasionally at a brass binnacle wherein an iron needle pointed at a round card immersed in a container of alcohol. The deck officer's sextant sighting at high noon that day put the ship at approximately twenty-eight degrees North Latitude by seventy degrees West Longitude. Officer Shipton lifted a water-tight lid hinged to a metal map table beside him. Commodore Bell bent over it to recheck his sailing charts. He muttered, irritated by the change in course.

"Shipton, Charleston is dead ahead. I have no choice. At twelve knots, we should get there in two weeks if not sooner. I'll unload this human scum there and be rid of them once and for all." Shipton was not convinced,

"But Commodore, isn't Charleston a slave port?"

Bell eyed the young man then slammed the chart case shut with a crash. He growled,

"Batten down the hatches Shipton and be quick about it."

The Connie II tied up in Charleston, South Carolina, berthed stern first at the foot of Market Street. Hours earlier, Commodore Bell had seen the tall steeples of St. Paul's and St. Michael's long before the city had come into view. Charleston was very important to the Confederate cause, as it was the fourth largest Atlantic port. For many years previously, its many warehouses poured rivers of rice and indigo while onto its streets flowed rivers of slaves destined for large plantations all over the South. Located on a low peninsula at the confluence of the Ashley and Cooper Rivers, Charleston managed to survive numerous floods and hurricanes for many years. Locals there said that these two rivers came together to form the Atlantic Ocean. Commodore Bell agreed.

He watched from high above on the poop deck as his prisoners were brought ashore in chains to disappear up Market Street to the nearby City Jail. The tinkling of their chains upon the brick streets receded whereupon he reflected,

'Good riddance! It'll take weeks before the stench of those filthy criminals will be scrubbed away. I do hope so.'

He turned and went below, glad to be in port, although crowds of onlookers outside were becoming openly hostile to his presence. Bell knew his guards would keep them at bay even if they managed to get through the locked iron gates of the customs quay. Bell put it behind him and entered his spacious aft cabin. Four rows of crown glass scuttles spread out before him across the ship's wide stern. Outside right below the windows, on a carved escutcheon was the vessel's name covered in gold gilt. Heavy anchor chains began rattling in the lazaret below the Commodore's feet. Soured by it all, he muttered,

"I do hope the crew is cleaning out the brig too. My God! What a stench! Well enough, there's always work to be done, even if this hell hole is hot and humid most of the year. Thank God I'm not stationed here!"

He took off his black chapeau-bras garnished by a long yellow swan feather and placed it on a chart table. His double-breasted dark blue frock coat found a home on a peg rack. Moments later, Bell lay back in his leather swivel chair, locking his long delicate fingers behind his bald head. He spun around to peer through the square window panes. Before him, sweating black stevedores pulled carts piled high with dry goods. After a few minutes watching them, they became animals. Shame swept through him. The Commodore stood up to clear his conscience thinking,

'This God awful place was better suited for criminals than for civilized company.'

Harley Blackstone trudged up Market Street, leading his messmates through throngs of free slaves, merchants and townspeople. He'd been there many times before. Harley hated the place for it was hot, humid and strangely enough, claustrophobic to him. His crew had suffered since they were captured as bad food, scummy water and constant taunting left them weak and vulnerable. Harley didn't like being helpless. His tawdry crew continued along dragging their leg irons, loudly proclaiming their presence to one and all. Iron links tinkled over yet another narrow brick street that bisected a sprawling black ghetto.

Blackstone eyed a growing throng of surly free blacks looking at him. He wondered if they knew who they were; apparently so, for an old black harridan began pelting him with small sharp stones. Others spit on him while many more followed suit. The embattled slavers began hobbling as fast as they could towards Charleston's City Jail on the corner of Franklin and Magazine St.

The newly built city jail was the pride and joy of the good burghers of Charleston. It was a massive stone octagonal structure, rising four stories surmounted by a forty foot tower. Flanking these impressive structures was a twelve foot high whitewashed brick wall spread out for some distance. Twenty feet along, two gated arches penetrated it. Through one of these archways, the slavers limped along as best they could. A cigar smoking gaoler herded them into a one acre rectangular rear yard surrounded by another high wall. An iron gate clanged shut behind them. They were led into the cooling shade of a grove of tall water oaks. Shortly thereafter, four black orderlies leisurely strolled by them to a nearby well wherein they began drawing up buckets of cool water. Harley and the others looked over thankful, for his mouth was as dry as a week old crust of bread. He thought,

'Oh! Thank God! Water at last! I could do with a cool one.'

Instead, the orderlies emptied their water buckets upon the helpless men then stood back laughing hysterically. Their overseer did nothing to stop them. Instead, he leaned against a water oak and watched. Harley sputtered, cursing all four in four different languages. They spit on him. He rose to defend himself but was dragged down by his crewmates on either side whereupon he raged like a lion in a cage but to no avail. Exhausted, he sank back against the hard stringy bark of a water oak tree. Harley glared about him. Without warning he lashed out at the men sitting on either side of him.

Blackstone and his crew were to remain incarcerated for nearly twelve months at the discretion of his Majesty's Navy despite the protestations of Charleston's city fathers. However, as civil war became imminent, Blackstone was transferred to Fort Moultrie in the spring of 1860. There, he and his fellow slavers along with a multitude of other prisoners failed in their attempts to adequately fortify it. In doing so, Blackstone suffered at the hands of a certain Corporal Riley who took it upon himself to torment him at every given opportunity.

Eventually, the Union was forced to abandon Fort Moultrie as being indefensible. On December 26th, 1860, one hundred and twenty-seven men including a regimental band were shipped to Fort Sumter directly across the channel. The slavers were not listed on the manifest for some had already succumbed to disease and ill treatment. Harley Blackstone was not amongst them for Riley had thrown him in irons just to make sure he didn't escape transfer. Strangely, early one morning, a small British yawl picked him up and took him away.

Harley woke up handcuffed and wearing leg irons connected by chain to another chain around his waist. Bilge water sloshed beneath him. More of it slopped over the gunwales of the small pinnace as it heeled over in a stiff breeze. He sat up. A boom swept by above him, barely clearing his head. He sat a little lower. Wary of it, Harley peered over the gunwale. Across from him, thousands of night lights in Charleston flickered about, distorted by a sea haze. Two barefooted sailors looked down upon him. One smiled crookedly,

"Well you rotten bastard, you finally woke up. Heard about you I did. So you're a tough one are you? Don't make any sudden moves matey or Charlie there behind you will blow your soddin' head off, right Charlie?"

Someone growled behind him. The metallic snick of a cocking revolver was heard. Harley held his breath, thinking,

'The bloody bastards are going to shoot me for sure, saying I tried to escape by diving overboard bound hand and foot with fifty pounds of chains. Christ almighty!'

At that very moment a large seabird flew over them. Harley wiped a blob of poop from his forehead as the vessel sliced through low swells and river chop. His minders laughed.

"Hey Charlie, he's goin' to be a lucky one indeed he is, well mannered too and from what I can see, the filthy bilge water below my feet is cleaner than this slaver sittin' afore me."

He laughed again as Blackstone bent over the side and washed his face. Once finished, Harley glared at him then cursed as a bare foot smashed into his stomach. He winced and looked ahead, his long brown hair streaming in the wind. Rising over chop and spray, the outline of a monolithic fort rose out of the water. He sat back to have a better look at the man sitting in front of him. Startled, he realized the man was a British sailor wearing a round tarred straw boater. Harley looked more closely at his blue and white striped Guernsey. Around his neck was a square cut white collar held up with a red serge scarf. A wide leather belt sporting a brass buckle held his black trousers up. Something emblazoned on his belt buckle winked at him but he couldn't see it clearly. Blackstone turned around. The sailors rowing behind him were dressed exactly the same. Harley exclaimed,

"Who are you?" The snotty laughed.

"Welcome to her Majesty's navy, arsehole!"

Fort Sumter swam into Harley Blackstone's vision very much like a fallen tombstone looming up slab-like through a thick London fog. Commenced in 1829 as a deterrent against naval ships, Fort Sumter squatted on a long wide sandbar. This served as its original foundation, one built with seventy thousand tons of New England granite. It was here that a small British naval tender arrived just as dawn was breaking. It tied up to a broad granite block wharf that jutted out from a vast bank of compact sand. Across from it, two long wooden scows sat low in the water piled high with oyster shells. A gang of soldiers were shoveling these mollusks into large ammo wagons. Blackstone watched as dozens of sweaty men pushed brimming carts back to the fort. Their wooden wheels squealed in protest as each one trundled over the stone blocks.

Midshipman Charlie Watts nudged Harley Blackstone with his pistol while the pinnace rocked in the river currents holding it tight against the quay. Watts was careful for Harley's reputation as a killer preceded him. He growled through broken teeth.

"Go ashore you big baboon. That's it matey, up you goes and don't fall in cause I ain't gonna git ye."

Blackstone didn't hear him and he would have cared less if he had. Right then he was sore all over. He swayed like a Sunday drunkard as he stepped out onto the pier. The stone slabs beneath his bare feet did nothing to assist him in regaining his balance. A hot sun rising and a dense haze lifting, promised a day like all the others before it. Harley turned about, his right hand shielding his eyes, the other lifting the chains attached to his leg-irons. Before him rose millions of red adobe bricks cemented together by a conglomerate of crushed oyster shells and seawater called 'tabby'. They formed a slab-sided structure rising fifty feet above the waters surrounding it garnished by numerous narrow vertical openings. Above them sixty cannon protruded along the top of each wall. Rounded corners defined its five sides. These manifestations gave the fort an impregnable facade. It didn't impress Harley at all.

Blackstone turned about. Watts had climbed out onto the dock. He stood there, his pistol pointed at Blackstone. Harley looked down into the pinnace. He was alone. Surprised, he wondered aloud,

"Hey, where's me shipmates?" Charlie laughed,

"What shipmates? Looks like you're the only one Harley."

"Hey!" The other one taunted, pointing his pistol at Blackstone,

"The big bugger here is all alone and already cryin' for his mother!"

Blackstone lunged at Watts but tripped, falling to his knees with a crash. Before he could get recover, Watts had leaped into the rowing boat and cast off; remaining a respectable distance from the granite jetty. Blackstone stood up swearing at them. However, he didn't notice an Army Corporal walking up behind him. Streaks of sweat were already soiling the Corporal's blue serge uniform. A small man, he carried a small riding whip in a small gloved hand. As the Corporal neared, Harley heard him, spun about and swore. It was Riley. The officer's weasel face pinched as he pressed the riding crop hard against Harley's Adam's apple.

"What did you just call me?"

One of the tars yelled,

"Well teach him some manners!"

Riley grinned, stepped back and laughed.

"Just like old times, eh Blackie!"

CRACK! Blackstone found the whip not to his liking and swore at Riley who promptly inflicted another cut across Harley's hairy backside. CRACK! Another strike got him hobbling towards the fort. Harley protested as he stumbled forward. Oyster dust encrusted upon the wharf rose up in floury clouds as his heavy chains disturbed it. CRACK! Harley moved faster, afraid now that he would be badly beaten. Futilely he cried,

"Riley, I'm goin' as fast as I can, you Yankee bastard!"

CRACK! Apparently this remark did not sit well with Corporal Riley. Harley hurried along. His calloused left foot stepped on a discarded plank. Harley cursed as a sliver drove deeper into his foot. The last thing he heard was laughter carried upon a river breeze. A Grey Gull swept up and over him heading straight for the fort's sally port on the Gorge wall where two tall double doors opened wide below a peaked dormer. Once through the portal, Harley skirted a ten inch Columbiad cannon then limped across the plank floor of a barracks building. Once through that, other three story brick barracks rose directly to his right and left. Directly ahead on the other side of the vast parade grounds were the right and left face comprised of arched gun embrasures rising two stories. No cannon were upon them. In front of that was a mountain of neatly stacked adobe slabs.

Next to it, near-naked men in chains were shoveling mountains of red clay into round wooden pits and centered by a vertical rotating wooden auger. Trudging in a circle around these pits were harnessed mules pulling four chest-high horizontal poles. Their sinewy muscles strained as the thick wet clay in the pits was thoroughly mixed with dirty straw and water. Upon reaching the right consistency, the pits were emptied by other prisoners using wooden spades. The clay was then packed into long shallow wooden molds. Once trimmed, each three hundred pound mold was carried by four men to a drying area where its wet slab was then delicately dumped on the court-yard's hard clay floor. Three beehive brick kilns squatted nearby, fiery with purpose. Rows of fire-hardened slabs leaned precariously along the walls of the courtyard waiting to be put into place. Once cured enough, they were put into ammo carts each pulled by two mules. These sturdy beasts slowly plodded up a series of inclined gun ramps to the unfinished left flank of the fort.

Across from the clay pits, mountains of oyster shells were being crushed by men wielding heavy sledges. As they worked, a gray cloying dust billowed up, covering each sweaty face with a death mask. A staved oaken vat bound by iron rings was filled with water. Ghostly apparitions shoveled pulverized oyster shells into it. After being thoroughly blended, the glutinous gray treacle was scooped into wheelbarrows. Gangs of sweating men trundled them up a steep wooden ramp to the top of the left flank of the fort's eastern wall. Thereon men cemented horizontal layers of slabs together, creating a wall over twenty-five feet thick. Down below them, the hideous squealing of wooden augurs in the clay pits, caromed about the courtyard like finger-nails on a chalkboard.

Harley began to sweat. Abruptly he stopped then moved forward again as Riley's whip bit into his bleeding right shoulder. Again he paused trying to make his mind grasp onto what his eyes were seeing. For the first time in his life, Blackstone believed in Hell. There at the foot of the slab pile were his shipmates hard at work. A half-hearted hurrah went up as they spied Blackstone dragging his chains towards them. A few were dipping a tin cup into a tepid water barrel. One thin looking specimen stepped forward. Through broken yellow teeth it hissed,

"Well blow me down if ain't Harley Blackstone himself. Hey matey, we thought youse was dead fer sure back at 'Old Moldy'. Bin a week now makin' slabs for the Yanks. What took ye so long?" Harley was short on patience.

"Shut up and gimme a cup of water will ya!"

CRACK. Riley's whip sent the tin cup and its contents flying. Riley snarled,

"Blackstone, come with me. Be quick about it!"

Harley straggled after the little Corporal. Behind him one of the chain-gang muttered,

"That bastard Riley will kill him afore the sun sets today." Another countered,

"Don't bet on it. Blackstone is a natural born killer and as long as he's chained head to foot, all of us have nothin' to worry about."

Major Robert Anderson, the Fort Sumter's commander, reached down and picked Corporal Riley up off his office floor. Harley had put him there a few minutes earlier. The Major was not pleased with Riley for whipping a prisoner, not pleased at all. He had ordered Riley to take off Blackstone's handcuffs. Upon completing this task, Harley promptly cold-cocked the Corporal, saying afterwards,

"Sorry Major, but I had to teach the bastard some manners!"

The Major promptly concurred, offering Blackstone a cheroot and a glass of sippin' whiskey. They watched as two orderlies dragged Corporal Riley out of the Major's office down to the infirmary. An amazed Harley went there an hour later, escorted by an armed orderly. Once there, Blackstone's severely injured left foot, ankle sores and whip welts were looked after. A few hours later, after a bath and fresh clothes, he would be sent to his new kingdom, the infamous slab yard.

After Blackstone had gone to the infirmary, there was a knock on the Major's door. A native of Kentucky, he drawled, "Come in."

In walked his second in command, a newly commissioned Captain Abner Doubleday; ten years younger, tall, with a pronounced military bearing. The Major returned his salute then motioned for the Captain to sit down at a small round table. Anderson's unpretentious office overlooked the fort's inner courtyard through two tall window casements. Wide pine planks sufficed as flooring while the unadorned plaster walls rose up to a ceiling ten feet in height centered by a coal oil lantern. Strewn about the untidy space were two folding map tables, a rocking chair and a stack of bound leather chests. Opposite the tall front door was a rather grand fireplace, its blackened slate hearth garnished by a long box of untidy kindling. The Major's personal effects; an umbrella, a Hardee hat and other items were scattered about as if thrown there in haste. A fastidious Doubleday looked around in disgust. In a lilting voice, he said.

"Permission to speak freely Sir?" The Major nodded.

"I hear Major, that our Corporal Riley used his little whip a bit too often. I understand a recently arrived prisoner of note; the infamous Harley Blackstone, cold-cocked him right here in your office. What are you going to do about it Sir?"

The Major sat back; a thin smile crossed his clean face shaven. He explained succinctly,

"Nothing. You see Captain, that animal Blackstone was First Mate on the slaver Wanderlust. Both he and his crew were transferred from the Charleston City jail to Fort Moultrie a year ago. Later on, he proved invaluable to me as a work gang leader when we tried to rearm and reinforce Moultrie. However, he had a serious falling out with Corporal Riley and was left in Moultrie to cool off. What's left of his crew are out there now on my slab pile. Blackstone will be their new overseer. His sole purpose will be to get enough slabs prepared to finish our left flank. These are desperate times Abner and our former artificer didn't know this crew like Blackstone. Their progress was too slow, way too slow, especially with the fort facing a Rebel town like Charleston. It was just a stroke of luck the 'Connie II' docked here two years ago with that lot in its brig. They couldn't stay on board as this town is a slave port. Those men for appearances only, were marched to the town jail where they stayed for nearly a year." The Major took another sip of whiskey, leaned forward and continued.

"You see Captain; their release would have displeased a British abolitionist government immensely. Secondly, the Limeys get their indigo from two places, India and here. In fact there's a large British windjammer in port right now loading up tons of the stuff as well as rice and other goods. She'll probably sail tonight on the flood tide."

The Major paused, and offered Doubleday a whiskey. It was accepted with alacrity. They settled back and lit cheroots as Major Anderson continued,

"The British consulate in Charleston found out that these slavers were going to be released from the city jail; so they threatened to embargo the indigo trade immediately if the slavers were not released into my custody. They were soon after and shipped to Moultrie. Because the British are considered neutral by the Rebels, the need for British gold by the Rebels was paramount.

He paused, sipped his whiskey while pointing his cheroot at his Captain like a rapier saying emphatically,

"You're aware Abner, that I abandoned Sullivan's Island because it was indefensible. River sand over the years piled up against Moultrie's walls so high that we couldn't defend it. Then that bastard Buchanan stopped the final completion of the walls here. It was a damned disgrace. Upon abandoning the fort, I spiked Moultrie's guns. War is coming Captain! You know it! I know it! We need labor now. Fate sent me twenty-five slavers. Blackstone came along later because he was out cold for two days. Some incident at Moultrie's jail I've been told. But Captain, our slab makin' will punish them well. Blackstone is a real slave driver!" They both laughed. The Major continued,

"Well Captain, we can always hang 'em later but not before the slab pile has gone." The Major stood up. He said,

"Captain, bring Blackstone here then I'll send him back to his crewmates. By the way, here's a key. Give it to Blackstone. Instruct him to free all of his men from their leg-irons immediately. Perhaps then, they'll move faster---- the poor bastards. Oh yeah, one more thing, give him Corporal Riley's riding whip too. I think our Corporal was too fond of it."

The Major picked up the whip from his desk, handing it to Doubleday. He laughed.

"Perhaps Blackstone will be more judicious using it."

Captain Doubleday started to protest as the Major threw him a small brass key.

"That's an order Captain, we're not playin' baseball ya know, now get goin' and bring him back here!"

Doubleday saluted, closed the door behind him and fled to the infirmary. A few minutes later, Harley Blackstone, followed by an armed Captain Doubleday walked stiffly in his leather slippers. As they hurried down the infirmary's tiled corridor, their footfalls boomed in Harley's ears. Sheer panic set in as once more as millions of red bricks closed in on him. He looked up at a white banjo wall clock. He whined,

"Christ Captain, I'm starved, when's lunch?"

Doubleday knocked on the Major's door, waited then opened it, stepping aside. Harley went in closing it behind him before the Captain could enter. Major Anderson stood up, went around his desk and shook Harley's calloused right hand. Harley was flummoxed because it had been a very long time since someone took his hand and that was usually when someone was going to sucker punch him or lay on the cuffs. They sat down facing each other. Harley was offered a whiskey and a cheroot. Not only was the Major civil but generous as well. Harley, always paranoid, waited for the Major to make the first move. There was another knock on the door. After the Major's response, Corporal Riley somewhat the worse for wear came in with a wooden tray loaded with food. He glared at Blackstone. The Major smiled as he returned Riley's salute. After he left, the Corporal stood by the door, trying to catch snatches of the conversation within.

Major Anderson sat back, motioned Harley towards the food and said expansively, "Help yourself Blackstone. Don't be shy!"

Harley sat down by a nearby window with the tray on his lap. He dived in and didn't surface for half an hour. Once he finished, the Major rang a bell. Riley took away the spotless plates, bowls and cups. Harley leaned back against a chair, lit another cheroot, burped, and said,

"Beggin' your pardon Major, but I'm not used to bein' treated so kindly. Now wadda ya want?" The Major stood up facing him, a refreshed whiskey glass in hand.

Harley eyed the Major suspiciously as Anderson paced back and forth. Blackstone noticed a large wall map hanging to one side behind the Major's large desk. He squinted at it, trying to get a better look while the Major gazed out a dirty window. Harley was surprised for on it was the positions of all the latest gun emplacements inside Fort Sumter. Harley knew that war was coming sooner, not later. He also suspected that after his work here was done, he and his crew would be hung. Harley had to have that gun map. The other side would treat him as a hero if he could ever escape with it before the first shot was fired. He sat there sucking his cheroot, completely oblivious to the major blathering away about teamwork, duty and dedication to the cause. The Major finished. He looked down at Harley quite satisfied.

"Am I right Blackstone?"

Harley dragged his eyes away from the wall map.

"Right as rain skipper!"

Blackstone rose out of his chair then took a blue slouch hat off a nearby clothes rack. The Major yelled for his Captain. Seconds later Doubleday burst through the door, Riley's whip in hand. He saluted. The Major yelled at him. The Lieutenant stood there as if he was pole-axed.

"I told you before Lieutenant, give him the damned whip." He obeyed.

Blackstone stuffed Riley's whip under his brawny left arm. Major Anderson stiffened as Blackstone stuck a cheroot in his mouth then calmly pilfered more from a humidor lying on the Major's desk. Harley smiled indulgently, raised his free hand and saluted leaving the two officers standing with their arms by their sides and their mouths wide-open in disbelief.

Harley Blackstone strolled nonchalantly out of the Commander's office wearing no handcuffs or leg-irons. Properly attired; he sported fresh clothes, a slouch hat, a cheroot in one hand and a small black whip in the other.

The chain gang on the oyster pile remained frozen in place as if Thor's hammer had struck them dead. The thin little man with yellow teeth, leaned on his sledge, cursing under his breath,

"Christ almighty! The 'Evil One' approaches, may God help us all!"

As Harley surveyed the stricken, he grinned, thinking,

'I'm gonna have fun with this lot before the day is out. There will be no wallopers or gadabouts in my territory.'

A man waddled forward in his leg-irons. He croaked,

"Holy Christ, Blackstone! How did you do it?"

Harley took a brass key out of his trousers and threw it at the man who barely caught it. He laughed,

"Now Jeffries me lad, unlock all these sorry lookin' blokes and be right quick about it."

CRACK! CRACK! Harley's whip snapped across Jeffries backside. He howled. Blackstone laughed,

"Gather round girls and listen good! From now on I'm the boss around this here yard. Major Anderson has wisely seen the light of day in these desperate times and has made me the foreman in charge of supplyin' tabby and slabs to finish this fort. My life and yours depends on gettin' it done by the end of next month. Any slackers will go over the side, chains and all... out there."

He turned about like a striking cobra, pointing his whip out towards the Sally Port. He growled, "Any questions ladies?"

BOOK ONE: CHAPTER 4
MAASAI ON THE RUN

Miss Bellefonte La Fontaine 'worked' at 101 Lower Line Street in Carrolton City, Louisiana. Most whites in nearby New Orleans, called this area 'Nigger Town' or in a more genteel parlance, 'Black Pearl'. Others, especially the black locals, preferred the area to be known as Carrolton City.

Belle was only ten years of age when she came to what was politely called, 'The House of the Rising Sun'. By the time she was twenty-five, she was an expert in her chosen field. Her clients came from every walk of life; lawyers, teachers, policemen and even men of the cloth. Belle, as she was known by her immediate friends was very popular. Besides her special skills, she was exotic; too beautiful to be real.

At the time, there were many beautiful women in New Orleans before the Civil War, for the Crescent City and its various cultural delights seemed to attract these women like bees to an exotic flower. Belle was special for she did not look like the ideal Victorian woman. Belle stood over six feet tall, was olive skinned, with long black hair, high cheek bones, large black eyes, aquiline nose, perfect teeth, large hard breasts, narrow waist and long legs. As such her beauty and skills as a courtesan was much sought after by her rich white clientele.

A Creole, Belle came from an upper middle class family living in the seventh district. Brought up as a devout Catholic; she was predestined by her parents to continue her education at the Ursuline Convent School for Girls on Chartres St. However, the strict rules of Mother Theresa Fargone were too much for the rebellious girl. Eventually, Belle ran away from home and found herself penniless on the front doorstep of 'The House of the Rising Sun.'

Over the intervening years, Belle worked there as a maid and kitchen helper; very rarely if ever going out. Over time, she grew up to be quite a beauty. Anna Prevost, the owner of the establishment, groomed the young girl for a career that would soon prove to very lucrative for both of them. Every night she would comb Belle's long lustrous black hair then let her experiment with heavy bottomed rouge pots. Under her tutelage, a pubescent Belle learned the proper decorum of the day such as the etiquette required at formal dinners, the new dances, and how to converse with her upper crust patrons. These were the staples of her soirees. She learned how to sew petite point and discern the finest of just about everything from clothes, to furniture and for that matter...men.

By her seventeenth birthday, Belle was fluent in French, Spanish and English besides her native patois. Anna made sure the legions of wealthy young beaux who frequented her

establishment did not become romantically involved with Belle but many had already succumbed to her charms. Every week, after Belle commenced entertaining, the house Doctor
came by to check all the girls for a variety of social diseases. Belle took her precautions and
remained unscathed.

At twenty-five, she was the highest paid escort in the city having amassed a fortune in
cash, gold, silver and precious gems. At thirty, Belle decided to buy her own 'house' on Rue
Conti, discreetly located in the more fashionable fourth district. The former owner was only
too glad to retire as a wealthy matron. Belle's establishment became known as 'La Belle
Maison'. However, there was another reason she acquired the house. Although, by far the
most beautiful woman in New Orleans, her days of entertaining were coming to an end.
She'd made amends with her parents after the birth of a baby boy. The last reason was more
personal. She wanted revenge on a fledgling Confederacy determined to uphold the odious
system of slavery. As such she became a spy for the Union and Allan Pinkerton was only
too willing to oblige.

A few years later, it was time to move out of 'La Belle Maison' into a proper family home.
Her son was named Marcus Jr. but his nickname was 'Cotton' because he loved to play with
a large cotton ball that Belle put in his crib. After four years, Cotton began asking questions
about all the people around him and what they were doing there. Belle decided it was no
place for an inquisitive child to grow up.

In due time, Belle bought another grand Victorian style house facing Rue Bienville that
backed onto her bordello. The owner, a rich client of hers, had been forced into bankruptcy
during the panic of 1857. Immediately after taking ownership, Belle installed a stout oak door
on the second floor that connected the two residences together as one. Thus, she didn't
have to walk around the block to attend to her growing business. She named it the 'Twixt'
door. A stout, middle-aged Scottish nanny was hired to cook, clean and look after Cotton.
Mary McPherson loved Cotton at first sight as if he were her own son. Belle wondered if that
tall, good looking Maasai, the boy's father, would ever come back as he promised too.

Over four years she waited patiently, perhaps too patiently; for many were the nights
she'd lay awake tossing and turning, her body aching for him. God! Sometimes she hated
him for not being there when she needed him. Her hot Creole temper would lash out at
Margery Briscoe her house manager or worse yet, her son. She hated herself for being
weak and undisciplined. It was not like her. Belle La Fontaine could hardly wait to sink her
sharp claws into that big man one way or the other for she was going mad with desire every
time she thought of him. Miraculously she remained chaste ever since the big Maasai sailed
away past English Turn down the Mississippi River.

The SS Anaona arrived at the Saxton warehouse beside the Canal St. levee near the end of October, 1860, heavily loaded; in fact so much so, the vessel had only a foot of freeboard. Luckily, the voyage south from had been through tranquil inland waterways and leagues of becalmed ocean. The nearby New Orleans Customs Office promptly sent an official, even as the ship was berthing. The vessel's mooring cables were thrown over iron bollards that lined the front of a long heavily timbered wharf. A short gangplank hoisted by a steam winch, rose high up into the air then was lowered with a thump onto the dock. Two steam cranes amidships hissed, squealed and spit as they unfolded skyward from their iron deck restraints. Immediately the ship's crew began lifting and stowing the ship's three cargo hatches.

A tall, lithe and muscular Customs Officer, a Captain Horatio Garrow, strode purposely towards the Anaona. Attired in a black double breasted frock suit adorned with large brass buttons, Garrow approached ghostlike through a thick morning river mist. While carrying a heavy canvas sack, he ran up the ship's gangplank throwing a spent cheroot into muddy waters below him. As he did so, he eyed Marcus sitting nearby on an iron bollard. The man glowered then turned away as he was greeted by Captain Wilkins who promptly ushered him down a companionway into his quarters aft.

The Custom's Officer had come aboard to inspect the ship's cargo of farm machinery stacked in the ship's cargo holds. They supposedly contained cotton gins, John Deere plows and McCormick reapers. However, the inspection would never happen as the Customs Officer already knew what was inside the crates in question.

Within minutes of his arrival, a company Supercargo paid a dock foreman a ground-age charge allowing dozen's of black stevedores to begin hoisting the cargo out onto large wagons lined up dockside. They did so and by noon these sweating roustabouts were ready to fill the ship with hundreds of heavy cotton bales. Long sinuous lines of heavy drays were waiting, each pulled by a team of Belgium mules. They lingered stoically in the early morning light, their long mulish ears twitching occasionally. Canal mist, thick and slow moving, rose up over the long wooden dock. It wound serpent-like through the open doors of the Saxton warehouses fronting the canal.

During a break, Marcus returned to sit on the bollard while smoking a thin cheroot. He mused about Thomas Saxton's new steam ship built not by Donald McKay but by Samuel Hall. Hall recently built a large yard at the end of Maverick St. in East Boston. There, the SS Anaona was fitted with twin Philip Petite propellers. The one hundred and fifty foot shallow draft coastal freighter had no sails whatsoever, just two iron cranes amid ships. To lower the ship's center of gravity, these steam cranes were pulled down and clamped and chained onto iron uprights before every sailing.

Marcus was intensely proud that it was named Anaona or 'We believe' in Swahili. Thomas Saxton held the vessel's christening party in early September 1860. Marcus did the deed. As the Anaona's hull chokes were knocked aside by men wielding sledges, the three hundred ton ship sped down the greased slipway into the water with a tremendous splash. A loud hurrah from the large crowd at the McKay shipyard erupted. Seagulls lifted from their pilings, swirled and dipped over dark waters as the whistles of other ships blew in loud exuberance. Even Donald McKay was impressed, although he tempered his enthusiasm by saying,

"The damned thing should have sails just in case".

After a smoke break, Marcus was content as he stood amidships, watching each cotton bale weighing over five hundred pounds, hoisted off its dray and swung aboard to vanish into the ship's expansive holds. Below decks, the bales were loaded onto push trolleys that took them to their appointed sections. Once there, they were rolled off into position. It was hard work. Two dozen black stevedores sweated as they struggled with the dirty bundles.

By noon, with one hundred tons of cotton bales already aboard, lowering the blunt nosed Anaona into the canal. As Marcus paced about the main deck, he remembered the early days when everything was loaded by hand. Oh, how he had prayed for death to release his aching body after his first day loading cotton here years before. Now he was content to swear at any dawdlers in rich Maa Swahili knowing full well that none of his crew could understand what he was saying. But that didn't matter, for they knew by the tone of his voice that they'd better not have 'Marcus the Maasai' mad at them.

Marcus returned to and once again sat on the iron bollard. Once again, his thoughts drifted to that of Belle, the woman he'd fallen in love with. He remembered her well, in fact too well. He became hard. Marcus ran up the gangplank, yelling,

"I'm going to kick your Matako's" at any stevedores who showed any signs of slackening off. His thoughts of Belle returned with even more vigor as he sat on a stack of hatch covers fondly remembering his lover.

After only a few nights together, they fell in love. It always seemed to him that the matters of ship and shore competed with each other. In the end he left a tearful Belle behind. She stood on the wharf like a waif, waving a white hanky at him as his clipper ship was pulled out into the canal by a small steam tug. The dusky smell of rosewater remained within his memory even after she became a small white dot. After he passed the Milneburgh Lighthouse, Marcus lost sight of the city as it disappeared round a bend into the labyrinthine expanse of the Mississippi river delta. Someday he would return, marry Belle and never go back to sea again. Until then, the heart of a vagabond lay deep within him, controlling every surge of lifeblood that coursed through his veins. Within minutes of entering the wide open serenity of the delta, all his aspirations concerning her became nothing more than wishful thinking.

The Supercargo's final paper work at the Saxton warehouse still had to be completed, delaying the Anaona's departure for another day. Marcus was anxious to see Belle after a messenger delivered a note to him that morning. The embossed linen paper smelled faintly

of rose water. Marcus read it once more. It simply said, "Meet me at the usual place at nine tonight."

Marcus would be late as always. It was already after nine but he knew Belle would understand. For a long time he wondered if he would ever see her again. Under the light of a gimbaled hurricane lamp, he polished his glistening head with palm oil and selected his best 'goin' to town' clothes. His eagerness increased as he bustled about his small cabin. While bending down to tie his new leather shoes, muffled voices in the hallway outside his cabin caught his attention. The door of the Captain's stateroom next door was unlocked, opened then snapped shut with a click. Marcus could barely hear the high pitched voice of Silas Wilkins Irish lilt. He tied his shoelaces then put a Philly derringer into a lower pocket of his double breasted overcoat. Marcus made sure his Sheffield Bowie-knife was fastened to his belt. The autumn nights were cooling but his thoughts of a lover's assignation were rudely interrupted by a verbal commotion going on next door.

Curious, Marcus rose to his full height and put his ear against a ventilation vent high up on an adjoining wall. His facial scars tightened as he listened in rapt attention. A finger of unease crawled down his spine as the full significance of the conversation took shape in his mind. He heard his Captain shout,

"I don't give a tinker's damn! But, if you really want to know what I think…." An exasperated Silas Wilkins was cut short as a deep voice replied,

"Pour me some sippin' whiskey Silas and listen carefully as you do it. You'd be better off if you never spoke my name again. There are spies everywhere in New Orleans. If any of this correspondence about 'Operation False Prophet' is discovered, we'll be swinging from a yardarm afore the sun rises." The voice stopped then Silas resumed on a more conciliatory note.

"Don't worry my friend, I'll be careful." Garrow was abrupt.

"Well dangerous times are afoot Wilkins. Here is the payment of five hundred Double Eagles I promised you for the latest shipment of guns and ammo."

He threw a black canvas sack onto a nearby chart table. It landed with a metallic thud.

Wilkins grabbed the sack and staggered over to a large wooden chest squatting on his roll top desk. Marcus heard the sound of coins cascading into it. The calm thereafter was broken as Garrow exclaimed.

"My dear Silas, I remember reading a very disturbing account in the Times-Picayune that reported that my father's ship, the Wanderlust was captured only because a certain Saxton clipper cut off its wind. I do believe that you were the Silver Ghost's skipper at the time. Right?"

He paused menacingly, looking like an adder ready to strike. He rose to his full height of six foot six, drink in hand pointing it at Silas. He hissed,

"You were her skipper at the time. Am I correct?"

Silas blanched. Garrow smiled, enjoying the Captain's discomfort immensely. He decided to turn the screws of guilt a bit more while twisting his fake waxed handle-bar moustache,

"My dear Silas, you a committed Confederate; let the Yankees kill my father, a true and stalwart champion of the South! How dare you!"

Garrow slapped Silas hard. Wilkins tried to rise but a large boot planted on his chest pinned him to the settee. A long steel marlin spike, hidden earlier under a cushion, lay there useless, just out of reach. Silas pleaded.

"For Christ's sake, the Conny was breathin' down my lazaret. It already fired enough ball and chain to disable your father's ship. In fact it signaled me to cut the Wanderlust's wind. My God Man! I had no choice!"

He slumped back on the settee as Garrow released him. Satisfied, but still suspicious, Horatio strolled over to the roll top desk, pulled out its hardwood chair and sat down with a thump. Clasping his hands together behind his head, he looked over at Wilkins.

"You're damn lucky I believe you Silas, because if you're lyin', I'll kill ya someday. He paused,

"By the way, I heard that John Saxton was aboard the Ghost. Who is he, this Saxton?"

He leaned back, sipped his whiskey and lit a cheroot waiting for an answer. Silas told him all he knew; leaving nothing out. Garrow stood up, savored his whiskey while looking down on a hapless Wilkins.

"Look me in the eye Silas. Tell me this Saxton boy won't give us any more trouble."

Silas could not. Captain Garrow grunted pointing his cheroot at Wilkins,

"I thought not sir. In the meantime, how about that 'Big Nigger', Marcus Brown that was the Ghost's First Mate"? I heard he's still workin' for Saxton Shipping?" Wilkins nodded weakly.

Garrow hovered over Wilkins like a mighty storm about to unleash its wrath. Wilkins shrank back when Horatio thundered.

"Is he aboard this ship?" Wilkins concurred.

"Good, for he'll never reach Boston alive. By the way, is he the nigger I saw sitting on a bollard as I came aboard?"

"Yes Captain that's him, seven feet tall and a face covered in scars."

"I saw him too and I must say he's a big bastard that one. Where's his cabin?"

"Why, right next door to mine..........My God, he's the only one I didn't hand pick.

Old man Saxton insisted he be aboard."

There was a long pause.

"Jesus H. Christ Wilkins! Got a pistol and a lantern?"

Marcus heard enough. He blew out a gimbaled lamp then moved like lightening to his clothes closet and stuffed his long frame inside it, shutting the plantation door behind him. He winced as hangers and clothes cascaded about him. The note from Belle was still lying on his bunk. He held his breath as two men entered his quarters, their lamplight flaring through the closet's wooden louvers. Garrow reached for the closet's brass handle. Marcus prepared himself to explode out of it, hopefully overcoming them. Just as the door was about to open, he heard Wilkins read Belle's note out loud.

"Well my friend, it seems that the nigger has a tryst tonight at nine."

He withdrew his fob watch from a vest pocket. He eyed it owlishly,

"My Hamilton here says ten past nine. He's gone, so our business is still our business and nobody else's, right?"

Horatio took the note, held up the lantern and looked at it. "Hummmm!"

It was handwriting he'd seen before. He held the note to his nose and in doing so, caught a faint essence of rosewater wafting upwards from within it. In vain, he tried to remember where he'd come across that scent. He shook his head saying,

"I have an uneasy feelin' about the whole thing Silas. Let's go back, conclude our affairs then deal with him later. By the way, I'm gettin' thirsty again. Is there any more Beam or Maker's Mark around? Christ, I need somethin' to cut through that god awful cotton dust?"

They strolled back to the Captain's cabin as Marcus uncoiled himself from within the closet, his derringer jammed into his groin. He laughed thinking how he might have shot himself by the simple act of breathing. In total darkness, Marcus returned to the vent. Within minutes, oddments of conversation that came to his ears sporadically through bouts of laughter and murmurings was enough to make him quite ill, enraged and resolute all at once. To Marcus, the nefarious "Operation False Prophet' had to be crushed at all costs, but how?

The Captain's quarters were rather palatial in comparison to that of Marcus Brown's. At least two hundred square feet in size; polished mahogany paneling covered all four walls of it. A rosewood double bunk sat upon a brass handled built-in dresser drawer. An oak roll top writing desk, large leather settee and a pull-out gumwood bar completed the décor. It was quite impressive. Gimbaled brass hurricane lamps lit the various framed ink prints of Saxton ships hanging on the walls with a lustrous light. Comfortably settled, both men lit Cuban cigars, freshened drinks in hand. They sat on a black leather settee looking down at a weapons manifest that Wilkins had received from Hans Larsen in Boston. It laid spread out on a large coffee table anchored on all four corners by shot glasses. A row of brass scuttles behind them were wide open, allowing lamplight through from two dockside lampposts. A light river breeze began ruffling the thick green curtains that covered them. It continued on, caressing the back of Garrow's neck. He looked back at the open portholes anxiously, demanding that they be closed but Wilkins disagreed.

"Look my friend, there are heavy curtains over them. No one outside can hear or see us. Besides, it gets mighty stuffy in here. I'm not going to choke to death just because you're paranoid. My God man! Look at you! You're a bundle of nerves to be sure! We'll just keep real quiet. OK?"

Both men resumed their close inspection of the ship's manifest with renewed interest. Horatio eyed Wilkins as he drank his bourbon, saying,

"This manifest and the correspondence that came with it, will help the South immensely! They'll pay you plenty in gold for these field pieces. It says here that this time, you've brought in:

A) Light artillery Pieces with caissons and firing accessories:
1. 7...... ten pound Parrot artillery pieces
2. 5......twenty pound Parrots,
3. 6.....twelve pound Napoleons
4. 10...Armstrong breechloaders.
5. 5.....Whitworth breechloaders
6. 20..3 inch Ordnance Rifles

Garrow paused then exclaimed, "My God, Wilkins, twenty Ordnance rifles! That's a coup indeed. I must say Silas that our Hans Larsen has been very busy."
He sat back impressed and watched as Silas went over the rest of the manifest, his voice at times incredulous at what he was reading. He said,

B) Ammunitions:
1. 30 crates of three inch Parrot shells
2. 20 crates of three inch Schenkl shells
3. 10 crates each of Reed and Amsterdam Shot
4. 5 crates each of twelve pound Blakely and Whitworth bolts
5. 20 crates each of four inch Hotchkiss and James shells.
6. 100 crates of three inch single and double case shot

Another section listed:

C) Miscellaneous:
1. 500 boxes of timed and percussion fuses
2. 10 crates of spare parts for powder mills in New Orleans, Nashville, Manchesterand Marshall, Texas.

D) Rifles/Small arms and their ammunition:
1. 1000....1855 Springfield muskets with 10,000 rounds of .60 caliber Minie Balls
2. 5000...1853 British Enfield rifle muskets with 50,000 rounds of .58 caliber
3. 150....Henry Carbines with 5000 rounds of .44 caliber brass cartridges
4. 50....56-56 Spencer Carbines with 5000 rounds of .52 caliber rim fire
5. 5....Crates of Blakeslee Cartridge boxes
6. 200...Burnside Carbines with 5000 rounds of .54 caliber cartridges
7. 500...Colt M1860s with 8" barrel and 10,000 rounds of .44 caliber cartridges
8. 300...Remington 1858 Army Revolvers and 15,000 rounds of .44 caliber

Garrow, satisfied that everything was in order said,

"Well done Silas. There must have been over eighty tons aboard. It's a miracle you didn't sink or blow up comin' down. Well I must say your timing couldn't have been any better, for everyone knows civil war is coming. However, I'm afraid that our next cargo from Boston will probably be our last until I figure out how to continue the operation after the war begins." He relaxed, sat back, drained his glass and exclaimed,

"Say, I have an absolutely delightful idea. Let's go out and find some ladies of easy virtue. I hear that a certain 'La Belle Maison' on Rue Conti is very accommodating to lonely and especially rich gentlemen these days."

Both men rose and put on their overcoats. Silas lifted the heavy chest containing the gold and put it inside his roll top desk. He locked both. After blowing out the cabin lamps, they left but not before Garrow put the manifests and their attendant papers into a long brown envelope. He tucked it under his left arm saying,

"Silas, I have to drop put this in my safe at home. My address is 1301 Rue Dauphin. I'll meet you there at ten tonight, OK? By the way Captain, just to reassure you, every cargo you unload is taken from the Saxton warehouse within hours of delivery to numerous secure storerooms scattered around the city. From there, the goods are sent to their various destinations within forty-eight hours. Nothing is left to chance and nothing is left to incriminate you or me for that matter. Now don't worry Silas, you and your cohort Larsen are worth your weight in gold, believe me."

After grabbing his coat and hat, Silas locked his stateroom door even though he still felt uneasy. As he climbed the companionway to the main deck, he called over two crew members and told them in no uncertain terms that no one other than himself was to enter his quarters. If anyone tried to, they were to detain them forcibly if need be. Wilkins was terse.

"Now guard both ends of the companionway and stay there until I return."

The burly sailors nodded. One, on his way to his post, picked up a belaying pin out of its pin rail.

As soon as he heard the two conspirators leave, Marcus ran to the Captain's stateroom. It was locked. However, unknown to Captain Wilkins, Thomas Saxton had given Marcus a spare key for such emergencies. Marcus entered the dimly lit room. He could barely see as he went over to the brass scuttles and drew back the curtains flooding the stateroom with the light. He knew that Silas kept important papers in his roll-top desk. He tried to lift its brass handle. It too was locked. No matter. Using his Bowie-knife, he jimmied open the roll top desk. Its crenellated wooden cover rolled back revealing the brass bound wooden chest. It too was padlocked.

'Jesus! Everything is locked.'

Frustrated, Marcus looked around the room for something, anything to pry open the lock. After searching the room high and low, he was about to give up, thinking out loud,

"There's nothing, absolutely nothing!" He paused then cried, "Wait a minute!"

A metallic gleam poking its way out from under a cushion tucked into a corner of a nearby settee caught his eye. Looking down, Marcus couldn't believe his luck. There, lying under a cushion was a steel marlin spike a foot long. He wondered,

'Yesiree, maybe Wilkins put it there if things had gone badly with that big fella?'

Who knew? Marcus went back to the chest. He inserted the marlin spike into the pad-lock's hasp then twisted it with all his might. With a loud SNICK, the padlock came apart. Marcus lifted the lid revealing thousands of gold Double Eagles basking in the glow of their own reflections. His large hands filled with coins. More money lay in front of him than he could make in a life time at sea. He thought,

'That traitor Wilkins and that Customs Captain are going to hang for this. I wonder what else they've been up to. Imagine! The Anaona's cargo is marked FARM MACHINERY when it's really contraband guns and ammo. No wonder it was never inspected. I've got to get into the warehouse and see for myself tonight before it's gone. Besides, how else can I prove Wilkin's collusion?'

Literally out of the blue an idea came to him. Taking his knife, he quickly incised double XXs into the soft faces of a dozen coins then mixed them back into the rest of the golden horde. Marcus hoped beyond hope that Silas would take them back to Boston and in so doing the double XX's would convict him at the very least of complicity. The only problem for Marcus was figuring out how to warn Saxton about Wilkins beforehand without anyone else knowing. That solution would have to wait. He had to jump ship and fast. Perhaps Belle would know what to do. He hoped so. With the chest closed and locked, he thought,

'I thank Enkai that it snapped shut cleanly.'

He closed the roll top desk using his knife to lock it up. He put the marlin spike back between the cushions and left the stateroom, locking it behind him.

Turning on his heel, he ran down the hallway as if chased by Simba himself. He stealth-ily approached the companionway. He climbed the stairs but tripped, falling onto the deck above with a loud crash. Marcus got up and staggered forward. Out of nowhere, a large man swinging a belaying pin rushed him. In one smooth fluid motion, Marcus raised his der-ringer. The man deftly knocked it out of his hand. The gun skittered across the deck into the scuppers. Momentarily stunned, Marcus drew his Bowie-knife. With a quick upward motion, he stabbed the man in the throat. The man screamed falling onto the deck. Marcus turned, smashing his left fist into the face of another sailor who appeared out of the shadows. The assailant went down, his head hitting a hatch coaming with a sickening thud. The Maasai leapt for the starboard bulwarks. Shots were fired. He felt hot lead whistling past his ears as he dived into the canal. Flocks of startled Laughing Gulls flew screeching away towards a paling horizon.

Down, down he sank, until his lungs were on the verge of bursting. With a tremendous effort he swam upwards under the stern of the Anaona as it rocked in the current. Strong undertows began pulling at him. A drifting log smashed into his head momentarily stunning him. Shouts and curses above him came seemingly from every quarter. They echoed with growing menace as his pursuer's lit torches. A yellow lifeboat splashed into the canal around him. One man yelled,

"We'll get 'Im boys. That black bastard is too big, too stupid and too slow to get away from us."

Marcus dog-paddled down the canal, keeping well within the shadows of ships moored beside the levee. If only he could get to Pirate Alley, he would be safe. Within minutes a large mob began patrolling the waterfront on either side of him. Holding their lanterns high, they shouted every time they saw something floating in the canal. More rowboats scoured the waterfront. A chorus of hate rose up all along the levee near him. A man screamed,

"The nigga raped and killed a white woman. He's round here somewhere!"

Something swam by Marcus in the dim light. Movement was visible all around him on the surface of the muddy waters. Rats, large brown rats, were swimming by him like lemmings heading for a cliff. By the dozens they rushed into some tall river reeds that lined the levee. He thought, 'Why were they swimming away and where were they going?' Marcus was about to find out. The air above him filled with harsh cries of human outrage. He decided to follow the rats into some thick reeds. After crawling part way up the levee, he saw it. A brick tunnel jutted out into the canal high up on the levee's muddy bank. Raw sewage spewed forth from it down beside him.

Marcus covered his face as the stench assaulted him. Physically sickened by the foulness around him, he staggered back down to the sanctuary of a thicket of river reeds. Hiding there, he sat down on a piece of driftwood, took off his leather shoes, tied the long leather laces together then placed the shoes behind the log.

It was fortunately a flood tide. Marcus crawled on his hands and knees back to the canal where upon he waded into the shallow water. He took off his overcoat and emptied its pockets, putting the contents in his trousers. A piece of driftwood lay nearby. He draped the sodden coat over it then slid the log up and over the muddy bank into the river. The momentum carried it out far enough to where the current carried it away from shore. Marcus returned to retrieve his shoes. He slung them over his shoulder. A few moments later, shots rang out. Someone cried,

"There's the black assed bastard! Get 'Im boys! Shoot to kill!"

Marcus parted the reeds, watching the log drift away. It began to jump about in the muddy water as bullets and buckshot pummeled it. Marcus smiled then retreated up a slimy embankment, foul with human excrement. Once again an indescribable stench assailed him. Marcus threw up. Upon regaining his senses, he hoisted himself up into the tunnel, not knowing where it went. He didn't care; he just wanted to survive.

Fighting total exhaustion, he crawled forward into near total darkness until occasional slivers of light from behind him disappeared altogether. After what seemed a lifetime,

Marcus heard an imperceptible pounding as he waded on his hands and knees further into the tunnel. He stopped. Faint thumping sounds were emanating from some infernal machine far ahead of him. There was no turning back. The Maasai continued to wade against a growing deluge of debris. Freshets of filthy water rushed forth past him at regular intervals. Filaments of light appeared, guiding him on like a lighthouse beckons a sailor lost at sea. They pulsated in time with the mysterious sound. After awhile, the roof of the tunnel rose up imperceptivity. Having floundered forward another hundred feet, Marcus stood up. He'd emerged into a gigantic brick sump.

Dancing light from street gaslights high above it streamed down through a circle of large iron grates inset into its flat roof. Twenty feet below that structure was a brick landing with a flat iron railing rising upwards alongside wet brick steps. The whole circular edifice was lined with squat brick buttresses designed to keep the massive structure from caving in on its self. A wide brick trough a few feet above the central cesspool gushed forth with raw sewage every few seconds. THUMP! WHUMP! The noise was deafening. Above this trough, wide metal paddle wheels swept sewage into it powered by a steam engine somewhere high above him.

Marcus staggered up a brick staircase until he reached a rusty iron door. He tried to turn its brass door handle but it was locked. Rat's eyes gleamed red in secret recesses. Desperation overcame him as he looked up at a circular walkway high above him. THUMP! WHUMP! The sound of the sump-pump was becoming catatonic. Methane gas rising from the cesspool below him made him light-headed. He vomited again. Barely able to stand upright, his only support was a rusted iron railing set into brick steps.

From somewhere deep within his conscious mind he heard loud voices coming from up above him. He moved quickly into the shadows afforded by a nearby buttress. Knife in hand, he held his breath and waited. An iron door above him opened with a crash. Two white men appeared in black overalls. One held a kerosene center lamp. Its harsh light illuminated the circular structure into which it had been thrust. The taller man held it up and peered into the gloomy confines of the sump. Satisfied that no one was lurking therein, he yelled angrily into the ear of the other man,

"George, what do you take me for, an idiot?" He pointed to the moving paddles.

"No one can get past those blades. The opening up there is just too narrow to crawl through. And besides, who in their right mind would ever crawl from the river through the outlet tunnel in this shit? It stinks to high heaven George. Besides, it's a dead end here anyway. Look man, that killin' nigga would never get out of here let alone leave here alive. You know what I mean."

He turned around and pointed upwards holding the lantern high above his bald head,

"And another thing George, those ventilation grates above us must be ten feet up. Even I can't reach 'em! The whole goddamn city is lookin' for him. Jesus man, I don't care what the Boss said! The lower door is locked tighter than a bull's ass in fly time. Let's go, I'm gettin' sick to my stomach from the fumes and deaf at the same time!"

The paddle wheel continued to turn relentlessly. The THUMP, WHUMP sound of its turning mated with a hissing and clanking noise emanating from somewhere behind the two men. Together they caromed about the brick walls like a hammer on stone. The iron door to the engine room slammed shut. Only then did Marcus come out of his hiding place. He looked up to where the men had been standing. He thought,

"I'm gettin' out of here while I'm still breathin' and can still hear! Perhaps the man was right."

He looked about him for a means of escape. Time was running out. Something caught his eye as shafts of light rippled across his scarred face. He looked up. Iron ventilation grates encircling the edifice above him beckoned. Alas, they all seemed so far out of his reach. Marcus concluded that perhaps, the mob had given up trying to find him. He turned and made his way back into the tunnel, his knife still clenched in his right hand.

While Marcus was running for his life, his paramour, Belle La Fontaine waited with growing impatience in the darker recesses of Pirate Alley. Her composure was, to say the least, not one of calm resignation. She realized that the very presence of a beautiful Creole woman wiling away her time in a venue of ill repute was fraught with danger. Belle once again, as she had innumerable times before, looked at her small Solis clip watch she'd extracted from the folds of a wide scarlet waist sash.

She turned the watch face this way and that to get a better look at the time. It was not to be. Voices of angry men mad with hate were heard running down the street towards her. Backing deeper into the blackness afforded by a small doorway, she literally stopped breathing as a white mob bearing torches and various weapons ran by her mere feet away. However her fear of being discovered dramatically increased as she felt someone or something move up from behind her. A male voice whispered,

"Don't worry none Miss. I won't give youse away."

Belle stiffened, her right hand gripping a derringer in her cloth purse. The voice continued.

"I'm just like youse Miss for I'm a hidin' out too. Best be scared I'd say for the whole town is a lookin' for the 'Big Nigger'. Seems he kilt a white whore down by the Saxton docks, he did. There's supposed to be a thousand dollar reward for his capture dead or alive."

Again Belle grimaced thinking that it had to be Marcus that they were searching for; it had to be. Her heart raced as her mind tried to come to terms with the news. She thought,

'Oh God, where is he? I'm sure he'll try to get to 'La Belle Maison' where he can hide out. But where will he appear?'

Behind her, the voice reappeared saying,

"The way, I figur' it, the only safe scape route for him would not be on 'Old Muddy' but on another one so to speak." Belle whispered.

"And where might that be?"

"There's a new sewer lyin' right below us. I should know, for I and hundreds of other poor devils like me built it. I hear tell that one can git here by tunnel from the canal. In fact Miss, see that street light right yonder; well right beneath it is a ring of man-hole covers lyin' directly over a sump-house. Perhaps he'll come up there."

Before Belle could say a word, a cold shadow passed by her into the street and vanished. Feelings of deep despair, counterpoised by hope, washed over her. She decided to wait. Whoever the mysterious stranger was, knew enough, that was obvious. So Belle remained; her black eyes glued to a ring of man-hole covers a few feet away.

Marcus's stomach churned as he slowly lowered himself into foul waters. Moving forward, he groped his way towards a stygian blackness until the sound of the sump-pump began to fade away behind him. Further and further he went, carried along by a current of hope. A smidgeon of light appeared ahead of him, flickering and dancing on the brick walls of the tunnel. Marcus stopped, tense, on edge. Eerie reverberations wafted back towards him. They were coming for him! He turned about in a panic. A shot was fired. Marcus rushed back, fighting each freshet as it surged towards him. The yelling behind him seemed to be getting louder. His breath came in sobbing gasps. More shots were fired, ricocheting off the curved walls around him. THUMP! WHUMP! For some unknown reason the sound became applause summoning him to freedom. He waded out of the tunnel onto a low parapet. His mind raced. Instinctively, he sheathed his knife. With his shoes slung around his neck, he rose to his full height and reached up to grab an iron stanchion above him. There was no other way up to the landing where the two men had stood only minutes before. Despite his best efforts, he could not reach it. Finally he took his shoes from around his neck. He held onto one and swung the other about his head. He let go.

"Yes! Yes!" he gasped. One had snagged on something! He grabbed a dangling shoe and pulled himself upwards with all his might. The thick leather laces held. Despite his exhaustion, he managed to get a leg over the high brick precipice. As he did so, he let go with one hand and grabbed an iron railing. Triumphantly, he climbed over it then lay breathless on the walkway totally spent.

THUMP! WHUMP! The staccato thud of the sump-pump kept on resonating within the brick silo. It seemed to grow in intensity as he lay there. He held both hands over his ears knowing without a doubt that he would go mad if he stayed any longer. The swish of the paddles was relentless. His mind raced back to the past as the resonance of it became legions of slavers beating him with their short clubs. The rhythmic crash boomed over the deck of the Wanderlust over and over as he was pulled forward, ever forward to the abyss. He rose up knowing that he couldn't go back. Voices fuelled by greed and propelled by hate were getting louder, even over the noise of the pump. The Maasai had to get out of the devil's workshop, but how?

He retrieved his shoes, got up, slung them over his shoulder and ran over to the door. Marcus pressed his ear to it. Muffled laughter mingled with the hiss and thrum of a steam engine came from the other side of the thick iron door. He tried to open it but was actually relieved that it was locked. Too tired to fight, Marcus slumped against it. Looking up, he noticed a faint light coming through the ring of iron grates above him. Jubilant, he climbed onto the railing. He balanced precariously. Using all his strength, he hooked his long fingers through a grate's lattice work then pushed it up and out of its iron collar. It ground loudly as it skid aside onto the cobbled street above him. After throwing his shoes upwards through the hole onto the street above, he reached up, grabbed the man-hole's iron collar and pulled himself partially up and out of his prison. The thump, whump sound of the pump diminished. Shots were fired from below. Something stung his right leg. Marcus winced as he made one last effort to escape. As he did so, the dusky scent of rosewater swept over him. No sooner was he out when he felt something hard poking into his shoulder. He froze. It seemed as if someone had a gun to his back. Turning about, Marcus looked up. Peering down at him was the angelic face of Miss Bellefonte La Fontaine.

Belle looked down at the foul smelling black man gasping for fresh air below her. Marcus reached towards her. She backed away saying coyly,

"One of the lost tribes of Israel I presume?"

Marcus stood up, brushed himself off, and shook his head. She stood there, her manicured hands on her slim hips. She hissed.

"You're late!"

"That's not funny Belle, not funny at all. I've been shot!"

He bent down, replacing the heavy grate with a loud CLANG! The noise echoed off the brick walls of that surrounded them. He picked up his shoes. Marcus was testy.

"I don't have time for niceties Belle; I'm hurt and I'm in big trouble. Captain Wilkins, my skipper and a Customs Officer are runnin' guns for the Confederates, we must....." Belle whispered, her voice emphatic, tinged with urgency.

"We don't have time to chat. As luck would have it, I live nearby. Let's get out of here because the whole damn city is looking for you. I hear there's a substantial reward on your thick head and I'm sorely tempted to collect it! My God, you stink to high heaven."

Two glowing gaslights on an iron lamppost bathed them in a pool of light. She stood before him in a revealing blue crinoline petticoat set off by deep blue satin drawers. The whole magnificence was crowned by a blue silk and taffeta feathered hat held in place by a long silver pin. Her feet were shod in matching blue silk slippers. Marcus smiled, looking down on her affectionately he said,

"I see you still hate wearin' shoes girl!"

The sound of harsh voices began ricocheting off the cobblestones of a street nearby. She grabbed his hand and pulled him into the shadows. After a few tense moments, Belle exclaimed,

"Quickly Marcus, I live four blocks away. We have to hurry."

They ran for their lives down Rue Chartres. Just in time, Belle opened a massive front door and dragged Marcus into the foyer, closing the door behind her. Her petticoat swished about while she put a solid iron bar across three iron brackets bolted into the door. It slipped into them with a metallic thud. Belle put her finger to his lips. In silence they waited. Before long many feet began pounding over the street outside. Shrill and strident voices were occasionally overpowered by the lower guttural shouts of ardent men looking for blood. Upon the drawn curtains of a nearby window, shadowy figures were silhouetted by flickering collages of light. The sounds of hate receded and the night became quiet once more. Marcus dropped his shoes on the floor, turned to Belle, tenderly drawing her to him. She backed away.

"Not now dear. I'm going to scrub you to an inch of your life. Undress here and then it's upstairs to the tub."

The next morning, a rising sun filled Belle's upstairs bedroom with dappling beams of diffused light. Her corner bedroom, large and well appointed, boasted cream crown molding bordered the high ceiling beneath which gilt mirrors covered the dark red walls along with oil paintings by black artists such as Robert Scott Duncanson and Joshua Johnson. Fashionable objects d'art, a hand carved Empire style French mahogany sofa and decorative nuances gave it a distinctly Parisian ambience. A pair of matching slipper chairs upholstered in chocolate chenille by John Belter fronted a bay window. On a Gerard Robinson cherry wood sideboard, sat a large, finely crafted Waterford porcelain wash basin with a matching jug full of clean water. An ornate soap dish, a thick Egyptian cotton towel and its matching hand towel were neatly arranged beside it. Across from the sideboard was a walnut four poster Chippendale canopy bed.

Marcus lay upon it partially obscured by a white mosquito net that bordered it. He parted the diaphanous veil to watch a naked Belle stride towards a tall, heavily inlaid Duncan Phyfe rosewood armoire. She stopped and turned to face Marcus, her hands on her slim hips. Her high, full breasts swayed slightly as she spoke,

"Oh mighty Maasai; impaler of many maidens, it's time to get up, once again!"

She looked down at him as he exposed himself saying,

"Oh mighty maiden, inhaler of many men, I salute you!"

Their laughter stopped. A child's voice could be heard on the other side of the locked bedroom door. Marcus looked inquisitively at Belle. She put a finger to her lips. Marcus pulled a cotton coverlet up to his chin, stacked two silk pillows behind his head then watched with amusement as Belle, in a growing sense of panic, tried to get into her green silk dressing gown and matching slippers all at the same time. She noticed Marcus grinning at her. She stuck her tongue out at him. Belle walked over to the door as a shrill voice on the other side of it began crying,

"Mommy! Mommmmmmy! Are you in there?" She cooed,

"Yes, dear I'm coming."

She unlocked the door. A small boy rushed into her arms followed by Mary McPherson who noticed Marcus lying under the bed's coverlet. Mary was nonplussed.

"I'm sorry Belle, but he's had his breakfast and we were wondering if you'd ever get up. Land sakes, it's ten already. I see you've got a skinny malinky longlegs with ye. I'll be back when lunch is ready. Come along Cotton, your momma is busy."

Belle closed her bedroom door. She turned around to face Marcus lying before her. Marcus looked up through the netting wondering aloud,

"Who was that little boy Belle? He's got your good looks and he's tall! Is he ours?"

Belle walked to the side of the bed, pulled back the netting and sat on the edge of the bed while taking his hands into hers. Her long black tresses fell down against his hairless chest. She bent down, her breasts pillowing upon it and kissed him. She looked deep into his coal black eyes.

"He's ours Marcus, all ours. He always will be my darling."

He held her close. Tears streamed down her face onto his. Marcus moved over as she lay beside him. She cried softly as he rocked her back and forth whispering,

"Oh, my precious Belle, you've waited all those years for me, all those lonely years!"

Marcus knew for the first time in a long time that he had a center to his universe. His moon was now circling her earth in perfect symmetry. They lay motionless for a long time. Finally Marcus got up, pulling the netting to a close behind him. He walked around to her side of the bed. Belle had fallen into a deep sleep. Carefully he covered her and pulled the netting shut. Marcus walked over to a Chippendale mahogany chest of drawers and opened it. He dressed silently in clothes he'd left behind years ago. Going back to the ship to get his working clothes was not an option. Belle had burned his soiled evening clothes in a hot kitchen stove shortly after he escaped from the mobs the night before.

Luckily, his leg wound proved to be just a scratch but the scar would remain forever as a reminder of just how close he'd come to dying. Besides he had to tell Belle more about what he'd heard aboard the Anaona. He had no one else to go to. He laughed thinking that Belle was probably the only person left in New Orleans that wasn't trying to kill him. He knew that getting back to the warehouse was impossible now. Maybe Belle could help him. He'd have to wait for the right moment.

Belle rolled over. From beneath the coverlet she devoured him with her eyes. She thought,

'God, what a beautiful man he is! There will never be another like him.'

A surge of moisture rose up from her loins. She snuggled even deeper into her soft world wondering how to introduce Marcus to Cotton. It had to be natural and loving. She knew Marcus cared about her immensely and loved her unconditionally. Every other man who professed love for her was conditional, power seeking, controlling and lustful. Oh how different Marcus was; how much more of a man he was compared to all the other men in her life. She giggled aloud. Marcus turned at the sound behind him.

"What's so funny Belle? Got the giggles have you. Well giggle away girl because it won't be the last time."

Marcus parted the netting and was upon her with only the coverlet between them. He started to tickle her unmercifully. She screamed, twisting, trying to hide under it. A door behind them flew open with a bang. The netting swished aside behind Marcus. He felt a small body slam down on top of him. It bawled,

"Leave my mommy alone! Leave my mommy alone!"

Tiny fists beat down upon him in a rain of rage. Marcus turned over pinning his assailant to the bed. Cotton struggled then bit Marcus on the hand. Marcus let go with a yelp. He jumped off the bed in shock becoming caught in the mosquito netting. With a crash Marcus fell to the floor, the torn netting draped upon him. Belle grabbed her squirming son and hushed him before he could do any more damage. She looked at Marcus trying to untangle himself while sucking blood from the wound. Belle laughed,

"Well I see that the lion's cub has teeth too, oh mighty Simba!"

Again she laughed as her son continued to attack him. Marcus now unfettered, looked down bewildered upon the boy. Before long a wide grin crossed his scarred face, his teeth shining like the pillars of the Acropolis. Belle sat up, her son squirming in her lap.

"Oh Marcus, this is your son Marcus Junior or Cotton."

Marcus bent down and gingerly put his hand over his son's head. He looked into his son's defiant brown eyes. They glared up at him. Marcus laughed, reached out for the boy who cried out as he hung onto his mother. Belle kissed the boy and nodded at Marcus. He lifted Cotton high up over his head then lowered him down gently as the boy touched his scarred face in wonder. They both looked at Belle naked beside them. She rose up to put her long arms around them.

BOOK ONE: CHAPTER 5
FALSE PROPHET

Silas Wilkins arrived at Captain Garrow's house exactly at ten. From there, they proceeded on foot west along Rue Decatur towards La Belle Maison. An unruly group of men rushed past them in the night carrying torches. Garrow grabbed one of them by the collar and spun him around effortlessly. The man gasped as he looked up into the reptilian eyes of the taller man. Garrow tightened his grip. The man sputtered; his eyes bulging out in panic. More men swept past them under the flickering gas lamps lining the brick street. Horatio swore.

"Goddamn it, what's going on man? Tell me or I'll throttle you here and now!" He nodded.

Garrow released him. The man staggered backwards, clutching his throat. He cried,

"The whole town is searching for a giant nigger who raped and killed a white woman down by Saxton's warehouse. There's a reward of a thousand dollars in gold to the first man that captures him."

With that said, he ran into the night followed by even more men. Horatio looked at a visibly shaken Wilkins, who croaked,

"Do you…? Do you think it's Marcus and if so, did he hear us in my cabin? My God, there were guards posted at either end of the companion way. Perhaps there was a misunderstanding, a struggle, a murder misinterpreted. I'm must go back to see if my gold is missing." Garrow was not amused.

"You're daft Wilkins to even contemplate such a series of events. Besides, who in their right mind would confuse a seven foot nigger with a white whore? You said yourself the he had left on a date. There was no one in his cabin; no one at all even before you posted the guards. Come on Wilkins, willing women await us for Christ's sake!"

Silas would not listen to reason. Panic gripped his mind as he fled into the night with Garrow close behind him. Both men ran through angry crowds. Never before had they seen such a lynch mob. They arrived breathless before the iron gates fronting the Saxton warehouse. There, a massive throng surged forward, more curious than anything else. Horatio hung back. Police officers wearing small yellow crescent badges on their black sleeves formed a human barricade in front of the gates. Behind it, the Anaona's Bosun, Sam Hillard ran up and spoke to a Police Sergeant. A few moments later, the beefy Sergeant approached Captain Wilkins. He said brusquely,

"Are you Captain Wilkins of the SS Anaona?"

Wilkins nodded. The gates opened. The Sergeant continued, grasping Wilkins' sleeve.

"I'm Sergeant Raines. Come with me Captain, I'll escort you aboard."

Garrow scowled as he watched the three men walk away through a deserted warehouse to the Anaona. He turned about and shouldered his way through the mob. Behind him, Wilkins walked up the Anaona's gangplank. Aboard ship, the scene was chaotic as Policemen were poking and prodding the vessel from stem to stern. On the main deck, the ship's crew huddled by the aft cabin. They looked pathetic. It was nearly midnight. A stiff breeze was sighing in the rigging. Far off in the night, a steam whistle blew. As Wilkins walked towards his cabin, he came across a sailor lying dead, a belaying pin next to his body. Silas blanched. Stepping carefully around the body, the Captain descended the companionway down into a short hallway. As Silas made his way to his stateroom, bile rose in his throat. When he reached his stateroom it was locked. Despite the dim light, he retrieved a key and unlocked the door. As he stepped forward, his heart began to beat like a piston in his chest. Light coming in through the portholes was just enough for him to see that the roll top desk was still shut. Silas yanked at its handle. It too was locked. While imagining Marcus trying to hide within it, he burst into hysterics. His reverie was shattered as Sergeant Raines knocked on the cabin door, a stove-pipe hat in hand. Silas asked,

"Where did you find that hat Sergeant?"

"It was lying on the bunk next door. Who's cabin is that by the way?" Silas blanched.

"My First Mate bunks there, Sergeant. He told me he was going out."

Silas remembered that the bunk had been bare except for the note. He was sure now that Marcus had overheard their conversation and escaped. He began to worry. The Sergeant sensed it,

"Is anything wrong?" He paused. Silas lied, realizing that the scuttle curtains had been pulled wide apart.

"No Sergeant, nothing at all." However, Raines continued, well aware that the Captain was lying. He said,

"Captain, I need a detailed description of your First Mate. I believe his name is Marcus Brown. Am I correct? Are you sure everything is alright?"

"Yes Sergeant, his name is Marcus Brown and no, there's nothing wrong here. Thank you. Nothing's amiss. Please leave me be. I'll write out what you want right away then meet you on the main deck in a few minutes. After that I will be very busy for the rest of the night. I do hope they catch that black bastard. Imagine, killing a white woman. What's the world coming to?" With that said he lit two cabin lamps then walked over and closed the porthole curtains.

Raines left the Captain to his thoughts. As soon as the Sergeant had left, Silas found a key to the roll-top desk and opened it. With relief he saw the chest was there and still padlocked. In his elation he didn't notice that its brass lock was already sprung. He retrieved a key from his breast pocket then put it into the lock. Twisting it viciously, the lock opened. Wilkins pulled up the lid of the chest. There in all its glory was the gold. He drove his stubby fingers into the coins, laughing hysterically as they cascaded back into the chest. Happily, he locked it and pocketed the key in his breast pocket. Pulling out a chair from under the desk, he sat down to write a short description of his First Mate. Finished, he rose up; put the note in a breast pocket, locked the desk, put on his black sea cap and a pair of black Moroccan kid gloves. Satisfied, he took one final look about then walked out. His cabin door swung about with a crash as the ship slowly listed to port. He turned and locked it.

Wilkins looked up the companionway, paused then entered the cabin next door. Other than the hat lying on the bunk, everything appeared normal until he opened the closet door. Inside was a shambles. Clothes had been flung off their wooden hangers and lay scattered about. Wilkins knew then that the Maasai had overheard them and was hiding there when Garrow and he entered the room. Wilkins looked up. A ventilation grate nestled high up on a wall separating his cabin from the Maasai's. He reached up and estimated that the vent was indeed low enough for Marcus to hear something. Wilkins was sure now. He ran out of the cabin to the companionway and strode out onto the main deck knowing he had to inform Garrow and soon.

Regaining his senses, he looked about. Fingers of torch light tangoed around him. Two black deck cranes highlighted by woven metal ribbing seemed about to pounce upon him like a Praying Mantis. Inwardly, his whole being was in chaos. His crew stood here and there waiting for his orders. The Sergeant instructed two of his men to move the corpse. They laid it out on No#1 hatch and covered it with a black canvas tarp.

Sergeant Raines saw the Captain talking to the Bosun. He walked over to them. The Bosun stood to one side avoiding the Sergeant's piercing blue eyes. Wilkins gave the Raines the detailed description of Marcus. He took the note and looked at it as his aide held a lamp over his head. Once finished, he looked down at Silas, his voice calm, controlled.

"Looks fine to me Captain, however, I'll have to get a sketch artist to interview you later for a reward poster."

Silas interrupted him saying,

"Jesus Sergeant, the 'Big Nigger' has wavy scars all over his cheeks and he's damned near seven feet tall! Isn't that enough?" Raines was curt,

"I see. Perhaps you're right Captain. By the way, I hear Mayor Monroe over at Gallier Hall issued a reward of one thousand dollars on behalf of the Customs House. I wonder why as the suspect is only a nigger, nothing more, nothing less? No, Captain there must be something else going on. No black is worth a thousand dollars. Was he a freeman?"

"Yes, Sergeant he was." Raines stroked his goatee thoughtfully. After a few moments pregnant with suspicion, he declared in a forthright manner,

"I have a few more questions for you Captain. I hope you don't mind. Please follow me."

Silas nodded reluctantly. He followed the Sergeant over to the body. Raines lifted a corner of the tarp revealing the waxen face of a crewman beneath it. He turned back while his aide took notes on a small pad. Sergeant Raines looked at Silas. This time he noticed that the Captain, like his Bosun before him was sweating profusely. Perhaps they both were hiding something. Still holding the tarp, the Sergeant looked down at the corpse saying,

"Who was he Captain and why was his body in front of the aft house door? Was he guarding something of value Captain?"

Silas nodded affirmatively telling him the man's name and his duties. Wilkins then explained that a large quantity of gold was on board for wages and other expenses. However nothing had been taken. Sergeant Raines dropped the tarp. He scratched his goatee again while he motioned for his aide to come closer. They whispered to each other much to Wilkins' annoyance. The Sergeant turned back to Silas as his aide wrote furiously on a yellow pad of paper while licking his pencil from time to time. Raines took something out of his pocket. It was a five shot Philly Derringer. He smelled the end of its stubby barrel.

"Now skipper, whose gun is this? It was found near the port side scuppers. It's still fully loaded. Well?"

Silas was given the pistol. He turned it over. On the end of it, the letters MB were inscribed on its silver butt plate. He replied.

"Sergeant, I'm sure this pistol belongs to Marcus Brown. His initials are on its butt plate."

"Captain, are there any other members of your crew with the initials MB."

"No, Sir."

Wilkins handed the derringer back, hoping that there would be no more questions but there were would be a lot more. The Sergeant continued after reading another report just handed to him by a departmental courier.

"Captain Wilkins, there is something not quite right here. This message I've just received, indicates a possible contradiction to the fact that your First Mate supposedly raped and killed a white whore near here. However, as I've been told by the guard, the gates to Saxton Shipping are locked after ten at night. To get out or back in, your crewmen apparently need a pass signed by you. Is that correct?" Silas nodded. Sergeant Raines became abrasive.

"Two guards are at the Saxton gatehouse twenty-four hours a day and they saw no one matching Brown's description. Why is that Sir?" He paused, eyeing Silas suspiciously.

"Secondly, no white whore or white woman for that matter has been brought to the Charity Hospital morgue tonight. Don't you find that odd Captain?"

Wilkins shifted his weight, looking down at the deck. Raines continued on, relentless.

"Thirdly, the dead man laid out beside us was either killed by someone else or by your First Mate.

So, this has left just the dead man and three others on dog watch during that time."

He turned and motioned another police officer to bring three crewmen forward. They straggled over unsmiling. Raines looked at them for a few moments then called the tallest one over. The man squirmed under the Sergeant's unflinching stare, his hands clasped behind his back. Clotted blood ran from behind his right ear while his left eye was swollen and black. The Sergeant held the young man's chin up then slowly turned his head from side to side.

"Looks like you've had some trouble son. Care to tell me about it?"

Wilkins' deck-hand related how his mate had been assigned guard duty after the skipper and his guest left the skipper's cabin. A few minutes later, he'd seen the nigger stab the dead man in the throat. He tried to stop him but was beaten up for his effort. The deck-hand tenderly touched the top of his head explaining that he'd been knocked out when he fell hitting his head on the corner of a nearby hatch cover. The young man pointed at some blood stains behind him saying that he remembered nothing until someone threw a bucket of water in his face. The man stepped back and the other two, the Bosun and the ship's carpenter were questioned with no positive results. They were told to stay on board for now. They returned to their duties. The Sergeant told Wilkins to continue loading. The Captain gave the order. Immediately dozens of black stevedores who had been standing idle on the wharf, swarmed aboard. In rapid succession, sling after sling of heavy coal sacks were lifted high above them. The ship's steam cranes hissed and squealed as tons of anthracite was maneuvered and stacked down into hold #2.

The clattering increased. Sergeant Raines motioned for Silas and his aide to follow him ashore. Down the gang-plank they went then away some distance from the long line of coal drays. Satisfied, the Sergeant stopped. He motioned Silas forward.

"Well Captain, just a few more questions and I'll be finished." He looked at Silas.

"Where were you when the deck-hand was killed? It seems that it happened at eight bells according to many witnesses. Where were you Captain?"

Silas had to be careful. He thought, 'This man is very smart and therefore very dangerous.' Silas became indignant. He rose to his full height.

"Well Sir, I've taken just about enough! Check with the guard at the gate. I left here at nine-thirty, well after eight bells!" He started to walk away saying curtly over his shoulder,

"I have far more important things to do aboard right now than stand here being harassed by you Sir!"

Sergeant Raines moved forward, grabbed him and spun Wilkins about before he could say another word. He hissed,

"Oh my, the Irish do have a temper don't they? Perhaps a murderous one at that! Now tell me Captain who was your guest? You know, just for the record."

Silas tore the Sergeant's hand from his shoulder, yelling, "Go to Hell!"

He turned and ran back to his ship. Raines watched him disappear through a gathering mist. The aide remarked,

"Well Sarge, do you want me to get him back here in cuffs or not?" Raines laughed,

"No Watkins, I'll let him stew awhile. He's lying because he's scared of something or someone. Whoever it is, it's not us.

"Who do you think it is?"

"Watkins me lad, who in this town besides me would ye be most afraid of." His aide without hesitation said,

"The Deacon gang of course, Sir."

"Watkins you're right as rain."

"Who's their leader Sarge?"

"I don't know Watkins. I've tried for years to find out but no luck." He looked towards the canal in rueful contemplation. His aide murmured,

"Well, I hope we find Brown before someone else does."

They turned as one, as the roar of a frenzied mob strung out along the levee assaulted them. Shots were fired. Raines grabbed his aide. He cried,

"Come on Watkins, if it sounds like trouble, smells like trouble, you can be damned sure it IS trouble!"

Both men shouldered their way through the mob milling about in front of the Saxton gatehouse. More shots were fired. Once through the gate, they ran towards the levee.

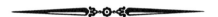

Upon his return to Boston from New Orleans, Captain Wilkins had grim news. He avoided young Saxton at the warehouse office by taking a company Phaeton directly to the Saxton House. Packard ushered him into the parlor. Muriel and Thomas entered a few minutes later. Both sat down across from a clearly distressed man. Muriel sent Packard away to get refreshments. Captain Wilkins, a squat little Irishman, appeared to be clearly unsettled about something. After a period of hesitation, he explained that Marcus was missing on shore leave while the Anaona had been waiting to clear customs in New Orleans. He turned his gold braided sea cap in his hands like a rosary, seeking solace but not finding it. He continued,

"Sir, a courier delivered a letter in Marcus's handwriting, telling me that he was through going to sea and that he was sorry for jumping ship."

Thomas asked to see the note. Silas wrung his cap again, "Ay! Tis a pity but it was lost at sea in a pea jacket I had carelessly left draped over a taff'rail."

Of course no one believed Marcus would forsake the family. The whole story about a strange note only increased their fears that something horrible happened to him. Captain Wilkins, cap in hand rose and stood before them. Muriel cradled Jack in her lap as Wilkins explained further,

"Mr. Saxton, I organized the crew into pairs. I sent them out into the streets and alleys to find him. But, I'm sorry to say, nary a lad come back with any news a' tall. I ask you Sir, how hard is it to hide a seven foot black with scars all over his face!" He paused for a moment then gushed,

"We inquired if the jail had I'm, but no they did not.

We searched the train stations. Nothing.

We went to every black church in the French quarter but no luck.

We inquired at the Charity Hospital, its morgue and again nothing was amiss.

We searched every dive, gin bar, music hall and whore house......"

He looked at Muriel, and blushed.

"Beggin' your pardon madam". She nodded grimly. He continued morose, agitated, full of emotion,

"We searched high and low nigh on twenty-four hours straight we did with no luck until we had to leave port. I must say, we were probably the last Yankee ship to exit New Orleans safely. The recent talk of succession from the Union is strong there and growing by the day. Some ships were even stormed by mobs and burned at anchor."

The Captain asked if he could sit down again. As he did, Muriel spoke gently, trying to sooth his frayed nerves.

"Now my dear Silas don't fret, for I'm sure Marcus had a very good reason for leaving his ship. Both Thomas and I really appreciate yours and the crew's efforts to find him. You know he's like a son to us. You all did everything humanly possible. We thank you. Please relay our gratitude to the crew."

She looked at her husband who apparently had made up his mind about something.

"And by the way Captain, tell Martin Smith he's your First Mate until such time that we get this matter straightened out." Silas nodded stiffly.

Thomas waited patiently, his face grim because he knew that they had to tell Saxton that his best friend was missing. He sensed that Captain Wilkins wanted to leave. They stood up. Thomas placed a hand on his shoulder.

"Silas, my wife is right. We both thank you and the crew. Now Silas, when the Anaona is unloaded, I want all of your crew to take a week off with pay. There's another shipment of farm machinery destined for Charleston, coming in by train ten days hence. I know it's risky, what with the southern states in a rebellious mood, but who really knows what will happen. As I said before in the panic of 57'; all it would take to cure it would be a good war. Sad but true isn't it."

"What's sad but true father?"

Saxton unbeknownst to them heard the very last of their intense conversation. Jack remained where he was wagging his stubby tail furiously. As the young man approached, his mother rose to greet him. She kissed him. His father clapped him on the back. Captain Wilkins shook his hand. After everyone was once again seated, young Saxton looked across the room at his parents,

"What's sad father?

What's going on?

Is it bad news?

What?"

Saxton sensed that something was terribly wrong for his father was leaning forward, his hands gripping the arms of his chair. Saxton's attention was momentarily diverted as Muriel brought her hand to her mouth unsmiling. She said gravely,

"I'm afraid my dear Sax, that Marcus disappeared in New Orleans and no one could find him anywhere."

Saxton asked the Captain what happened. Poor Silas had to relive the search for Marcus all over again. After a few minutes of interrogation, the Captain appeared to become physically sick and begged to be excused. He fled. Moments later, the wheels of the Phaeton could be heard grating on the pea gravel driveway as he left the estate. Saxton got up and walked over to the heavy drapes that fronted the parlor. He drew them further apart. In doing so he noticed the Captain was not going to the harbor but rather in the opposite direction. He wondered why.

So it was that John Saxton heard about the note from Marcus and why it had 'conveniently' disappeared overboard. Although Irish, Captain Wilkins had faithfully served the Saxton family for many years, Saxton was beginning to wonder if the current opinion about the large Irish population in Boston was true. Many old Boston families here adhered to the 'know nothing' movement. They considered the flood of Irish immigrants escaping a potato famine as, 'unintelligent, disloyal and dangerous bog hoppers' as quoted in one of the editorials in the Boston Post. Saxton turned and pulled the nearby service cord twice. Packard appeared. John Saxton said lightly,

"Well bad news is always more palatable on a full stomach. Let's have lunch shall we! I'm starved."

John Saxton approached his father in his study after lunch telling him that he suspected Captain Wilkins was involved with Marcus's disappearance. At first his father refused to believe him but was willing to let Saxton carry out his investigations in his own way. Both men agreed to make discreet inquiries wherever they could. Saxton left immediately for the harbor. Thomas rose from his chair and locked his office door. He walked over to a portrait of his wife and pulled the hinged painting away from the wall. Behind it a Chubb safe contained many interesting items, one of which was a recent telegram from Washington DC. Thomas Saxton had received it two weeks earlier in code. Young Saxton didn't know the half of it for Thomas had been of service for two Presidents. His contact was the famous Chicago detective, Alan Pinkerton or 'Pinky' as his intimate friends called him. Thomas knew Wilkins was lying and that Marcus was in hiding. He had a telegram to prove it.

"Marcus Brown of the SS Anaona in hiding
STOP N. Orleans police want him for murder
STOP Do not interfere with False Prophet
STOP Next shipment on time STOP Pinky"

Thomas realized that the time had come for his son to see the telegram. It was a matter of necessity. 'Operation False Prophet' was nearing fruition. All the players were accounted for but one. Thomas realized that the 'family tradition' of serving the nation on a clandestine basis had to continue at least for another generation. Anything could happen. War was on the horizon and the enemies of the Union were very busy preparing for it. Thomas had a bad heart. Doctor Wilson, Muriel and Allan Pinkerton knew about it. No one else did, not even his son John Saxton. Late that afternoon Saxton was ushered into the presence of his father by Packard. As the office door closed, Thomas walked over to the bar and offered his son a drink. He accepted. His father lit a cigar. Saxton settled into a comfortable chair, drink in hand. Thomas retrieved Pinkerton's telegram and gave it to his son. It was undated. Saxton read it. He had only one question.

"Tell me father, how long have you known that Marcus was safe and in hiding?"

Thomas rolled a whiskey glass between his rough hands, as if coming to some terrible decision. He looked at his son straight faced and lied.

"Why son, I just received it today from Allan Pinkerton."

"Pinkerton, father? Why he runs a detective agency in Chicago. What does he have to do with you and this so called operation 'False Prophet'? More's the point father, is what's not said in the telegram. I have a feeling you're involved in this whole matter and have been for some time."

John Saxton jumped out of his chair and angrily accused his father of abusing his trust, saying,

"Father, please tell me what you know. I promise that whatever you say will stay private between us. Obviously Marcus is in danger because of what he possibly stumbled upon down in New Orleans. He's in hiding there and needs our help. Are you and Allan Pinkerton connected in some other way father? I've heard tell that the Pinkerton Agency often works as a private investigator for the railways and the office of the President occasionally. Is it poss...?"

Thomas rose and motioned for his son to sit down as it had become quite apparent to Thomas that his son's questions would be left unanswered for now. He put his cigar in a nearby ashtray, turned and said evenly,

"Look Sax, what you say is true to a point but there are some things that I cannot reveal to you at this time for your own protection and peace of mind. However, I have left a packet in my safe that will explain everything to you in the event of my demise. Your mother has the combination. Trust me son for I'm just as worried about Marcus as you. However, for his safety and yours, I cannot reveal what 'Operation False Prophet' is at this time. I do however want you to conduct your own investigations on Marcus's disappearance and find out why he's on the run. If you do find out, keep me informed. Do not mention 'False Prophet' to anyone but me. Why? It's for reasons I'd rather not divulge right now. So my son, search for the why of it and keep me posted." Saxton started to protest.

"Father, I'll abide by your wishes for it seems to me that there is a far bigger picture here than I know about. I love you father and trust you. Thank you for your confidence. I'll take my leave now with your permission Sir." Thomas nodded.

Saxton shook his father's hand and left the room, closing the door behind him. Thomas sighed as he reached for the telegram. He placed it in the large ashtray on his desk, picked up his discarded cigar and sucked on it. Its round tip glowed brightly as he held it under a corner of the paper flimsy. Within seconds it became a meaningless blot in an ashtray. Thomas closed the wall safe and left his office, locking the door behind him.

Thereafter, Saxton would leave the mansion on the hill every morning and over the next nine days he interviewed every crew member who was on leave. All of them seemed evasive. It was very strange. Something didn't seem quite right. Meanwhile, Thomas keeping up his charade confided in his best friend Donald McKay to keep a weather eye open for any shred of news. He also asked his colleagues in the shipping business to keep their ears close to the taff'rail as well.

One evening after Muriel retired for the night, a black boy arrived at the mansion with a note in hand. Packard formally delivered it on the usual silver salver to where father and son sat in the Grand Salon. Thomas unfolded the one page note. It was a mysterious message from Marcus. He read it slowly, shook his head then handed the note to his son, who exclaimed,

"Father, it is from Marcus to be sure. I'd know that handwriting anywhere. It's dated two days after he disappeared in New Orleans. How did it get here? Look at the bottom of the letter, those are blood stains, I'm sure of it."

Thomas moved a coal-oil lamp closer to the letter and confirmed his son's observation. It was certainly unlike anything he'd ever seen before; for capital and lower case letters were seemingly printed in random order, arranged in twelve columns vertically and twelve columns horizontally. Near the center of one side was a crude drawing of the Saxton Maasai shield, chevrons and all. Both were perplexed about what the message contained. Saxton exclaimed,

"Father, Marcus knew this message might be read by someone he did not trust, or by someone who definitely would try to kill him if they found it. Also, the condition of the paper is a clue. It looks expensive. It also looks like it has been handled by many people along its journey. But as you can see, there are no cuts on it or pieces missing from it. There was no envelope for it and it was hand delivered to us specifically and not to Larsen. Why? Didn't Packard see the messenger? Let's get him in here. I know it's late but we have to do it. Please ring him now."

Thomas got up and pulled a nearby service cord. As he did, Saxton walked over to an alcove. He reached in and pulled downwards on the wooden handle of a gas igniter. The room lit up even more so as another row of gas jets sputtered then caught fire. Both men sat down just as the French doors opened. A sleepy Packard in a black silk nightgown entered the room. Thomas motioned the curious butler where to sit then rose and walked to the crackling fire place. He put a hand on the wood mantle below the spear and shield. Lovingly, he reached up and touched the spear, reading its inscription. He turned, casting himself into a halo of gas light. He paraphrased,

"Gentlemen, the sailor has returned from the sea but I'm afraid that Marcus is being hunted in the hills wherever he is. May God protect him."

Thomas sat down and leaned towards his butler.

"Dear Packard you've worked for our family since you were a boy and not once has a cross word ever passed between us or was there a trust ever broken, am I correct?"

"Yes Sir and I appreciate that comment but how can I be of service?"

Thomas pondered for a moment then leaned even closer as did Saxton. He continued carefully, fully aware of the significance of what he was about to ask of his long time man servant. He looked into Packard's coal black eyes.

"Packard, is there any possibility you knew who delivered the note tonight, any possibility at all?"

"Why Sir, the messenger was a young black boy whom I've never seen before now."

"Can you describe him? Was there anything unusual about the boy at all, anything that might help us?"

"Why, I do declare that the boy was about ten years old and dressed proper like. Good clothes and leather shoes. Maybe he worked for some rich white folk in town."

He paused and wrung his hands as if something else was bothering him. He cleared his throat.

"Yes I do remember something else rather odd about the boy. He had the nerve to ask me for money, in fact he asked for a quarter. Needless to say I was hesitant to give him a days wage but I did so with some reservations."

Thomas reached into his pocket, took out two quarters and gave them to Packard saying,

"Packard, here are two quarters for you. I've given you another just in case the young scamp appears again."

They all laughed and Packard was given permission to retire which he did with obvious relief. Saxton turned to his father.

"Well father, how generous of you. However, it is rather late. You'll need a good nights sleep to say the least. I'm afraid this business will be more of a challenge than we ever imagined. I hope not but we'll see."

Saxton reached over, took the note and carefully looked at it again. As he did so, his father rose, saying,

"Well Muriel awaits and I do feel exhausted. I'll see you in the morning son but don't stay up too late."

He paused to affectionately clap his son's back.

"I know how much Marcus means to you and we both know that the best way to help him is to decipher that infernal code he sent us. We know he's safe so the note is probably about why he's hiding." Saxton agreed. His father paused by the door, his hand on the door knob.

"Staying behind are you?"

"Yes Father, the ills of youth are upon me and one of them is impatience and another is curiosity. See you in the morning. I'm going to your office where I can use your library if necessary. I'll let you know if anything turns up."

Thomas nodded, turned about and strode through the French doors on his way upstairs to Muriel.

Saxton sighed. Ever since he returned home, he never really recovered from the incident with the Wanderlust. The Connie II had taken the slavers aboard then blasted the slave ship out of the water. In effect, the evidence of their crime was deep-sixed once and for all. Later, Saxton learned from the Shipping News, that because of bad weather, the Connie II sailed to Charleston, South Carolina. Thereafter for some strange reason, the slavers were incarcerated in the city jail. Did this incident have something to do with Marcus? Perplexed, Saxton picked up the note, extinguished the gaslights of the Grand Salon, and left for his father's office down the hall.

Before long he was hard at work, a glass of whiskey his only comfort. Trying to understand what Marcus trying to tell him was important, very important. Marcus was safe somewhere, probably either in New Orleans itself or near it. It was obvious he'd had time to get pen, and paper together and compose a code. Saxton reasoned that Marcus would use a code they both were familiar with. No semaphore, no foreign language was going to give him the answer. He pulled an Aladdin lantern closer and studied the parchment once again. At first he didn't see it, but then he noticed the spear pointing to the right. The shield was dead center at the top of the page where north is at the top. Saxton orientated the note so that the shield was at the top, thinking,

"Ok, so far so good, what next?"

Saxton began to wonder aloud about the messenger.

"Why did he want just a quarter? Why wouldn't he take anything but a quarter? Poor Packard must have been fit to be tied. Imagine a days pay for a note."

Again Saxton's thoughts turned back to the task at hand, namely,

'Why a quarter?'

He dug into his pocket and found one. He inspected both sides of it with a magnifying glass but could find nothing that would help him. Exasperated, he put the quarter back on his father's desk. Saxton leaned back in his swivel chair thinking about the code. Abruptly he sat forward. He cried,

"The note's in Morse code. The capital letters are dashes. The small letters are dots and the letter 'A' sequentially through 'Z' separates each word."

Eagerly Saxton started translating the code from left to right but after the sixth row across, the code turned into gibberish. Now what? Again he looked at the note trying to decipher it at all angles. Once again he ran into difficulties after the sixth column no matter how he arranged the note. Frustrated, he looked up as a Chauncey Jerome wall clock chimed twice. He was astonished. It was two o'clock in the morning.

Bending to the task at hand, Saxton's agile mind began to pick up speed. Again the mystery of the quarter tantalized him. He knew that everything he needed was in front of him but what and where? The code was in Morse but its orientation was still a mystery. The key was the silver quarter and Saxton knew it. After a long pause he reasoned that a quarter was a quarter because it was a quarter of a dollar. The creased note lay in front of him. Suddenly he saw proverbial trees despite the forest. He cried, "Yes! That's it!"

The note was creased into quarter sections. He hadn't really paid attention to the creases before now. Reaching into his father's writing desk, Saxton took out a pair of scissors. But, before he cut the note into four pieces, he numbered the four sections of the note. Carefully he cut along the creases of the note. He arranged the four pieces by number, four, two, three and one from left to right. It still didn't work. For the next two hours he fiddled with the four squares. Some worked upside down, others not. With four squares, in various rotations, there were hundreds of possible combinations. Exasperated he stopped. Finally, he started noting down all the combinations. An hour later he had a note that was twenty-four columns wide and six deep.

Within minutes, Saxton deciphered the note. He was astonished as to what it revealed. It read,

"SWCREWRGUNRUNNERSEAGLESXXANAONA"

Carefully, Saxton laid the severed sections out on the desk top. He thought,

"Was this what my father had alluded to? Was it 'False Prophet? I cannot believe it! Captain Wilkins and his whole crew are spies for the Confederacy."

He now suspected that all the crates stenciled FARM MACHINERY, packed into warehouse No#3 probably contained light artillery and their attendant ammunition. Unknowingly, he had stumbled upon 'False Prophet', or part of it. The other half unbeknownst to him was being worked out by Pinkerton in the White House. Pinkerton however had only half of the information he needed. Saxton unknowingly held the other half in his hand. He could only guess what his father really knew about the entire operation. He prayed that his father wasn't in any danger. Saxton was uneasy as he concluded that the sooner he got to the bottom of this, the better.

Saxton thought about Captain Silas Wilkins carefully. It did seem strange in light of what had happened that ever since Saxton returned home a year ago, Wilkins acting as a Supercargo, had personally supervised the loading and unloading of every Saxton ship that sailed south of the Mason-Dixon Line. This was especially true when the port of call was New Orleans, Mobile, Wilmington, Charleston and other coastal cities loyal to the South. He also remembered that Wilkins was always asking questions about Boston's harbor and the many Union naval yards that were scattered up and down the eastern seaboard. When asked why, he merely said he was writing a paper for the US Navy on how best to increase the effectiveness of its ship building facilities. Wilkins also visited the Charlestown Navy Yards across the channel from Boston on a regular basis.

Saxton's deliberations turned back to the mysterious message. He reasoned that Wilkins had been paid in Double Eagles; that much was evident. Most spies were paid for their services; but the XX's puzzled him. Why would Marcus restate the obvious? XX meant twenty in Roman numerals. Each Double Eagle was worth twenty dollars. He knew the Anaona was involved and possibly Hans Larsen. The very thought of Larsen's treachery appalled him. He remembered his Father explicitly telling him to tell no one about 'False Prophet'. Why not Larsen, a trusted employee who for many years was in charge of the books and crew assignments? He pondered a few more minutes. Saxton got up to wander aimlessly about the room. The walls seemed like they were closing in on him, telling him to hurry up. Time was running out. The TICK, TICK, TICK of a large white banjo wall clock became a metronome, keeping time to some malevolent composition. It began to beat on his mind as if he was a slave being beaten before he went overboard. Saxton had to have proof of Wilkins' complicity; enough rock solid evidence to convict him of treason. He stopped, shaken by a sudden revelation. It seemed that Marcus was talking to him again as he did years ago, saying, "Don't look down, don't look down."

As always young Saxton disobeyed him and now years later, he did look down at the message one more time. But this time he saw a possible answer.

Marcus had marked some of the Double Eagles with a XX. Saxton knew now that they were on the Anaona. He had to get to the ship and arrest Wilkins and his crew before they left for New Orleans on the flood tide that very morning! Another thought crossed his mind. Rummaging through his father's desk, he found the tide tables for the Atlantic seaboard. Saxton thumbed the pages until he came to the section marked BOSTON. He looked closely at the date and columns of numbers. His finger stopped. There it was. He looked up at the wall clock. The next flood tide was in two hours! Was he going to wake his father? No, there was no time.

Saxton jumped up and ran over to his father's gun cabinet. After taking out two matching Colt .44s and a box of ammunition; he raced out of the room, turned down the hallway, and ran through the kitchen. In the mud room; his fur lined boots, hat, overcoat and gloves flew onto his body. He lit a lantern then ran through the back door forgetting to close it. The night was pitch black. An early storm had hit the eastern seaboard. Heavy snow and intense cold surprised everyone. Snow with the consistency of Talcum powder clung to him like a funeral shroud. He smashed his way towards the stables. Wilkins and his crew had to be stopped at all costs!

Very early that morning, Thomas Saxton put on a red silk housecoat. While doing so, he decided to check in on his son, expecting him to be fast asleep but his knocks on the door of Saxton's bedroom went unanswered. Thomas opened the heavy door and peered into the gloom but Saxton was not there for his bed was still made up. Somewhat perplexed, Thomas hoped that his son was still in his office trying to figure out the coded note. Down the padded dark upper hallway he went, picking up speed. While descending the grand staircase, he ran ever faster. By the time he passed a startled Packard, he was sprinting. Ahead of him the door to his office was wide open. He called out his son's name but there was only silence. Once inside, no Saxton greeted him. However, something else caught his eye. There on his desk lying in the fading lamp light was the note, cut up and arranged into four pieces. Another piece of paper lay beside it. Thomas bent down and held it to the light. After a brief moment, he cried,

"No, no, he mustn't stop…."

He clutched his chest in agony then staggered backwards right into Packard's waiting arms.

BOOK ONE: CHAPTER 6
A WHIFF OF GRAPESHOT

John Saxton held the lantern high as he waded through deep snow towards the carriage house. Once there he quickly harnessed a horse to a small cigar-box cutter. He threw in a heavy woolen horse blanket, checked to see whether or not his guns were loaded. They were. He then tucked them under the driver's seat along with some ammunition. He thought,

'God it's cold! Perhaps this storm will delay Wilkins departure just long enough for me and God knows who else to stop the bastards. I hope so!'

He put on his woolen mittens then grabbed a halter and led his horse out of the stable and into a freezing blizzard. Once aboard the cutter, he covered himself with a thick buffalo robe. Grabbing a horse whip out of its holder, he lashed out and hung on as the little cutter flew through the gates then down Snow Hill Street towards Boston Harbor far below. In the dim light of dawn he got only one glimpse of the steam ship. To his horror, a whiff of shredded black smoke escaped from her stack. Desperately lashing his horse again and again, he raced down Copps Hill. Laying in wait were ribs of wind driven snow cutting across his chosen path as if trying to warn him of the futility of his mission.

Meanwhile, Captain Wilkins was busy, very busy. He stood on the frozen deck watching the last few sacks of coal being loaded aboard. His engineer and colliers were raising a head of steam. Wilkins was starting to feel apprehensive. He thought,

'Goddamn it all! These infernal steam engines take a hell of a long time to get going! Look at the snow! Never in my life have I shipped out in October in such conditions. It's my last trip, I swear.'

He yanked a fur lined hat down over his frozen ears then motioned for his new First Mate to come over. Wilkins looked down on the pinched red face of the young man.

"Now Smith, get the crew below. Make sure they get breakfast. God knows when we'll mess up again. The tide will be flooding soon; we have to catch it. Now off you go. There'll be hell to pay if the old man sees us in port at sun up!"

Martin Smith ran off to the aft crew quarters. Wilkins lit a new cheroot, throwing the old stub over the side. He peered through falling snow towards the outer harbor. Moments later the blizzard ceased, its hoary breath whimpered and died about him. All around the harbor, dozens of ships were getting ready to depart. On the surrounding hills, yellow and white coal smoke rose straight up from houses stacked like cordwood above him.

He grumbled aloud,

"One more trip to New Orleans and I'm finished. I'll turn this ship over to the Confederacy and hopefully I'll be given a command of a real ship...maybe a frigate with many guns. Once more he stamped his boots. "God it's cold!'

Wilkins crossed a slippery deck to his cabin for breakfast. On his way, he looked up at the Saxton Chevrons flapping in an errant breeze high above his head. The small silk burgee crackled, sounding exactly like small arms fire. Silas shivered involuntarily, stomping his sealskin sea boots free of snow then closed the door behind him. Outside, the snow started falling once more, piling up into terraces that came to rest against the windward side of the cargo hatches.

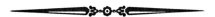

Packard held on grimly to Thomas Saxton. It seemed as if everything happened in slow motion. In one instant, his master had gone from busily reading something on his desk standing up, to suddenly collapsing like a tree downed by a sudden gust of wind. He dragged Thomas to a couch. Packard struggled to lift his master onto some cushions. Carefully he laid Thomas out and put one under his head. Turning slightly, he pulled a silver cord twice then ran out of the office, past the foot of the grand staircase into the kitchen. At five in the morning it was deserted. Grabbing a large metal jug, he pumped it full of cold spring water. He thought,

'Thank God the well hasn't frozen solid like it did two years ago!'

He snatched a dish towel off a nearby drying rack as he ran past it. The butler arrived back at the office just as Millie appeared in her housecoat. She looked aghast at Thomas lying apparently dead on the couch. Packard said curtly,

"Please move aside Millie. I'm going to wake him up."

Packard poured some cold water on his master, who by any measure of the word was shocked as he sputtered,

"For God sake Packard, what the hell are you doing?"

Thomas wiped his face with a towel proffered by his awkward manservant. Shaking his head, he stood up as Packard assisted him. Millie retreated to the kitchen where she commenced brewing a large pot of coffee. She wondered what had happened.

'Why wasn't young Saxton there to help out?' She looked at a Seth Thomas hanging on the kitchen wall.

"My Lord, it's after five in the morning!"

For some reason, she turned about. The kitchen's side door was wide open. A blast of cold air hit her as she went into the mud room to close it. Before she did so, she noticed foot prints on the steps. Further out towards the stables, barely visible through the driving blizzard was a narrow trough in the snow. It was rapidly being filled in by swirling snow. She cried, "My God, may the saints preserve us, young Saxton has gone out into this storm! It has to be him!" She then quickly closed the door as another frigid gust tried to force its way past her.

Thomas was worried. He looked nervously at Packard then walked over to where Saxton's message had fallen out of his hand to the floor. As he bent over a wave of nausea overcame him. Thomas struggled to stand up, waving Packard off as he did so. Taking another deep breath, he successfully retrieved the crumpled scrap of paper. Thomas spread it out flat on his desk and looked at the message again. Just then Millie came running into the room. She was upset.

"Oh Sir, Master Saxton has gone out into the blizzard tonight. The mud room door was wide open. I saw tracks leading to the stables."

She sat down on a couch. Thomas walked over to comfort her, giving her a handkerchief from his pocket. He told Packard,

"Wake up the stable boys and get my personal cutter ready at once."

Packard fled downstairs in the basement. In moments, Thomas heard his stable boys shouting outside in the driving snow and bone-chilling cold. The conditions were hellish. Thomas walked over to an oak gun cabinet. Its long glass doors were unlocked. His heart leaped as he noticed that his prized pair of gold inlaid Colt .44's was missing, as well a box of ammunition. Gathering his wits about him, he realized that his son was well armed. Relieved, Thomas took out a Remington double barreled .410 shotgun and a box of shells. Thomas turned to leave. There in the doorway stood his wife Muriel with Jack in her arms. She put Jack down, walked over and held her husband with both hands. She asked him,

"And where are you going Thomas Saxton with that shotgun at this hour and in this blizzard?" Her husband kissed her lightly.

"I'm going to rescue Saxton before he gets into real trouble at the warehouse." She became adamant.

"Trouble Thomas--- what kind of trouble is our son in? Tell me this instant!"

He pushed her away gently, grabbed the shotgun and fled down the hallway to the foyer. Therein he put on his boots, overcoat, hat, gloves and scarf. She ran after him, calling out, "Thomas, Thomas come back, you can't go alone."

The front door opened then slammed shut just as Muriel entered the foyer. A blast of air wrapped its frigid arms about her as she opened the door and stepped onto an icy threshold. Her husband had already left. It was only then that she realized he was still wearing his housecoat. Only a faint cutter track was visible until it disappeared into oblivion. Muriel felt someone come up behind her. She turned about. It was Packard. He said,

"Perhaps Madam it has something to do with this." He handed her the note Thomas had left behind. She read it and gasped,

"Oh my God! My son and husband need help and quickly. Packard, get some boys to run over to the McKay's right away. I think they still live on Prince Street nearby. I do hope they haven't finished moving to Eagle Hill! Ask them for help and tell them to hurry to the Saxton wharfs. Tell them to get the police too! Now hurry! Hurry! Please Packard go now before it's too late. Tell them to go to the warehouse armed. May God help and protect them."

Stylus Packard ran back into the house; dressed and waded out to the stables. There he relayed the message to two stable boys who put on snow-shoes. Packard watched as they tramped away as fast as they could through deepening snow.

John Saxton's horse slowed as the drifts on Snow Hill Street got progressively worse. The poor beast was covered by a thick white lather that fell off in frozen slabs as it staggered forward through mountains of fresh snow. Wisps of steam rose from its withers. Saxton saw a small house emerge from the storm just down the hill from him. Once there, he pulled back on the reins, stopped, jumped out then waded through the snow to untie a pair of snow-shoes strapped to the backside of the cutter. He took off his mittens then struggled putting on the bear-paws. Finished, he went to the front of the cutter, reached in and unwrapped his twin Colts. Being careful to keep the snow away from them, he jammed the Colts into his deep overcoat pockets. Taking the stiff leather reins, he led his exhausted horse over to shelter in the lee of the house. He threw a buffalo blanket over the shivering animal, tethered it then went around to the side of the house and knocked on its back door. A few moments later, a lamp flared inside. A shrill woman's voice said,

"Henry, there's someone knockin' on our kitchen door." A deep resonant voice responded,

"Christ almighty woman! What the hell is goin' on?"

Moments later, the back door opened a crack. An old man peered through the screen door, his breath white and cloudy about his grizzled face. He held up a sputtering coal-oil lamp. He growled,

"Whadda ya want mister?"

Thomas explained quickly. The door slammed shut. As he turned to leave, Thomas heard the wife cry out,

"Who was it Henry? What did they want?"

"Quiet Martha and go back to sleep! I'm gittin' dressed. I'll be awhile. Where's my musket? I wouldn't miss this for the world!"

Silas Wilkins finished his breakfast and headed for the wheelhouse upstairs. The inside of its small windows were frosted over. His breath hung in the cold air like a forgotten promise. Slabs of frost came off a nearby windowpane as he scratched it with a fingernail. He peered out. The storm had abated once again. Crystalline stars splayed out high above him. Wilkins tried to open the portside door leading outside to the flying bridge but it was frozen shut. He cried out in exasperation,

"God almighty, it's like an ice box in here."

A long brass speaking tube stuck out just to his right. Its chipped cork stopper swung back and forth as. Wilkins leaned over, his breath vaporous.

"Morgan, send someone up here to the wheelhouse; the damn radiators are frozen again."

Wilkins stood back and kicked the door open with a crash. He stepped outside, closed the door, and lit another slim cheroot, drawing in a sweet sharp mouthful of smoke. He coughed. As he spit out a piece of tobacco into the snow, he put on his mittens. Martin Smith came running across the wharf from the warehouse, down the gangplank, across the main deck below him then clattered up ten iron steps to the bridge. Captain Wilkins leaned over a railing. Smith came over as Wilkins stamped his sealskin boots. Martin exclaimed,

"Christ its cold! Is the ship ready to sail?"

He backed off. Wilkins was not paying any attention to him. Martin turned and peered through the few drifting snowflakes that swirled down through the cold night air. He became very alarmed, for a sinuous line of torch lights were weaving down Copps Hill towards them. They flickered and flared as if there was a procession of Druids marching towards Stonehenge. He looked back at Captain Wilkins who seemed mesmerized. His cheroot had dropped onto the icy main deck below him. Martin was shocked. He reached over, shaking Wilkins out of his trance.

At that very moment, John Saxton tramped through deep snow thankful the blizzard was over. Above him a full moon shone brightly. After struggling over what had seemed to be endless high drifts, he could see that he was only a short distance from the Saxton warehouses at the foot of Snow Hill Street. More white combers lay before him like an endless ocean. The silence was eerie. Not a soul, man nor beast was about. Something however, electric and undefined caused him to stop and turn about. Instantly he became jubilant, for behind him a long line of flickering lights were descending the hillside. Saxton turned around, staggered over the last few drifts then collapsed completely worn out. He lay in the snow looking up at a universe under which he'd just turned twenty-one. He was exhausted. How ironic! He laughed as someone began pulling him up. It was Eddie Finch. He cried,

"Hey, look Charlie! It's Mr. Saxton. Look at 'Im. He's half froze to death he is!"

Two grinning fur lined faces gazed down at him. They were Charlie and Eddie Finch, identical twins Thomas hired to command the Saxton Shipping gatehouse. Over the years, it had become a running joke that Saxton Shipping was guarded night and day by the same man. Saxton grinned back at them. He quickly brushed himself off.

"Eddie, has the Anaona left yet?"

They nodded no.

"Good!"

Saxton explained what was happening. They appeared shocked. He took off his snow-shoes, leaned them up against the gatehouse and began to issue orders. As he did so, Saxton's breath rose straight up in white clouds as if they were ominous smoke signals erupting from beneath an Apache blanket. Saxton continued.

"Charlie, I want you to run to the nearest Police station. Tell them we'll need all the help we can get, for there must be at least twenty Confederates gun runners on board ship and they're fully armed. Here, put on my snowshoes." He did. "Now get going!"

As Charlie reluctantly snow-shoed away through deep snow into the night, he knew that if the Police never arrived, he would be implicated, found out and hung for treason. He ruefully considered becoming 'Galvanized" as he trudged towards a Police Station three blocks away. Saxton then turned to Eddie. He became emphatic, saying,

"Wait here Eddie for the others. As soon as they arrive, direct them to warehouse No#3. I'll be waiting there. Remember Eddie, no lights, no noise and don't talk to anyone else but me, not even Mr. Larsen." He too ruefully obeyed as he watched Saxton run past the Gate house down to the waterfront.

Saxton knew that Warehouse No#3 would block out any sight of any advance towards the Anaona. He also realized that any attack would have to be coordinated, quick and completely overpowering. That much he had learned from Marcus as they wiled away many hours aboard the Silver Ghost becalmed in tropical doldrums.

Silas was stunned. He looked at Martin wild-eyed. The crew below him was just emerging into the cold from their breakfast. Wilkins leaned out over the railing and screamed,

"Cast off all spring lines! You there! Release the stern line then the bow line!"

Three crewmen ran down the gangplank onto the wharf to a row of iron bollards. They began lifting various frozen tie-up lines over them, throwing them overboard. Drift ice caught between the pilings sounded like gunshots as the lines smashed into them. Round manila bumpers were pulled aboard and thrown on deck. By now the rest of his crew had emerged onto the main deck. Their Captain continued yelling orders. A loud vibration shook the ship from stem to stern as its twin propellers started to turn over. Black smoke mid-ships punched its way upward through the single smoke stack. Without warning, the gangplank slipped off the wharf into the harbor, throwing a column of black seawater high above it. Three crewmen still ashore, leapt over an ever widening chasm onto an icy deck. One of them screamed as his right leg popped out at the knee. He lay there in agony. Another crawled towards the aft cabin, leaving a thin trail of blood behind him in the snow.

Saxton made it to warehouse No#3 unseen. As he did so, he watched the Anaona's crew tumble out of the aft cabin. Captain Wilkins was going out to sea into an early dawn. His heart raced as he heard the ship's engine turn over then its propellers began thrashing drift ice into smithereens. Seconds later, a violent prop wash slapped against rows of tarred pilings underneath him. Saxton knew he had to do something fast or the smugglers would escape. He was too far away and it was too dark to shoot anybody with his Colts. Besides, its crew was probably trained soldiers with an extensive armory at their disposal. In fact, he knew that the whole ship was an arsenal. He had to do something fast, but what? Frantic, he looked about him in the gloomy warehouse for anything that might give him an idea, an advantage, anything. Unbelievably, there in a dark corner were two wooden crates. On each was stenciled FARM MACHINERY. He ran towards them. On the way he grabbed a long crow-bar lying on a work bench. He thought,

'Is it possible that light artillery might be inside those crates? God all mighty, I hope so!'

Thomas Saxton was also frantic. He could see the Anaona cast off. Half-way down Snow Hill, he passed the house where Saxton left his horse and cutter. The way was clear as other early risers had already bulled their way through the deep snow. His sleigh's steel runners hissed as he drove on towards Boston harbor. Thomas arrived in an explosion of ice and snow at the Saxton gates. A police constable came running over, tugged at his black billed helmet then assisted Thomas out of his cutter. Eddie Finch told him that Saxton was already there. Thomas Saxton was too late. He retrieved his Remington shotgun, cracked the breech open, took two shells out of his coat pocket and carefully inserted them. He closed the breech with a snick.

Saxton attacked the larger of the two wooden crates with his crow-bar. He pried off a large side board, then another. From behind him he heard voices echoing within the large empty warehouse. Soon there was a sizable group of men about him. Saxton told them what was happening. Someone ran away then came back moments later shouting that their quarry was fifty feet from the dock and picking up speed. Desperately, Saxton and the men about him tore the two wooden crates apart. Hans Larsen, hearing the commotion from high up in his office, ran down the stairs into the warehouse. He stood back in feigned shock as a crate marked FARM MACHINERY revealed a three inch ordnance rifle. Saxton ignored him. Unfortunately the rifle was in pieces. A gun carriage with two wooden wheels was packed on either side of it. A ram-rod, worm tool, boxes of wadding, a trail spike, leather water bucket, a caisson containing canisters of grapeshot, boxes of shells and a firing lanyard were in the smaller crate next to it. Someone else shouted that the ship was one hundred feet away from the dock, and slowly turning down harbor.

Silas Wilkins was desperate for speed, for speed meant escape. He also knew that any naval ships nearby would take hours to get up enough steam up to chase them. If only he could get more speed. Wilkins stood in the wheel house turning the helm to port. The Anaona loaded down with heavy weapons responded sluggishly. Someone on its main deck shouted then pointed towards the Saxton warehouses. Silas picked up his new Galilean binoculars from out of their wall rack. He walked out onto the starboard flying bridge. Two highly polished lenses rose to his eyes while he turned a brass knob to focus. He was horrified. There in front of warehouse #3, were dozens of men desperately shoveling a wide path through snow drifts to the edge of the wharf. Something else caught his attention. Being wheeled out of warehouse No#3 was the ordnance rifle he didn't have room for.

Within the warehouse, John Saxton's men had quickly put the ordnance rifle together under the expert direction of a man called John Gibbon. Luckily, Captain Gibbon was visiting relatives in Boston on Charter Street on leave from Camp Floyd in Utah. He'd been up late that morning, reading his newly published manual 'The Artillerists'. A long time artillery instructor at West Point; he became curious when he saw three Boston Police officers running by his bedroom window at six in the morning. They looked exactly like London Bobbies wearing black-billed pith helmets perched precariously above deep blue double breasted frock coats. It seemed as if the Policemen trudging through the snow down Hull Street were following a red haired man attired in a strange uniform. His curiosity aroused, Gibbon dressed then followed more police as they ran downhill towards the waterfront. Once there, Captain Gibbon and a steady stream of armed men were directed into warehouse No#3 by Eddie Finch. Captain Gibbon ran through the cavernous warehouse towards a mob of frantic men.

Once apprised of the situation by a distraught John Saxton, Gibbon with military efficiency started to assemble the ordnance rifle. He knew the long barreled cannon had a range of over eighteen hundred yards and was renowned for being extremely accurate. Within a few minutes of his arrival, the nine hundred pound gun was trundled onto the wharf. There hadn't been time to clean out its packing grease. It had to work as is despite the cold. The armed men took cover then began to lay down a steady rifle barrage on the nearby but rapidly receding SS Anaona.

Silas ducked instinctively as a bullet smashed through a wheelhouse window beside him. Leaving Martin Smith at the helm, he ran out onto the portside flying bridge, leaned over the railing and yelled, "Return fire!"

A steady crackle of small arms and rifle fire resounded across the inner harbor. An occasional 'BOOM' from Thomas Saxton's double barreled shotgun was heard over the din. Its pellets however, fell harmlessly into the harbor far short of its target. Minie balls zinged over the vessel like bees in a bonnet. One crewman screamed and slumped dead; his body rolling into the scuppers near a cargo hatch. The ship was just out of range of all small arms except for rifles. Silas ran through the wheelhouse and out onto the starboard side of the flying bridge and looked across the harbor towards the Charlestown Naval yard. There, one of its patrol boats was trying desperately to get up steam. He looked the other way. Boston's Harbor Police had just left their Sergeant's wharf station in two large rowboats. They seemed to crawl through the harbor's drift ice like crippled pond skimmers. Other ships cowered at their moorings. None made any attempt to intercept him. Silas thought of trying to use them as cover but already any ship near him was steaming away in panic. He returned to the wheelhouse. Silas smiled. The worst was over.

Captain John Gibbon was worried for he had reason to be. He couldn't use explosive shells because Saxton told him that the fleeing ship was a virtual powder keg. If it exploded, it would devastate any ships moored around it. In response, Gibbon chose grape shot that would explode above the Anaona while not penetrating it. There were two problems with choosing grapeshot; its range was less than four hundred yards and the target was rapidly moving away, zigzagging as it did so. Gibbon would have only once chance, maybe two at the very for the fugitive vessel was at the very least two hundred yards away from him and quickly steaming out of range. He looked over at a Navy patrol boat a mile away. It wasn't moving despite frenetic activity on its gun deck. Once back to the task at hand, Gibbon began directing his gun crew with military expediency. They secured the gun with a trail spike driven by a heavy sledge into thick wharf planking. They finished cleaning the fuse hole with the worm tool and then affixed its firing lanyard. Gibbons began yelling instructions.

"Wet sponge the bore!" A man shoved a wet sponge attached to a pole down the gun barrel then retracted it. Gibbons yelled again,

"Dry sponge the bore!" Another behind him put a dry sponge on a pole down the bore right after that and withdrew it smartly. A three pound case shot was taken out of a leather haversack. Gibbons shouted, "Load and hold!"

The canister filled with powder and .50 caliber grape shot slid down into the smooth bored barrel and rammed into place. The charge was seated, the vent primed and the marked oak rammer extracted. Another man stood twenty five feet away with another canister in a leather haversack. Gibbon elevated the gun sights. Satisfied, he stood back well off to the side and yelled,

"Ready to fire!" After a few seconds, he pulled the long lanyard hard. A tremendous blast of heat and smoke erupted as the canister sailed far out over the inner harbor exploding well astern of its target. Wintering black gulls and white winged scoters rose in feathery clouds from every nearby dock and piling. They shrieked as they flew above the harbor through a blanket of frigid sea air. Quickly, Gibbon corrected the elevation. The loading and firing process was repeated. Again the rifle roared.

Silas heard the scream of a case shot after he saw a puff of white smoke erupt from far off on the Saxton wharf. Everyone dropped to the deck as a deadly cargo of grapeshot exploded one hundred feet off their stern. His crew stood up and cheered. Silas prayed for more speed. At least three hundred yards away, his ship was making ten knots on a flood tlde. Agaln he screamed a warnng as another puff of white smoke appeared. Wilkins froze. A missile hurtled towards him releasing a deadly shower of hot lead right above him. The Anaona staggered through the water as if a giant iron fist had come down upon it. Silas Wilkins looked up into a dawning light. He smiled, thinking about all that gold just before a minie ball smashed into his skull, killing him instantly.

Gibbon's gun crew reloaded the ordnance rifle but was told to hold their fire. For there, out in the harbor, their quarry was turning ever so slightly towards them. A white flag appeared from her flying bridge. The smugglers were surrendering. A loud hurrah went up all over the inner harbor. Whistles, horns and bells blew with wild abandon. In fact, hundreds of curious spectators crammed every vantage point the waterfront had to offer. Gibbon's gun crew grabbed him and hoisted him high on their shoulders. He protested to no avail, for the men holding him aloft would not listen. What they didn't notice was a growing web of hairline fissures radiating out across the bottom of the ordnance rifle's wrought-iron chassis.

The 'Battle of Boston Harbor' as it was to be known thereafter, was over. Many claimed later that Captain John Myron Gibbon fired the first shot of the Civil War. Everywhere, grown men were happily dancing about hugging each other. A Navy Patrol ship was alongside the defeated vessel; its crew arrested without resistance. They sat in leg irons on the patrol boat's main deck. A small steam tug came out to tow the disabled Anaona back to the Saxton dock. As Saxton looked on with pride, he was overcome by a deep sense of relief. His father ambled up behind him, his red silk house coat dragging in the snow. The breech of his shotgun was broken open over his left shoulder. Thomas, red faced and shivering uncontrollably, stammered,

"Well done, done... son! We showed... the bastards, didn't we?"

BOOK ONE: CHAPTER 7
THE STATE OF THE UNION

It was the afternoon of New Years Eve, 1860. The Saxton House on Copps Hill was still decked out in all its Christmas finery. Into the Grand Salon walked Muriel and Thomas Saxton. He stopped and pointed an accusing finger at his wife saying,

"Muriel my Dear, you're up to something aren't you?" She parried.

"Why not at all Thomas, whatever do you mean?"

"You know what I mean Muriel. You and Packard have been scheming about something ever since the 'Battle of Boston Harbor' two weeks ago."

Packard stood behind them in the salon. Within the massive granite fireplace, a fire crackled and popped loudly. Behind them Packard was grinning from ear to ear. Thomas pointing to a green settee and said,

"Please have a seat dear."

Muriel looked up at Packard, her eyes lively as she instructed him.

"By the way Stylus, if you can find that hero son of ours; tell him to get down here promptly."

Packard left, adroitly closing the French doors behind him. Thomas reached over and patted a plump silk cushion. Muriel sat down primly, carefully arranging her bright white and blue silk gown. It was decorated with lace cuffs and a matching neck piece by Ernest Lefebure. Her graying hair was held back in a sever bun impaled by a long silver pin. She wore no rouge or powder. Three strands of matched black pearls hung around her long neck. Her tiny feet were shod in blue silk house slippers for Muriel hated those high hook and ladder leather boots she was forced to wear for Sunday service in the presence of Boston's high society. Ever since Saxton returned from overseas, she hadn't worn her black satin dresses or 'Widows Weeds' as she called them. Thomas was shocked when she bought the first of many colorful outfits. Muriel Stamford Saxton's remarkable recovery was the talk of every tea parlor in the city.

John Saxton entered and walked over to a red leather wing chair. His parents looked up as they sat side by side holding hands. Saxton was thrilled at the transformation of his mother and happy that his parents had made amends, prepared to live once again in harmonious concert.

Thomas reached over and pulled a service cord twice after which Muriel adjusted his black bowtie one more time. She remarked,

"My dear Thomas, please, no fretting over your new suit. I know you don't like it but wear it for me dear."

Thomas muttered something about 'married and buried'. Packard appeared to announce that a formal buffet dinner was about to be served in the dining room. Both men waited for Muriel to rise. She did. Then arm and arm, Thomas and Muriel proceeded to walk into the dining room. There, before them awaited their guests seated around a massive mahogany center table. Thomas, somewhat surprised, turned to say something to Muriel but she put a finger to his lips. Thomas thought,

'Ever since our Saxton has come home, everyone I know has been putting their fingers to my lips shushing me. Is Jack next?'

Muriel stepped forward, her arms stretched out before her. The assemblage rose, each in turn warmly expressing their delight at her remarkable recovery. After the introductions, she introduced her son as one of the 'Heroes of Boston Harbor'. They cheered heartily. After a few moments, Thomas signaled for everyone to take their places. He whispered in Muriel's ear,

"What's this all about darling? I must say everything looks absolutely fabulous!" Once again Muriel put her fingers to his lips, her voice light and lilting.

"Why dear, it's a New Year's Eve party replete with total strangers that Saxton invited, some of whom I hear are quite famous. It is too bad that our dear friends the McKay's went to Canada for Christmas and New Years. But I'm sure we'll celebrate with them next year as we have in the past."

The Boston Herald printed the Saxton's guest list the next day. Its editor waxed poetic over who had been invited. The notables included the rich and famous of American society. A glaring omission from this list was that of Minister Dexter Norland. Thomas would not invite him. In fact he quit attending his old Church soon after the second anniversary of his son's disappearance. Muriel however, continued to go there without him. She couldn't bring herself to desert her peers, friends and the Stamford clan. Instead, much to everyone's shock, Thomas Saxton began worshiping at the First Free Baptist Church led by the 'Good Reverend' himself, Nathanial Clover.

Apparently Thomas Saxton could no longer stand Minister Dexter Norland's racist opinions about black Americans. From the pulpit, the Minister had a more perverse opinion. To him, the Creator's prophets Moses and Abraham amongst others, his Noah, his Adam and Eve, his Apostles, and Jesus Christ himself were all white not black. Therefore, any 'educated person' knew right away without hesitation that God was white. Even his angels were white except Lucifer; a fallen arch-angel come Devil, who many swore was black. Thus, his evil minions had to be black too. So, if these observations didn't convince 'the chosen' that they were inferior then the Declaration of Independence, the Constitution and the Supreme Court of America would. So incensed by Norland's blatant racism, Thomas became an ardent abolitionist.

It became the talk of Boston, for Thomas was the first and only white man that ever attended that church. At first its black congregation was unsettled, but the unassuming Scot found a release for his pent-up grief amongst other grievers especially after worship. It was the 'Ring Shout' that moved the holy spirit within the man. As the congregants shuffled their feet in a counterclockwise direction around a second alter set up in the middle of the church, they broke out in spontaneous clapping, shouting, singing and praying aloud. Thomas thought it appropriate that the church was on Joy Street. They in time accepted and loved the dour scot. Reverend Clover knew John Saxton was lost at sea and that Thomas was assuaging his grief both for him and his depressed wife. The elder Saxton had found a sanctuary of peace in a time of crisis. He belonged there. However, after Saxton returned from his ordeal; the Saxton family as one attended the Old North Church once more despite Thomas's dislike for the minister. As a family once again, they returned, sitting in their square white pew box at the fore-front every Sunday.

The weather for the New Year's Eve festivities was cold yet somewhat clear outside. Despite the deep snow, the roads were passable. The carriage house was full, as busy stable boys tended to a few dozen horses and sleighs. All of the household staff had been feted earlier in the day. There had been a sumptuous lunch held for them in the Grand Salon. Therein each of them was content to treasure a single golden Double Eagle in their pocket. Suitably incised with a double XX, Thomas had given them out as a reward for serving the cause. Four large potbellied iron stoves filled with hot coals warmed the stables. Pots of coffee were brewing in the kitchen to eventually make their way through the rear mud-room of the Saxton House out to the stables behind it.

Inside the Saxton House's dining room; pots of coffee, tea, hot chocolate and mulled cider warmed over tea candles on a long rosewood sideboard. A granite fireplace at one end blazed away giving the dining room a welcoming ambience. Two gaslight chandeliers hung down over a massive Chippendale mahogany table. Thirty feet of exotic floral displays decorated it'd mid-section from one end to the other. Against one wall, stood a narrow mahogany veneered pier table with gilt-bronze mounts. Sitting upon its red marble top were two crystal bowls filled with Medford punch. Rows of crystal cups and two silver Crespin punch strainers completed the set.

Thomas Saxton was relieved that his normally gregarious wife was back to her former standard as a hostess. The three years that Saxton was absent had indeed been somewhat funereal. It was if Muriel was shunning her world and not the other way around. Thomas gave up musing about the past as he pulled an Ethan Allan chair out for his wife. Every one of the men stood and waited for her to be seated. Gracefully she sat down. The room immediately filled with laughter and earnest conversation. Muriel motioned for Thomas to put his head near hers.

"I do hope Thomas that you won't be cross with Saxton and me. You know how we once loved formal dinners". She paused then continued brightly.

"Everyone has to dress up and act civilized; you know dear, best behavior and all that. By the way my dear, don't wander off to visit your old cronies. You'll have plenty of time to do that in the smoking lounge later."

Thomas was quite content to bask in the glory of his son's heroism and his wife's recovery. A vacant side chair had been set aside for Marcus. A name card was placed before it. Upon it written in a neat calligraphic hand was, 'Marcus the Maasai'. On a signal from Thomas, everyone carried their plates to the sideboard buffet. Once there, the dinner guests began loading up as if starvation was imminent. Thomas pointed them out to Muriel who was still holding his hand. She laughed lightly at them. All at once she leaned over and kissed Thomas full on the lips.

"I love you Thomas, I really do!" She kissed him again for good measure.

Startled, the usually stern Scot responded in kind. They kissed again much to the delight of the guests who saw it. Someone tapped a cut crystal champagne glass with a silver fork. Immediately a tinkling of Swarovski filled the room. Thomas with a twinkle in his eye grabbed his startled wife. He proceeded to give Muriel a long kiss to much applause and laughter. A guest shouted, "Speech, speech!"

Muriel let go of him. The crowded room became quiet as Thomas stood up. He looked down at Muriel, his face still flushed. He prefaced his remarks by saying,

"I must say thanks to all of you for coming here on New Year's Eve despite the horrid weather. My lovely wife Muriel and her staff, I'm told, have worked hard to ensure your happiness here at Saxton House. I also offer my apologies to any Democrats who might have mistakenly come in from the cold. You all know of course that for the first time a Republican President, Abraham Lincoln has been elected, taking office early next year."

He paused for the hoots and hollers to subside then continued,

"My dear friends, it's New Years Eve and as such I propose a toast to the New Year ahead and may it be blessed by peace!"

Everyone rose and in so doing raised their fluted champagne glasses; touching their neighbor's in kind, wishing them well. As soon as all were seated, Thomas continued lightly,

"It seems that we have been terribly remiss in the fact that grace was not said before dinner."

He paused for the merriment to slacken then jovially continued.

"And to make things worse, I've been terribly torn between who is going to say it." More laughter erupted.

"It seems that we have in our presence tonight, three men of the cloth, whom I've heard through reliable sources, are all well qualified for the task."

There was even more laughter as Bishop John Bernard Fitzpatrick, Rabbi Saling and Reverend Clover looked at each other.

"So my friends, I've decided that a Bishop outranks a Rabbi and a Reverend and as such I welcome his Holiness to say the grace."

Thomas sat down bowing his head as Bishop John Bernard Fitzpatrick rose solemnly. In his early thirties, the Bishop had been approved by the 'Brahmins' or old style Protestants of Boston. It was because he was a 'cultured' and learned Irishmen, unlike the rabble that poured into Boston after the 1849 potato famine. Dressed in a scarlet cassock, held up by a scarlet sash, the Bishop's bald head was topped by a scarlet zucchetto. The tall and elegant man looked about bemused then closed his eyes. He intoned gravely,

"May God protect us and may his holy word comfort us. Thank you Lord for what we are about to receive, Amen."

Visibly relieved, his Holiness sat down. Thomas rose and thanked him for his brevity. More laughter erupted. The Bishop squirmed but managed to smile albeit somewhat unconvincingly.

So the diners enjoyed the lavish repast and after dessert was served, the satiated throng was ushered into the Grand Salon. Photographer Mathew Brady and his assistant Timothy O'Sullivan were waiting for them. They'd set up a daguerreotype camera for a group picture. Brady's instrument was supported by three adjustable cherry wood legs sporting a series of brass knobs. The camera was large, housed in a cherry wood box affair fronted by a black leather bellows capped by a large glass lens. Mathew politely smiled as some of the guests kidded him about whether or not their group picture would be included in his next volume entitled, 'A Gallery of Illustrious Americans'.

After much ado, Brady got them together. Under stern instructions to hold still for at least two minutes, Brady readied his colloidal dry plates, focused the camera then dove under a black shroud. His assistant held onto a short wooden handle that supported a narrow, V shaped metal flash pan. In his other hand was a fob watch. In the flash pan was lycopodium powder. After two minutes precisely, on an electrical signal, the pan flared and the picture was completed. However, there was a problem. As Brady ducked under the shroud, Jack seated on Muriel's lap, started to growl and just before the powder flashed; the dog launched himself forward, ears back, fangs bared.

Immediately, everyone was in an uproar. Jack had one of Brady's pant legs in his jaws and was hanging on, growling fiercely. Packard had run into the salon and was trying to get Jack away from Brady. O'Sullivan, Brady's assistant, was desperately hanging on to the flash pan with one hand while at the same time trying to keep the large camera from tipping over. Order was restored, although barely. Regaining his composure amid many profound apologies from both Saxtons, Brady still somewhat flummoxed, took one picture after another. Eventually everyone relaxed. Brady and his assistant hurriedly packed up their equipment and left. It was said later, that Muriel's favorite photo was that of Jack, whose launch, fangs and all, had somehow been miraculously captured.

The Grand Salon once again filled with laughter, polite talk and the clinking of champagne glasses. Packard wheeled out a serving table into the center of the room. Resting upon it were three purple velvet coverlets hiding three mysterious objects; two small ones and a large rectangular one. Thomas leaned over to his wife Muriel.

"Well my dear, you're not the only one full of surprises tonight, are you?"

With aplomb, Thomas stood up and asked his somewhat bemused son to stand up as well. Saxton did. Thomas hushed everyone to be quiet. They did so reluctantly more out of curiosity than anything. Thomas exclaimed solemnly,

"Ladies and Gentlemen, there are many here tonight who fought in the 'Battle of Boston Harbor' a few weeks ago and I for one thank them. However, there are three men who performed beyond the call of duty in that deadly enterprise and two of them are here with us today. The first is my son John Saxton who broke the code and led the charge against the enemy. So without further a due, I present this token of our esteem to my son John Saxton."

Thomas reached out, lifted off the velvet shroud that covered the first object and instantly there were cries of delight and astonishment. Thomas shook his son's hand as he handed him a gold plated telegraph key on a highly polished oak base. Two Double Eagles marked by a XX were positioned on either side of a brass plaque on which were inscribed the words,

'TO JOHN M.SAXTON FOR PERSEVERANCE
BEYOND THE CALL OF DUTY, DEC. 16, 1860.'

Everyone stood up and applauded as "Hear, hear" and "Well done lad," resounded around the room. Saxton thanked his father and sat down; the trophy resplendent before him. Although the room rang with "Speech, speech", Thomas realized his son would remain silent. He raised his hands for quiet and everyone sat down. Thomas motioned for Captain John Gibbon to rise and come forward. With great reluctance, a naturally shy Gibbon did so, resplendent in his formal dark blue Army dress uniform trimmed all around in scarlet piping. Thomas turned to him and shook his hand. Embarrassed, Captain Gibbon waited patiently for the ordeal to be over. Thomas continued oblivious to the poor man's obvious discomfort, saying,

"In everyman's life there comes a time to step up and do what's necessary so that life, liberty and justice can continue for others. Captain John Gibbon stepped up." The room rang with "Hear! Hear!" Thomas continued,

"Without the Captain here, the traitors would have gotten away. There is no doubt about that in anyone's mind here today. So, with heartfelt thanks on behalf of everyone here, I present to you, Captain Gibbon of the US Army 4th Artillery, with this."

With a flourish Thomas whipped away a second velvet coverlet revealing a perfectly cast metal model of an ordnance rifle on a black granite slab. Inscribed on a polished brass plaque were the words,

'TO CAPTAIN JOHN GIBBON, FOR ACCURACY
BEYOND THE HUMANLY POSSIBLE
DECEMBER 16, 1860.'

Once again everyone stood and applauded heartily. The Captain blushed then shook Thomas Saxton's hand. After giving his thanks, he too made a strategic retreat to his seat where he tried to regain his composure. This gave him reason for further embarrassment as everyone laughed. Thomas waited for the uproar to die down then he moved behind a vacant chair. His guests went silent. Thomas grasped the high backed chair from behind with both hands. He paused, trying valiantly to contain his emotions.

"Sadly, the third recipient for bravery is not here to receive our approbation and applause. However, I do have here in front of me a small token of our love and respect for him."

Everyone seemed to hold their breath. Thomas, once again with a dramatic flourish, unveiled a brass bound oak chest. He lifted the lid, reached in with both hands and brought up a gleaming horde of gold Double Eagles. They cascaded back into the chest with a delicious clinking sound. His audience was stunned. They'd all heard a rumor that the SS Anaona carried a golden treasure but until now, it had never been revealed. Thomas motioned for Boston's Police Chief, Robert Taylor, to step forward with two of his Captains. Chief Taylor did so as Thomas sat down.

The Chief looked magnificent in his new formal blue coat replete with tails. He looked down at the open chest then up again saying,

"Ladies and gentlemen, it took two of Boston's finest to lug this thing all the way up Copps Hill to the Saxton House."

Laughter erupted as he looked at his two Captains attired in blue dress coats with tails, standing at attention on either side of him. Both men appeared very tall because their pressed black pants, light buff vests and enameled black top hats anointed by a single gold star gave that impression. Chief Taylor waited. A skilled politician, he too was quite aware that civic elections were just around the corner. He continued drolly.

"Ladies and gentlemen, we all agree that heroes have to be recognized and rewarded for their heroism. Tonight, it gives me great pleasure to announce that the City of Boston, the State of Massachusetts and the federal government who are aptly represented here tonight, have agreed to bestow these twenty thousand dollars in gold coins to Marcus Brown."

Everyone stood and clapped then sat down as Chief Taylor continued his remarks. He winked at his audience and as he did so said,

"Of course the constables who brought it up White Hill told me that there are a few marked coins missing which I'm told were unfit for circulation."

He paused as more laughter ensued then raised a nearby crystal flute of Mumm's champagne,

"A toast to Marcus Brown my friends!"

Everyone stood up glasses in hand and applauded, especially Reverend Clover who cried and stomped his feet as well. After the commotion ceased, the Chief continued,

"It was the property of all three governments but after due deliberation, all three decided that a legal battle over the spoils of war would consume it all and only the lawyers would get rich!"

He closed the lid and the two Captains put the chest on a side table. There they remained at attention guarding it.

"Hear! Hear!" again resounded around the room. With that, the Chief returned to his seat. Packard came back into the room smiling broadly as he gave Thomas a telegram. The elegant butler backed away and stood by the open French doors. All of his household staff crowded in behind him. Somewhat puzzled, Thomas put on his pince-nez reading glasses. With a touch of gravitas, he angled the paper towards a nearby gaslight and said,

"This is from the Office of the President of the United States, and is addressed to me. It reads as follows ladies and gentlemen,

"It has come to my attention that a certain Marcus Brown of Boston risked his life to expose a gun-running and spy operation led by a Captain Silas Wilkins. It is my great pleasure to announce that the Congress of the United States has deemed Marcus Brown to be forevermore a citizen of these United States, effective immediately.

By order of James Buchanan,
President of the United States."

Not a sound came from within that room. Reverend Clover was the first to regain his wits. He stood up clapping. Soon everyone stood up and followed suit. For many minutes thereafter, two Swarovski crystal chandeliers above the entourage tinkled and shimmied as sounds of passionate applause ricocheted off them. Never had a black man been so honored before. Everyone sat down except Clover. It was a poignant moment for him as tears were streaming down his black face. The Reverend reached up with both hands, and turned facing the open French doors of the dining room. Through them everyone could see a Maasai shield and spear prominently displayed over the mantelpiece. Inspired, Clover turned about and cried out joyously,

"Praise God almighty, for his Shield of Righteousness and his Spear of Justice shall prevail against the wicked! Halleluiah! Halleluiah! May the Lord protect Marcus and bring him home to us very soon!"

The Reverend sat down and bowed his head in prayer. Again Thomas rose and waited for his guests to settle down. The Mayor elect, Joseph Milner Wightman, spoke briefly to his neighbor former Chief Justice Lemuel Shaw. Both men nodded. So instructed his Worship rose and walked over to Thomas to whisper in his ear. Thomas smiled as he gave the floor to the Mayor, who with practiced aplomb looked every man in the eye waiting for the right moment. With a large measure of pizzazz, he said,

"I, being the Mayor elect of the great City of Boston, will hereby give Marcus Brown the key to this City if he ever honors us with his presence again."

More hurrahs erupted. His worship waited for a propitious moment,

"It also gives me great pleasure to introduce a dear old friend of mine, his Honor, Lemuel Shaw former Chief Justice of our great State of Massachusetts. Your Honor, please come up and say a few words."

Wightman shook hands with Shaw and sat down.

The former Chief Justice using every bit of his venerable reputation to great effect rose phoenix-like from his chair. He too was a past master of many political enterprises especially in a year of state elections. Both he and the Mayor used such occasions to their best political advantage. Everyone there knew it and accepted it. Lemuel Shaw was even more of a master at public speaking than his wily predecessor. He began his voice sonorous and commanding.

"It has come to our attention today that our great nation and the City of Boston have been magnanimous in their acclaim for one of our own Marcus Brown. However, the great state of Massachusetts will not stand idly by and be outclassed by anyone."

Applause and laughter again made the room tinkle with sound. His Honor waited for silence.

"So in my capacity as former Chief Justice, and one with unprecedented experience in twisting arms…,"

There was even more laughter. Again he waited, then said with amazing conviction,

"I, Lemuel Shaw, formally pronounce that Marcus Brown will be forever immune to the Fugitive Slave Act of 1850. And…," He paused,

"I include any other persons if so indicted under its unconstitutional provisions. Although my wishes are probably without any shred of legality, I will however instruct my fellow Justices current or otherwise by telegram at the earliest possible moment as to my intentions." He continued buoyant,

"You see, I know where all the skeletons are buried."

His Honor sat down amongst the uproar around him and hugged his wife Hope.

No one spoke. No one breathed. The air within the room like outer space seemed to hold no capacity for sound whatsoever. It was as if the dinner never existed. Their hunger was erased not by copious food and drink about them but by an historical moment of importance where very powerful men were being moved to do very powerful things. They knew what was right, and most importantly, they knew what was just. John Saxton stood up and announced to the shocked multitude before him,

"Ladies and gentlemen, these men here have shown us that an 'Age of Reason' can again be evident within their ranks despite their opponent's best efforts to thwart it." He paused dramatically,

"So, seize this moment and hold this time and this place in your hearts forever. It was here that future generations will say that the seeds of change were planted. It was here that the emancipation of men despite their race, creed or religion took place. Leave this place tonight with new eyes and look to the future with great expectations in high and low places. I alone brought you all together tonight." He faced his parents saying,

"I apologize to them for using the Saxton name to encourage, cajole or downright bribe you all to come to this place, all expenses paid."

Saxton continued, his voice strong, inspired,

"Never before, and perhaps never again, will all this talent, enterprise and political will, be in one place at the same time in our history. I invite you gentlemen to retire to the drawing room down the hall, while I'm sure you ladies in our absence will have more intelligent subjects to discuss than ours."

Saxton waited politely until all the men, including Harriet Stowe had left. He noticed that Stephen Foster Collins stayed behind with the ladies in the Grand Salon. A few minutes later, he heard laughter. Someone on his mother's Grehorne piano was playing 'Camptown Races'. The merry music followed him as he made his way down the gas-lit hallway to the drawing room. As he entered it, the men and the fervent abolitionist Harriet Stowe stood; cigars and brandy in hand. They all applauded, shook his hand or patted the young man on the back. Mayor Wightman and others had previously decided amongst themselves, that the young Saxton showed an early talent for public speaking and with his name, wealth and Republican leanings; could possibly become President someday.

Quite suddenly, it was all over. Most of their guests had left a few hours before. Muriel and Thomas had gone to bed but Saxton remained seated in the den reflecting on the events of the evening. The Saxton House was quiet as snow continued drifting downwards upon it in icy spindrifts. Saxton got up and went to a frosted stained-glass window that spanned one end of his father's den or for that matter his world as only he knew it. Saxton scraped away some frost with his hands and peered uneasily through shards of seemingly blown glass. An arabesque pattern of stained glass lay imprisoned in lead before him. He was intrigued by its strong yet whimsical workmanship. His father had commissioned a well known English artist, William Morris, to design a square rigged sailing ship in full bloom as it scudded across some imaginary sea towards some distant unknown land. There was no horizon evident. No North Star was there to guide the great ship. All around it were large panels of clear glass through which one could look down upon the inner harbor below. A cold north wind picked up somewhat reminiscent of the recent storm he'd struggled through. Saxton became uneasy and with a sigh, he drew the window's thick curtains close together. A relentless sowing of snowflakes upon hummocked grounds outside the Saxton House continued well into a starless night.

To Saxton's mind, what had been was no more, and what was no more came into being. It seemed a natural world was trying to prevent a human world from going forward into oblivion. But no drifts, no amount of ice or blizzard winds could stop mankind's thirst for power. Powerful men and woman; of politics, of literature, of commerce, of law, of the arts, of faith and of military might had gathered to debate in the Saxton House. Yet despite their words, despite their prayers and most of all despite their vanity, Saxton learned one thing. Knowledge was power, pure and simple.

Many of his distinguished guests left earlier, either to catch a train, coach or ferry in time to crawl into their warm beds safe and sound. Others stayed to discuss politics, slavery and other contentious topics as they were wont to do. The oppression of and the recent resistance to the Fugitive Slave Act was debated vociferously. The Reverend Clover reminded them that he rejoiced in being a freed slave; but according to 'The Great Compromise' of 1850 was no longer in theory able to walk the streets of Boston or anywhere else for that matter. Congress had abolished his constitutional right to do so. Thereafter on many occasions, he railed from the bully pulpit against the 'Act of the Devil' as he called it. This heinous crime guaranteed every federal jurisdiction's right to assist slave owners in the recovery of their slaves who had fled to Free states such as Massachusetts, California or New York. Therefore, only an affidavit was required by slave owners while their fugitive slaves were not entitled to a jury trial to defend themselves. Any person caught assisting the escape of a slave or caught hiding them was subject to heavy fines or jail.

Some expressed support for slaves rescued by black mobs. William and Ellen Craft, and Shadrack's escape to Montreal, amongst others were talked about. They were horrified over former President Millard Fillmore sending Federal troops into Boston itself to remove a captured slave, a Thomas Sims, into the 'loving' care of his owner from Virginia. It was a disgrace and a perversion of the Declaration of Independence itself. Henry Wheeler Shaw rose up solemnly and summed up their wholesome sentiments most succinctly when he gravely intoned, "No one can disgrace us but ourselves."

Saxton sat in silent rapture as one after another they espoused their views to a captive audience, namely each other. Harriet Beecher Stowe was perhaps the most elegant of them all in her denunciation of slavery and all it stood for, but in turn it was said that she was also the most naive. Of all the cities in America, Boston was the center of a political hurricane as it became the 'eye' of abolitionist activity. It was here that Stowe published her famous novel, 'Uncle Tom's Cabin' in 1852. It became an instant sensation all over the world. What it did for all Its slmpllstlc moralizing was to expand the average person's insight into the horrors of slavery. It also fanned the flames of Southern rage into violence a short time later.

Reverend Clover, Rabbi Saling and Bishop Fitzpatrick were certainly the most practical. As men of the cloth, they were closer to the mark than most. They were reasonable, humble men who were powerful in inspiring hope and in reaffirming a wondrous faith in those who were weak. But, by having a more pragmatic view of humanity; they knew within themselves that they were powerless to stop powerful men from being powerfully self-serving.

The one man everyone listened to with serious concentration was the founder of the Free Soil Party, Congressman Charles Sumner. Sumner stood up; a fine figure of a man, his aquiline nose thrust itself out from a strong clean shaven visage topped by a brown mop of unruly hair. Sumner fingered a gold fob watch on a chain that hung down over a blue silk vest. As he spoke, his black bowtie wiggled like a fly caught on a sticky roll of paper. Despite this distraction, his voice and diction commanded attention.

A few years before, after making a speech against pro-slavery groups in Kansas, the Senator was nearly killed by Preston Brooks, a congressman from South Carolina. It was only recently, that Sumner had been able to resume his Senatorial duties. All those present in the soiree were aware of Sumner's ordeal but a few still rejected his radicalism. Former Chief Justice Shaw was against slavery but was inclined towards a separate but equal equation for blacks in America. Even President Buchanan himself after signing the 'Great Compromise' of 1850 where many States could have slaves, firmly believed that the expansion westward of the Mississippi River was a 'Whites Only' affair. The Chief Justice concurred.

Sumner, as the evening progressed, became somewhat vociferous in his denunciation of slavery in any form. Harriet Beecher Stowe took umbrage at his assaults on her book, 'Uncle Tom's Cabin'. Not only was she a woman, but she was a pacifist, or so Sumner expounded. As he leaned forward off his chair, brandy glass waving about, he said in a blatantly condescending tone,

"My dear Harriet; be that as it may, slavery must be crushed in America by force if needs be. Do you really think the southern states could survive without it after relying on it for the past two hundred years? Well for one, I don't! Once freed, the slaves would take over their master's plantations or at the very least seize their own farms as a fair return for their prolonged suffering."

He paused and leaned back, quite satisfied with himself. Mrs. Stowe smiled and rose to her full five foot height, her unruly locks of blondish hair swirling about her. She adjusted her pince-nez glasses carefully. With a steely resolve, the diminutive woman retorted angrily.

"I do believe Senator, that your thinking is somewhat flawed. I realize that your sentiments are flowing with the prevailing current of southern opinion but I for one believe that it takes more courage to go upstream against the violence of that current than sit back and let caution blow away in the wind. Lincoln is using the anti-slavery ticket to great advantage and I predicted that he would become President on such a platform. However, he is far more moderate than you and is willing to compromise with the South as evidence in his debates with Stephen Douglas a few years ago. South Carolina has seceded and many more will probably follow sooner than later; I hope not. If they do, Civil War will destroy the Union, God forbid."

She sat back down and turned to her husband Calvin, her face pinched and flushed with anger. She took his hand and said to him sweetly,

"My dear, I'm really quite tired and since we are staying here overnight, I think we should retire."

As she rose, the men did too; all except Sumner who remained seated staring into another snifter of brandy. Packard closed the door behind them then escorted them to their room upstairs.

An avid reader of many books on American history his father had given him before his voyage on the Silver Ghost began; Saxton had been as many Americans at the time were, somewhat ambivalent on the issue of slavery. After his return, he was convinced that to capture, imprison, torture and transport another human being away from their home and family had to stop. The incident on the Wanderlust sickened and disgusted him. The frequent nightmares he suffered from drained him emotionally. He knew that human beings were not animals to be bought and sold like cattle. It was not Christian, it was illegal and the Declaration of Independence said so. Saxton recalled that even Thomas Jefferson as President said in a private letter,

"I have sworn upon the alter of God, eternal hostility against every form of tyranny over the mind of man"

Saxton wondered if Jefferson should have included the body of man as well.

So, throughout New Year's Eve, these men of education, political ambition and religious fervor, continued to put forward their support for various versions of the anti-slavery question. The 'Age of Reason' within the room was short lived as no real compromises or solutions offered were practical. In fact, the views that Abraham Lincoln espoused in 1850 during his great debate with Frederick Douglas on equality, were acceptable to all of them except John Saxton. To him, Marcus was his brother, equal in every way.

Civil War was eminent to everyone there and as the New Year came about, those who remained went into the Grand Salon. A French mantel clock tolled midnight. Packard pulled back the drapes just in time to reveal an outburst of fireworks leaping up from Hoosac pier into a leaden sky over the harbor below. With cigars and brandies in hand, the group watched through a light dusting of snow; red, white and blue rockets burst into fiery fans of power and glory. Someone on the Grehorne piano began to play 'Auld Lang Syne'. The old song spread its melancholia throughout the room. Everyone there sang it as if it was the last time they would ever sing it together. The music died away. Somehow, everyone knew that this would probably be the last New Years Eve party they would attend for a very long time.

Thomas returned from seeing his wife to bed earlier. He bade his guest's adieu as numerous gas lights were extinguished throughout the upper floors of the Saxton House. It was but a foretaste of what the nation was about to experience as men of reason became unreasonable and men of the cloth extolled from the pulpits of the nation that their God was the only true God in which their nation could trust. So divided, Americans like the slaves aboard the Wanderlust, were dragged, chained and helpless towards the abyss of Civil War.

BOOK ONE: CHAPTER 8
THE MASTER OF MAYHEM

Belle La Fontaine sat in her parlor reminiscing about past events. She thought,

'Imagine! It's been six weeks since I dragged a wounded and foul smelling Marcus into my parlor. What an experience, overhearing Wilkins and a Custom's official discussing gun running for the Confederates. It's a good thing I wired 'Pinkie' right away about it for further instructions. Land sakes, we've known about 'False Prophet' for a long time now. Perhaps it's better if Marcus left town before he gets into more trouble and lets the cat out of the bag.' She continued her reverie thinking,

'It's better that way. The Confederates get defective weapons and ammo and I get a defective paramour, just like before. God almighty, I'm always caught between a rock and a hard place.'

Within weeks of his escape, Belle had recognized the old familiar signs. Marcus was restless to get out of New Orleans. She knew that by doing so, he would protect her and Cotton by drawing away those few men still roaming the streets of New Orleans looking for him. At least she had other reasons; reasons that had to remain secret.

She got up and walked over to a nearby window and stood beside it peering through its plantation shutters. As she stared down at the red brick street below her, Belle remembered how Marcus had met her son. She chuckled as it all came back to her.

She'd let go of Marcus and Cotton when Mary McPherson ran panting into the room. Without a word being said, Mary scooped up the boy and carried him protesting out into the hallway. Unknown to Belle, Mary smiled as she kicked shut the bedroom door. Belle was brought back to reality when Marcus went over and held her from behind. He kissed the nape of her neck. She stiffened slightly. He backed away releasing her. Belle turned around and looked up into his face, tears wet upon her cheeks. Marcus went to wipe them away but she walked around him, saying,

"Marcus, we have to talk. Come here and sit down beside me on the bed dear. It's important, really important."

Marcus did as he was told. He frowned as his mind raced to think of what Belle was about to say. He thought,

'It's been hard cooped up here for nearly two months. Her house is big but not big enough for a seafaring man like me. I've spent all my life either on the wide open plains of

Africa or the high seas of the world. I love Belle and Cotton, I really do. In fact I'd give my life for them but I know that I put them at risk every day that I stay here.'

Marcus reached over and held Belle to his chest. For the next two hours the couple talked about the perilous situation they were in. In the end they agreed to a course of action. Marcus was leaving New Orleans and soon. Only the how and where of it remained unresolved. Marcus told Belle the rest of the story about his eavesdropping escapade aboard the Anaona. She listened intently, nodding her head in apparent sympathy, knowing all along she had to stall Marcus yet satisfy him at the same time.

She immediately got in touch with her friends who knew other friends of friends involved with Harriet 'Minty' Tubman, a black Union spy. Tubman and others had organized an underground railway meant to assist runaway slaves escape north to Canada in response to the Fugitive Act of 1850. Many slaves on the 'railway' waited nervously for their 'Conductor' to lead them ever northward from one safe house or 'station' to the next. Thus after 1850, no person of color was safe anywhere in America, even the so called Free States within the Union.

In the first few days after Marcus fled from the lynch mob, he insisted that Belle send a message to Saxton, hoping beyond hope that it would get there safely. Apparently, Marcus was afraid that all telegraph machines at all the Western Union offices were being tapped by Confederate agents. Belle agreed and went to work on a coded message assuring him that she had used it many times in the past for sending messages to her rich clientele who for obvious reasons wanted their liaisons with her kept secret from their wives.

At the time, Marcus was astounded at how Belle cleverly devised a simple system of arranging the quarter panels of the note. He realized she was smarter than she let on. She was, for Belle had another secret that would have shocked him in that she and her 'soiled doves' were spies for the Union and used such a code every day to convey telegrams to Pinkerton. As such, she could have wired Pinkerton but decided to appease Marcus knowing full well that 'False Prophet' could not be compromised by exposing information that Pinkerton already knew about. The missing piece was the identity of the operation's mastermind in New Orleans. All Marcus knew was that the man was dressed as a Customs Officer whose name was never mentioned. For Belle, her country came before anything else therefore 'False Prophet' could not be endangered in any way. She also knew from Marcus that John Saxton was very smart, perhaps too smart. Hopefully, he wouldn't decode the message in time and consequently upset the apple cart. There was no way of knowing.

Every day, Belle sent Mary to buy the latest edition of the Times-Picayune newspaper.

America was heading towards Civil War. The papers screamed of it. Lincoln was campaigning for the Presidency and it looked like his abolitionist message would get him into the White House. South Carolina had seceded. Jefferson Davis was proclaimed President of the newly formed Confederate States of America a week earlier. Marcus wanted to stay but he knew that he could not. He steeled himself as Belle took his hands in hers. She looked up at him and said sweetly,

"Marcus, I'm pregnant."

Marcus couldn't believe his ears. He held onto Belle's hand while the other gently explored her slightly rounded belly.

"Oh, Belle my darling, how wonderful! I never noticed until now."

They leaned together as one, neither saying anything but at the same time saying everything. They remained that way for a long time until there was a polite knock at the door. It opened. Mary and Cotton came into the room. Immediately, Cotton ran to Marcus who held him high over his head. The boy giggled as Marcus put him down between him and Belle. Mary looked at Belle expectantly, saying,

"Lassie, have you told him yet? You have! Congratulations!" Mary hugged Belle and kissed Marcus. Cotton cried,

"When's lunch Auntie Mary?" Belle took his hand and said,

"Lunch is ready upstairs in the kitchen

Cotton struggled to get away. "Lunch is ready. Let's go Papa!"

He tugged at both of them then let go, turned and opened the bedroom door. He stood waiting impatiently. His parents got up, kissed then followed their son up the stairs.

Belle's kitchen was enormous. A large cast-iron Franklin coal stove sat at one end. Above it a blackened stove pipe ran upwards and into a high tin plated ceiling. A wooden coal bin squatted beside it. A coal scuttle lay upon it. Beside it was a large cast-iron sink flanked by a water pump. Clapboard cupboards covered the walls all around. An immense wooden chopping block centered the room. A flexible drying rack stood beside another wall. Pine floorboards, highly polished and waxed, ran throughout the room. A substantial cooling room and an even larger pantry were on the other side of the stove. However, this pantry was unusual, for behind its rear wall was an opening that led to a secret escape route out of the house down a staircase to Pirate Alley four blocks away.

A former owner with many enemies used it often over the years. Belle discovered it after some of her gem jars filled with preserves fell down and shattered. She wondered why their watery juice was disappearing under the bottom of a tall shelf. As she began cleaning up the mess, curiosity got the better of her. On a hunch, she tried to pull the heavy shelving aside. Nothing moved. She then tried rotating it, her hands gripping either side of it. It moved slightly. She tried harder. Slowly the shelving rotated on an upper and lower metal pintle just enough to let one person slip through at a time. Belle tentatively explored its dark recesses but had not gone the whole way into what seemed to be a dangerous, steep and unfathomable stairwell. Perhaps Marcus would. She showed it to him one day. Taking a lamp and a pistol, he crouched down and entered its darkness. An hour later, he returned covered with cobwebs. He agreed with Belle that someday the escape route might come in handy.

Over the next few days, Belle and Marcus stashed lanterns, money, canned food, weapons, clothing and medical supplies in an alcove at the end of a very long tunnel. They had to, as dozens of bounty hunters were still looking for Marcus and time was running out. What he didn't know was that Garrow and his gang were looking too.

Mary moved about with matronly purpose as she set their lunch down before them. After it was finished, she put Cotton to bed for his nap. Mary returned, washed the dishes, putting them on a wooden rack to dry. She retired to her room leaving Marcus and Belle alone but not before she returned with a copy of the Boston Daily Advertiser. It laid on the table in front them. While sipping his coffee, Marcus adjusted himself, allowing light from a nearby bay window to stream down over his broad shoulders. He picked up the paper. Across the first page, a black headline screamed,

'CONFEDERATE GUN RUNNERS DIE IN BATTLE OF BOSTON HARBOR'

Marcus couldn't believe his eyes. He yelled, "He did it! He did it!"

He shoved the soiled newspaper across the table towards her. She read with suppressed glee that fourteen Confederate spies had either been killed or captured. Silas Wilkins was dead. His body and those of his dead crew were bound by train for New Orleans for burial. The others who survived would be tried in Boston and would surely hang for treason for running guns for the Confederates. Marcus knew that the Anaona's cargo had been a lot more dangerous than farm machinery. He sat back stunned by the audacity of the smugglers and the betrayal of a man who once saved his life off the coast of Africa. Marcus asked himself, why had a man he'd known for over twenty years betrayed him, the Saxtons and most of all, his country? Was it just for gold or was it something else?

Belle slid the paper back across the table to Marcus. He laughed as he recalled his escape but stopped as he remembered Belle's note he left behind on board the Anaona. Since the incident with the Wanderlust, Marcus had read newspaper reports about Josiah Garrow, the dead slaver. Apparently his son Horatio was a Custom House official in New Orleans. Marcus wondered if it was he who had boarded the Anaona that fateful morning. The very thought disturbed him, for with this newspaper and others, Garrow would know that he, Marcus, was to blame for killing Josiah. As such his son would never rest until he avenged his father's death. Marcus became increasingly worried, for Belle's note might have implicated her in some way. Perhaps Garrow would try to track down the courier who came aboard with it. In any event, he was now a sworn enemy who might have had enough time to figure it all out. He looked over at Belle reading the paper and said,

"Belle, have you ever heard of a Captain Horatio Garrow?" Belle's face went chalk white. Marcus was shocked. He reached over and took both her hands in his.

"Belle darling, what is the matter, you're so pale. You look as if you've seen a ghost?"

She trembled uncontrollably. Tears streaked her cheeks; she looked up into his face and cried out.

"Captain Garrow was a customer of the 'Rising Sun' many years ago when I had just turned seventeen. I was a virgin at the time. One night when the owner was out, Garrow and three of his goons came into the House demanding service. At the time I worked in the kitchen and laundry. I heard a commotion in the foyer. Some of the girls screamed. Curses and sounds of severe violence always frightened me, but over time, I tried to get used to it. I had no where else to go. As the commotion began to get out of control, I realized I was trapped in the kitchen. Tommy, our house bodyguard told me to hide in a pantry. Soon after that I heard a shot. Someone shrieked. I hid. There I was in the pantry looking out through the louvers of a closet door. I heard the kitchen doors swing open. A large white man came in. He acted like an animal, sniffing and prodding the dark recesses of the room. All of a sudden there was silence. I swore that the pounding of my heart could have been heard at twenty paces."

Marcus stood up to put his hands on her shoulders.

"Belle darling, you don't have to tell me the rest. You really don't. It doesn't take much of an imagination to realize what happened next. No Belle, don't tell me. Please don't or I'll go mad. I think the man I overheard talking to Wilkins was Horatio Garrow."

Belle was inwardly elated. Perhaps Garrow was the mastermind behind 'Operation False Prophet'. She had to find out and soon. However, Belle had a deeper secret buried within her. She couldn't tell him. She began sobbing in his arms. He caressed her gently. The two of them held on to each other for what seemed like forever as they rocked back and forth in the kitchen. Marcus swore that if he ever had the chance to kill this man, he would do it the old Maasai way. Unknown to him, Belle was thinking exactly the same thing.

Horatio Armstrong Garrow sat in a high backed Windsor chair at his slant front desk in the Custom's House. He was furious, his rage uncontrolled and deadly.

"Christ almighty, it's been six weeks now after the Anaona incident and still no one; no one has captured Marcus Brown or whatever the hell his name is. My boys have scoured New Orleans from top to bottom literally, but no giant nigger has been found. Time is running out. I'm positive he knows what I'm up to! Silas told me so. Imagine hiding in a closet. If only I had opened that damned door we wouldn't be in this mess."

He lit up another Cuban cigar, leaned forward in his wing-backed chair, and reached for a copy of Times-Picayune lying before him on his desk. A bold headline screamed,

'SOUTHERN PATRIOTS DIE IN BATTLE OF BOSTON HARBOR'

He chewed his cigar while searching the paper for any other details that might have escaped his attention. The front page diatribe went on as it raged against the death of Captain Silas Wilkins and most of his valiant crew. The actions of one Captain John Gibbon, a West Point Academy artillery instructor were ruefully mentioned. Further down the page, one John Saxton, the son of the shipping magnate was vilified in livid detail. Horatio muttered evilly,

"I knew that Saxton kid was going to be trouble! I knew it!" He paused, took a puff on his cigar, exclaiming,

"Well, it says here that Captain Wilkins died with honor for the 'cause' in battle."

He continued to read further with renewed interest. There at the very bottom of the article was mentioned one John Saxton, who learned of the plot. Another paragraph told how Marcus Brown, First Mate of the Anaona had escaped from a lynch mob in New Orleans. Apparently he made his way back to Boston with help of an underground network. The marine news of the same paper reported that Brown upon his return to Boston became Captain of a Saxton Co. clipper ship, the Katanga. It sailed for China three weeks after the 'Battle of Boston Harbor'. Garrow grumbled aloud,

"So that's why no one had seen the bastard for the past six weeks!"

Little did he know that Thomas Saxton called in favors from the owners of two of Boston's largest newspapers namely, The Daily Advertiser and its cross-town rival; the Boston Globe. Thomas and his son agreed that this ruse might possibly give Marcus a better chance of making it home safely. Garrow continued to ponder. Marcus Brown was gone. Anyway, it really didn't matter. South Carolina seceded from the Union December 21st and Major Anderson deserted Fort Moultrie shortly thereafter. Fort Sumter was reinforced with a company of Moultrie's artillerists a few days later. At least Silas Wilkins had been reliable. The Captain put his big feet up on his desk, leaned back, and took another sip of Jim Beam while puffing mightily on a cigar. He enthused,

"Little do those blue bellies know that General P. Beauregard, our 'Little Napoleon' will attack Fort Sumter and soon."

Horatio planned to be there or die trying. He jumped up, donned a long frocked overcoat and left the Custom's House for his residence.

Horatio Garrow walked from the Custom's House at 423 Canal Street to his modest Victorian home at 1301 Rue Dauphine in the 5th district of New Orleans. It was only six blocks north of the Customs House on the levee. The residence was small but that was all he needed. His son Lucas was home on vacation from 'The Old War Skule'; a new all male military school for boys in Pineville, Louisiana. Lucas was nearly thirteen, and Horatio's only chlld. He always told the boy that his mother died in child birth. Lucas believed him. It was just as well, for Horatio's first wife Melinda, disappeared one night. Apparently, when infant Lucas was brought home, she rejected him and Horatio at the same time. Her body was never found.

Working incognito as a spy and gun runner for the 'cause', Horatio was adept at changing lies into palpable truths. Right after Melinda's disappearance, Horatio employed a white nanny, Marie, to look after Lucas. He decided early on to run his son's life in a military fashion as he himself did albeit as the Captain of the Customs House. Horatio was determined to instill in the boy a dedication to the southern way of life and the discipline required to do its bidding when the time came for preserving it. Garrow was sure that that time was coming very soon indeed.

At home in his paneled study, Horatio sat at his desk smoking a cigar. His cigar died. He stubbed what was left into a nearby glass ashtray, leaned over and retrieved Belle's note from his desk. He held it up and smelled it. A slight tincture of rosewater was still impregnated within it. He was positive it was Belle La Fontaine's and that she knew where the Marcus was hiding. The idea of renewing his sordid relationship with her hardened him up as he thought more about it. He lit another cigar then rose carrying the note out into his salon to a small mahogany bar. After pouring a whiskey, he sat down in a padded rocking chair next to an ornamental brick fireplace. Within it, a small coal fire smoldered in a cast iron grate. Horatio put down his drink on a side table. He stoked a mound of glowing coals with a brass poker. Red and yellow spikes flared upwards. Horatio closed his eyes and smelled the note one last time then carefully put it upon the fiery coals. Once thereon, the note flashed and popped as the rosewater within its porous paper boiled. He prodded it until the note curled up in seeming agony before it was completely consumed.

Satisfied, he leaned back, cradled his old fashioned whiskey glass upon his chest and rocked back and forth thinking about what he was going to do next. He didn't have long to wait. There was a knock on the door. After a few moments, he replied,

"Come in."

Lucas Garrow walked in dressed in a grey military styled school uniform. His father stood up returning his salute. The tall, black haired, olive skinned boy said,

"Captain Sir, I've just received a telegram for you."

He gave it to his father. The boy saluted, turned smartly about and left the room closing the door behind him. Horatio opened the sealed telegram. It read.

"By the Order of the Confederate President elect,
Jefferson F. Davis STOP Captain Horatio Garrow
formally of the New Orleans Customs Dept. STOP
has hereby been promoted to the rank of Captain
CSA STOP to be effective immediately STOP He
Is to report to Major Douglas H. Cooper, Baton Rouge
immediately STOP Leroy P. Walker, Secretary of
War STOP February 07th, 1861."

Horatio was elated. He jumped up, thrusting the brass poker about like a cavalry sword in a mock battle. He was going to the Gulf Divisional headquarters in the Baton Rouge state library building, then on to Memphis with a Major Cooper by steamboat. He put the ornate poker on its stand then sat down somewhat disappointed realizing he was heading in the wrong direction. But, he reasoned that he was now a Captain in a real army. His training as a siege specialist was about to pay off. He was elated, for it was a step up from his lowly work at the Customs House. There was one problem. Someone else would have to run the Deacon gang. But for now he put these thoughts aside, reached down and raised his whiskey glass on high, crying,

"Oh, please God, let the war games begin!"

Before he left New Orleans, Horatio Garrow was going to pay a visit to Belle's new residence adjoining La Belle Maison. It was well after midnight and all been arranged. He'd finally come to a conclusion, after weeks of trying, to understand how a seven foot black man with numerous facial scars could simply disappear in a 'White' city. His gut feeling was that Belle La Fontaine had something to do with a lot of unexplained mysteries in New Orleans. He knew damned well she was most certainly involved with the disappearance of the 'Big Nigger' whose knowledge of 'False Prophet' although minimal was too risky to ignore. Garrow, a master of deception, knew when someone was trying to conceal his prey. He had only two days left before his son went back to Military School. After that he would be leaving to join Major Cooper in Baton Rouge. Besides, Horatio still didn't know if the 'Big Nigger' had somehow compromised any of his other smuggling operations in New Orleans or elsewhere. He had to act fast for time was running out. Abraham Lincoln, the old hypocrite, had become President of the Union, February 9th and was apparently dead set against slavery. Horatio thought ruefully,

'Surely there will be hell to pay now that Jefferson Davis, President Elect of the CSA and Lincoln are about to have a pissing contest over it.'

The Captain left his house just after midnight. From there he walked a short distance to Pirate Alley where he was joined by three other armed men. Standing in the shadows, they lit cheroots and discussed their plan. They'd been in Belle's house many times before on Rue Bienville looking in vain for its former occupant. After talking it over, their plan of attack was laid out with military precision.

Belle and Marcus were in bed. They'd finished their love-making hours earlier and were lying entwined under a cotton coverlet. The bedroom window's plantation sashes were wide open allowing a soft warm breeze to flutter about the room. An intricate four poster mosquito net swished back and forth as gusts of air clung to it then released it every few moments. Belle was fast asleep. Her full breasts rose like two storm waves coming ashore onto a tropical beach. Occasionally, she would flinch as if someone or something was tormenting her subconscious mind. Her long black tresses trickled across her paramour's naked chest like ocean spindrift. Marcus lay there musing in an uneasy trance, not asleep but not quite awake either. His inner ear however, awoke to the imperceptible sounds of voices.

He sat up disorientated. As his eyes and ears became alert, he heard low voices outside a nearby window. From down on the street below him, harsh guttural whispers, followed by a grating sound of metal on metal rose to assault him. Marcus slipped out of bed like a Tvaso lion moving low through red grass. He quickly dressed then peered through the shutters to the street below. A moonless sky was further darkened by the fact that a corner gaslight had been extinguished. Marcus was sure he heard a familiar voice say, "Be careful lads! Easy does it. That's it, use the drill."

Marcus strained to see what they were doing but could not. What they were doing would have shocked him. They were drilling a hole in the green door right beneath him. The drill was withdrawn. A specially designed iron pry-bar was inserted down into the small hole then slowly raised upwards, lifting the bar inside up and over two of the three brackets. A metallic clank from downstairs meant the door was now unbarred, the bar lying useless on the foyer carpet. Marcus closed the shutters tight knowing he had only a few minutes before the front door lock was picked.

He ran over to Belle, pulled the netting aside and put his hand over her mouth. Her eyes flew open with alarm. Marcus whispered in her ear. She understood and leaped naked out of the bed towards the armoire. Once there, she lit a nearby Aladdin lamp, leaving it on a nightstand. She opened the armoire and took out raggedy cotton shift and slipped into it. Barefoot, she fled out of the bedroom and down a short hallway. Meanwhile, Marcus hurriedly dressed. Once finished, he opened a narrow drawer in his nightstand. From within it he withdrew a Colt .31 dragoon pocket revolver. He checked to see that it was loaded. It was. Then he retrieved his Bowie-knife from under his pillow. Fully armed, and barefoot, he grabbed a lantern and headed for the bedroom door.

Belle had already entered Cotton's bedroom. She roused him and Mary McPherson sleeping on a cot across from him. As soon as she understood what was going on, Mary told the boy they were going to play hide and seek. He was overjoyed because it was his favorite game. She looked up at Belle grimly, knowing that she could flee with her. She said,

"You take Cotton. Don't argue with me. Marcus needs me and more than that, Cotton needs a mother. Now lassie off you go and be quick about it dearie." Mary bent down and kissed Cotton. Belle nodded to her son.

"Cotton, take my hand. We're going to hide while Mary counts to ten. OK?"

The boy's face shone with anticipation. He pulled at his mother whispering,

"I know the perfect place we can hide Mommy. No one will ever find us!" Belle replied,

"Yes son I know a place too."

She looked at Mary who knew exactly where they were going. Mary whispered,

"Now off you go"; she paused then slowly said,..."1.......2.......3......4.......5."

Belle chased Cotton down the hallway towards the kitchen. Once she'd counted to ten, Mary ran down the hallway to her bedroom in the back corner of the house. Once there she lit a lamp, leaving it on a nightstand. She ran barefoot to her armoire, unlocked it then pulled its tall doors wide open. Her white cotton housecoat was hanging from a hook on the door next to it. She put it on over her night gown and tied its cotton belt tightly around her ample waist. Reaching once more into the armoire, she pushed a few garments aside, and pulled out a double barreled sawed-off Whitmore shotgun. It was loaded with No#3 buckshot. She called it 'The Peacemaker'.

Holding the weapon straight up in one hand and a lantern in the other, Mary left the bedroom and advanced down the darkened hallway towards the downstairs staircase. As she got to the top of it, Marcus was lurking at the foot of it, a revolver in his right hand. The front door below her was wide open. Just then, pistol shots were fired from outside the house. A return fire erupted. In its muzzle flash, Mary saw Marcus slump to the ground. A man staggered through the door falling upon him. Mary put down the lantern and ran down a few steps. She lowered the shotgun just as another silhouette came through the open door. Her shotgun roared, knocking her backwards. The target screamed as it was literally blown back through the open doorway. Mary recovered her wits and ran down the stairs. With one hand, she rolled a body off of Marcus. He groaned trying to get up. Mary used all her strength to get him to his feet.

Meanwhile, Belle had run into the kitchen with Cotton ahead of her. He turned to hide behind the stove. Belle grabbed him and pulled him towards the pantry. Cotton protested, "Mommy, mommy; I had a good place to hide. Mary always looks in the pantry!"

Belle smiled and whispered, "Son, I have a better place to hide. Just you wait and see!"

Shots were fired downstairs. With that as instant motivation, she rotated some shelving and together they vanished behind it and waited.

Horatio Garrow stood in deep shadows across the street. He saw his men drill a hole, raise an iron bar behind the green door then pick its lock, all within minutes. They threw their tools behind some rose bushes, opened the green door wide and advanced through it, guns drawn. Garrow continued to smoke his cheroot quite satisfied with himself, as shots were fired from within the house, he thought,

'Good, they killed the 'Big Nigger'.

His satisfaction evaporated with the roar of a shotgun. Horatio watched incredulously as one of his goons was blown out through the open door and onto an iron cornstalk picket fence that faced the street. The body lay impaled before him, its life blood gushing into a brick gutter. Garrow was momentarily stunned.

Belle heard more muffled shots as she lit another coal-oil lantern. She thought that Mary might be right behind her but she wasn't. She called out for her but there was no answer; just the sound of Mary's shotgun blasting away at the intruders. Belle then understood that Mary and Marcus were sacrificing themselves, giving her and Cotton precious time to escape. Slowly she rotated the shelf to its original position. With a prayer on her lips and a lantern in hand, she tugged Cotton along behind her headlong down a narrow staircase.

Mary McPherson knew that more men would come, for cowards always came in packs. Slowly, she and Marcus climbed back up the staircase. A trail of blood followed them like a jilted lover. Upon reaching the top, Marcus collapsed, breathing hard. A bullet had barely grazed his left leg. Mary turned as a shadow crossed the lower threshold. It stopped, looming in the semi-darkness at the foot of the staircase. She felt the hair on the nape of her neck rise. Below her, a deeper blackness took the form of yet another man. She raised her shotgun to fire but as she did so, Marcus got up, deflecting the blast. It shredded a wall beside the darkened figure. Marcus pulled her around a corner just as two bullets zipped past them. Still gripping his Colt, he fired back until his gun was empty. Below them a man grunted in agony while another began climbing the staircase. Mary cursed, holding her empty shotgun. She looked Marcus in the eyes without any hint of fear. Her fate was sealed and she knew it.

"I'll stay and teach the bastard my version of the Highland Fling. Now get goin' Laddie and don't look back!"

She pushed him towards the kitchen. Holding empty shotgun by the barrel, she turned to meet her attacker. Marcus reluctantly hobbled off towards the kitchen dragging one bleeding leg behind him. He stopped and turned about. In the glow of a lantern by her feet, he saw Mary swing the shotgun at a man. She screamed, "RUN LADDIE RUN!"

Her assailant swore for she'd bashed his face in with the gun butt. Garrow staggered backwards under the onslaught. In a rage he rushed forward. A knife slivered down upon Mary McPherson again and again.

Marcus dragged himself through the kitchen. Once there, he jammed two shells into his Colt and turned towards the pantry. The man was upon him before he could get any further. Both grunted as they hit the floor. Marcus fired his revolver into the man as his assailant's knife found its target. The man went limp. Marcus felt searing pain in his left shoulder. His ears rang from the gun's explosion. After regaining his senses, he rolled out from underneath the body lying upon him. Marcus bent down to retrieve his gun then groped in the dark about the kitchen until he found a lantern sitting on a counter. In his pocket was a tin of matches. Seconds later a glowing lantern highlighted a body sprawled on the floor in a pool of blood. Marcus was shocked. It was the Customs agent he'd seen going aboard the Anaona. The man's face would be forever etched into Marcus's memory. Holding the lantern high, the Maasai limped down the hallway to Mary but she was dead. There were no signs of anyone else about. He reloaded his Colt then came back to the pantry. The shelf was still in place. Knowing that Belle and Cotton were safe, he went to the kitchen, took off his bloody shirt and hung it on a chair. Marcus staggered to the sink where he washed his head wound with lye bar soap then packed it with a brown sugar poultice from a cupboard nearby. The dressing stung sharply. He did the same to his bleeding leg and shoulder, wrapping each of them with a clean kitchen rag, then ripped an end in two and tied it off tightly. Marcus looked at the floor leading towards the pantry. It was clean. Miraculously, he hadn't left a blood trail.

Garrow awoke just as Marcus spun the pantry shelving shut. Horatio got up and groped in the dark towards a kitchen chair, sliding blindly about on the bloody floor. He knocked over a lantern sitting on a table. Picking it up, he lit it using matches from his pocket. He peered about the kitchen. His head throbbed for he was bleeding from a severe head wound and his ears still rang from the shot that nearly killed him. He was lucky that the 'Big Nigger' thought he was dead and he knew it. Never had he fought someone as strong. For the first time in his life he was afraid of someone. A sick feeling emanated from every pore of his body. He hated it. Garrow groped around for a towel and found one balled up lying in a sink. It smelled of blood. He thought,

'I've wounded him. Good! I hope that bastard dies sooner rather than later. As for Belle, I'll deal with that bitch, all in good time. I'll keep this rag though. One never knows, it just might be useful trackin' 'em down.'

Satisfied, he stemmed his bloody head wound long enough to put a clean rag over it. Tying it off, he bent down, and after searching in the gloom, retrieved his dagger. Garrow while holding a lantern high stumbled down the hall towards a shadow laying prone on the floor ahead of him. Horatio stepped over Mary but as he did so, he remembered her bravery. He paused, looked down, saw her shotgun laying there, picked it up, checked the breech and strangely enough stood at attention above her. He thought,

'Here's to you woman. You died unafraid of death.'

Mary's killer instinctively knew that the rest of the house was empty although he tried to force open Belle's 'Twixt' door but found it locked. Garrow ran down the stairs, Mary's shotgun in his hand. He didn't stop to examine his partners in crime. They were dead, that much was obvious. Horatio closed the front door behind him, and turned towards Pirate Alley. Therein, he ran past a narrow metal plate inset into a brick wall unaware that a tiny ray of light was flashing low down from within it. Its rusty hinges began squealing moments after he rounded the corner onto Rue St. Anne.

Belle and Cotton were waiting quietly when Marcus got to them. He told Belle about Mary. Belle wept. However, he didn't tell her about his struggle in the kitchen with Garrow. He didn't have to, for he was bleeding through his bandages. She was upset.

"Marcus, you're hurt bad all over aren't you?" He nodded.

"Let's have a closer look."

Belle's lantern hovered above him. Her fingers grazed his head. He winced.

"I'm ok. Let's get out of here to somewhere safe before sunup."

Marcus bent down and put his ear to a tiny hole drilled through an iron plate. He heard someone running past followed by silence. The big man put his hand on a metal lever, pulled it downwards then pushed. The small room was filled with an angry screeching as two rusty hinges on the door gave way. His heart stopped. Marcus put his ear again to the hole. Nothing seemed amiss. Encouraged, he pushed harder against the metal plate. The narrow door swung open into the night. Marcus with great difficulty slipped through its small opening because its door was pushing against him as if it was spring loaded. It was. Once outside, he looked both ways down Pirate Alley. They were alone. Marcus turned, pulled Belle out who in turn pulled Cotton out. Cotton looked around.

"Mommy, Auntie Mary will never, ever find us, will she?"

Belle looked down at Cotton, took his face in her hands and whispered,

"No son, she will never find us again."

Cotton looked up puzzled. His attention was diverted as Marcus reached back into the hole and pulled out two burlap sacks of supplies. He blew out the lantern and put it back through the door. It shut with a sharp clang. Marcus hoisted a heavy sack over each of his broad shoulders. With Belle in the lead holding onto Cotton, Marcus hobbled after them as they exited onto Rue Chartres. After two blocks, they reached Rue St. Louis and turned right. Marcus whispered,

"If only we can make it to Lafayette Square. At least there we can hole up in some shrubbery and rest awhile."

Belle agreed. After fleeing down Rue Decatur they reached the square, where they concealed themselves in dense brush. Once settled in, Belle turned to Marcus.

"I have an idea. There might be sanctuary for us at the Ursuline Convent nearby. I know it well, believe me. Their church, Sainte Marie de Archveche is next door to it. However, I've heard that the Bishop Grodine there is sympathetic to the Confederacy."

Marcus was alarmed. He grabbed her shoulders.

"Belle, are you crazy! He'll turn us in for sure!"

She laughed at him. Marcus released her, somewhat bewildered.

"The Bishop was a private customer of mine years ago. I would meet him in his quarters instead of at the 'Rising Sun'. He paid very well. I'm sure he'll be glad to take us in and even gladder to get rid of us as soon as he can."

She bent down. Cotton looked up at her, his eyes enormous with anticipation. Belle whispered,

"You two stay here and be quiet; especially you Cotton. This is no longer hide n' seek, but a game called, 'Who can be quiet the longest'." She laughed,

"I'm sure you'll win Cotton."

Belle kissed both of them then crept out of sight. It seemed like an eternity but a few minutes later several bushes nearby rustled. Marcus held a hand over Cotton's mouth. Belle crept forward on her hands and knees, her belly hanging down ever so slightly. As she came forward, Marcus kissed her. Cotton whispered, "I won Mommy! I won! Hurrah!"

Belle hushed him and sat down, putting him on her lap. Marcus looked at her, pleading with his eyes for her to say something, anything. She took a hand written note out of her dress pocket. It was on fine white linen paper embossed with the official gold seal of the Bishop of New Orleans. Belle gave it to Marcus. He held it up to the light from a nearby lamp post. In neat copper plate script, it said,

"TO: Mother Superior Theresa Fargone.

You are hereby instructed without prejudice, to assist these penitents, a Miss Belle La Fontaine, her escort Marcus Brown and her son Cotton in their journey from our parish north to the next parish and so on as soon as they see fit. You and the other sisters are also instructed to abide by a vow of silence on this matter, during their stay and after their departure. You are also instructed to send through the Church courier service, a note to Bishop John Fitzpatrick of the Archdiocese of Boston, telling him that he is to forward it to Thomas Saxton of Saxton Shipping Co. at his Holiness's earliest convenience. Lastly, this note will be given to these penitents and it will act as a mark of safe conduct if they so choose to avail themselves of the protection of the Holy See. Please see to their protection and comfort immediately.

In Christ's name and that of the Holy Mother,

His Holiness, Bishop Jean Michael Grodine.

Sainte Marie de Archveche,

February, 17th, 1861."

Marcus gave the missive back to Belle, covered his mouth and rocked back and forth trying not to laugh too loud. His laughter was cut short. Loud angry voices carried on a warm evening breeze swept towards them. The trio tensed. The voices got closer and closer. One swore,

"I'll be Goddamned if I'll let him get away again!"

Belle, her eyes wide with terror, recognized the voice of Horatio Garrow. She couldn't believe it. Here they all were, so close to safety, so close. Marcus saw her distress and lay low in the bushes clutching his knife in one hand and his Colt in the other. Lanterns flared, driving shadows away in spurts as if the very air was riven by hatred. Another man cried,

"I'm goin' to get that reward if it kills me."

"Clem , in your condition it probably will!" Garrow yelled at them.

"Shut up you idiots and keep looking. God! My head hurts somethin' awful. It's bleeding again. Now keep a look out. This nigger is smart, fast and as strong as three of us put together. Shut up and keep looking you two! They're holed up here somewhere. I know it 'cause I seen 'em runnin' down Decatur in this direction."

They were very close now. Cotton was afraid, very afraid. For the first time he realized what happened tonight was not a game and never would be. His heart raced in his small chest. Marcus parted a bush far enough to see where their pursuers were. Garrow stood mere feet away. He cried,

"You two stay here; I'm going over to Dirk Burton's and get Cain and Able. They'll get I'm for sure once they smell this here nigger's bloody rag! And also, don't tell anyone you're hunting him or we'll never see that reward. Do you two pecker heads understand me? Now hole up in the bushes somewhere and stay out of sight. I'll be right back."

After a few moments, one said to the other,

"Jesus Christ Clem, I've never seen him so jumpy and when he's jumpy, he's deadly."

Disbelief crept over the fugitives for their pursuers decided to hide right next to them. Marcus looked at Belle and nodded. She mouthed the words, "Be careful, I love you."

Marcus was used to stalking his prey, as he had done the same thing many times hunting game in Africa. This was no different. His prey was armed and dangerous too. Before Belle knew it, Marcus had crawled away into the night. The two pursuers put out their lanterns. Belle could hear them whispering and smoking. Her hand was clamped firmly over Cotton's mouth whose eyes were like two large moons orbiting Jupiter. An evening breeze ruffled the bushes. One man jumped up in terror. His partner pulled him down.

"For Christ's sake Bubba, sit down and shut up! Here's some more liquid courage."

As Bubba raised his whiskey flask, his blood sprayed all over it. Before Clem could even react to the horror beside him, his throat was slit too. Marcus sat their bodies' upright against a tree as blood and corn liquor mingled on the ground between them.

After what seemed an eternity to Belle, Marcus reappeared. He growled.

"Simba hunted well tonight. Let's be going."

Together they ran to the Ursuline Convent nearby. The trio silently approached a great bronze door marking its front entrance. It lay under a square portico fronting a white three story building. Belle lifted an ornate iron knocker. BANG! BANG! BANG! A hollow metallic sound crashed about them like thunder as Marcus was sure it would wake up half the city. Minutes late a small metal slot was pulled back from a small square inset in a smaller trap door. From within a woman's voice intoned,

"What do you want at this late hour my child?"

Belle shoved the Bishop's note through the narrow slot. After a few moments the smaller opened. The trio entered just as the baleful sound of blood hounds on a scent came wafting towards them.

Dirk Burton hung on grimly to his two bloodhounds and a bloody cotton cloth. Both dogs bayed as they approached a verge of bushes on the edge of Lafayette Square. Their vocalization increased as they stopped, sniffed the ground then surged forward once more. Garrow lifted a sawed-off shotgun to his waist just as Burton let go of the hound's leads. The dogs ran into some bushes. Their baying became hysterical. Burton stood back as Garrow parted dense foliage with his gun's stubby barrel. There, before him lay his cohorts. Astride them, Cain and Able were happily licking the bloody necks of two dead men.

Margery Briscoe knocked on the 'Twixt' door that connected 'La Belle Maison' to Belle's house next door. It was very early on a Sunday morning. There was no answer. Margery wondered.

'Belle is usually having breakfast coffee with me by now.' She straightened a yellow house coat that hung about her thin body like a funeral pall. Again she knocked on the door.

Once again there was no response. Taking a brass key from her pocket, she unlocked the door. It opened silently revealing a tomb. Acrid airs within the hallway smelled strangely of gunpowder. All was dark and dim. She called out. There was no reply. Briscoe walked nervously to the sitting room at the front of the house. Its long curtains were still pulled tightly together. She drew them apart flooding the room with light. Something was not right. Margery turned a corner leading to the kitchen. She nearly tripped over a woman's body sprawled out at the top of the staircase. Before her lay Mary McPherson covered in blood, a cold lantern quiescent beside her. Margery dropped the brass key and began screaming.

Sergeant Milford Raines sat at his duty desk listening to an excited young constable who'd found a man dead in front of 509 Rue Bienville. Twenty minutes later, Raines arrived there in a police paddy wagon. Its matched team of Belgium mules stomped their iron-shod hooves on the red brick street, for they smelled a body impaled on an iron picket fence directly across from them. As they stomped, the sounds were reminiscent of gunshots ricocheting between rows of nearby brick tenement houses. A man's gruesome remains had been found an hour earlier by one of the night patrols. A constable had waited for his arrival. He led Raines to the body. The Sergeant looked down at the bloody torso. On the left wrist of the corpse was tattooed a large letter 'D' with a dagger thrust through it. A patrol officer beside him observed wryly,

"Well Sarge, it looks like buckshot got one of the Deacon boys. I've run into this bastard before down at the docks. Has the dagger tattoo on his wrist he does. Nasty lot that gang is. Sure looks a mess doesn't he, guts hangin' out n' all? From where he's lyin' it looks like someone inside the house blasted him with a shotgun at close range." Raines stepped closer to the body.

"Well son, I suppose you're right, but the door is closed. So let's first get him out of here. He's starting to smell."

Raines looked about, spying two junior constables nearby.

"Here you two, lift him up, lay him out in the wagon and cover him up. Wait a minute, there's a pistol lying over in some rose bushes over by the doorstep."

The two officers paused then went to the paddy wagon, opened the rear iron door, reached in and took out a canvas stretcher, placing a black tarp upon it. They strolled back across the street, one of them at either end of the stretcher. Meanwhile Raines left the door closed until the area around it was searched thoroughly. Something sparkled at him. He bent down and retrieved a short barreled Colt .44 belly gun from amongst some rose bushes. He examined it carefully. He opened its breech. The gun had not been fired. All six balls and caps were still there. Strangely it was brand new. Packing grease could still be seen in every crevice. He handed the gun to another policeman as he walked over to the building's large green front door. Raines kneeled down to inspect a small hole drilled into it. Minute bits of sawdust lay below on the stone threshold. Raines began to say something, but something caught his eye. He walked over a few feet to his right. Once again he parted some rose bushes. Behind them lay a strangely shaped iron pry-bar. He had seen one before. In an instant, he knew what had happened.

Behind him, the litter was laid out on the stone sidewalk that fronted the narrow brick building. Two policemen pulled the impaled body upwards off the short iron spikes of the cornstalk fence. As they did so, the body made a sucking sound as if it was still alive. One policeman vomited upon it. Sergeant Raines turned about. He remembered his first day as a patrol officer too. He walked over and put his hand on the young man's shoulder boards.

"Walker me lad, it's alright, for everyone does it once you know. Now get goin' and forget about it."

The body was laid out, covered up then loaded into the paddy wagon. The skittish mules pranced nervously, the smell of death flaring their nostrils.

The older officers were teasing Walker but stopped instantly as screams erupted from inside the house. Sergeant Raines ran to the green door. It was unlocked. He flung it open, withdrew his pistol and charged into the house. In the gloom he tripped over two bodies lying at the foot of some stairs. He fell to his knees. Cursing loudly, he looked up as Margery Briscoe screamed high above him. Regaining his composure, Raines ran up the stairs three at a time. Briscoe, hands to her face, stood over the body of a dead woman dressed in a bloody housecoat. Two policemen ran up the stairs behind him. They stepped around their Sergeant. Raines nodded. Immediately, one of them moved the distraught woman away from the body to a sitting room nearby. In fact, he literally carried Briscoe there. The Sergeant picked up his black billed hat. It had fallen on Mary McPherson covering her face. Numerous knife wounds in her upper torso still oozed. He bent down and lifted her left arm to reveal deep defensive cut marks upon it. Raines released it. The fleshy arm flopped onto the bloody floor beside her. She had powder burns on her face. Mary's pale blue eyes seemed to be looking down the hallway as if trying to tell him something important. A blood trail, thin and sinuous led away from him. Seconds later he and another officer stood in the kitchen. Morning light streamed into the room, harsh and definitive revealing telltale signs of a titanic struggle.

Blood was strewn about all over the kitchen's floor boards. To Raines it seemed that someone had thrown blood deliberately about the room. A broken chair over there and a smashed dinner plate on the floor beside him amongst other items caught his attention. He walked carefully over to the sink. Blood was all over the countertop. He dipped a finger into it. It hadn't completely congealed yet. This meant that the murder must have occurred sometime late yesterday evening. He looked at his Baume fob watch. It was eight in the morning. A dish cloth ripped into long bandages lay in a pile on a small side table along with a bowl of brown sugar and a bar of yellow soap. The air smelled of gunpowder.

Raines knew that Belle La Fontaine and her family lived here. Whoever killed her housekeeper was wounded. He looked at the floor again. There were two sets of footprints, both large in themselves. One of the combatants was barefoot while the other wore shoes. That much he could tell. As for who they were, he could only guess. He'd heard rumors that Belle had a lover; a tall Maasai named Marcus, the Anaona's First Mate. The footprints were very long and narrow. Was he the 'Big Nigger' everyone was looking for? There still was a substantial reward out for his capture. Perhaps the Deacons wanted to settle an old score. Whatever the case, Raines was sure that the matter would land in his lap sooner than later. Perhaps the woman knew something.

Raines finished his inspection. He told his young assistant to make sure no one other than he was allowed into the house especially the pantry. He turned about and went back down the hallway. Mary lay there, her eyes wide open. Raines reached down and closed them. In a nearby sitting room, Briscoe was laid out on a settee, apparently unconscious. Raines motioned for a constable to approach him. He did so. Raines whispered in his ear. The young man nodded and went back to his position just outside the door. Raines stepped back then noticed the 'twixt' door was wide open. He walked through it into the adjoining bordello. After checking all the rooms on the top floor he carefully inspected the lower suites. No one was there. Why? Then he remembered. It was Sunday and the bordello was closed. He checked the front door. It was barred and locked from the inside. Raines ran back upstairs and exited through the 'twixt' door. Stepping carefully around the housekeeper's body, he ran down the stairs to the lower foyer and out the front door. He walked over to address two of his men outside. The Sergeant lit up a cheroot, took a silver flask out of his breast pocket. After taking a strong pull on both, he said,

"A nasty business indeed boys for we've just found two more of the Deacon gang and one very dead housekeeper."

Both of them walked over and looked through the open front door; however they were distracted by a distant figure running pell mell down the street towards them. It was another policeman. A young constable rushed up. Raines tried to calm him by grabbing his shoulders.

"Now, now Freddy, easy does it. What is it now lad?" The young man sputtered,

"Sarge, a patrol just found two Deacon Boys in Lafayette Square with their throats cut!"

Margery Briscoe recovered from her trauma. A day later, she was summoned to the local jailhouse on Rue Royal a block north from 'La Belle Maison'. Upon entering, a desk Sergeant directed her down the hall to Raine's small office, wherein she was told to wait. Sergeant Raines entered the room a few minutes later and sat down behind a battered desk. After shuffling some papers, he looked up at his aide standing behind her then back at the middle-aged woman sitting before him on the edge of a small wooden chair. Briscoe was dressed in a black silk mourning gown crowned by a stylish black silk hat. Somehow it seemed to flutter above her head like a murder of crows. The matron sat stiffly but after a few minutes of silence, she began to squirm under the Sergeant's intense scrutiny. While pretending to peruse a memo he'd retrieved from a nearby wooden tray, Raines carefully adjusted his wire-rimmed pince-nez reading glasses. After a few humms and hahhs, he looked at her intently for a few pregnant moments, then drawled,

"I apologize, Miss Briscoe, for dragging you down here like this. I do hope that we can clear up a few things today if not sooner." She smiled bleakly.

"It seems to me that 501 Rue Conti is advertised as 'La Belle Maison'. Am I correct?" She nodded.

"And it is always closed on a Sunday, correct?" Briscoe nodded once more. He continued drolly,

"And 509 Rue Bienville adjoining it is also owned by a madam by the name of Miss Bellefonte La Fontaine. It serves as her principal residence. Am I correct?"

She nodded again, straightening up as if she was sitting on an anthill. Sergeant Raines continued, while his aide behind him continued taking notes.

"Now Miss Briscoe, you've told me that you are an employee of Miss La Fontaine. In what capacity may I ask?" Briscoe stiffened and looked away.

The Sergeant leaned over and said, "Now don't be shy." She grimaced,

"I'm her business manager, bookkeeper and night matron."

"I see, and the dead woman, was a Mary McPherson I believe?"

"Yes."

Raines took off his reading glasses, putting them on the desk. He moved closer, peering at her as if she was an exotic bug in a specimen jar. Marjory slumped in her chair, put her face in her gloved hands and cried piteously. Abruptly she stopped, took a lace hanky from under her right cuff and delicately dabbed her dry eyes. She simpered,

"She was a dear friend who looked after Belle and her son Cotton for over four years. She was taken in by Belle you know. Never knew why, but I can tell you that she loved them both. She was from Scotland methinks or perhaps Ireland."

Briscoe continued to dab her eyes, then sighed as she put the soiled hanky back beneath her right sleeve. A telegraph key chattered in the next room. It stopped after a few seconds. Another officer entered the room, gave Raines a piece of paper while he whispered in his ear. Marjory squirmed again. Raines never for one instant took his eyes off Briscoe. He frowned as the officer left, closing the door quietly behind him. The telegraph key next door chattered then stopped. Raines looked indulgently at Marjory Briscoe. He ripped open a brown envelope. Five small daguerreotypes spilled out before her onto his desk. He carefully arranged them in a row facing her. He said.

"I have here a rogue's gallery so to speak Miss Briscoe, of criminals who operate here in the quarter. One gang in particular is the Deacon gang; ever heard of them?" Marjory bristled.

"La Belle Maison has a respectable clientele Sir, and no, I've never heard of them!"

She had, but she wasn't going to rat out her well paying clients. The Sergeant slid all five pictures closer. She couldn't help but look down at them. Raines persisted, his tone somewhat sharper than before.

"Miss Briscoe, do you recognize any of these men?"

"No." She lied. She knew all of them. He looked at her lower lip. It trembled. He could tell that she was lying but realized Briscoe was scared, really scared of someone. He thought to himself,

'If it isn't the Deacon gang, who on earth is it?' He continued on stolidly.

"One more question Miss Briscoe. Do you know the whereabouts of Belle, her son and her paramour Marcus Brown?"

Again she lied. An Ursuline novitiate had delivered a note that very morning to the Rue Conti address. It was still in her pocket. She prayed that the relentless Raines wouldn't search her. Her focus regained some clarity as he stood up, leaned over the desk, putting his beefy hands flat out in front of her. He purred pleasantly,

"That'll be all for now Miss Briscoe although you have I think been rather economical with the truth. For now madam, you can clean up the mess as you please but, don't leave town and don't open for business until further notice. Do you understand?"

BOOK ONE: CHAPTER 9
MANHUNT ON THE MISSISSIPPI

Captain Horatio Garrow headed up 'Big Muddy' for Memphis on a steam boat piloted by the legendary Horace Bixby. The Captain left Baton Rouge along with the rest of Major Cooper's staff a few days before. The hurricane deck of the SS. D.A. January became his domain where he often enjoyed smoking a cheroot. The wind of the steamboat's passage caressed his face. Flatboats, keelboats and faster packets swept by him loaded with hemp and cotton. Others struggled upstream avoiding the sandbars and other hazards lurking under its muddy waters. He choked on a piece of tobacco stem. Angrily he threw it into the river three decks below him. The wide Mississippi river swallowed the brown speck as it splashed upon its bosom.

Garrow had been on this river many times before and each time it thrilled him. 'Old Miss' seemed to be a world of its own. The river's riparians gathered on the edge of the flowing waters. Crowned by cottonwood trees, a ghostlike world slid by in an early light. White Crested Egrets stalked its reedy shallows for their breakfast. Opportunistic ospreys circled above them ready to steal it. River otters frolicked nearby, their sleek bodies sliding with wild abandon down the river's muddy flanks. Enormous snapping turtles, basking mute and menacing on deadheads, sunned themselves. In the rising heat of dawn, thousands of diaphanous veils began spiraling upwards far and wide from languid waters hidden deep within the river's secret recesses.

Rhythmic palpitations of the steamboat's monstrous red paddle wheel pounded behind Garrow. Its rotations flung a hissing aqueous veil far out over the boat's wide wake. This however did nothing to lull the volcanic demon of hate centered deep within Horatio. Unable to contain the furies within, he leaned over the railing and yelled,

"Goddamn it, all to hell! I had that bastard within my grasp then those two idiots let him get away!"

His fists pounded the thick oak railing so much so, it quivered slightly. Garrow continued to vent his spleen on any and all objects that caught his attention. He grabbed his sore hand, rubbed it, vexed and flummoxed by his failure. Again, his vile curses were directed at anyone who showed up along the river's wide expanse. It made him even madder when they waved back oblivious to his rants.

The steamboat, D.A. January was making three knots upstream while skirting sand-bars and numerous deadheads. Its two insatiable boilers forced it to stop ever so often for cordwood. Above the distraught Captain, a brass whistle blew two sharp blasts into cool winter airs. Horace Bixby guided the steamboat to a shuddering halt beside a narrow rickety wharf jutting out into the river like a loose tooth. Behind it, a monstrous pile of pine cordwood was stacked in long evenly spaced rows which stretched back as far as the eye could see. Horatio joined Major Douglas H. Cooper on the boat's boiler deck.

Cooper was exploring the possibility of raising a regiment of plains Indians loyal to the fledgling Confederacy. Born in Mississippi, Cooper was a veteran of the Mexican-American war and had served with Jefferson Davis at the Battle of Buena Vista. President Franklin Pierce appointed Cooper as a Federal agent to the Choctaw tribe in 1853, whereupon he was instrumental in peacefully removing them to Indian Territory. In 1856, he became an agent to the Chickasaws who made him a member of their tribe.

In May of 1861, two months hence, the Major's dream would come to fruition when Confederate Secretary of War, Leroy Pope Walker authorized him to raise an Indian regiment later known as the 1st Choctaw and Chickasaw Mounted Rifles. At that time, Cooper would be promoted to a full Colonel.

Garrow offered the diminutive Major a cheroot. From inside his vest pocket he withdrew a small metal tin of safety matches. Cooper took the proffered cheroot. His subordinate, reached down and quickly lit it. The Major nodded then asked to see the tin of matches. He looked closely at it as he turned the small green tin over in his black leather gloves. He murmured,

"Made in Sweden; what will they think of next? Do you mind if I keep these?" Garrow complied.

Cooper lit his subordinate's cheroot and in so doing asked him if he'd ever dealt with any Indians. The Captain replied no, he had not. Cooper leaned on the railing, watching gangs of sweating black stevedores trundle tons of cordwood aboard and stack it on the main deck below him. The tall man beside him made him apprehensive. He didn't like being uneasy. In fact his whole mission was fraught with uncertainty. Major Cooper was a careful man and one who had prepared for every possible crisis except one, namely Captain Horatio Garrow. The Major, for some reason instinctively sensed that the man standing beside him was trouble. He wondered why? He knew General Beauregard promoted him to a full Captain because he'd trained at West Point as a siege specialist. Cooper pondered.

'What the hell is he doing here? He should be in Charleston not in Memphis. God damn it! The sooner he's gone the better.'

The Major puffed on his cheroot, looked up and drawled,

"I guess you'd agree with me Captain, that a good Injun is a dead one."

He waited like a rattler under a rock. The Captain sensed a trap as if its tinny rattle was directly in front of him. He paused, knowing a gull when he heard one, turned, looked down at the Major.

"Well now Sir, I suppose you're right but only after that Indian has killed three or four blue bellies first."

Cooper looked up sharply, realizing his card had been trumped. He pulled on his cheroot with even more vigor.

"Glad to hear that Captain, I'm very glad to hear that indeed!" He lied, saying,

"You and I just might get along well together after all."

Major Cooper began telling Horatio about why he was going to Memphis. He wasn't going to kill Indians. Instead he was going to enlist them to the Confederate 'cause' before some Yankees did. Garrow laughed but Cooper did not.

Captain Garrow climbed to the steamboat's hurricane deck once more. There, he stood in a stiff breeze watching the stevedores return ashore. A steam whistle blew as the boat's crew cast off its mooring lines. The great boat backed slowly out into moving water. Immediately the river's brawny shoulders pushed it downstream. However, as the boat's wheel bit into the river's backside, it moved slowly ahead gaining momentum. Within moments, the spindly wharf and long piles of cordwood lying behind it disappeared around another bend.

The D.A. January picked up speed. The thrashing sound of its efforts echoed eerily wherever the river bank rose steeply beside it. A previously bare main deck was once again piled two decks high with a fresh load of dry cordwood. Sweating blacks began throwing four foot logs down a chute to the boilers below decks. The process was repeated innumerable times on both sides of the steamboat accompanied by a sonorous work holler. 'Got a Woman up the Bayou' rang out, as the laborers sang it with joyous abandon.

On the port side, a rising sun cast its golden glow over a vast expanse of murky water. Garrow smoked, listening to the holler while savoring the river's magical reflections. He actually was content, enjoying himself as a watery world swept past him. A steam whistle blew from up ahead around yet another bend. Moments later a majestic steamboat splashed by him heading downstream at over ten knots.

The Mississippi river was at its lowest level. Numerous channels had changed since previous floods. Sandbars had shifted. Deadheads, snags and sweepers were prevalent. However, aboard the D.A. January, Horace Bixby had been on the river for many years. His pup pilot, Samuel Clemens, found out soon enough that this older man knew every twist and turn, every sand bar and shoal of it. Bixby's encyclopedic knowledge of the Mississippi River included nearly three thousand miles going up and nearly three thousand miles coming back.

That evening, Garrow heard the cook ring an iron below him. The Captain was starved. At least the food on board was better than he imagined it would be in the field. He was tempted to stay and enjoy more of a peaceful world going by him but he could not. The boat's whistle blew. White Egrets rose up in shredded clouds from dead cottonwood trees surrounding a small bayou. The great steamboat gradually turned away from the river bank. As it did so, it nearly collided with a small keelboat hugging the low shore line. Garrow watched it slide by. The little craft began rocking gently as the steamboat's bow wave came upon it. One of its two black pole men was tall, very tall. Something flashed through Horatio's memory like a bolt of white lightning. He looked again. Then he was sure. Garrow started to run down the hurricane deck keeping abreast of a tall black man fifty feet away from him.

Horatio ran while struggling to unholster his Colt .44 revolver. Unrestrained, he commenced firing again and again at the tall black pole man. He missed. Ever faster he ran as the distance between them grew rapidly. The heavy firearm jumped as black powder exploded within it. He missed again. Desperately Horatio pounded down the hurricane deck to where the great wheel was thrashing about. WHUMP! SWISH! WHUMP! SWISH! His gun clicked loudly. The Major was out of ammunition. Defeated, he slumped against the boat's taff rail. WHUMP! SWISH! WHUMP! SWISH! Like a metronome, the sound of the paddle wheel thrummed through his brain. It continued relentlessly. He looked up as the great boat began rounding another wooded bend. Behind him, the tall black man jumped straight up and down with his legs together, hands at his sides on the flat roof of the keel boat. A sinking sun tinged the steamboat's muddy wake with lines of rolling fire. Captain Garrow looked back one more time, turned around and walked away as another world vanished behind him.

Marcus had heard the steamboat rushing up behind him. Sensing trouble, he pushed hard against a thin cypress pole with all his might while walking down the port side of the keel boat as fast as he could. His partner Nate did exactly the same on the other side. The river's current slowly released its grip upon them. As it surrendered, they poled towards a slack water bayou just ahead of them. Both men leaned on their poles sweating in the dimming light. Marcus looked up at the steaming behemoth bearing down upon him. While wiping his sweaty brow with a rag from his trouser pocket, he turned to Nate and said, "Well Brother, it looks like we made it just in..."

He never finished. A lead ball smashed into the keelboat's cabin right beside him. Another whistled past his right ear. Not yet comprehending what was happening, he looked up at the enormous boat coming abreast of him only fifty feet away. There, high up on its hurricane deck was a tall man in a grey uniform firing down at him. A puff of white smoke appeared. Another lead ball smashed into the keelboat's planking beside him. Nate yelled, ducking out of sight. Marcus threw down his pole and stood there, immobile, unwilling to move. The shootist began running pell-mell down the hurricane deck towards him, firing in desperation as the steamboat approached the little keelboat. Moments later the sound and fury of it crashed ashore like a tidal wave.

Marcus knew who it was. He would never forget that face in Belle's kitchen. Never! He leaped up onto the flat roof of his keelboat and began the traditional Maasai warrior's 'Jumping Dance'. He screamed,

"Mkundu! I'll see you in hell first, you monster! I'm gonna make sure I kill you next time. Do you hear me?"

His wild antics continued unabated. High above him, Horace Bixby swore as the steamboat swung out into the river. Beside him a young man grappled with a massive helm. Bixby swore.

"Jesus H. Christ Clemons, did you see that? We just missed that black son of a bitch! I wonder why he was yellin' and jumpin' straight up and down like that?"

Horace watched his young pilot swing the helm back to starboard. He smiled at the lad thinking, 'Maybe he's gonna be alright, alright indeed!' Clemons shouted over the noise at another man next to him.

"Lights fadin' fast Captain. We'll have to tie up in the next five minutes or we'll run aground fer sure."

Captain Thomas P. Leathers laughed at the young man still struggling with the ship's great wheel, half of which protruded below the floorboards of the wheelhouse. He drawled,

"Don't worry Sam, I know a place; it's just around the next bend."

Captain Leathers walked over to an open window on the starboard side. He reached above him and pulled a braided whistle cord twice. Two long blasts rent the air. Up ahead around a bend, a black man ran down to the end of a small wooden dock and lit tarred torches. The D.A. January came into sight moments later, its high twin stacks belched clouds of dense black smoke as it slowed down then glided ever so sedately into the tiny landing. The vessel's mighty paddlewheel thrashed in reverse nudging its charge to a quivering halt. Crewmen scrambled about tying it up just as an orange sun dropped below a cobalt horizon with a fiery splash.

A river and a steamboat lay together as lovers in a liquid embrace under a starry night. Two brass coal-oil marine lamps on either side of the boat's wheelhouse glowed green, the other red. Silhouetted against a green light; three figures dressed in white leaned over the starboard railing, their cheroots winking in the lamp light that embraced them. A relentless river slid seaward below them, gurgling, and pulling past thin cypress pilings. After a few moments, Bixby flicked an ash overboard then turned to appraise the younger man standing beside him while jamming a stubby cheroot back into his mouth. He drawled, "Nice work Sam. Not bad for a pup pilot."

Captain Leathers nodded in agreement. The younger man smiled while leaning on the railing. He nonchalantly gazed at the wharf below him, thinking,

'My! My! That's the first time ever that the Old Man has called me by my first name. Things are looking up.'

Nate picked himself up as the small keelboat rocked wildly in the passing swells. Two long whistle blasts sounded upriver. He looked up as Marcus danced up and down on the roof screaming, "Kikulacho kinguoni muvako!"

The great steamboat vanished into twilight; its thrashing and swishing gradually faded away into silence. Moments later, only small waves rippled through the black bayou beyond him. A few cattle Egrets landed in nearby trees squawking loudly.

Marcus taunted his enemy as he had many times before a battle on the plains of his homeland. Blood ran like a river of fire throughout his body as if he was in heat. He stopped dancing but the keelboat continued to rock. The Maasai yelled once more then jumped down onto a narrowing deck, grabbed his pole and walked to the bow. He exclaimed,

"Come on Nate; let's tie her up for the night. Grab your pole. I'll tell you all about it over supper."

Nate picked up his pole and began pushing hard against it as he walked towards the keelboats' bow. They tied the keelboat to a cottonwood branch hanging low out over the bayou. Marcus prepared a cooking fire in a small three legged cast-iron fire box. After a supper of cornbread and beans, the two men sat down on some gunnysacks. They leaned against a low cabin as their keelboat drifted back and forth over black waters. Nate filled a small clay pipe, while Marcus smoked his usual thin cheroot. The fire cast leaping shadows about them as dry cottonwood therein popped and hissed. After a few moments, Nate looked over at Marcus dozing under a paling moon suspended behind a frieze of cottonwood trees. Nearby, a barn owl hooted in a willow thicket waiting for a sugar squirrel while a whippoorwill cried for its mate in the darkened piney woods behind them. Nate nudged Marcus with his big toe.

"Well supper's over Marcus. Why don't you tell me bout the white idiot back there that was tryin' to kill two innocent niggers mindin' their own business!"

And so for the next hour, Marcus recounted the story of his family's escape from certain death. Nate was enthralled as time after time he'd exclaim,

"Ya don't say! Imagine that! Or I'll be damned!"

Marcus related with relish how he and his family were let into an Ursuline Convent just as a pack of hounds began baying hysterically a short distance away at La Fayette Square. Just in time, a sleepy novitiate nun closed a little metal grate and locked a little wooden door behind them.

The plain diminutive young woman in her grey and white habit stood before Marcus. She looked back up at him in the glow of a flickering lantern shocked by wavy scars dancing on his face. Fear fawned in her eyes for a brief moment then he reassured her.

"Thank you Sister. You just saved our lives."

She relaxed and turned away to speak to the Mother Superior who'd mysteriously appeared behind them. Marcus scared her too. Belle gave her the Bishop's letter. After reading it, the older woman regained a measure of control. She handed the letter back and said,

"Sister Angeline, please show our guests to their quarters?"

With that, the Mother Superior opened a side door and vanished. Sister Angeline turned about. Without a sound she ascended a wide spiraling stone staircase. Belle carried Cotton who was already asleep. Marcus followed with their belongings. The tiled staircase spiraled upwards through a silo of stained glass. Arriving at their tiny garret, they collapsed unconscious on three tick mattresses. Sister Angeline smiled as she closed the door locking it behind her.

Marcus continued his story as Nate filled his pipe with another plug of tobacco, his black eyes fastened upon Marcus. He wondered aloud saying,

"Jesus man, you were locked in a room. What happened when you woke up the next mornin'?"

Nate struck a match and lit his pipe. Marcus finished his cheroot, flicking the butt into the lagoon. He stood up and stretched.

"Look Nate, it's late. I'm too worn out for more bedtime stories. How bout tomorrow night? Ok?"

Nate was disappointed but it had been a long day and he knew Marcus was tired. He stood up then damped his pipe with a calloused thumb. Olapa, the Swahili one eyed moon goddess beamed down upon them. The whippoorwill was no longer crying for its mate. The barn owl caught a sugar squirrel in mid-air as the little flyer neared its nest. All was well with the world. Nate doused the fire box with a bucket of river water. Both men crawled into their tiny cabin and lay inside it wide awake. Fingers of river currents entered black waters around them, gently lulling them into a deep and abiding sleep.

Dawn heralded a new day but the two men were still dead to the world. A thin river mist lay low on the wide river as it had done for millennia. Another steamboat came upon them, thrashing its way up river. Twin blasts of its steam whistle warned weary wood crews ahead that they'd better be ready to load it. Its passage rocked the little keelboat. Moments later, a fuzzy black head appeared as Nate emerged from his cabin. He looked around, yawned and stretched his muscled arms. Marcus appeared soon after. He likewise yawned and stretched. Both men slept in their clothes as they had always done. While standing side by side on the wide aft deck, they unbuttoned their flies. They laughed and kidded as they tried to out-piss each other. Two yellow streams splashed into obsidian waters, frothing it into ever widening circles of iridescent foam. Finished, Nate returned to the boat's bow and untied it. Once again slim cypress poles set to broad shoulders as they'd done thousands of times before. Breakfast was still two hours away. Nate paused, looking at his friend.

"Ya know Marcus, ever since I caught you a hidin' in my keelboat; I've had a darn good time. Mind you; you damn near kilt me with that pig sticker you got there in your belt. I wet my pants when you held it to my throat thar in the dark an all. You were quite a sight, scars an all. Anyways, you paid for your trip to Memphis by workin' like a dog here on the big muddy and then some."

He looked past his friend at a vast riverine expanse as if trying to get a mental grip on it. He shook his head, put his pole into the silty bottom of the bayou and pushed hard. Marcus did the same and once again their keelboat was on its way to Memphis, many hard miles upstream. Marcus looked over as Nate began singing,

"What a friend we have in Jesus, All our sins and griefs to bear!"

Marcus joined in. Their voices rose over the river like swans in flight then settled down into perfect harmony as Nate's deep bass complimented Marcus's rich baritone. Their voices soared out over a river of mists warmed by a rising sun. Marcus knew he'd made a good friend; as good as young Saxton ever was or ever would be. That night after supper, Marcus continued telling Nate his story. Both men reveled in it as Marcus had someone to talk to and Nate had someone to do his talking for him. Marcus sat smoking his cheroot and Nate his clay pipe. Like so many times before, another fiery sunset flooded the vast river kingdom with ruddy light. Rolling lines of fire once again swam ashore rocking their little boat as another passing steamboat bulled its way upriver. Life was good. Marcus settled down to recount how he and Belle were married by the Bishop of New Orleans.

After a few days in the convent of the Ursuline Nuns, Belle and Marcus were summoned to the Bishop's office next door. They were ushered into the august presence of his Holiness, Bishop Grodine, by Mother Superior Theresa Fargone. Cotton was left behind in the care of Sister Angeline who in a short time took a liking to the little boy. His Holiness rose pompously from behind his desk as the trio entered his opulent chambers. He walked towards them then stopped. A solid gold symbolic ring was thrust forward to be kissed. Belle and the Mother Superior knelt before him and kissed it. Marcus did not. A patient man, the Bishop returned to sit behind his desk where he waited until Belle and Marcus were comfortably seated. He asked Mother Superior Fargone to remain standing. She kneeled then rose up, her chest bereft of any distinguishable features. The old nun crossed herself then waited piously to one side, standing behind the couple.

His Holiness sat in a red leather wing chair behind a massive oak desk. Twenty feet above him, a paneled ceiling of polished mahogany, intersected by ebony ribs, rose spreading like a spider web over his immense office. An alcove containing a six foot plaster statue of Christ on a golden cross lurked directly above and behind him.

Bishop Grodine, covered by a scarlet cassock bordered in gold embroidery, began fingering a stunning filigreed gold cross suspended from a thick gold necklace. A scarlet silk zucchetto perched on his bald head matched the complexion of his fat and florid face. A nervous tick betrayed inner furies as his eyes tried in vain to stray from Belle's voluptuous cleavage. In a calm but struggling voice, he wheezed,

"And my children, I understand that you are ah, pleased with your accommodations?" They nodded.

"And you my dear Belle ah, have some questions for me?"

He laughed nervously, his mouth dry. A nearby crystal water glass beckoned. As he was about to take a sip he enquired warily,

"And what may they be young woman?"

Belle's eyes blacken into two bottomless pits, reminding him of how she looked at him long ago. Then, she growled like a she leopard, the way he wanted her to before she leapt on top of him. The Bishop despite himself was aroused. He put the glass down hard upon his desk thinking,

'May God forgive me for still lusting after her body.'

Belle aware of his discomfort spoke seductively,

"Your Holy Eminence; Marcus, Cotton and I, thank you for saving our lives last week. As a young girl, I went to school here. I remember Mother Superior Fargone very well, for she was at the time, my teacher. Since then life has been kind to me although I have strayed from the teachings of the Church. Lately however, I have been to confession for the first time in many years and have as of this moment returned to the blessings of the true Church."

His Eminence nodded. Belle continued more contrite and demure, saying,

"It is a sin to live in sin. Therefore, I ask your permission to marry me and Marcus at once."

She humbly bowed her head and waited. Surely his Holiness was also aware of her condition. She smiled inwardly knowing how difficult it would be for him to refuse. She tried to suppress any laughter. Bishop Grodine visibly paled, fingered his necklace with some measure of agitation, thinking,

'The whore is in heat, gets pregnant, has a child and remains miraculously chaste. Her lover returns from God knows where, knocks her up again then comes here to get married by me! How preposterous! It's sacrilege! I won't do it!'

He looked up sternly at his Mother Superior whose pallor matched the liturgical candles standing behind her. Belle smiled sweetly. He croaked,

"Of course my child I would be delighted. Would two o'clock today be alright?" Belle nodded coyly. A gasp was heard behind her.

"It must be here in your office, officiated by Your Holiness?"

He nodded weakly without malice.

"Any more questions my child?"

He waited, steeling himself for more revelations. The Bishop was sorely tempted to take off his zucchetto and dry off his head, but he did not for he had succumbed completely to her will. A glass of water appeared in his hand. Gulping it down, he sputtered, the glass falling from his hand to the desk where it rolled this way and that spilling water everywhere. Helpless, he looked for support from a stricken Mother Superior but did not receive her blessing for she was at that very moment staring off into space in the direction of the statue of Christ behind him. Grodine swallowed hard as Belle intoned,

"Thank you your Eminence. I accept. We will be here at two with our son Cotton acting as best man. Would that be alright?" Again he nodded. Belle next enquiry startled the Bishop.

"As for my next request, I would have you know that I am with child again." He nodded.

"And as such, both Marcus and I feel that in the best interests of our child, I should stay here where we would be protected by sanctuary law. For here we would be safe from intruders who might want to harm us. I wish to stay, have my child then leave soon after. Do you agree your Holiness?"

She sat back and rubbed her rounded belly provocatively. She stared into the Bishop's eyes all the while opening her lips slightly, wetting them with just the tip of her pink tongue. Marcus was stunned. Even he didn't have a clue what she was up to. He agreed with everything she said, thinking, "What a woman!"

Bishop Grodine sat back as if his groin had been hit by a mallet. He leaned forward.

"What about Marcus, your husband to be, my child? What is to become of him whilst you are staying here?"

Before Belle could speak, Marcus stood up, all seven feet of him. He scowled at Grodine who shrank back as if he was being assaulted by the devil himself. The Bishop thought,

'May the Holy Mother protect me, for this savage is surely a born again killer or at the very least a cannibal.'

Marcus continued standing, while horrific scars twitched all over his face. His luminous black eyes were shot through with wide yellow streaks, a terrifying sight to be sure, and the Maasai was going to use it too his full advantage. He turned suddenly and growled. Mother Superior Fargone shrieked, fleeing the room in a panic. Marcus swung his undivided attention back to the Bishop whose scarlet zucchetto had been flung onto the floor beside him. Grodine began wiping his shaved head with a linen napkin embossed with a symbol of the Holy See. They locked eyes. Belle looked on thinking,

'What a perfect man Marcus is. He really is Simba incarnate!'

Marcus sneered at the stricken man cowering in front of him. He snarled,

"In my culture, the Maasai deal with their enemies in hand to hand combat. They do not hide behind the skirts of their woman! I, Matari Simba of the Kisongo Maasai will leave my wife and son in your care. I will hunt down and kill any enemies who threaten my beloved. I have spoken."

With that he turned to Belle, pulled her up from her chair and kissed her full on her mouth. The Bishop remained in his seat aghast, unable to speak, think or move.

Belle and Marcus were married punctually at two that afternoon. Cotton was their best man and Sister Angeline for the first and only time in her life was a bridesmaid. Their wedding night was spent in the Bishop's quarters. Belle gave the Convent School a substantial donation from funds secreted away in her 'Gettin' out of town dress'. Bishop Grodine was pleased and suddenly very forgiving of the whole ridiculous situation. Marcus left New Orleans a few days later in the dead of night. He'd found out from Nate that a Major Horatio Garrow had left New Orleans on a steamboat, the D.A. January, for Baton Rouge two days earlier.

124

Another evening came to a close exactly as it did every night before it. Nate enjoyed laughing about the Bishop and the Mother Superior. However, before long he became quiet, smoking his pipe as he reflected on his life upon the river. He was exhausted from another hard day's work for he wasn't getting any younger. At times Nate felt like dropping anchor but he couldn't do it. Inside him was a thirst for adventure slacked by action and nurtured by fear of a past that just might catch up to him. In effect he was running away from life in the city, the farm; wherever normality resided. Only wide open waters offered any solace to him. The 'Big Muddy' had been Nate's partner in life for many years. It was the only place where he felt he belonged. As such, he remained alone and happily married to 'Old Miss' where the consequences would take care of themselves.

In turn however, where once only oceans could ever satisfy Marcus, he knew now he'd never go back to sea for Belle's love was too strong. Any demons that might try to persuade him otherwise were banished to the nether regions of another life. He had to live with that, hoping their love for each other would be enough to conquer all. For now Marcus was content to chase Garrow, the one threat to his family. After learning that he'd left Baton Rouge for Memphis aboard the D.A. January, Marcus knew his quarry was elusive but not impossible to find. For many nights thereafter while rocking to sleep on still bayous, his last waking thoughts were,

'I will kill Garrow once and for all or my family will never be free. I'm a patient man. I'm Matari the Maasai of the Kisongo. I am Simba!'

Memphis, Tennessee, lay beside the Mississippi River eight hundred miles upriver from New Orleans. The imposing Chickasaw bluffs below the city, ran along a crescent of river very much like that of New Orleans but much shorter. It was here that Nate and Marcus sat on their keelboat's cabin roof enjoying their usual pipe and cheroot. It was a comforting and pleasant routine they'd gotten used to at the end of every day. Marcus stood up and pointed across a narrow channel at Mud Island. His long shadow cast a rippling pointer towards a gaggle of riverboats nesting there. Marcus turned and looked down at the stocky river man sitting below him, saying,

"Well my friend it looks like the end of the trail. It seems we were on 'Old Miss' for a long time. Got to know each other pretty good I'd say, not that I liked who I was bunkin' with n' all."

Nate pointed a long clay pipe back at Marcus smirking above him.

"Now youngin' don't sass your elders or you're liable to be a swimmin' pretty damn quick. I've been on this here river longer than you've bin' alive son and don't you fergit' it. Why I remember when Memphis here...,"

He pointed his pipe up at the bluffs behind him,

"Was nothin' but a tradin' post facin' a wild and wooly west just over yonder. Had a fort here once upon a time but the injun's burned it down nigh on forty years ago."

He puffed furiously then lowered his voice, enquiring,

"By the way, ya never did tell me why ya didn't kill Garrow when ya had half a chance. Looks like ya shouda! Musta bin connected to that idiot shootin' at us a while back some. You've bin mighty edgy ever since, lookin' at the January over thar like its some sort of beast that's gonna git you one night. Care to tell me about it? I mean what you've served up so far has bin mighty tasty to say the least!" Marcus sat down beside Nate to explain.

"I thought he was dead Nate. Guess I shoulda shot him again but you see I was in kind of a hurry and out of bullets."

Nate looked at Marcus and understood. As to lift the pall that hung between them, Nate rose and slapped Marcus on the backside.

"My, My, what a hell of a woman you got there boy!" Marcus laughed.

"Well now Nate that's the most you've said at one time since we met. I guess we bring out the gab in both of us. Well I've gotta get goin'."

He got up and jumped down on the narrow fore deck.

"I'm all packed up. Maybe I'll be seein' ya round a river bend some time."

They shook hands. Marcus picked up a large canvas knapsack, slung it over a shoulder then turned and ran down the gangplank onto the river bank. He climbed upwards to a willow thicket and was gone. Nate jumped up onto the keelboat's flat roof and sat down on a bale of dry goods. Minutes later a loud 'halloooo' came from on high. He looked up squinting into the sun barely making out a tall figure standing on a bluff above him. It was Marcus, bigger than life. Nate stood up and waved his broad felt hat until Marcus was gone. He returned to his seat where a powerful feeling of loneliness overcame him. It was a cold void never to be warmed up by Marcus again. He cried out to no one in particular, knocking the cold ashes out of his dead pipe as he did so.

"I'm gonna miss him fer sure. Best man other than me on the river, I ever saw. Never did tell me where he was a goin' to do once he got here or why for that matter. Oh well, I better unload Nelly before it gits too hot. Work, work, work! Goddamn it all to hell!"

Marcus waved goodbye to his friend and shipmate for the last time then yelled "Halloo" at the top of his lungs. Far below him, Nelly was just a bug on a puddle. He turned and began walking towards Memphis, using the wharves lining the river as a highway. He was tired and his pack was heavy. The Maasai cut a green sapling and was leaning on it as he stood before a Harrison and Sons warehouse. Behind it, large drays, similar to those in New Orleans were lined up, their mule teams placid. The drays were stacked with cotton bales going east while others were filled with dry goods going west. A Baldwin locomotive chugged across a river bridge to somewhere beyond the western horizon. Marcus continued walking then stopped as a shrill voice threw itself upon him.

Around a corner were a dozen black dray men were listening to a skinny little black man who cried like a country preacher on a Sunday,

"Step right up brothers. There's nothin' to it. Here son you do it. Pick a shell, any shell and you'll win fer sure. Shy aren't you, well here I'll show you."

His black hands flew back and forth across a small wooden crate as three large walnut shells were moved back and forth faster than one's eye could follow, let alone one's mind could fathom. Within seconds, all three shells were in a row. He turned over the middle shell revealing a pea. He laughed, saying, "Now son, see how easy it is."

He spied Marcus hanging back between two drays. The little man knew a mark when he saw one. Licking his thin lips, he crooned,

"Well lookee there boys!" He pointed at Marcus, saying with relish,

"There's as fine a specimen of the chosen race I ever did see. Now friends, I'd say this big boy is intelligent." As his tip turned about, they were astonished by the size of a man standing high above them. The shell man cried out,

"Say Big Brother, come on over here and join in the fun."

Marcus ambled over, knowing exactly what was going to happen.

"Wanna double your money mister?"

The shell man looked around confidently at the others turned back to Marcus who towered above him. He laughed seductively,

"How about it big fella, wanna try your luck? Just pick any shell with a pea under it, and son, youse an instant winner!"

Marcus put aside his pack and cane. He stepped forward grinning for he'd played this game many times before in Kisongo. Playing the role of an initiate, he drawled,

"Well if you don't mind Sir, I'll give it a try. How much is a bet?"

"Two bits. Got the money? Let's see it first!"

Marcus took out two bits but held onto them. He said,

"I think I'll hang onto my money, you can have the pea." Every one laughed. The little man thought,

'So, he's gonna be a wiseacre is he? I'll show the big nigger. I'll let I'm win a few rounds then hit I'm real good; he'll see!'

The shells flew back and forth in a blur. Time after time Marcus picked the right one. In twenty minutes he'd made five dollars. Everyone was amazed. The shyster was terrified about losing his touch; therefore he decided to not put a pea under any shell. Three shells were rapidly laid out in a row, beckoning seductively. Marcus pondered the situation knowing exactly what had happened. He looked around at everyone and said,

"Boys, I need some information about the D.A. January that tied up at Mud Island a week ago. Does anyone know if any of its passengers was a Captain Garrow and if so where did he go? I tell you what. I'll pay a dollar for the information, what do you say?"

The shell man motioned for Marcus to bend down. He whispered in his ear. Marcus nodded while two long fingers dipped into the man's coat pocket. He smiled then looked around at the group draymen standing around him.

"Well boys, the little man here deserves to be rewarded for the truth."

Marcus gave him a silver dollar then started to saunter away, his duffel bag in one hand, and his walking stick in the other. After a few steps, the tall Maasai turned about and came back. He paused then reached down towards three walnut shells lying on top of the crate. As his hand hovered above them, Marcus grinned, saying.

"Oh, one more thing boys, he deserves this too."

Marcus turned over all three. None of them had a pea under them. The shell man jumped up and ran for his life, chased by a mob of angry draymen. Marcus went another way. The dock walloper screamed once. Marcus smiled; a pea lay in the palm of his hand. He threw it far out into the river.

Evening shadows grew longer as Marcus waited where engine #49 would slow down as it came to grade. An hour later the train appeared. Marcus swung aboard as the front of a baggage car slowly came abreast of him. He climbed an iron ladder to its domed roof. Moments later behind a large roof vent, his body was securely wedged against it. Marcus prayed to Enkai that no one had seen him. All through the night he slept fitfully as from time to time the train slowed down, or came to grade. Wood smoke and sparks blew down upon him in a fiery turmoil threatening to set him alight. At dawn the next morning, it began to spit rain heralding a coming storm. An hour later, a downpour drenched him through and through.

He stood up. Marcus decided that he'd better head towards the locomotive to keep warm and dry out. Once there, he'd hold the engineer and his fireman at gunpoint. To enter any of the cars would have been sheer suicide for many armed men were sleeping below his feet. Marcus sensed this train was special because it didn't stop at any station. But he thought his plan might work as he pondered the consequences.

'Perhaps at the first fuel or water stop I'll set the baggage car on fire; create a diversion then kill Garrow. It'll be very risky.'

At that precise moment, the train was again at grade, going slowly around a sharp bend. Marcus stood on the roof of the first coach behind the tender, his pack strapped to his back. He was about to jump onto a high load of cordwood piled up in front of him. Thick black smoke blinded him just as he leapt forward. In an instant, Marcus was thrown back then swept off the train. His body had slammed chest high into an iron beam that spanned a low bridge over the Tennessee River. He landed in soft mud twenty feet from the track, unconscious and injured, his knapsack still strapped to his lifeless body.

A week before; the D.A. January delivered Major Douglas H. Cooper, and his staff including Captain Garrow to Memphis, Tennessee. Their temporary divisional headquarters, a colonnaded anti-bellum mansion called the Hunt-Phelan Mansion an imposing, tall, red brick building on Beale Street, six blocks east of the river. Cooper was very pleased to be off the vast Mississippi. For some reason its size and strength was irksome to his ego. The Major at forty-five was full bearded, sporting a thick crop of salt and pepper hair. He projected a commanding appearance to all who met him despite his size. But the Major's diminutive stature bothered him. In such a condition he was envious of anything or anybody that was more significantly significant than he.

"Big Chief Cooper" as his staff called him behind his back, began wondering about the mental condition of one of his subordinates, namely, a Captain Horatio Garrow. It seemed that Garrow, somewhat peckish of late and was not concentrating on the job at hand. To Cooper, the Captain was competent enough in a criminal sort of way; meaning shifty, devious and down right scary. Major Cooper didn't trust the tall man or for that matter all tall men. Cooper was sure he would regret General Beauregard's recruiting Garrow at all. How, he reasoned over a brandy in his new office, such an obviously covert personality could be put to better use. He sipped as he made plans to entice the Choctaw and Chickasaws to join the Confederate cause. He looked up, downed his drink, his concentration shattered by a knock on his office door. He grunted,

"Come in and close the door behind you."

In walked Captain Garrow who stood at attention, then saluted, his cover tucked under his left arm. Major Cooper saluted in return but remained seated. As two reptilian eyes bored into him, Cooper drawled.

"And what can I do for you Captain?"

Despite himself, Cooper stiffened, slightly uncomfortable in the presence of the 'Presence' as he thought about it. Garrow replied,

"Sir, There's been a change of plans."

He handed the Major a telegram. Cooper sat up and put his pince-nez glasses on. It read,

"Captain H. Garrow, proceed to my
Charleston HQ immediately STOP
Commanding Gen. P. Beauregard."

The Major enthusiastic over the news, stood up, reached out and shook Garrow's hand vigorously. He gushed,

"Well I'll be Goddamned Captain! It looks like you're headin' to Charleston. Hallelujah! Thank God there's a railway all the way. Arrange your accommodation on the next train out of here, and make it an express. No stops! And, that's a direct order!"

Two days later, a powerful Danforth & Cook 4-4-0 steam locomotive, No#49 of the Norfolk & Petersburg Railway Line, pulled out of the Memphis station with Captain Garrow aboard. Other officers requested by General Beauregard were on it too. As the five car train pulled away, there was another passenger on board. He hadn't bought a ticket. Marcus Brown was riding on top of the baggage car. Two cars down, his sworn enemy was lying in a bunk reading a copy of the Memphis Daily Appeal.

Horatio removed his leather Jefferson boots, grey slouch hat and grey field jacket but otherwise remained fully dressed. He was going to war; feeing it in his bones as the train wobbled along. It was his destiny to rise in the ranks. A single gold star was sewn onto each lapel of his field jacket lying beside him. Horatio reached over and fondled them thinking of greater things to come.

Engine No#49 puckered and clicked over jointed iron rails as it pulled itself towards the Tennessee River over three hundred miles to the east. Its brass whistle tooted every time it approached a crossing or a bridge. Horatio looked out his bunk window as lamp light from his coach spilled through it out into a starry night. A black rolling roof line floated magically up and down by his windowpane on the occasional cut bank. The Captain could see it very clearly. He looked back at a newspaper lying on his chest. Its headlines screamed back at him about imminent war. He was tired of it all, although elation deep within him pleasured his mind. Horatio decided to read something else, anything else for that matter. While he flipped a few pages, he didn't notice a furtive shadow rise above the black outline of the coach roof outside his window because Horatio's attention was focused on the society page. There before him, buried at the bottom of it was a wedding announcement. In clear bold type it proclaimed,

SAXTON-ROWLAND NUPTIALS

"Mrs. Muriel S. Saxton, owner of the Saxton Shipping Co. and Mr. and Mrs. Cerile Rowland, of Boston, Mass. are pleased to announce the engagement of Mr. John Manley Saxton to a Miss Virginia Rose Rowland. They plan to be married March 14th, 1861, by Reverend Nathaniel Clover of the First Free Baptist Church, Boston. Their reception will be held at the Saxton estate. After a honeymoon in Bermuda aboard a Company ship, the SS Anaona; they'll be residing on the Saxton family estate for the time being."

The Captain put his paper down, reached over and extracted a half spent cheroot out of his breast pocket. He struck a match against the window frame next to him. Flicking the dead match onto the floor below him, he lay back and took a deep drag. He smiled evilly, thinking,

'My! My! My! The bastard is getting married to a nigger. That should be interesting!'

He sat up and read the article one more time. It seemed not too long ago that his father died because of the Saxtons. He murmured aloud,

"Old man Saxton must have died too! Good riddance I say!"

He threw the paper at the foot of his bunk. Sitting up, he undressed then blew out a small Dietz lamp behind his head. Once laid out covered by a thin wool blanket, he was instantly asleep. The metallic cadence of the train increased in volume as it barreled headlong over yet another iron bridge. After refueling and taking on water in Chattanooga the next morning, the express train crossed over Allegheny Pass that day then barreled south for Charleston, South Carolina and destiny.

Big Willie looked down at Marcus in awe. His son, Hudson sat beside the bed. The boy reached over to touch the Maasai's facial scars that seemed to jump out at him. Hudson was fascinated as the big man twitched and twisted about on the narrow tick mattress like a wounded bird. His father standing behind him put a hand on his shoulder.

"Now Hud just leave him be. I know he's a sight, be'in a giant n' all. Why look at his face scarred all over. I hope his bones bin set right. He musta broke some ribs. Lucky thing that deer ran down to the tracks and holed up there or we neber would a found him, no siree! Took him back we did 'cross the Tenny to our mountain. Good thing too, we had a wagon waitin' there to take him up to my Sweet Daphne."

A stout black lady smiled down at 'The Giant'. She bent over to unwind a long cotton bandage wrapped around Marcus's rib cage. A brown poultice smeared all over black and yellow bruises covered most of his chest.

Despite many years of experience as a mid-wife and a backwoods doctor, Sweet Daphne was horrified at his condition. She prayed while her ministrations were performed under a lantern held above her. He'd been in her clapboard cabin for over two weeks while her husband scoured the forest floor for the healing herbs she'd asked for. Somehow, they knew that Marcus was important for they'd found his knapsack still strapped to his body, the letter from the Bishop of New Orleans inside it.

Hudson ran to his mother out in their dirt yard a week later while she was busy feeding his prized Barred Rock chickens. He screamed,

"Momma! Momma! Come quick. The giant is awake and talkin' strange like."

Sweet Daphne carried her woven reed basket of chicken feed back to the clapboard cabin. She put it on a small wicker table sitting on a wide veranda. A shaft of light streamed through a small crack in a front window, its source peeking over low mountains directly across a wide fertile valley below them. Big Willie heard Hudson too. He and his son, 'Little Willie' ran from the barn, crossing a wide yard to the ramshackle cabin.

Therein, Marcus tried to rise up. Sweet Daphne hushed his groans while gently pushing his head back against a soft feather pillow. Her round smiling face beamed down at him. To Marcus, it was like a sensation of sunshine reflecting down upon him from beneath the surface of a becalmed sea. He moaned again. Sweet Daphne dabbed his sweating forehead with a cool damp cloth. A drizzle of cold spring water ran into his sub-conscious mind as if he was being baptized. Floating above his body was an effervescent shape-changing form of a beautiful black woman, the goddess Enkai. He thought, 'How beautiful she is. The light flowing about her is like that which lays upon the Mississippi's breast on a summer's day.'

He was on a river of drifting souls. A radiance beckoned to him whilst an angelic voice within it beseeched him, crying seductively,

'Come with me and be at peace. Be whole again as I have rescued many lost and lonely souls drifting on the river of life. Power and glory are within your reach. Come, abide with me now.'

But, Marcus could not obey. He wept as the light slipped away, setting on a tropical sea. The luminescent aura faded then blacked out completely. Within him, the sub-conscious soul of his mind slipped into the presence of his body. Hurt and healing mingled within him, fighting each other for dominance until the struggle was too much to bear. Marcus opened his eyes, reached out for Sweet Daphne and cried joyfully,

"Oh! Belle! Oh! Belle! You've come for me. Oh sweet Jesus, you've come for me!"

He closed his eyes murmuring, "Ngai Ndeithya! God help us! Ngai Ndeithya!"

Sweet Daphne backed away as tears streamed down over his scars into the fresh bandages wrapped around his face. After a few moments, he opened his eyes again and looked up into her face then the faces of the others looking down in wondrous rapture upon him. He shivered, the words spilling forth in a torrent. "Where am I? Where am I?"

Big Willie kneeled down beside him and held an immense hand in his, saying,

"Hallelujah! Hallelujah! You're safe now. You're on the mountain. May the Lord be praised for your merciful deliverance?"

BOOK ONE: CHAPTER 10
A MAN OF SURPRISES

For the umpteenth time, Muriel Saxton was severely pestered by Jack, her Russell Terrier. Jack demanded attention, barking constantly until she threw his red rubber ball. Early that morning, her son had left for Warehouse#3, whereas Thomas told her he had some pressing work in his home office. So there Muriel lay propped up in her four-poster bed watching Jack at the foot of it wagging his tail, looking at her with his pink tongue hanging out, the red ball between his paws. His deep brown eyes sparkled in the soft window light. However, Muriel was quite content to lie in bed reading the local papers. Dark and ominous headlines screamed out from every one of them. It was Valentine's Day, 1861.

Lincoln, inaugurated the week before, had barely escaped an assassination attempt in Baltimore. Another paper raged against the Fugitive Slave Laws, while another put out dire warnings about the coming Civil War. Muriel prayed that saner heads would prevail at the Willard Hotel in the Nation's capital, where negotiations between the Confederates and the Unionists were taking place. Hopefully a workable compromise would be found; she was sure of it. Nobody wanted war but nobody wanted a perpetuation of slavery either. Thomas and his rich friends had tried to exert their considerable political influence and bring these two obstinate parties to their senses but to no avail. She mused further, thinking that if woman such as herself and Harriet Stowe were in charge, the world would be a far better place to live in. Men were so stupid. She cringed.

Jack began to whine, jolting Muriel out of her reverie. Irritated at being dictated to by a male dog no less, she took his red ball and threw it out of her bedroom. It bounced off an open door to carom down the hallway. Jack took off, a white and brown spotted streak. Muriel heard him bark as he ran away.

'Oh, Jack!' She thought. 'How I've come to love the rascal.'

She laughed inwardly remembering the famous photo episode six weeks earlier. It was the talk of the town. Apparently every one heard about it and wanted a signed copy. Brady was stunned as he sold hundreds of them. Muriel looked at hers in a metal frame she kept beside her bed. It was signed, 'To Jack, with many thanks. MB'.

Jack chased his red rubber ball down the long hallway to the grand stair case. It disappeared over the precipice. The dog ran after it, snapping at it as the ball bounced hither and yon down the risers. Once the ball was deftly caught, Jack turned and trotted past the billiard room to his master's office. He stopped. A telegraph's loud metallic TICK! TICK! TACK! TICK! TACK! TACK! caught his attention. It continued for a few moments then stopped abruptly. Jack dropped his red rubber ball. He ran into the office and over to Thomas. The dog licked his master's limp hand that hung down above him. He licked it again. There was no response. Jack backed away and sat down to whimper softly. After a few moments, he threw his snout high into the air filling the room, the hallway outside, the whole house, with a cacophonous wail. Loud, sharp, staccato barks were followed by more howling. It was if the very heart of the dog had been split in two.

Packard was in the nearby warming room sitting at his butler's desk. He'd heard Jack go by him chasing his ball. He liked Jack but was not his master; not even Saxton was; only Muriel and Thomas were. Stylus Packard continued with his duties until he sensed that something was out of order. Packard was a stickler for order. His reputation demanded it. He pursed his thin black lips thinking, 'That damn dog isn't going to quit.'

Irritably, he put down the daily work schedule he was composing. Rising, he entered the hallway Therein, he nearly ran into Muriel dressed in a blue housecoat. Stylus Packard followed his mistress like a ship of the line. Jack's howling and barking was verging on the hysterical. Muriel screamed. Both of them started running.

Thomas Clifford Saxton was dead. He'd been found in his office, dead of an apparent heart attack. He was fifty-six years old. At the time of his death, his son was communicating with him on the company telegraph. Immediately, Saxton became alarmed when his father did not respond to his efforts. Something was very wrong, terribly wrong. Saxton conferred with Larson, apprising him of the suspected emergency then fled in his cutter up Copps Hill to the house. Saxton arrived on the run leaving the cutter and its exhausted horse outside in the cold winter air. He pounded up the front steps, flung open the front door, threw off his heavy parka onto the floor and fled out of the grand foyer. He could hear his mother keening in his father's office. His heart skipped a beat, for he knew then that his worst fears were confirmed.

Muriel Saxton had not touched her husband's body for she could not. Thomas was slumped, face down on his desk. She and Packard stood there in mute silence, holding onto each other. It was the first and last time they would ever do so. Packard was stunned at the sight of his master who appeared so peaceful, his eyes wide open. Thomas Saxton's right hand was still on the Morse key pad. Beside it was an open Esther Howland Valentine card wherein a hand written poem in a large fine script said,

"To my Darling Muriel,
My loving arms are around you.
Companion of my soul,
Our hearts now beat as one not two,
True love has made us whole.

Love Thomas"

Saxton slowed down as he neared his father's office. He had to look composed, in control of his emotions. He remembered what Marcus said to him. The words rang in his head like a liberty bell,

"Sax, on this side of the door you are still a boy but on the other side you must be a man."

Saxton knew he had to be more than a man for now he was his father's successor.

Muriel looked up as her son entered. She released Packard. Saxton came over and wrapped his arms around her. It seemed that they stood there forever, grieving as one, over their common loss. Saxton said to Packard, standing behind them,

"Packard, please take my mother back to her rooms. I'll be up in a few minutes. Take Jack as well. Ok?"

As he motioned to Packard, he noticed Millie standing in the doorway with one hand to her mouth. Millie was crying but she knew Packard needed her to help him with their mistress. After they left, Saxton turned, walked over to his father, bent down and kissed his bald head. Carefully he took off his father's steel pince-nez glasses. He closed his father's eyes. In doing so, it was as if a fragile light had been extinguished, a life snuffed out. Saxton sat Thomas up in his leather chair then reached over putting his father's Valentines card in his breast pocket. In his mind, he composed a message to Larsen but paused before the brass telegraph key, his hand trembling. He stopped, took a deep breath then deftly tapped out,

"Thomas is dead. Halt all Co. dealings immediately
until further notice. Flag half mast. Notify Leonard
Keys Re will, Cerile Rowlands Re: Burial and Minister
Norland Re: Funeral. Get Doctor Wilson here now.
All staff are off today. Bring everyone aforementioned
to the house tomorrow noon. John M.Saxton."

Packard returned shortly to assist Saxton. Together they carried Thomas into the warming room where they laid him out on a long couch, covering him over with a wool blanket. Saxton stood up. Packard closed the drapes then lit a coal fire in a small grate inset into a rear wall. Once finished, he turned around to speak but Saxton was gone. Packard left to inform the rest of the household staff but he needn't have bothered. They were all sitting around a long kitchen table looking quite miserable.

Saxton ran up the grand stair case, padded down the hall and knocked on his mother's bedroom door. After a few moments, Millie opened it. She stepped aside as Saxton entered. The maid left the room, closing the door behind her. A coal fire burned in a fireplace grate at one end of the room. Muriel was propped up in her four poster bed, with the morning's newspapers scattered about her. Jack wagged his short stubby tail halfheartedly. He had crawled into Muriel's arms. Saxton walked over to the edge of her bed, looked down into his mother's eyes then bent down taking her hands in his. To Saxton, she'd aged over the past few moments; somewhat older but somehow much wiser. Muriel looked up into her son's blue eyes as if he'd just been born then released him and patted the bed, indicating for her son to sit beside her. He did. She looked upon him fondly.

"Saxton dear, please forgive me but I have to ask you something. Do you mind if we have a heart to heart talk?" He nodded and squeezed her hand. She smiled.

"I know it's been dreadful but your father's death was not unexpected. Dr. Wilson and I have known for some time that your father has not been very well; his heart, you know."

Saxton started to say something but he thought otherwise. He'd just let his mother get it out, and then she would go to sleep, alone in her grief. She continued bravely,

"Yes my dear, his heart was weak. It runs in the family amongst the men folk. I do hope you understand that I worry about you. Please be careful son and don't run away to war where you could be under a lot of stress yet alone get shot."

He stood up and went to a window, his back to her, saying without conviction,

"I won't mother, I promise. However you know, I've been boxing for a while and I'm in great shape."

He turned to face her lying wan and spent upon her bed. He walked over, bent down and kissed her forehead. He laughed,

"I'll be careful mother, I promise." She smiled knowingly and closed her eyes.

He left the room, shutting the door behind him. An hour later he returned. His mother was fast asleep. Saxton took the Valentines card from his vest pocket, opened it and placed it on a side table facing her. He patted Jack then closed the sheers around the four poster bed and left the room. Packard was waiting outside in the hallway. Saxton closed the door, paused, and turned about. He looked up at his tall elegant butler, who intoned solemnly,

"I've informed the household staff Sir. Are there any instructions you might give me at this most unpleasant turn of events?"

Saxton Informed hlm of Dr. Wilson's imminent visit. A light lunch was to be prepared at noon the next day in the dining room. He continued evenly,

"Tell the staff that no one will be relieved of their duties."

With that, Packard bowed, turned about and fled downstairs to the kitchen. Millie appeared out of the shadows. She too waited for Saxton's orders. He simply said,

"Look after my mother night and day."

He was nearly twenty-one years old and had to tell everyone what to do. He felt like a weathervane exposed to the elements. Saxton leaned against a wall and sighed. A shiver ran through him. He thought again of Marcus.

'So this was the measure of a man!' Oh how he needed the big Maasai. He thought, 'Where was he?'

That afternoon, John Saxton climbed to the 'widows walk' on the roof of Saxton House and lowered the Saxton Co. flag to half-mast. He looked out over the harbor below. In moments as far as he could see, ships of all descriptions began lowering their flags too. He shivered in the winter air and turned to leave. His ears however, caught a growing chorus of horns and whistles screaming their respect and grief over the loss of his father. A blanket of cold air that lay over Boston's inner harbor was torn asunder as thousands of seagulls and terns swept over the ships in shredded grey clouds. It was as if Mother Nature was saluting his father too. Tears froze on Saxton's cheeks. He stood to attention and saluted.

Doctor Wilson confirmed what his mother had said about Thomas Saxton's heart condition. C.W. Rowland's Funeral Parlor would prepare the body. A private funeral service would be held that coming Saturday at the Old North Church on Salem St. Saxton knew the family crypt was waiting in Copps Hill cemetery nearby. Generations of Saxtons were already interred there.

John Saxton showed Doctor Wilson to the front door. Saxton stood on the large front veranda watching his 'Doctors' or Top buggy make its way at a fast clip over the frozen gravel driveway. A cross breeze blew, flushing Red Polls and Goldfinches out of nearby holly bushes. They flitted about in alarm, their bright plumage reminding Saxton of semaphore flags waggling from the upper deck of the 'Conny II' as she closed in on the slave ship Wanderlust only a few short years before.

Hans Larson, Leonard Keys Esq., Cerile Rowland and Minister Dexter Norland arrived punctually at noon the next day. A light lunch was served in the dining room. Norland said grace after which they all conversed in sober desultory tones except Cerile Rowland the undertaker, who with his assistant Harvey Copeland was busy loading the body of Thomas Saxton into a horse drawn hearse. Minister Norland, after some direction, was given written instructions before he left. A few minutes after the minister departed, Saxton watched the hearse containing his father's remains wend its way down Hull Street until it disappeared. Packard directed everyone to the Grand Salon where comfortable chairs and couches were arranged around a low teak coffee table. Refreshments were served. Everyone tried to relax. Muriel thanked Larsen and Keys for their sympathy and condolences. She looked very regal in her black mourning dress. Unbeknownst to Saxton, it was the same dress she sat in everyday on the 'Widow's Walk' waiting for him to return from overseas. Muriel motioned for her son to speak. She'd decided it was best that he do so as the new patriarch of the Saxton House. John Saxton knew what he was about to say was very important. He spoke, his voice fitting the solemnity of the occasion.

"Thank you for coming gentlemen. My mother and I find your presence assuring and comforting as we all grieve for my father. I know that each of you knew him for many years and as such, he trusted your judgment and valued your opinions greatly. All of you have served the Saxton family well for many years therefore, I thank you both on behalf of myself and my mother. I'll now ask Leonard to read the will. I do hope it contains no unsavory revelations although my father was known for being unusual at times."

After reading the will, their barrister suggested a tea break. Packard, on a signal from Muriel, brought in more refreshments whereupon the barrister reached down and brought out an envelope from his leather grip. To everyone's surprise he apologized, saying,

"Dear Muriel, I have one more task to accomplish. For the life of me, I do not know what is in this envelope but I have been instructed by your late husband to follow whatever instructions he may have for you inside it. Do you mind?" They both nodded. Keys opened the envelope and shook out a single handwritten letter. It was a codicil to the will. He began to read it slowly word for word. As he listened to the preamble about Thomas being of sound mind and body, Saxton put down his tea cup and leaned forward. The barrister's demeanor was becoming somewhat serious. The document was dated February 20, 1857, four years previously. Keys continued.

"Dear Muriel, Saxton and family friends;
When you hear what I have to say, it will mean that I have passed away, hopefully in my sleep. First of all, I love you Muriel, although right now you and I are going through a very hard time. Saxton is still missing at sea. Lately, I've begun to reassess my role as a Christian in our society. I'm ashamed at how many so called white Christians have treated those of a different color, race or creed rather shabbily.
Although the Old North Episcopal Church is where I have worshipped for many years,
I've become appalled and distressed at the blatant indifference shown by many in its congregants to the suffering of our black, our Irish and our Jewish immigrants. So, it is my belief that my church leaders have failed in their mission of promoting peace on earth and fellowship between all men, especially here in Boston."

Their barrister paused as shock swept the room like grapeshot sweeping the deck of a ship. Muriel clutched her son's hand. Keys waited then continued to read.

"As a result, I request that a private funeral service be held not in the Old North Church but in the First Free Baptist Church on North Joy Street, Pastor Nathanial E. Clover presiding. A guest list I've prepared is attached. You might be shocked about who is on it and who is not on it. However, my next request is for a public memorial service and subsequent reception to be held in warehouse No#3, and, it will be open to all of my friends, company staff, business associates and politicos who have cared about this old reprobate. I'm sure that Saxton will keep the wretched, ink stained 'Fourth Estate' at bay and Packard will do the whole gaudy affair justice in preparing it.
On a more sober note, the theme of my memorial service will be from one of Boston's most famous historical events. In lieu of what I've aforementioned, I will leave the Reverend Clover to figure it all out. If not. I'm sure Saxton will.

"One by land, two if by sea, please oh Lord, what do you see?"

At that very moment Saxton sensed a sea change. Steeling himself for a bolt from the blue, Leonard Keyes paused, took a deep breath and said,

"And to that Church I bequest ten thousand dollars immediately. My next request I know will upset my beloved Muriel. For that I beg her forgiveness. As to Saxton, who I hope and pray has returned home safely, don't laugh too loudly. Therefore, in conclusion, I have been a seafaring man all my life and as such I want to be buried in the middle of Boston's inner harbor opposite Hudson's Point. I have spoken."

There was dead silence. Saxton laughed inwardly, thinking,

'That old bugger, he's really upset the apple cart now!'

The barrister put the letter down. Muriel remained seated. She sputtered,

"He can't! I won't. It's a sacrilege! Why I've never heard of such a thing." Saxton noted his mother's reaction, thinking, 'Neither I nor anyone else has for that matter.'

He rose leaving his mother frozen on the couch as he escorted the silent entourage to the grand foyer. There, Packard helped them get ready to leave. Their sleighs and carriages waited in the driveway at the foot of the front stairs. Horses stamped their hooves as they ate oats from canvas feedbags slung under their muzzles. Flocks of Red Polls and Goldfinches swooped down. There, they squabbled over stray oat grains falling on the snow around them.

Saxton shook hands with everyone and thanked them for coming. Before his barrister left, Saxton asked him,

"Leonard, could you please send Reverend Clover back here right away and secondly, contact our Chief of Police and our Mayor to see if it is legal to bury Thomas at sea in the middle of the goddamned harbor!"

Keys nodded then motioned Saxton to follow him into the nearby parlor. Once there, he closed the door. He turned and took something out of his briefcase. He handed it to Saxton. It was a large brown manila envelope sealed with the Saxton Crest pressed into a red blob of hard wax. Not a word was said as Keys left the room, closing the door silently behind him. Saxton looked at the writing on the envelope's cover. It was in his father's distinctive copper plate script. On the front was a printed message,

"TO BE GIVEN AFTER MY DEMISE BY MY
BARRISTER, TO JOHN SAXTON, MY SON
IF ALIVE. MARCUS BROWN, IF HE'S NOT."

'True to form.' thought Saxton. 'A man of surprises. What's next?'

He went to his father's office and put the envelope in his wall safe behind an oil painting of his parents. Other than his mother, he was the only one who knew the combination and had a key.

Later that same day, after being informed by the taciturn barrister that he was wanted up at the Saxton House, the Good Reverend Clover sensed that perhaps something was amiss. He thought despairingly,

"But what could it be? Perhaps it had something to do with the recently deceased Thomas Saxton."

It was a point of pride with the 'Good' Reverend that he followed the Good Book's teachings to the letter although in a small capital sort of way. Most white churches in Boston were free to measure up to a more capital way of biblical interpretation, if they so desired. However, their worship was too straight laced, too joyless and too unforgiving of any human frailties for the Good Reverend to stomach. Thus the Reverend and his wife Miriam of thirty years sat before him every Sunday, their seven children sitting next to her in a tidy row.

The skinny Reverend scrambled aboard his black Surrey sporting a scarlet fringe that garnished the edges of its canvas roof. The long fringe swayed violently as Clover lashed out at his skinny horse for the first time in his life. By the time he arrived at the Saxton House, he was in a panic for Leonard Keyes Esq. had not revealed anything more to him. Clover was literally sweating bullets as he ran up the front stairs three at a time. A solemn Packard was waiting for him. He ushered the panting preacher into the parlor. Once the Reverend was settled in a comfortable chair, Saxton rose to speak, his hands clasped firmly behind his back. His mother Muriel, newly recovered from her recent fit of pique said quietly,

"Go ahead Saxton. Do as your father wished, God rest his soul."

Saxton began to pace back and forth in front of the Reverend, his hands clasped behind his back. He turned and stopped.

"As you well know by now Reverend, my father has passed away. His funeral will be held next Friday at 10 AM. Do you have anything planned at that time?"

Clover pulled a small notebook out of a breast pocket, opened it up, read for a moment, then looked up and shook his head. Saxton continued.

"Good. Now, how many people can you accommodate in your church?" He paused as Clover said,

"I'd say two hundred souls, more or less."

"Well, it may come as a shock to you but my father wants a private funeral to be held in your Church next Friday and he has willed your Church ten thousand dollars for the privilege."

Saxton paused as Reverend Clover for the first and apparently the last time in his life was at a loss for words. He gasped.

"I, I, I....don't know what to say! I, I, I ....think I'm going to faint."

He did just that, slumping over in his chair. Saxton laughed. Packard swept in with a glass of cold water and a wet rag. Both he and Saxton suspected that it would be needed.

They'd even considered getting Doctor Wilson but decided that the Reverend was young enough to survive.

Leonard Keys got up and left the new Mayor's opulent fourth floor office on School Street. Upon hearing Thomas Saxton's request to be buried at sea in the middle of Boston's inner harbor, Mayor, Joseph Wightman and Police Chief Robert Taylor, were beside themselves. Nothing like this had been so exciting since the 'Tea Party' or the 'Battle of Boston Harbor' for that matter. Wightman rose and looked out over the harbor. His receding forehead, flanked by curly brown hair reflected in the window. Grasping his drink in one manicured hand and stroking his clipped beard in the other, he cried.

"Jesus H. Christ, Bobby, old man Saxton was a real character. Why I still remember him firing his goddamn shotgun at the Anaona way out in the harbor. BOOM, BOOM!"

Chief Taylor stood up. Wearing pressed black pants, a buff Marino vest over a white shirt, the Chief was impressive indeed. His long blue dress coat with tails hung on a nearby coat-rack, the top of which was crowned by his black top hat adorned with a gold star in rosette. Taylor, quite jovial, stood there watching the Mayor. He said.

"I hope his son John is a chip off the old block."

They both sought legal advice from the city's lawyers and sure enough neither was disappointed. Thomas Saxton was to be buried as he wished.

BOOK ONE: CHAPTER 11
MEMORIAL FOR THE MASSES

Thomas Clifford Saxton's impending funeral became a cause celeb for two reasons. A rich white man's funeral was being held in a poor black man's church. Secondly, the City of Boston's lawyers were according to the local scribes,

'Legal eunuchs when they tried in vain to prevent a Christian burial in Boston's inner harbor, of all places'

Boston's newspapers were having a field day. Arguments for calm and collective common sense took a back seat to vile invective and spurious gossip. It was said with authority that Thomas Saxton had been a slaver and that his conscience had gotten the better of him, thus his generous bequest to a black Church or African Meeting House as it was called. Some even went so far as to suggest the Good Reverend Clover was Thomas Saxton's long lost son he'd fathered in Zanzibar. Supposedly, it occurred according to reliable sources, on one of his trading missions years ago when he was a young buck on the high seas.

Muriel Saxton took it all in stride as she read her morning papers. After showing some baseless headlines to Jack, he'd put his head between his paws. She agreed with Jack that all the papers toed the line on libel but none dared cross it, not yet anyway. She had stayed in her room ever since Thomas died. There were only three things that she treasured; namely Thomas's last Valentine card, her son and Jack in that order. Her mind had not been crippled by grief this time because the aforementioned comforted her.

Saxton on the other hand was not as genteel as his mother. He was more of a 'grab the bull by the horns' type of person like his father was. Oh how he missed him. He knew that Muriel did too but in a more spiritual way whereas an elemental connection had existed between father and son. Saxton struggled valiantly against a mounting flood of things to do, most of which should have been done yesterday. During this period right after his father's death, Maynard Keyes and Hans Larsen the company's comptroller, kept Saxton's financial ship afloat allowing him time to deal with the onerous task of burying his father.

Moreover, the memorial arrangements were becoming quite tedious. Endless meetings with Boston's Mayor and its Police Chief muddied still waters. These two egotistical public servants tried at every opportunity to divert unwarranted attention away from each other. Saxton blew up. He told them both to go to hell and walked out. They looked at each other quite shocked by his bad manners.

Saxton was fed up as he walked down a crowded street towards the harbor. Throngs of thrill seekers had come to Boston to see the 'Saxton Show'. He blamed himself for agreeing to his father's wishes. There was no going back. He hailed a Hansom cab, directing the driver to C.W. Rowland's Funeral Parlor on Traverse Street.

Cerile Rowland was gracious and serene as he extended a large black hand to Saxton. The undertaker ushered his client into the quiet confines of a formal sitting room set aside for quiet consultations with grieving relatives of the recently deceased. Everywhere, black ding balls hung from every window, wall, table and archway. As he took a seat, Saxton thought that black was certainly in poor taste for the dead, especially since the living thought that Heaven, God and this attendant Angels were all attired in blazing white. These thoughts evaporated instantly as a mellifluous voice from somewhere behind him purred,

"Would you care for some Darjeeling tea and a biscuit, Mr. Saxton?"

He turned around, looked up and saw before him the most exquisite creature he'd ever seen. She was a black beauty of the first order. Saxton politely accepted her offer. After tea was served, John Saxton stared at the stunning young woman across from him. He wondered why Cerile had left them alone. Saxton sipped his tea, completely mesmerized. While gazing into her coal-black eyes, he sputtered, choking on a Frean. Tea went everywhere, on him, on her and the settee he was sitting on. Saxton was beside himself,

"I say, I'm so sorry Miss. Look at the mess. My, how careless I am. Please forgive me."

Before he knew it, the gorgeous girl magically appeared with a dry cloth. She began soaking up spilled tea from his black frock suit and vest. He stood there paralyzed looking down at her. Slim and tall with fine features, she blushed, her eyes flashing as she dabbed away at Saxton. He could feel her body heat as they remained close just for a few moments. She smelled faintly of lavender. To Saxton it seemed like a delicious eternity. Cerile Rowland came into the room. He paused seemingly trying to collect his thoughts. By pausing, he made the two youngsters even more awkward. He stuttered,

"I heard a, a co, co, commotion from next, next door. Is, is everything alright?"

He looked at a stricken Saxton then at his daughter Virginia. He started to laugh. It was a big generous deep rumbling laugh. He threw back his black bald head.

"My Lord girl, leave the, the poor, poor man alone. Harvey will clean, clean up the mess. Here now Mr. Saxton, let's go, go into my office and, and finish our, our arrangements."

Cerile Rowland was somewhat taken aback by the burial arrangements outlined in Thomas Saxton's will; however, he knew Reverend Clover would concur. All the while, his beautiful young daughter took notes as they talked. Their business concluded; Saxton rose to leave. He looked closely at Virginia while shaking hands with her father. It did not go unnoticed. Saxton was smitten. Not only was she lovely but she was probably smart, compassionate and honest. He stepped out of the Rowland's Funeral Parlor onto a busy sidewalk then hailed an approaching cab. He was going to his warehouse to see Larsen. Saxton climbed aboard. The driver recognized his passenger by tipping his hat slightly. With a flourish the cab headed for the harbor down Washington Street. After a few blocks, Saxton had a sudden urge to get out. He thought of going back because he'd forgotten to ask for her name. But he did not.

Larsen was sitting beside his telegraph key as Saxton made a rather buoyant entrance into the small office. Larsen thought at the time that young Sax was being somewhat irreverent so soon after his father's death. However, as Saxton blurted out his plans, Larsen saw that something else had taken place in the young man. What he saw was a young man in love for the very first time. Larsen smiled. He remembered the first time he met his first love, Ingrid. He thought, 'Perhaps a little love would take the edge off a whole lot of grief.'

And so it was arranged that Thomas Clifford Saxton's memorial would take place in the Warehouse #3 at 10AM, on Saturday, two days hence. On that day, a new sign went up in front of the First Free Baptist Church. It was put up during the early hours of that morning.

"MEMORIAL SERVICE TODAY 10 AM
FOR THOMAS C. SAXTON.
INVITED GUESTS ONLY."

Saxton reasoned that at least the puissant press and its ink stained scribes would be harassing the First Free Baptist Church instead of warehouse#3 wherein the memorial service was really taking place. He laughed aloud thinking about the reporters twiddling their pencils for hours waiting in front of the little church. Saxton hoped that this white lie would give invited guests time to proceed down to the harbor before his ruse was discovered.

Reverend Clover was overjoyed as he heard about the change in funeral plans from John Saxton. He was especially pleased that the young man had invited his entire congregation. Of course, what he did not know; was that Saxton was taking no chances on having that special girl miss the memorial.

Clover's church choir had to be at the warehouse by five AM sharp. Their scarlet choral gowns, hymnals, choir risers, piano and everything else they needed would be shipped there the day before disguised as cargo. A gang of warehouse stevedores were already busy cleaning out the massive building. Any cargo already there was moved into empty Saxton ships berthed nearby. Over one thousand rented folding wooden chairs, one hundred trestle tables, linens, cutlery, crockery and everything else that was needed, arrived incognito just after midnight loaded aboard an express freight train from New York City. It steamed into the vast interior of warehouse #3 via a spur line right on time and was unloaded forthwith.

Packard was given the challenging task of looking after the memorial service in the front section of the warehouse. Millie's task was setting up a memorial reception that would take place in the middle third of the warehouse. Rodney was in charge of utilizing the rear of warehouse No#3 specifically set aside for dozens of carriages, wagons, and livestock that needed to be housed and fed. Thankfully the winter weather miraculously warmed up to above freezing. The streets and alleys around the city were mostly free of snow. Work crews were busy shoveling the last remnants from the walks, byways and driveways of the Saxton Company property on the waterside. Even the massive wharf had been swept bare. A stiff cool breeze still blew over the harbor from time to time but an early spring seemed to be in the offing.

Pinkerton's security guards agreed that the Saxton Shipping property's iron fences topped by lethal metal spikes would kept the city's denizens at bay if continually patrolled. Alan Pinkerton would see to that. Invited guests would be checked off by name as they went through the massive iron gates fronting the Saxton Shipping Co. property. One guest, Mathew Brady, was told not to bring his camera. In reply, he said he was relieved knowing that Jack would surely be there. Saxton laughed when he remembered Brady's response.

John Saxton had been very busy in his home office on the 'infernal' telegraph machine for nigh on ten hours. An uneaten lunch sat on a small side table across from him. The telegraph spewed endless tributes to Thomas Saxton from all over the eastern seaboard. One was from President Abraham Lincoln, who called Thomas Saxton a great patriot. Saxton was very proud of his father, but very curious about a certain mysterious packet in his father's wall safe. He wondered, 'What's in that package anyway?'

He decided that he would disobey his father and find out. Saxton locked the office door. Minutes later he knew all about 'False Prophet' and his father's role in it.

Saxton was in effect, instructed by his father to carry on as if nothing was amiss especially concerning Hans Larsen. Further more, he knew that Allan Pinkerton was working closely with his father and the War Department in Washington, and had been for sometime.

Pinkerton was running nearly one hundred agents across the northeast looking for Southern contraband, on the major railway lines of several large companies. Operation 'False Prophet' was an arms smuggling scheme devised by a group of Confederate sympathizers known as the 'Knights of the Golden Circle'. Their sole purpose was to arm the South in preparation for Civil War. Their members held important positions in railway and shipping companies. Hans Larsen was suspected of being such a member. There were many more like him all over the Atlantic seaboard known as 'Copperheads'.

John Saxton was expected to be as patriotic as his father. A quote from a friend of the family, Samuel Clemons, was inserted at the very end of his father's long letter to his son.

"Each man must for himself alone decide what is right and what is wrong, which course is patriotic and which isn't. You cannot shirk this and be a man. To decide against your conviction is to be an unqualified and inexcusable traitor, both to yourself and to your country. Let men label you as they may."

The words struck Saxton to the core. What his father had done was pass on the torch of patriotism to his son, nothing more and nothing less. It was a profound moment for he would do as his father had hoped. Saxton in partnership with Pinkerton would thwart the smugglers nefarious schemes. 'Operation False Prophet' would continue until the mastermind behind it was exposed. However, since even before the 'Battle of Boston Harbor', the 'Farm Machinery' had been sabotaged beforehand. Faulty firing pins, cracked gun mounts, worthless ammunition, improperly machined gun barrels, poorly cast wrought iron gun carriages, broken fuses and other mischief designed to plague the enemy were rampant amongst the boxes and crates labeled 'Farm Machinery'. Saxton was astounded that Gibbons and his crew survived firing the ordnance rifle.

Instructed to destroy all the papers within the packet once he memorized their salient points, he did so immediately by burning them in the fireplace in his father's office. All that is, except his father's letter. He just couldn't do it. It was if his father was still talking to him. Somehow comforted by his father's words, he put it back into the wall safe, amazed at his father's complicity in the whole affair. He wondered if Muriel knew about it. Perhaps she did, for she always insisted that her Thomas was a man of surprises. Now Saxton knew why.

The Saxton family held an intimate service in the Good Reverend's church the day before the memorial. It was attended by less than a dozen of Thomas Saxton's immediate family and close personal friends, excluding Reverend Norland. The press though persistent, was not invited. The public memorial of over one thousand invited guests would take place in warehouse No#3 the next day.

These guests would arrive there in small groups every few minutes, starting at four AM. The Finch twins would deal with the arrivals. Saxton laughed as he knew the Finch brothers would preserve their reputation, of being on the job twenty-four hours a day. As for any weak security points, it was namely the company dock fronting the warehouses where Pinkerton deployed most of his agents. Boston's Harbor Patrol was enlisted to assist him in securing that area. In the interim, the SS Anaona had been completely repaired. Several obvious scars inflicted by Gibbon's grapeshot that shattered its wheel house and flayed its decks were gone. The rejuvenated vessel would do the honor of taking Thomas Saxton to his final resting place, escorted by two Navy Patrol boats.

All funeral plans demanded total secrecy from the curious rabble; especially a slanderous press. Saxton and his cohorts in deception, finalized a plan to get His Worship, the Mayor of Boston, his Council, the Police and Fire chiefs and their wives, and other dignitaries down to the funeral, unseen and hopefully unheard. Every Saxton employee, at the Mansion, on the Saxton ships, at the Saxton shipyard, docks, offices and in the warehouses was sworn to secrecy by their superiors the next morning. The plans for the memorial and its subsequent reception were to be carried out with strict military precision. It was total victory or nothing.

Hundreds of Saxton employees, black and white, had been considered family by Thomas for many years. Thomas knew everyone by their first name as well as their wives and their children's. He bailed them out financially in times of disaster but never asked for a penny back. Their employer even paid for any medical bills they incurred thus being generous to a fault. Everyone worked extra hard for Thomas Saxton. In plain words, he was loved by one and all, rich or poor. His memorial would be a testament to a man who many believed would never be replaced. As Saxton thought of this, he knew that his father's shoes might be impossible to fill, but by God he was going to try!

Precisely at four in the morning, an army of invited guests began to arrive in small groups of ten or less. The Finch twins were kept very busy checking the guest's credentials before admitting them. Despite the often hilarious confusion caused when there seemed to be one of the twins in two places at once, the admittance of the chosen few proceeded for the most part, quite smoothly. Twenty Pinkerton agents were busy patrolling the Saxton waterfront property. Boston's Harbor patrol rowed around the Saxton wharves in dark choppy waters. The Anaona began raising steam hours earlier while tied up in front of Warehouse No#3. Its spring lines strained trying to hold her snug against the wharf while it bounced about in a winter chop.

Thomas Clifford Saxton's body was smuggled out of Rowland's Funeral Parlor at midnight disguised as a load of embalming fluid. Saxton knew his 'Old Man' loved surprises and practical jokes. He would have been pleased indeed, if he saw all the shenanigans going on because of him. It wasn't a funeral; it was a spectacle, an event, a celebration of a life well lived and a man well loved. A dray wagon with Thomas aboard arrived just after 1 AM at the gatehouse then was immediately driven down to the Anaona. A few minutes later, a weighted canvas sack containing Thomas's body was put into a wooden coal chute atop hatch No#2. A cool sea breeze ruffled the fringes of an American silk flag draped over it.

The memorial service started with a mixed race choir singing popular hymns such as 'Amazing Grace' and 'Oh what a friend we have in Jesus'. Black African spirituals followed such as, 'Elijah Rock', 'Swing Low, Sweet Chariot' and 'Oh Mary don't you weep'. These spirituals were accompanied by thunderous clapping and hallelujahs from the black audience. However, after a few moments of cultural restraint, the white throng joined in on the happy celebration.

Saxton, his mother and Mathew Brady with Jack the terrier on his lap, sat in the first row on padded chairs. Stretching out on either side of them and in many rows behind them, were all the dignitaries, politicians, immediate friends and senior employees of the Saxton Shipping Company. On a raised dais decorated with white roses and black tulips, sat Reverend Clover, Rabbi Saling, and Bishop Fitzpatrick. Minister Dexter Norland from Muriel's Old North Church had not been invited. This in itself was cause for considerable speculation amongst the social elite in Boston, as to who was invited or not.

Before the congregants, an elaborate empty coffin sat upon a shrouded chromed gurney. A large American Flag in the 'Great Star' design lay draped over it. A Naval honor guard stood at attention on either side for Thomas had graduated from the Naval School at Annapolis then served honorably in China for ten years, eventually being promoted to the rank of Commodore. Saxton was very pleased with everything. Packard had done a magnificent job. Throughout the huge warehouse, portable kerosene heaters vented through tall stacks piercing the metal roof high above, warmed the interior. The SS Anaona lay serenely berthed, extensively decorated in red, white and blue bunting, but not black. A colorful floral wreath was tied to a steam crane raised high above the ship.

All music ceased as Reverend Clover rose up dressed in a black frock suit, covered by a black gown. A long scarlet cope around his neck completed the ensemble. Raising his arms high, he began to lead the assemblage in prayer, shouting joyfully from beside the pulpit. He commenced to give a short invocation.

"My Brother Thomas Clifford Saxton has passed on to the hallowed land! Hallelujah! Hallelujah! Yes my brothers and sisters, he was your brother too. May the good Lord bless him and keep him forever in our hearts. We are here today to celebrate a life well lived and a man well loved. Mourn not for him but mourn for yourselves for we now have to go on without him; without his compassion, generosity and moral integrity. He was a man's man, a family man and our man. My dear friends, he was a champion of the common man. Dear Lord, please ease our suffering today, especially that of his immediate family. Oh Lord above, look down upon this righteous man and lift him high above us into your waiting arms. Hallelujah! Hallelujah! God Almighty, bring him home; bring him home to eternal life and glory, Amen."

A stately Chickering grand piano thundered out the opening chords of 'Onward Christian Soldiers'. The Good Reverend Clover directed his audience to stand and join in as both black and white choirs on either side of the dais rose to sing. The warehouse shook to its very rafters as the famous marching hymn was sung with religious fervor. Jack had to be muzzled by Brady to prevent the beast from howling. Muriel smiled.

'Surely, Thomas would be waiting for her in Heaven asking where Jack was and if the little scalawag was still getting into mischief.'

The hymn finished. Everyone sat down exhilarated. Reverend Clover introduced Bishop Fitzpatrick and Rabbi Saling.

They rose as one, adorned by their traditional vestments. Standing at the pulpit together, they gave their eulogies in alternate orations of praise. It was a singular event. Never before had two disparate religious leaders stood side by side, rejoicing as one, over the life of another who was from neither faith. It was sensational to say the least. Both men were long in their praise for Thomas, for he had been a bridge that brought people of all races, creeds and religions together. They recounted the many times that Thomas brought them together as friends and compatriots, blessed by his compassion and willingness to listen. Bishop Fitzpatrick and Rabbi Saling sat down in total silence. Virginia clapped then the whole congregation rose as one. Their approbation was electric with significance. After many long moments they sat down. Reverend Clover came back to the pulpit. Overcome by a revelation of conscience, he simply motioned for Saxton to come to the dais.

Saxton came forward to give his eulogy. As he approached the pulpit, he looked out over a vast assembly waiting expectantly in front of him. Before he even uttered a word, he took his time looking for her. He thought,

'She's there on the left, twenty rows back; the girl of my dreams.'

Their eyes met. Even in this moment of grief, he felt a rush of adrenalin sweep through him. She smiled. Tears began running down his cheeks, not from grief but from pure joy. Standing tall, his shoulders squared, John Saxton began to speak clearly, forcefully and most important; truthfully.

"Dear friends, family and invited guests. Thank you for coming here today under such difficult conditions." His audience murmured, willing him on.

"As you have heard, my father was a special human being and we all mourn his passing today. My mother Muriel and I have no words at our disposal to describe to you the extent of our personal loss. No, my friends, no such words are in my heart that can describe our pain as I stand here before you. But, I am secure in the knowledge that Jesus Christ will make our pain his own as he did on Calvary's cross for all of us long ago."

Saxton paused as the Reverend Clover, stood with his hands in the air crying,

"May the Lord God erase my brother's pain and his terrible sorrow!"

Many of his congregation in the audience stood, raising their hands high in the air, joyful and exultant. One of them was the girl. Saxton waited as they and the Reverend sat down. He continued, steeling himself, his resolve welling up within him, ready to erupt.

"There are many in our community, who go to Church and hear about the Golden Rule, 'Do unto others as ye would have them do unto you'.

However, they hear it but they do not practice it. In life, my father Thomas Saxton practiced the 'Golden Rule'. In his will he wanted Reverend Clover to expound on the theme of, 'One by land, two, if by sea. Tell me Lord, What do you see?'

I pause to apologize to Reverend Clover for I'm going to take the wind out of his sail today by telling you what I think my father actually meant."

Behind him, the Good Reverend nodded his approval. Saxton continued, driven on by his father's sentiments.

"As you well know, my parents worshiped at Boston's Old North Church all of their lives. That Church became famous for its tower where, a signal about the coming of the British was sent long ago; one lamp by land and two lamps if by sea. My father hated bigotry with a passion. He said many times that slavery in America was being replaced with bigotry, a far more subtle, more illusive, and more insidious slavery because it separated races as brutally as any whip in the cotton fields ever did. So my friends; one by land is bigotry and two if by sea is slavery for our land nourished bigots while the sea brought slaves from Africa to America. Bigotry and slavery are the evil twins flourishing within our nation and our neighborhoods right here today." He paused, ready to deliver a telling blow.

"My dear brothers and sisters, the shame of it is, we do NOTHING about it!"

Saxton paused again, letting the guilt of his audience rise to the surface. He could see shame, anger and disbelief on their faces. Black or white, it didn't matter. He continued on, poignant in his delivery as he spoke from his heart.

"Our nation today is divided over slavery. We here in the North will die fighting to abolish it and those in the South will die trying to preserve it. Will we be as willing to die fighting bigotry after slavery is banished? I think not."

Saxton stepped down off the dais to stand by his father's casket, his hand upon it. Tears streaked his cheeks. His captive audience remained hushed, paralyzed by his passion, his poignancy. John Saxton continued on resolutely, sweeping his other arm in an arc, proclaiming,

"Today, I see black and white folks here because they loved and respected my father. But, as I look out over the multitudes gathered here in this building, I see that they do not respect each other. Until they do, America will never heal, will never be free."

He returned to the dais. His audience stricken, riveted to their seats, looked straight ahead. Saxton's voice became icy, unforgiving and relentless in its veracity. He swept his right arm in an arc and shouted, "LOOK AT YOU!"

He paused dramatically, beseeching them, venting his grief and rage upon them like delinquent children before a teacher. He beseeched them,

"Before me today, I see two solitudes where my black brothers and sisters sit on one side of this vast building while my white brothers and sisters sit on the other. WHY? My father Thomas Saxton is asking you, WHY? We must love each other. I quote John 1 Verse 18. 'There is no fear in love, for perfect love casteth out all fear.'

We must not fear each other. Show it, I beg of you, before it is too late to love one another as the Lord himself intended."

The mourners sat stunned until Virginia stood up. Her father tried to stop her. She threw off his hand, looked about her, turned and walked out to the center aisle. She stopped, saw who she was looking for then walked over and sat down on a vacant chair beside an old white man. He never moved a muscle as his wife next to him jabbed him in the ribs. He sat there like he was carved in cold marble. His portly wife rose, looked around and made her way to a vacant chair beside a young black man. Presently, others began doing the same thing. No one shouted, no one spoke, no one cried. It was as if a silent session of musical chairs or a macabre racial charade was taking place. After a few moments many had changed sides. Finally it ceased. Saxton stood there the whole time, his arms stretched out like Moses parting the Red Sea. He lowered his arms and his voice, saying,

"Thank you all, for courage is your watchword and love is your reward. My father lived many years on earth but I know he will live much longer in Heaven. His life recently has been accurately reported by few and falsely reported by many. Today however, the truth will prevail and the truth will set him free. Goodbye father, I will not say, but hello father I will say when we will meet again in Heaven. God bless you and keep you. Amen."

Saxton bowed his head as he returned to his seat between his mother and Packard amidst thunderous applause. Reverend Clover motioned to Captain Stephen Carter to come forward. As the Reverend sat down, a tall bewhiskered, blonde headed Captain in his formal dress whites came up one of three aisles that parted the audience. His gold braided cover was under his left arm as he strode purposefully towards the dais. Stepping lithely onto it, he carefully placed his white sea cap on the pulpit. In a strong clear voice tinged with pent-up emotion, he said.

"Dear friends, Thomas Saxton and I were and still are shipmates. His life was the sea and then his family. As a seafaring man he traveled the world as I and all his Captains have. We all respected him and will miss him dearly as we go back to our ships and sail once more."

He took out of his pocket a small piece of paper, for he'd written a poem especially for the occasion. It was entitled, 'Our Captain'. As he began to read it, he would occasionally look down at the coffin in front of him. The cavernous room became very quiet as the poem's words rang from the rafters.

"Oh, Our Captain of the seas, you left for distant lands,
God trimmed your sails before the gales; he had you in his hands.
Oh, Our Captain of the seas, reefs nearly broke your keel.
But you stood as skippers should and spun the clipper's wheel.
Oh, Our Captain of the seas, your life at sea's no more.
On through the night past Heaven's Light, God brought you safe ashore.
Now your sleeping body lies at peace within the deep.
Above waves rise below calm skies, God knows you've earned your keep."

Captain Carter put on his cover and stood saluting the coffin. Other Captains rose in their dress whites and saluted as he laid the poem on top of the coffin then sat down. Reverend Clover rose and stood before the pulpit with his bible upon it. He flipped a few pages and began to read Psalm 91:1-2. He spoke as if he was at a revival somewhere in the backwoods of Kentucky, his home state. He thundered,

"He who dwells in the shelter of the Most High will rest in the shadow of the Almighty. I will say to the Lord. He is my refuge and my fortress, my God in whom I trust."

Nathaniel held the pulpit prisoner with both hands, firmly grasping either side of it. He started to jump up and down as the Holy Spirit gripped his rail thin body in ecstasy. He shouted. "He who is taken away shall return. He who shall return will never be taken away again. Amen, Hallelujah!"

Bishop Fitzpatrick and Rabbi Saling behind him rose up and cried 'Hallelujah'! They remained standing as the Good Reverend continued oblivious to what was going on behind him. However, he was totally aware of what was going on in front of him. For, both Saxton and Muriel had risen clapping their hands. Behind them like a tidal wave, the rest of his congregation stood up and clapped. The two choirs rose as one and started singing a raucous version of an old spiritual, 'Go down Moses'. Their voices rose in a wail of hurt as the slave song echoed throughout the vast building.

Poor Reverend Clover never did finish his sermon, for his choir left their risers clapping in time to the music. They walked singing in twos past a startled Reverend followed by the Bishop and the Rabbi. They filed past Thomas's coffin on either side then down the center aisle towards the exit. As one, his black congregation rose up and followed, clapping and singing at the top of their lungs. Meanwhile, the white mourners sat stunned until some of them also rose up in ragged groups and joined the happy procession.

Outside, a long row of Saxton Company sailors were lined up from one end of the wharf to the other. As the singing crowd spilled out, they spread out on either side. The Anaona's steam whistle gave out a tremendous blast. It was reported later, that there were as many skiffs, boats, ships and anything else that could float than there were people on the long Saxton wharf.

Saxton and his Mother Muriel remained standing as the choirs swept by. After the warehouse emptied, Saxton stepped forward to apologize to those who remained behind. However, the Good Reverend intervened, his hand on Saxton's shoulder.

"Oh don't worry Mr. Saxton. Any sermon I could give today would never compare to the miracle we've all just witnessed. Besides, after the eulogy you gave here, I might just be out of a job."

Muriel delicately wiped her flushed cheeks with a large linen handkerchief as Jack bounded about her feet. Her voice tinkled, delicate yet strong.

"Well Gentlemen, let's give Thomas his due; Saxton take my arm. Mathew Brady, come here this instant and carry Jack for me."

The crowd parted as Muriel and Saxton exited the warehouse. Men doffed their hats respectfully as the small group walked slowly past them. An honor guard of Saxton Captains stood along the port side of the Anaona's lower deck, their covers stuffed under their left arms. A crackling Saxton flag flew at half-mast as were all civic flags over Boston.

Captain John Gibbon was on special leave. His West Point gun crew stood at attention dressed in Army 4th Artillery fatigues. A chromed ordnance rifle brought down by train from West Point, gleamed in the sunlight, pointing out to sea. Three white doves were released. They flew away then returned back over the crowds standing far below them.

A Navy Patrol squad in dress whites stood shivering at attention, their breath rising in tremulous white clouds. They stood on either side of a wide gangplank amidships that led to the Anaona's main deck. A veiled Muriel Saxton wearing a black sable fur coat went aboard followed by Saxton then Mathew Brady who was trying to hold on to a squirming Jack. As they did so, they were bag-piped aboard to the tune of 'Amazing Grace'. Once there, a Naval Honor guard stood at each corner of hatch No#2. Only Reverend Clover, Bishop Fitzpatrick, Rabbi Saling, Mathew Brady, Donald McKay, their wives and Packard were allowed aboard. Moments later, two spring lines were let go, then two stern lines, followed by a bow line. Slowly the ship pulled away from the Saxton wharf.

The crowd beside it surged forward. Someone at the back pulled out a large white hanky and began waving it. Others followed suit. In an instant, every quay and jetty around the harbor was covered by blizzards of white linen. Ships in the harbor blew their whistles; their flags at half mast. This cacophony of various sounds spread over the harbor. Once again, sea birds rose in panic over cold choppy waters. Captain Wainwright steered straight for a red buoy anchored mid-harbor. As the vessel slowed, two Navy cutters came out to meet it. A sailor in one tied the Anaona's painter to the buoy, while three sailors aboard the other saluted as their little boat backed away. The funeral ship swung bow first into the wind, its engine idling.

Bishop Fitzpatrick wearing a golden miter, matching cope and grasping a golden crosier, stepped forward. In an act of aspersion, he blessed Thomas Saxton. An acolyte held his crosier as the Bishop shook a short handled aspergilla. From it, holy water was sprinkled over the flag shrouded canvas sack that contained the body. As he did so he chanted the Prayer of the Dead,

"God our father, Your power brings us to birth, Your providence guides our

lives, and by Your command we return to dust. Lord, those who die still live......"

Once his ministrations were completed, the Bishop crossed himself, retrieved his crosier and braced himself with it. Rabbi Scaling, an elaborately embroidered tallit draped over his shoulders, stepped forward. Speaking in English, he too blessed the body by singing the first few lines of the burial Kaddish,

"Exalted and sanctified is God's great name. In the world which will be

renewed and he will give life to the dead and raise them to eternal life....."

Upon concluding, he immediately turned and pinned a black ribbon upon Muriel and Saxton then stepped back as the Good Reverend went forward to lay a large black and white floral wreath upon the flag draped canvas sack. He too stepped back, remaining where he was, unmoving in body but not in spirit. Four crew men stepped forward onto the hatch cover to lift one end of the heavy wooden coal chute over and onto the starboard gunwale. Dark waters waited. John Saxton bowed his head. Together, the crewmen raised one end of the coal chute. A weighted canvas sack containing the earthly remains of Thomas Clifford Saxton slid from underneath the Stars and Stripes into the harbor with a splash. Muriel's wreath floated away through thin plates of drift ice caught by a capricious wind. For a long time Muriel watched until it gradually drifted out of sight. She reflected, 'Thomas is finally at rest where he wanted to be.'

Saxton held his mother tightly. Two sailors expertly folded the flag military style. One of them held the bundle forward to Muriel. She accepted. They stood back and saluted. As church bells tolled noon, Gibbon's ten gun salute rang out over the harbor. Behind her black veil Muriel was crying. She was amazed because she'd never cried before, never. Overhead, flocks of seabirds wheeled and shrieked. The Anaona was untied from its buoy then proceeded like a ship of state back to the Saxton wharf. After it was secured and its gangplank put in place, the deck party went ashore to a reception waiting in warehouse No#3. They were led by a bewhiskered bagpiper playing 'Scotland the Brave'.

Saxton and his frail mother walked into an area where they would be receiving their guests. They stood together, as he, his mother and the luckless Mathew Brady holding Jack in his arms, received condolences from well over a thousand guests. An hour later, Packard took Muriel home to Saxton House. Her son would follow hours later, completely exhausted. There was a good reason for this. Saxton had found out who that mystery girl was. She was Virginia Rowland; Cerile and Miriam Rowland's only child.

BOOK ONE: CHAPTER 12
AGAINST ALL ODDS

The memorial service and the reception thereafter lasted well into the afternoon. It was here that Saxton had been drawn to Virginia like the proverbial moth to a flame. He knew it was blatantly risky to expose his feelings to her in public. His friends, family and employees were all about him. However, over many glasses of the infamous Medford punch, they managed to say what all young people say when thrown together by chance, or in Saxton's case by design. Still rather shy as he had led a sheltered life, John Saxton never really had to fear anything or anyone. At the moment, he was afraid of losing Virginia.

They sat across from each other sipping punch at a long covered trestle table piled high with various desserts and plates of assorted finger foods. Amidst the laughter and conversation of those around them, it became evident especially in Virginia's case that still waters did run deep. Finally out of exasperation, John Saxton broke the ice. He'd just finished eating another distasteful Frean. Nervously he leaned forward, his blue eyes fixated upon her, saying obliquely,

"My! Virginia, the crowd here is so very loud today. You'd think it was a wedding reception rather than the opposite. Don't you agree?"

Virginia put aside a silver punch strainer. The woman in her wanted to shout out,

"Everyone can go home now, just go and leave me with this wonderful man." She replied coyly,

"Why Saxton, it is loud but your father was one who loved a party. I'm quite sure he wouldn't mind at all if we had some fun at your expense if you know what I mean?"

"Virginia! Did anyone ever say you're smart as well as beautiful?" She thought,

'How nice, he put my brains before my looks.'

She adjusted her black dress then sat up a little straighter. His big blue eyes bored through his facade. She blushed slightly as if thinking about something erotically funny.

"Saxton, I do hope you don't mind me calling you that but, we do live in different worlds, as far apart as two people can get without actually going to separate poles. You know we could never have anything more than what we have right now. Look, we can't even sit side by side. My parents would have a fit!"

"Why?' He queried.

"Well because for you, it would be unseemly. Secondly, for me it would be somewhat dangerous. Imagine, a woman of color talking to a white man, especially a rich, good looking one like you." He feigned,

"Like me?"

"Yes you--I mean rich."

"You think because I'm wealthy, the world is my oyster. Perhaps you probably think I don't bleed, don't worry, and don't put my trousers on one leg at a time. Virginia, it's true, I'm rich and you are not. It only means I've had more opportunities than you to acquire material things in greater abundance than you. Love, honesty, loyalty, commitment and a host of other positive qualities can be found in people like you who are not rich. Greed, dishonesty, immorality, hate, bigotry and a host of harmful qualities can be found in rich people all over the world." She threw back her head coquettishly.

"Like you?" He laughed. She continued to banter.

"I'm glad Saxton that you don't have many if any negative qualities despite an obvious-burden of being wealthy. I know you will be like your parents and use your wealth wisely for the greater good." Saxton brightened.

"Yes Virginia, for the greater good of all races, creeds and religions. Slavery is the antitheses of freedom."

"You're starting to sound a bit like Lincoln. I've heard the stories Saxton, of your experience with the slavers a few years ago. It was the talk of the town. It's very obvious that experience left deep, horrific scars upon your mind. Perhaps they are even more horrible than those upon my father's backside." He was shocked.

"Oh my God Virginia, is that true?" She nodded.

"Yes, hate will consume you Saxton if you're not careful. I too have seen the results of white hate, black hate and just plain old fashioned hate lying on the marble slabs in our funeral parlor. These victims were stabbed, beaten, hanged, or drowned. Yes--- even suicides including any other form of death you can think of. I have to bring their bodies back to life so at least they're presentable as they lay in an open coffin. It's very distressing. I might be only nineteen years old Saxton but I've seen a lifetime of grief. Thankfully, there is a place of solace where I can go to get away from all the pain, bigotry and violence."

"And where's that Virginia. What place is there that will cleanse one's mind and restore It so that one doesn't go mad? Please tell me Virginia!"

Saxton leaned across the table to hold Virginia's hands in his. Just as he was about to speak, the Good Reverend Clover came over, and interrupted them. Once more he praised Saxton for his eloquent 'Sermon in the Warehouse'. He said that he might ask him to preach some Sunday. Saxton declined. Clover turned about slightly, his attention focused solely on Virginia. He cooed,

"Oh, my dear child, what can I say? I'm always so busy; a funeral here, a baptismal there, and a wedding on the nearest horizon. Why my goodness gracious, one never gets to have a good time with one of their own now, do they my child?"

The Reverend kept looking straight at Virginia waiting for an answer; his black eyes demanding that she acquiesce to his wishes. However she did not. Instead, she glared back at him in defiance. Nathaniel Clover was not pleased that she was having a good time talking to John Saxton. Virginia didn't answer. She watched the Reverend look about furtively then hustle off towards her parents.

From time to time the young couple was interrupted as people gave their condolences to Saxton. At the same time they were eyeing the beautiful colored girl across from him. Saxton's thoughts reflected on how his fellow parishioners could give him human warmth as well as sympathy on one hand but on the other project a bigoted menace towards Virginia. His father was right. It made him wonder about the veracity of the living. No wonder Cerile Rowland was more comfortable amongst the dead for at least their attention was unconditional.

Virginia reached across the table and shook him, saying,

"Saxton, what on earth are you dreaming about? You haven't heard a word I've just told you. Why I declare; that you're either deaf, uncaring or in love." He was startled,

"Was it that obvious?"

Again he leaned towards her, the word 'love' ringing in his head like a wedding bell.

"Virginia, I'm not deaf and I'm not uncaring either. As for that refuge from pain you were just talking about, I don't agree with you at all." Virginia was ruffled,

"Why John Saxton, my Church is the only place right now that people of color can go to get away from the pain of discrimination and hate. There's a sense of belonging. It's a safe place, a comforting place that keeps us strong, together, and bound by faith." Saxton countered.

"Perhaps so Virginia but my ancestors came here on the Mayflower, landed at Plymouth Rock, endured hard winters, witch hunts, starvation, disease and bigotry. They escaped persecution in England only to do exactly the same thing here in America. They erected their churches, prayed together as you do, but they failed as you will. Believe me Virginia, if you don't reach out, rid yourself of fear and invite other races into your homes and churches, your black society here in Boston will rot from within like an apple. You wait! You'll see!"

John Saxton sat back exhausted. He'd talked too much and had accomplished nothing but feel frustrated. In the end their words meant naught. Virginia could sense that Saxton was spent mentally and physically. She was angry. They were going nowhere. All the arguments in favor of separate but equal as the only way races could live in peace together, was gospel to white Bostonians. Her church was all black. The local synagogue was all Jewish. The Catholics were all Irish. Not even just laws would bring them together. Only one thing ever brought any two races together temporarily, was a mutual crisis that forced people to put aside their religion or politics. Most likely, that was when they had to fight Mother Nature or a foreign invasion. But, another powerful connection bringing diverse cultures together was love, pure and simple. Saxton's eulogy moved Virginia deeply. His challenge to the assembly to love each other without fear was climactic to her. John Saxton was unlike anyone she'd ever met. His message of love lay before her like a gift. In her heart of hearts while thinking about him, she realized that,

'Love is colorblind. Love is unconditional. Love is the antithesis of racism. Love is a healing balm.' Saxton became petulant as he reached over and shook her saying,

"Virginia, are you listening to me? I've been talking about us."

She leapt out of her mind as his words touched her heart. Saxton was in love with her. He was giving her a chance to free herself from the shackles of her race. They would fight the battle against bigotry together. It would come from a stronger position, an educated and politically powerful position built on a foundation of mutual respect and unlimited love. Saxton was right. Slavery would be replaced with bigotry. Virginia could see it in the eyes of the whites who fawned over Saxton across from her. She could see it in those same eyes that seconds later either looked at her lustfully or in contempt. The slavery of the black body would be replaced with the slavery of the black mind. The leaders of her own race were only protected against the slavery of the soul. Their minds and bodies could not be whole until they were educated enough to gain political power. Virginia reasoned, knowledge was power, but a political power based on a mutual respect for all people. She laughed inwardly, thinking,

'Good gracious, now I sound like Lincoln.'

Saxton looked at her, as a play of emotions swept across her face. He was wondering what was going on in that head of hers. He guessed, saying,

"Yes my dear Virginia, I was thinking the same thing!"

Their table became a wide turbulent river flowing between them. But somehow, Saxton's words crossed over into Virginia's heart. Suddenly he was sitting next to her, holding her tight as her tears flowed like 'Old Miss'. Virginia became aware, very aware of what she wanted and what she must do. Those around them; blacks and whites were either appalled or bemused at the display of affection that radiated out from within these two young people. Saxton let go of Virginia, took a linen hanky from his trousers and gave it to her. As she dabbed her eyes with it, he said,

"I'm so sorry Virginia. I can see clearly what has really gone on around us tonight; the fawning, the scraping, the jealousy. I want to change all that. I need someone that will walk that path, fight that battle and savor victory with me. Although we haven't known each other very long, I do know you feel the same way as I do."

He gently put his arms around her shoulders. Their eyes met.

"There will never be a right moment for us Virginia. We don't have the luxury of taking time to know each other."

Virginia stood up. As she did so, she pulled Saxton to his feet. She knew he was the one for her. They belonged together. Love would protect them. Knowledge would lighten the path before them. She whispered in his ear,

"I love you Sax. I'll always love you but it hurts all the same." She kissed him tenderly.

Saxton buried his face in her hair and thus it was into this cauldron of hate that young Saxton fell totally and exquisitely in love with an undertaker's daughter. He declared,

"I will from this moment on always love you Virginia! You will be the constant companion of my soul."

Without warning he felt her being pulled away. John Saxton opened his eyes, sensing a deathly silence around him. Everyone was standing still looking at them, their mouths wide open, their faces frozen by shock. It was as if Saxton was in an accident as everything and everyone was moving about him in slow motion. He raised his arms out to her as she was slowly, oh so slowly pulled away from him. Virginia's face was a mask of anguish. Her dress rippled as if in a slow breeze. Her long black hair flowed like spring water around her black face. Saxton tried to move towards her but his legs were frozen. He was losing her as if she was going over the side of the Wanderlust, her screams of "Kwaheri, Kwaheri!" unheard.

Virginia's parents had come over. They quickly hustled their distraught and defiant daughter out of the building accompanied by Reverend Clover, his wife Miriam and most of his black congregation. It was cause enough for the closing of ranks on both sides. As young Saxton watched in dismay, Alan Pinkerton shook him out of his nightmare. He pulled Saxton aside.

"Mr. Saxton, I'm afraid there's going to be trouble, I've got twenty agents I brought into town just for the funeral. Do you need them?"

Saxton reflected inwardly.

'You can stop my heart from going out and pursuing her.'

Saxton regained his composure. He directed Pinkerton's attention to the Rowland family as they hurried towards their waiting carriage.

"Yes Mr. Pinkerton, find a rooming house for your men in town and make sure nothing happens to Virginia Rowland, her family, their business, the Reverend Clover, his family or his church. I want unobtrusive, twenty-four hour protection for all of them. If you need more men, get them. I'll inform His Worship, Mayor Wightman and Police Chief Taylor. You're now on a monthly retainer to cover all your expenses as of this moment. Guard the Saxton House as well as Saxton Shipping. Can you do it?"

"Yes Sir!"

"By the way Allan, I want you to deliver a message to the C.W. Rowland Funeral Parlor at nine tomorrow morning for Virginia Rowland's ears only. I also want two of your agents to begin following her immediately at a discreet distance." Pinkerton nodded.

"Then tell her parents Cerile and Miriam Rowland that I'll be there at seven tomorrow night with or without their consent."

Saxton took Pinkerton further aside and whispered,

"Tell Virginia to meet me at the First Free Baptist Church rectory at ten tomorrow morning. Tell her to bring its key."

After the memorial service was over, Virginia had been taken to the vestry of the First Free Baptist Church. Therein she waited patiently for Reverend Clover to finish lecturing her while she sat seething beside her parents. They in turn were horrified upon hearing that she and John Saxton were interested in each other. To them, any liaison, platonic or otherwise between a black woman and a white man, especially a rich white man was untenable and most certainly fraught with danger. More so now than ever, was such a union doomed to failure. The Reverend had stood up somewhat triumphant, all the while looking down indulgently at Virginia as she sat on a settee before him. His reedy voice intoned,

"We are all children of God, my dear Virginia and as such we are the creation of the Almighty. Moreover my child, you are too young and naïve to understand that the real world is quite different from what God intended. Lucifer himself has soiled the Lord's creation and it is my responsibility as your Pastor to lead you towards the light of God's infinite wisdom."

The next morning, Saxton left the Saxton House to meet Virginia at the rectory of the First Free Baptist Church. Virginia had arrived early. As she opened a side door, a voice behind her, nearly scared her to death. It was Saxton. She turned to scold him but she couldn't for she was instantly in his arms. They kissed long and tenderly. Virginia gasped, "Oh Saxton, let's go inside before someone sees us."

Saxton agreed knowing full well two discreet figures were watching them from a distance. Virginia closed the rectory door behind her, heart racing. It seemed as if she was dreaming and feeling reality about her all at the same time. Again they drew together and after many heartbeats slowly parted. Errant bands of sunlight glimmered through tall windows above them like wind through a keyhole. It was spectral, as if a holy sepulcher was their only sanctuary. They were alone but not alone. Saxton brought her over to a leather settee beneath these high windows. They sat down together, their arms about each other. After a while, Saxton put her at arms length, saying tenderly, his eyes fervent in the soft light.

"I love you Virginia and always will. I know last night was just a taste of what we can expect if we are to be married."

Virginia snuggled into him and countered coyly,

"Dear Saxton, are you proposing marriage to me? Why we hardly know each other!"

He laughed gaily while holding her once more away from him. Saxton looked at her intently as young people are wont to do.

"We don't have the luxury of time darling as you found out last night. I want you to know that I'm exactly like my father was or ever would be."

She retorted, her black eyes teasing him.

"You mean stubborn, bull headed, outspoken and domineering." He laughed, as if expecting something else from her.

"Yes, Virginia, all those and others you haven't heard about yet." She snuggled into him once again.

"Perhaps loving, committed, loyal, smart, brave, very responsible and witty thrown in for good measure."

He kissed the top of her head. She looked up frowning.

"Saxton, our parents will never agree to our relationship? Reverend Clover reprimanded me last night. It was terrible to see a 'Man of the Cloth' so bigoted. It was as if I had committed some horrible sin. He said it was dangerous to love a white man let alone a rich one. How could he say such things and preach the opposite? I love you Saxton not only for what you are as a person but what you stand for as a human being." Saxton kissed her full on her lips, his passion unabated.

"Now my dear, don't get too poetic or I'll want more of it: Just calm down and listen to me."

He held her while trying to sort out his emotions.

"My dear Virginia, you are a firebrand! Still waters not only run deep but hot as well. Look my Darling, be at my house at five tonight. Tell your parents that I've invited you there to meet my mother. I'll have a coach pick you up and bring you back. You'll be safe believe me. Only you, no one else, do you understand?"

She looked at him, waiting. He continued,

"Packard will show you to my office. Stay there until I call you in. By the way, will you marry me?"

Virginia rose up and as she did so, drew him up to her. She looked up into his sea blue eyes. He looked down into her radiant face. She kissed him and purred, "Maybe!" He pretended to pout.

"I take it then that a 'maybe' is highly suggestive in this case."

He released her and sat her back down on the settee. He knelt before her. Again he asked her to marry him. Again she looked deeply into his eyes looking for love. She realized he was serious, very serious about her; about their families and about their prospects. She saw a future with Saxton and no one else, for no one else would ever love her as he did right now and forever. Virginia bared her soul to him.

"Yes of course my dear. Once and forever till death do us part."

Saxton reached into his gray frocked jacket and brought out a black ring box, handing it to her. Virginia gasped as she opened it up. Therein was an engagement ring of large alternating round black sapphires and round white diamonds inset into a white platinum band. It sparkled seductively on its own, back lit by soft light streaming down upon it from somewhere high above them.

The next day, Saxton told his mother about what had happened at the reception after she'd left. They entered the parlor together. Muriel rang for refreshments. Promptly her butler appeared.

"Please Packard would you bring us some tea and those horrid Peak Freans. I'll ring you when we're ready."

He bowed and departed. As he entered the kitchen, his staff rushed forward and said,

"What's the news Packard? Tell us all about it, I'm dying of curiosity!" cried Millie. Another gushed,

"Imagine John Saxton in love with an undertaker's daughter and black to boot! My God! I can't believe it! All of Boston is agog!" A scullery maid cried,

"I understand the Pinkertons are guarding her night and day as well as her home and here at the Saxton House, imagine that!"

Packard's patience was exhausted by the melee. He raised his white gloved hands in exasperation,

"Enough everyone, please get back to work! Millie, we'll take the tea and Freans to the parlor when the bell rings."

Meanwhile, the battle lines were being drawn. Muriel still dressed in widow's weeds, sat on a Louis XV carved settee, Jack upon her lap. She leaned forward looking sternly at Saxton sitting across from her. She enquired somewhat exasperated.

"Do you really love her Sax? Will it be real, lasting and immutable? Will it withstand the hate, the bigotry, the gossip, the lies, the taunting that will be inevitable? Your wealth will not protect you. Your business will suffer, your health will too and God forbid; your children will suffer as well. There'll be nowhere to hide but here or at sea for no place else will be safe. You'll stand out as a couple like two scarecrows in a rose garden. My son, listen to me. You belong with your own kind. Do you really understand the ramifications of your actions Saxton? Are you really, really sure about Virginia?"

After his mother's opening salvo, Saxton decided to unleash his heavy artillery by announcing,

"Virginia and I are engaged as of today. I've given her an engagement ring. Is that sure enough for you mother?"

Muriel blanched, her thoughts piled up like cumuli beneath a thunderhead.

'She weathered many storms waiting for her Thomas to sail past Boston Light.

She waited nearly three long years for her son to come home.

She had endured beyond endurance.

She lost Thomas, her one and only love.

She would be losing her only child to whom, to what?

She realized that she didn't have the heart to bully him. It was against her nature.

She would, like her sailor husband try another tack.

She put Jack down, rose and stood looking down at her defiant son.

Muriel's second attack began by not using another frontal assault. That tactic had failed miserably. Instead an attempt at securing victory through subterfuge began in earnest. Obviously she knew what she was talking about as it had been her life, her only life for nearly fifty years.

"My dear son, don't you think that your recent funereal rhetoric has gone to your head?" He parried.

"Whatever do you mean mother?" She thrust back hard.

"Well it seems rather far fetched that someone in your position would even consider courting, let alone marrying some one below your station, don't you think so my dear?"

"My station in life you mean mother, as you seem to know exactly where you and all your so-called friends want me to be. Is that it?"

"Yes dear."

"And what station might I be worthy of mother?"

Muriel courted his reputation within the inner circles of political power by saying,

"Why a station of respectability, of decorum, of financial responsibility is what I mean. You'll need all three if you ever aspire to throw your hat into the ring. Why I've been told by many at our last New Year's Eve party that an erudite young man such as your self could go far in the national arena. Charles Sumner amongst others in power would support you if you ever decided to run for Congress. But my dear son, having a colored wife would certainly make that happy prospect quite impossible. Think of your future and hers for that matter. My dear Saxton, the girl's family is obviously bereft of what I mentioned earlier; namely decorum, respectability and financial means and always will be. Can't you see that or at the very least understand the implications of it?"

Saxton played her little game but now he'd had enough. He rose up, hands on his hips and glared at his mother. She stepped back and sat down heavily. His voice hissing like cold water over hot steel, said,

"I'm only going to say this just once mother. Virginia and her family are as respectable as you, as knowledgeable about social graces as you and as financially solvent as you. But, those qualities are outshone by those possessed by Virginia alone."

Muriel Stamford Saxton knew then that she was losing the battle. As such she looked up at her recalcitrant son and began speaking with a forced sarcasm bordering on hysteria.

"And pray tell, what might they be my son? What possible qualities could she ever have, that would make her one of our own? My God, she is colored! Therefore no matter where you two would go, no matter where you might hide; her color alone will crucify both of you on a cross of white hatred." Finally, completely spent, she whimpered,

"I'm only trying to protect you and her." Sensing capitulation, Saxton stormed the gates of her meager defenses.

"No mother, I think you are only trying to protect yourself from the shame of it all, if Virginia and I marry."

Saxton pressed his argument not caring about his mother's discomfort although he knew what he was saying was unpleasant. But, his future with Virginia was at stake, for without his mother's approval, any chance with them having a life together in Boston was doomed. He had to leave Muriel no choice but to submit to his wishes. Saxton continued his offensive, giving no quarter and certainly taking no prisoners.

"Yes mother, your humiliation by your peers awaits you. Imagine if you will just for one moment; no more high society tea parties, no more formal Christmas dinners, no front pew in the 'Church of Bigotry', and no more trips into town to shop at your 'by invitation only' stores. The complete and utter shame of being ostracized within your own hypocritical community would be too big a price to pay, wouldn't it mother?"

He sat down beside her, completely exhausted. But, he loved his Virginia pure and simple, mother or no mother.

Muriel Stamford Saxton seethed, as if her son was a slaver flaying her conscience with a leather lash. The sting of truth was unbearable. She reached deeply into her store of vocabulary for a rebuttal but none was to be found. She delved into all the sermons she'd ever heard for a rebuttal but none was to be found there too. At last Muriel Stamford Saxton knew what her husband had found in the little black church long ago and what her son now found in Virginia. They'd found pure love; colorblind, unconditional and everlasting. Muriel looked at her son with new eyes, a new heart. Knowing that her son was cleansed by love, his mother took his hands in hers and said softly,

"Thank you Saxton. I understand now. Truly, I do. I'll love her as if she was my very own child. Yes indeed, thank you son for setting me free. Thank God for setting me free!"

She reached over and pulled a service cord beside her. Moments later, Packard, followed by Millie entered the carpeted hallway and as they moved along it there was only silence. Nothing was heard coming through the closed door of the drawing room before them either. Packard stopped and put his ear to it. Nothing! Not even a murmur.

'Very strange indeed!' thought Packard for he'd fully expected a heated exchange between Muriel and her determined son to be ongoing and at full volume. He knocked twice then opened the door, standing aside for Millie and the tea tray. As they swept into the room; there before them, were mother and son, sitting side by side smiling at each other, talking in a calm civilized manner. Millie set the silver tray down and left as Packard poured tea. They finished, left and quietly closed the door. Packard pressed his ear to it. Muriel waited a few moments then spoke out loudly,

"Stylus Packard, don't you have things to do other than eavesdrop?"

Saxton rose, put his fingers to his lips and opened the door connecting the drawing room to his office. He returned with Virginia on his arm. His mother was momentarily at a loss for words.

"John Saxton, you are a man of surprises just like your father"

Muriel rose, and immediately walked forward and kissed Virginia. Both women hugged each other. Saxton waited then beckoned his mother to sit in a wing chair with Jack on her lap while he and Virginia sat on the red settee holding hands across from her. On Virginia's left hand was the engagement ring Saxton had given her. It was Saxton's turn to enter the crucible. Virginia had told him to be at Rowland's Funeral Parlor at seven o'clock that evening.

Some said later, considering the bigotry that surrounded them that Saxton and Virginia were like Romeo and Juliet; two star-crossed lovers doomed never to have their love requited. John Saxton had thought long and hard about the racist ramifications people of color endured in his America. It was bad enough that women were denied their right to vote as suffragette Susan B. Anthony decried all over America. But at least white women had some rights whereas lovely Virginia and her race had none, especially after 1850. As a young man, John Saxton might have been forgiven for being rash, impulsive, ignorant or simply irresponsible. However, he was by no means an ordinary young man with flights of fancy in his head and puppy love in his heart. No, John Saxton was mature beyond his years. His wealth, his political potential, his common sense approach to everything had matured him very quickly. Others observed wryly that the Saxton family tree was indeed known by its fruit.

And so Virginia, her parents and the Clovers sat down in the drawing room of Rowland's Funeral parlor waiting for John Saxton to appear. Her parents had remained silent as the Reverend lectured their daughter that morning in the vestry. They were reserved people who went about their unsavory business in a white world as invisible as possible. They dealt with the dead and stayed away from the living except in church. There, a kindred spirit moved them and others around them to jubilation. Their church on Joy Street was their freedom ground, a common denominator of joy other than slavery, their former common denominator of grief.

Once again the Reverend continued to lecture Virginia in the upstairs drawing room as they waited for her paramour to appear. When the Good Reverend had finished, he sat down and waited for Virginia to respond. She did so with steely resolve. She looked at a Seth Thomas clock sitting on a nearby sideboard then stood up sharply and told them all to be quiet. The Reverend sputtered and her parents remained silent as it was their habit to do so. Virginia walked over and kissed both of them. She stood back then stamped the floor twice. A few moments later, sweeping the ever present ding-balls aside, a very confident John Saxton entered the room. He'd been waiting in a viewing room downstairs amongst the newly dead.

Everyone rose as Saxton walked under rows of black ding-balls into the Rowland's drawing room. He shook hands with everyone then sat down on a Tete a Tete rosewood sofa opposite four adults sitting sphinx-like across from him. Virginia sat next to him, her engagement ring sparkling like a morning rainbow on her ring finger. Miriam Rowland pulled a nearby service cord. Moments later Harvey appeared. Miriam said,

"Harvey, would you please get us some tea and Freans."

Saxton thought, 'Not again!'

Harvey departed. Saxton began by saying,

"Virginia and I are deeply in love and are engaged as of this morning." The Good Reverend said curtly,

"I noticed." Saxton continued, his confidence rising.

"I do hope we'll have the same support from all of you as that given to us by my mother Muriel. I would like to read a letter that she wrote to you. She apologizes for not inviting you all to the Saxton House for tea but she is still indisposed, as you might imagine. Do you mind?"

The silence was deafening. Virginia squeezed his other hand as he withdrew a letter from the breast pocket of his new frock suit. He began reading in a clear and vibrant voice.

"Dear Cerile and Miriam. Thank you both for your sympathy as I grieve the recent loss of my husband Thomas. I'm sure you know from experience that grief can cripple one's judgment and afflict them with prolonged bouts of despair. I hope you will consider me to be of sound judgment as I now affectionately count you and Miriam to be part of my family. I realize the future will probably be grim not only for our nation but for people of color and especially for Saxton and Virginia.

I know the differences between us are obvious and the distance between us socially is vast, but I know now that their love can conquer all. Love can liberate a nation, a people and the human heart in a way that no other force on earth can do. I have loved, been loved and have given birth to love. Virginia and Saxton deserve better from us, from our friends and from our race. Let them together, sow seeds of love and in turn harvest the fruits of that love. We are all equal in the eyes of God and therefore have nothing to fear if we trust him to protect us. I quote Mathew Chapter 8, verses 25 and 26,

'And his disciples came to him, and awoke him, Saying, Lord, save us: we perish. And he saith unto them, Why are ye fearful, O ye of little faith? Then he arose and rebuked the wind and the sea; and there was a great calm.'

I welcome Virginia as my own, regardless of what you or anyone else will think. She is my daughter now and always will be a wonderful and loving addition to our family. God bless you all.

Muriel Stamford Saxton,

February, 18, 1861."

The silence was prolonged. Saxton gave the letter to Cerile who could not read it as he was illiterate. Tears began running down his face. Virginia was shocked. She'd never seen her father weep before. The Good Reverend reached for the letter as if it would strike him dead. He was, for the second time in his life, at a total loss for words. But his silence didn't last long. After he finished reading the letter, he jumped up and cried,

"Glory to God for the righteous have spoken the truth and the truth has set us free!"

The wedding banns were published a week later. The Saxton wedding took place March 14th, 1861, at the First Free Baptist Church in Boston. Pinkerton's security was everywhere about and it was needed. Protesters of all political and religious persuasions paraded two blocks away on either side of the little clapboard church. The ceremony inside it was raucous, jubilant and yet somehow a happy fusion of two divergent cultures. As the wedding guests arrived, their racial biases surfaced. White guests tried to sit on the right and black guests tried to sit on the left. However Muriel and Miriam would have none of it. Saxton's funeral eulogy had had a pronounced social and spiritual effect on both women. Soon the little church was packed with a polyglot audience experiencing culture shock, new religious revelations and a fair measure of soul searching. Satisfied, Miriam and Muriel sat down holding hands in the first pew.

Virginia was radiant and late. Saxton was nervous and early. Her bridesmaids were black and his groomsmen were white. Behind a raised dais, a mixed choir sang the Angelus with a joyous rendition never before heard before by either side. The whole church was awash in colorful floral arrangements, while black and silver satin bows graced both ends of every polished pew.

One might have said quite honestly indeed that it was a second chance for everyone there in that little old church that day. On the dais, Bishop Fitzpatrick and his good friend Rabbi Schindler sat on either side of their good friend and colleague, the Reverend Nathaniel Clover. The wedding was traumatic, especially for Boston's social elite. Many of both races boycotted it because of who was getting married but not because they hadn't been invited. However, everyone knew the latter reason was the truth. Reverend Clover was sorely tempted to sermonize but did not do so under strict orders from his wife. Instead he tempered his enthusiasm with a poem composed especially for the occasion by Virginia. He read 'Another Chance' with vigor.

"Within this Baptist church we stand, we're side by side, we're hand in hand.
God gave us both another chance; at life, at love, at sweet romance.
For out of hatred into the light, we know true love, we know what's right.
Was it luck or circumstance? We thank our Lord for a second chance.
We'll leave this little church today to face a world of bigotry,
But our pure love will conquer all. We will not falter, will not fall.
Down through the years as side by side, we will not run, we will not hide.
Whatever happens from now on is in God's hands when we are gone."

The Good Reverend concluded; his emotions ready to burst forth despite Miriam's dire warnings.

"Thank you Virginia for composing this beautiful and very moving poem of love. It certainly outlines the challenges ahead of you. Yes, my friends, we all know the road of life will be challenging for them but we also know that their love for each other and the radiance of it, will blind the bigots around them into submission. Hallelujah! Hallelujah! May God bless you and keep you!"

Virginia looked knowingly at Saxton, remembering Clover's sorry demeanor at the funeral reception when their love and the radiance of it did little to quell his bigotry at the time. Perhaps, he had seen the light. Virginia hoped so.

Reverend Clover soberly proceeded with their wedding ceremony after the church organist played the traditional, 'Here comes the Bride'. The happy couple was married and as they left the church, long lines of Saxton Captains flanked them on either side, their white covers held high above them. The newlyweds ran to a white Barouche wedding carriage through a veritable blizzard of flower petals thrown from all sides. Their wedding night was spent in the master bedroom of the Saxton House. Packard's household staff was discreet as they silently went about their duties. Millie guarded their privacy like a lioness guarding her cubs. Not even Packard escaped her wrath as he tried to attend to their requests. Defeated, he swaggered back to his station in the kitchen muttering "Women" as he did so. His staff worked feverishly, preparing for the wedding reception to be held later that evening in the Grand Salon of the Saxton House.

Early the next morning, the SS Anaona was building up a head of steam beside warehouse No#3, in preparation for the couple's honeymoon cruise to Bermuda, often referred to as 'A place of eternal spring.' Axel Benson, a short, sinewy Creole, had just returned on the Silver Ghost from Canton China with a cargo of tea. Saxton immediately informed him that he was promoted to be the Anaona's First Mate. Benson had missed the 'Battle of Boston Harbor' but was delighted to ship aboard as he was a confirmed bachelor with no family waiting for him ashore. A senior Captain, Ian Wainwright would be his skipper. For the first time, Saxton hand picked a crew instead of Hans Larsen. Hans was not pleased, not pleased at all.

The newlyweds boarded at noon. On the wharf, Muriel and Miriam held hands. Larsen, Packard and Millie as well as Virginia's parents waved goodbye. The Good Reverend offered up prayers and salutations. Jack tore back and forth between two large bollards chasing his red ball. A blizzard of white linen from hundreds of Saxton employees once again swept the dock side as the Anaona pulled away. A large 'JUST MARRIED' sign set up in a yellow lifeboat was towed along behind it. Virginia and Saxton held each other tight as the little lifeboat bobbed and weaved about from side to side in a turbulent wake. A steam whistle high above them blew through clear cool airs. Other ships in the inner harbor began to salute them. The Anaona plodded up the shipping channel towards Castle Rock accompanied by two naval patrol boats. Saxton House on Snow Hill receded far astern. An hour later, the patrol boats blew a parting farewell and headed back, picking up the 'JUST MARRIED' lifeboat along their way.

As the newlywed's steamship passed Boston Harbor Light, intermittent Atlantic swells began to caress the ship as it pushed against the steady north bound current of a warm Gulf

Stream. Hours later, the couple, were bundled up, sitting in folding teakwood chairs on the aft deck. Beneath them, the ship's steam engine throbbed along quite contentedly. They gazed about, watching each headland gradually disappear as a settling sea haze obliterated them. Their attention turned to their ship's foaming wake being rent asunder by a stiff westerly breeze. Virginia turned to Saxton, took his hand and cooed,

"Oh my dear, at least now we'll have some peace and quiet."

BOOK ONE: CHAPTER 13
THE HONEYMOON FROM HELL

The SS Anaona proceeded at five knots through Hell Gate, a narrow shipping channel connecting New York City's harbor to the Atlantic Ocean. It was dawn. The happy couple missed seeing the skyline of Manhattan swing into view. The island's granite fist thrust outward as if Moses was parting the Harlem River to starboard and the much larger Hudson River to port. The ship swung into the Hudson River chugging upstream towards the Saxton Shipping Co.'s Manhattan warehouses sited at the foot of Fifth Avenue. Captain Wainwright stroked his thin white beard instructing his helmsman to correct his course to "Starboard two". A faster Staten Island Ferry steamed past loaded with office workers headed for Wall Street. Its wake rocked the Anaona. Below decks, there was a discreet knock on the couple's stateroom door. Virginia was still in bed. Saxton was in the head shaving while trying unsuccessfully to regain his balance. He poked his head out and said,

"Come in Rodney. Put our breakfast on the side table please. Be careful, the ship is still bouncing about."

Rodney, a black bodyguard and former boxer, was the newlywed's coach driver recently hired for the trip by Saxton. He carefully put the silver breakfast platter on a sideboard. Without eyeing Virginia, he backed up, leaving as silently as he had arrived. The stateroom's brass door lock clicked shut. Virginia leaped out of a wide bunk bed, ran over to the sideboard and lifted up two silver lids revealing her favorite breakfast of bacon and soft boiled eggs. She was delighted, crying in ecstasy,

"Oh Sax, how wonderful it all has been for us!"

Virginia ate a piece of bacon as she danced naked over to a large scuttle through which a round shaft of sunlight splayed across the spacious stateroom. Her lithe body glistened in the morning light. Throwing back her long black hair, she leaned through sunbeams to look outside. She cried,

"Saxton, we're in New York City! Oh, I can't stand it I'm so excited."

She backed away when she realized that the dock was closer than she'd imagined. Virginia pulled two heavy curtains together just as the ship's propellers began thrashing in reverse. The ship nudged gently against the wharf's bumpers. Shouts of crewmen echoed about. Spring lines were cast ashore followed by the sound of a heavy gangplank as it dropped onto the dock with a thud. Seagulls began mewling nearby. Heavy swells from passing ships slapped the port side of the ship as if someone was patting a wet granite headstone. Virginia cringed. She reached for her red chiffon peignoir, slipped into it and cooed,

"Saxton, my dear, I need you now if not sooner!"

Saxton stuck his head out of the head and looked at Virginia lying back on the bed, her peignoir open, revealing all. He moved naked towards her, his arousal quite evident. She giggled as his face was still covered in shaving cream.

"How sexy!" she squealed as Saxton lowered himself into her.

Later that morning, Captain Wainwright stood on the portside flying bridge. He lit his meerschaum pipe. Below him the Saxtons had minutes before disembarked straight into a Company coach. Driven by Rodney their personal valet, it swept past the gatehouse and up Fifth Avenue. Behind Rodney, an iron luggage rack was crammed with half a dozen monogrammed green alligator suitcases. His charges would be staying at the St. Nicholas Hotel on Broadway for the next three days. Unsightly warehouses and a dusty coaling wharf stretched out beside the Anaona. Captain Wainwright didn't blame the newlyweds for leaving so soon, as coaling was a long, loud and dirty operation. His observation concluded as their black Landau coach pulled by a matched foursome of grays turned a corner and disappeared. Unbeknownst to the Captain, two other men were watching it too. One of them put his brawny arm on the shoulder of his shorter companion and as he did so, a tattoo appeared on his left wrist. Thereon was a large capital 'D' with a dagger thrust through it.

Saxton had made an early morning appointment at Mathew Brady's 'Gallery of Daguerreotype' located at No.785 Broadway. Along the way the newlyweds were astounded at seeing sidewalks as wide as streets in Boston, crowded with jostling window shoppers, repulsive beggars, screaming news boys, sidewalk vendors hawking their wares and businessmen in a hurry to get nowhere fast. About them, in endless streams, hordes of horse-drawn street cars on iron tracks clattered about, their bells constantly ringing. The city smelled of horse manure and urine. A constant buzz could be heard as millions of flies settled upon every mound of equine excrement piled up on the cobblestone avenues.

The couple arrived before Brady's shop. A tiny copper doorbell above them tinkled as they entered. Moments later a long black curtain was pulled aside by Brady's assistant, Timothy. He stood there momentarily stunned by Virginia then bounded forward to shake Saxton's hand exclaiming,

"I must say Saxton you have a real eye for women. Who is this lovely creature?"

Virginia moved forward as Saxton introduced her. She offered the thin little man the back of her kid gloved hand. Eyes sparkling, he took it and planted a slow extravagant kiss upon it. He backed away as she coyly announced that she was 'THE' Mrs. Virginia Saxton herself of Boston, no less. Timothy feigned mock surprise then hugged a startled Virginia. She blushed, turning to Saxton.

"It seems that you're full of surprises like your father." Timothy winked at Saxton.

"Why yes my dear he is. We've known about your plans for a few days now and everything is ready in the studio behind me." Virginia stopped and sputtered,

"But I'm not ready Sax! My gowns are still packed in my luggage."

Saxton pulled her to him, looking into her eyes. He teased,

"Perhaps you'd rather be naked!"

She boxed his ears gently then stood back a few paces and pouted.

"John Manly Saxton, you can be really cruel. Why look at you; sporting a grey silk top hat, black silk double breasted suit, scarlet vest, a gold fob watch on a gold chain, a black silk cumber bund, creased grey trousers, spats and highly polished patent leather shoes, carrying a silver headed walking cane in one hand and over your arm a black cotton overcoat in the other. Here I am in a very ordinary dress looking like a wastrel in a washroom. I'm getting the vapors just thinking about it." She paused for effect,

"Oh Saxton, how could you?"

Virginia sat down on a plush velvet settee completely at her wits end. Saxton grinned, turned, walked out of Brady's shop and returned with a suitcase which he laid upon a counter top. He unsnapped two brass clips, leaving the lid closed. Her husband motioned for Virginia to approach it. She got up and walked over to him. He kissed her, saying gaily,

"My dearest Virginia, I brought it along a surprise for you my love. I think it will suit this occasion quite nicely."

He stepped aside as she opened the suitcase. There in all its shining glory was her wedding dress.

The happy couple was handled expertly by Mathew Brady who was delighted that Jack was no where near him. The little man with the goatee at the end of a pinched face was polite and as professional as ever. After selecting a number of metal frames and picture albums, John and Virginia left Brady's shop for the St. Nicholas Hotel just down the street. They would return the next day.

The St. Nicholas was considered to be the most luxurious hotel in New York City. The 'Home Journal' recently gushed,

"Comfort, convenience, magnitude and luxury seemed to have attained their climax.... in the vast and magnificent St. Nicholas. The hotel embraces every requisite of personal comfort and luxurious ease, which the most exigent of Sybarites could desire."

As their coach approached the six story marble monolith, the couple was indeed awestruck. A long white canvas awning fronted the hotel under which numerous fashionable shops were located. Rodney eventually found two black porters who stacked the Saxton's pile of luggage onto brass dollies. After tipping the porters; the newlyweds, two black bellhops and the dollies were crammed into a newly installed Otis steam freight elevator; the only one of its kind in New York City.

Later that morning, after settling into their opulent honeymoon suite on the top floor, the couple planned on shopping for a wedding ring. At their wedding, Virginia had worn

Muriel's ring on the promise that Saxton would buy Virginia a proper one on their honeymoon. Nothing suitable had been found in Boston. Besides, for Saxton, only Tiffany's would do. Gifts, silver ware, bedding and other baubles were waiting their undivided attention just down the street at 295 Broadway.

After a light breakfast, away they went, walking hand in hand down Broadway. Many people, black and white stopped and stared at the newlyweds. Some had the temerity to make rude remarks. The couple ignored them for they were totally enamored of each other, quite oblivious to the glares coming from those around them. Besides, Rodney was just behind them on their coach, his long horse whip at the ready to discourage any physical indiscretions that might be directed towards his two charges.

They arrived unscathed at Tiffany's with a regal flourish. Saxton, bowed to Virginia as a doorman dressed in a robin's egg blue uniform opened the large blue and gilt doors for them. The two potentates swept regally into the most exclusive shop in town. Hours later, they left for the most exclusive hotel in town, with Rodney in tow. Their coach's luggage rack was piled high with blue boxes covered by a canvas tarp. They'd spent well over twenty thousand dollars not only on themselves but on their families, friends and employees back in Boston. Virginia pulled off her left kid leather glove to admire her new wedding band. It was a stunning five carat black sapphire surrounded by ten white brilliant diamonds set into a wide platinum ring.

After their arrival back at the St. Nicholas, they were served lunch in their room. They ate it stark naked. After a few hours of strenuous physical activity, the newlyweds were once again fully refreshed. Elegantly dressed, they descended the hotel's grand marble staircase into the lavishly appointed lobby of the 'St. Nicks' as the locals called it.

Virginia decided to browse the quaint little shops lining the front of the hotel. Rodney, adequately armed, guarded her and her ring. Saxton went to Phalon's Hair Dressing Establishment, the city's most fashionable barber on the hotel's ground floor. It was to be a unique experience. Gleason's 'Pictorial Drawing-Room Companion' summed up the merits of a visit to Phalon's:

"The American who visits New York and does not go to Phalon's Hair Cutting saloon, is in infinite danger….of departing this life without having had the slightest idea of what it is too be shaved."

Saxton was not to be disappointed after which he did more shopping unbeknownst to anyone but himself and Allan Pinkerton, or so he thought.

The St. Nick's concierge, the fastidious Piree Lafite, had known Thomas Saxton well and was beside himself when he heard about the death of his old friend. He spent the rest of the couple's stay there, placating their every whim although he'd been told in no uncertain terms by the hotel's management to send the couple elsewhere. Apparently several complaints from various white guests about a Negress prowling the sacred halls of the hotel was unsettling. Lafite informed his superiors of his guest's Boston connections and the matter was quickly dropped. It seemed that 'new' money had been trumped by 'old' money. And so over the next few days, Saxton and Virginia were amused every time they entered the hotel lobby as Piree would rush up to Virginia and gush,

"Oh, Mon petite choux, how may I help you two love birds? Ah love, the elixir of life! Ce la vie mon amour!"

He would then take Virginia's hand and kiss it extravagantly. As his kisses started to migrate, Virginia would gently smack his bald head, saying,

"Non mon amour! Arête, already!" He would enthuse,

"Mon Cherie, perhaps sometime later on, Mon amour. Zut alors! Je suis très misérable."

They would all laugh at the joke. Piree would bow then pirouette off to the hotel lobby's monstrous front desk. Once ensconced, he would ring a brass bell while looking around for a bellhop to harass.

Their second day in New York City was spent touring the city in a white, horse drawn caliche. They explored the newly opened Central Park. It was a lovely winter's day and their new driver Sidney had been hired because he knew New York like the back of his very old black hand. Rodney as usual was never far away. They toured the Battery then later on, after a picnic lunch in an ornate gazebo, they stopped by Mathew Brady's to pick up their pictures. They were delighted. Saxton gave a humble Brady a gold stick pin shaped like a small barking dog. Timothy his assistant loved his Adolph Nicole pocket watch suitably inscribed. It was Saxton's way of saying thanks for their compassion and sympathy over the death of his father.

After dinner that evening at the hotel, Rodney drove them to the Wallach theatre a few blocks away at 485 Broadway. As they alighted from the coach, two men watched from the shadows of a doorway across the street. The larger man with cauliflower ears muttered,

"We'll get him soon my friend. There'll be no escape for Mr. Saxton. Both of us have followed him quite closely these past few days. Christ Tinker, they've shopped and toured all over New York City; Tiffany's, Phyte's, Central Park, the Battery, you name it." Tinker laughed,

"Yeah, when do they find time for pokin'?"

Garrett ignored the crudity and continued saying,

"Harrison searched their hotel suite, their luggage and their cabin on the Anaona but still no packet was to be found, only a brown suitcase containing a doctor's and a nurse's uniform. But that's not all Tinker. Under their mattress was a long oak board upon which was screwed brass letters that read RMS Folkstone. I wonder why an American ship would be renamed under a British moniker. Strange it is Tinker, strange indeed. I'm gettin' an uneasy feelin' about all this." Tinker finished his cheroot, throwing the dead stub into a gutter. He exclaimed,

"Well go on Garrett, I'm listening!"

"Harrison even tried cracking the ship's safe but the Captain nearly caught him at it. Incredibly he believed Harrison was the foreman of the coaling gang sent aboard to get sailing instructions from the office. Damnable luck! Perhaps it's hidden in the Landau. That would be the last place anyone would look. Besides it would be guarded night and day by that boxing nigger, Rodney. I've heard he even beat Hyer once. We'll have to do the deed and soon Tinker. Time's a wastin' my friend." His feral-looking companion agreed as he nervously lit another cheroot. Garrett eyed him, appraising his partner's antics with a practiced eye. Tinker sputtered,

"Yes, Garrett, it helps enormously to have someone on the inside workin' for the cause. I hope Larsen knows what the hell he's doin'. Christ almighty, he nearly got caught after that Boston Harbor incident on the Anaona. I hear the Finch twins are now workin' for him." He laughed,

"Imagine, gettin' two agents for the price of one! Christ, some people will do anything for money even us." His partner was not amused for he grabbed his accomplice's collar and snarled,

"Don't ever accuse me of working just for the money. I live for the cause like Harrison Listen good Tinker; he says that the Confederacy will be a nation soon and damn any Yankee who stands in its way. Do I make myself clear?" Suitably impressed, Tinker exclaimed,

"I wonder if Saxton's nigger wife knows what her husband is up to."

Garrett's attention was abruptly diverted. Tinker followed his gaze paling visibly as a dapper looking man in his late twenties ran through busy trolley traffic towards them. It was Henry Thomas Harrison, their Confederate contact.

Both men stayed put waiting for Harrison to walk by them. He did so without making any eye contact with them what so ever. Tinker and Garrett followed from a discreet distance as Harrison walked to a cab stand. A Hansom rolled up. Harrison climbed aboard. The duo waited then took another. Garrett instructed its driver to follow the cab just ahead of it.

Two cabs stopped at McSorley's Old Ale House cab stand on east 7th street. Tinker and Garrett alighted as Harrison entered the Tavern. Once inside the raucous confines of the saloon, Harrison commandeered a private booth in the rear. Tinker and Garrett showed up a few minutes later. Once the trio was comfortably ensconced, they ordered beer, closed the privacy drapes and proceeded to make new plans.

That evening, Saxton and Virginia sat in a box seat where they enjoyed a production of 'Rob Roy', starring the very debonair leading man, Lester Wallach himself. Upon leaving the theater, Virginia turned to Saxton ignoring the well dressed throngs pushing by around them.

"Dear Sax, I do feel a chill in the air. Can you get my wrap please? For some reason, I feel that we've been watched from the very moment we set foot in New York. I can't explain it dear. Perhaps you wouldn't understand."

Saxton retrieved a sable wrap from their nearby coach. As he did so, he looked down at Virginia sympathetically.

"Don't be silly my dear, I do understand indeed. Women are very prescient, meaning they have better developed and more prolific imaginations than men. I'm quite sure your unease is unwarranted."

He laughed outwardly but inside, a foreboding coldness entered his subconscious. It unsettled him. He thought, 'Perhaps she is right.'

Virginia put the wrap about her as Rodney took her arm. She shivered slightly as she stepped up into the coach. Later that evening they went dancing in the St. Nick's extravagant ballroom. The next day, they prepared to leave for the Anaona completely exhausted. Their Company coach was actually quite empty of boxes and sacks as it made its way back down Fifth Avenue. Everything else other than some jewelry and clothes would be shipped later to Boston on the next Saxton ship out of New York City.

Washington Square Park; a thin rectangle of heavily wooded land was located just up the street from the Saxton docks. It was late morning, and a heavy fog had not quite lifted. Two figures emerged from behind some bushes as the coach approached them. They ran towards the back of it. Saxton felt the coach sag as the intruders climbed aboard. Startled, Rodney looked back drawing a revolver as he did so. Seeing nothing but highly aware that some form of danger was present, he lashed the horses into a fast trot. Faster and faster they went as the Landau caromed over wet cobblestones. Sensing danger, Saxton reached for the door and swung it open.

Virginia saw him go through it then his legs disappeared above her. Immediately the coach began to career about wildly. Shouts and vile curses were heard. Virginia heard a body hit the cobblestones with a loud thud followed by another. The coach slowed down as it approached the high iron gates fronting the Saxton gatehouse. They swung open. Two uniformed guards tipped their black cloth hats. The team clopped into a cavernous warehouse. It stopped, the horses breathing heavily. Rodney jumped down. He opened a coach door and offered a gloved hand to Virginia. She took it, stepped out onto the footplate and looked up. Above her Saxton lay injured. He reached down, and grasped her hand in his.

John Saxton was carried aboard ship on a litter. Captain Wainwright sent Benson by coach to New York Hospital on Broadway with strict orders to bring back a Dr. Stewart immediately. Stewart was on retainer. The Doctor complied immediately, leaving a nervous patient under the care of a very nervous intern. The dapper Doctor and his nurse arrived one hour later. They ran up the gangplank and were met by Captain Wainwright who immediately led them into the Saxton's stateroom. A distraught Virginia sat beside her stricken husband. Dr. Stewart gave her a sedative while assuring her that he would do all he could. His nurse led her away to another cabin down the hall staying with her until she went to sleep.

Saxton awoke a few hours later. He sat up and gazed through a porthole beside him. A hazy New York City skyline was receding in the distance. The Anaona was sailing for Staten Island with Doctor Stewart and his nurse still aboard. Saxton lay back as the door to his stateroom opened. Doctor Stewart told him the good news. Nothing was really wrong with him other than a few superficial wounds, a black eye and a minor bruise on his stomach. Fortunately the assailant's knife was deflected by a large brass belt buckle. Thereafter, Saxton always insisted that it was his lucky charm.

That night Virginia slept fitfully but awakened early the next morning to return to her husband. Doctor Stewart and his nurse felt that Virginia had fully recovered from her hysteria. They watched her hold her husband's hand, saying gently,

"Oh Sax, I was so worried. I nearly died of fright when you went to fight those blackards on the roof of the coach."

Saxton opened a swollen eye slightly and groaned loudly. The Doctor looked knowingly at his nurse. Both backed out through the stateroom door as the Doctor said,

"Well if you don't mind Mrs. Saxton, my nurse and I will be in the Captain's cabin if you need anything. I'll check in on him later, say in one hour."

Saxton's recovery however was prolonged. When Virginia realized he was feigning, she tried to smother him with a pillow but he fought off her feeble attempts. They kissed then enjoyed each other making up. Later, Doctor Stewart noticed a 'DO NOT DISTURB' sign hanging on the stateroom's door knob. It obviously had been written by Mrs. Saxton. The Doctor and his nurse disembarked at the Staten Island Hospital wharf an hour later. From there they took a horse tram then a ferry back to Manhattan.

A few hours later, Captain Wainwright picked up a sealed telegram lying on his desk. On the front of it in large letters was printed, OPEN AT SEA. It was time. He carefully unsealed it. The message stated,

"To Captain Wainwright of the SS Anaona STOP
Sail to Annapolis Spa Creek immediately STOP
By order of Simon Cameron, Secretary of War."
Wainwright muttered, "Bloody hell!"

BOOK ONE: CHAPTER 14
LINCOLN UNLEASHED

President Abraham Lincoln's long boney fingers were clasped behind his large head, as he listened intently to Allan Pinkerton. Simon Cameron, Secretary of War, and his aide Edwin M. Stanton sat across from Lincoln. Pinkerton had just been congratulated for foiling an assassination attempt on Lincoln at his recent inauguration.

Pinkerton, a small man, paced back and forth in front of a brick semi-circular fireplace trying desperately to stay warm. His hoary breath hung in the air like a mistake. While stroking his full black beard thoughtfully, he continued.

"As I was saying Mr. President, our agent in Memphis confirmed by telegram yesterday that Marcus Brown was there. He apparently was asking about the passengers of the steamboat D.A. January, in particular a certain Captain Garrow under a Major Cooper's command."

Lincoln rose from his leather chair and walked over to a tall window that overlooked a grove of mature white oaks fronting the White House. He swung about like a ship at anchor, his face mottled from lack of sleep.

"Is this Garrow the same man who smuggled guns from Boston into New Orleans?" Pinkerton knew the signs. He waited.

Lincoln again turned about, looking through another narrow window at an unfinished Washington monument and the Potomac River just beyond it. His black silhouette stood there like a dagger portending doom. Feral pigs scattered about on the grounds below him, foraged amongst the oak trees. Lincoln continued staring at them then raised his hand. Pinkerton obliged.

"Yes, he was Mr. President at that time Captain of the Customs Office there using it as a cover for operation 'False Prophet'." Lincoln continued his vigil.

"Was anyone else involved?"

"Yes Mr. President, a criminal organization called the Deacon gang. However, Brown killed a few of them the night our agent there escaped with him and her young son."

"Is she still alive and if so where is she?"

"Mr. President, she is alive. A telegram to that effect came in from her late last night. It was strange though, because it came in under the auspices of a Bishop Grodine of New Orleans."

Lincoln silently nodded, his interest piqued. He continued his vigil.

"What happened to her Allan? She's been invaluable to us." Pinkerton was positive,

"She returned to her house with her son. A Sergeant Raines of the local Police has given permitted her to reopen her former business. I also understand that she is now Mrs. Brown."

President Lincoln turned about, his eyes fixated on the detective. He inquired somewhat obliquely,

"Will she be working for us again in the same capacity as before Allan?"

"Yes, Mr. President, her former employees will resume their work for the Union." Lincoln chuckled,

"My, my gentlemen, it seems our Union will once more be serviced by other unions. Imagine that!" He questioned Pinkerton further.

"Where is Marcus Brown? We could use a man like that!"

Pinkerton warmed his hands again with his back to Lincoln,

"We don't know Mr. President. Our Memphis agent tried to follow him but couldn't." Lincoln queried,

"Why not?"

"Apparently, he was beaten by a mob of draymen on the riverfront. He barely survived but he's alright." Lincoln replied,

"Send him a coded telegram immediately. Give him my thanks for a job well done and tell him to find Brown. We're in need of both their talents. Don't you agree Allan?"

"Yes, of course Mr. President. I'll have him find Brown and send both of them on to Boston for 'Operation Insertion'.

Lincoln broke away from the depressing scenes outside the window. He walked over and looked at Pinkerton who turned to face him. Lincoln's demeanor was lively and attentive.

"What do you mean, 'Operation Insertion', Allan?"

Pinkerton sat down on a black horsehair settee and leaned back, his small hands clasped in his lap. He was thinking about an idea fermenting in his mind ever since Saxton told him about it. He swallowed hard. This opportunity would never come again. Pinkerton looked up at Lincoln directly,

"Well Mr. President, from what I've been able to ascertain, Marcus Brown has proven many times before that he can handle himself as we well know. Secondly, his loyalty is impeccable. He's also a natural born leader, smart, quick to action and innovative to say the least. A family friend, John Saxton of Boston, came up with an idea that you might just be interested in, especially with war looming on the horizon. Saxton thinks that Brown could quite conceivably command a lightly equipped, highly mobile, guerilla company of black Americans. They would operate behind enemy lines armed with Spencer and Henry repeating rifles using hit and run tactics used in the revolutionary war by Butler's Rangers. Camouflaged sniping, sabotage of railway lines, bridges and the capture or killing of senior Rebel officers, military maps and other documents would be their mandate. John Saxton's willing to finance and organize the whole operation if need be. Secondly, they could use shallow draft freighters such as the SS Anaona to drop off and pick up mounted saboteurs along the coasts and rivers controlled by the South. The ship in question Mr. President, might have to be armored and refitted to take up to thirty horses, men, their equipment and supplies. We would need at least six to eight months to get ready. What do you think Mr. President?"

"Six to eight months you say? Well we'll probably be at war by then. You'll have to find Marcus Brown first and get him to Boston right away." He paused,

"Of course Allan we'll will have to tell him that his wife Belle has been one of our agents for three years, right?"

"I agree Mr. President. I'll send her a coded wire right away as to our plans about Marcus." Lincoln approached Stanton.

"What do you think of Saxton's idea Edwin?"

"Mr. President, he has my backing. It sounds as if it could be done. However, finding two or even three dozen qualified blacks would take time, I don't know if he could do it, but come to think of it, Virginia Saxton, his black wife I'm sure could find them and quickly. I also know where they could train for their operations."

"And where is that Edwin?"

"At West Point Academy, Mr. President, fifty miles up the Hudson River from New York City. Once there, the Army would provide all the training facilities they'll need. It's on the river and would be ideal for the Anaona. There, they would be easily supplied. Lincoln responded,

"Why not use the Marine Academy in Arlington, Virginia?

Pinkerton intervened,

"Mr. President, I'm sorry to say this Sir but I've heard that Southron sympathies are strong there, thus any operation there would be compromised. Secondly, West Point is closer to Boston by sea and by railroad. Perhaps the Marine Corps could send up an instructor for the sea operations and a 'Pointer' could instruct them on the land operations." The President became more animated.

"It's a good idea Pinkerton but getting the Army and the Marine Corps to work together may take a real diplomat! But, as luck would have it, I happen to know just such a man. He arrested abolitionist John Brown at Harpers Ferry last year. Would have killed him too if his sword hadn't bent. Ceremonial it was I think, too bad. Anyway, he's our man; Marine, Lieutenant Israel Green." Stanton raised his hand,

"Mr. President, I've heard of him too. He was with General Robert E. Lee who arrested Brown; therefore he'll know Lee very well. By the way Mr. President, I hear you offered General Lee a commission and he refused."

"Yes, Edwin that's true. General Lee is a loyal Southerner. It was very difficult for him but I understand. If war breaks out, we'll have our hands full if Jefferson Davis appoints him Chief of Staff."

Lincoln returned to the window. The pigs had moved on out of sight. He remained in place gazing at the Potomac River in the distance. He said without turning around.

"Simon, find Lieutenant Green and send him to West Point immediately. By the way Allan, you have the honor of giving a name to the guerilla operation if it ever comes to fruition."

Lincoln continued looking out the window, his back to them. After a few moments of contemplation he turned about, looking even more haggard and drawn yet earnest, saying,

"Well gentlemen, any ideas for a moniker?" Pinkerton replied.

"Mr. President, since Marcus, a native Maasai will be leading a group of black operatives into battle, I believe an appropriate name would be the 'Maasai Rangers'."

Lincoln agreed. He returned to his seat. Once settled, he threw back his head, finger tips together and cried,

"Splendid! The 'Maasai Rangers' they will be! But first find Marcus Brown. Now Mr. Secretary, I understand that you have something on your mind."

Lincoln's Secretary of War, Simon Cameron rose to his full height of nearly six feet. President Lincoln was glad that Stanton was there. Cameron was proving to be a liability. Lincoln would tolerate him for now until he knew more. He turned in his swivel chair and hoped that the frivolous Cameron would not be too verbose. He thought,

'Oh how I hate politicians full of them selves. Thank God my Mary always brings me down to earth.'

Cameron, clean shaven, with a crown of white hair adorning a head that looked remarkably like Lincoln's, started to pace about on the black oil-cloth flooring of the small room. As he did so, his new shoes squeaked in the gloom. He glanced up at an engraved portrait of Andrew Jackson hanging above a brick fireplace. Below it, Pinkerton was warming himself. He wasn't moving for anyone either not even the Secretary of War. He didn't like the man and it showed. Cameron steered clear of him. Pinkerton was in Lincoln's favor now, but there would be a time when he would not be. Cameron, a pompous man, declared,

"Mr. President, in my capacity as Secretary of War, it has come to my attention that Fort Sumter has not quite finished being built. Buchanan saw to that. However, construction has resumed albeit hastily. The Rebels however, have stopped the supply of clay and tabby from reaching the fort. I'm afraid Major Anderson will have to find another way to finish the left flanking wall. It's a desperate situation indeed as Brigadier General Beauregard sent another demand for Sumter's surrender just this morning. I think that's the fourth one in three months. From what Captain Fox has told me, Anderson's garrison will be out of food by April 15th. There are only eighty-five effectives from the E and H companies of the 1st US Artillery manning sixty cannon. The 'Star of the West' tried valiantly to bring relief to Sumter last January 9th but as it sailed past the battery on Morris Island it was holed twice and was forced to retreat. The fort's situation is becoming more desperate by the day Mr. President. Thank God the woman and children were evacuated February 3rd." Pinkerton spoke up.

"I've also just been informed that a certain Captain Garrow arrived in Charleston by special train from Memphis last night. His arrival means only one thing; apparently, he's a siege specialist trained at West Point, therefore Beauregard will probably attack Fort Sumter very soon. He has the support of South Carolina as it has seceded from the Union."

The President was getting very weary suing for peace. He had proposed abandoning the fort and promising not to collect revenues from southern ports if war could be avoided. Instead the Virginia Convention ridiculed his efforts. Lincoln was purported to reply, "It may be necessary to put the foot down firmly." The delegates were enraged.

On April 4th, Lincoln gave a naval Lieutenant Gustavus V. Fox, written permission to equip and organize an armed fleet to relieve Fort Sumter. Lincoln was convinced that it might work even though his Generals especially Scott thought the idea was ridiculous. Ideas born of desperation were not his forte. The President was looking forward to a hair cut right after his lunch. At least all he would feel was the soothing touch of William's scissors, brush and razor. He looked up at a Seth Thomas clock near him. His voice became querulous.

"Get on with it Cameron, we're running late as usual."

Cameron proceeded onward, ignoring Lincoln's pleas for brevity.

"As you know Mr. President, a Thomas Saxton of Boston, died recently."

"Yes, I know, I've sent my condolences."

"Anyway, his son John Saxton recently married to a,...a,"

"Miss Virginia Rowland, an undertakers daughter of exceptional beauty and poise for a nineteen year old, I must say." said Pinkerton gleefully as Cameron sputtered,

"Yes, Rowland's the girl's name! They are honeymooning aboard the SS Anaona, a steamship of three hundred tons with a top speed of over ten knots I understand." Pinkerton watched Cameron carefully and said,

"You're not thinking what I'm thinking are you?"

Cameron petulantly slammed a map table, crying,

"Yes, of course. Fort Sumter MUST be resupplied and reinforced with more guns especially the deadly accurate Ordnance rifle and the new rifled Blakely."

He paused and looked icily at Pinkerton, saying,

"I understand, a certain artillery instructor at West Point, a Captain John Gibbon was uncannily accurate with one such gun at the 'Battle of Boston Harbor'." The President nodded,

"Incredible, Cameron, I read all about it. Quite a feat indeed I'd say for I understand he laid down grapeshot at nearly four hundred yards. Outstanding! We could use him at Sumter. Is he available?" Pinkerton stepped forward, eager to be vindicated.

"No, Mr. President. He's currently stationed at Camp Floyd in Utah. However, one of his colleagues, a newly minted Captain Seymour Truman of the Ist Artillery is available. Although he was a minister and a drawing instructor at West Point, his military record in the Mexican War before in '48 and his fight against the Seminoles in '56 were exemplary. In fact he and his gun crew disguised as medical orderlies will rendezvous with the Anaona at Norfolk. Ten Ordnance rifles, ten Blakely rifles as well as fifty cases of Spencer and Henry repeating rifles and all appropriate ammunition are heading by rail to Annapolis as I speak. They will be loaded aboard the ship when it arrives there sometime in the next two days along with eighty tons of food and medical supplies. No offense intended Mr. President but I do believe that one small ship can get in whereas the relief fleet you've authorized will not." Cameron started to protest but Lincoln cut him off saying,

"Well done Allan. Well done indeed, don't you agree Stanton? I need men of initiative as long as it doesn't cost the Treasury an arm and a leg."

The President laughed when Pinkerton drolly replied that the whole scheme would cost nothing because John Saxton had paid for it all. Pinkerton had one-upped Cameron. It was a coup. As Stanton enjoyed Cameron's discomfort, Lincoln got up and approached the fireplace. Pinkerton moved away. Lincoln looked down into the flames. He mused, his back to the three men.

"Has anyone heard if the Peace Commission down at the Willard Hotel has been successful yet?"

"No progress of note Mr. President," replied Stanton.

Stanton, who up until then had remained in the shadows sitting on one of the horsehair sofas, got up, stretched his arms and approached Lincoln who continued to stare into the fire. Stanton was a man of few words. His high forehead, steel rimmed glasses and a longish black beard streaked with white, made the rotund little man somewhat bookish and professorial. However, this impression evaporated as soon as he opened his mouth. The man was all business and to the point. He was totally opposite to Cameron. He spoke without vacillation, his voice clipped, precise.

"Mr. President, time is of the essence here. Operation 'Mail Packet' will be the perfect cover. More than one ship will raise suspicions. The SS Anaona will ostensibly be carrying only medical supplies and food to Fort Sumter. It will fly the Union Jack, and be renamed as the mail packet RMS Folkstone out of Bermuda. From what I understand, the Rebs are about to cut off all mail to the fort very soon. We must hurry and get the supplies there and soon."

Pinkerton cut in, as Stanton paused

"Mr. President, we've already spread disinformation to that effect in Annapolis. As for its intended cargo, every crate is marked FIELD DRESSINGS, and or MEDICAL SUPPLIES. It should work very well." Lincoln countered,

"What about the newlyweds? Are we going to hijack their ship and send them back to Boston?"

Stanton explained,

"I think not Mr. President. They will appear on the ship as it docks at Annapolis as a Doctor Morris and his wife. She will be his nurse." Lincoln became skeptical.

"Have they agreed to go along with us Stanton? I must say it could be very risky coming into Charleston under the very noses of Beauregard's artillery, to say the least."

"Saxton has but I'm not sure about his wife."

"You realize that they're supposed to be on their honeymoon. My God Stanton, how on earth did you ever do it?"

Stanton smiled, not saying a word. Lincoln was back in his chair, leaning forward, studying Stanton like a newly discovered insect. His estimation of the man had increased immeasurably indeed. Pinkerton cut in on Stanton's behalf.

"I know Saxton received your envelope containing the salient details about 'Operation Mail Packet' the day after Thomas died. While in New York, Saxton was attacked by two armed men whom I believe were after the aforementioned details. Lincoln interjected, his voice tinged with concern,

"Did they get it Allan?"

"No Mr. President, Saxton fought them off but he was slightly wounded in the attack. Fortunately, the envelope was in the ship's safe."

"Good, I'm glad to hear he's alright." The President came closer to Pinkerton, his black bushy eye-brows fully arched.

"Well, has he read your letter Allan?"

"I do believe so Mr. President for he sent me a coded telegram from Boston before he left." The President leaned closer.

"What did he say Allan, for God's sake, you're trying my patience!"

"He said that the family tradition would continue."

"Good! He's a true patriot like his father before him. I hope he can convince his new bride to be one too! We'll better be there in Annapolis to meet him when he arrives. Besides I have to convince that slave-owning Governor Hicks to stay in the Union."

Lincoln looked up at a small photo of the great English orator and reformist, John Bright for inspiration. He simply said, "Make it happen Simon."

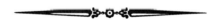

Captain Ian Wainwright set the telegram alight then ground its ashes into a glass ashtray lying on his desk. He muttered, "Well, that was interesting."

He pulled a cord nearby and waited. As he did so, he remembered how Thomas Saxton used his services many times in the service of his country. He remembered the time that..... He was interrupted by a light knock on his cabin door. Wainwright put on his braided black sea cap and said curtly, "Come in."

His first Mate, Axel Benson walked in, a sea cap under his left arm. He looked worried, "Captain Sir, you wanted to see me?"

"Yes, Axel, there's been a change of plans. Set a new course for Spa Creek, Annapolis then give me an estimate of how long you think it will take us to get there. That is all."

Benson was really worried. Something in the Captain's voice was dire, evoking mystery. He didn't like mysteries. Axel hurried back to the bridge.

Saxton and Virginia were disturbed by the Bosun rapping lightly on their stateroom door despite a 'Do Not Disturb' sign hanging from its brass door knob. After discreetly slipping a note under the door, he heard someone from within say,

"Virginia, there's someone at the door." Saxton spied the note, picked it up and read it. With note in hand he exclaimed,

"We're wanted by the Captain darling. Can't I ever have some peace?"

She laughed, rising naked from the bed. Picking up her peignoir she went to the clothes closet and opened a lower drawer. She said coyly,

"But my dear, you've already had your piece so to speak."

He ran over to her. She squealed as she evaded his clutches. Finally, she was caught. He held her tight, teasing her.

"Virginia my dear, let's get dressed and see what the stuffy old Captain wants, shall we?"

Captain Wainwright waited for the newlyweds to be seated. He remained standing, puffing on a meerschaum pipe while looking out a brass scuttle. He tried to stay calm but inside a storm was approaching his vocal cords. He turned to face them saying,

"I'm sorry to inform you that the Secretary of War ordered me to sail to Spa Creek at Annapolis, Maryland as soon as possible. I do not know why. I wish I could tell you why."

He stood there looking down expectedly at Saxton.

"I know why Captain, but I'll let the President himself explain it to you when we reach Annapolis. One more thing Captain, your ship will be renamed the RMS Folkstone when we're further out to sea away from prying eyes. I'm sorry Captain but that's all I can say for now."

Captain Wainwright was aghast. He thought. 'Good grief what have we here, another man full of surprises? One was enough, but two? I need a drink.'

Virginia was taken aback too but recovered. She laughed.

"Well gentlemen, at least we'll meet the great man himself. I can hardly wait!"

Saxton spent the better part of that afternoon in their stateroom explaining Stanton's 'Operation Mail Packet' in detail to Virginia. He told her that he received the details via one of Pinkerton's agents at the St. Nickolas Hotel. At first she was upset at Saxton for not telling her. However, this passed as he explained what services his father had provided for his country before he died. Saxton would carry on with or without her. After thinking it over, Virginia wrapped her arms around him and quoted Ruth Chapter 1, Verse 16. "For wither thou goest, I will go; and wither thou lodgest, I will lodge."

Saxton kissed her forehead and motioned her to sit on their double bunk. He went to the closet and took out a brown cardboard suitcase she'd never seen before. He laid it on the bed beside her. In it were uniforms for a doctor and his nurse. He lifted up a dark blue nurse's linen cape and put it over her shoulders. She stood up and pirouetted about the stateroom. He laughed, "Well dear, does it suit you?"

"Yes Doctor, it will do very well indeed."

"Now try the on the rest of it. I'll be a while instructing the Captain about changing the name of his ship."

He reached under their bunk mattress and took out a long plank of polished oak with the brass letters RMS FOLKSTONE screwed into it. Virginia said,

"And I suppose that was waiting in New York for you as well my dear?" He nodded

"Yes my dearest, courtesy of our new friend, James Phyfe himself."

Two days later, RMS Folkstone entered Spa Creek near the Annapolis Naval base and tied up. The ship kept its steam up, for there on the dock were stacks of crates upon which was stenciled MEDICAL SUPPLIES and FIELD DRESSINGS waiting to be loaded aboard. Alongside this mountain of crates was another mountain of anthracite coal in one hundred pound burlap bags. Doctor Morris stood on the flying bridge and wondered if it was going to be enough. The ship's two steam cranes began to clank and hiss after their restraints were released. They looked like a metal Mantis had died on deck, its two articulated legs rising crookedly into the air. Captain Wainwright and his crew watched as black stevedores began slinging the crates and coal sacks into the cargo holds and coal bins.

Before arriving at Spa Creek, it dawned on Saxton why he'd been attacked in New York City. He concluded that the thugs were looking for the envelope containing information about 'Operation Mail Packet'. Upon reflection, he also surmised that his suite at St. Nick's had been searched as well. Nothing of any value was missing. It therefore had to be the sachet for only Confederate agents would have been interested in that. Did they also suspect that his father had been an agent let alone his son?

The newlyweds barely had time to disembark before a large carriage pulled up to the RMS Folkstone. Its sole passenger alighted to greet them. It was Allan Pinkerton himself. Doctor Morris and his nurse were glad to see him. They shook hands. Everyone including a perplexed Captain Wainwright climbed aboard the Barouche. Once settled in, they sped away followed by two armed Pinkerton guards on horseback.

While the coach's team of four clip-clopped over the wide firebrick streets of the State Capital, Pinkerton informed Saxton that his mother was well. Everyone else who was still under the protection of his agency was safe and sound. Saxton was grateful. He didn't learn until much later how grateful he should have been. They arrived on the State Circle concourse that surrounded the red brick State House. Four white, smooth round columns supported a long and narrow portico. A colossal white dome, the largest ever built without nails rose high above them. The party walked up a wide red brick pathway bordered on either side by tulip trees in bloom. Saxton and Virginia raced ahead hand in hand to an expansive granite staircase.

Virginia gushed,

"Oh Sax, this day will be a perfect day, won't it darling?"

Saxton wanted to agree with her but he could not because he knew what they were being called upon to do for their country. He muttered,

"Yes, dear it is perfect for now."

He pulled her up wide brick steps then through the tall white double doors of the State House into an immense Georgian foyer. The floor sparkled as black and white marble tiles criss-crossed diagonally in front of them. Above them a chandelier was suspended. A uniformed aide beckoned them to a sweeping marble staircase rising to a second floor. Hand in hand the newlyweds ran gaily up it, followed by the rest of their retinue. There, in the House of Delegates, the Treaty of Paris ending the Revolutionary war had been signed. Next door, immense Boston & Sandwich crystal chandeliers sparkled within the senate chamber. Dozens of red leather chairs sat behind polished oak desks in orderly rows. A central red damask carpet led one's eyes to four darkly veined white marble columns supporting a triple bay gallery. In fact, most of the room was fronted by scalloped marble. Underneath the gallery squatted a long double tiered rosewood Speaker's Desk. Virginia was thrilled and impressed. However her reverie was cut short by Saxton's preoccupations. He was trying to figure out what more surprises Lincoln had hidden in his stove pipe hat. He already knew it involved his ship in that they were sailing south to Fort Sumter. However, he was very afraid for Virginia despite her willingness to persevere in the face of certain death.

Lincoln arrived the day before to convince Governor Thomas Hicks that a strong hand was needed to keep Maryland in the Union. He barely succeeded. Lincoln, Stanton, and Secretary of War Simon Cameron were waiting in the Governor's lavishly appointed office also decorated in heavily veined marble. Governor Hicks, his long mutton chops quivering, rose as the Saxton party was led in. Tall double doors clicked shut behind them. Sunlight poured through numerous tall windows revealing the city's skyline beyond them. Introductions were in order after which Virginia and Saxton sat together on an overstuffed settee. The others made themselves comfortable. Governor Hicks announced that he was leaving them alone. If they needed anything, they were to pull a white braided cord by his desk. Armed Naval guards stood outside the doors as others patrolled the grounds around the building. Pinkerton agents roamed the polished marble halls. Allan Pinkerton was not going to risk another attempt on Lincoln especially here, where Southern sympathy was high. Pinkerton motioned for the Governor to leave. It had all been prearranged. Hicks bowed slightly to Virginia. The President rose to meet him. Lincoln shook Governor Hick's hand saying with emphasis,

"Governor, the Union owes you and the citizens of this great State, an eternal debt of gratitude that will never be forgotten." Hicks grinned.

"I'll hold you to that Mr. President."

Hicks turned and walked away. The tall oak doors opened wide then clicked shut behind him.

The President strode forward, stove pipe hat in hand. As he approached Virginia and Saxton he paused. Virginia blushed, rose from her seat, curtsied and held out a gloved hand. Everyone else rose as well to greet Lincoln. Virginia blushed again as the President took her hand, his grip firm yet surprisingly gentle.

"Mr. President. It is indeed an honor to meet you. You're even more magnificent than any photos Brady might have taken of you."

She demurred seductively, her black eyes teasing him. Lincoln looked down upon her, kissed her hand then threw his head back laughing. Saxton was paralyzed as well as everyone there. However, all of them started laughing and slapping their knees. Virginia sat down. Lincoln took out a small white hanky and dabbed his eyes. He stood back with both long arms akimbo, looking down at her.

"Well gentlemen, I must say, Isn't she a brave and honest corker. Our nation needs more of her. Thank you Madam."

With the ice broken, the meeting started in earnest. The couple was reminded about the dire situation at Fort Sumter. Virginia actually scolded the hapless Cameron for suggesting a woman's place was in the home and a colored woman's place was being subservient. She asked Cameron if he was ready to go and die for his country. She did not receive an answer. Virginia had had enough of spineless plotting politicians. The meeting continued however in a more sober tone after her outburst. Saxton thought,

'What a woman!' Unbeknownst to him, so did Lincoln.

They learned that the British consulate in Charleston agreed to go along with the scheme on humanitarian grounds only. Lincoln explained,

"The SS Anaona has been renamed the RMS Folkstone of the Royal Mail Service, after a registered British ship long since sunk but, let's say, raised from Davy Jones locker for this one occasion. Fortunately for us, it looks very similar to one of those fast British mail packets out of Hamilton, Bermuda. It will fuel up again in Norfolk's Gosport Naval yard which is a refueling stop for the RMS service anyway. There it will pick up Captain Gibbon and his gun crew disguised as medical orderlies. Luckily, two Coehorn mortars are already aboard the ship to persuade pirates and other brigands from soiling Her Majesty's Royal Mail pouches." They all laughed. Lincoln countered.

"Questions anyone?"

There were none. Stanton rose and gave a curious Captain Wainwright a sealed envelope containing his sailing orders. The Captain held them in his lap. Stanton patted the Captain's shoulder boards, exclaiming,

"Well Captain, you might as well read about 'Operation Mail Packet' right here and now in case you want to go back to a Boston tea party instead. We all hope you will not."

Wainwright broke a wax seal, extracted a letter and started reading. His whiskered face blanched. He sputtered,

"I dare say Mr. President; you want me to sail right up to the Charleston Customs quay as bold as brass and ask permission to send this cargo, ship and crew to Fort Sumter?" Lincoln chuckled.

"That's exactly what I want you to do Captain."

"But Mr. President, the cargo manifest says Medical Supplies and food, NOT guns and ammo." Lincoln persisted.

"From what I've been told Captain, Ordnance and Blakely rifles and their ammo are hidden under false bottoms. The crates of medical supplies and food will cover them up. Besides, they are not going to unload a cargo that took all day to stow aboard, are they?"

The President became quite jovial. He turned to Pinkerton urging him to speak because Lincoln sensed that Captain Wainwright was having serious doubts. He knew Wainwright was a civilian Captain and under no compunction to serve his nation and as such could leave the ship high and dry but Lincoln knew he wouldn't. Lincoln signaled Pinkerton once more, this time without pretense, saying,

"Now, Captain you needn't worry. Pinkerton will explain it all in more detail."

Pinkerton's address was forthright.

"Captain, you needn't worry because I will meet you at the customs quay disguised as a Major E. J. Allen. Once there, I will as some would say, 'facilitate' a speedy processing of the paperwork."

Saxton was impressed, thinking,

'Either Pinkerton is a brave idiot or a genius of note, maybe both. God help us!'

Captain Wainwright was eventually satisfied but concluded warily,

"I think you're all bloody bonkers, but I'll do it. If someone has to look after the lot of you, it might as well be me. By the way, I might have come across someone diddling my cabin safe while coaling in New York. Said he was a coaling foreman waiting in my cabin for sailing instructions. I believed him at the time but now, since I know more, the man did appear to be shifty and somewhat devious." Pinkerton asked Wainwright for a description. The Captain complied, concluding drolly,

"And here I thought I was on a peaceful honeymoon cruise to Bermuda."

Even Lincoln laughed. They patted Captain Wainwright on the back and joined in shaking his hand along with all the others. The deed was done. All that remained was the doing. Pinkerton however was very worried. He thought,

'It's Harrison. It's got to be. If it is God help us. Perhaps a certain Major Allen can foil him.'

Before the meeting broke up, the President put his stove-pipe hat on a nearby side table and pulled a white service cord. Immediately, refreshments were served as well as something else quite special. Governor Hicks returned. Lincoln waited for everyone to rise with glasses in hand. He then proposed a toast to the happy couple and their crew, saying sincerely,

"The Bard in Twelfth Night once said I believe, and I quote,

'That some are born great, some achieve greatness,

While others have greatness thrust upon them.'

Therefore, the Bard and I salute you all for serving your country in a most difficult time while having greatness thrust upon you, willing or otherwise. A grateful nation thanks you."

Of course, everyone except the Governor knew exactly what Lincoln was talking about. As Saxton's party were about to leave, Lincoln motioned Saxton and Virginia over to a secluded alcove whereupon he looked down at Saxton fondly,

"Son, your father, Thomas Saxton, served two Presidents in the service of his country. I'm proud that you John Saxton, as young as you are, are very much like your father, willing to serve your nation. I like your ideas, and your willingness to take command. I take your hand now in a solemn vow, that whatever happens at Fort Sumter, before, during or after; America will salute you and treasure your service to it. And may I say that I am whole heart-edly behind your plan to form and back the 'Operation Insertion', now under the moniker 'Maasai Rangers'. This nation will support you in any way it can. Sadly, I fear war is coming and we must be vigilant and prepared. Expect my fullest cooperation and support young man. All we need now is for Marcus, wherever he is, to come home to Boston."

He stepped back as Virginia was taken aback thinking,

'Maasai Rangers, hummmm, never heard of them. Perhaps, my mysterious Saxton will tell me.'

She recovered her composure then looked up at the President who duly noted her for-mer confusion. Virginia confirmed the President's initial estimation of her by saying,

"I'm sure my husband and all the others will do their duty as best they can. Thank you Mr. President."

With that said, Lincoln bowed after them as they left the room with the others. He turned and faced those who remained. The President's façade was aged by premature sorrow. It was as if the whole weight of a nation was upon him let alone the office of Commander in Chief. He rose to his full height, his voice grasping the moment succinctly.

"I wish all of you good luck gentlemen. Hopefully common sense will prevail at the Willard soon, but gentlemen, while I am President of these here United States they will stay united, no matter the cost, no matter the sacrifice we have to bear, so help me God!"

Lincoln retrieved his hat. His retinue departed, boarding a special express train for Washington, and destiny.

The RMS Folkstone left on a flood tide a few hours later. She lay quite low in the water. As the famous white spire of St. Philips church receded behind it, the stubby ship made slow headway. A day later, she was far out to sea plowing through waves birthed off the coast of Africa thousands of miles to the east.

An unhappy couple stayed in bed only because they were horribly seasick, especially Virginia. Their ship gradually turned landward pushed by a following sea as it approached the eastern seaboard of America. Once there, it hugged that shallow coastline to avoid the northward-flowing current of the Gulf Stream. Disguised as an Imperial mail packet, it flew a British flag of convenience. After a crew meeting as to 'Operation Mail Packet', all of them practiced their English accents or a variation thereof much to the amusement of everyone especially Captain Wainwright. He would say,

"Now you blokes, get a bloody move on if you're goin' to the loo. Now matey, look lively there. It's not a bleedin' tea party we're havin' here. You're all quite daft ya know!"

The RMS Folkstone refueled in Norfolk, Virginia, at sunset a few days later on schedule. It was raining hard but her coaling chutes were covered. The rain didn't bother Henry Thomas Harrison at all. He glassed the ship from a grove of trees as Naval Commander Roland Sykes came aboard. Sykes shook hands with Captains Wainwright, Seymour and Saxton. They entered Wainwright's cabin to dry off as Benson stood by the helm. Leather lounge chairs under warming lanterns provided a welcome refuge from the elements. While drinking hot toddies, Commander Sykes handed Wainwright an envelope stamped with the presidential seal and signed by Abraham Lincoln. Wainwright opened it up, hopeful that the mission had been cancelled. Instead, the telegram within it simply said, 'GOOD LUCK'.

Sykes took the note offered by Wainwright and said drolly,

"Once again as always Captain, our political masters are making the decisions; but we still have to carry them out, good or bad. So I say to all of you, a toast to Fort Sumter gentlemen. Down with the Confederacy and its hideous legacy! God bless America!"

Shortly before, RMS Folkstone left Norfolk, Captain Seymour and his gun crew disguised as medical orderlies scrambled aboard. From then on it seemed that the Anaona was constantly fighting storm winds, riptides and lofty larboard seas all the way. It was as if nature itself was trying to turn them around but they did not deviate from their chosen course. They were sailing to Fort Sumter into the valley of the shadow of death. Every man-jack of them knew it too, including Virginia.

The storms passed. Troubled waters became calmer; a morning sun arose, spreading its radiance upon the bosom of an obsidian sea. After settling in, Seymour's gun crew began firing one of the Ordnance rifles at canvas targets set adrift on the ocean. Saxton and Benson were drilled on the operation of the Anaona's two Coehorn mortars christened 'Lincoln' and 'Packard'. Virginia took a fancy to firing them off, shrieking every time she did so. After a few days, the trio became quite proficient at laying down grapeshot on targets bobbing merrily away nearly three hundred yards astern. The heavy mortars were attached to a round plank platform that rotated on ball bearings. This allowed the guns to shoot from any angle. As to rifle practice, it was said of the sixteen shot Henry rifle that, 'One could load it on Sunday and fire all week'. Before long they were all quite proficient, firing nearly two dozen rim-fired rounds a minute.

After two days at sea, Saxton decided to read the letter his father had written him before his death to Virginia. Virginia sat beside him in their stateroom as her husband opened it up once again. He had decided that Virginia should know what a patriot his father had been and more to the point what his father expected of him. Saxton gave her the letter, sat down and watched the play of emotions that crossed her face as she read it. Yes indeed, she was amazed at how Thomas Saxton led a secret double life serving two Presidents. She also wondered,

"Did Muriel know about 'False Prophet'? Perhaps there are more surprises up my husband's sleeves."

She handed the letter back to Saxton realizing for the first time just how committed her husband was to destroying slavery. She also knew that the letter was the last living link to his father. Virginia took him in her arms. He held onto her weeping, the letter in his hand. She said softly, her head on his broad shoulders,

"It's alright darling. I understand how hard it is to let go of someone you love. Believe me Saxton, I know." He held her away from him. He said, "Yes, I believe you do."

Virginia watched Saxton burn his father's letter. They left their stateroom for the aft deck. It was still dark. Once there, Saxton dumped the charred remains over the stern, its scraps devoured by the ship's roiling wake. When it was all over, they held each other tight as the Milky Way sparkled high above them. Virginia was thankful that they would be given a meaningful chance to serve their nation. Thomas would have been very proud of them. They rejoiced in the strength of their love and commitment to each other. It was an affirmation of life not death. Virginia looked up, kissed her husband, saying, "I love you Sax. I'll always love you."

BOOK ONE: CHAPTER 15
ESCAPES

Harley Blackstone's slab pile was shrinking too fast. Major Anderson was very pleased, for the work on the left flank of the fort was nearing completion despite many setbacks. Harley Blackstone was not happy for a lack of slabs meant an early hanging. Working too slow would have the same effect thus he planned to escape before either event took place. Harley cajoled the Major into giving the slavers better working conditions, food, water and medical care. Anderson reluctantly agreed, however what he didn't know, was that Blackstone was planning to escape with Fort Sumter's newest gun map.

It was early April, 1861. The weather was warming up. The temperature inside the fort's courtyard was by high noon insufferable, notwithstanding the added heat emanating from a trio of kilns baking hundreds of adobe slabs within them. As a result, many of Harley's crewmates were ending up in the infirmary from heat stroke. There, the fort's medical superintendent, Surgeon-General Wylie Crawford was at his wits end. Medical supplies were dangerously low and in his view of priorities, slavers should be dead last or just dead. But Major Anderson insisted that the slab-makers be given top priority. Crawford reluctantly obeyed.

Blackstone suspected that the Major would hang the slavers unless they became 'galvanized'. Harley and his mates hated the Yankees and to a man would never switch sides. Scuttlebutt within the rank and file told of the Rebs taking over all the Federal forts around Sumter. After a few weeks, Palmetto flags flew over Fort Moultrie, Fort Johnson on James Island, a floating battery due west of Fort Moultrie, Cummings Point on Morris and the Castle Pinckney battery on a small Island called Shute's Folly located at the confluence of the Ashley and Cooper rivers. The arsenal in the City of Charleston was taken over by a detachment of the local 17th Regiment. Fort Sumter was surrounded. Harley Blackstone was surrounded. In both instances they were desperate for help. Miraculously, help steamed down Ship Channel late on the afternoon of April 11th. Alas, for Harley, it was a British mail packet, the RMS Folkstone.

A robust twenty-four pound battery on Morris Island commanded by a Major Stevens declined to fire on a vessel flying the flag of her Majesty, Queen Victoria. He glassed the ship's colorful pennants flying from her yardarm. They indicated she was on a mercy mission from Bermuda. A telegram from the British Consulate in Charleston to General P. Beauregard the day before said that she was bringing medical supplies and food to the sick and starving in Fort Sumter. Semaphore signals from the fort on Morris Island told the RMS Folkstone to report to the Customs quay in Charleston. Immediately, a crew member standing on the Folkstone's aft deck wigwagged yellow and red semaphore flags in a positive response. Nurse Morris appeared on deck dressed in her Florence Nightingale uniform; a blue cape, white cap, white gloves, black shoes and socks set off by an ankle length black dress. Saxton on cue strolled out to stand beside her, looking quite the Doctor, attired all in white. The Rebs looking on were duped.

The Folkstone met no resistance as it sailed under the heavy guns of the Confederate forts looking down upon it. As it approached Fort Sumter on its port side, Virginia held Saxton tight. She shivered in the rain as if two cold hands of impending doom were bearing down upon her shoulders. Fort Sumter, the insolent brick monolith swathed in low clouds slid by secure and seemingly impregnable. Shortly thereafter, 'The Holy City' appeared, looming through a veil of pouring rain.

RMS Folkstone after battling a storm at sea berthed at the end of Laurens Street below the cannon battery overlooking the Ashley River. Immediately, a delegation of Customs officials, assorted military personnel and including Governor Francis Pickens marched up the Folkstone's broad gangplank. Pickens was determined that another Union sleight of hand was not going to happen. Apparently Major Anderson the commander of Fort Sumter had literally smuggled men, food and arms from Fort Moultrie into Sumter a few months before. The Governor was also worried about a Federal relief force fighting a storm off the mouth of the shipping channel. An immaculate Captain Wainwright calmly presented his forged credentials while First Mate Axel Benson gave his forged cargo manifest to a Mr. Humphries, the Customs Agent. A Major E.J. Allen was in charge of securing the ship while it was in port. Technically, everybody aboard it and everything in it was under arrest. The hatches were opened. The black canvas tarp over 'Packard and Lincoln' was removed. All crew members were interrogated thoroughly, British accents and all. The crates stacked below deck were pried open. Nothing seemed amiss so after paying an exorbitant groundage fee in gold coinage, the ship's cocket was signed off.

As the assemblage milled around on the Folkstone's aft deck, Major Allen took off his field hat and bowed to the good doctor's beautiful wife, Nurse Morris. As she held onto an umbrella, he kissed her proffered hand. In a deeply accented southern falsetto, he said in a rush of emotion,

"And I thought our Southern belles had beauty dear lady, but I and the others here are stunned by yours. I must declare Madam that I'm in a state of complete surrender!"

Every Southron there about was shocked at the Major's inappropriate performance. And, as they were so distracted, Virginia felt him slip a rolled note into her hand. She closed her white cotton glove around it smiling coyly, whilst scared to death. Her fellow shipmates were sweating as well but not Saxton, Wainwright or Seymour. They were cut from the same cloth; cool, calm and collected.

'Thank God!' Virginia thought as the entourage walked down the gangplank and departed. Minutes later, the Folkstone slipped her lines, turned about and sailed at top speed for Fort Sumter. A tumultuous harbor chop slapped the vessel as it wallowed about once again in the confluence of the Ashley and Cooper Rivers. The stormy weather had dissipated but briefly. As it did so, a very distraught Henry Thomas Harrison and a squad of soldiers ran down to the custom's dock. They were too late. After rushing back to General Beauregard's headquarters, he discovered that someone had cut all its telegraph wires. From a third floor balcony of the General's quarters, Harrison watched helplessly as the mail packet turned to port, then steamed straight for Fort Sumter. Below the Confederate's heavy guns at Fort Johnson it raced, disappearing into a rain squall before anyone could fire a shot.

Virginia gave the note to Captain Wainwright as soon as the ship left the Customs quay. It read, "LOOK IN SAFE". The Captain promptly did so, wondering how someone had 'cracked' his new Chubb safe. What he didn't know was that Pinkerton had been taught safe-cracking by Hobbs of New York City. Captain Wainwright swung open the safe's thick steel door. Inside was a brown manila envelope. He cursed,

"This takes the biscuit! Not another one."

The Captain took it out and looked at a thin red wax seal pressed upon it. He was relieved, for written on the envelope itself were the words,

"FOR MAJOR ROBERT ANDERSON'S EYES ONLY"

What he didn't know was, inside it were updated maps of all the recently installed Confederate gun positions surrounding Fort Sumter; in fact all forty-three of them.

Major Robert Anderson was half asleep at his table taking a siesta. A bluebottle fly buzzed by his head. He swatted at it. He'd had a tough day and every time he looked out his office windows, he was rudely reminded by former President James Buchanan's stupidity. Fort Sumter derided as 'The Bastille of the Federal Union'. Facing seven thousand Confederate soldiers, it was woefully undermanned and outgunned two to one. A native of South Carolina, the Major had been vilified by every newspaper and orator in the south. Considered a monstrous traitor, Major Anderson, still unshaven, rubbed the sleep out of his eyes and walked over to a dirty window once again. Somewhat depressed after sending his 'Glorious' wife back to New York City, he peered out through the cheerless rain. Nothing had changed. He grabbed a cigar from a tin humidor then sliced the end off with a Barlow knife. After first breaking a match on the seat of his pants, he finally lit the stogy. Frustrated, he cursed.

"Goddamn that Buchanan! The son of a bitch was a coward and a weak-kneed arm-chair President to boot. His back- stabbing compromises and now this debacle here at Sumter have proved it. Old Abe must be having a fit of pique trying to get his Secretary of War, Cameron off his skinny ass. Thank God, Stanton is Cameron's advisor. Now there's a man's man!"

The Major continued his reverie as squadrons of flies droned overhead. They hovered over a half-eaten sandwich lying dead on a cracked wooden tray beside him. Papers, maps and other detritus littered his small office. He was not a neat man like his second-in-command, Captain Doubleday. A loud rap on his door aroused his rage even further. To his surprise, a disheveled Peter Hart, his personal manservant, messenger and provisioner ran in, stopped and cried,

"Sorry Major but a ship's approaching the dock and it ain't a tabby boat either. It's flyin' a Union Jack!"

Corporal Riley just happened to be in the hallway. Major Anderson flew out the door forgetting his Hardee hat. The Corporal tore after him. Upon passing the slab yard, the sweaty men working there stopped and gawked at the two officers running for the Sally-Port. Something important was happening. Harley sensed it. He growled,

"Stay put girls! I'll be right back."

He ran off through the rain and joined a throng of soldiers looking through the Sally-port at the granite jetty lying low over a long wide sandbar. One cried,

"Holy Moses, it's a ship; a Limey one at that."

Blackstone's heart stopped beating. He swore under his breath,

"Christ almighty! The Brits have come back to hang the lot of us!"

Harley spun around bumping into a large cannon. He cursed and limped back through the fort, positive he was going to be hanged along with his crew. At the slab works, a swarthy man with big yellow teeth ran up to him.

"Tell us Blackie, what the hell is goin' on?"

He stood back as Harley summoned the rest of them forward. A small group of ragged men surrounded him. Harley swatted at a fly that had the misfortune to land on his neck. He wiped the blood off onto a man's frayed shirt then stood back pointing his whip at the wharf saying,

"Well lads, looks like the jig is up. It's a British Mail Packet and I think they're here to hang us!" One of the men cried,

"But we haven't finished Blackie!"

"SMACK! The man fell back under Harley's backhand.

"Shud up stupid and listen well. Everyone go back to makin' slabs but be ready to act as a group when I give the signal. If I take off my hat, rush the guards, kill em', grab their guns and follow me on the double. We'll storm that limey boat down there and get over to Charleston real quick like. I hear the girls there take slavers out to dinner then love em' later!" Harley laughed. They did not.

Major Anderson ran down the pier as fast as he could with Corporal Riley right behind him. He knew that every spy-glass the Confederates had was upon him. He slowed down, brushing bread crumbs off his blue uniform as he walked towards the mail packet. He fumed.

"Damn it all Riley, I've forgotten my hat again and the Limey's are sticklers for decorum, manners, spit and polish."

He looked down at his soaked salt-caked black leather boots while buttoning up his shirt and his fly. 'Ok,' he thought, 'I'm as ready as I'll ever be.'

A British flag flapped from the mast-head of a mail packet tied up at a long cross pier. Its uniformed crew was busy with two spring lines that checked the ship's lateral movement. A wide gangplank swung into position, landing with a thump on the stone wharf. A steam whistle blew, its staccato echo smashing into the walls of the colossal fort like cannon shot. A tall, distinguished and bewhiskered Captain Wainwright dressed in a newly pressed white uniform, walked towards the Union officers seemingly impervious to the inclement weather. The distinguished Captain saluted then held out a white gloved hand.

"Hello, I'm Captain Wainwright of her Majesty's mail packet, the RMS Folkstone, and you are?"

Major Anderson was escorted aboard for 'Tea' in the Captain's cabin while Riley was sent back to the Fort to report to Captain Doubleday. Shortly thereafter, a Dr. Morris and his nurse took their leave for a tour of the fort, escorted by Captain Truman Seymour. To Virginia, Fort Sumter was indeed impressive. Standing nearly fifty feet above the low tide mark, each side of the fort was over two hundred feet long. Once inside, two arched tiers of red brick on the right and left flanks were crowned by numerous gun emplacements. It reminded Seymour of the coliseum in Rome. A large group of near-naked men were making thousands of red adobe slabs over to one side of the expansive two acre courtyard. One of them saw Nurse Virginia. A chorus of wolf whistles erupted. Virginia shivered as a large white man whipped one of the slab makers who called her a nigger. To Saxton, the man who meted out the punishment was all too familiar. John Saxton grabbed his wife, spun her around, and whispered.

"My Dear, I know that man. He's the slaver I told you about I saw aboard the Wanderlust years ago." Saxton approached Captain Seymour standing nearby, his voice sotto voce.

"Truman, my good fellow, would you come back to the ship to supervise the unloading. Besides, it's getting dark and I think I hear 'Cookie's dinner bell ringing. What do you say?"

Later, Saxton found out from Corporal Riley that the big mean man with a little whip was Harley Blackstone, former First Mate on the slave ship Wanderlust. Saxton knew what death looked like in the flesh as he escorted Virginia out through the Sally Port. They passed a very happy Major Anderson as he made his way back from the wharf.

Dusk fell like a gravedigger's shovel within the walls of Fort Sumter. Cliff swallows flipped through the humid air like acrobats dressed in white and blue tights. Thousands of their red clay nests hung precariously from the inner fascia of Sumter's right flank. Within hours, their aerial world would be shattered forever.

Corporal Riley walked up to Harley Blackstone who along with his crew was waiting to be hung on the spot. They watched intently as the two men talked for a few minutes then both men sauntered towards Major Anderson's office. Ten minutes later, Harley ran out of the Major's office. Blackstone was all business as he sidled up to the slab pile. His men were waiting, expecting the worst. Harley laughed at them, knowing full well what they were thinking. He said cheerfully,

"Well me hearties, we're gonna hang but not today. You see girls, we've got chores. Looks like Captain Doubleday wants us to unload that ship! So let's mess up then get some ammo carts down there on the double! Let's go."

CRACK! His little black whip touched Jeffries neck like a bee sting. He yelped. The little man with big yellow teeth would feel even more pain before the night was out.

Major Anderson and Captain Abner Doubleday looked at the maps extracted from the manila packet Captain Wainwright had given them. Maps, large and small littered the Major's office like pirate's treasure on the bottom of the Spanish Main. After an hour of perusing them, both men were ecstatic.

"Imagine Abner. Here before us are forty-three Rebel gun positions, most of whom we knew nothing about!"

Anderson didn't care how they got to him. He would use them well. Doubleday stood back, acting as a Devil's advocate, his moustache quivering as he talked.

"Well Major, what if they're counterfeit and the Rebels want us to waste our shot on marsh land?"

"Listen Captain, I thought of that too but the Folkstone's skipper assured me that these came from none other than Alan Pinkerton himself." However, Doubleday persisted.

"I'm still not convinced but I guess we'll have to take him at his word for Pinkerton's proven in the past to be reliable. Christ, he just saved Old Abe from certain death up in Baltimore two months ago. What a way to start a presidency. Anyway Sir, we're outgunned and outmanned."

"Not quite Abner, for that ship out there holds ten-- count 'em twenty cannons, their ammo, fifty Henrys, Spencers and eighty tons of food and medical supplies. I'll get the maps to Seymour while you supervise the unloading of the ship before the Rebs catch on. By God, Beauregard might have been one of my artillery students at West Point but I didn't teach him everything, not by a long shot!"

Both officers grabbed their Hardees and ran out of the office. After they had left, they didn't notice someone sneak into the office and replace Fort Sumter's newest gun emplacement map pinned on a wall with another similar looking paper that listed the fort's medical needs written up by General Crawford.

The Folkstone's cargo holds lay ready to be unloaded. Corporal Riley led a detail of slavers hauling empty ammo carts down the jetty on the double. The steam cranes were up and alert. Directed by Benson, they rapidly loaded large and small crates onto a row of ammo carts waiting dock-side. Sweating slavers pulled these carts back up the long wet wharf whose salt-caked granite stones splintered as heavy wheels trundled over them. As the afternoon progressed, the Folkstone's three holds emptied one by one until they were bare. The ship's cranes were clamped and chained down; the gangplank pulled aboard and stowed.

Meanwhile, inside Fort Sumter, Captain Seymour and his gun crew were busy putting the Ordnance and Blakely rifles together. They'd practiced these maneuvers before until their hands were raw and bleeding. After each gun was cleaned and assembled; mule teams pulled them up steep brick cannon ramps to their designated positions. Dozens of flaring torches inset into the brick walls around the inner courtyard cast macabre shadows that danced about like surefooted devils. It was indeed the devil's workshop as dozens of men struggled mightily into a wet spring evening. On the upper battlements, Captain Truman Seymour directed each rifle into place, making maximum use of the 'Magic Maps' as he called them. He knew time was running out. He thought confidently,

'If the Rebs ever fire the first cannonade, by God they're going to get more than they bargained for!'

By two thirty in the morning, all was quiet aboard the Folkstone as it rocked in the river currents flowing around the wharf. Aboard ship, Captain Wainwright went into his cabin to get his pipe, but as he opened the door, a hulking shadow emerged from the gloom. It was Harley Blackstone, a belaying pin in his right hand. He snarled,

"Now skipper, don't do anything rash now or I'll smash ye sure! We wouldn't want to soil that nice clean uniform yer wearin' now would we?"

"Don't call me skipper!"

Harley roughly pushed the elderly Captain away from the door. Blackstone hissed,

"We're goin' for a ride in one of your pretty yellow lifeboats Captain. Well, How about it?"

Down below decks, Virginia and Saxton were asleep still dressed in their uniforms, totally oblivious to a life and death situation happening directly above them. Virginia rolled over, knocking an empty water glass from a nightstand onto the cabin floor. The glass broke into pieces with a crash. It woke her up instantly. Saxton grunted, turned over and continued to snore undisturbed. Virginia was grateful that he did. She got up, lit a swinging chain lamp above her then carefully put all the shards in a linen napkin. She padded barefoot to a large brass porthole across the cabin. As she was about to throw the bundle out, Virginia heard a strange man's voice above her whisper,

"What was that?" This was followed by Captain Wainwright saying,

"Step aside and I'll have a look."

She heard a loud shout, followed by a thud and silence. Heavy footsteps pounded above her. The linen bundle dropped to the floor. She ran over to wake up Saxton. He groaned, "Virginia, for Pete's sake, not now!"

She whispered in his ear. His eyes flew open. Jumping out of the bunk in one fluid motion he reached into a bedside drawer and retrieved two small derringers. Virginia was startled, saying, "Where did you get those?"

He reminded her of the attempt on their lives in New York City. He continued.

"I went shopping in Norfolk while you were sleeping; sorry dear. Know how to use one of these?"

"Of course I do!"

He cracked the breech. It was loaded. He gave it to her just before she disappeared through the stateroom door. In seconds, she was busy waking up the crew sleeping down the hallway.

Meanwhile, Saxton clutched his derringer. With consummate stealth he crept up the companionway towards the wheelhouse. Next to it the Captain's door was wide open. He thought, 'That's very odd.'

He stood still, his senses on full alert. Not a sound was heard except the soft slapping of some passing waves on the ship's hull. He peered into the gloomy cabin. A man's body lay on the floor. Saxton moved closer. It was Wainwright. Blood oozed from a small head wound. Saxton bent down and shook him. He groaned. Saxton stood up.

'Good!' he thought. 'The Skipper's not dead.'

He ran out the way he's come in. Halfway down the companionway he ran into Virginia. Behind her were five crewmen armed with guns and belaying pins. First Mate, Axel Benson whispered,

"What's up Mr. Saxton, is there trouble afoot?"

"We've got boarders men! Virginia, you go to the Captain's quarters and bandage his head wound. There's a medical kit in his locker. Lock the door. The key's hanging on a hook next to it. Don't leave the cabin no matter what happens. I'll rap four times if everything is ok. Three times will mean someone has a gun on me. Do you understand? We'll check him later to see if he can still command the ship. If not, Axel you're in the wheelhouse. Yates, you go to the engine room and get up steam. I think we're going leave immediately. Remember everyone, be quiet and no lights. In the meantime, Axel, you come with me. You take the port side, I'll take the other."

After Harley knocked out the Captain, he rushed out onto the main deck. Amidships, a yellow lifeboat hung from its davit. Blackstone untied it, then swung it out and down onto choppy waters. Without warning, a deep voice behind him growled,

"And just where are you going Mister? Don't move.....Don't even breathe, or I'll blow your head off. It's been a long time since I saw you throwing slaves off The Wanderlust, you murdering son of a bitch!"

Harley knew instantly who it was. He'd seen Saxton earlier but couldn't quite place him. Blackstone turned around slowly,

"Nice to meet you 'Doctor, but I've got a boat to catch."

With that said, his belaying pin lashed out, knocking Saxton's derringer away to the side across a rain swept deck. Harley was on him instantly, his hands around his throat. As Blackstone's long fingernails bit into Saxton's neck, he rolled just enough to put the larger and far stronger man off balance. A hard right cross came straight up slamming Harley's head backwards against an iron railing. Saxton twisted away while Harley staggered to his feet shaking his head. Saxton, now on his hands and knees, looked around frantically for the derringer. It was nowhere to be seen, but Harley had already found it lying in the scuppers. He stood over Saxton pointing it down at his hapless victim. Harley growled.

"I'm gonna kill ya boy just for the simple reason I ended up here. The Ghost cut our wind. Woulda' got away too. Cost me money, and my freedom. Now you're gonna pay boy! I need a hostage. Get up, and jump into that lifeboat!"

He waved the derringer in Saxton's face. Both men felt the ship come to life as a ton of burning coal began heating up the ship's massive boilers. Saxton lowered himself into the lifeboat very slowly, playing for time. The lifeboat's painter became taut in a sea breeze. Harley spat,

"Now, go aft nice and easy matey and no sudden moves or I'll blast ye!"

Saxton did so. The lifeboat rocked from side to side while still tied to the ship. Harley waved the derringer about. He hissed.

"Don't move a muscle."

Saxton stood still facing certain death only a few feet away. Blackstone backed up, grabbed a rope and despite his size, nimbly swung down into the yellow lifeboat. He raised the derringer. Saxton's veins went cold. From out of nowhere a belaying pin flew through the air knocking the gun out of Blackstone's right hand. In an instant, Saxton dived overboard. In doing so, the lifeboat was thrust violently aside snapping the painter. A passing river current caught the lifeboat, carrying it away. Axel rushed up and looked over the side at Saxton treading water below him. He cried out,

"Mr. Saxton, are you all right?"

Saxton nodded, swam over to the ship, grabbed a knotted bumper and climbed aboard. Both men peered about but Blackstone was gone. It seemed as if the night had reached out and swallowed him whole.

Harley's right hand hurt as he recovered his wits. The lifeboat rocked in the water when he sat on a wide seat. After putting two long oars against the wooden tholes, he rowed away towards James Island, slicing easily through the water. An outgoing tide pushed him away from the confluence of the Ashley and Cooper rivers to the south-west of the fort. A vicious storm, born far to the east off the coast of Africa has come ashore upon the eastern seaboard from New York City to Jacksonville, Florida.

Torrential rain and high winds battered Fort Sumter. Wavering lines of rocket lightning illuminated the leviathan. Harley dug his oars into black water. The blades bit viciously as they scalloped through it. Silvery splashes leaped up every few feet as the clinker-built bulled its way through a stiff rain soaked chop. With the tide and wind going against him, Blackstone pulled with all his might, his glistening muscles rippling with abundant power. Sonorous rolls of thunder boomed across the waters like cannon fire. Harley looked up and grimaced. Afraid of lightning, he began to row like a man possessed. The craft was supposed to be rowed by four men, but Harley alone equaled that with ease. After an hour, he stopped rowing, caught his breath and turned about. A dark sinuous shoreline loomed up behind him. He resumed rowing, satisfied.

Closer and closer he clawed his way towards it. Black shadows seemed to gradually lighten. After rounding a low point of land, the wind and chop died down. The lifeboat glided smoothly onto a wide muddy bank. Harley stowed the oars, leaped out then pulled the heavy lifeboat through thick reeds into dense shore bracken. Harley was free. He checked the waterproof map pouch hidden under Captain Wainwright's overcoat. It was dry. A twig snapped behind him. Startled, he spun around. The muzzle of a Colt .44 was pointed right at him. Captain Horatio Armstrong Garrow barked,

"And were the hell do you think you're goin' mister?"

While Harley was confronting a certain Captain Garrow, the RMS Folkstone was rumbling all over as Yates its engineer and his two black colliers, Abraham and Theo frantically tried to get up a head of steam. Saxton and Axel ran to the wheel house. Benson went to the engine room speaking tube while Saxton ran to Captain Wainwright's quarters. He knocked four times on the door. Virginia opened it then rushed into his arms. She cried out,

"Oh, thank God Sax you're ok. I was so worried!"

"More is the question dear. How's the skipper?" A gruff voice replied,

"I'm quite alright and don't call me skipper."

Captain Wainwright stood up uneasily, his head heavily bandaged. Traces of blood oozed from beneath it. He staggered slightly as he left for the wheelhouse followed by the Saxtons. Axel was there at the wheel bent over the speaking tube listening to Yates tell him that steam was up but not enough for full speed ahead. Saxton told the Captain about Blackstone escaping. His voice rose.

"If the Rebs find out Captain, there'll be hell to pay."

Wainwright took the helm and ordered all lines to be cast off immediately. Saxton and Benson ran out to slip them. As heavy lines splashed into the choppy waters, Saxton heard someone pounding down the wharf from the fort. Benson looked up, letting a thick manila spring-line slip through his fingers. A lone figure was running through the rain hell bent for leather. It was Captain Truman Seymour.

Saxton dropped his line and ran to meet him. He put his hand on Truman's shoulder saying, "We're leaving. You must come with us now." Seymour replied,

"I can't Saxton. The fort's gun map is missing. The Major suspects that the slaver who escaped has it. I have to go back and reset the batteries. The Rebs have given us one hour to surrender or all hell will break loose at 4.30 this morning."

St. Michael's bell began ringing. Four times it rang. Seymour screamed,

"There's little time left. You have to go now."

The RMS Folkstone was leaving. Benson ran out onto the flying bridge directly above them. He screamed at them to jump aboard. Saxton turned and ran, just making it aboard. Truman ran to the end of the dock, cupped his hands around his mouth and yelled at both men standing on the aft deck high above a boiling wake,

"Remember what I said about mortar elevation. It's tricky but you can do it. Don't forget to swab after every shot. Good luck. Any trouble, I'll try to cover you. If you make it home, tell them what happened here. Tell them. Tell them."

With that, the three men straightened up and saluted each other. In the wheelhouse Captain Wainwright pulled the brass lever on the engine room telegraph to SLOW AHEAD.

Harley Blackstone raised his hands over his head slowly, very slowly. A rather large Colt .44 encouraged him to do it. The man holding it emerged. He was tall, well muscled and every bit as dangerous looking as Harley.

"Your name mister and be quick about it."

Harley was quick about it. He started talking and didn't quit until Garrow told him to shut up. Blackstone gingerly retrieved the oilskin pouch and offered it to Garrow. The Captain backed up, his gun never wavering.

"I see it and you say you've got maps inside it detailing every new gun position in Sumter and they are genuine."

"Yes Captain, they are. I got it off Major Anderson's office wall I did. Yes sir. Bin there, bossin' the slab yard for a short time I have! You see, we came off the slaver Wanderlust onto the Connie II as prisoners. They kilt our skipper Josiah Garrow; threw him overboard they did. After a year cooped up in the city jail, myself and my fellow shipmates were taken over to Fort Moultrie to help rebuild it. Stayed over a year in that hell hole too, we did. From there, the Brits took me to Sumter. Strange it was indeed Captain."

Garrow holstered his Colt revolver, and grabbed the oilskin pouch. He Looked at Blackstone thoughtfully as if he was watching a violent storm sweep away before him. He seized both of Blackstone's shoulders laughing as he did so.

"You see Blackstone, Josiah Garrow was my father. I'm Horatio Garrow. It's your lucky day Blackie. My father talked well of you. Let's go and get this map to 'Little Napoleon' right away."

Blackstone however wasn't so sure. He'd heard all the stories. He thought,

'Christ, out of the fryin' pan and into the fire.'

Exactly at 4.30 AM, April 12, 1861, a red signal flare exploded over the water near Fort Sumter. This was immediately followed by a single mortar round fired by a Lt. Henry S. Farley from Fort Johnson. Shortly thereafter, several large Columbiad shells began arching through the night sky, bursting over Fort Sumter. Blackstone and Garrow stood watching the barrage. Harley remained transfixed by the intensity until a large hand grabbed his arm. He was roughly pulled back into deep shadows.

That first mortar burst over Fort Sumter just as the RMS Folkstone rounded its port side. Captain Wainwright rang FULL AHEAD. He grabbed a brass speaking tube and yelled, "Connor, for God's sake give it all you've got man!"

Artillery shells flew high over the Folkstone, now a hundred tons lighter. It raced down the channel past Cummins Point on Morris Island towards the Atlantic and safety. Captain Wainwright had a rough sketch of the main shipping channel before him, courtesy of Major Anderson. On it were the approximate positions of four submerged hulks that the Rebels had sunk in the channel two days before and where the sand bar was at the mouth of the channel. The Rebels had removed all the marker buoys that evening. It seemed that every fort surrounding Fort Sumter was firing at once. Sea airs about Fort Sumter heavy with rain squalls, were shattered by shot and shell from forty-three Confederate artillery batteries. A break in the weather revealed a flotilla of Rebel picket ships bearing down the Anaona. Coming ever closer, their bow cannons began spitting flames and white smoke. On one of them stood Henry Thomas Harrison determined to settle an old score. Saxton, hearing the explosions turned about. Not believing his eyes, he screamed, "Oh my God, they're onto us."

Saxton, Virginia and Axel ran down from the flying bridge then across the main deck to 'Packard' and 'Lincoln'. Saxton tried to remain calm. He cried out,

"Virginia, take off the tarp, stow it between the mortars then wet swab em' good. Axel, get a crane up and running. Hook up the #3 hatch cover and stack it onto hatch #2. Hoist up a few crates of case shot on the double. I'll be back shortly, but first, I've got something to do."

RMS Folkstone on an incoming tide and buffeted by high winds and high seas was making barely over eight knots as it fled eastward down the main shipping channel. As it did so, Axel and two crewmen unencumbered one crane, powered it up then began hoisting crates of grapeshot out of the hold, slamming them onto the deck. It was dangerous work as the top heavy ship yawed from side to side. Once finished, the heavy crane was clamped down. With the center of gravity lowered, the Anaona continued on more of an even keel.

Atop Fort Sumter's battlements, Captain Seymour watched the Folkstone weave back and forth across the channel through a hail of shrapnel. He focused his Porro binoculars to get a closer look. Incredulous at what he was witnessing, he shouted out to others about him glassing the ship.

"They're raising the Stars and Stripes! They'll really get hell now!"

He continued his vigil from the uppermost gun tiers of Fort Sumter as another cannonade bracketed the ship. High geysers obscured it. For many moments his heart stood still. The Folkstone disappeared into virtual Niagaras of water, but it always emerged unscathed. Its thin wake jinxed this way and that as Captain Wainwright swung the helm back and forth to avoid the hulks. He watched as the Anaona disappeared out of sight behind the low headland of Sullivan's Island. It seemed that they were being followed by the grim reaper, whose gleaming scythe was cutting a swath of death just behind them.

Saxton had run to the main-mast. The Union Jack and the other pennants were pulled down. Saxton stowed them then took the Stars and Stripes out of its metal can. He ran it up. The wind flared it out. As John Saxton ran astern to the mortars, the flag snapped to attention.

Benson cheered as he carried more canisters aft. Virginia wet and dry swabbed the mortars while Saxton lifted the heavy canisters and rammed them home. He elevated the barrels as Seymour had taught him. Virginia lit the fuses with a cigar. Twin canisters arched high overhead, exploding directly over the Rebel fleet. Deadly missiles of lead rained down upon it. The hunters began to zigzag after realizing their quarry had sharp teeth. Some steamed safely past the hulks, while others were not so fortunate.

Again 'Packard' and 'Lincoln' fired; this time however, it was to starboard. The swivel platform performed flawlessly as the greased rollers beneath it carried the heavy mortars easily in that direction. Mortar shells began leaving the Folkstone at a rapid rate. A sweating Benson kept up a steady supply of canisters. Thunder and lightning continued to explode in the dark above, illuminating the picket ships behind them. Packard and Lincoln barked like mad dogs crazed for a kill, spraying grapeshot above the Rebel fleet only three hundred yards behind them. The batteries on Cummins Point and Fort Moultrie fired upon them from time to time. Their shells shrieked towards the mail packet, only to fall short of their target. After a few more attempts, they quit as the Folkstone sailed out of range to the north-east.

Virginia continued to swab as Saxton lifted the canisters into the tubes then rammed them home. Virginia fired over and over again. Despite her best efforts, the lighter Rebel sloops were two hundred yards away and closing fast. Fountains of sea water rained down, drenching the Folkstone's aft deck where the mortars lay. Saxton yelled for Benson to come up out of the hold. He did. Together they threw the large black mortar tarp over a crane. All four corners were securely tied down to the railings around it. For now the mortars could be kept dry and still fire. Ever closer, the enemy came down upon them. Again and again the packet fought back.

Once calm and collected, Saxton began to sense something uncontrollable, deep down and primeval growing within him. It was a feeling of fury born of helplessness, of desperation and of fear. John Saxton began jumping up and down shaking his fists at the oncoming sloops. He didn't care as he screamed at them, insane with rage, his soul shriven by hate.

It seemed to be the culmination of everything he stood for and everything that he hated. He cried out.

"No! No! You bastards you're not going to take her away from me!"

He felt her arms clasp him. It was as if he was a boy all over again, deep into an ocean of rage. It was no longer day but a terrible night that descended down upon him. It was a night with no end, no beginning, but a continuous roar of blackness pulling him ever deeper into the nether regions of his mind.

'They would never take him alive. He would fight them to the death.' Again he screamed. "Virginia! Virginia! I'll never let them take you away from me."

She backed away, shot through with love and amazement. 'Packard' and 'Lincoln' continued to roar. Ball and bullets fell all around them. Waterfalls rained down upon them. High explosives deafened them. Blasts of heat, hotter than the breath of hell itself beat upon the tarp above them. Deadly shrapnel rattled off the decks around them. To the end, it seemed as if the hand of God was protecting them. Suddenly artillery shells screamed over them towards the Rebel sloops. Nine inch Dalhgren cannons from Lincoln's relief ships; the steam cutter USS Harriet Lane and the steam sloop USS Pawnee began firing on the Rebel sloops. It was a fortunate rescue indeed for the Anaona. The two man-o-wars and the merchant steamer 'Baltic' had just weathered a fierce storm and were lying off Sullivan's Island waiting for the rest of the fleet to appear.

The end for the fugitives came about as they sallied forth into a new day, a new life, a new beginning. The last of their pursuers eventually turned away; spent, defeated. Virginia and Saxton stood on the aft deck clinging to each other. They waved at the relief ships as they slid by them at close quarters. Two hundred recruits aboard the 'Baltic' began cheering them on. Their hearty huzzahs drove a nightmare back into the dark cave from which it had emerged. It was over. The Anaona's whistle blew in triumph over the bosom of a vast ocean as a rising sun burst over the eastern horizon.

Saxton's blonde hair was plastered to his face; black smoke and powder burns ran down his arms. Both his and Virginia's white uniforms were soiled by black streaks of gunpowder. They looked at each other, laughing hysterically as their wet clothing flapped about them. Saxton turned to Virginia, a mortar ram in his hand. The image of his father firing his shotgun at the Anaona came back to him. It was like yesterday. He looked down tenderly at Virginia whose eyes looked up at him gleaming wetly in the light of dawn. The ram dropped with a thud from his hand to the deck. It rolled into a scupper. Saxton held Virginia tight.

Captain Wainwright walked onto the flying bridge, his head bandage loose, fluttering about in a freshening sea breeze. An opaque sun came out from behind scudding clouds high above him. He was yelling something but his words were being blown away by the wind. Axel ran over to talk with him. After several minutes he came back. Saxton and Virginia stood together looking astern as a thin wake curled up beneath them. It was 7 AM. In the distance twenty miles away, they could hear the 'BOOM' of the rifled Blakely cannon firing from the iron clad-battery at Cummins Point. In response they heard the sharp 'CRACK' of Seymour's Ordnance rifles. The distant headland of Sullivan's Island obscured the battle but they could tell it was fierce and fought with no quarter. Virginia turned to Saxton. She was weeping,

"I do hope Captain Seymour is safe. What a brave man he was. Thank God for him or we never would have made it!" She trembled as Saxton held her close.

"I know darling, I know. He was the bravest of men indeed."

Benson came up to them. They turned to face him. Captain Wainwright was still on the bridge trying to say something. Saxton looked at Axel.

"What does he want?"

"He received a semaphore message from the USS Harriet Lane. They want to know if we need further assistance and secondly the skipper wants to know if we are still going to Bermuda?"

Saxton turned to Virginia, his hands on her shoulders.

"Well Nurse Morris, I know we're alright but where are we going?"

She reached up, held his face with both hands and said,

"Home, darling, let's go home."

END OF BOOK ONE

'SACRIFICE'

"Vita havina macho---War has no eyes"
A Swahili proverb.

BOOK TWO: CHAPTER 1
THE SHELL MAN

The Tsavo lions lay under a thorn bush waiting for their prey to approach from downwind. The big cats had traveled for many weeks from where their former hunting range lay. As a drought there intensified, it left them no choice but to seek food and water elsewhere. All around them columns of hot air spiraled upwards, creating shimmering mirages of yellow light upon the savannah far below.

Ambling along towards the lions hidden in the brush, a tall Maasai boy prodded an old cow with a stick. Behind him, a dozen cattle followed in single file. It was the dry season. Water was scarce and precious. A tribal water hole lay a mile further on through the thorn bush and Acacia trees.

The boy was Nimsi of the Kisongo Maasai, an ancient people who had populated the Maasai Mara of East Africa for thousands of years. Nine years old and newly circumcised, his groin hurt as he shuffled along thinking about his recent 'emuratare' ceremony. Ahead of him, the lead cow stopped abruptly. It sniffed the hot air, pawing the dusty ground as it did so. The other cattle coming up from behind bunched together, refusing to move any further.

Matari heard his little brother scream in the distance. He ran forward, his leather shield clutched in one hand while his broad bladed throwing spear balanced in the other. A loping gait moved his tall body quickly and silently between the grasping thorn bushes. His red Shuka cloak swung like a clipper's top gallant before a stiff wind. As he rounded a stone kopje; he saw a male lion dragging his brother by the head through the grass towards some thick thorn brush. The cattle had run off, bawling their way towards the water hole nearby. Matari ran silently in a semi-circle hoping to intercept the maneless lion. He stopped, sensing that it was close, very close. There were no more screams. Nimsi was dead.

With his right hand he raised his six foot long steel tipped Isiphapha and gripped his longo with the other. He began moving forward, his mind on edge, his legs like steel springs. A tawny form exploded out of the brush fifty feet to his right, just outside his peripheral vision. The man swung about as the lion knocked him aside. However, it miscalculated its attack and only scratched Matari's face. Bush pigs in the nearby underbrush fled as the lion crashed to the ground, rolled in the dust, sprang up and whirled about. The Maasai wiped his bloody face with his Shuka being careful not to get any on his hands. He stood there fighting back the pain of the lion's attack, his throwing spear raised. Twenty feet away, his bull-hide longo lay useless in the dust behind him.

Matari's heart beat like a trip hammer. The 'spear to claw' encounter he had dreamed of as a boy had arrived. He never killed a lion before. If he did so, he would become a Moran or warrior. Strangely though, the lion did not roar or snarl at him. It crouched down, its sulfurous eyes hypnotic. The lion's tail stopped twitching. In a heartbeat the beast leapt forward thirty feet.

The man threw his Isiphapha into the big cat. The force behind it drove the spear deep within the lion. The beast fell to the ground, breaking the spear's red wood shaft in two. The Tsavo lion was dead. The Maasai staggered away leaving a blood trail in the dust. He retched when he realized just how close to death he had been. While his thirsty cows bawled in the distance, Matari returned to the lion. After much effort, he pulled the shattered spear out of its body. The long hand hammered blade shed its gore as the Maasai wiped it clean with some red oat grass.

He picked up his longo and began searching the brush for his brother's body. A blood trail wound its way to a thorn bush where the lion had dragged the boy. Matari picked up the body and carried it to the waterhole. After slaking his thirst, he washed the corpse. A grossly bloated baobab tree sheltered his cattle; their brown and white bodies tense, skittish, ready to bolt. A broken spear prodded the lead cow forward. Matari looked up. Already scissor-tailed kites were wheeling in tight circles high up above the waterhole.

To make his claim as a Moran, he knew the lion would have to be taken back to the village Enkang soon or not at all. The cattle ambled after the old lead cow. Draped across her boney backside was Nimsi's body. It was late afternoon. Long shadows skittered about the underbrush on all sides of him. A pair of Helmet shrikes twittered in alarm nearby. The Maasai never knew until the last second that the lioness was upon him. He screamed just once.

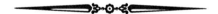

Tyler Wicks received a coded telegram from 'Pinky' that afternoon. The little black Plnkerton agent stlll hurt from the terrible beating he'd received two weeks previously in Memphis. He was incredulous about having to find the 'Big Nigger' and accompany him back to Boston. He thought,

'Christ! I'm getting too old for this business.' Besides, he'd sworn to get even for the humiliation of it all. But he took orders, distasteful as they were. His mission in Memphis now over, he had another; find Marcus Brown!

Wicks through the efforts of another agent in New Orleans found out that Marcus was somewhere on Elder mountain in Marion County, very near the Tennessee River Gorge. For some unknown reason, the Catholic Church courier service was used as a conduit to relay the information to Wicks. Whatever the case; Tyler Wicks finally managed to track down Marcus Brown deep within the hardwood forests that crowned the mountain. His journey there had been interesting to say the least.

Tyler boarded the next train east out of Memphis like Marcus before him, he had no ticket. He too rode up on the roof of the baggage car behind an air vent then jumped off on a steep grade just before a low railway bridge near Chattanooga. Now he was standing over his quarry looking down on its tormented scars. However, his prey was not the fearsome Tsavo lions of the Serengeti. Still, the effect was startling to Tyler as Marcus dreamed about his brother Nimsi and the Tsavo lions. Marcus tossed, turned, lurched, twisted and shook violently on his cotton tick mattress while the 'shell man' waited patiently. Tyler smiled inwardly as he remembered how he had first met Big Willie two days earlier.

Tyler Wicks had begun to sweat as he followed a narrow trace ever higher through a massive hardwood forest. Occasionally he'd stop and mop his brow with a red neckerchief. The scars of his beating were still visible. Limping slightly as he trudged along, his pain was forgotten as he looked around in awe. Hardwood trees big and beautiful surrounded him. Their grandeur diminished him. A Mountain Skullcap nearby began twittering in the underbrush for its mate. Cathedral oaks, both red and white, towered high above him. Sweet-gum and Ash danced in grassy glades freshened by a spring wind. His path was dappled by bolts of light that pierced a greening forest canopy. A freshet in a nearby creek gushed under a log bridge. Tyler drank in the beauty of it all.

Big Willie watched Tyler Wicks from behind a thicket on a bright spring morning in late March of 1861. He smiled as Tyler walked past him. As he did so, Big Willie prodded the little black man with the long barrel of a squirrel rifle. Tyler stopped dead in his tracks. Big Willie exclaimed,

"Where youse headed brother?"

Tyler stared straight ahead, unmoving until he squared his thin shoulders, raised his head and lifted his nose ever higher.

"T'aint none of your business brother; it's a free country tain't it? Besides I'm out for a stroll lookin' at all these big trees. I just might try livin' hereabouts one day."

"Youse seem pretty cool little man for somebody about to be lookin' down the barrel of this here gun. Now turn round real slow like. No sudden moves boy."

Wicks did as he was told but as the big man moved closer, Wicks spun around like greased lightening. Before Big Willie knew it, he was on the ground flat on his back, his old hunting rifle and slouch hat lying beside him. Wicks stood over him pointing a pepperbox derringer at Big Willie's head. He crowed.

"Well big man, I guess it looks like youse takin' a nap in the middle of this here road. Let's get up now real slow like. Gimme your rifle mister for safe keepin' cause I sure don't want youse a shootin' up the neighborhood."

Big Willie reached over and held it up butt high. Wicks took it and leaned it against a tree beside him. Big Willie stood up, retrieved his hat placing it at a rakish angle over his balding head. He laughed as he looked down on his adversary.

"I bet you'se come lookin' for the 'Big Nigger'. I bet you'se are too mister!" Wicks countered.

"What makes you think so?"

"I heard that everybody's bin lookin' for him. Seems he killed five men down in New Orleans then taught a little nigger in Memphis a lesson or two in honesty as well." Big Willie's eyes widened.

"Say now, just a minute here, yes, I'll bet a jug of home brew that you ain't one of the aforementioned five cause you'se still alive. I bet you'se the little uppity nigger that cheated folks at the shell game."

Wicks raised the derringer slightly as if it was a teacher's pointer in a classroom.

"And what makes you think that?" Big Willie said,

"Why look at youse. Eyes still a bit red. You limp slightly. Yessiree Bubba, you'se come to kill im' with that pea shooter ain't you boy?"

"I have a mind to shoot you mister if you keep on talkin' like a turkey lookin' for love in a holler." Big Willie grinned.

"Well, what ya gonna do? Can't stay here all day or my missus will come a lookin' with the dog. Don't want that now do we?"

Tyler reached over and picked up the rifle. He threw it to Big Willie. Wicks put the derringer away in his mackinaw jacket then held out a little black hand as Big Willie dusted himself off.

"Name's Tyler Wicks from Memphis. I'm glad to meet you."

Big Willie shook Tyler's hand then stood back and laughed. Wicks looked up at the big black man saying,

"What's so funny, I coulda kilt you?"

"Look Tyler, I can see you meant no harm or my boy Little Willie over yonder woulda shot you sure." Tyler turned as a boy's voice said,

"Papa, kin I come out now? I've got him good. By the way, are youse alright? Seems mighty quick, ain't he papa?"

"Now son don't you ever tell your momma what you just seen or I'll whip ya good. Ya hear me boy?"

"Yes papa, but it sure looked funny n' all."

Little Willie stepped out of the shadows. He was big framed like his father, tall and husky and not more than fourteen years old. An old musket was tied at either end by a leather strap. It hung in his hands like a dead fish. The boy said politely,

"I'm known as Little Willie round these here parts mister."

Big Willie pushed the boy aside and looked down on Wicks.

"So, wadda ya want with the 'Big Nigger' anyways? Must be real important to traipsy all the way here from Memphis. Well speak up! Don't just stand there with your foot in your mouth."

They started to walk up the winding road, their voices rising into the cathedral of leaves high above them. Tyler told them,

"The 'Big Nigger's name is really Marcus Brown. I work for the Pinkerton Detective Agency back east in Chicago. President Abe Lincoln wants Brown in Boston real quick like. That's all I know. Honest to God, that's all I know. I do believe that you can help us get there 'cause this is Johnny Reb country as sure as God made little green apples. I guess I'm real lucky youse a brother or I'd be hangin' out to dry right now." Big Willie looked down at the little man,

"Marcus Brown eh? Nebber did say his last name. Yeah, he's bin here nigh on two weeks now. He musta fell off a train, got hurt real bad too. My oldest boy Hud and I found him down by the Tenny and brought him 'cross to the mountain here. His face was smashed in and my Sweet Daphne suspects that he has some broken ribs. Sure is a lotta hurtin' for one man, I'd say; but my Sweet Daphne's bin healin' him up some." He stopped and laughed,

"I nebber seen nothin' like it. My Sweet Daphne keeps feedin' him herbs 'n sich. It's the Lord's work afoot I think; his wonders to perform. Hallelujah!"

The narrow track ended amongst chestnut trees that ringed a clapboard cabin. Wood smoke rose lazily into the greening canopy high above it. An old redbone hound barked and ran towards them wagging its tail. A barefoot boy ran after it across a dusty barnyard. Chickens scattered like tumbleweeds before a hot prairie wind as the boy ran through them. He cried,

"Papa's home momma! My papa's home!"

The boy flew into his father's arms; the old dog laid down in the dusty yard wanting a belly rub. A stout moon faced black woman came out onto the sagging porch wiping her hands on a cotton cloth. She laughed; her voice lyrical, young as sunlight.

"Land sakes, we's got company agin'. Lordy! Lordy! We haven't had so much folks visitin' us since we got hitched!"

A deep pounding laugh that spoke well of her character resonated across the barnyard. She looked over at her older boy, Hudson, scratching the dog.

"Lord have mercy child, leave Cooder alone and come here. Your momma needs your help gettin' food on the table."

She wiped her worn hands on a torn flour sack apron.

"My name's Sweet Daphne. I'm the other half here abouts." Tyler stepped forward, his small black hand thrust out like a tarred stick.

"Name's Tyler Wicks; I've come for the 'Big Nigger'."

BOOK TWO: CHAPTER 2
AMBUSH

The SS Anaona slipped into Boston's inner harbor at two in the morning. For three weeks it had been an uneventful voyage home from the battle of Fort Sumter. The 'Honeymoon Heroes' were feted by Allan Pinkerton in Annapolis albeit quietly. The President wired his congratulations while they were there. The Civil War started poorly for the Union. Fort Sumter fell and the Confederates were victorious nearly everywhere. Even the Capital, Washington DC was poorly defended and was soon under imminent threat of invasion. Times were desperate for Lincoln. He issued a Proclamation April 15, 1861 calling for seventy-five thousand militiamen. In response, eleven States and two territories eventually rallied to the Confederate cause. Lincoln then issued a Proclamation of Blockade permitting the Union Navy to blockade over thirty-six hundred miles of Confederate coastline from North Carolina to Mexico on the Gulf. From then on the South was handicapped in trying to supply itself with vital war materiel. The industrialized North would have no such problem. General Robert E. Lee resigned his commission from the Union Army April 20th. He said to Lincoln,

"I cannot raise my hand against my birthplace, my home, or my children."

He then went home to Virginia to command their military and naval forces. The nation was split asunder.

Virginia and Saxton were still asleep in their stateroom below decks. Their ship weathered shot, shell and rough seas but had sailed home relatively unscathed. Upon its arrival, pouring rain dampened Boston's Inner harbor as if a black depression had fallen upon it, its waters beaten into submission by the incessant power of the elements. No crowds greeted the returning heroes. No waving white linen from one end of the Saxton wharf to the other welcomed them—nothing. Muriel Saxton, Jack the terrier, and whistles of salutation were absent. Only flocks of sullen gulls greeted them as they slept atop the pilings, their heads tucked under wing. Even they seemed to have been quarantined by the rain. It was if the whole universe was in mourning over the state of the Union. The Anaona docked silently in a sea of tears and remained mute until the break of dawn four hours later.

Captain Wainwright was awakened by the rocking of the ship. His inner ear over the years had become acutely alert to any disruptions in the atmosphere around him. Any change in engine cadence, waves slapping the hull, or noises from the wheelhouse, were all part of a litany of warning sounds that would disturb a sailor's sleep. The Captain rose, putting on leather slippers and a black cotton robe which he tied at the waist. Dawn was breaking, for a watery light had found its way into his stateroom. The Captain wended his way to the bridge, the aroma of coffee wafting along behind him. 'Cookie' was up making breakfast. Wainwright looked at a brass Seth Thomas above the massive ship's helm. It was 5.40 AM. The port side door opened and in stepped his First Mate, Axel Benson. A small man, his close cropped black hair was juxtaposed by an enormous beard. At 27 years old, Benson had only been at sea for less than five years. Energetic and endearing, Captain Wainwright had a soft spot for him but rarely showed it. Benson chirped,

"Mornin' to you Captain. Looks like you didn't get much sleep either. I took a tour then walked up to the office and left the message you gave me for Mr. Larsen. I understand Mr. Saxton wants to see him in his office at 0800 hours right?"

The Captain nodded, knowing the message was confidential. Benson continued oblivious to his faux pas. The Captain lit his morning pipe. Benson leaned against the helm eying the Captain, trying to gauge his mood. Satisfied, he reflected,

"Seems strange after what we've been through that no one was killed, not even injured during our escape from Fort Sumter. A miracle I'd say. I thought we were goners for sure. My, with all the shot fallin' round us, we still zigzagged our way out of hell. Right Skipper?"

"Don't call me skipper son."

"Sorry Captain, I forgot. But really, it musta bin hell for ya too Sir? I didn't have much time to worry though. I was too damn busy feedin' our mortars, 'Packard' and 'Lincoln'." He laughed. The Captain did not, saying brusquely,

"The Captain's job is to run the ship despite the crew, the weather or the threat of attack. It's been that way throughout naval history. While at sea nothing is strong enough to break the bond between a captain and his ship."

"Would you have gone down with the ship Sir?"

Wainwright stood tall. He scowled fiercely, pointing his pipe at Benson in reprimand.

"Of course, Mr. Benson, now get along and rouse the crew and wake up the newlyweds."

Shortly thereafter, the crew was eating their breakfast in the ship's galley. Saxton and Virginia had finished theirs earlier in their stateroom. Saxton was getting ready to disembark. It was nearly six. He kissed his new bride Virginia goodbye and left the ship headed for the company office perched high atop warehouse #3. Hans Larsen its comptroller was already there with his perpetual pot of coffee. Saxton ran across the rain swept wharf. Nothing had changed. Everything looked normal. It was hard to believe that men were dying by the thousands somewhere a few hundred miles south of him. How could it be that America for nearly a year now, was at war with itself? In despair he ran up the rickety steps to the office then strode into it like a flushed grouse. Hans Larsen rose to greet him, looking remarkably like an elderly church deacon. Saxton shook his sodden raincoat as he hung it up to dry on a coat hook. His cloth hat sailed through the air landing on a hook beside it. Larsen grinned. He extended a boney hand.

"My, it's great to see you again Sax. What an ordeal you've been through. Some honeymoon!" He laughed, stood back and admired the young man.

"Your father would have been proud. Too bad Sumter fell. But it was through no fault of your own. However, I have good news Sax. Captain Truman Seymour survived the action at Sumter. Miraculously so did everyone else there. He's been promoted to Major. A remarkable man, quite remarkable he was. From what I've heard from Pinkerton, Seymour saved your lives."

Saxton walked over to a pot bellied stove in the corner and poured himself a coffee. He stood there for a few moments savoring the bitter brew then sat down. He said.

"That's true Hans. He did. He was the bravest man I've ever met. I'll miss him. I have more good news from our mutual friend 'Pinky'. Apparently, there's going to be a new medal awarded to those in the Navy who have shown uncommon bravery in battle. A Senator, James Grimes of Iowa, has been working on a draft paper to present to Congress next year. Pinkerton is probably involved in some way I'm sure, as well as Lincoln. Supposedly, it will be the highest honor for the Navy. But I'm sure it will later include the Army if the Generals have their way. He says it might be called the Congressional Medal of Honor. Damned politicians! Always have to have their name on anything worthy. I guess they got the idea from the Victoria Cross, you know, that the British award. Anyway, Captain Seymour's name is apparently on the list of future recipients. According to the Boston Globe, he deserves it."

Hans sat down for a brass telegraph key began chattering beside him. Saxton couldn't believe his ears.

"Marcus Brown will disembark at Fitchburg
RR station May 07 at 2PM STOP Meet him
STOP Come armed STOP A. Pinkerton."
Saxton started to have uneasy feelings all over again.

A special express train of the Fitchburg Railroad arrived at the downtown Boston terminal on the north side of Causeway Street precisely at two o'clock. Pinkerton agents watched as Saxton, his mother Muriel, Virginia, her parents, and Hans Larsen, waited on the long wooden platform. Virginia and Saxton had spent the morning reuniting with their parents. Saxton took everyone up to the Saxton House for lunch. The Anaona's happy crew was given a week's shore-leave with pay. Everyone including Jack was ecstatic about the Maasai's homecoming.

After a light lunch, the rain which had tormented the city over night suddenly stopped. A catholic sun spread out over the Irish city of Boston like a benediction. The welcome party left the Saxton House for the train station at 1 PM arriving on time with not a minute to spare. A Baldwin 4-4-0 approached. The Saxtons grew anxious for Marcus had been gone for nearly five months. Clouds of wispies hissed from Engine #321 as it came to a squealing stop. It tooted twice. Black smoke issuing from its slim black stack dissipated quickly. Passengers began disembarking, their luggage carried by black uniformed porters wearing red hats. The aging conductor, reported to the station master Tilson Porter at his office inside the impressive Victorian stone train station. After everyone aboard had left, one of the Pinkerton agents waved the little group forward. They were ushered into the private coach of the railway President, Alvah Crocker. Marcus rose to greet them apparently none the worse for wear despite his injuries. Sweet Daphne had performed a miracle. As Marcus moved forward, his head touched the domed ceiling. He took Saxton into his arms then hugged Muriel saying,

"I'm so sorry about Thomas. He was my father. I owe him so much."

Muriel reached up and caressed his broken face then pulled away saying,

"Marcus, I want you to meet my new daughter-in-law, Virginia."

He turned to greet her exclaiming in delight.

"Now Saxton, is this the gal you've married. Why, I as a Maasai warrior can have many wives but after seeing this young beauty, I wouldn't trade her for thirty cows." He paused, his black eyes looking down upon her mischievously,

"But, for fifty I might!" He laughed uproariously.

Virginia retorted in jest,

"My dearest Sax, now I know for sure that I'm worth at least thirty cows, maybe even fifty." Saxton wisely stayed mute.

She turned to her parents Cerile and Miriam Rowland.

"Marcus, I'd like to introduce you to my parents."

She stepped aside as Marcus shook hands with them. She could already see the mind of her father trying to figure out how long a coffin would be needed for the giant man in front of him. Marcus had lost a lot of weight but seemed to be fine physically. Time would tell if his mental acumen was still as astute as ever.

Their black Landau coach came right up to the railcar. They were ushered into it but were told not to raise the blinds. Marcus carried a small brown canvas sack over his shoulder. They were off. Occasional shafts of light pierced the gloom inside the coach as it bumped over the brick streets of Boston. Marcus knew about the precautions. Tyler Wicks had been quite specific. Wicks detrained a few miles outside of Boston as other agents took over. Before they parted, they had one last shell game. This time Marcus let Wicks win. Tyler was pleased but suspicious just the same. On their journey by train, riverboat and on horseback, they'd become fast friends.

The Rowlands were dropped off at their funeral parlor. A few blocks further on, the coach continued up Thatcher Street towards the Saxton House far above it. After a few moments, Marcus realized that Cerile had been sizing him up. He murmured to Virginia discreetly.

"I wondered why your father was looking me up and down. My coffin will be on the next train for sure, ready and waiting." Muriel heard him.

"I know for a fact, he has mine with my name on it, bought and paid for." Saxton was appalled,

"Really mother, that's so depressing. Can't we talk about something else?" Saxton agreed. They were just passing Louisburg Square situated atop a low hill. He turned to Virginia and said,

"My dear Virginia, do you know what the British called Louisburg Square in 1775?" She replied, "Why no dear I do not." Saxton grinned.

"They called it Mount Whoredom." His mother sputtered, "Why I never...!"

Their coach continued awhile longer, the horse's hooves clopping a seductive rhythm on the cobble stones. Without warning, the coach lurched forward violently as pistols were fired nearby. Saxton jumped up, grabbed Virginia and put her beside his mother. Virginia reached into her bag and withdrew a two shot derringer. Muriel nodded approval. More shots were fired. Their driver screamed. The coach fled totally out of control. Saxton put a .31 Colt baby dragoon in his pocket. Muriel still remained calm. Marcus nodded at Saxton as the coach slewed from side to side. Both opened the coach doors on either side and swung their bodies out into blinding sunlight. In an instant they were gone. To Virginia it was déjà vu all over again.

Marcus grabbed the roof's iron luggage rack, swinging easily up and onto it. Saxton hit the ground running straight for some black alder bushes. The driver tumbled off onto the road into a ditch just down apace from him. Meanwhile Marcus took over the reins, flaying the team with renewed vigor. The Saxton House loomed above him on Copps Hill. Marcus wedged his Colt .44 between the edge of the driver's padded seat and the back board. A large man stepped out of the bushes brandishing a sawed off shotgun. At that moment another on horseback rode by the coach. He fired twice. The shotgun flew into the air as the man went down. Two more horsemen raced by to disappear around a sharp bend of Margin Street ahead. Gunshots echoed. A body fell across the road just in front of the coach. Marcus could not stop. The man was crushed where he lay. Sparks were flying as the heavy coach began sliding around another hairpin bend, its team in full flight.

Saxton rolled into the wayside brush completely hidden within its dark fastness. Next to him a few yards away was Simpson his driver. They locked eyes. The man groaned but indicated he was alright. Saxton heard the coach rattle up the cobbled hill. Shots rang out and then silence. He looked at his driver, signaling him to be quiet. His driver nodded, shrinking back into the shadows under the alder bushes. Voices from somewhere near them became louder; excited. One stood out in particular for it had a slight southern nasal drawl to it. They were very close now. Saxton searched for his gun. It was gone. One voice exclaimed,

"I'm sure I saw two of them leave the coach. I'm sure of it." Another voice cried irritably,

"Keep looking until you find them Hillard or there'll be hell to pay. Twice now we've failed to kill Saxton and that nigger bride of his. Christ! Can't anyone do it right? We had em' in

New York, had 'em cold but that Saxton clocked us good. You there, go back to their ship and keep an eye on things. We'll meet later where we always do. Now get goin'."

Saxton couldn't believe his ears. Sam Hillard, a spy? It was unbelievable but at the same time plausible. Hillard was Bosun on the Anaona. Larsen wanted him on the honeymoon voyage but Benson was selected instead. Larsen was furious. Was Hillard really a spy? Again Saxton was faced with more questions than answers. Saxton became angry, very angry.

Meanwhile, Marcus could barely control the four horses galloping in front of him. Saxton House hove into view, a sanctuary of granite and brick. Beneath him, Virginia was holding Muriel Saxton close to her breast. Blood trickled over Virginia's lemon yellow satin dress. The coach rocked back and forth. Muriel Stamford Saxton was dying, shot by a stray bullet. Virginia looked down upon the woman she'd known so briefly but strangely it seemed for a very long time. Muriel opened her eyes and tried to speak over the clatter of the coach. Virginia bent down. Muriel whispered,

"Tell Saxton I love him. Oh Virginia I'm so happy for you both. Don't cry dear. Not now or ever. Hold him close to you and never let him go, never! Remember, he's full of surprises just like his father before him."

She closed her eyes then opened them again as if a new day was dawning over the harbor below her. Virginia's tears were the last rites of Muriel's final moments. She caressed her face. Muriel whispered,

"Thomas! Oh my Thomas! Yes my dearest, we'll soon be one not two."

As the coach turned up the long curving driveway below the Saxton House, a lone rider rode in front as two more followed close behind it. This entourage was met by two more Pinkerton agents as the coach came to a shuddering stop below the mansion's front steps. Marcus jumped off, landing like a cat. He ran to its door and swung it open. He couldn't see through the gloom as the curtains inside were still closed. A wailing heart torn in two assaulted him. Marcus swept aside a curtain revealing Virginia, holding Muriel Saxton in her arms. She rocked back and forth, her face a mask of blood and grief. Virginia looked at Marcus, her mouth open but no sound was forthcoming. He moved forward. Muriel was not breathing, or moving. He reached in, lifted her into his arms and then backed out of the coach carefully. Packard ran down the steps towards him crying,

"Oh Mother of God! No! No! Please Lord not her, not her!"

Marcus carried Muriel up the stairs, crossed the veranda, pushing the front door aside with a boot. He turned towards the warming room followed by Packard. They laid Muriel out on a long couch. Millie ran into the room, her hands to her mouth. Packard told her to get hot water and rags. She ran out. Jack the terrier wandered in pushing his red ball in front of him with his nose. Packard scooped him up.

"I'll put him in Mrs. Saxton's bedroom, besides her bed will need fresh linen. I'll report back to you when I'm finished."

While Packard carried Jack upstairs, Millie returned with a jug of hot water and clean cloths. Virginia came into the room, her dress covered in blood. She was weeping softly. Steeling herself, she said,

"Marcus, leave Millie and me alone with her. I've done this many times, sad to say but it needs to be done. We have to redress her, clean her up and get her upstairs before Sax gets here. He's in great danger Marcus. Go find him. Please hurry!"

Marcus ran out of the warming room. Virginia began to gently wipe thin streaks of blood off Muriel's face.

Saxton and Simpson lay hidden beside the road as the angry voices receded. A few minutes later, a posse approached. Saxton and his driver looked out from their hiding place. Luckily it was a mounted column of Boston's finest led by Chief Robert Taylor. Saxton emerged onto the gravel road holding Simpson erect. He yelled,

"Hold up there Chief, my coach was ambushed and my driver here has been shot." Taylor replied.

"I can see that Saxton." He looked down at Simpson's bloody shoulder.

"I'll have one of my men take him back to Doctor Wilson. He'll be ok, so don't worry."

Simpson was put on a horse behind an officer. As they galloped away, the Chief said,

"We heard shooting so we came right over. Who were your assailants and where they were going?" Saxton remained strangely silent. Finally the Police Chief inquired,

"What do you want us to do?" Saxton was released from his inattention. He apologized then began to issue orders.

"With your permission, perhaps some of your men could come with me up to the house and you could take the other constables to the Saxton wharf.'

Taylor agreed. Saxton continued.

"Tell the Finch twins that no one leaves or enters without your permission. I want you to arrest a Bosun by the name of Sam Hillard. He's a contederate spy. Send a man down to the Harbor patrol and put them on the lookout for anyone in a small boat that's acting suspiciously. Search the Anaona, the warehouse and the offices for Hillard and three others wearing long black trench coats. Be careful, they're armed and dangerous. Don't kill them, I want them alive. Now Chief, please get me a horse and I'll be on my way.

Saxton didn't have to wait long. Police Chief Roberts exclaimed with a flourish,

"Mr. Saxton, I do believe your steed has arrived on time Sir."

He laughed. A saddled horse was wandering down the hill. It stopped, neighing nervously. Saxton calmed it down, reached up and took the loose reins. The horse, a chestnut bay became skittish but relaxed as Saxton scratched under its chin. The English saddle on it was new and the animal had been well fed and groomed. Perhaps it belonged to one of the assailants? Saxton swung easily into the saddle and watched as the Police Chief galloped up and over Copps Hill to the waterfront.

Halfway up the hill, Saxton and his posse stopped. A man's body lay in the middle of the road. Saxton dismounted and ran over to the crushed remains of a man. A white face glared back at him. It was one of the men who tried to knife him at the Washington Park. Saxton rolled up his left sleeve. A "D" with a dagger through it was tattooed onto the man's left wrist. Saxton's gorge rose as he thought of his mother and Virginia. He ran back to his horse, and swung up into the saddle in one fluid motion. He galloped madly up the hill rounding a sharp curve just as Marcus galloped down towards him. Saxton reined in.

"Thank God Marcus, you're alright. Is everyone else ok?"

Before he could get an answer, Marcus turned around and galloped back up the hill. He just didn't have the courage to tell his friend that his mother was dead. It could wait. Further on, Saxton looked down at another body lying on the hill. He dismounted. This man too had a "D" with a dagger through it was on his left wrist. Saxton looked at the pug nosed face of a man who attacked him in New York City.

Muriel Saxton was laid to rest inside the Saxton crypt in Copp's Cemetery as she had wished. Minister Norland conducted an austere service, while Saxton gave an equally reserved eulogy. Pinkerton agents patrolled the grounds outside the church. Muriel's open coffin was slowly lowered into a marble grotto. It started to rain heavily outside. Within the cramped confines of the mausoleum, a dozen wreaths were scattered about. Saxton, with Jack in his arms, put a little red rubber ball in between his mother's clasped hands. He looked askance as he closed the lid. Two men slid a heavy marble lid into place. Jack whined as his mistress vanished.

After Muriel's internment, the funeral party arrived back at the Saxton House without incident. Packard had preceded them. The reception lunch was wasted on the dismal group sitting before it. Saxton was beyond grief, totally consumed by hate. Virginia knew her husband was firmly within the grasp of disbelief. Only her love could temper the steel within his heart. She listened carefully as Allan Pinkerton explained what happened in more detail. He stood up puffing on a cigar. Saxton sat before him. Pinkerton spoke gravely,

"My dear Saxton, I got your wire about Hillard. We'll get him. I'm so sorry about Muriel. I guess we didn't have enough men to do a proper job. They were obviously gunning for you." Saxton looked up. Pinkerton pressed on quite aware any questioning could be distasteful at such an occasion.

"Now Sir, you're absolutely sure the two men on the road were the same men that attacked you in New York?" Saxton nodded.

"And these men all had the same tattoo, a capital "D" with a dagger through it?"

"Yes."

Marcus slapped the table rattling the heavy silverware lying upon it then sat back exhausted. He cried,

"I've seen that tattoo in New Orleans on two of the men who hunted my family. It was exactly the same, a "D" and dagger. Their leader was a Customs Captain, a Horatio Garrow. It was his gang that attacked my family. I'm sure of it. I tracked the bastard all the way to Memphis. He damned near killed me on the river getting there. I jumped his train but got knocked off near Chattanooga. Would have died too if it hadn't been for Sweet Daphne and Big Willie. Tyler Wicks found me and brought me here." Pinkerton explained.

"Indeed he did Marcus. I wired Wicks to find you and bring you here because we need you badly. Garrow and his Deacon gang will have to wait. It's the war. We've bigger fish to fry now. President Lincoln and Congress have as of two days ago, authorized 'Project Maasai Ranger'." Marcus was startled. He rose up and replied,

"Don't keep me in suspense my friend. Just what is this so called 'Maasai Ranger Project'?" Pinkerton looked up.

"All in good time Marcus, all in good time." His response didn't sit well with the big Maasai.

"With all due respect Sir, I have to get back to New Orleans. I haven't seen my wife and son in over five months. Belle's in extreme danger. Tyler told me she was a spy for the Union, and has been for three years. I never had a clue. God knows where Garrow is. With the blockade of New Orleans by the Union, Belle will be in even greater danger if there's any panic. I'll need a ship." He faced Saxton expectantly.

"You don't have to ask Marcus, the Anaona is yours. I mean literally yours." Marcus looked puzzled.

"What do you mean Sax?

"Thomas willed you the ship. It's all yours to do with as you please."

Marcus was stunned,

"All mine?"

"Yes, all yours and that's not all. Stay here. Allan, come with me please."

The two men rose and left the room. A few minutes later, they returned carrying a large wooden strongbox between them. Marcus recognized it instantly.

"It's Wilkin's chest of double eagles. How did you get it?"

"It's a long story."

Virginia rose and cleared away some dishes on the table to make room for it. The chest landed on the table with a thump. Marcus stood up.

"May I?" Saxton nodded. Marcus lifted the lid. Before him, lay the golden treasure. Saxton put his hand on the Maasai's shoulder.

"I have something to say my friend. You'd better sit down."

Marcus sat down wondering what was next. Saxton continued to stand as he explained.

"Last New Years eve, here at the Saxton House, a company of esteemed citizens from government, the arts and others were here. They'd come to honor the heroes of the 'Battle of Boston Harbor' and to address the state of the Union. Myself, and a Captain Gibbon, now deceased, were so honored. Sadly, Marcus you were not here. So, to be brief, in recognition of your heroism in New Orleans, and your exposure of 'False Prophet', you have been deservedly rewarded. Former President Buchanan has made you a full citizen of these United States, you are immune to the Fugitive Slave Act, you are going to get a key to the City of Boston and you have been given clear title to the Anaona. And now to top it all off my friend, I give you the golden spoils of battle. What do you have to say Marcus? Speak up; don't be modest!"

Marcus tried but he didn't have the mouth for it.

BOOK TWO: CHAPTER 3
THE BEGINNING

Two days later. Saxton, Virginia, Marcus, , Allan Pinkerton, Captain Wainwright, John Ericson, Commander Franklin of Boston's Charlestown Naval Yard, and a Colonel Robert Shaw spent most of the day, fleshing out the details of 'Operation Maasai Ranger'. Hans Larsen was included in the entourage. Pinkerton told Saxton he had his reasons and that patience was a virtue. Saxton and Marcus were not happy but they had learned to trust the little detective.

After much discussion back and forth, it was finally decided the Rangers would use a specially outfitted ship as their base of operations. From it, they would infiltrate behind enemy lines wreaking death, destruction, disruption and distraction. Thus the Rebels would be forced to reassign valuable assets to try and stop the Ranger's depredations. Only Marcus or Saxton would reveal to the Rangers where they were headed but not until after they'd sailed. Their lives depended on secrecy. West Point Academy on the Hudson River, fifty miles upriver from New York City would be their training grounds. Marcus immediately volunteered his ship but was politely turned down. Pinkerton looked across at him,

"I'm sorry, Marcus but this ship will have to be built from the keel up. It'll be one hundred and fifty feet in length by thirty-two feet wide. You'll understand why soon enough." Marcus leaned forward.

"Could it be called the Nimsi in honor of my little brother who was killed by a lion many years ago? The name means 'Commander or Colonel' in Swahili." They all agreed. Pinkerton continued.

"Before I begin, I'm here at the express wishes of the President and Secretary of War, Stanton. I speak for them and as such convey their best wishes to all of you here today. What I'm about to tell you is strictly confidential. Do all of you here understand the implications of that?" He waited then continued, satisfied as to the veracity of their allegiance.

"Splendid, let's get started shall we? Remember, no taking notes for security reasons. Thank you. Mr. John Ericsson, the designer of the Nimsi, would you fill us all in on the details please. I dare say these plans are unlike anything I've ever seen before."

Saxton pulled the service cord twice. Packard arrived soon after with more refreshments. Ericsson, a short muscular Swede sported magnificent mutton-chop whiskers. He laid out some design drawings on the dining room table. The plans were astounding to say the least.

The vessel would be fitted with a double expansion steam engine from the Etna Iron works of New York City. The double ended hull was to be camouflaged; streaked with brown, green and black splotches of paint. The wheelhouse; a round turret encircled by rectangular windows, lay low, barely two feet above the deck. Because the ship was capable of sailing backwards or forwards, the watertight wheelhouse could rotate through three hundred and sixty degrees. An armored escape hatch mounted on top of it allowed egress and ingress. Submerged and muffled exhaust pipes, one at either end of the ship, would emit invisible fumes. Coolant for the steam engine would be sea water/fresh water filtered through sand ballast before it ran through the boiler's two hundred pipes. The sides of the ship would have no railings or gunnels. In fact, when submerged, the ship would lie just below the water undetectable even to the most astute observer.

Despite the added weight of men, horses, guns, ammunition and supplies; its maximum draft was a mere fathom. The half inch steel hulls would be water-tight to such an extent that it could lie submerged with only a dozen air vents and its wheelhouse showing. Submerging the vessel would be accomplished by pumping water into its unique double hull. Water pumped out of the hull by engine or by hand would elevate it six feet above the waterline. Once done, watertight rubber rifle ports around the perimeter of the ship could be opened. The two Coehorn mortars inset into waterproofed wells aft and fore decks will be mounted on swivel platforms used so successfully on the Anaona.

Pinkerton watched the group pore over the plans, talking excitedly amongst them selves. Finally he rapped the table for silence saying,

"Please everyone sit down. There's much, much more". He paused, while holding up an enlarged photo before him. The group leaned forward.

"Here's the latest photo of a new gun, called the Gatling gun. It's being developed by a Doctor Richard Gatling of North Carolina. His prototype fires fifty caliber bullets from six multiple barrels at once if it doesn't jam. Apparently Gatling is trying to solve the problem but I hear that one of these guns can hold off a whole regiment. It's a real improvement over Ager's single barreled 'Coffee Mill' gun. An arsenal of Spencer and Henry rifles will also be aboard. No more single shot muskets gentlemen. Watertight drums inset into the deck would hold the ammo, wadding, ram and anything else needed for the mortars and two Gatlings."

He gestured for Ericsson to continue. Again, everyone was amazed as Ericsson explained the intricate drawings. Finally, after two hours he sat down exhausted. Pinkerton took over.

"My friend here, John Saxton, has generously agreed to finance the whole project. I do know that it will cost a dear sum, probably around five hundred thousand dollars to build and equip it for the first year of its operation." He looked directly at Saxton, saying emphatically,

"You're very sure it won't be a financial burden?" Saxton nodded no then said with a measure of hesitation,

"Mr. Ericsson. What about fuel? Coal and wood will take up too much space. The boiler will need firemen to shovel it. The noise will be deafening inside the ship. How will you solve those problems Mr. Ericsson?"

Ericsson, an inveterate inventor, stood up then paced the room. After a few moments he replied.

"I'm glad you asked. A new fuel called oil has recently been discovered at Oil Creek on the Tarr farm in upstate Pennsylvania. Apparently, it can be distilled like kerosene into a fuel that burns hot. Stored in a tank, it's fed by gravity into a boiler where it's ignited. There's no need for wood or coal. Apparently five thousand gallons could get the ship right into the center of Confederate territory, carry on raids and refuel at a number of places. As to noise suppression, there will be three feet of compressed coconut fiber packed between the engine room and the rest of the ship. We're testing other fibers right now, but coconut is the most promising."

He looked around for more questions. There weren't any. He continued.

"Good. The next thing will be where is it to be built? I suggest that it be built right here at the Charlestown Naval Yards where Saxton can keep an eye on it." Ericsson waited,

"Commander Franklin and Captain Wainwright, you've both looked at the plans and have approved them."

They nodded.

"You'll both be working closely with me. The War Department has given 'Project Maasai Ranger' top priority along with another ship I've designed. It is an ironclad called the USS Monitor. If that's all, I'm sure Mr. Pinkerton has more on his plate."

Ericsson walked over to the window. He parted the drapes, opened the window as the room was getting quite stuffy. He returned to his seat. Pinkerton rose behind him.

"Thank you John. Well gentlemen and Lady, if any of you have any suggestions for the War Department, I'll forward them along through channels. The President is taking a personal interest in this unique project. I'm sure any suggestions we have will meet with an instant and favorable response."

He looked over at Saxton and Virginia as he strolled about smoking his perennially ragged cheroot. He motioned them to rise and step aside, away from the others. He whispered,

"I must say, I've never witnessed nor want to witness another shelling like you two, and your crew endured as you escaped down the shipping channel away from Fort Sumter. For I, disguised as a Major Allen was invited to watch the battle from the widow's walk above General Beauregard's headquarters in Charleston. My, what valor under fire! My hat's off to you both. The President is thinking of some reward for the crew; a civilian award perhaps. Even though the fort was captured, your timely insertion of weapons, ammo and medical supplies into Fort Sumter was daring to say the least. It's too bad an escaped prisoner named Blackstone I believe, rowed ashore with a detailed diagram of all its gun emplacements. Tit for tat in the end I'd say. A certain Captain Garrow used them well. Both he and

Blackstone are extremely dangerous men. Garrow has taken Blackstone under his wing. I'm sure they're both up to no good. My agents are looking for them as I speak."

The trio returned to the dining room. The others were stretching their arms, engaged in small talk. Once they settled down, Pinkerton continued; a large drawing of the Nimsi lay on the table before him. He passed it around.

"As for the inside of the ship, it will be designed to hold twenty mules, thirty Rangers, a doctor, medical supplies, military equipment, sleeping quarters, kitchen, larder, mess hall etc. By the way, all the Rangers and crew will be black volunteers from the Boston area. Saxton considered a mixed bag but decided against it." Commander Franklin interrupted.

"Why not Saxton? I'm sure the Navy would be glad to supply men already trained such as those on the Monitor? Why reinvent the wheel? And, if I may say so, why not have a mixed group of Rangers? We are all fighting to end slavery you know." Marcus stood up.

"May I speak on this matter? I know what it means to lose one's freedom for I was once a slave in Dars es Salaam. I was nineteen years old when I escaped from the slave bazaar there. Today, I'm still a slave while you are not. For all intents and purposes, you're fighting this war solely over the economic control of this country. Whoever wins will not really matter to my brothers because after the fighting is over, I as a black man will still not be free like you or have the same economic opportunities as you. To the South, as slaves, we are indispensable while to the North as soldiers, we are expendable. Therefore, fighting for the North is the lesser of two evils. By having 'Operation Maasai Ranger' an all black unit, it serves many purposes. The Rangers will have to be twice as good as any White unit. Secondly, the very fact that we are black will send a message to the enemy that as blacks, we are willing to fight for an imperfect democracy that can liberate millions of our brothers and sisters rather than a perfect dictatorship that imprisons them."

Marcus sat down not to applause but to dead silence. Pinkerton walked over and shook his hand saying,

"Well said Marcus; well said indeed. I do believe that the only possible leader of the Maasai Rangers is my friend here, if he so wishes. Ay laddie the truth will out indeed. Saxton told me that you are a Maasai warrior. I believe it after what I've heard about your exploits in New Orleans. Well what do you say?" Marcus stood up,

"Thank you Mr. Pinkerton, I accept on one condition."

"What is it?"

"I want to rescue my wife, son and baby before 'Operation Maasai Ranger' begins." Pinkerton agreed with the rest. Marcus was gratified, saying,

"Thank you all; I accept the honor and I know my men will look up to me no matter what I do." They laughed.

Pinkerton turned to Commander Franklin of the Charlestown Naval yard asking him to say a few words. The Commander stood up; a splendid specimen, dressed in naval whites, sporting a large head of dark wavy hair and a handle-bar moustache with dazzling effect.

"My fellow compatriots, we are at war and as such, our sole aim is to win the war at all costs. The future of our great nation is at stake. Therefore, I commend the efforts of all of you in launching this unique and hopefully successful project. I know the Navy will do its part. Captain Wainwright and I have served together before and will do so again. Shipwrights and metal artificers are at this very moment coming here from all over the nation and abroad. Slipway No#3 is being cleared as we speak. Materials, supplies and machinery are on order and have been given delivery priority for this project. If we do not suffer any major setbacks, we should have the Nimsi ready in twelve months from start to finish. Our mutual friend, Donald McKay has agreed to lend his manpower and expertise if needs be as advisor to the Navy. However, he's sick in bed right now and couldn't come today. Are there any questions?"

There were none. The Commander sat down. Pinkerton asked Captain Wainwright to rise then said,

"Before you start Captain, may I say on behalf of everyone here that your considerable seamanship meant the difference between life and death when you and your brave crew escaped Fort Sumter. I therefore heartily congratulate you and I must tell you that you are definitely our choice to Captain the Nimsi."

"Hear, hear!" echoed around the room. The impeccable English born Captain rose gracefully. At well over six feet, he too had a commanding presence and an equally imposing voice, heavily accented by a cockney dialect.

"I must say chaps, that the only war wound I've suffered so far is a rather nasty cut on the head given to me by a lout with a rather large knife as I was leaving the loo." He continued drolly,

"As for my navigational skills at Fort Sumter, they were taxed to the limit. I was screaming 'Bloody hell' at the time while being forced to zigzag hither and yon trying to avoid sunken hulks, reefs and Rebel hell fire all at the same time.. Yes, my friends, fear and fear alone, drove me forth in a panic all over Charleston Harbor."

His audience laughed.

"Besides, I'm too bloody old for more daring do. I'm pushing sixty. In this man's Navy I'd rather be an Admiral sitting at a desk littered with paper boats. No, I have to decline. Get someone young, dashing, daring and completely devoid of fear or even common sense. May I suggest young Saxton, for he might not be black but he who pays the piper, plays the tune."

Saxton had gone very pale. Wainwright eyed him.

"Marcus told me that you've been taught all the skills necessary by our former Captain Wilkins while aboard the Silver Ghost. I myself saw your uncommon bravery while escaping Fort Sumter. Besides, you dreamed this project up, are ready to finance it yourself and you probably would be very quick to learn how to effectively use the Nimsi to its fullest potential. My dear boy; with you as Captain of the Nimsi and Marcus as Captain of the Maasai Rangers, you both would make a formidable team."

He sat down to loud applause looking rather relieved. Pinkerton concurred. Saxton rose,

"It would be my humble honor to serve our nation. However, I fully agree with Marcus, for other than myself, and Yates the engineer, every man aboard will be a black American volunteer committed to fight the Confederates and their specious racial practices. I hope my courageous wife Virginia here will forgive me for not asking her permission."

As he sat down, Virginia rose to speak. The room went very quiet. A hard rain had started up again. It beat a tattoo on the crown glass window panes behind her. Virginia had been visibly moved by what Marcus said earlier. It was apparent in her demeanor as she spoke.

"My husband Saxton and I had what you might call, a rather short, violent and extremely risky honeymoon. To appreciate life, one has to face death."

Her audience sat sphinx like in rapt attention. She paused, well aware that as a black woman, it was very rare indeed to be addressing such an august assembly of white men. Gathering strength from a beaming Saxton, she forged ahead, strong and resolute.

"However, we're both glad to be home. Saxton and I are stronger as a couple because we faced down the forces of fear together. We wed under difficult conditions, we honeymooned under very calamitous circumstances and we will probably raise our children in even more perilous times. But, we persevered and will continue to do so. I agree with Marcus totally, for it is amazing that our nation has through its short history, continued to persecute black Americans while at the same time allowing them to defend it."

Virginia consulted some notes extracted from her dress pocket. From time to time she became very animated, pacing about while the men remained mute, respecting her will and her passion. She cried out, empowered by the moment.

"Five thousand black Americans fought bravely in the Revolution. In the War of 1812, the 26th US Infantry Regiment fought with valor, many within its ranks, Black Americans. Recently, in the Mexican-American War of 1848, from the First Regiment of volunteers New York, the 4th Artillery, and the 9th, 10th, 11th and 13th infantry Regiments fought for America were Black. I'm sure they're dying in this war as well with honor and valor. Let us pray for them gentlemen." She concluded joyously,

"May God Bless them; may he raise them up in glory from the battlefield and may he silence the bigots that will surely await them as they return home victorious to their families. Amen."

Virginia sat down emotionally drained. Saxton took her hand, saying,

"And now gentlemen, you know why I love her so much."

Pinkerton rose, chagrined by Virginia's outburst.

"I'm sure gentlemen that we've all been chastised before but never like this. I thank you Virginia, as I'm sure everyone here does. Black Americans are still hurting, are still being hunted like animals, and are still living without basic rights that we enjoy. 'Project Maasai Ranger' must be one hundred percent black American; Saxton and Yates excluded of course. With that in mind, I'd like to introduce Robert Shaw of the 7th New York National Guard. Welcome Sir."

Robert Shaw rose as Pinkerton strolled to the window, where rain drops streamed down over the glass very much the tears of a grieving nation.

Shaw, the son of a wealthy and prominent Boston family, was charming and quite handsome. His parents, Francis and Sarah were strong abolitionists. They joined the Anti-slavery Society in 1838 and Francis was involved in the Boston Vigilante Committee helping runaway slaves escape to Canada. Robert was older than Saxton but not by much. He did however share Saxton's hatred for slavery. Only its total abolition would redeem the honor of America in the eyes of the civilized world. He spoke evenly as the rain striking the window panes behind him rose to a deafening crescendo. Pinkerton closed the heavy drapes, muffling the storm's outrage allowing the soft-spoken young man to be heard. Shaw nodded at Pinkerton and continued.

"It is indeed an honor from what I've read in the Post and Herald to be included in this august company of true and valiant patriots. Saxton and I have met in social circles from time to time, but our parents knew each other very well, not only socially but in business. Presently, I'm serving as a volunteer in the 7th New York National Guard. I was fascinated as Virginia listed the regiments that Black Americans served in. I've been told that very few of them were used as fighting troops but rather as cooks, clerks, latrine troops, transport troops, camp deployment troops etc. I, like the rest of you, know it's time for black Americans to fight not just on the front lines but fight the enemy behind those lines as well. To this end, this enterprise has my unqualified support. My parents I'm sure will contribute their considerable resources to this worthy project. I do believe that in your briefing a few days ago Mr. Pinkerton, you wanted Virginia to assist me in finding suitable volunteers for this venture."

"That's correct Robert. She knows people who might help us. Isn't that right dear?"

Virginia straightened up and addressed him directly.

"Mr. Pinkerton, that is correct. My family, through our business and our church connections can I'm sure be of assistance."

She paused, turning her attention to Shaw seated directly across from her.

"However, I do caution you Robert. This recruitment must be kept secret as to its purpose." Shaw agreed.

"You're quite right Virginia. In fact, they will be sent to West Point where they will be trained by a Lt. Israel Greenleaf. To be blunt, this project could only go ahead if it was trained by white offices. As to leadership in the field, the Rangers will be led by Marcus Brown. Every Ranger will become a master of camouflage, tracking, cold-bore sniping and hand to hand combat. They will all be of superior intellect, of good moral fiber, exhibit excellent physical stamina and horsemanship. They must be able to move fast under cover of darkness, strike hard without warning and live off the land. At no time will they ever execute the unarmed or the helpless. There are other guerilla groups on both sides as we speak but the

Masan Rangers will be the only group operating from a ship. They will, so to speak, be true Marines but clandestine." He grew more serious.

"However, if they are ever captured by the enemy, they are NOT to expect rescue. All seriously wounded will be left to their own devices. The simple reason is; that unlike regular troops they won't have the luxury of a field hospital following them over hill and dale. If they can get a wounded Ranger back to the ship, I'm sure that they will try their hardest to do so. However, because they are so few, they cannot and will not unnecessarily put each other at risk. So gentlemen, it will probably take months to find thirty such men who are single, preferably orphaned and willing to take the risk. They can expect to be away for two years maybe more if this damnable war drags on. By the time the Nimsi's sea trials are over, their training will be concluded. At that time they will embark at West Point. I expect that their final training aboard her will take less than one week. Suitable mounts will be selected at West Point. These mounts will probably not be horses but mules instead." Pinkerton interrupted,

"I'm curious Robert, what's wrong with horses?"

"Mules won't eat or drink to excess. They can't be driven to exhaustion, have greater tolerance to heat. They're fed and watered once a day as a group, are more responsive to voice commands, are more sure footed over difficult terrain, have a steadier temperament, are less skittish, are ill less often, and they don't need stalls because they don't fight for dominance. I rest my case; any more questions?"

There was only silence. Shaw sat down. It was now very dark outside for the storm had reached a crescendo. There was a loud knock at the door. Saxton said, "Come in".

After shaking his rubber poncho in the foyer, police Chief Taylor walked in. He excused himself then said,

"Mr. Saxton, I have some news. The Harbor Patrol found a man's body floating in the bay. One of the Finch brothers identified it as Sam Hillard. I personally looked at the body. His throat was slit. By the way as per your instructions, I looked for a tattoo but none was found anywhere on his body. He lies on a slab at Rowland's. Are there any instructions for me, as he was one of your employees, I believe. Apparently, he had no immediate family."

Saxton was shocked. This news meant only one thing to him. The killer was still out there and very close to home. Little did he know just how close he was; in fact Hillard's killer was in the same room sitting right next to him.

Two large oil tanks were installed within the SS Anaona at the Charlestown Naval Yards. After a complete refit, and subsequent sea trials, it steamed for New Orleans via Fort Jefferson in the Dry Tortugas in late January of 1862. Laden with ninety tons of medical supplies, it was on a mercy mission once again. Marcus was the proud Captain of his own ship. His crew was a seasoned mixture of black sailors from Boston and Gloucester. Saxton stayed home to be with his pregnant wife Virginia, ostensibly to keep an eye on the progress of the Nimsi. Its keel was laid earlier in June of 1861, under the supervision of

Donald McKay and John Ericsson. The slipways upon which it lay, was covered over with heavy canvas tarps to prevent prying eyes from finding out anything about it. The work on the vessel proceeded quickly; its top priority status notwithstanding.

On October of 1861, thirty handpicked Black American volunteers arrived at their West Point facility. A strict and strenuous regimen awaited them. During the process of recruiting the Rangers, a number of events took place concerning the affairs of the Saxton House. Captain Wainwright sailed the Silver Ghost to China. Months later it was reported that he and the ship were lost in a typhoon somewhere in the South China Sea. It was a sad end for an illustrious career. Meanwhile, Saxton continued to look for the traitor that killed his mother but without success. The attacks on him, his friends and family mysteriously stopped. Allan Pinkerton returned to Chicago. Saxton House was guarded by four huge mastiffs twenty four hours a day. Rodney, who served Saxton well in New York City lived in the Saxton stables and looked after the mastiffs. Jack the Terrier however, was still the boss and took instant umbrage at any mastiff foolish enough to cross the line. Flocks of Goldfinches and Red Polls still thrived in the hedgerows that bordered the circular driveway that fronted the Saxton House.

BOOK TWO: CHAPTER 4
LA BELLE MAISON

La Belle Maison was in operation once more, much to the relief of Belle and her rich clients. It had been closed since her family left the Ursuline Convent two months before. In early January of 1862, New Orleans, the largest Confederate city was in a state of panic. The Union Navy stationed in Key West at Fort Taylor and at Fort Jefferson in the Dry Tortugas, commenced attacking Confederate forts along the entire gulf coast. The city's defenses guarding the mouth of the Mississippi River would surely come under fire and soon. It was into this dangerous world that Rufus Brown was born.

The happy event took place upstairs in Belle's house on Rue Bienville. Maybell Clegg, a local Creole mid-wife, attended the birthing as Belle cursed every man she'd ever lain with except her husband. She missed him terribly and had done so for many months. After it was all over, the brown baby boy lay swaddled in her arms. Her son Cotton was let into the bedroom by his new nanny, Nancy Dixon. Cotton ran to his mother's bedside.

"Momma! Momma! Can I see the baby?"

Belle held the newborn towards him. Nancy crowded in behind. They both peered down in wonder. Nancy remarked,

"Oh Belle is it a boy or a girl?"

"It's a beautiful boy to be named Rufus after my grandfather." Cotton moved closer saying,

"When can I play hide and seek with Roophas? Can we play today?" Belle stroked his head gently.

"No son, not now son. Perhaps when he's as big as you, you can."

Cotton stood back pouting,

"What good is a baby brother if he won't play hide n' seek?"

The boy turned and ran out of the room with Nancy right behind him. Belle lay back as the baby's feeding time approached. She thought about all that had happened after Marcus left the sanctuary of the Convent for Memphis. The last she'd heard of him was through the diocese of Memphis. He had reached that city but then disappeared. Since then she was unable to telegraph 'Pinky'.

The nation had been at war for nearly a year but it had been a very successful year for Belle. Sergeant Raines allowed her to reopen the La Belle Maison. Apparently he didn't want to, but his superiors did for obvious reasons. He had no choice. Belle recruited her former 'soiled doves' and a constant flow of military intelligence once again kept her very busy.

Many frequent customers were high ranking Confederate officers in charge of defending the crescent city and others on the western theater of war.

Forts Jackson and St. Philip, seventy miles downstream would come under siege by Admiral David Farragut's Union fleet. If his fleet got past these defenses, New Orleans would surrender without a shot being fired. Belle sent her purloined information by trusted couriers to a secret central agency set up in the basement of Gallier Hall. From there it was coded and dispatched by Harriet Tubman's contacts via the 'underground' railway to wherever it was needed. Belle suckled Rufus, as more memories of the past came back to her.

The Convent had been home to Belle and her son Cotton for nearly six months. In that time Sister Angeline became very fond of Cotton. The Mother Superior allowed the young nun to look after him on a daily basis, teaching the five year old to read, do simple sums and indulge in finger painting and other childish pastimes. In the meantime Belle was free to wander about. It happened one evening after dinner while the nuns were busy cleaning up and getting ready for evening prayers. Belle finished her kitchen duties and was sent to the root cellar to tally up how many sacks of vegetables there were, for the Convent's large garden fed thirty nuns.

The air grew cooler as Belle made her way down the moist brick steps to the root cellar. She lit a coal oil lantern. The scene before her always gave her the 'Willies' as she called them. It reminded her so much of the escape tunnel from her own pantry at La Belle Maison. She pulled back a thick door and walked in. Shelves of Mason Gem jars filled with fruit and vegetables were stacked in tidy rows all around her. Belle wondered if there was a secret 'priest's hole' nearby. She'd heard of them in school when she was a student there long ago. Everything looked normal. Nothing was out of place. The darkness about her frightened her but she persisted. Over the next few weeks, Belle made sure she was assigned to retrieve food supplies from the extensive root cellar. Each time she went down into it, she expanded her search.

One day, quite by accident, she stumbled and fell. Luckily she'd already put her lantern on a tall barrel of sacramental wine nearby. As she was about to get up and brush herself off, she noticed a tiny shaft of light coming from underneath what seemed to be a solid brick wall. She was five months pregnant. She had to be more careful. Moving closer to the sliver of light, she put her head upon the cool brick floor. Belle squinted, trying to see or hear anything. A wide shadow broke the beam of light in front of her. Someone was moving about on the other side of the wall. She moved closer. Faint voices emanated from beneath it. She strained to hear more but a voice above her poured down upon her like hot lead.

"Belle Brown, whatever are you doing lying on the floor?"

Mother Superior Fargone stood looking sternly down upon Belle's prostrate body. She rose slowly and moaned.

"Oh Mother Superior, I'm so glad you've found me. I fell hard on the floor when I tried to reach for a jar on the top shelf over there. May I go to my room? Please help me up the stairs. I don't feel very well."

"Here take my arm child. That's it. Careful now, up we go."

Belle knew that the old Convent built in 1745 had a few secrets even the nuns never realized were there. Somehow, the voices, one in particular seemed familiar to her. She had to find out who it was and soon.

Although the Convent had been a safe haven for many months, it was beginning to feel like a prison. Belle gathered her few possessions, thanked the Mother Superior and left. She hailed a Hanson cab, taking Cotton back to 509 Rue Bienville. Margery Briscoe opened the 'twixt' door, for Belle had no key. Dust motes swam through sunbeams, settling on muslin sheets that covered all the furniture. Cotton ran by her to the kitchen wanting something to eat but the cupboards were bare. Frustrated, he wailed,

"Momma, I want somethin' to eat. I've had enough of nun's food momma. Please momma!"

Margery and two 'Doves' returned later with enough food to stock the barren larder for two weeks. Belle was lucky, as food stocks in the city were beginning to dwindle. The restrictions of the Union's naval blockade on everyday life were just beginning. That night, the new nanny that Margery hired, arrived and settled into her room. Nancy Dixon was a devout Irish catholic with flaming red hair and a matching tongue. Over the next few months, Belle spent most of her days in bed as her time neared.

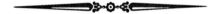

Major Horatio Garrow arrived back in antebellum New Orleans in the fall of 1861. He had been promoted to Major then reassigned by General Beauregard to the staff of General Mansfield Lovell. The Major's mission as a siege specialist was to improve the defenses of Forts Jackson and St. Philip that guarded both sides of the lower Mississippi River's approaches seventy miles south of New Orleans. The Confederates could ill afford to lose their largest city. However, Horatio Garrow and Harley Blackstone had other priorities to consider. Both men had met before the attack on Sumter, in fact only a few minutes before the shells started arching towards the Fort. Harley escaped with its gun map. This map proved invaluable to the Confederate's success in taking the fort. Harley was a hero for the first time in his life. But, he was even more. He was a kindred spirit Horatio could trust.

Major Garrow was given another task by General Lovell and that was to facilitate any blockade runners trying to slip past the mouth of the Mississippi River. 'Operation Anaconda' was strangling the flow of cotton leaving the Confederacy for export, and the flow of munitions going in to the Confederate war machine. Blockade runners were using high speed craft carrying small cargoes of contraband war materiel. They were primarily manned by

British Royal Navy officers on leave out of the Bermudas. Five out of six such craft successfully made their journey to New Orleans by way of shallow river channels flowing like arteries through the vast heart of the Mississippi delta. Unknown to General Lovell, Garrow and his Deacon gang were hijacking this contraband then selling it for huge profits on the black market.

During the crisis, La Belle Maison was very busy. Its customers were the very rich upper class of New Orleans. It was because of this elite clientele that Belle learned that Major Horatio Garrow was back in New Orleans. Even more ominous, was the news that his Adjutant, a former slaver, Harley Blackstone was his partner in crime and the new leader of the once dreaded Deacon gang. Belle considered the news of Garrow's arrival in New Orleans, his complicity in the black market and his resurrecting of the Deacon gang. She wondered if General Lovell knew of his criminal activities or if he even cared. Perhaps the General was in on the action as well. She didn't know but she was going to find out sooner than later.

BOOK TWO: CHAPTER 5
FLIGHT TO FREEDOM

The SS Anaona cruised southward towards the Gulf of Mexico. Once there, it set sail for Fort Jefferson in the Dry Tortugas located seventy miles south-west of Key West. The hexagonal fort, constructed of sixteen million adobe bricks in 1846, was still unfinished although it protected a deep water port guarding one of the world's busiest shipping lanes. Built amongst outlying shoals, its three tiered gun embrasures of up to 477 feet in length sat atop fifty foot high walls. With over four hundred guns and nearly two thousand troops, it was five times bigger than Fort Sumter. Fort Jefferson also housed hundreds of military and civilian prisoners stricken with dysentery, malaria and cholera. As the only source of precious drinking water thereabouts, six enormous freshwater moats fronting each of the fort's outer walls became polluted. The fort's numerous tidal toilets stopped working. Garbage instead of being burned, was constantly being thrown into the moat-like cisterns where it stagnated, breeding malarial mosquitoes.

The Anaona, awash with medical supplies, arrived much to the relief of the fort's commander, Major Lewis G. Arnold who had reoccupied the fort in January of 1861. The vessel arrived under a hot tropical sun at mid day. Marcus and his First Mate Edward Nelson supervised the unloading of dozens of crates stacked deep within the Anaona. Marcus looked up at the massive sides of the fort, each one ending in a corner bastion. He was in awe for it was much larger than any fort he'd ever seen. However, what really impressed him was its inhospitable location. The fort literally rose out of the Gulf of Mexico, its stone foundation strewn across a colony of eleven coral reefs. He thought,

"Desperate men built it, desperate men man it and desperate men have died trying to escape from it."

Major Arnold met him at the ship. Marcus invited him into his stateroom. After settling in, Marcus offered him a whiskey. The Major accepted saying with a large measure of curiosity,

"I say Captain, who owns this vessel?"

"I do free and clear." Arnold was taken back, exclaiming,

"I believe I'm in shock! You're the first black I've ever met who actually owned anything of value." He laughed.

"I do want to thank you though, for coming to our rescue with the medical supplies. I say, half the garrison is sick with dysentery. Many have died. The damn cisterns are impure and the garbage in them is most foul!" He raised his glass.

"Here's a toast to a total Union victory! As you know the whole coast is in a state of siege. Commodore Farragut is assembling a fleet of ships at Ship Island off the mouth of the Mississippi in preparation of an attack on New Orleans as we speak."

Marcus jumped up visibly alarmed. The Major sat there glued to his chair fascinated by the Maasai's facial scars. They seemed to leap like a lion from his face. Marcus was to the point.

"Are you quite sure Major that the Union is preparing a naval assault? If so, I'd like to volunteer this vessel. It's armed, has a shallow draft and can carry over one hundred tons of supplies and men. Could you contact Admiral Farragut or at least tell me where the Anaona can go? Please Major I beg of you. My wife and child are in New Orleans. If the city is shelled they'll be in peril."

The Major placed his glass on a nearby table. He stood up.

"Well Captain, you've scratched my back, perhaps I can do the same. Although very precious to me, please take aboard any fresh provisions you may need. You can refuel over there at the oilers dock. An aide to Admiral Farragut arrived yesterday. He needs passage back to the Union fleet as his ship is disabled."

Withdrawing a small piece of paper from a breast pocket, the Major handed it to Marcus.

"Here's a requisition chit signed by me. Could you come to my chambers tonight for supper Captain, say around nine. I know it's late but at least it will be cooler."

Marcus accepted. The Major left the ship through the shimmering heat towards the Fort. Marcus wandered out to the flying bridge. A squadron of grey pelicans sailed past him. There was no motion, no effort as the birds glided by. He prayed that Belle and Cotton would remain safe in the convent of the Ursuline nuns. The Anaona's steam cranes ceased their chattering. Minutes later they were clamped down, ready for sea duty. Marcus threw the bitter end of a cheroot into azure waters. A blue fish rose, sucked it in then swirled ever downward towards a white sandy bottom. Marcus ducked inside the wheelhouse, making his way to the galley. Sooty terns flew by, their passage marked by an obese sun being gobbled up by a voracious orange ocean.

Later that evening, Marcus and his crew sat in the galley talking; their ship rocking gently beside the fueling dock. The supper with the Major had been simple fare but a welcome change from what he'd been eating on board. The SS Anaona was to become part of Farragut's fleet paid for by 'Uncle Sam'. The Commodore's aide, Jason Wells welcomed the ship for many reasons. It was armed, had a shallow draft, was fast, and was expendable. The only condition Wells imposed, was that Marcus had to obey orders. This condition would be rescinded once his ship docked at the Saxton wharf in New Orleans. Marcus asked the crew if they were willing to enjoy a bit of adventure and a whole lot of danger. To a man, they all volunteered. However, Marcus wasn't about to obey any orders especially if he and his crew made it safely to New Orleans eight hundred nautical miles north-east.

They sailed the next day into a stiff wind. The Anaona plowed through turquoise waters which turned a milky cream then muddied a day later as they sailed for Ship Island. Three days passed then Farragut's fleet appeared spread out all along the low shores of the island. The Admiral's aide, Jason Wells disembarked. That night the Anaona stole away from the fleet and crossed the bar at Pass au d'Outre without incident. During the night of February 25th 1862, the Anaona crept by Forts Jackson and Phillips just south of New Orleans.

At the same time, as Belle rejoiced with the rest of the city's black population, rumors spread like wildfire confirming that the Union fleet was about to leave the Gulf in five weeks for the city. The air became festive from 'Nigger Town' to the French Quarter. Within hours, black joy was being replaced by white rage. Unruly white mobs began torching parts of the city along the river. Panic stricken white residents were preparing to leave the city. The Stars and Stripes were torn down over Gallier Hall and the Customs House. The Anaona eluded the Rebel river patrols by sailing only at night. It slipped into the crescent city's outer harbor unnoticed then laid up hidden between a derelict paddle wheeler and an outer levee. Into this vortex of violence, Marcus Brown would attempt to rescue his family.

Belle stayed inside her house. She had closed down La Belle Maison a week before, not because her girls were afraid, quite the contrary. The simple reason was that the elite clientele she serviced were fleeing the city. So there she sat in the dark watching mobs run down the streets venting their anger at anything that even smacked of federalism. The Customs House was torched but the fire was soon put out. However, more flames flared across the night sky along the river front. Cotton and Rufus were blissfully asleep quite unaware of the chaos growing in intensity around him. Both children were being watched over by an increasingly nervous nanny. Down the hall Belle lay in her bed but she couldn't sleep. The light from the fires four blocks from her house splayed out across the bedroom's lace curtains. Two Colt .44's lay one on either side of her. She prayed that her parents and little sister were safe. A growing sense of unease grew within her as the rioting spread ever closer. A Remington shotgun leaned against the nightstand next to her. At two in the morning horses and carriages began careening past her house in full flight.

She felt comforted by thoughts that ranged from her early childhood, to her romps with the Bishop, to her meeting Marcus. Her family was growing up without a father. Her mood changed as a familiar moistness flooded her lower regions. She bit her lip, rolled over and started to swear.

"Marcus Brown you son of a bitch, I need you now."

She put the other pillow between her legs. Her body started to rock back and forth as her desire for him increased. She cried out for him. Oh how she loved that man. The air around her grew warm. Clothes rustled nearby. A familiar musky scent swept over her as she lay naked on the bed. Her fevered brain realized that someone was in the room with her. Was it Marcus? She couldn't tell for the room was dim, and gloomy. A gun lay gripped by her right hand. Meager moonlight within the room diffused as a tall shadow crossed her mind. The mosquito net opened then closed with a swishing sound. Her bed sagged deeply. She held her breath as familiar hands caressed her full breasts. The pillow between her thighs vanished. Soft lips kissed her belly then traveled slowly upwards. Her gun dropped to the carpet with a thud. Hot breath lay upon her heaving body like a summer's fog on a distant shore. Two bodies met with passion as he entered her. Hours later, their ardor spent, they succumbed to a deep sleep. Simba had returned to the pride and the pride was whole again.

A crackling of shattered glass in the early morning hours woke them up. Marcus roused Belle. She became aware that something terrible, something dark had just happened. Light, harsh and more intense than any sunlight, crawled past their bedroom window. Joyful voices rose as one as someone in the street below yelled,

"Yer gonna burn boy! Yer gonna burn in hell tonight 'Big Nigger'!"

Marcus parted the four poster mosquito netting and ran to a window throwing back its heavy silk drapes that covered the plantation shutters. Silver light glistened off his sweating black torso like drops of liquid mercury. Below him Harley Blackstone waved a flaming torch. Their eyes locked as it did long ago on the Wanderlust. Harley laughed looking up at Marcus frozen high above the frenzied crowd. He yelled,

"Well boys, we might as well fry the nigger bitch too and all her little whoring spies in one go."

A ragged cheer cleft the night air. Roaring along like a freight train, the house fire's intense heat shattered the lower floor windows. Other houses nearby were set ablaze. Fear and hate, the evil twins of chaos hung in the air above the mob. The first floor curtains went up in a fiery swoosh. Snaking tongues of flame crawled up the front of the wooden façade like a hag fish looking for a way into a victim. Garrow came out of the shadows; unbridled glee gripped his entire being.

Belle didn't panic. She took her time putting on a rather raggedy old cotton dress. Marcus ran to get his two sons out of bed. Nancy had Rufus wrapped up already. Marcus opened the 'Twixt' door to rouse the working girls boarding upstairs at La Belle Maison. Margery Briscoe was already dressed. The front of the bordello had been torched as well. Seven panic stricken girls huddled together in the 'Arabian Nights' bedroom. Briscoe was Irish and as such had faced exactly the same thing in Ireland as the British burned her Ti down one winter night leaving her homeless. She slapped Naiomi across the face to stop her hysterics. It worked. They had to move fast or they'd all be burned alive. There wasn't much time to dress. The lower floors of both houses were ablaze. Dense black smoke began to seep into the second floor. The girls screamed as another brick shattered an upper window. A fiery torch sailed through it, alighting on a bed. A loud 'SWOOSH' was enough to get the girls moving through the 'Twixt' door to where Marcus and his family were waiting.

Garrow was in his glory. He reveled in violence and destruction like a termite enjoying a tasty piece of wood. Mother Superior Fargone had been sympathetic to his cause as was the Bishop. He knew Belle found sanctuary there but couldn't do anything for the Bishop prevented it. Why? He was livid, certain that Marcus Brown had wiped out most of his old gang. But now things had changed since the war started.

Horatio was back with a new gang bossed by Blackstone and business had never been better. The Major surmised that Belle was probably a spy for the Union and a good one too, for it seemed that many Confederate clandestine operations for one reason or another was either compromised or defeated. He didn't take his suspicions to his superiors, for Belle was a prize that only he would take. Her exposure and elimination would be a feather in his cap, suitable he hoped for further promotion. He would drive her out into the open where his lust for her and the 'cause' could be consummated at the same time. Garrow guessed correctly that the La Belle Maison bordello was a very clever front for gathering information from an enamored high ranking Confederate clientele. Besides, Fargone had discovered Belle with her ear to the convent's cellar floor. Belle had probably guessed that Garrow's gang was quartered there. No one would ever have suspected that the Ursuline Convent's basement was being used by his Deacon boys. However, another enemy of Belle's had surfaced.

Mother Superior Fargone hated Belle for despoiling the Bishop's honor with her wanton behavior. She hated Marcus for scaring her so bad that she hadn't slept in months. But most of all she hated both of them because they'd peeled away the layers of false platitudes, and false beliefs that hid her bigoted soul. Thus exposed for who she really was, her hate was like an open book that anyone could read from ten paces. Revenge would be a dish best served cold with her lover Horatio Armstrong Garrow.

Marcus coughed again as the thick black smoke clawed at his lungs. He herded the terrified women and children towards the kitchen. Flames crackled behind them. The roof of the La Belle Maison next door fell inwards with a fiery crash. Surrounded by shrieking women, Nancy and Belle held on to the children. Marcus ran ahead into the pantry and pulled aside the secret door. From within the blackness confronting him, not a wisp of smoke appeared. Guided by Marcus holding a coal-oil lamp, one by one the fugitives rushed away into a black void. Moments later the roof of Belle's kitchen crashed down behind them. Marcus lit another lantern, giving it to Belle. At the bottom of the staircase, a narrow brick tunnel ran forward away from the burning houses. The runaways emerged into a stone alcove fronted by a narrow iron door. Marcus touched it. It was cold as a corpse. He pushed the door outwards. It squealed as if it was a pig getting its throat slit. Marcus slid through the narrow opening, holding the spring loaded door aside as the group made a hasty exit. Pirate Alley was deserted but not for long.

A large Landau coach wended its way down Rue Royale. It slowly turned left into Pirate Alley then picked up speed. Many hooves pounded the cobbles, the sound of which cannonaded off the brick buildings on either side. Marcus stood before it and waved his arms. The driver of the onrushing coach reached for a pistol but pulled back hard on the reins as

Marcus drew out his Colt. The coach clattered to a halt. Marcus motioned the driver to get down. He did so and was disarmed. A tattooed "D" with the dagger through it was on the man's left wrist. Marcus guessed that the man was stealing the coach for the Deacon Gang. He was. The thief managed to twist out of the Maasai's grasp and run away down Chartres Street. He did so as if the devil himself was after him. Marcus shot him. His target fell down heavily then got up and staggered forward clutching a wound in his thigh. Marcus grabbed the reins, calming the horses. The coach was empty.

Marcus climbed up onto the padded driver's seat and gathered up the lead reins. He steadied the four horses as thick smoke swirling towards them from some buildings burning nearby. Marcus pulled back on the thick leather reins with all his might, allowing Belle to usher everyone into the coach. Once inside, she closed the door and the coach lurched forward. Every leather curtain inside it was pulled down and snapped shut. The coach swayed like a drunk as it turned right on Rue Conti. Marcus headed for the Saxton docks. Meanwhile, the coach thief, although gravely wounded ran straight for a mob throwing flaming torches into 509 Rue Bienville. Garrow saw him coming. The man collapsed on his knees in front of him. He pointed back down the street.

"They're gettin' away Boss; they're gettin' away!" Garrow eyed him like an insect crushed underfoot. He yelled,

"Who's getting away man? Who?" The man spit blood. He screamed,

"The 'Big Nigga' is, that's who; the 'Big Nigga'!" Garrow reached down and grabbed the man by the throat dragging him up to face him.

"Where damn it? Where did they go? Tell me this instant."

He slapped the man. Blackstone came running up with the gang close around him.

"What's up?" Garrow whirled around, threw the man to the pavement and cuffed Blackstone across the head.

"They've escaped you idiot. They're probably running to the levee. We'll head 'em off. Follow me."

Garrow ran towards Pirate Alley, his gang in hot pursuit. Smoke pouring out from around the edges of an iron door inset low into a brick wall caught his attention. He stopped.

"Damn it all to hell. That's how he got away! Well he won't get away again. Come on men, a hundred dollars in gold to the first man jack of you that slits the 'Big Nigger's' throat!"

With a howl, the pack ran off past Pirate Alley towards the waterfront.

The heavy coach rocked back and forth as it flew over red brick streets. Multiple house fires blazed a trail ahead of it. Down Rue Conti it fled towards the levee. A scattering of angry men running about in front of Marcus were thrown aside like chaff in a strong wind. As the coach neared Rue Decatur, Garrow and his gang burst out of a nearby alley at a dead run. They leapt upon the coach from all sides like wolves on a moose. Marcus kicked a man in the face. He fell bawling into a gutter. Meanwhile, Blackstone gained a foothold on the rear of the coach. He drew himself up onto the iron luggage rack, a knife in one hand and lunged at Marcus, his knife flashing in a deadly arc. Marcus twisted just as the blade slashed into the horsehair seat beside him. Blackstone was caught off balance. Marcus reached back and grabbed him by his coat collar. The coach rocked violently. A shot was fired from within the coach itself. Another body hit the bricks, bouncing into the shadows. Another shot rang out from the other side. Garrow himself flew off onto the roadway, landing hard with a sickening crunch. He picked himself up and limped after the coach. No one stopped to help him. Cursing, he fired shot after shot at the coach as it careened down the street.

Meanwhile, Marcus used every ounce of his strength to throw Blackstone over his head onto the galloping horses in front of him. The horses spooked. They neighed and whinnied, panic stricken as Harley hung on grimly to the traces, his body prostrate upon the long bouncing tongue. Marcus gathered up the loose reins and lashed the team's flanks. Blackstone was gradually losing his grip as his big body bounced violently from side to side. The coach careened to the right down Rue Toulouse towards the Saxton warehouses. He looked over his shoulder as a bullet zipped past his head. A mounted troop of 2nd Dragoons had rounded a corner three blocks back. A few blocks further on, Marcus came to the Saxton docks. He couldn't believe his eyes. The company gates were smashed open and a mob was looting anything and everything they could lay their black hands on.

Two hours before, as dusk settled over the harbor, Edward Nelson, the First Mate, wished Marcus well as the big man lowered himself into a lifeboat. Marcus would go to La Belle Maison first, just in case Belle had moved back in. His decision happened to be fortuitous indeed. Edward lost sight of Marcus rowing through the river mists entombing the harbor. The Anaona remained in hiding near the hulk, ready to make a mad dash for the Saxton docks a short distance away. Its crew was armed and dangerous. 'Packard and Lincoln', the ship's Coehorn mortars were loaded with grapeshot. Meanwhile the crew took cover, their rifles ready. Two crewmen manned a Gatling gun protected by a thick steel shield mounted on an iron post. It could be swung full circle. Below decks, Connor Yates and his firemen kept the ship's steam pressure up. Marcus had said that he was going to be back by sun-up with his wife and children. Time passed then dawn broke over the crescent city.

Edward, high up on the masthead, watched as fires swept all along the levee. The Customs House was torched, its Stars and Stripes lowered. He reached for his Porro binoculars and focused on the Saxton warehouse overflowing with cotton bales and dry goods. Dozens of drays parked side by side covered the wharf which to all intents and purposes appeared to be completely deserted. Satisfied, he climbed down the mast to the flying bridge. Zip! Zip! Bullets started flying past his head. He ran inside the wheelhouse, pulled the handles of the engine room telegraph to FULL SPEED AHEAD then grabbed a brass speaking tube. He screamed,

"Give her all you've got Conner. The bees are in our bonnet!" He then ran out onto the flying bridge yelling,

"Take in all lines, we're under attack." The Anaona lunged forward, her twin propellers frothing the murky waters of the harbor.

Crewmen fell prone to the deck as the ship leaped ahead. Hot lead whipped the ship's bulwarks. Winking muzzle flashes from along the levee were targeted as the Anaona swung out from behind its hiding place. At once, a roaring hail of incoming fire was directed at them from every wharf and warehouse. The crew's Gatling gun spit lead at the attackers with devastating effect. Rebel bullets smacked into its steel shield. As the ship steamed towards the Saxton docks out of range, only an occasional bullet zipped by into a breaking dawn. Finally all was silent. The Anaona slowed to a dead stop, rocking gently in the river swells, a hundred yards from the Saxton wharf. It didn't have long to wait.

Edward resumed scanning the levee for any sign of Marcus. He glassed the warehouse again. There was movement inside it followed by a fiery explosion. Someone had torched it. Other buildings all over the French Quarter began burning as well. It seemed as if the whole levee was on fire. Edward looked closely once more at the Saxton warehouse. Shadows were tearing apart wooden crates loaded with dry goods and sundries. As they came into focus, he realized to his horror that they were black just like him.

Harley hung on for dear life, the terrified team still in full flight. Through the open doors of the warehouse they flew. Sparks from their hooves ceased as the team raced over wooden planks within the burning warehouse. Therein, blacks, their arms full of loot were swept aside. Blackstone was still trapped in the traces. Marcus looked down at him and threw his head back. He laughed. Strangely, Blackstone realized how ridiculous he looked, bouncing on the tongue like a rubber ball. He started to laugh as well. The scene was ludicrous indeed.

The Anaona began steaming towards them only three hundred feet away. Marcus pulled mightily on the reins, his right foot locking the brakes. The team came to a shuddering halt, quivering in fear, breathing hard and ready to bolt at any sudden movement. Marcus slid across the padded driver's seat them stepped down onto the front wheel. He jumped onto the wharf, ran back and opened the coach door. A pepperbox derringer stared him in the face. Marcus pulled Belle out into his arms. She cried,

"Thank God, you're safe."

Belle looked over his shoulder and screamed. Marcus whirled just in time to deflect a fist aimed at his head. Belle shrank back. Marcus yelled,

"Belle, get everyone out. A ship's coming to pick you up. Get going!"

Marcus squared off against Blackstone. They circled each other like two wary alley cats at midnight. Harley growled,

"I'm gonna kill you nigger. You won't get away like you did in Shanghai." Saxton replied,

"I don't think so Blackie. I see by your tattoo that you've made a pact with the devil. Now I'm gonna send you straight to hell to collect it, you murdering son of a bitch!"

Marcus stepped back and feinted to the right striking Blackstone in the face with a left hook. In response, Harley lashed out in a duo of uppercuts, catching Marcus by surprise. Staggering back under the blows, Marcus dropped to his knees. Harley moved forward and kicked him in the ribs hard, very hard. Marcus rolled away. He leaped up clutching his chest. Blackstone took out his Buck-knife and moved in for the kill. As he did so, the horses next to him bolted. As the coach's brake shoes locked up, a shattering explosion resounded across the wharf. Harley was distracted just long enough to give Marcus a chance to rush him. They collided like bull elephants. The Maasai's momentum carried them over the edge of the wharf into the canal. Belle shrieked. She ran forward to peer into muddy waters below her. A swirl of water, a black arm and a Bowie-knife rose up from the turbulence then were gone. Belle strained to see more but there was nothing. Deep below her in the depths, two giant men twisted and turned, sinking ever deeper.

Edward had seen the Landau careening down Rue Toulouse. His ship was a hundred yards from the docks. The First Mate telegraphed FULL STOP. As he did so, the ship shuddered, its two large propellers thrashing in reverse. Meanwhile, the coach flung itself through the mob and disappeared from Edward's sight. Within seconds he saw it shoot out of the open loading doors heading across the wide wharf straight for the water's edge. There, it slewed to a halt just in time. He watched as Marcus leapt down and opened a door. A woman got out just as another man appeared from nowhere. Instantly, the two began slugging it out on the wharf before him. Edward reasoned that the tall black woman was Belle. Other women tumbled out from within the coach. In the twinkling of an eye, the two men had fallen into the canal and disappeared. Edward watched the coach depart, pulled by a runaway team. As it fled into the warehouse, a troop of Dragoons appeared in hot pursuit. They fired at the Anaona whose momentum slammed it into the wharf with a grinding crash. The crew had no time to throw out a gangplank. The ship's mortars threw a duo of canisters towards the warehouse. They exploded directly over the Dragoons, cutting man and beast down with a terrible roar. More crewmen leapt forward, literally manhandling women and children aboard. No sooner was that done when the ship started backing away from the dock in a thrashing moil of propeller wash. Everyone aboard dropped to the deck. Wounded and bloodied, the Dragoons retreated to the confines of a Saxton warehouse. Their muskets blazed in response. Minie balls zipped by the Anaona's bridge. By now the Saxton warehouse was totally engulfed in flames, trapping looters and Dragoons alike. One of Belle's black harlots, Rebecca, screamed. She slumped dead in a pool of blood. Rufus squalled in Nancy's arms. Margery Briscoe grabbed a discarded rifle and started shooting at any movement on the levee. She yelled,

247

"You bloody bastards. I'll see you in hell first!"

She kept firing as Belle herded the rest of the group towards the safety of the wheel-house. By now the ship was headed back to the harbor. The firing stopped, replaced by the sounds of utter and overwhelming anguish as the warehouse hellfire consumed its helpless victims. Metal shell casings rattled across the Anaona's deck, tinkling in the scuppers as the she began to pick up speed. An acrid smell of gunpowder and burnt human flesh lingered in the air briefly but dissipated as a freshening river wind swept across the main deck.

Marcus surfaced just astern of his ship. Its wake slapped his face. He could see its Gatlings spit fire and the mortars throwing grapeshot through the dawning light. The Gatlings kept firing then one of them jammed as he swam down the channel. The Anaona steamed out of sight, black billows of smoke marking its passage as it pulled itself around a bend. Only the top of its smoke-stack was visible over the levee. Marcus knew it would seek safety in the harbor. He also knew that his crew would begin searching for him. Very tired, he rolled onto his back and floated, carried away by the current. Strangely, he was at peace despite the chaos flaring up on the levee beside him. From the shore he looked exactly like a black log floating through the morning mist. That was just fine with Marcus. He'd drift right out into the harbor where Belle and his sons were waiting for him.

A column of muddy water boiled to the surface of the canal. Harley emerged gasping for air. He choked, "That damned nigger nearly killed me again,"

He reached up and grasped a slimy crossbeam under the Saxton dock. Heavy footsteps pounded above him. Someone shouted his name. He recognized Garrow's voice. Harley cursed. There was blood on his right hand. He'd been stabbed in the left shoulder. He cursed even louder. Garrow called out again, insistent.

"For Christ's sake Blackie, are you down there? Come round to the ladder. You can get up there."

Harley let go and slid back into the water. Tremulous bands of aqueous light flickered all about him. He breast stroked to a ladder twenty feet away. A small skiff was tied up to it. It had been crushed. The name SS Anaona was neatly painted on its bow. Harley grabbed it, pulling it towards him. A hand appeared above him as one of his gang reached down for him. He grasped it and was pulled painfully up the ladder onto the wharf where upon he lay spread eagled. Garrow sneered down at him.

"Well Blackstone, are you having any fun yet?"

With that said, he administered a vicious kick to Blackstone's groin. Harley writhed in agony. Garrow hissed,

"That's for letting the nigger and his spying whores get away Blackstone." He kicked him again, this time in the ribs, saying

"And that's for not waiting for me after I was thrown off the coach, you disloyal son of a bitch." Harley screamed.

Garrow stood back laughing then whirled about like a wounded hyena on the rest his men cringing behind him. He snarled,

"That's what will happen to you bastards if you ever get out of line."

He unholstered his Colt .41 and leveled it at them. Harley moaned behind him.

"I have a mind to shoot the lot of you incompetent pricks. But I need you. We're gonna track down the 'Big Nigger' down no matter what it takes!" His gorge rose as he spit at them.

"Yes siree boys, we're gonna have fun when we get em' alive. We're gonna have so much fun you'll all think you've died and gone to Heaven. Well let's get a move on. Those harlets will look after us real good if you know what I mean." No one said a word.

Garrow looked back at Blackstone sitting up clutching his groin. He laughed. Two very nervous young men waited for orders.

"Get over there you two and help Harley up. Just remember he'll be really pissed off when he recovers." Garrow limped away, yelling.

"Harley should keep you boys on your toes for a while."

His demonic laughter was lost on a thick river mist that crawled up and over the wharf. It swirled around him as he limped through the Saxton gates down the levee. The Saxton warehouse was a crumpled mass of charred timber, smoking bales of cotton and human remains that lay behind him. After walking a few hundred yards downriver his attention was drawn to a black log floating way out in the canal. He stopped, watching it with interest then with a growing sense of disbelief. As it rounded a bend, the log moved slightly. It disappeared. Garrow screamed,

"You black son of a bitch, I'll kill you if it's the last thing I ever do!"

He fired wildly where the log had been an instant before. Bullets ripped the muddy water into tiny spouts that twinkled in the morning light. It seemed like yesterday. He was running once again down the deck of the D.H.January firing and firing until he was spent. And once again he could go no farther as the WHUMP, SWISH, WHUMP, SWISH of another steamboat passing by, pounded through his brain.

Marcus heard bullets shred the water behind him just as he was stretching his arms high above his head. Rolling over, he dog-paddled into tall reeds lining the opposite shore. A steamboat, the SS Saladin was fast approaching from down river. It brought back memories of him and Nate just two innocent niggers on a keelboat mindin' their own business. The five-decker smashed its way towards him. It was brimming with rich whites fleeing the city. Marcus waded to the levee then sat down on its muddy flank. The steam boat continued to bore down upon him. Aboard it, hundreds of whites lined every deck railing while looking out over his head towards the harbor. There the Anaona lay waiting. Its crew hoisted a three inch ordinance rifle out onto deck and spiked it down amid-ships.

Marcus moved deeper into the reeds for some of the passengers were armed with rifles and hand guns. Women in flounced dresses cheered as the men began firing at the Anaona. As they did so, a puff of white smoke obscured it then the port side of the SS Saladin's wheelhouse exploded into splinters. Marcus watched the hapless vessel veer sharply to starboard towards the opposite shore. Another shell flew over his head hitting the Saladin's red paddlewheel. Still many yards away, pieces of thick red planking rained down next to him. The last thing Marcus saw was the steamboat hitting the levee at full speed. The doomed vessel vanished as its immense boilers exploded in a ball of white death. Marcus was hurtled back against the river bank, deeply embedded within its muddy bosom.

Only the fact that an ebbing river had exposed a thick layer of muck saved him. Minutes later, a yellow rowboat bulled its way through the reeds near him. His unconscious body was carefully lifted into it by two crewmen. They rowed back down the canal past the wreckage of the shattered steamboat. Burned and broken bodies drifted past them, blown apart by the horrendous force of the blast. Alligator turtles began feasting, making the scene even more horrific. The rowboat made its way to the Anaona. Lining its taff'rail were Belle, Cotton, Nancy and the rest of them. Cheers rang through the air as the yellow rowboat bobbed towards them then tied up. More crewmen jumped down to help lift Marcus aboard. His broken body was laid out on the nearest hatch cover. Belle cried out then moaned deeply. She sat beside him and cradled his head in her lap, keening into a river mist that gently gathered around her.

BOOK TWO: CHAPTER 6
THE UNUSUALS

Boston Harbor lighthouse on Little Brewster Island flashed to starboard every twenty seconds as the Anaona neared Long Island in mid March, 1862. Its final destination lay directly ahead past the frigid waters of President's Roads nor-west of it between Castle Island and Governor's Island. Darkness cloaked the outer harbor as Boston twinkled in the distance.

For those aboard the Anaona it had been a narrow escape as they fled New Orleans. Well hidden in numerous sloughs during the day, the fugitives avoided every Confederate patrol. Their ship raced down the Mississippi River to the Gulf, passing unseen over the bar at Pass au d'Outre two days later as dawn broke over the eastern horizon of the Gulf of Mexico. They were free at last.

Marcus reported to Admiral Farragut at Ship Island. Marcus's ship, crew and its passengers were paroled with one proviso. The Anaona would report back for duty as soon as possible. The Admiral received vital information about the enemy's defenses not only along the river but in the city of New Orleans itself. He thanked Belle and her 'Doves'. Rebecca, the dead harlot, was buried at sea.

At sea for nearly a month, the Anaona made stops at Fort Jefferson, Key West, Norfolk, Annapolis, and New York City. Marcus was examined by a surgeon at Fort Jefferson. Except for a few cuts and bruises, he was fine and also very lucky. Over five hundred people perished in the Saladin explosion. A large section of waterfront shops and warehouses bordering the levee were destroyed with many more casualties reported. Sections of red paddle wheel had landed near SS Anaona. Marcus would keep a piece as a souvenir. The cataclysmic explosion of the Saladin had allowed the fugitives to escape unnoticed as they sailed down river for English Turn and freedom.

Hans Larsen and John Saxton were waiting as the Anaona tied up at the Saxton dock. They stood in deep shadows just inside warehouse No#3. The night was clear and cold. A full moon rose high in the night sky, bathing the inner harbor in a luminous light. Hans smoked his briar pipe and stamped his feet. After the ship tied up, its gangplank was run out onto the wharf. Hans tamped his pipe, put it inside the breast pocket of his woolen jacket and watched while Saxton strolled across the wharf. His long shadow rippled over the planks behind them in the moonlight. Marcus hallooed from the flying bridge. Below decks, Connor

Yates damped the boiler. The ship gave out a long steamy sigh of relief. Once again it had come home unscathed from another perilous journey.

Marcus was proud of his ship. His good nature augured well for him as his crew stayed in Boston or at the Saxton House. The surviving 'doves' had disembarked in New York City. Belle bought clothes and set them up in the St. Nicholas Hotel for a month, all expenses paid. After that they were on their own. Marcus wondered where Belle had gotten all the money to pay for everything. He asked her that very night after their departure from New York City. Their stateroom glowed in the light of gimbaled oil lamps as she walked over and reached into a closet. A raggedy black cotton dress was laid it out on the double bunk. Carefully she turned it inside out revealing a garment lined in thin yet strong sail cloth. Dozens of zippered pockets lay in neat rows. Some were larger than others. Belle laughed as Marcus stood there stupefied.

"Well my Simba, open any one of them. Some contain deeds to my New Orleans properties and other important papers."

He gingerly reached down and unzipped the smallest one nearest the bottom of the dress tipping it in such a manner as to expose its contents. Inside was a card-board packet sealed in yellow wax. He broke it open and spilled its contents onto the bed cover. Precious gems lay glittering before him like a peacock's fan in a warm rain. Dozens of cut and uncut diamonds, sapphires, emeralds, and rubies took his breath away. He gasped,

"My Lord girl, where did you get these?" Belle held a large uncut diamond up to the lamplight. Its crystalline soul glittered between her thumb and forefinger. She laughed as she put it back.

"Darling Marcus, you might say they were gifts from grateful clients for services rendered many years ago. I call this my 'Gettin' out of town real quick dress.'"

She held it up and postured for him. Her eyes gleamed like cut jewels in the soft light. She laughed as his arms wrapped around her. He held her close. The scent of Rosewater wafted over him. Gently, oh so gently, he laid her on the bed. She lay there naked waiting. In the Saxton House, Virginia also lay in bed with Saxton curled up against her.

The day after the Browns returned to Boston, Virginia met Belle for the first time at the Saxton House. A tall black beauty dressed in a yellow satin gown piped in black satin, stepped easily from a Saxton coach assisted by Marcus. Instantly Virginia was jealous, if not envious. Belle Brown was exotic, turning heads wherever she went for her stature and her clothes were stylish and classic. Atop the coach, pale blue Tiffany boxes containing gifts were handed down by Rodney to Packard's household staff. Marcus, dressed in a sleek dark blue jump suit piped in silver crowned by a tall black silk hat formerly introduced Belle and her two sons, Cotton and baby Rufus. Nancy Dixon and Marjory Briscoe were then introduced. Rodney jumped back on the driver's seat and swung the coach around towards the stables. He had to feed four Bull Mastiffs. They bayed loudly in their pens as he approached them.

A few weeks later, Virginia lay once more upon her four poster bed upstairs in the Saxton House. Jack whined whenever she moved about. She remembered how happy her parents were, especially since their first grandchild was due in five months, just in time for Thanksgiving. The Nimsi was taking shape faster than anyone dared or dreamed. It would be ready for sea trials by the end of the year. Saxton had spent most of his time at home communicating with Larsen over Company business by telegraph. He was also linked to the Charleston Naval yards. The happy couple was content.

Virginia dreamed of redecorating the entire lower floor of the Saxton mansion. The walls of the Grand Salon were recovered by a bright striped yellow wall paper rising vertically above a light green wainscoting. Gone were the heavy tasseled drapes. Instead, light off-white silk curtains gathered on the top, hung from floor to ceiling. All their old furniture would be replaced by a lighter, cleaner style they'd found in New York City. Duncan Phyfe had recently died but his son James delighted both Saxton and Virginia while in his furniture shop. The newly-weds were sick of overstuffed French furniture such as that of Charles-Honore Lannuier. Virginia's thoughts ended abruptly as someone tapped lightly on her bedroom door. It was Packard announcing that breakfast was being served. Jack barked and jumped off the bed. He could smell food.

Nancy Dixon stayed on as Belle's nanny aboard their ship until Belle and Marcus could find a house in town. Marjory Briscoe left shortly after she arrived, gaining employment as an office manager at a local tannery. Six months later she married its owner. A telegram arrived from New York City from one of Belle's former doves. All six were successful escorts, pandering to New York's rich and famous. They operated out of the Saint Nicholas hotel owned by one of their rich clients.

The Good Reverend Clover and his wife Miriam arrived one evening for supper just the Brown's escape from New Orleans. Virginia, despite Saxton's misgivings invited them to meet Belle and Marcus at the Saxton House where a formal dinner had been prepared. Virginia hoped that the Brown's would join her every Sunday at the Reverend's First Free Baptist Church. His church was beginning to attract some of Boston's influential white residents such as Francis and Sarah Shaw, the city's leading abolitionists. The significance of their attendance there was not lost on Boston's upper crust.

The diners sat down to an intimate repast, replete with Virginia's finest Christofle flatware, Waterford crystal, Stevenson & Sons linen and Royal Dalton china. During the course of the evening, the Reverend Clover watched Belle and Marcus very carefully, especially Belle who wore a stunning gown of yellow silk garnished with pouffed sleeves and trimmed in cream Chantilly lace. It certainly had not been bought in any of the shops in Boston. In fact, Belle had acquired it from a renowned couture in New York who in turn imported it from Paris. A rather large blue sapphire necklace magnified the whole sensuous effect.

Thus inspired, the Reverend began building up a head of steam both physically and mentally. Miriam Clover, being quite aware of her mercurial husband's shortcomings, stayed close to him with her hand on his skinny right knee giving him not so subtle signals whenever she detected his behavior becoming errant.

After dessert, everyone retired to the drawing room. Once comfortably ensconced, the Good Reverend was allowed to speak his mind. He rose up and with both thumbs firmly thrust under the lapels of his gray frock suit. He solemnly intoned,

"Dear Saxton and Virginia, thank you for inviting my wife and me here tonight. As you well know, the past few months have been difficult for all of us."

He turned to Belle like a weathervane signaling the approach of a sudden squall.

"Yes, difficult indeed especially for you my dear Belle, for you lost everything you possessed including your parents to the fires of hatred in New Orleans I've been told. I grieve for your loss. But, right here in Boston, we might be far from the war but we're right in the middle of another war, a war against bigotry. New Orleans has a reputation if I may say so, where the unusual is the usual. However, here in Boston, the unusual is like putting a bull in a pasture lined by red flags." Belle looked up at him and sweetly asked,

"Why Reverend Clover, what exactly do you mean?"

Marcus bowed his head and started praying for he knew what was coming. Nathaniel Clover was given an icy stare by his wife but now the poor man was in the grip of his own undoing.

"It has come to my attention Belle, that in the past you profited from, what should I say, the more puerile side of life. As such, do you plan to continue giving your special services to the citizens of this city? Secondly, the influential city fathers in Boston can be very dangerous when fully aroused. They do not accept people who are black such as you and Marcus. Especially a couple who are wealthier than they, are not willing to accept their place in Society, and are so physically different that they are perceived as a moral threat to those who for want of a better word, 'run' this town."

The Reverend sat rather abruptly for Miriam had grabbed his coattails and literally pulled him down beside her. Belle started to rise but Miriam beat her to it. She stood over her husband like Vulcan, the Roman god of fire. She glared at the poor man who shrank into the settee then turned and smiled at the Browns.

"I apologize for my husband's remarks. I'm sure he meant no harm but was only trying to protect you from dangers you two know nothing about. You are new to Boston but Boston isn't new to you. All cities I'm sure are basically the same, run by the same type of people, are afflicted with the same bias and bigotry. New Orleans, Boston, it really doesn't matter. My husband and I as well as all other black Americans living here, realize we are only tasty minnows swimming in a sea of hungry white sharks."

She paused, catching her breath, her emotions waiting to appear as her common sense was about to leave.

"Women have no rights and as women of color we have even less. My dear Belle, you are beautiful, wealthy, and a mother of two sons. You are unusual. You could never live here in Boston because you are too unusual. Could you run for Mayor? No! Could you get a loan from a bank? No! Could you become a doctor? No! Could you attend the new Boston Theological Institute on Pinckney Street? Certainly not! So your world is very limited not only as a black but as a woman. What are your plans Belle? Please tell us now so that we might be able to help you avoid any pitfalls here."

Miriam sat down. Belle reached over and took her hand in hers, then turned and smiled salaciously at the Good Reverend. He blanched. Belle leaned back and started laughing. It was a good old fashioned belly laugh from the heart that saved the Reverend from a severe verbal beating. Marcus was steeling himself. Saxton and Virginia looked at each other grinning. Belle dabbed her eyes with a hanky, daintily sipped some Jim Beam from an old fashioned glass, coughed then asked Marcus for a cheroot. He quickly obliged thinking,

"What a woman! But what the hell is she up to now? God help the Reverend and may God rest his soul."

He lit Belle's cheroot. She rose and paced the room, sucking on the five inch cheroot while rolling it about in her mouth. She continued smiling down at the Reverend. Despite himself he was being aroused and she knew it. Finally she stopped as she realized they were all as mesmerized as a flock of chickens facing a fox. She pandered to the minister's baser emotions,

"Dear Sir, I've had many experiences with lay preachers over the years. I must say you're the first one that was honestly trying to help me not lay me."

Marcus and Saxton could barely control themselves. Virginia became more animated, squirming in her chair while Miriam was needless to say, appalled. Belle continued blithely.

"My dear Reverend you have been forthright in your appraisal of my situation as well as extremely accurate. Perhaps I should make a substantial donation to all of Boston's white Churches. Or maybe I should dress in something provocative and stand on a corner of Scollay Square soliciting for a living. Would that make me less unusual and more acceptable? I ask you Reverend, would it?

I will never be usual like you. Usual to me is like servitude, you know how it goes don't you Reverend? You'll enjoy your usual dinner, give your usual Sunday sermon and read your usual newspaper.

Yes, everyone is enslaved by the usual pleasures and may I say from vast experience, the usual sins. Marcus and I and our two sons will never be usual but instead will be unusually blessed with unusual talents that an unusual creator gave us. Yes indeed, the usual things in life are unusually safe, that's how you survive and for what end? I ask you Reverend, for what end?"

Belle continued to casually stroll about the room. Only the soft footfalls of her new yellow slippers were heard in the deathly silence. Sensing that the right moment had come, Saxton jumped up, reached for Belle's hand and led her to her place beside Marcus. Miriam Clover on cue arose and dragged her sullen and obviously aroused husband out of his seat. She thanked Saxton and Virginia for their hospitality. They were escorted by Packard to their waiting democrat. Saxton ran over to the double doors fronting the drawing room's veranda. He opened them wide. He ran out and leaned over the railing, joined by the others. Even over the sound of buggy wheels grating on the pea gravel driveway below them, they could hear Miriam Clover giving the Good Reverend the tongue lashing of his life.

On the long voyage back from New Orleans, Belle became very interested in 'learning the ropes', so much so that Marcus, Edward, as well as Connor Yates, began to teach her. She quickly absorbed all the intricacies of navigation, using a sextant, flag semaphore, high pressure steam control, reading naval charts, and the actual running of the ship and crew. Belle blossomed under their attention. She took copious notes, never getting in the crew's way and never complaining as she swabbed the decks and took her turn at the wheel. By the time Belle reached Boston three weeks later, she was in love with the sea and 'her' ship.

Eventually, Belle decided not to buy a house in Boston but rather live aboard the ship. Connor Yates was quite taken by her efforts to learn all she could in such a short time. One day in the ship's salon, just before he was about to depart for a week of shore leave; they were all having a drink. Connor rose to his feet and said,

"Ay, Marcus, Belle's an Irish colleen to be sure; smart, beautiful and full of life."

He turned to Belle, doffed his oily cap and bowed from the waist, his lilting voice as light as a four leaf clover.

"Ay! Tis' an honor to ship aboard with ya dearie! As many have said afore me,

May the road, rise before you. May the wind, always be at your back.

May the sun shine warm upon your face. The rains fall soft upon your fields and,

Until we meet again, May God hold you in the palm of his hand."

Belle's eyes moistened as the old man spoke. She stood enthused and kissed the top of his bald head. The trio ascended to the main deck. After saying goodbye, Connor's words were carried away by a warm wind as he skipped nimbly down the gangplank as if he was crossing the Half-Penny Bridge in Dublin. He slowly walked across the wharf whistling, 'The Rose of Tralee'. They watched him turn about, doff his cap and bow once more. He paused, turned around then clicked his heels together. His laughter hung in the air like baby's breath long after he disappeared into Warehouse No#3.

Thereafter, living on aboard ship was what Belle and Marcus both wanted and most importantly, needed. At least behind the locked gates of the Saxton waterfront property, they would be invisible to the bigoted burghers of Boston despite the fact that the Maasai while in full tribal regalia received the key to the city as promised. In chambers at city hall, the Mayor and his retinue of astonished Burghers conducted the induction ceremony on a level of 'flabbergastation' never seen before or since. The next Sunday, the Browns, their boys and their nanny, Nancy Dixon, attended mass at the Cathedral of the Holy Cross on Franklin Street. The mass was presided over by the venerable Bishop John Fitzpatrick. Marcus and Belle although a social oddity, felt right at home surrounded by Irish immigrants who were equally discriminated against. The Browns had a double burden to bear; they were both black and Catholic.

Belle finally came to terms with her distaste for Boston society. It was preferable in a circuitous sort of way that she was willing to go to war with her family to get away from what she called, 'The bigoted burghers of Boston'. Marcus at first was against the idea, saying,

"For God's sake please listen to me Belle! The war has been raging for nearly a year. You and especially our children have no place on the battlefield or anywhere remotely near it. The very idea is insane."

Belle caressed his scarred face, trying to settle her husband down. She stood up to confront him,

"When you were a Moran, wasn't it true that the Maasai women and children followed their warriors into battle? Why not now? Why can't women fight for what they believe in? I certainly don't want our two boys growing up in Boston. I detest everything it stands for. On the one hand the abolitionists are all for getting rid of slavery at a Saturday rally on the Commons then they deny any black admittance to their churches on a Sunday. No, Marcus my darling, the war for us has two fronts not one and I'm sure that once this war is over, blacks will not have any more rights than they have right now. And, my dear as I've heard you say many times before, we'll fight for the Union because it is the lesser of two evils."

In the end, the two compromised to some extent. The family would go to war but Marcus would have the final say on how much war his family would be exposed to. While in Boston, the Anaona lay on McKay's slipway for two weeks. There, the ship's living quarters were enlarged. Forward hold No#1 became a private suite for the Brown family. Nancy lived in the master stateroom cum nursery. The Captain's cabin became Engineer's and First Mate's living quarters. A secret hidey-hole designed by Belle lay just behind the master head below decks.

The wheelhouse was completely swathed in steel plate. Iron plantation shutters protected its windows and could be instantly opened or closed from within the wheelhouse itself. The new additions included more water ballast which lowered the ship's center of gravity, controlled its trim and making its profile even more difficult to see from a distance. As soon as it left McKay's shipyard, it sailed for West Point, New York, averaging well over ten knots.

BOOK TWO: CHAPTER 7
THE MAASAI RANGERS

The Nimsi was launched without fanfare in the dead of night on December 27th, 1861. Her sea trials were conducted from a secret location on Deer Island, east of President Roads. Camouflaged during the day at the Charleston Naval Yards, her successful sea trials over the next two months were successful in every way except for a stuffing box leak for her aft propeller shaft. After repairs and more testing, the Nimsi sailed for West Point in late March of 1862. With Duncan Toller as First Mate and Saxton as Captain, both ship and crew looked forward to a safe voyage. The Anaona, fully refitted and commissioned by the Union Army, sailed a week later. Her role was to be that of a tender, supporting the Nimsi with spare parts, fuel, munitions and medical supplies.

Six months earlier, Marine Lieutenant Israel Greenleaf arrived at West Point Military Academy on the wide Hudson River by train from Annapolis. He had strict orders, to get along with its feisty Superintendent, Colonel Alexander Hamilton Bowman. Greenleaf's mission was to train thirty black Americans to wreak havoc behind Confederate lines then come back alive. It was a tall order but Israel Greenleaf was the right man for the job. Acclaimed as the hero of Harper's Ferry, he was intimately knowledgeable about General Robert E. Lee's military mind. Greenleaf had served under his command at Harper's Ferry. Both men were of the same age and temperament, namely calm, cool and collected.

A Saxton steamer, the SS Sea Rover, had arrived a week earlier at the Saxton docks in New York City. Thirty prime specimens of black American manhood duly disembarked. They were met by Allan Pinkerton who gave them furlough to recover from their voyage and see the sights of the great city. Slightly the worse for wear two days later, they boarded a Hudson Railway train to West Point Academy fifty miles upriver.

It was at West Point that Lt. Greenleaf and Superintendent Bowman met the new recruits and their recruiter, Captain Robert Shaw. They both watched as the youngsters scrambled off the train all the while being yelled at by a tough little Prussian Drill Instructor; Sergeant Heinz Leitzell. A cold breeze blew in off the Hudson shivering the young men lined up side by side at attention on the train station's platform. Captain Shaw stepped forward to return the Sergeant's salute. The Captain and Pinkerton walked over. Introductions were made all around.

The Sergeant waited, then strolled down the line, a short leather riding crop gripped firmly in his right hand. He'd occasionally slap his thigh with it. Although thoroughly briefed before hand by Lt. Greenleaf, Heinz Leitzell was going to make a memorable first impression. After asking every man where he was from, he was amazed. They were from all from Boston. He finally stopped, looked over at Lt. Greenleaf, Captain Shaw and Superintendent Bowman and barked,

"Gott en himmel! Thirty men, one city; I don't believe it! What next, the second coming of John Brown?"

The recruits rocked back and forth tittering. The officers grinned. The Superintendent nodded. Leitzell continued,

"Well now, before me are the finest specimens the 'chosen' race has to offer. We will see. In the meantime, listen to Lieutenant Greenleaf well, because if you 'Esels' screw up, you'll have to deal with me. I will be responsible for your accommodations here at the Point when you're not in the bushes eating grubs and getting shot at. You will wear an Army uniform while living here on the base but in the field your dress is up to the Lieutenant who I understand is an expert in Indian warfare. You must not fraternize with anyone at the Point other than with yourselves. And stay the hell away from Benny Haven's Tavern!

Your leader, Captain Marcus Brown, is not here yet to hold your hands, but from what I've been told, those who have met him will ever forget it. Apparently, he's over seven feet tall, twice as strong as an ox, faster than a cheetah and more cunning than my mother, God rest her soul. I also understand he's a savage from the darkest heart of Africa. While barely out of his crib, he started killin' lions for a hobby. His favorite beverage is Rebel blood mixed with milk. He also killed five good old boys from the dreaded Deacon gang in New Orleans with a paring knife. Cut their throats in broad daylight he did when they were sittin' side by side talkin' in front of a Priest on a Sunday. Rumor has it that he likes to chew on human flesh especially black flesh. So ladies, you have been warned. Now here is your instructor, Lt. Greenleaf."

He turned smartly about and saluted a very serious looking Lieutenant. He got right to the crux of their assignment by saying,

"Welcome gentlemen. Listen well, for after today you will be nothing like gentlemen. You will learn to kill by hand, by knife, by gun, rope or any other damned thing you can get your bloody black hands on. Just kill the enemy, if not, terrorize the enemy, if not, give the bastards nightmares, if not, have them cryin' at night for their mommas. You will run, swim, climb, jump, crawl, hide, freeze, and damn near fly by the time I'm finished with you. Anything you can do I will do better. Anything I can do, that flesh eatin' monster Maasai will do even better.

There are thirty of you now but in all probability there will not be thirty of you alive when this damnable war is over. So, to stay alive you must stay alert, stay smart, and stay hidden. Patience is a virtue; never more so than from now on. Remember ladies keep your pecker in your pants. Get the pox and no amount of pokeweed, zinc sulphate, mercury, or even a life time supply of elderberries will keep you in the Rangers. Do I make myself clear?" The recruits yelled,

"YES SIR!" The Lieutenant continued; his resolve unchanged.

"The Rebs are winning this war right now. Go south-west a few hundred miles if you want to see thousands of our brave men lying dead at Bull Run. Washington itself right is presently in grave danger. President Lincoln is relieving Generals right and left who are too timid to attack. Well ladies; timidity, defeat, retreat and surrender, are not in our vocabulary and never will be. However, stealth, patience, surprise, attack and victory are words that we will learn to live by. Do I make myself clear?"

"YES SIR!"

He turned abruptly, saluted Superintendent Bowman who stepped forward. In a more conciliatory tone he said,

"I welcome you to West Point Academy. You are the very first black Americans to train here as fighting men. As you well know racism, prejudice and bigotry are the three sisters that feed on hate, jealousy and misunderstanding. The Civil War will not change that. I'm sorry but it is true. However, you all have a chance to rescue millions of your brethren due south of here if we win this war. Today your presence here honors thousands of black Americans who have served America well since the Revolution. As I stand here, I know that you will serve her well again. I congratulate you all. Every man here is already a hero, already a champion; ready to be the best of the best. I will not tolerate any abuse of you by my staff or by my cadets. I tolerate total victory and only total victory. Do I make myself clear?"

The recruits yelled, "YES SIR!"

Colonel Bowman stepped back as Lieutenant Greenleaf saluted then cried, "At ease men, at ease!"

The sky clouded over as a stiff river breeze continued to sweep across the station platform. The recruits stamped their black leather bootees to limber up. Sergeant Leitzell saluted Greenleaf then spun about smartly. Dressed in a light green tunic and riding breeches, he stood back a few feet from the line of recruits. Leitzell snapped his little riding crop across the top of his high leather Jefferson riding boots. He yelled,

"Ten Hut!" The men instantly stood at attention.

"Well Ladies and I will keep calling you Ladies until you prove me wrong. Yes, Ladies it will be supper time in the mess in a few hours. So before you enjoy roasted grasshopper omelets and other delicacies, pick up your luggage from the baggage wagon over there and follow me. We're going on a short ten mile hike my little 'halbdackels'. Before that happens, Lieutenant Greenleaf wants to know what possessions you've lugged along from Boston that you'd consider essential in the field. For those of you dumb enough to even consider taking anything at all, our medical staff at the end of the run will be here to check the living. Our gravediggers will bury the dead wherever they have had the misfortune to expire. We'll be sure to notify your loved ones right away."

All thirty men stood, as if they were carved in ebony. The Prussian Sergeant smiled indulgently, put his fingers to his mouth and whistled shrilly. From around a corner, a beautiful black Arab stallion galloped towards them. It clopped up the station's wooden cargo ramp and stood beside the Sergeant who put one highly polished black leather boot in a silver stirrup and effortlessly swung aboard an equally polished black McClellan cavalry saddle. He looked down sternly at the recruits standing stock still, each looking straight ahead. He barked,

"Now my lovelies, you have two choices, grab your gear or don't grab your gear. You've got thirty seconds to make up your minds because that will be all you'll ever have in the field. Now move it!"

The Sergeant's steed reared up as some men ran to their gear. Others still stood at attention. Others began opening their luggage, frantically throwing clothing and other sundries away. Heinz checked his Hamilton fob watch and yelled,

"Time's up 'Heidenei's'. Follow me!"

He whirled his horse about, and as it reared up, he saluted the officers below him then trotted down the ramp to disappear around the corner. The ragged recruits followed carrying their gear. Some tripped over debris already thrown away. Others were still sorting through their luggage. But within minutes the Officers and Pinkerton were left alone. Lt. Greenleaf laughed,

"Well Gentlemen, is there an Officer's Club around here where we can get a stiff drink? I think I'm going to need one now if not sooner. My God, I've never seen such a splendid display of vitriol since I captured John Brown at Harper's Ferry."

The Nimsi berthed at West Point's North dock at twilight on April 15th, 1862. Fort Arnold loomed over Gees Point guarding the narrows but no one saw the ship tie up inside a canvas covered wooden boathouse erected to keep any prying eyes from seeing what Pinkerton called, "The Union's sinking weapon". It was only by chance when a soldier on dock duty took a leak into the Hudson River that the ship was discovered. There it lay in the shadows of the boathouse below him barely visible above the slow moving river. Saxton was quietly sitting beside the open wheelhouse hatch looking about. The young cadet nearly pissed on him. Saxton looked up and waved. The startled young man threw down his musketoon and scrambled up the dock ramp screaming at the top of his lungs.

"We're being attacked! The Rebs are here! The Rebs are here!"

A squad of unarmed infantry ran out of their mess hall towards the river. They jumped over the railway tracks and high tailed it towards the North dock. Their Commanding Officer ran after them, his dinner napkin clutched in his hand like a white flag of surrender. He yelled at them to stop. They didn't. Meanwhile, the Nimsi's crew had lined up along the lip of the dock standing at ease under a string of shining lanterns. All of them wore black fatigue caps, black cotton trousers, and yellow V necked jerseys covered by a light black cotton double breasted field jacket. Their rubber soled black bootees prevented sparking an explosion below deck. One of the crew held up a small American flag behind Saxton.

As the soldiers rushed down the dock's ramp towards them, they stopped like cattle trapped by a prairie fire. They pointed and whispered while waiting for their commanding officer to catch up. He did, puffing like a steam engine. Saxton grinned. The 'attack' on West Point was successful. He knew by gaining respect from the 'Pointers', he had a better chance of impressing the brass in Washington. Besides, his ship had sailed up the Hudson River for fifty miles undetected even though Union gunboats swept past them in the river mists barely twenty feet away.

Saxton's ruminations were interrupted as a squad of armed troops raced towards him with fixed bayonets. They stopped at the top of the ramp, rifles leveled. Their commanding officer walked briskly down the ramp, gun in hand.

Saxton yelled "Ten Hut".

The Nimsi's crew snapped to attention. Saxton saluted smartly. A clearly flustered Lieutenant man came to his senses, stopped, holstered his Colt .44, and saluted. Saxton moved forward, his right hand extended,

"Lieutenant, Captain John Saxton of the SS Nimsi at your service Sir." The man stood flummoxed. He croaked,

"Yes of course. I'm Lieutenant Walker of the 4th Artillery. I guess I'm pleased to meet you Captain. I had no idea that you were coming for we were at mess."

He turned and waved at the squad of infantry lined up along wharf's railing above them, their muskets ready to fire. Their Corporal yelled something. Instantly the soldiers lowered their rifles and marched onto the dock single file. They arrayed themselves in front of the Nimsi's crew. In seconds, the racial tension between the ranks became palpable. Saxton knew that anything could happen at any moment. It could get ugly very quickly. He stepped forward and whispered in the Lieutenant's ear. Shock registered upon the young man's face. He stepped back and saluted. Saxton faced the Lieutenant.

"Lieutenant Walker, I'm here on orders of President Lincoln. Here are my authorization papers."

Saxton took a brown envelope out of an inside breast pocket. He withdrew some papers from it carefully. He gave them to the Lieutenant who read them then perfunctorily handed them back. Saxton saluted. He addressed the Lieutenant saying,

"I would appreciate it Sir, if you could set a twenty four hour guard here on the dock."

The Lieutenant stood back and saluted.

"It would be a pleasure Sir." He yelled, "Corporal Diggins, on the double!"

Diggins ran up and saluted. Walker whispered in his ear then stood back as the Corporal turned on his heel and led a squad to the far end of the dock. Once there they halted, standing at ease while their Corporal explained. Moments later, they split up into pairs, patrolling the North dock with fixed bayonets.

A knock on Israel Greenleaf's door woke him up. It was after dinner and he was resting in his leather desk chair. He said gruffly,

"Come in and close the door behind you!" The door opened. Superintendent Bowman walked into the tiny office. Lieutenant Greenleaf jumped up. Bowman returned his salute.

"Sorry Sir, I thought it was Davis Sir." Bowman smiled.

"The Nimsi has arrived Lieutenant. Apparently, it's tied up at the North dock right now. All one hundred and fifty feet of it somehow sailed up the Hudson River through the picket sloops completely undetected until now. Amazing! Some green cadet on guard duty was taking a leak from the pier and didn't see it. When he did, he messed his pants, dropped his musket and fled. I'm sure his parents will understand why I'm sending him home. This man's Army has no place for cowardice. Follow me Lieutenant."

Within minutes, Lieutenant Greenleaf and Superintendent Bowman tramped down the dock ramp. Standing under the row of glowing kerosene lamp standards, everyone came to attention. Lieutenant Walker and his soldiers not on guard duty marched away to their mess hall. Colonel Bowman returned Saxton's salute. After introductions, the ship's crew was inspected closely by the two officers. Saxton was very proud of them for they answered all questions simply and directly. After the inspection was over, Saxton dismissed them and sent them back to their duties. As one, they saluted, spun around and marched back into the ship. The Colonel exclaimed,

"I must say Captain Saxton that this might be the finest crew I've ever laid eyes on for they're a lot better than the scurvy laggards I had to deal with when building Fort Sumter."

"Thank you Sir. I remember Fort Sumter well." The Superintendent grinned.

"I've heard. Well done young man. The President has spoken fondly of you. I understand that 'Project Maasai Ranger' is your idea."

"Yes Colonel; mine as well as that of a lot of other people such as Lieutenant Greenleaf, Captain Robert Shaw, Alan Pinkerton, President Lincoln and others."

"The President you say. I'm impressed. Do you have your authorization papers Captain?"

"Certainly Colonel." Saxton presented them. The Colonel surveyed them under a hurricane lamp while carefully riffling through the sheaf of papers.

"Indeed Captain, I see the I's having been dotted and the T's crossed, I'll take my copies and give you back the rest now. However, we'll both sign off on these tomorrow in my office." Saxton returned them to his inside vest pocket. He thought,

'Well the politicians have had their say, the bureaucrats will have their papers signed in triplicate and then the military, hopefully will get out the hell out of my way.'

Saxton invited them aboard for drinks. They accepted. Once comfortably seated in Saxton's cabin, they relaxed. Lt. Greenleaf spoke up,

"Congratulations, Captain Saxton, it's quite the ship you have. Don't believe there's another like it, so be careful and don't sink it on us while it's here." Bowman laughed, took a sip of Beam and said,

"Captain, you and your crew are to be commended for a job well done. Tomorrow you'll berth below the Marine Battery just across from us."

Lt. Greenleaf picked up the conversation as Saxton reached for the bottle of Jim Beam beside him. He explained further.

"The Army engineers have built a camouflaged berth over there for your ships. For the past five months, the Rangers have trained here and over there depending on ice conditions in the river. Their last week of training will start tomorrow on Constitution Island. Right now however, they're in their main camp at Delafield Pond. The poor devils have endured Sergeant Leitzell, and the mules for what seems to them to be an eternity. No one has dropped dead so far but I dare say half of them still want their mommas." They laughed. Saxton refreshed their drinks saying,

"Thank you Colonel Bowman and Lt. Greenleaf, I'm sure the Rangers have been working hard. I'm really anxious to see them. However, their real leader is Captain Marcus Brown, not I. I'll have to just wait for him to show up. Knowing Marcus, his introduction to the Rangers will be different to say the least. So, where were we Lieutenant? Ah yes, as you were saying, there's a special training camp across the river."

After breakfast the next day, Saxton stood on the Nimsi's deck looking across the broad waters of the Hudson River. Half a mile away and directly across from Gees point lay Constitution Island. In reality it wasn't an island at all but a peninsula; the eastern half of which was Constitution Marsh and the western half a low rocky bluff. Fort Constitution was not a fort either but was actually a series of redoubts and artillery batteries scattered across the high ground facing the river from Redoubt #7 to the north and Gravel Hill Battery a mile downriver from it. Owners of the island since 1849, the Warner family voluntarily vacated their two story house to live in West Point during the course of the Ranger's training. The white two story clapboard house served as an infirmary.

Visions of Virginia's unease in New York on their honeymoon abruptly came back to interrupt Saxton's musings. His sudden discomfort increased even more so as a tiny glint of sunlight on glass twinkled back at him from across the river.

His First Mate came over bringing Saxton back to earth.

"Captain, do you want the ship to remain in low or high position?"

"Wait a few minutes, I'll let you know. Get the crew below and mess up. Be ready to sail at any time. Keep her just turning over. That's all thank you."

"Yes Captain."

The First Mate hustled the deck crew back aboard the boat. It lay there like a whale basking in the sun, its twin exhausts sputtering into the river fore and aft of it.

The Anaona arrived at West Point a few days later also at twilight. It backed in stern first into the canvas hangar and tied up across from its counterpart where it lay languidly in the slip stream of the Hudson River. Saxton ran over to meet Marcus and Belle. Belle, dressed in dark blue denim dungarees, had come out onto the flying bridge. Saxton jumped aboard and climbed up to the bridge. She hugged him then released him as Cotton, Rufus and Nancy appeared behind her. After Saxton and Cotton rough-housed a bit, Nancy took the boys down to the main deck to sit in the weak spring sun that tried to penetrate the canvas roof above them. Saxton and Belle leaned over the oak railing side by side as the two boys played below them. Belle turned to Saxton,

"You were wondering why Marcus isn't here Sax. Well, I let him off between Gees and Noah's Point. I think he said he wanted to know how the Rangers were doing. Last time I seen him, he was in a black loincloth, red Shuka and nothing else. He had a big spear and a bull hide shield. God it's chilly. I don't know how he stands the cold but he looked comfort-able though. A real warrior; he's my Simba incarnate. God Sax! What a prime specimen he is! I love him just the way he is, wild and free."

Saxton laughed for he now knew full well what was going to happen. He said,

"God help them Belle." She laughed and continued to smoke her cheroot while looking out across the river.

Later that afternoon, Allan Pinkerton came over to the Anaona along with Lt. Greenleaf and Colonel Bowman. The latter two were quite astounded to see Belle with her two children, and their nanny. The two officers asked where Marcus was. Belle told them. They guffawed loudly. Lt. Greenleaf smiled knowingly.

"Well Gentlemen, you and I better get over to their camp pronto by dark. I don't want to miss the fun. Thank you Belle, and stay here please. You'll be sailing over to the island yonder in the morning at 0600. The Army will supply a pilot for you. But, stay alert and be ready for anything. You can shut her down now. However, I don't want you or your crew to leave the ship. Guards have been posted all around." He paused,

"Is it alright Belle for two guards to be posted on board?

She nodded. She thought, 'It's just like old times.'

Belle had been a Union agent under Pinkerton for many years; a hazardous secret she'd kept all to herself. After inspecting the ship, Colonel Bowman and Lt. Greenleaf disappeared up the dock ramp. Saxton watched them, remembering when they had climbed aboard the Nimsi earlier in the day for a closer daylight inspection of his unique ship.

Saxton had reached into a box lying on the dock. He had them put sail cloth slippers on over their boots, saying,

"Something called static electricity Colonel. I can't explain it but it's for safety's sake. Sorry gentlemen."

They stood back as the clam-shell deck hatch slowly opened. The curious entourage de-scended down a wide cleated mule ramp into the ship. Lamplight flooded the whole interior.

Greeting them was an empty mule corral replete with tack, feed and other necessities. In one corner there was a blacksmith-Ferrier shop and a tack room. The rest of the ship was taken up with living quarters, mess hall, Officers quarters, medical room, two heads, weapons storage rooms and larder. Designed as a double ender, the aft stern contained the engine room, oil tanks, and steering mechanism. At the fore stern were the floatation pumps, water tanks, machine shop and storage rooms filled with ropes, anchor chains, barrels of packing grease, lubricants and other supplies. Colonel Bowman wondered how everything had been stowed away in such a small craft. He was impressed,

"Double hull you say. Sinks and rises too. Amazing! I can't even hear the steam engine. Packed coconut fiber! Really! No exhaust fumes. Out under the water! Incredible! I can hardly wait to see it in action Captain." Saxton stepped forward,

"I'm sorry Sir but you never will. Oh I'm sure you'll hear about it soon enough. It will take a few days before the Rangers and their mules get used to it enough to be ready to go into action."

After Lt. Greenleaf and Colonel Bowman had disembarked, Saxton's reverie vanished as he closed the wheelhouse hatch shut, climbed down the ladder and went to join his crew in the ship's galley.

On the way back to Colonel Bowman's quarters, Lt. Greenleaf suggested,

"Perhaps we could mess up say in one hour. I don't want to miss 'Marcus the Maasai' in action. What do you say Gentlemen? Shall we?" The Colonel demurred.

"Lieutenant, I'm sorry but my wife Marie has other plans. She pulled rank you know. I wanted her to meet this 'Marcus the Maasai' as you call him. I heard he's quite the lion killer."

They both laughed. Bowman returned the Lieutenant's salute then walked to his quarters high on a bluff that fronted the river.

Meanwhile back on the North dock, Pinkerton looked down at the canvas boat shelter. He could hear Belle's sons laughing in ragged delight as they ran helter-skelter around the Anaona's broad deck between the hatches playing hide-n-seek. However, he knew their innocence combined with their imagination, allowed them to see the game for what it was, just a game that they could play again and again. But he also knew that war was also a game that was played time and time again with similar imagination but most certainly without innocence. Another game of hide-n-seek was in store for the Rangers that night. He turned, walked across the upper landing and joined Lt. Israel Greenleaf. The two men slowly made their way across an open field to the Officer's mess hall.

An hour earlier, Marcus climbed into a yellow lifeboat and rowed ashore a hundred yards upriver from the North Dock. He pulled the heavy lifeboat through thick reeds, flipped it over and covered it with brush then crawled underneath it and went to sleep as night fell upon him.

Marcus had been curious to see his recruits. While in Boston, Pinkerton suggested that Marcus raid the Ranger encampment shortly after his arrival. He also suggested that any introduction to his men be spectacular. Apparently the Rangers were divided into three squads. The squads were being drilled into a cohesive team by Lt. Greenleaf and Sergeant Leitzell. Captain Shaw stayed for a month until he became quite satisfied with the recruit's progress. He returned to Boston by train as the sea made him seasick.

Sergeant Leitzell doubled the guards around the four tents the men and their officers lived in for five long cold months. The men knew something was up. Their 'flesh eating' Maasai giant was coming soon, very soon. The eighteen hundred acres around the Ranger's camp was large enough to conceal them well. Located near a small creek in a grassy glade, their encampment was nestled down low, out of the winter winds along the shores of Delafield Pond. There, a plentiful supply of firewood, kept them occupied. Each canvas tent lay under a roof of branches covered by sod. The sides of the ten by twenty foot enclosures were horizontal logs packed with moss inside and covered by live brush on the outside. The enclosures formed a large rectangle with the cooking fires in the center of it.

It was a tough life compared to the relative comforts of the nearby barracks but the Rangers had grudgingly gotten use to it. After awhile, the inter-squad rivalry so prevalent at the beginning disappeared. All three squads became one cohesive group. They could march in formation, hike fifteen miles each day, handle any and all ordinance with ease and kill anything, two legged or not with consummate skill. But Greenleaf and Leitzell knew they were not quite ready. They still had yet to meet their commander Captain Marcus Brown. They would be breaking camp tomorrow at 0400 hours for Constitution Island where their final two days of training would take place.

The camp remained tranquil as the men lounged about cleaning their equipment, talking quietly or catching some much needed rest. After supper was over, late afternoon shadows began creeping down the hills towards them. The guards sat beside nearby t in special cloth blinds, their Porro binoculars sweeping every inch of the surrounding area. After darkness fell, they communicated with each other using bird calls. Thereafter, the sounds of the Wren and Warbler occasionally wafted through the cool air of the night. The Rangers were ready to meet 'Marcus the Maasai' head on.

Marcus slept until midnight before he crawled out from underneath the camouflaged lifeboat. River patrols regularly sailed past him every hour, their main sails stiffened by the river wind as they tacked back and forth across the wide Hudson River. They didn't see him slither up the high river bank, dash across the railway tracks, climb a steep bluff then run through gloomy hardwood groves that sprinkled across the West Point cemetery. After skirting a few more barracks and other buildings; he climbed to the top of the rocky bluff overlooking Delafield Pond. A steel-tipped throwing spear rested across his shield, as he ran through the dark fastness. He knew where the camp was as wood smoke from its campfires below him betrayed its whereabouts. It would have been a fruitless exercise for any other man because the Rangers were constantly on the move from their main camp by a creek to their temporary bivouacs elsewhere. But Marcus was not just any other man; he was Simba.

After weeks of preparation, they were ready for the Maasai's arrival or so they thought. The first inkling that anything was awry was the absolute silence coming from all four guard outposts. Sergeant Leitzell had heard nothing for twenty minutes. It was well after midnight when the short hairs on the back of his neck rose, the hot breath of Simba upon them. Heinz froze; his guts turned to water. His skin crawled. Marcus gagged and bound him all in one silent moment. The Sergeant looked up into a terribly scarred and broken face. The scars smiled back while he was slowly being dragged into deeper shadows out of sight. The same thing happened to Lt. Greenleaf and Alan Pinkerton himself even though they'd hidden in dense underbrush overlooking the camp below. Twittering Warblers and Wrens once again performed their requiems. The Rangers relaxed and went about their business, until one of them cried out.

Out of nowhere right in the middle of the encampment appeared a long spear, its steel point buried in the ground beside the fire pit. The spear was still quivering. One man reached forward to touch it. At that precise moment, a mighty explosion of light and heat erupted from one of the cooking fires. Blinded by its intensity, it increased the recruits panic. A fearsome figure emerged, goliath-like amongst them. It bellowed,

"I am 'Matari the Maasai'. I have come for you!"

BOOK TWO: CHAPTER 8
TRIAL BY FIRE

The night lay upon West Point like a lover. Colonel Bowman had been asleep for two hours. An Army cadet, scared out of his mind about waking the Colonel up, nevertheless delivered a hand written message. The Colonel was not amused. However, the message was marked urgent, its portent ominous.

"Colonel Bowman, report to the duty desk now. The President is waiting." He sputtered,

"This must be a joke. I'll kill the son of a bitch that dreamed up this one. Christ! It's just after one in the goddamned morning." Bowman's wife, Marie rolled over,

"Alexander Bowman, do you know what time it is?"

"Go back to sleep dear. You'd never believe me."

"Believe what Alex? Believe what?"

"I have a note here from the duty desk that says that Abraham Lincoln is waiting for me. How ridiculous. I can't wait to court mar....!" His wife interrupted him.

"Alexander Bowman, the President just might be here. Since the war started, he's been here, there and everywhere. Get your white's on Colonel." She slipped out of bed, gathering a robe about her.

"I'll put the coffee on. I hear he likes gingersnap cookies."

Lincoln had received Pinkerton's wire the day before. The Anaona was spotted by one of Pinkerton's agents at the narrows leading from the Atlantic into the Hudson River. Agent Wicks had been eating his lunch high on a cliff overlooking the narrows while glassing every passing ship. Something odd was churning upriver. He quickly refocused his binoculars. It looked like a metal mantis was eating a ship. Flipping through his notes for confirmation, he found it as the strange looking ship disappeared around a bend in the river. The 'Shell Man' passed the information on to Pinkerton who had recently returned to West Point. Pinkerton immediately wired the White House. 'Redstone' would be at the North Dock West Point station after midnight the next day. For security reasons, only Pinkerton would meet him. However, there were two problems. Colonel Bowman was not be prepared for the President's arrival and secondly, Allan Pinkerton at that time, was bound, gagged and lying in the bushes.

The President with stovepipe hat in hand, stood as Colonel Bowman ran through the open door of the Duty Room. His mouth opened wide in amazement for standing beside an awed cadet was Christ himself, all six feet four of him with his hand out. Lincoln approached smiling.

"Glad to meet you Colonel. I've been waiting for you. I do apologize for showing up unannounced but the less my itinerary is known by the enemy on both sides of the Potomac, the better I like it." Bowman sputtered,

"Yes of course Mr. President."

"Just call me Abe please Alexander; yes Abe will do nicely. Do you know where Pinkerton is?"

"He was to have been back from the Rangers camp over two hours ago. You see Mr. President he was expecting a surprise visit from 'Marcus the Maasai' tonight. Would you like to wait? He might show up at any minute."

"No Colonel. Just show me the way. I'm here to see the Rangers, the Maasai himself and the ships. I hear they're both unusual." The Colonel finally gathered his wits about him. He replied.

"Yes, Mr. President, without question they are indeed."

The President summoned a young cadet forward. Lincoln looked down upon the lad fondly. He laughed as he put a large hand on a scrawny shoulder, saying,

"I hear you're the bravest cadet at West Point. No one else but you was courageous enough to wake up the Colonel let alone his wife." The cadet grinned.

"Yes Sir, they made me do it or else."

"What's your name son?"

"I'm Thomas Blanchard from Chicago, Illinois."

Lincoln stepped back approvingly and cried, "Bully for you son!" He turned to the Colonel.

"Alex, do you know where the Rangers are camped?" The Colonel nodded. Lincoln was relieved.

"Good enough; now Thomas perhaps you can get us some lanterns and we'll be off."

Marcus waited patiently as the Rangers recovered from their temporary blindness. He pulled the spear out of the ground, pounded it on the shield then motioned them to gather around. His deep voice, soothing yet commanding said,

"I salute you Maasai Rangers. In my land far away, warriors are known as 'Moran'. Their camp is called an 'Emanyatta' where they learn many skills necessary for their survival. My people have a saying which I think you'll understand when you engage the enemy,

"Life has meaning only in the struggle. Triumph or defeat is in the hands of the Gods. So let us celebrate the struggle."

The change was remarkable. At one instant he'd been the devil incarnate and in the next he was one of them; their master until they'd mastered themselves. He put a long finger to his full lips. All thirty Rangers leaned closer to hear him. Marcus whispered,

"Listen carefully men. A group of perhaps eight people are at this very moment crossing the creek one hundred yards away to my right. From the sound of their footfalls, one is very tall, two are short and overweight. Only one of them is a cadet. They will be here in two minutes. Stay still and wait for them. I'll be right back."

The Rangers watched the flickering apparition slip away into the bushes. Moments later four guards appeared amongst them. Right after them, Pinkerton, Greenleaf and Leitzell emerged slightly the worse for wear. When they all turned back to where Marcus had disappeared he was squatting there beside his bull-hide shield. They shrank back thinking as one, 'the Maasai is a magician'. Their attention was sharply diverted, for to their right, hurricane lanterns floated towards them like fireflies on a summer breeze. A cadet, followed by Colonel Bowman, President Lincoln, two Pinkerton agents and three soldiers emerged out of the dark forest, each one holding a lantern high above their heads. Sergeant Leitzell saluted his superior officer and barked,

"Rangers, form ranks now!"

The Rangers formed three rows, each in front of their squad's shelter. Marcus walked towards the President, his spear and shield in one hand, the other thrust out before him. The Maasai spoke.

"Mr. President, it is indeed an honor." Lincoln doffed his famous hat. He shook the Maasai's hand saying,

"The honor is all mine, Matari of the Kisongo Maasai. Without a doubt, the honor is all mine."

Marcus was immediately taken aback by the courtesy shown by this remarkable man standing in front of him, saying,

"Mr. President, I've never met a man whose shadow was longer than mine, until now. How can I be of service? The President looked up at the scarred face above him. He grinned.

"I've heard many tall tales about you Captain and I believe they're all true. May I say a few words before I leave? Your ships await my inspection then I'm off again. By the way, what does the word 'Anaona' mean in Swahili?" Marcus replied,

"We believe." Lincoln grinned, his eyes lively yet somehow drawn back deep into his face. He said,

"How appropriate Marcus; we all have to believe in ourselves, our cause and our nation. The pursuit of victory is our common burden."

The President began inspecting the Rangers by casually laughing and talking with each of them. He then conversed quietly with the three officers. Marcus watched as the old railsplitter worked his magic. The Maasai people too would have succumbed to Lincoln's all embracing humble charm. Finally, the President stood before them, stove-pipe hat in hand. He humbly bowed his head saying,

"Gentlemen, my hat's off to you. You are the bravest of the brave. If you are captured by the enemy, they will certainly kill you. If you are severely wounded by the enemy you may be left to die on the field of battle. May God Bless you and keep you. I will never forget you, the Maasai Rangers. Let us pray."

All heads bowed as the great man intoned,

"Give us the strength Dear Lord to forgive our fellow countrymen who beset themselves upon us. Let not thy protection Dear Lord, desert us in our time of peril. Let not the purpose of our mission become lost in the night that will surround us. Let us stay as one, united by faith, strong in will and all enduring for a nation depends on us. Lord, protect each and everyone one of us as we walk through the shadows of the valley of death. Forgive those who rise up against us for they know not what they do. And, with the dawn before us, let us reunite as a whole nation forever and ever, amen."

With that the President, like Marcus, disappeared as quickly as the he had appeared.

Early that morning, before 0600 hours Belle waited for the Rangers to board the Nimsi. As she did so, she laughed about what happened a few hours earlier. A commotion on the dock had awakened her, so she had quietly dressed and rushed up to the bridge. There, to her surprise, holding lanterns on high was an entourage including the President himself asking the guards for permission to come aboard. She went down to meet him. The President doffed his hat and bowed as Belle ran up to him. He was charming but appeared terribly sad. President Lincoln put out a knarled hand but Belle reached up and kissed him on an unshaven cheek. He turned to Colonel Bowman exclaiming, "Ain't she a Corker?"

They all laughed. The President's party strolled over to the Nimsi whose crew had been forewarned. A gangplank was thrust out onto the dock. Saxton and his crew though half asleep, stood at attention on either side of it. They saluted as the President was piped aboard. The gangly Lincoln scrambled down the mule ramp. Again and again, the great man was amazed at what he saw. He was especially interested in the underwater flushing toilets. Saxton explained how they worked and suggested that Lincoln try one out. The President wisely demurred saying,

"I think that Allan should do the honors before me. One never knows if the Rebels have a bomb waiting for me in a most unexpected place."

Pinkerton gritted his teeth as gales of laughter came down upon him. Saxton rescued the poor man by taking the President to see the ship's unique pantry.

This watertight room was twenty by twenty feet and its walls, floor and roof were packed with sawdust through which pipes cooled by river water flowed back and forth. The whole edifice was extra ballast. Lincoln was impressed. But Saxton saved the best till last. The piece d' resistance was the observation balloon built by Thaddeus Lowe and its gas generator stowed in a watertight compartment inside the ship.

Lincoln remembered Lowe well. They'd met on July 17, 1861, whereupon Lowe rose five hundred feet above the Capital and used a telegraph to communicate with the ground. A portable gas generator was used to inflate the hydrogen balloon. Lowe himself had come to West Point to train the recruits on how to operate them. They were hauled down by a steam winch on board the ship or by hand winch and could rise up to a thousand feet.

They had been installed at West Point under the direction of the newly formed Bureau of Topographical Engineers with Lowe as chief balloon operator. Lincoln was so inspired that the Balloon Corps was established later that summer. Aerial exercises were done during the day but later on night practices would commence. Every Ranger became conversant in Morse code, semaphore, the Portuguese heliograph and the Caton telegraph key. During dinner, they would sometimes tap out humorous messages to each other. They were very surprised when Saxton and Marcus joined in. Morse code was used at night while on their exercises. It would prove quite effective later on.

The President after inspecting both ships, exclaimed confidently,

"Captain Saxton, I do believe that 'Operation Maasai Ranger' will be successful. Right now however, the war going against us, I do need some good news and soon."

Lincoln reached out and held Saxton at arms length.

"You are very much your father's son. I'm so saddened by the death of your mother Muriel. You have my sincerest condolences. By the way, I hear that you're the proud father of a baby girl, Felicity, I believe." Saxton nodded.

"I'm glad it wasn't a boy for if you ever do have a boy, don't call him Abraham. The poor lad will probably be pestered like me for miracles the rest of his life."

They all laughed. An agent came over and whispered in the President's ear. He turned to Saxton.

"Well Captain Saxton I have to go. My masters await me at the Capital. I'm weary of the bickering, the guile and the incessant grasping for power. The politics of war is like an unwelcome house quest. After a few days it has worn out its welcome if you know what I mean."

The President accompanied by Allan Pinkerton, climbed aboard an armored train coach a few minutes later. Inside it, Lincoln slumped exhausted into a leather lounge chair. He lit a cheroot, removed his stove pipe hat, and took off his long boots. A muscular black attendant came forward with a gift wrapped box in his white gloved hands. He said,

"Mr. President, this came by way of cadet, a Thomas Blanchard, a few minutes before you boarded Sir." Lincoln was curious. He looked up.

"What is it William?"

"I have no idea Mr. President." Pinkerton reached over and took the box.

"Mr. President, I'll do the honors."

He carefully untied the red ribbon, unwrapped some red paper to reveal a plain white box. He opened the lid. He handed the box to Lincoln. The President laughed for inside were two dozen freshly baked gingersnap cookies with a note from Mrs. Bowman.

The President's train pulled away from the North Dock Station. It tooted twice. A long face appeared in the window. She waved. A tall gaunt figure appeared soon after on the rear platform of the private car. Belle waved again. Lincoln waved back. The 4-4-0 Baldwin locomotive slowly gained speed, pushing towards a dark and brooding tunnel. Lincoln stood there until he disappeared. Belle returned to the wheelhouse. She hadn't slept since the President's arrival. In three hours, soldiers would be clambering aboard to be taken across the Hudson River.

Cotton was asleep in her bed. He murmured "Momma I love you" as Belle slid in beside him. Within seconds she fell into a deep sleep.

Meanwhile, Sergeant Leitzell and Lt. Greenleaf decided that the Rangers had had enough excitement for the night. They ordered them to their shelters then posted guards around the camp's perimeter, rotating them every two hours. The trills of Wrens and Warblers began to twitter around the glade. The officers returned to a fire pit where only a few glowing embers remained. Marcus sat between them. He offered both a cheroot. The Sergeant accepted, lighting his with a fire stick. Greenleaf drew out a long stemmed clay pipe from a breast pocket. He lit it. As they puffed away, clouds of lazy wood smoke spiraled high through flickering light. The Sergeant looked down at his trousers. He cried,

"Gottdammerung Marcus, you made me piss my pants, nearly crapped too. Never bin so scared in my whole life. Guess I'm not cut out for killin' people. My specialty is to kill their bad habits. A drill instructor is what I am, nothin' more, nothin' less. I have to appear tough as nails with a thick hide to boot. That's me." Marcus sympathized,

"I had to gag you Sergeant, or you'd a had me marchin' pretty damn quick. I hate marchin'. Sorry about that, I won't do it again." Lt. Greenleaf sat back amused, saying, "I can tell you both right now, I'm glad I'm not going with you Marcus. I've done all I can to train them to survive. They're still not wild animals; you are but I'm not. Looks like you're stuck with them at 0600 this morning. I know you'll do a good job, you certainly did on me. My God man! How the hell do you do it?" Marcus lay back on his shield.

"Well gentlemen, I'm still in your territory. I'm leaving now because I've got a skiff to find. Tell the men to bring only what they need. They're still babes in the woods. But from what I've seen, they're no longer Ladies, correct Sergeant?"

"Correct, Captain."

Both officers stood up. Marcus returned their salutes then picked up his spear and shield. As he did so, he noticed every enclosure was filled with heads looking at him. He moved forward to face the two men. In a strong voice, tinged with emotion, he solemnly declared,

"Gentlemen, may I show my deepest appreciation for your efforts to change these men into real freedom fighters. To you Sergeant, I present this Maasai shield or Longo. To you Lieutenant, I present this Maasai spear or Ishiphapha." He stood back, saying,

"I salute you and I thank you."

Both men stood stock-still, the gifts of respect in their hands. A thunderous applause erupted from the enclosures. It quickly grew into a roar. Marcus felt good.

He ran back through the woods listening to the approbation rise and fall behind him. Finally, it became quiet as he swept through the cemetery. The sacrifice of those who's fought before him lay all about him, honored, respected and immortal. He continued running, silent as a lion seeking prey. The railway tracks lay below a steep bluff. He stopped and surveyed the river. Its waters had passed this way for millennia. Born upon the breast of a dry and parched land in Africa; to Marcus every river symbolized eternal life; a living thing that would carry him away to a better world. He climbed down the bluffs to the river. The lifeboat was still there. Sweeping aside the brush covering it, he rolled it over then pushed it out through tall reeds into the river. He jumped in, grabbed the oars and started rowing leisurely downstream close to shore. Within minutes he tied up to his ship. Belle felt another warm body in her bed. Her Simba had come home from the hill.

Thirty Rangers tramped along single file towards the North dock, arriving there at exactly 0600 hours. The Anaona's flying bridge rose high above the Nimsi. Belle leaned against its oaken railing. The Rangers marched forward led by Lt. Greenleaf and Colonel Bowman as Sergeant Leitzell harassed their starboard flank. The Nimsi's crew stood at attention in their black and yellow dress uniforms waiting for them. Captain Saxton stood at the foot of the dock ramp. The Rangers dressed in their dark green field uniforms hustled single file down it into the hangar. Therein, the wharf's planking shook as they formed a sinuous line in front of the Nimsi berthed directly across from them. With the echoes of their Sergeant's barking still ringing in their ears, their attention was diverted by something even more spectacular than Leizell's histrionics.

The Rangers had heard scuttlebutt about the Anaona's beautiful skipper. This was very evident to the diminutive Sergeant as he noticed his charges looking up admiring Belle's magnificent cleavage.

He yelled, "About face!"

Instantly, the line of men spun about to stand at attention facing the Nimsi's crew. They saluted as Colonel Bowman passed between the lines inspecting them with Lt. Greenleaf in hot pursuit. To Saxton, the Nimsi's crew was absolutely splendid in appearance and bearing. The wide river flowed behind them, gurgling and pulling around the tarred pilings beneath the boat house. Cooling April airs washed over them as if they were about to be baptized. It was over. There were no speeches; no eulogizing made about the duty that lay ahead of them. Their little Sergeant barked at them for the last time.

"By the ones, forward March!"

Belle watched them board the Nimsi in two's as if they were entering Noah's Ark. An Army river pilot jumped aboard ship as the crew cast off all lines. The Nimsi slowly backed away from the wharf, its two exhausts burbling just below the surface of the river. Another pilot came aboard the Anaona as its crew let go its lines from the small bollards lining the dockside. Marcus came out onto the flying bridge. He looked down at Belle fondly, however his attention was diverted, as a dozen manila bumpers were pulled aboard and stowed.

Puffs of black smoke rose up through open vents in the canvas roof above. Like the Nimsi before her, the Anaona backed out into the river. At first the ship was momentarily pulled downstream, gripped by the force of the current.

However it slowly gained headway as both ships began crabbing their way across the narrows towards Constitution Island.

Located on a strategic 'S' curve in the Hudson River, Martelaer's Rock or Constitution Island, was first fortified by George Washington's Revolutionary Army in 1775. Their earth and stone redoubts were destroyed by the Americans in 1777 before the British under General Burgoyne could take them. Burgoyne destroyed what was left. The next year, Thaddeus Kosciusko, a Polish engineer, commenced designing West Point, a series of redoubts and five forts. On Constitution Island, a barracks, three stone redoubts and four batteries were constructed; the latter to protect a great iron chain strung across the river. Supposedly this chain weighed over eighty tons and was supported by log floats. Each of its massive iron links weighed one hundred and fifty pounds. For five years this impenetrable obstruction prevented the British from sailing any further up the Hudson. Nearly a hundred years later when the Maasai Rangers arrived, the chain was gone and the fortifications protecting it were in ruins.

Two ships berthed under the canvas roof of their camouflaged boathouse below the Marine Battery. A long finger dock that separated them ended in a ramp that rose and fell with the river. The cove into which they had entered provided adequate anchorage. It lay a few hundred yards west of the old Gravel Hill battery. After tying up, the Nimsi's crew joined the Rangers for some shore time together. Saxton, Belle and Marcus watched them from the Anaona's flying bridge. Belle held Rufus in her arms as Cotton played on the deck below them. Nancy was in the galley preparing their breakfast. Aboard the Nimsi, 'Cookie' was also messing breakfast. Saxton turned to Marcus.

"Well my friend, we leave for Fort Monroe in two days. We'll be in the thick of it soon enough, I'm sure. We must have been crazy to get ourselves in this situation. My God, look at them, chickens before the slaughter to be sure."

He flicked a cigar butt into black waters. Marcus disagreed,

"I don't think so Sax. They're not boys any more. After I finish with them, their own mommas won't recognize them. This is total war, winner take all. Even your crew will have to train in the little time we have here as well." Saxton turned abruptly,

"What do you mean Marcus? We're trained to crew a ship, not crawl on our bellies through enemy lines and the opposite is true. Your Rangers could never crew the Nimsi; they'd sink while tied to the dock. I'm appalled at the very thought of it." Belle intervened.

"Listen you two. It might be a good idea to train everyone together. Inter-squad rivalry is fine to a point but what would happen if by some chance, the lives of the men depended on everyone or someone knowing what to do. Emergencies do happen. Besides, Sax, your crew can't be kept aboard while the others are out there killin' Rebs. They would go crazy, believe me, I should know." Saxton reluctantly agreed.

"You're right Belle. Besides I could do with a few more lessons on how to kill using my fists."

He backed up facing Marcus. They exchanged playful punches. Belle intervened again like a mother scolding two sons.

"Ok you two, enough of your shenanigans for now. Perhaps the Rangers can learn how to operate the Nimba on the voyage down to Fort Monroe. They'll have a week or more won't they? She sniffed the air.

"I smell breakfast. Marcus, go with Saxton. Be there for their first meal. I'm sure you two will fight over who's going to say grace. Now go, both of you!"

Both men smirked and saluted, saying, "Ay! Ay! Madam Admiral!"

Belle harrumphed on her way into the wheelhouse.

The next day, the Nimsi was still lying at her berth fully raised. However, her steam was up. The Rangers stood on the finger pier, fascinated when the main deck split upwards into two twenty foot long sections. As each ten foot wide section flipped open, anyone emerging would be protected by walls of armored decking. Indeed a camouflaged water-proof canvas roof covered the open hatch automatically as the two sections were pulled apart and secured by chained hooks on either side. A mosquito net could be thrown over the opening when needed. A thick vulcanized rubber seal designed, made and installed by Henry Goodyear ran around all the edges of the opening making it water tight when closed. The weight of the water and armor upon it when submerged made it even more so. A wide ramp, ribbed with cross cleats, allowed man and beast to exit or enter the ship's cavernous hold. Rollers set into a circular track located dead center on the floor below allowed the ramp to be reversed. Saxton remembered the first time the Rangers set foot inside her a day before.

It was down this ramp that the Rangers walked in their new rubber soled bootees to the lower deck of the Nimsi where its crew had lined up to greet them. They were led into the galley which also served as sleeping quarters. Bound hammocks were strung out taut above them. Everyone stood at ease wherever they liked, waiting for their Captains to sit down. There were no squads here, just one team. Saxton stood beside at a unique canvas trestle table facing four similar tables placed lengthwise. He nodded. Everyone sat down on folding canvas benches strung out beside them. Oil lamps in brass gimbals orbited above them. The air was ventilated by round metal stacks turned about to catch the breeze. Fine wire mosquito netting covered the bottom of each pipe thus allowing them to be replaced from within the vessel. Each opening could be sealed with a water proof rubber plate. There were a dozen such vents bringing fresh air in and exhausting stale air out.

A simple breakfast lay before them in tin plates, mugs and bowls. Metal spoons sharpened on one side with a fork on the other end served as their only utensil. Saxton remained standing while everyone sat down. After all was quiet, he bowed his head.

"Gentlemen, may the Good Lord bless this food. May it nourish our hearts, minds and souls, in your holy name Amen."

Afterwards, the men stowed their gear, then lined up in the galley standing at attention waiting for further orders. Saxton paced back and forth in front of them. Every Ranger had changed into their clothes of choice, their weapons at their sides. Some preferred Spencers, others Henry repeaters. Both fired a .51 caliber rim-fired two hundred grain bullet. Saxton noticed that none of the men carried anything that would rattle, reflect light or smell. Marcus ordered weapons inspection. He cruised up and down the lines. Amazingly, all weapons were in excellent working order. At random he selected a Ranger to come forward. After being blindfolded, he told the man to kneel down and field strip his rifle then reassemble it. The man did so in two minutes flat. While at attention, the Ranger offered his weapon for inspection. It was perfect. Marcus returned the Ranger's salute and motioned another to step forward. After ten such perfect performances, he was satisfied. One of the Rangers approached Saxton with a rifle in hand. He stood at attention, saluted then enquired innocently,

"Perhaps Captain, you could show us all how to strip this weapon without a blindfold." Saxton got the point.

Months before, a firing range had been set up behind redoubt #7 a half mile to the north of the boathouse. There, with their backs to the river, the Rangers practiced cold bore shooting at still, moving, and camouflaged targets. Scores were diligently recorded. Some recruits were naturally comfortable, others not so much. The remains of redoubts #5 and #6 were used to practice ambushes, tracking, explode the new land mines and play a more deadly form of hide and seek. All activities were conducted at night. During the day, the Rangers cleaned their weapons, wrote letters, listened to Marcus's battle tactics or engaged in hand to hand combat on the straw floor in the mule corral.

During the previous winter months at Delafield Pond, they practiced snow-shoeing, cross country skiing, winter camouflage techniques, and surviving alone and without anything but a knife and flint in the frozen forests of the military reserve. Miraculously no one froze to death however, there were broken bones, cuts and scrapes but no deaths, only near deaths that didn't count anyway. All the Rangers used these incidents to practice setting bones, and applying medicinal herbs they scavenged, all under the stern eyes of 'Bones' Barstow, a West Point Doctor assigned to them. For fun, they played hockey on the frozen pond against the 'Pointers', rarely winning but it didn't matter as the game released their tensions in a constructive manner. It was fun, pure and simple.

The Ranger's Appaloosa racing mules, intelligent and tough; arrived at West Point two months before. The men picked their own animals. While riding and shooting without a hand on the reins; the Rangers rode through hardwood forests, brush, over bluffs and open glades near their encampment. In the final weeks, they rode only at night. The days were left to rest in ambush exercises concealed under a specially designed sniper blind; or under a rock, a bush or buried in the snow. Their mules lay near them camouflaged under a net. It was a tough life but they survived. Sergeant Lietzel was amazed.

The twenty mules adapted well to the confines of the Nimsi. Over the next two nights, they practiced entering and leaving the ship many times along the shores of nearby Foundry Cove. While aboard ship, the mules appeared to be totally oblivious to any and all strange sounds around them as they stood stolidly in their corral apparently fast asleep. While the ship was in a raised position, the mule corral was mucked out into large metal dumbwaiters fitted with clamshell doors. When loaded, these dumbwaiters were pulled up through a watertight hatch by steam winch or by a chain pulley then swung over the side to be dumped overboard. High pressure stream hoses and lime were used to disinfect them and clean up the mule corral afterwards. A wide central gutter flowed through the corral then out through large scuppers located just over the fore and aft propellers. These scuppers were shut tight whenever she lowered herself into the water. Roof vents brought fresh air into the 'Mule Carousel' as Saxton called it. Heat from the boilers was not needed to warm the crew's living quarters. The body heat of men and mules was sufficient.

The night before the Rangers were to set sail for Fort Monroe, shots rang out from somewhere in the hardwood forests above them. At the time, two squads were bivouacked within the ruins of old Fort Constitution. A third was aboard the Nimsi as it lay raised up inside the camouflaged boathouse. More shots rang out. Saxton knew it was enemy musket fire. He rang the alarm bell. Rangers piled out of their hammocks fully dressed. He yelled,

"This is not a drill! This is not a drill! Battle stations everyone. When the deck hatch opens up, you all know where to deploy. Now grab your weapons and get to the skirmish lines at the Gravel Hill and Hill Cliff batteries on the double. Make sure the 'Pointers' don't shoot you. The password tonight is 'Maasai'. Stay alert Rangers!"

Saxton ran to the wheelhouse and peered through the bullet resistant windows. There was nobody but soldiers hiding behind the metal roof vents. Saxton ordered Connor Yates to put on more steam. Slowly, the armored deck hatch rattled open. Ten Rangers ran up the mule ramp, out onto the dock, up its ramp and into the forest. Meanwhile, the Nimsi began to shake as Yates and his black oilers brought steam pressure to bear. The Gatling's and mortars were manned, their crews crouching behind armor plate. Saxton patrolled the deck like a new father in a maternity ward knowing his crew was well prepared for just about anything.

Meanwhile, Marcus had run over to the Nimsi just as Belle came out onto the Anaona's flying bridge above him. After conferring with Saxton, he raced back. Four Army guards on deck duty saluted. One said,

"Any orders Captain? We heard gunfire." Belle looked at Marcus below her. She was worried.

"What's going on? I heard musket shots. What do you want me to do?"

"Get under way as soon as you can and take Nancy and the boys to West Point. The Colonel's wife Marie will look after them. Bring back as many soldiers as you can get. Something's not right. Any trouble, three short blasts on the whistle. Remember, only running lamps when you get well out into the river. Sax will follow you out. I've got to get back to my men Belle. I love you!" He turned to the soldiers.

"Ok men, this is NOT a drill. Be ready for anything. Keep a sharp lookout. I want one of you on the end of each flying bridge and the other two manning the Gatling's. Is that clear?"

"Yes Sir!" He returned their salutes then ran back past as its crew cast off the tie-up lines. The Anaona slid out of the hangar. The Nimsi lowered itself then followed suit. Far above them more shots rang out. The Ranger's Spencer's replied, spitting lead through the night air. Meanwhile, two squads of Rangers had ridden like the wind back from the old fort pinning down intruders holed up in redoubts #5 and #6 due west of Fishkill Creek. Corporal Cornel Wright's squad fanned out well forward on their left flank near a perimeter on the bluffs overlooking the moorage. There they joined the 'Pointers' in a prearranged defensive position. Fifty soldiers and Rangers were dug in amongst the stone ruins of four batteries from Roman's to Gravel Hill.

Marcus appeared, appraised the situation then with two of his Rangers ran around the right flank of the attacking force. From there they could hear the enemy moving away from them towards the Ranger's moorage. A grove of hardwood trees loomed large around them. Shadows flitted in and out amongst them. Marcus whistled the 'tut, tut' piping alarm of the Wood Thrush twice then once. On his command, his Rangers moved to his left and lay in ambush. A long column of armed men moved single file by them, the last of which was taken out, gagged and bound. The Rangers carried him towards Marcus whereupon they interrogated their captive using knives to loosen his tongue. The man dressed in butternut fatigues would give them nothing, not even under torture. Marcus wondered,

'Who are these guys? The man's clothes has no markings, he wears no insignia, has no identification, nothing.'

Marcus peered into the charcoal blackened face of the man bleeding to death. Finally the man groaned, closed his eyes and died. Marcus rolled up the man's sleeves. There on his left wrist was the dreaded "D" with a dagger thrust through it. At that very moment, three short blasts shattered the night air. Marcus started running.

Minutes before, the Anaona slipped its lines and backed out of the boat shed. As the ship pivoted about, the four guards took their assigned positions. From inside the wheelhouse, Belle stared nervously through the metal shutters. Her anxiety increased as more shots were fired behind her. The dark narrow waters of the Hudson River in front of her lay dappled with moonlight. A quarter mile away was the North dock. She closed the shutters and peered through viewing ports cut into them. Her knuckles bled white as she gripped the ship's helm. The passage across the narrow river in daylight had been fraught with challenges enough let alone at night. Even with a full moon above her, it was still very hard for Belle to see clearly especially within the confines of the wheelhouse.

Meanwhile, Nancy and the two boys ran to the secret hiding place just behind the ship's aft head. Once there, she slid some wall-paneling aside and entered with Cotton and Rufus. Belle had often told her,

"I guess no matter where I am a hidey-hole will always be nearby just in case I need it."

She also kept food and weapons in it. A large bullet resistant glass scuttle provided light and an escape route. The tiny room was sound- proofed with coconut fiber so that her children could never give themselves away. A special quartz lens secreted in a wall allowed a 180 degree view into the head. It was also armored. Belle thought,

'Nancy and my boys will be safe there.'

As her ship began making its way across to the North Dock at West Point, Belle didn't see four slim canoes leave the reedy shorelines on either side of her. Within minutes, a dozen black figures climbed up amidships. A shot was fired. Both flying bridge pickets were distracted long enough to die quickly, their throats cut. The aft Gatling gun turned about and burst into life.

A swath of bullets swept across the wheelhouse from left to right. Belle was thrown back by the impact of lead slugs smashing into the iron shutters in front of her. However those shutters and the bullet resistant glass behind them saved her life. Recovering quickly, Belle set a course straight for Noah Point. She looped the steering rope ties over spokes on either side of the helm. Sounds of battle punished her as her Gatling's opened up on the Nimsi cruising far astern. With both hands, she pulled the brass engine room telegraph controls to AHEAD FULL. Moments later, the ship surged forward. She barely had time to pull the braided whistle cord three times before she was sapped from behind. Her body slumped unconscious to the wheelhouse floor.

Saxton heard Belle's ship being attacked far ahead of him. Alarmed, one of the his crew yelled out,

"Look over their Captain, there's canoes coming towards us." Saxton crouched down behind a Gatling and screamed, "Fire at will! Fire at will!"

In response, enemy rifle fire twinkled in deepening twilight. Minie balls began pinging off the Gatling's armor plate in front of him. The Nimsi's forward Gatling opened up cutting a canoe in two before the gun jammed. Screams filled the air. It was all over as suddenly as it had started. Not one raider had even come close to boarding her. Except for a few superficial wounds, his crew had been blooded. Saxton yelled, "Cease fire." He was more than pleased but not for long.

Marcus ran as he'd never run before, two Rangers flanked him on either side. Twice, they killed intruders as they rushed ever onwards to the four redoubts cresting the bluffs to the west. Both victims wore the "D" tattoo. The Maasai cursed himself.

"The whole attack had been a goddamn diversion. How could I have been so stupid?"

His family and crew were in trouble. Hopefully Belle was still alive and the rest were in the hidey-hole. Bullets zipped past him. He yelled "Maasai". The firefight had settled down to a stalemate. Four long whistle blasts rent the night air. The raider's rattling musket fire stopped as quickly as it had started. The enemy was withdrawing, their mission apparently accomplished. Within minutes two squads of Rangers emerged out of the forest shadows. They flitted across the moonlit glade, gave the password then stood in front of Marcus. He asked them if anyone was hurt. Two Rangers had been wounded, but none were dead. The commander of the 'Pointers' ran up. Two of his men were dead and five were wounded. Marcus looked downcast saying,

"I'm sorry men but we were tricked tonight. The assault was a ruse. Our ships were their real objective, I'm sure of it now. He turned to their commander.

"Lieutenant Halsey, take the wounded to the Warner house and bring any dead back here. Secure this area and the docking berth. Send a squad to scour either side of the island along the river banks. Split up your remaining men to defend the barracks and the stables and see if the bastards are lurking about watching us. Be careful Lieutenant. By the way have your men camouflage their tunics. I can see 'em a mile away."

The Lieutenant saluted, turned and barked out his orders. The soldiers disappeared into the night. Marcus ordered the remaining Rangers to the ruins of the fort and dig in. He ordered Lt. Wright and his squad to follow him to the stables. There, the 'Warden', Marcus's mule and ten others were saddled up. Moments later, Marcus rode out into the night with ten Rangers riding on either flank straight for Foundry Cove where he suspected the raiders had come ashore.

They rode into the forest and vanished. The highest point of land; the old fort beckoned. In minutes they arrived. Marcus raised his binoculars just as the Nimsi emerged heading to West Point. He cursed, "Where the hell is the Anaona?"

Marcus wheeled about. He seemed defeated, but one of the Rangers was not. Upon seeing his Captain's dejection, he rode over and mentioned,

"Captain, one time a few months ago, we were on maneuvers. We came to a place called Garrison Landing. It's right across from the South Dock about a mile downstream from us. It was there that the river's main current will pull most boats close to shore. There's nothing but five miles of deer trails and logging roads from Foundry Cove over the bluffs to the Hamlet.

It's a rough go and nearly impossible to navigate at night. But, with a full moon we just might get there before they do and somehow swim out unseen and board her."

Marcus agreed. Nothing was impossible. As the Rangers thundered away he wondered just how they were going to be that lucky.

BOOK TWO: CHAPTER 9
PURSUIT ON THE HUDSON

The Nimsi slid into the Hudson three hundred yards astern of the Anaona as it steamed upriver. Saxton saw nothing amiss until hot lead started hammering thick armor plate around him. He reached for a bell cord. Instantly the crew battened down the hatches and the Nimsi began to lower itself into the river. The message was clear, 'Don't get too close or we'll kill all aboard'. Saxton prayed that Belle and the rest were safely hidden. He climbed up the ladder into the wheelhouse. Peering through the portholes, he saw a shadowy vessel ahead of him. Four empty canoes floated past him, bobbing about on a rippling bow wave. By their size alone, he estimated that at least a dozen men had boarded the Anaona. He lost sight of his quarry for it lay in Foundry Cove, completely hidden as Saxton passed it by on the river. An hour later after an incoming change of weather obscured the full moon, the Anaona glided back into the river, picking up speed as the current beneath it carried it along downstream towards New York City and safety.

Eleven mules raced past the old fort and down its rocky flanks towards Foundry Cove. Marcus had seen the Nimsi enter the river and head for West Point. There was no sign of the Anaona until Marcus pondered. 'Where was it?' At that moment, dark clouds obscured the moon and the Anaona slipped into his view heading downstream. If it ever reached New York City, it could hide anywhere in the warrens of wharfs and jetties that littered nearly two thousand miles of shoreline. Marcus had only one chance to catch it and that was where the river curled close to the hamlet of Garrison five miles downstream. Once there, he could swim out and board it unseen while his Rangers created a diversion. He needed a miracle.

As he rode forth, the 'Warden' beneath him seemed tireless. Foundry Cove disappeared behind him as a silver wedge bathing in a pool of moonlight. Trees flew by as the Rangers descended a series of low rocky bluffs onto a flat northern shoreline. They rode out along a thin finger of land then splashed across a small creek that flowed from Constitution Marsh to the river. Onward up a steep bluff they climbed then trotted south along a series of flat benches, skirting the vast and treacherous marsh on their right side. A wondrous ballet of jack-o-lanterns played over the face of the marsh. It beckoned them but they resisted and kept to the higher ground above it. Rising above them, the flinty flanks of one steep bluff rose one after another. After two miles, they crossed Indian Brook then a mile further on Philipse Brook. The ground flattened out, allowing the muleteers to gain even more momentum. A half mile further on they scrambled down a steep draw into the hamlet of Garrison Landing itself. Marcus's prayed that Connor Yates had sabotaged the steam engine in some way, giving the Rangers precious time to catch up.

Even above the surrounding clanking and hissing of the ship's steam engine, Connor Yates heard three sharp whistle blasts. He turned to his black oilers, Abraham and Theo saying,

"Well Laddies, trouble's afoot. I'll...." Before he could finish Blackstone burst into the engine room, followed by two ruffians, guns drawn. One shouted in Yates's ear,

"Keep her steam up matey or one of youse is dead turkey meat and I'm not fussy whether it's white or dark."

His attentions were interrupted as someone in the wheelhouse rang, 'SLOW'. Blackstone nodded as Connor pulled the brass lever of the engine room telegraph three clicks back as ordered. After a few minutes another engine order asked for 'FULL ASTERN'. Seconds later the aft propeller thrashed violently. Connor and his oilers knew what was coming. They braced themselves but their assailants did not. The ship staggered backwards. Blackstone and his accomplices lost their balance and their weapons at the same time as they crashed to the floor. Abraham, a lithe young man, leaped upon the prostrate Blackstone. Theo Smith tackled the other two. Connor, seeing a golden opportunity reached over and engaged the emergency valve that prevented the fuel oil from reaching the boilers. Another order from the wheelhouse ordered 'STOP ENGINE'. Connor complied just as the engine wheezed and quit. Connor felt the ship nudge against something solid. The sound of boots pounding over the deck above him was followed by dead silence. A shot rang out in the engine room. Connor gasped as Blackie, gun in hand, stood over Abraham Stringer. Stringer was dead, shot through the heart. Smith lay unconscious beside a work bench. Connor screamed,

"You bloody bastards, you killed them! I'll see you in hell first!" Blackstone laughed,

"How about it Irish, the sooner you go the better maybe? At that moment another engine order demanded 'SLOW AHEAD'. Connor waited, watching the steam pressure gauge next to him. The engine struggled, sputtered and died. The steam pressure fell from 800 to 100 PSI within seconds. Blackstone grabbed Connor by the scruff of the next.

"What the hell is goin' on Mick?" Connor laughed,

"Wait and see you dumb son of a bitch!" Blackstone pistol-whipped the feisty little Irishman. Connor slumped to the floor just as Garrow ran through the door.

The Nimsi glided alongside the North dock and tied up. A Corporal ran forward followed by a squad of soldiers. He listened in alarm as Saxton told him what was happening. A Private ran up the ramp and disappeared. A few minutes later, Sergeant Leitzell followed by two squads of armed cadets raced down the dock towards him. Saxton waved them to a halt. As the ship began raising itself up above the water, they watched in awe. Once fully raised, the ship's clamshell hatch sprang apart, stopped and was chained back. Spencer Rifles and their ammo were carried up the ramp from below. Sergeant Leitzell saluted Captain Saxton then conferred. Once all the details had been agreed to, the Sergeant saluted smartly, wheeled about and barked,

"Climb aboard, take cover and follow my orders. We're goin' to war boys!"

A loud hurrah went up as the 'Pointers' clambered aboard.

Suspecting a ruse, Saxton headed upstream for Constitution Point. There was no traffic on the river as Noah's Point passed to port. Constitution Point lay straight ahead to starboard. The Nimsi bulled its way through rip tides that scurried the river's surface with jagged lines of foam. Constitution Island loomed above them as they sailed past then turned sharply to starboard, the ship slowing as it entered the narrows. Upon exiting it, a vast silvery expanse stretched out before them. Two river patrol sloops lay drifting dead ahead. The Nimsi slowed to a stop, rocking gently in the river chop as the smaller boats glided towards her. Saxton climbed out of the wheelhouse and hallooed into the night, his voice skipping like a flat stone across the pewtered surface of the river.

"You Captain. Come closer. I need your help. Have you seen the Anaona tonight?"

"No Captain, we haven't seen it. We've been here at the bend all night. What's going on?" Saxton yelled,

"It's been captured by Rebels. Don't get too close if you see her. There's Gatlings and mortars aboard."

Pointing to one of the sloop's officers, he shouted,

"If you could return upriver to Cold Springs and get whoever you can to help block the river there in case they turn back. It would really help us."

Saxton turned to the other sloop bobbing nearby, imploring its Captain.

"Please go to West Point and get more soldiers, then go down river and check the coves and bays on the Gees point side, I'll do the other. Good luck and thanks."

The Nimsi heeled about and raced downstream towards the hamlet of Garrison ten miles away.

Marcus and his men galloped over narrow deer traces, winding logging roads, across meadows, around lakes and rock outcroppings that bordered the bluffs above the river. Miraculously, their night riding had paid off handsomely. No one, man nor beast was injured in any way. They fled down a widening valley that wended its way to the little hamlet of Garrison Landing. Emerging from the forest, the Rangers headed for a small dock thrust out into the river. They came to a shuddering halt then dismounted, rushing to the wharf where they untied several skiffs. Two Rangers were left behind to hobble the mules and guard them. As they did so, oil lanterns started blooming in nearby houses. A few villagers emerged cautiously then came over to gather about the two men. One of them strode forward, his battered musketoon pointing at the Rangers.

"Say, hold on there darkies, what's goin' on at this hour?" Another came up behind him and blustered,

"Is there trouble on the river? Hey, my skiff's missin'! Whad ya two niggers do with it? Who are you anyways? I've never seen your kind round these parts before."

The man's attention was diverted by something moving upon the river. He squinted into the darkness, his free hand over his forehead. After a few moments another man shouted,

"Who are those guys rowin' out on the river?"

The Rangers raised their weapons. The crowd backed off. The mules stood tethered to a picket line. Finally one of the Rangers explained. Some villagers ran home and returned armed, ready to row out and fight the Rebels. The Rangers again had their hands full. One explained,

"Now folks, try to remain calm. The men in your skiffs are Maasai Rangers. They know what they're doing. Stay behind cover and only fire when one of us tells you to. Now get down! I've heard that the river here will force most ships to hug this shoreline. Now get down." He pointed upriver and yelled, "There she is boys, she's movin' fast."

Everyone took cover as the Anaona plowed around the bend towards them, a hundred feet off shore. The river's current had been strong but slowed down considerably as it spilled into the little bay fronting the hamlet. As the ship came near, Marcus slipped into cold waters. The remaining skiffs drifted away from him, forming a floating picket line. The Rangers were not to fire until Marcus boarded his ship.

The river's undertow tried to turn Marcus around as the fugitive's vessel rushed towards him. He lay back and stretched out. From its wheelhouse, he looked exactly like a black log bobbing upon the river. He thought of New Orleans. Marcus rolled over face down as the bow came upon him. The helmsman never saw Marcus grab the bumpers tied along its side. Someone had forgotten to stow them aboard. Marcus hung on desperately as the rushing water tore at him. Painfully he pulled himself up onto and over a wide gumwood gunnel. He peered about. It was very strange. Only the Gatling guns fore and aft of the wheelhouse were manned. No one else was on deck.

The Nimsi rounded the same river bend as her prey had minutes before. Its crew cheered as the Anaona came into sight a quarter mile ahead. The Nimsi was slightly slower so it stayed out in the middle of the river trying to intercept the other ship. As they veered closer and closer, rifle bullets began to flick off the Nimsi's armored hatch covers. Sergeant Leitzell barked,

"Take cover men, the bastards are onto us, fire at will!"

The soldiers began firing. The Anaona's aft Gatling gun spit a steady stream of lead that ricocheted off the Nimsi's armor plated sides. More minie balls and bullets zipped overhead. Both ships were only one hundred yards apart. The Anaona slowed, gripped by the river undertows swirling about in the bay. Sergeant McCarthy screamed,

"Prepare to board."

The crew crouched down, ready to throw grappling hooks as they came alongside their quarry. Steel claws flew through the weak light of dawn landing with a clang. After the lines were pulled in, the two ships crashed together with a sharp jolt. 'Pointers' leaped upon the enemy with a mighty yell. Shots rang out as both sides came to grips with each other. One of the Anaona's Gatling gunners was already dead. A dark figure ran out onto the starboard flying bridge and jumped over its railing in one graceful motion. He landed lightly on the main deck like a big cat.

Harley Blackstone started killing cadets with ruthless efficiency. His broadsword flashed, bloody in the dawning light. Cries of terror and triumph split the air on both sides. The river Rangers drifted up to the action, tied up, then scrambled aboard and joined the fray. Over sixty men began fighting to the death on the wide bloody deck of the Anaona. Saxton fought his way to Blackstone. They squared off. Saxton's broadsword was easily deflected. Harley looked down on his puny adversary and laughed,

"Well now Mr. Saxton, we meet again and this time I'm not inclined to jump into a god-damned rowboat."

Meanwhile, Marcus hid behind the ship's aft deck crane housing. Deep shadows concealed him as a squad of raiders ran past. A sense of foreboding overcame Marcus. He turned about. Garrow was there, knife in hand. Marcus unsheathed his Bowie-knife and stepped out of the shadows to face him. Belle's rapist growled like a man possessed. He spat on the deck.

"Well lookee here! It's 'Marcus the Maasai', master of the 'chosen race', and the killer of my boys in New Orleans." He snarled,

"You should have killed me when you had the chance you nigger bastard."

They circled each other warily as Garrow continued to rant. It was as if he was addressing convocation of defrocked priests. He yelled,

"Before me stands the 'Devil of Darkness' who killed my father Josiah. 'Big Nigger', you're a dead man." He laughed hysterically, spitting the words out like a viper's venom. He leapt forward and continued his tirade, saying,

" Marcus, I hear that your precious Belle lies exhausted below us. Apparently her recent love life was too much for her. I guess she's not seventeen any more! Has she told you we're going to have another son?"

An all consuming rage exploded from within Marcus. He leapt forward, roaring his hatred at Garrow. They clashed as titans. Both strained mightily against each other, looking for any weakness, any advantage. However, they were evenly matched. After a lengthy contest, both men were completely unaware that they had a rapt audience of cadets, crewmen and Rangers. For all intents and purposes the larger struggle was over. The finale was now before them as Marcus and Garrow continued to cut and thrust. The partisan crowd screamed and yelled as both men sought any advantage. Horatio leapt up onto a deck crane. Marcus followed, bobbing and weaving on its narrow metal cross ribs. Precariously, fifteen feet above the crowd, the two adversaries continued to parry and thrust. As Garrow feinted with his knife, he foot swept Marcus off his feet onto a hatch cover below. Marcus lay there bloodied, unmoving. His adversary pounced for the killing blow. It never happened for his intended victim rolled away, and stabbed Garrow in the chest.

Dropping to his knees into a widening pool of blood, Garrow groaned and rolled over. Everyone's attention however, was immediately refocused on a small man who staggered out from behind an air vent clutching his chest. It was Sergeant Leitzell covered in blood. He fell, got up and grabbed Marcus, ripping the Maasai's bloody shirt with his small hands, his eyes, his face stone cold. He sputtered,

"I'm sorry Maasai. I was never very good at killin' anyone. Shouda stayed a Drill Instructor."

Leitzel loosened his grip as if any life left within him was slipping away. But something brought him back momentarily. Marcus held onto him, bringing Leitzell's body to attention. The Sergeant gasped,

"Rangers come forward!"

He spoke again, his voice barely audible as Marcus continued to hold him up. The Sergeant continued,

"Form a line Rangers." They did.

"Ten Hut!"

As they did so, he saluted, and with one final effort shouted, "I'm proud of you men......."

The little man with a big heart died at attention. His Rangers rushed forward and caught him. Behind him, Leitzell's Rangers fell upon Garrow's body, picked it up and threw it overboard. Marcus stopped, and watched it bob about beside the ship. A squad of soldiers began rounding up prisoners. Marcus turned, ran into the aft cabin, down the hallway and swung open the stateroom door. There before him, lay Belle strapped to the bed, groaning under lamplight. He cut her bindings. Belle moaned as Marcus gathered her in his arms and kissed her tenderly,

"I'm here my darling, I'm here."

Her eyes flew open, her lips moved. Silver tears came forth like a spring of holy water. He said,

"Garrow is dead. His body's in the river like so much garbage."

She smiled wanly then closed her eyes. Soon, only her rhythmic breathing could be heard. Marcus covered her up and ran to get Nancy and his sons. He held the three of them in his arms. He whispered to Nancy. She immediately took the two boys to her suite, telling Cotton to look after Rufus. She locked the door after her then ran back to the main stateroom. The door swung listlessly back and forth as the vessel yawed in the river current. She crossed herself before entering the room. Immediately she began washing Belle. Marcus hovered above her. Nancy screamed,

"God almighty, may he strike them all dead! They were animals all of them. I could hear them. Oh Marcus, Oh Marcus. I'm so sorry. I could do nothing, nothing! Here now stay with her. I've finished." She backed away, her hands to her head and wailed, "Oh my poor Belle!"

Marcus stood there absolutely shattered by it all. Nancy stood up, threw the wash cloth on the bed then beat her fists upon his chest crying,

"How could you leave her alone? How could you?"

She stopped, her head against his heaving chest, her sobs breaking his heart in two. Marcus stood like a statue carved in black stone, unable as a man to comprehend the extent to which Belle had suffered as a woman. After a few minutes, Nancy regained her senses. She released him, backed away from the stricken Maasai and said,

"I've locked the boys in my room. I don't want them to see their mother or you for that matter like this. Oh God in Heaven, please help her!"

Nancy put her hand on Marcus's face to wipe away his tears. In her immutable Irish lilt, she crooned,

"You poor man, oh you poor man! Please send us home I beg of you!"

With that, she crossed the room leaving Marcus alone with his wife.

Nancy closed the door behind her. Marcus came out of his stupor as he felt the ship pick up speed. Someone else was at the helm. Belle lay asleep under the coverlet. He slowly pulled a pale green bed sheet from beneath her body. Its sweet wetness clung to him as if begging for forgiveness. Gathering it to his chest, he walked over to an open porthole and pushed it out. He watched it float upon the river as the ship's wake lifted it up then rolled over it. He ran back to Belle and held her in his arms. He wailed,

"Oh Belle, there's always been a river of tears between us. How could it ever be otherwise, how could it ever be otherwise? I'm sorry! I'm so sorry! Ninatokea samahini! Ninatokea samahini!"

Nancy returned to the stateroom. Its oak door swung from side to side as if waving her away from the suffering within. She found Marcus clutching Belle tightly to him. He was murmuring something in Swahili over and over again. Instinctively, she knew what he was saying. Nancy closed the cabin door quietly making sure it stayed shut.

During the fight between Garrow and Marcus, a battered and bruised Harley Blackstone used the diversion to escape unseen in one of the village skiffs tied to the ship. He jumped in, cut the painter then lay down within the skiff out of sight. As it drifted down river, he swore,

"Goddamn it all to hell, every time I meet that little bastard, I end up in a rowboat. Where the hell did he get that derringer? Well, the next time, I'll make sure I'm as far away from water as I can get!"

After a while he peeked over the skiff's starboard gunwale, squinting into a rising sun. He shaded his eyes with a beefy paw. Something on the river caught his attention. Looking closely, he saw a man's body hung up on a floating log. It looked familiar. Harley sat up, and grabbed the oars. He thrust them between the rowing tholes and crabbed his way over to it.

The body bumped up against the skiff. Harley stowed the oars, reached down, grabbing a man by the scruff of the neck. Harley rolled it over. It was Garrow.

Harley hauled him aboard for he realized that Horatio was barely alive, a deep and bloody knife wound in his chest. A pale green bed sheet floated in the river nearby. Harley reached over and pulled it into the rowboat. He wondered,

'Where in the hell did that come from? Oh well it's better than nothing.'

He immediately ripped it into wide bandages then carefully wrapping them around Garrow's chest. The bleeding stopped. But Harley knew that Garrow didn't have long to live. If he died, Blackstone's chances of escape were diminished considerably for Garrow knew the way back to Rebel lines, Blackstone did not. A house at Mystery Point appeared around the next bend. Harley rowed towards it with all his might. He was lucky or should one say Garrow was even luckier. An hour later, a very nervous doctor began preparing potions and applying them to Garrow's wound. Of course the doctor had no choice. Harley had bound and gagged his terrified wife.

The Nimsi steamed back to Garrison Landing and picked up the two Rangers and the mules. It then headed to its berth below the Marine battery to load up the rest of the mules and every Ranger there. It sailed for West Point at noon. Belle was taken to the Point's infirmary where Doctor Barstow attended to her. Nancy and the two boys stayed with the Bowmans. The next day, Sergeant Leitzell, five soldiers and ten raiders were given a military funeral at the Point. A few days after that, "Bones" Barstow pronounced Belle fit for travel. Belle and Marcus never said a word about what had happened. All Marcus knew was that Belle would never set foot upon any ship again. For her, her private war against slavery was over. Her private peace was now between her and God. Marcus could only hope that Belle would fully recover. For Cotton, the whole episode was no longer just another game of hide n' seek. For Nancy, her prayers were answered as she watched Belle and her two sons board a private train coach for Boston, courtesy of the Union government.

That very day, Colonel Bowman received the Ranger's new orders from Secretary of War, Edwin M. Stanton. A day later, their ships refueled at the Saxton dock in New York City. The next morning they left for Fort Monroe, Virginia, arriving there on May 5th, 1862. Both Captains now knew for certain from what Garrow told Belle, there was a traitor in their midst. All communication with Pinkerton, Belle, Virginia, and especially Hans Larsen was terminated. The Rangers were headed for a war where there would be no quarter asked for and none given. Only victory mattered.

A Fitchburg express train arrived at its Causeway Avenue train station right on time. Virginia, her parents and the Clovers were there to meet Belle, her sons and Nancy. Baby Felicity remained at Saxton House under Millie's maternal care. The greeting party arrived

back at the Saxton House in time for lunch. The day was warm but there had been showers earlier that morning. Another generation of red polls and gold finches flitted about in the hedgerows lining the driveway as the Saxton's passing carriage disturbed their little world.

Belle was grateful to everyone but told them she was tired. Her room was ready as well as Nancy's. Cotton stayed downstairs playing with Jack. They ran outside to play in the back yard. Rodney penned up the Mastiffs before Jack could attack them. The four massive dogs howled for they wanted to play too. At this time, Packard was serving lunch in the drawing room. Even though the Saxton House was full, to Virginia it had been empty for a long time.

She missed her husband who had run off to war. Now she was cut off from him altogether. However, she too realized that a cunning and resourceful traitor was in their midst; someone who knew everything about 'Operation Maasai Ranger'. Well, she'd talk to Belle about it. Since the police had failed to find whoever it was that was trying to kill them, then perhaps it was time for female brains to solve the riddle.

After lunch, Virginia listened to Reverend Clover drone on about what Belle had gone through until it made her physically ill. She was glad when everyone left. Now her thoughts were to herself. Virginia too lay in her bed that night, waiting for her hunter to come home from the hill. She remembered the day when Saxton accepted the Union's commission to Captain the Nimsi. She hated war with a passion few women ever experienced. America was at war with itself. She wondered why? It was so unnecessary, so self-destructive, and so expensive. Brothers fought each other, fathers killed sons, where after wives and mothers cried over their graves. Whole generations were swallowed up into a maw of hatred. Would time really erase all traces of it? Where were the peacemakers? Would there be any room left for love and forgiveness when this terrible war was over?

Virginia Saxton had given birth to a baby girl just before Saxton and Marcus left for war. Of course, everyone was ecstatic, especially Belle who couldn't keep her hands off the new child. She smiled as she lay dreaming about how Belle found the name for the child. They'd been sitting around the long pine table in the kitchen drinking tea and eating those horrid Peek Freans. The war had been raging for eight months. Belle leaned back in her chair, tea cup in hand expounding as usual. She said with authority,

"I'm sick and tired of calling babies after characters in the Good Book. Land sakes girl, aren't there enough Mary's, Ruth's, Naomi's, Hannah's and Abigail's already? Why all my doves at La Belle Maison were named after women from the bible. Somehow it comforted my church-goin' clientele to know they were sleeping with a girl from the Good Book itself. It relaxed them in a way which was good, because believe me some of those bible thumpers needed a whole lot of relaxin'! Ever see their wives? God, I've never seen such a bunch of stiff necked, pious pouters in my whole life. Imagine tellin' their husbands that once the appropriate number of children were born, there'd be no more sex Herman."

They laughed as she continued her discourse. Virginia thought Belle could out-preach anyone once she got rolling. Belle continued undaunted. Her tea refreshed; she lit a cheroot and leaned back, her fervor undiminished.

"You see, a man has needs. It's born in him and dies with him. Women gotta understand that. Believe me; a thirsty man will go to any well that will slack his thirst."

She looked around. Virginia was tapping her nails on the table top. Marcus and Saxton were looking up at the ceiling. Belle suddenly remembered what they were all there to name the baby. She changed the topic, for she was used to holding people in the palm of her hands, so to speak.

"As I was sayin'" She sipped some tea as if relaxing at a church bake sale.

"As I was sayin' before I got carried away; why not give the girl a name like…say…Felicity." Marcus leaned over.

"What does that mean Belle? He waited sipping the bitter tea he hated. Virginia grew excited.

"Why Belle, I think Felicity is a wonderful name for a girl. I do believe it means a state of well-founded happiness. Yes, that's it, a state of well-founded happiness. What do you think Saxton?" Saxton was dreaming. She punched his shoulder saying,

"John Saxton! Are you listening to me? Good Lord Belle, he did this when we first met at his father's funeral reception. I'd talk and he'd be off in some other world completely oblivious to me or any one else for that matter." Belle laughed,

"Oh Virginia, he's now probably in love with the Nimsi. All men love their projects, believe me." Saxton came out of his trance,

"Sorry dear but you're right when you say that I never listen to you. At least I think that's what you said." After the laughter subsided, Saxton continued.

"The war and the Nimba have been on my mind a lot lately. I'll try to pay more attention." Virginia kissed him saying,

"My experience with men and their projects has been rather limited. The only men I've ever gotten close to were as one might say already passed on. I mean, I'd talk to them as I prepared their bodies for their funeral. They never talked back or complained while I worked my magic." Belle laughed, sipped her tea and said coyly,

"My dear, that sounds very familiar to me, please continue." Virginia did.

"Now my Dear Saxton, please tell us, will it be Felicity or some other name?" Saxton roused himself again.

"Whatever you say dear is fine with me." Virginia scowled, "Men!"

Belle looked at Marcus and said, "Amen to that Sister!"

Both women looked at each other, got up and left the kitchen. Their husbands were left there alone, wondering what on earth was going on.

S.A. Carter

Hans Larsen was upset, very upset; for all telegraph communications concerning 'Operation Maasai Ranger' had been cut off. No longer was he or anyone else for that matter, able to have any idea what Marcus and Saxton were up to. This worried him as others higher up the chain of command would be demanding information. Had he been found out? Did someone close to him know he was a Confederate agent? So far 'False Prophet' had worked superbly well for his masters. There had been major coups because of his complicity. Hans considered himself a patriot of the South. He had been very careful. If he ran, his guilt would be evident. If he stayed, he stood a good chance that his complicity would be uncovered. Hans Larsen was indeed worried. It drove him deeper into a depression that only copious amounts of alcohol seemed to relieve.

Although born in Sweden, Hans Larsen grew up in New Orleans. In fact Thomas Saxton found him there when Hans applied for an accounting job in the Saxton Co. office on the levee. The panic of 1857 hit America hard, especially the Southern states. Cotton prices dropped through the floor. Shippers were pressed to lower their rates. Thomas Saxton needed financial help just to keep his company from going under. Interest rates were usurious.

Hans Larsen literally appeared in the proverbial nick of time. Immediately, he began cutting costs by firing staff, selling off ships too old to avoid costly repairs, changing to steam power instead of relying on sail, eliminating unprofitable sea routes, employing new labour saving technology in the warehouses, consolidating debt and so on. Within three years the Company was back in the black. A grateful Thomas Saxton made Hans the company's comptroller replete with a large stock portfolio. Despite this largesse, Hans was bitter even though he would receive five percent of the Company's net worth upon Thomas's death. At that time, John Saxton would become the company's sole owner. Larsen was incensed,

'Imagine! Five percent of a company that I have built, not the Saxton's but me; Hans Larsen! Without me there wouldn't have been any company at all. I'll get even with the Saxtons if it's the last thing I ever do. They live above me in their mansion while I live in a coldwater garret off Boston Commons. It isn't fair at all, not at all!'

Larsen's opportunity came in the person of Silas Wilkins, Captain of the Silver Ghost who listened attentively one afternoon as Hans got drunk in the Warren Tavern in Charlestown. The Warren, a three story red brick building on the corner of Main and Pleasant Streets, had been a popular watering hole ever since the British burned the town in 1780. There, Silas plied Larsen with mugs of strong ale. As Silas poured ale in, Larsen poured his heart out. Wilkins was also a true Southron from New Orleans. Both felt persecuted as men, as professionals and most of all as Southerners. They found common ground from which to launch their verbal attacks on the Saxtons. They also found another common ground; pure unadulterated greed.

Passed over as Captain for many years, Wilkins had considered other shipping Companies but they rejected him on his one physical impediment; namely he was blind in one eye. He never wore an eye patch and learned to compensate well for his disability. Thomas Saxton

294

never found out. A short, rotund man, with a pinched clean shaven face, Wilkins was physically bereft by the social standards set by the Cunard Line either; in other words he wasn't tall, white whiskered, debonair or loquacious. However, he was a superb sailor of the old school, for tall ships were his specialty. After twenty-five years with the Saxton line he finally became Captain of the Silver Ghost upon which young Saxton sailed to China. However a series of calamities beyond his control plagued the voyage for nearly three years in which time both Muriel and Thomas Saxton suffered greatly. Although not implicit in the Silver Ghosts' misfortunes, nonetheless the blame rested squarely on its Captain. So, two desperate men; Wilkins and Larsen became inseparable. In their fifties, too old to fight, they were however young enough to serve the 'Cause' in other more insidious ways.

Silas Wilkins first met Customs Captain Horatio Garrow in New Orleans in 1857 just before Wilkins captained the Silver Ghost. A cargo of sundries and dry goods in to the Saxton warehouse awaited inspection. Silas had heard about the Garrow's, especially its patriarch, the notorious slaver, Josiah. Hours later, while trying to reason with Horatio Garrow inside his Custom's office, Silas became enraged. That small part of an impressive stone edifice fronting the levee at the foot of Rue Bienville figuratively shook to its very rafters. There in, Garrow stared down at a florid little man shaking a long ship's cargo manifest in his face. Silas sputtered,

"I say Captain; do you rob everyone that docks here in New Orleans? These groundage charges are outrageous and you know it. The Rover's skipper's is sick, lying on his bunk. Christ man, these charges will kill him fer sure. Wadda ya say mate, there must be some other way to accommodate both of us?"

Horatio remained mute, staring down at the livid penitent standing before him. The Custom's officer's reptilian stare had worked well before and it was doing so again. Oh, how he loved his job. It wasn't the highway robbery so much that he enjoyed, but the complete arousal he felt when he had someone completely in his power, man, woman, child or animal. It didn't matter to Garrow, for he was a man without a conscience just like his father. He purred,

"What did you have in mind Silas; perhaps something naughty? For a man with one good eye, perhaps your employers know nothing about, I'm sure we could come to an agreement." Silas blanched thinking,

'How on earth did this awful man know I'm blind in one eye?' He collected himself.

"And which eye might that be?"

"Your starboard runnin' light matey! It never moves to port. A one eyed sailor you may be; but a First Mate lookin' to be a Captain, never!"

He was right and Silas knew it. Garrow offered the stricken man a cheroot. He accepted, bent over and lit it. Silas became wary, very wary for no longer was he in rough waters, instead he was sailing right into a hurricane. Garrow, sensing his advantage, pressed forward.

"Come to think of it Silas, there is something you could do, not for me mind you, but for the 'Cause'.

"The 'Cause',"

"Yes, the 'Cause'."

Garrow stood above the hapless Wilkins like a hawk hovering over a desperate pigeon. He continued thinking aloud.

"Definitely, the 'Cause' my dear Silas as you and every other astute man knows full well, there's going to be Civil War in a few years and there will be nothing civil about it. We Southrons need arms now in order to fend off the greedy grubbing Yankees, whose only goal is to strip us of our livelihood and our manhood at the same time." Silas brightened, puffing on his cheroot with renewed vigor.

"I must say I heartily agree. Do press on Sir."

"Thank you. Might I suggest that the Saxton Shipping Co. could very well be used as a conduit for the funneling of essential war materiel into New Orleans, Pensacola, Mobile, Wilmington or, perhaps Charleston. My contact knows Jefferson Davis, President Pierce's Secretary of War very well. As a true Southron, I'm sure the Secretary's inner circle would be very interested. I'm also quit sure that we would be paid well for our astute patriotism, don't you think?" Silas agreed. Garrow concurred saying,

"As to our previous disagreement, the normal duties owed this office will suffice. How about sealing our business deal with a glass of Jim Beam's finest?"

Garrow speedily filled two old fashioned crystal glasses. The conspirators toasted their future success. The Custom's Captain returned to his black leather chair and rested his six foot six frame by putting his black leather riding boots upon a polished mahogany desktop. He raised his glass, looking through its amber depths as if it was a crystal ball.

"Any ideas, partner as to how we can smuggle arms right under the noses of the bible thumpin' Saxtons?"

Silas began roaming the room, glass of Bourbon in one hand, a cheroot in the other. He replied,

"I think so, but we need a third man."

"Who's that Silas?" Silas waited, relishing the moment.

"Well, he's the business manager of Saxton Shipping at its Boston headquarters. His name is Hans Larson. I've been working on him for months, getting to know where he stands on the coming war."

"And where does he stand, my friend?"

Silas turned to put some ash into a large glass ashtray. He continued.

"Let me explain something first. He was born in Sweden but spent most of his life in New Orleans working in his father's furniture factory in the French quarter. From there he trained as an accountant in Boston. He was very successful until the panic early this year when they summarily threw him out on his ear. Needless to say Thomas Saxton has taken him to Boston where in past three months he's saved the company from bankruptcy. Amazing really; he's very smart but has been very depressed. He's been drinking a lot lately."

Garrow asked, "Why's that?" as he refreshed their drinks.

"Well apparently Thomas Saxton's will has prevented him from ever owning any part of the company which I understand is worth over ten million dollars. It's pissed him off I'd say because Saxton's only child, John Saxton, will inherit a company that Larsen basically built from scratch, sacrificing everything; his marriage, children, and lots more. He's even got a cot in Saxton's office to be there at all hours receiving telegraph messages and incoming ship's manifests." Garrow jumped up nearly spilling his Beam.

"You say he's got a telegraph machine in his office?"

"That's correct. It's also connected to Thomas Saxton's office at his mansion. Why do you ask?"

Silas sat down. While he sipping his whiskey, Garrow was enjoying this exchange immensely. Thus enthused, he exclaimed.

"Don't you see man, that telegraph will allow us to arrange cargo pickups, dispersals, and arrivals of say," He paused,

"We'll label the cargo farm machinery." Silas laughed.

"Yes of course, well I'll be damned!"

"Silas, we have to get Larsen on our side. See what you can do when you get back to Boston. Let me know by telegraph. Shall we call our arrangement 'False Prophet'? I like the double entendre you might say. By the way, my code name will be, Belle's Poker. For me, it has a certain delicious ring to it. We'll flesh out the details later Silas after I've made some contacts. From what I've heard, the Confederacy has only thirty-five field pieces. We need more and their ammunition. With Larsen involved, his connections will be invaluable."

In the ensuing three years from the time the Silver Ghost sailed to the Far East until Captain Wilkins died, Hans Larsen had filled many Saxton ships with cargoes supposedly destined for federal ports. Larsen really didn't need much convincing. He would serve two long range causes, one was to the South and the other was to Larsen himself. Thus the Saxton cargoes would leave under a false invoice Hans made sure looked legitimate. No one ever checked the cargo in Boston because any shipping manifests were handled by Larsen who acted as a company Supercargo. In 1861, after the Civil War began, a plethora of Saxton ships manned by Larsen's handpicked crews would steam far out into the Atlantic then turn south headed for the Bermudas. After being paid in gold by Confederate agents, the Saxton Shipping Co. office in Hamilton, Bermuda would purchase loads of cotton, indigo and rice warehoused there destined for New York or Boston. As for the military and medical contraband smuggled from Boston and later New York City, fast steam packets would run their illicit booty up the Mississippi delta to New Orleans where Garrow's gang of thieves awaited.

False shippers and an assortment of counterfeit documents were used. In Boston and New York City, the Saxton Shipping Co. was paid for storing and shipping the goods through agents posing as Union shippers. Besides, the Finch twins were part of the smuggler's stew, keeping Larsen well informed as to who was asking too many questions at the front gates. Unbeknownst to Larsen, every defective gun, and artillery shell casing had been previously marked, stamped and recorded beforehand where they were manufactured because captured artillery and other material were often used by the victors after a battle on both sides. Lincoln and his Secretary of War didn't want any captured Confederate cannon blowing up afterwards. Therefore, Government agents set aside a portion of the Metro Archives on 'D' street in the nation's capital for storing all files pertaining to 'Operation False Prophet'. By the end of the war, the building's basement it was full.

Luckily, after Wilkin's death and the discovery of the illicit weapons after the 'Battle of Boston Harbor', Hans Larsen, although suspect was never implicated until much later. Before that happened; he successfully presented false documentation that for all intents and purposes appeared to be genuine. Mysteriously, Confederate shippers in Boston, Bermuda and in New York disappeared when 'the poop hit the propeller' only to reappear again after the hue and cry had died down. After Thomas Saxton's death, a rewritten codicil signed a week before he died, relieved Larsen of his lucrative partnership. John Saxton kept him on by doubling his salary because Pinkerton as head of the Union's Secret Service at the time wanted it that way. Every shipment of 'Farm Machinery" became compromised in such a way that during the war; firing pins shattered, cartridges jammed, cannon barrels cracked, ammunition was plagued by misfires, gun carriages came apart, and spare parts were susceptible to minimal wear and tear. Pinkerton also knew Larsen was playing a dangerous game as long as Garrow was alive. If he fled, Garrow would kill him. Pinkerton counted on Larsen's predicament to keep him in Boston. The detective was playing the same game in New York City with a Saxton Company shipping agent under the thumb of the 'Tiger of Tammany Hall', William Marcy Tweed Jr.

As for 'Project Maasai Ranger' the very fact that it was incommunicado made Larsen very nervous indeed. Pinkerton would feed false information to Larsen, Tweed, 'Copperheads' and Confederate spies about 'Project' when the appropriate time came. With the project now incommunicado, Pinkerton waited to see which of the aforementioned would pop up.

SACRIFICE: CHAPTER 10
THE PACKET

Corporal Harley Blackstone was transferred to Richmond, Virginia, after the battle of Fort Darling in late May of 1862. Summarily demoted to buck Private for cowardice in the face of the enemy, he was put to work on the construction of the Howard Grove Military Hospital. While there, Harley hated taking orders especially from a certain foreman named Sergeant Morgan.

Morgan was the son of a rich plantation owner whose estate stretched for miles along the James River south of the city of Richmond. Like Corporal Riley at Fort Sumter, Morgan was short, stocky and full of himself. It didn't take long for matters to come to a head.

The first of seven hundred patients began to arrive at the hospital just as the paint dried. Therefore, Surgeon in Chief, Dr. James Bolton, had no time for petty disruptions from his 'inferiors' as he liked to call them. The acrimonious and volatile situation that existed between Blackstone and Morgan for months finally came to a violent conclusion. Simply put, Harley killed Morgan with his bare hands late one evening in front of a dozen witnesses. Blackstone, however escaped from the hospital's so called jail under mysterious circumstances.

It had taken five strong men to put him there. Apparently, a tall, good looking Major, recovering in an upper ward from a severe chest wound, heard about the incident. He asked to see the prisoner. No one was about to question a Major. After he left, Blackstone produced a gun, killed a guard and escaped along with the Major. Now AWOL, they were being sought not only for desertion but for murder.

Garrow and Blackstone escaped to New Orleans only to find that the Union blockade had completely destroyed their smuggling business. Instead of one in nine blockade runners being caught by Union ships, it was now one in three. The Deacon Gang was not only on the run from the law but the military forces on both sides. It was too risky for them to stay in New Orleans. Mother Superior Fargone in the interim had became repentant after Garrow jilted her. In due course, she confessed her sins to Bishop Grodine. Steps were immediately taken by the Holy See to correct the situation. The Bishop was transferred to a remote Catholic outpost in the Algarve region of France. Soon after that, Fargone was found floating face down in the canal. She'd been strangled.

The murder of Fargone had been impulsive and rather foolish on Garrow's part. Sergeant Raines suspected that the Major committed the murder but couldn't prove it. New Orleans had a new Union commander, General Nathaniel P. Banks. Like his predecessor 'Beast

Butler', Banks took umbrage at anyone disturbing the status quo. Within months, most of the Deacon Gang had been killed or captured with only Garrow and Blackstone remaining at large. The dogged Sergeant Raines posted a guard at Garrow's former residence on Rue Dauphine. With the basement hideout at the Convent no longer available, Horatio remembered the secret door in Pirate Alley. He and Blackstone holed up there, living off the charred remains of Belle Brown's stash.

It wasn't long however, before a certain Canadian blockade runner by the name of Alexander 'Sandy' Keith Jr. came looking for Garrow one night on the levee. Horatio's luck was about to change for the better. Keith had been sent by a confederate spy, Henry Thomas Harrison to find the Major. Keith and Garrow had done a lot of business together before and the war. Keith's ship, the sixty foot steam cutter SS Reliant was fast. After finding Garrow, both climbed aboard while Blackstone stood guard outside its main cabin. At the time, the cutter's crew of four was fast asleep below in the foc'sle. The main cabin was surprisingly large, warm and private. Keith had a message for him from a Major William Norris, head of the CSA Signal Corps who was coordinating the activities of dozens of agents operating along the 'Secret Line'.

This 'Line', was an underground espionage system that stretched from Richmond, Virginia, to the Washington DC-Baltimore area. Run by the Confederate Secret Service Bureau, it used a system to get letters, intelligence reports and other documents across the Potomac and Rappahannock Rivers to confederate officials. Norris directed intelligence networks along the Potomac River. It was one of his operatives working as a custodian at West Point who had run across 'Operation Maasai Ranger'. Norris's assistant, 2nd. Lieutenant Charles Cawood recruited Major Garrow to lead the attack on the Rangers while Confederate Colonel John S. Mosby's Partisan Rangers created a diversion.

It was Mosby's Partisan Rangers first expedition behind enemy lines. The Confederate Congress in Richmond, Virginia, had just passed the Partisan Ranger Act on April 12, 1862. Mosby's Rangers narrowly missed killing Lincoln as well. By taking control of the Anaona, Garrow and Mosby would have shelled the President's party as they approached by train. But the Rebels failed on both counts.

Keith gave Garrow a sealed packet. A desperate Garrow tore away the red wax seal stamped with the letters CSA, hoping its contents offered a way out of his current dilemma. He sat before Keith looking like a scarecrow in a cornfield. The knife wound to his chest still hurt although it had healed completely. Keith had not seen him for nearly a year. The Major was gaunt, his face sallow, unshaven. Sandy was shocked,

"My God man, were have you been? Holidaying on Ship Island?" Garrow scowled,

"Look Sandy, a lot has happened to me and none of it pleasant. Leave me be while I read this message."

After a few minutes, he visibly changed for the better. Sandy Keith, a wizened old man, noticed this miracle saying,

"I do say old chap, the news must be good. Do you mind telling me?" Garrow reached for two cheroots in his breast pocket and gave one to Keith. They both lit up. Garrow relaxed.

"All I can say Sandy, is that Major Norris wants me to go to Boston right away."

Garrow jumped up and strolled about pensive and somewhat agitated. He turned to Keith.

"Sandy, tell me where you're headed to next?"

"Back home to Halifax. Another fellow and I have an idea about infecting Yankee uniforms with cholera. We did it to the injuns, why not the blue bellies too?" Garrow was impressed.

"Christ almighty Sandy, you're a brilliant bastard indeed. Imagine Cholera. Anyway, my partner and I must go to Boston and I want you to stay there awhile. We'll need your ship in case we have to escape to Canada. Do you know Boston Harbor well?"

"Of course, we 'Blue Nosers' all have relatives there. If Norris wants you, it must be really important. I'm all for the 'Cause" as long as it has a silver lining."

He rubbed a thumb and forefinger together. Sandy was needed and he knew it. Garrow would have to pay a lot. Keith looked up at him towering above like a cobra facing a mongoose. He also knew the Major was deadly for he'd heard all the stories in every seaside bar from Canada to the Keys. However, he was known to pay well and keep his word. Sandy smiled.

"How much are you willing to pay me for my, ah, unique services old chap?" Garrow was cagey.

"You tell me old chap. It's your ship, crew and neck on the line. Yeah, Sandy, you tell me."

He puffed his cheroot and waited. Keith looked up into reptilian eyes. The effect was startling. He croaked,

"I want one thousand dollars in silver, half of it now and half on delivery."

Garrow tried not to smile, for according to the letter, five thousand dollars in silver waiting at his old digs in the Customs House three blocks away. He replied, somewhat reluctantly,

"I don't like it but I guess I've no choice in the matter. Ok, you've got a deal Sandy. Shake on it." They did.

Horatio said goodbye to Keith. They would be leaving in the morning on the flood tide.

Harley and Horatio sauntered up to the Customs House. A massive structure, three stories high and a city block in length, it was indeed impressive. An Egyptian Revival style gave it an air of dignified importance. Built in 1848, by the very man that promoted Garrow, General Beauregard; its narrow windows and impressive Doric colonnaded portico looked down as if frowning upon anyone bold enough to approach it. It was two in the morning on a moonless night. The occasional bat swept past as Garrow jimmied a side door and crept in.

He knew every inch of the interior, thus he did not need a light. Blackstone as usual stood guard in the shadows under a portico outside.

The Customs House had been torched a second time a year earlier after Admiral Farragut fired on the city, forcing it to surrender. The interior of the small office was still a shambles. Broken windows had been boarded up. Burned papers and smashed furniture were scattered about. The message from Keith had said to go there and wait.

Effete and quite dapper, Harrison was already inside sitting in the dark watching Horatio break in. His small feet rested on a canvas bank sack filled with silver coins. Harrison had robbed the New Orleans mint on Rue Esplanade earlier that morning. Actually the silver was left behind in a secret room by accident as Confederate forces fled in panic when Farragut's navy cruised into the harbor. The room remained undiscovered until one of architect William Strickland's employees became a spy for James Seddon, the Confederate's Secretary of War. It was this employee that contacted Seddon about the hoard of silver dollars.

Garrow froze as he sensed movement in the shadows behind him. He spun around, knife in hand. A gun cocked loudly in the dark silence of the small room. A deep voice uttered,

"Don't make a move Garrow. Put the knife on the table over there very slowly. There are other scoundrels who love money too my friend, so don't make me shoot you. Easy does it. That's a good boy."

Garrow did as he was told. Henry Thomas Harrison came out into the dim light of a nearby street lamp. He put away his gun and reached out to shake hands. Seconds later, he found himself on the floor with a knife at his throat. He sputtered,

"Easy does it Garrow. No need to get rough. I'm only here to get you on your way old chap. Now let me up. Carry a second knife do you now? I've heard you're deadly with a blade. Glad to know you can handle yourself. Seddon knows all about you and wants you to know that all the murder and desertion charges against you and Blackstone will be dismissed if you do as you are told by me and others."

Garrow let him go. Harrison stood up and brushed himself off as he considered himself somewhat of a gallant. He picked up an overturned chair, sat down and came to the point.

"It seems that you and a certain Hans Larsen of Boston successfully smuggled, should I say, farm machinery from Boston into New Orleans before the war. I believe it was called 'Operation False Prophet'. You worked as a Captain of Customs here and through deceit and cunning handled the cargoes Captain Silas Wilkins brought to you. That operation was very successful, therefore very profitable for everyone until a certain Marcus Brown uncovered the whole scheme. Am I correct?" Garrow growled,

"Get on with it. We've been here long enough. The tide turns in one hour. My colleague and I will be shipping aboard the Reliant for Boston. Give me my orders, the silver and I'll be off." Harrison laughed.

"You are impatient aren't you? Well let's not be too hasty. Anyway, Hans Larsen recruited two identical twins, the Finch brothers as accomplices. They are waiting now for a

Saxton steamer to come back from Sweden. On it are agents that have, let us say, liberated a certain packet of information that will mean victory for the 'Cause' if we can get it to Richmond without incident. It will be your job to get it to Richmond quickly and safely. However, your old nemesis Belle Brown is currently living at Saxton House in Boston with Virginia Saxton. Their husbands are in command of the Maasai Rangers whom I understand you will never forget. So, I not only give you a golden opportunity to serve the Confederacy but an opportunity for another rendezvous to satisfy your unbridled lust for the lady. Indeed it's a silver lining to be sure."

Harrison produced a heavy canvas bank bag marked with the letters CSA NEW ORLEANS MINT. It clinked deliciously. Harrison continued,

"Major Garrow it's in the bag so to speak. You will get the other half once Nobel's packet gets to Howard Grove's Military Hospital in Richmond. By the time you get there, the Hospital will be certified as a small pox lazaret. However, it really is a cover for the many interesting experiments the Confederacy is carrying out. I've brought you a pass. That's all I can say because I don't know any more. You will be escorted to safety by an agent named 'BB' who will pose as your wife."

He reached into his breast pocket and withdrew a brown envelope.

"Here are your new identification papers. You are now a Mr. Anthony Crawford from Bermuda. You are aboard the SS Reliant as a British representative of the Camrose Trading Co. based out of Hamilton, Bermuda. Blackstone will play the role of a mute sailor. Avoid the Union blockade by the usual routes until you round Florida. You have just three weeks to get to Boston in time to meet the SS Night Hawk. Once Larsen has given you the packet, you and BB will proceed by the B&O Railway to Washington DC supposedly on business with the Union. The Night Hawk's crew will be your bodyguards. If there is any hint of impending trouble along the way, you will escape to Richmond, Virginia along our own 'underground railway'. He paused,

"Upon your arrival in Boston, Blackstone will stay at the Finch garret at #112-1020 Canal Street. A block away, your domicile will be Larsen's apartment at 967 Friend St., suite 108. Your 'wife' BB will be there waiting. A word of caution my friend and I'm being serious now. Never underestimate, abuse or betray her Garrow, or she will kill you."

He proceeded to tell Garrow more about his future wife. Needless to say, Garrow was intrigued as he heard more about the 'romping' girl. After a few more details, Harrison got back to business.

"Now my friend, memorize this information. Do not write it down or tell anyone. Don't leave here for ten minutes. I'll tell your mute companion to cover you as you make your way back to the Reliant. By the way, do not go back to Pirate Alley tonight for any reason."

Garrow wondered how Harrison knew about the hiding place at Pirate Alley. What else did he know? He started to ask for an answer but Harrison resisted.

"Have you left anything incriminating there Garrow?—papers, personal items. No? Good, then get going and good luck."

Harrison drew back into the shadows disappearing as mysteriously as he had appeared. Garrow waited ten minutes, took the silver then walked back to the levee. Blackstone made sure he wasn't followed.

They arrived in Boston three weeks later in late October after an uneventful voyage. The British flag had fluttered all the way from the Reliant's main mast. Everyone's papers were in order even after being checked many times by Union blockaders stationed along the Atlantic seaboard. Once in Boston, Garrow went directly to Larsen's apartment, while Blackstone went to the Finch garret.

Garrow knocked on the door of suite 108. It opened. Before him stood a tall, blue eyed, full figured woman smoking cheroot. Her long light brownish hair crowned a pleasant face that sported a strong prominent nose. He was stunned by her beauty. She curtsied gaily, saying suggestively,

"You must be my husband I presume, please come in sir." He nodded.

Before Garrow knew it, she grabbed his hand, pulled him into the room, closed the door with her boot and proceeded to kiss him passionately. They made love all afternoon until Garrow was totally exhausted. The woman was insatiable. Horatio was more than a little satisfied. Finally he'd met his match. He looked at her nubile body as she pranced about the room. They had not even exchanged names, it had happened so fast. Garrow lay back on the bed, his groin in full salute as she got dressed. She laughed as he asked her name.

"My friends call me La Belle Rebella or BB, like in honey bee."

Garrow was at a loss for words. She looked at him curiously as he lay there apparently tongue tied.

"Anything wrong lover boy?" she chirped.

"Why, not at all my dear. Please call me Anthony when you're mad at me and Tony when you're not." She giggled.

Horatio was instantly infatuated. BB's reputation, well deserved, had preceded her.

Only nineteen years old, BB's outgoing personality, her rumored nymphomania and her complete disregard for any danger were already legend. She indeed captivated Horatio. His only real concern was his own outrageous streak of insane jealousy. Garrow kept reminding himself that he had to be very careful with her as she was his only means of getting back to Richmond where another pot of silver awaited at the end of the Confederate rainbow. He mused as BB dressed. It seemed that Howard Grove Military Hospital would make his journey come full circle. How ironic. BB was reportedly brave and resolute but Garrow surmised instinctively that she was a 'loose cannon' and therefore unpredictable. He would play along with her until he was paid off then move on.

She finished dressing and sat on the bed beside him smoking a cheroot. Her other hand stroked him until he moaned in exquisite release. Her mouth engulfed him. He cried out. She rose up and cooed into his ear,

"Now, come again with me sweet knight."

Later that day they rendezvoused with Larsen at the Ship's Tavern for lunch. Blackstone as usual remained out of sight, sipping his mug of ale. He made very sure that he sat beside a large window near the tavern's front door. Hans Larsen although completely captivated by BB, pretended to be reserved. Every other male eye in the place feasted on the girl as she laughed gaily with her two companions. Finally, Garrow reached over and closed the heavy curtains of their private booth. BB pouted, saying that her admirers were being deprived. She laughed when Larsen said they were more depraved rather than deprived.

While eating lunch, the trio got down to business. The SS Night Hawk had been sighted off Boston light two hours before. It would be docking soon, luckily for them, a week late. An hour later a plan of action was agreed upon to everyone's satisfaction.

Hans Larsen would retrieve the packet secretively from a crewman aboard the SS Night Hawk and then bring it to the Saxton Warehouse office. An unsuspecting Captain Owen Sound would never see it. Larsen would receive the ship's cargo manifest from Sound as he did with every Saxton ship that docked there. After returning to the office, Hans would put the packet on top of a filing cabinet in plain sight. However, once the office door was locked, blinds drawn; he would immediately make up an identical packet filled with shredded newspaper. Later that afternoon, an hour before the Fitchburg train left at three, the Finch brothers carrying identical packets would leave the Saxton Shipping together. Larsen would stay at the gatehouse until one of them returned. Taking circuitous routes, Eddie Finch would go to Larsen's house where Garrow and BB waited while Charlie Finch would go to the apartment on Main St. where Blackstone waited just in case they were being followed. They laughed about one spy being in two places at once.

The SS Night Hawk docked two hours later. Hans Larsen greeted the bosun then asked for the ship's cargo manifesto. A few minutes later, Larsen was given a waxed packet by one of the crew. At that moment; Garrow, BB and Blackstone were waiting, ready to entrain. They knew that the other party would catch the Fitchburg train no matter what happened, packet or no packet. The Night Hawk's crew would also be on the train, fully armed ready to protect them at all costs. All went according to plan until the telegraph machine in Larsen's office started to chatter while he was wrapping the counterfeit packet.

It was just after two o'clock. Hans was alarmed at what was coming over the wire. It was from the Customs House across the harbor. He had to get down to the SS Night Hawk but not until a half hour from then when the Customs Officials would arrive. Larson thought that there had been a dreadful mistake. Somehow, someone thought that contraband was on board the Night Hawk therefore as a representative of the company, only Larsen could deal with it. Unbeknownst to him, Belle Brown sent the telegram from Saxton's office to the Boston Customs House. She was calling in a favor from one of the officer's there. That officer in turn telegraphed Larson at the Saxton Co. warehouse then Saxton House, telling Belle that the deed was done. Both she and Virginia immediately boarded a waiting carriage for the Saxton Shipping office in warehouse #3. Rodney drove the team hard to get there in time.

They arrived forty minutes later in a driving rain storm. Charlie Finch let them through the iron gates then retreated to the warmth and shelter of the gatehouse. He was very nervous, for Larsen told him that he and his brother had to be in Larsen's office in thirty minutes to get their packets. He wondered why Virginia and Belle told him that they wanted to see the new steam ship, the SS Night Hawk and talk to its handsome Captain, Owen Sound. Why? Their arrival was most inopportune indeed. Something wasn't right. Charlie watched as the two ladies hustled into warehouse No#3 and disappeared. Meanwhile, their driver Rodney climbed down from the coach and ran into the gatehouse, slamming the door behind him. Both men watched the carriage horses stand stoically, a heavy rain streaking their black bodies. Charlie tried not to show it, but Rodney knew the man was on pins and needles about something. He reached for a blue enameled coffee pot warming on a small pot bellied stove. As he did, he turned saying,

"Say Charlie or is it Eddie..."

"Charlie." Rodney laughed as Charlie kept looking out the window.

"Never could tell the difference boy. Got a mug somewhere? I need to warm up. Christ, the weather is comin' down on us in buckets." Rodney persisted as Finch stood there still looking out the window.

"Want a coffee Charlie?"

"No!" Rodney was curious. He said,

"Jesus Christ boy, you're sure jumpy 'bout somethin'! What is it man?"

Charlie continued to stand unmoving in front of the small window, looking out at where the two women had gone into the warehouse. Rodney shrugged his broad shoulders, found a clay mug, filled it and sat down. He wondered. 'What the hell is going on?'

Inside the gloomy confines of the warehouse, two frantic women ran upstairs to Larsen's office. Virginia's heart was racing as she knocked on the door. There was no answer. She tried the door. It was locked. A sign hung from the door knob. It said,

"BACK IN 20 MINUTES, PLEASE WAIT IN THE GATEHOUSE"

Belle moved Virginia aside, took out two metal lock picks from her pocket; deftly inserted them into the door lock and jiggled them around. Virginia watched in amazement as Belle opened the door and stepped into the empty office. They both knew that time was precious. Belle picked all the locks on the filing cabinets, the roll top desk and Larsen's desk. There were manifests, invoices, bills of lading, legal papers, crew lists, vessel repair surveys and so on. Nothing was incriminating. Then it happened. Virginia turned to Belle to say something just as a bolt of lightning flashed followed by a long sonorous rumble of thunder. Startled, Virginia knocked a large ledger off Larsen's roll top desk including two identical waxed packets. On impulse and nothing else, Virginia bent down and picked them up. She'd never seen anything like them in Larsen's office before. On both were labels, neatly printed with the words, 'PROPERTY OF ALFRED NOBEL'. Belle instantly recognized the famous name. She cried,

"Alfred Nobel. Let's have a look inside. You open one Virginia, I'll open the other. Be quick about it. We haven't much time."

They ripped open the sealed packets. Inside Virginia's were shredded newspapers. This made both women very suspicious. Inside Belle's packet were dozens of pages of chemical formulas and other scientific data. She cried,

"Look at this!" Virginia came over taking the papers from Belle. She thumbed quickly through them saying,

"Why would Larsen have these? It's all about explosives and their manufacture?" Belle was testy,

"We're at war my dear Virginia and from what I've been told, our dear 'Pinky' suspected that Hans was involved in smuggling operations hereabouts long before the war even started."

Some what startled, Virginia looked at Belle, wondering how she knew. She'd ask her later but not now. Perhaps Belle's past was more colorful than she ever imagined. Virginia had watched Belle pick all the locks. How did she ever learn that? Her thoughts came to an abrupt end when Belle said,

"Look girl, we've got our proof. Let's get out of here. We can always clear up any misunderstanding with Hans later."

Both women fled down the rickety wooden staircase forgetting to lock the office door behind them. Thunder and lightening boomed and flashed around them as they hurried through the deluge to their carriage. Rodney was waiting for them. Charlie had opened the gates and had watched the women run out of the warehouse towards him. He mistook their haste as being the result of the horrid weather. Little did he know that their panic was caused by something entirely more urgent. Virginia, with the Nobel packet tucked firmly under her overcoat, climbed aboard the coach completely breathless followed by Belle. Rodney sensed that they had to leave quickly. He whipped the skittish horses into a fast trot. Their carriage threw up a spray of water as it fled through the tall iron gates. Charlie stood there watching them leave wondering why they were in such a hurry. He closed the heavy gates then locked them. He started running. The rain turned into freezing sleet just as he slammed the gatehouse door behind him.

In the interim, Larsen had just returned from the ship. It was a false alarm. Now he knew he had been duped. A few minutes before, while hidden behind a crate in the warehouse, he watched helplessly as Virginia and Belle left his office with the packet. Larsen choked on his fear. He had to get the packet back before the Fitchburg train arrived at the Causeway Station at three o'clock only an hour away. Hans Larsen ran for his life up to the Saxton gatehouse. He arrived there quite pale, cold, out of breath and soaking wet.

BOOK TWO: CHAPTER 11
THE MAN WHO NEVER SLEEPS

Thirty minutes earlier, Pinkerton knocked on the front door of Saxton House. Packard opened the massive door and stood aside as Pinkerton entered. Packard took his wet hat and coat and ushered him through the grand foyer into the dining room next to the Grand Salon. Pinkerton went straight to the bar, poured himself a Beam and sat down. Packard appeared, waiting as Pinkerton made himself comfortable. The detective lit a cheroot, while inquiring politely,

"My Dear Packard, could you please inform Mrs. Saxton that I'm here."

"Why Mr. Pinkerton, she's out with Mrs. Brown. I don't know when they'll return. Perhaps if you'll wait, I can get you some lunch and coffee?"

"Packard, some lunch and coffee would be fine indeed. I'm starved. By the way, did the women say where they were going?"

"No Sir, but come to think of it, I did overhear Mrs. Saxton say that they were going to catch a Swedish rat. Strange it was Sir as most things around here have been very peculiar lately."

"Whatever do you mean Packard?"

"Well Sir, there's been odd comings and goings on lately. Mrs. Brown for instance, has been using the telegraph in the office at all hours of the night. Pinkerton teased,

"Been eavesdropping again you old bugger!" Packard puffed himself up indignantly,

"Most certainly not Sir! A butler never stoops to such unsavory activity! I'm shocked!"

Pinkerton smiled knowingly at Packard's discomfort as if he was caught with his hand in the cookie jar once again. He laughed inwardly thinking, 'Muriel Saxton was right about Packard, he's a nosey Parker to be sure." He continued.

"Anyway my good man, anything else that I as your trusted guardian should know about?" Packard began squirming,

"If I have to Sir, only if I have to."

"You have to Packard. It's my business to know. Go on man!"

"Well Sir, Rodney the coachman came home all excited. He said there was trouble afoot. I asked what trouble. He didn't exactly want to say. Said it was none of my business. He came across to me like one of those uppity uptown niggers from New York City. What he knew would be too complicated for a small town nigger like me to fathom, if you know what I mean Sir." Pinkerton nodded. Packard plodded on.

"Anyways, I persisted despite him. Rodney asked me to follow him out to the stables. Once outside, those awful Mastiffs came charging towards me. I thought I was done for but he whistled and the beasts stopped in their tracks. Thank God! Anyways, Rodney led me into the stables. First time in years since I've bin there; too dirty and smelly for me you know." Pinkerton became impatient,

"Well-- what happened Packard? Cut to the chase man!"

"He took me to one of the horse stalls. It belonged to a horse named Charger. Inside the stall, some boards were covered in blood. I asked him what happened. He said, the evening before, the dogs went wild, bayin' an all. When he ran out armed to the teeth looking for intruders, there was no one about. However there were some blood stains inside Charger's stall and oh yes, I nearly forgot, a piece of blue cloth was hanging from a nail head some six feet up the wall. Bizarre it was to say the least, for both of us mentioned it to Mistress Virginia. We showed her the torn blue cloth too. She never said a thing. Just took it, thanked us and went upstairs to her room. Peculiar indeed Sir! Peculiar indeed! Perhaps she'll tell you about it. By the way, do you still want lunch?"

"Yes, thank you Packard, perhaps a sandwich and a cup of coffee will do."

Packard bowed, closing the door quietly behind him. Pinkerton got up drink in hand and walked to a window. Outside the sky was slate grey. He lit a cheroot then continued to gaze out the window. Down below him, the Red Polls and Gold finches flitted through the hedgerows that lined the long gravel driveway. Pinkerton muttered out loud,

"There must be someone coming up the drive. I hope it's the women, however I smell trouble brewing."

A company coach swept into view and grated to a halt below the front entrance. Rodney jumped down, lowered the metal footstep, opened the door and reached in. Out stepped Virginia and Belle. Both looked terrible. Pinkerton was aghast. He swung around, put down his glass of whisky and cheroot then ran out of the room and down the hall. Packard opened the front door and stood aside as two very wet women crossed the threshold into the foyer. It was a few moments before they noticed Pinkerton standing there. They stopped dead in their tracks. Virginia took a packet from underneath her coat and put it on a side board. She off her coat and handed it to Packard then strode forward to kiss Pinkerton. Belle followed suit. She said,

"Just the man we want to see. Any news from that good for nothin' husband of mine?" Virginia laughed saying,

"Make that two good for nothin' husbands Allan." He smiled, saying,

"Ladies, I have letters for both of you. They send their love and both of them can't wait to get home. But please forgive me but I do need your utmost and undivided attention right now. So, please join me in the sitting room where my cheap cheroot is getting cold and my cheap Beam is warming up as we speak."

He politely stood aside as the two women walked down the hallway towards the sitting room. Packard followed everyone like a loyal old dog. Millie ran down the stairs with Rufus in her arms. Packard stopped and whispered something in her ear. Millie shook her head, saying

"It's Rufus's feeding time Packard. I'll give him to his mother and then keep Cotton busy upstairs." Packard disagreed,

"I'm sure that Mrs. Saxton, Mrs. Brown and Mr. Pinkerton don't want to be disturbed. I'll bring them all minced egg sandwiches and a pot of fresh coffee as soon as possible. I think Mr. Pinkerton will be here for supper, but who knows. Strange things are afoot." Millie became incensed.

"Look Stylus Packard, a woman knows. This child needs his momma now. Don't get uppity on me mister."

With that said she brushed him aside, entered the room and gave baby Rufus to Belle. Upon closing the door behind her, Millie gathered her skirts about her and ran upstairs. Packard headed for the kitchen muttering something about women, and Millie in particular.

Meanwhile in the sitting room, the quartet was just settling in. Pinkerton preferred to patrol the room's perimeter like a Tsvaso lion. Meanwhile the two women sat side by side on a plush velveteen settee with Rufus between them. They looked very much like two wary Meerkats sitting on a termite mound. Finally, Belle perked up,

"Come on Allan, why are you really here in Boston. Land sakes, you probably have your usual contingent of agents staked out somewhere. Perhaps they're upstairs on the 'widows walk', armed with a big cannon." They laughed, he did not. Pinkerton got to the point, saying,

"Packard informs me that trouble might be afoot. What's all the fuss about blood in the stables and a mysterious piece of blue cloth?" Belle laughed,

"Poor Packard can't help telling tales out of school. He's a lovable old rascal, that dear, dear man."

Virginia stood up and went to a mahogany writing desk. She pulled out a small drawer and withdrew a bloody piece of blue cloth wrapped in a napkin. She gave it to Pinkerton. He unfolded the napkin and examined the bloody cloth within it carefully. A monocular jeweler's loupe attached to a thin chain became his instrument of inspection. After a few moments, he pulled out a pair of brass tweezers to pluck a white hair that was embedded in the blood. He plucked out another hair but it was thicker and brown in colour. The women were mesmerized. He asked Virginia to light an Aladdin lamp nearby. She did so. Pinkerton held the cloth up to it, murmuring all the while. The women leaned forward breathlessly. Virginia couldn't bear it,

"Well Allan, what is it? I'm dying of anticipation. Please tell us what you think."

He put everything down carefully on a nearby coffee table. Just then there was a knock on the door. Packard entered with a large silver tray upon which were a plate of sandwiches, a carafe of coffee, a cream pitcher, a covered bowl of sugar and three coffee mugs. Before

Allan could react, he'd put the tray on top of the evidence Pinkerton had so painstakingly collected. The tweezers and cloth were swept to the floor in an instant.

Pinkerton gasped and rushed forward. The women were horrified. The baby woke up crying piteously. Belle once more cooed and rocked the squalling child in her arms. Poor Packard was dumbstruck, not knowing what he had just done. His shoulders sagged.

"Is there something wrong, Mr. Pinkerton? What did I do?"

He stood back as Pinkerton took the lamp and crawled about on his hands and knees under the table. Virginia looked up at her stricken butler,

"It's alright Packard. No harm has been done I'm sure. Go about your duties. I'll ring if I need you. We might be going out to the stables soon. Don't be alarmed. Now off you go."

Packard fled closing the door behind him. Virginia watched the little man crawl about then inquired,

"Allan Pinkerton, just what are you doing?"

Pinkerton rose with the cloth and tweezers in his small hands. He stood up and held the tweezers to the coal-oil lamp. He smiled and turned to look down upon them. In his thick Scots brogue he remarked.

"No harm has been done lassies. By Saint Andrew! Tis a miracle, for I found the hairs I collected." They leaned closer. Pinkerton looked at Virginia and held up a tuft of hair, saying,

"These short white hairs are from your dear Jack while the brown hair is from your steed Charger and the blue wool cloth is from someone very tall but not well to do. Now ladies let's eat while I think about what to do next." As they began reaching for napkins, Pinkerton casually inquired,

"Belle and Virginia, where were you today? Your shoes are not muddy but your clothes are streaked with dirt. What have you two sleuths been up to?"

Belle looked at Virginia and giggled,

"Virginia, should you tell him or should I?"

Pinkerton sat back chewing away, waiting for the duo to make a decision. Virginia nodded, then approached the subject rather obliquely.

"Alan, we've all heard of gun cotton, correct?" Pinkerton replied,

"Yes of course my dear, its dangerous stuff to say the least. It was invented by Christian Freidrich Schonbein in 1846. However, it's highly unstable and wears out gun barrels after a few hundred rounds are fired." He waited, eating another sandwich as Belle continued,

"That's true Allan. Have you ever heard of a scientist by the name of Ascanio Sobero?"

Pinkerton finished his lunch. He reached for the silver carafe and poured himself a coffee. The two women waited politely as he poured cream and sugar into a large mug. He took a sip while eyeing the women intensely. Satisfied, he wiped his moustache delicately with a linen napkin. His dissertation commenced.

"Sobero, Sobero. The name does ring a bell. Oh yes, I have Ladies. I must say you've done your homework. I'm impressed. Anyways, I think he invented an explosive called pyroglycerine. That's right he did, in fact it's highly unstable, so much so that Sobero kept it a secret for over a year until 1848. It scared him to death. I believe it is now known as nitroglycerine. Wonderful stuff but very unstable, so it only comes as a liquid. Many scientists around the world have tried everything to stabilize it but to no avail. It's banned all over the world because making it has been extremely risky to say the least. Factories here and abroad have blown up and other calamities have occurred recently."

He finished another sandwich, wiped his beard with a napkin then sat back eyeing them. He stood up and said,

"What are you ladies really saying?"

Pinkerton's voice was stilled as lightning flashed across the windows. The deep sonorous boom of a thunder clap followed it into the room. Rufus woke up squalling once again. Belle comforted her son by softly crooning an old lullaby, 'My Merlindy Brown'.

Her rich contralto filled the woman within her with a satisfying sense of purpose as the melody of the old negro serenade lulled the child into a deep sleep. Pinkerton and Virginia were mesmerized by the words pouring forth from within her. They gradually realized that Belle was undergoing an act of contrition. The soul of the song was the healing balm that she'd prayed for ever since that terrible time on the Hudson. As the lightning and thunder flashed and rumbled outside, Belle closed her eyes and sang her heart out.

"O, de light-bugs glimmer down de lane, Merlindy, Merlindy.

O, de whip' o-will callin' notes ur pain, Merlindy, O, Merlindy.

O, honey lub, my turkle dub, Doan' you hyuh my bango ringin'.

While de night-dew falls an' de ho'n owl calls,

Be de a ba'n gate Ise singin'".

As she finished another verse, the total innocence of the child in her arms baptized her, forgave her and cleansed her. The child's unconditional love swept over her. Belle remained transfixed, at peace within herself. The war was no longer important, only the child was, for the child was the truth, and the truth had set her free. The whole episode was in stark contrast to the purpose of the meeting. However, both her friends knew what she had gone through and so as witnesses to this remarkable event condoned it. Belle smiled wanly as she came out of what seemed to be a deep trance. She excused herself, saying she was going to feed the baby in her room upstairs and that she'd return shortly.

After Belle left, Virginia walked out of the room and came back with a thick paper packet bound by string tabs. She handed it to Pinkerton. He untied the strings and opened the packet on a nearby side table. He reached within it and pulled out pages of notes neatly organized under various headings such as propellants, binders, stabilizers, de-coppering additives, flash reducers, wear reduction additives and other additives. Under some of the headings, various chemicals were listed such as nitrocellulose, ethyl acetate, diphenylamine and so on. Pinkerton looked up at Virginia in amazement.

"Where on earth did you get this Virginia?"

"I found it in Hans Larsen's office an hour ago. Belle and I went to his office to see him but he was out. While there, I accidentally knocked a ledger off of his desk. Two identical packets fell out from beneath it. One was full of shredded newspapers whereas inside the other were pages covered with scientific formulas and so forth. Why would Larsen have something like that for he wasn't a scientist? Across the front of this packet was "Property of Alfred Nobel." He jumped up.

"Alfred Nobel. Hmmmmm! He and his brother own an iron foundry in Sweden called Boofors or Bofors. I also believe Alfred was a student of Theophile-Jules Pelouze of the University of Turin. Alfred Nobel; some say is a real genius with explosives. His company is currently selling 'Swedish Blasting Oil' made from gunpowder and nitroglycerine. Apparently he's been working on something quite secret, some sort of new explosive for commercial use or more to the point, military applications."

Abruptly, Pinkerton stopped. He looked at the notes once more then ran out of the room and thundered down the hallway towards Saxton's office. Virginia followed. A metallic maelstrom of dots and dashes clamored for their attention as Pinkerton hammered away on a telegraph key. Just as he had finished, Belle ran into the room wondering what was going on. Pinkerton consulted a black notebook as he was working. Obviously, what he was tapping out was in code. Finally he finished, looked up and said,

"Belle, come over here please. Do you know Larsen's fist very well? I mean have you ever used Morse code?" Exasperated, he cried.

"What I really mean, have you and Larsen talked to each other on this telegraph? You know, sent messages back and forth since Marcus and Saxton have gone to war?" She nodded yes.

"Good. Come here please and send this message for me."

Pinkerton took a pencil off the desk and wrote furiously on a piece of paper. He handed it to Belle who tapped it out. They waited. There was dead silence. She tried again, still dead silence. She wondered. Larsen always answered night or day. He even slept by the telegraph from time to time. No, something was terribly wrong. Belle sensed it. She said,

"Allan, something's not right. You'd better get down to Larsen's office right away." Pinkerton agreed. He cried,

"Right away indeed! Now stay here by the key Belle and don't use it. I hope I'm not too late. I'll explain later. My, my ladies, you just might have accidentally uncovered what our Hans Larsen was up to. Now don't leave the house for any reason. I'll put Rodney and his mastiffs on high alert. Virginia, please inform Packard of the situation but tell him to watch for any of the staff who might leave here after I'm gone. Don't try to stop them if they do.

My agents will handle the rest. I'll try to get back by telegraph as soon as I can. By the way, here's your mail."

He ran for the foyer. Once there, he jammed on his bowler and overcoat; put the packet under his arm and fled out the door. Lightening lit up the sky to the east. Thunder, close and dangerous rumbled over the bosom of the harbor and up the hill towards the Saxton House. The two women stood on the veranda and watched him ride away flanked by four agents. The sound of hooves ground loudly on the pea gravel driveway then gradually faded. The Red Polls and Gold Finches continued to flit about then settled down deep within the boxwood hedges. The two women went back into the house. After a few minutes all was secure. Another storm spawned torrents of rain that pummeled the Saxton House with an uncommon fury.

The two women waited by the telegraph key for what seemed an eternity. The room was deathly quiet until the telegraph key started to hammer away. It stopped. Belle reached over and tapped out a response. The key stilled. Virginia looked expectantly at Belle who put her fingers to her lips and reached for a pencil and a pad of paper. She tapped out another few words. The key responded violently. It seemed a long time but finally the chattering stopped. Belle signed off and turned gasping for air. Alarmed, Virginia rose and walked over to her,

"What's wrong?"

"You won't believe this but Hans Larsen was found hanging in his office just a few minutes ago. Perhaps he'd seen us leaving with that packet under your arm. At that moment, Larsen knew the jig was up, so he hanged himself. Well I guess we were right, he was a traitor. But why would he betray us and his country?

An hour earlier, Charlie Finch had been on duty playing solitaire. His concentration was shattered as a distraught Hans Larsen opened the door of the gatehouse with a crash followed by a gust of ill wind. He listened in astonishment as Larsen blurted out what had happened. Larsen unlocked a desk drawer and took out a pocket Colt. He gave it to Finch. Charlie was to go to the Saxton House post haste, saying he had a message from Larsen because the telegraph lines had been damaged by lightening. Once there he would have all the staff assemble in the Grand Salon on the pretext that Captain Sound of the SS Night Hawk was about to bring them gifts from Sweden as was the custom of many loyal Saxton Captains. With Packard in tow he would knock the butler out in the foyer then open and close the front door, pretending to let the Captain in. Out of sight from those waiting around the corner in the Grand Salon, he would sneak into Saxton's office, open the safe and disappear with the purloined packet. If he could not find the packet, he was to take Virginia Saxton as hostage and force Belle to telegraph Larsen as to what occurred. Larsen would get Garrow and Blackstone to ride up there and retrieve the packet knowing that Pinkerton's agents would never interfere as long as there were hostages involved.

Larsen looked at Charlie Finch hopefully. He gave him a small brown envelope. Inside it was the combination for the safe as well as its key for Larsen had stolen Muriel's key and the safe's combination the day after she had died. With a wax impression of the safe's key, and a copy of its combination in his pocket, no one was the wiser. Besides, an errant remark from Saxton had given him a clue earlier as to where Muriel had hidden it. It seemed that Muriel in a panic had forgotten where it was but Saxton knew. Larsen had overheard him telling his mother as to its whereabouts. It lay in an envelope behind Thomas's valentine card on Muriel's bedroom mantle. Larsen had opened the safe later on but to his chagrin had found it empty. Perhaps the packet was now in that safe. Larsen had to find out and quickly.

Thus, after explaining what to do, Larsen said,

"Now Charlie, your brother's shift starts in five minutes. I'll stay here and wait for him. Take my horse and off you go. Do exactly what I've told you. Good luck!"

Charlie jumped up scattering playing cards all over the floor as he fled out into the storm to the nearby stables. It didn't matter to Larsen. He had a plan. Eddie showed up five minutes later right on time. He was surprised to see Larsen there let alone picking playing cards off the floor. He inquired,

"Where's Charlie?"

Larsen told him that he had sent him on an errand before he went home. Now he wanted Eddie to go and get Garrow down to the gatehouse right away. He gave Eddie cab fare and watched as the young man ran through the pouring rain to hail a passing Hansom cab. Larsen was sure that both Finch brothers would carry out their assignments capably. They were considered to be 'soft' patriots rather than 'hard'. The 'hard' patriots like himself and others did not want money. Their only reward was victory for the 'cause' at all costs. Both Finch brothers had been well paid in silver for their cooperation and Larsen had promised them even more.

Sam Hillard however, had been both 'soft' and greedy. He threatened to blackmail Larsen. It was a fatal mistake. Although it was extremely dangerous and quite distasteful, Larsen lured Hillard aboard one of the Saxton ships docked at the warehouse. The ship was locked and deserted except for a watchman whom Larsen dismissed. The man ran off, glad to join his shipmates ashore. Hillard was grabbed from behind then Larsen slit his throat. He threw the body into the harbor.

Larsen abruptly recovered from his reverie and closed the gatehouse door. A deluge of pea sized hail rain beat a thunderous tattoo upon the tin roof above him. Hans looked down at the scattered playing cards on the floor in disgust. Larsen was neat. He bent down to pick them up. The last card he touched was the Ace of Spades.

As Larsen sat in the gatehouse looking out at the hail storm he resumed his daydreaming. Hans Larsen was smart. He'd send Garrow and Blackstone to assist Charlie at the Saxton House. With Virginia as a hostage, any Pinkerton agents thereabouts would be powerless to stop them. Belle and Virginia would be tortured until they revealed where they had hidden the packet. To escape, the women would be used as shields as Garrow and Blackstone escaped. At least they might give Garrow and Blackstone enough of a head start to escape with the packet and vanish. Belle and Virginia would die after they were no longer of any use. Meanwhile, Larsen would hide out until Garrow left town then he, Hans Larsen would vanish, disguised as a wealthy passenger sailing for Shanghai, China.

Larson tried to remain calm, for without question Garrow was an insane killer, capable of any depravity who would relish torturing the women, especially Belle. Larsen knew she was a Union spy. Her husband Marcus foiled 'Operation False Prophet' and Saxton dreamed up 'Operation Maasai Ranger' to bedevil the Confederacy. To Larsen, the retrieval of Nobel's packet was paramount. Even if Garrow was being well paid, it didn't matter. The South had to win the war at all costs. Nobel's new explosive meant victory. Only victory mattered. He looked up. A Hansom cab had clattered up to the front gate.

Eddie Finch, Garrow, and Blackstone stepped out the cab and ran to the locked gate. Larsen heard Eddie yelling. Quickly he grabbed his overcoat and hat. The hail storm had passed on but a steady rain had replaced it. Larsen ran out into the storm and unlocked the main gate. Garrow and Blackstone pushed him roughly aside in their haste to get out of the inclement weather. Larsen locked the gate, followed Eddie through the open door of the gatehouse, closing it with a bang. Garrow shook the rain off his overcoat then turned to Larsen, saying pleasantly,

"My dear Hans, you don't look well. Perhaps a stiff drink is in order. Harley, you stay here. Don't let anyone in and I mean anyone. Eddie my lad, you come with us."

Before the stricken Larsen knew it, he was in his office pouring Garrow a whiskey. Larsen tried to remain calm as Garrow looked about the office. Inadvertently, he spied a waxed packet lying under the office desk. Larsen had missed it in his panic. Shredded newspapers within it hung out of it as if they were intestines. Garrow put down his drink, retrieved the packet, turned about and raised it above Larsen's head. Garrow shouted,

"It seems that the genuine packet has flown the coop? Where the hell is it?"

He grabbed Larsen. Long steely fingers closed around his windpipe but not enough to choke him. Hans wheezed; his face dead white.

"It must be at the Saxton House. I've sent Charlie to get it." Garrow grimaced. He looked at Eddie cowering in the corner.

"Did you know this Eddie?"

Eddie cried that he didn't know anything about it. Garrow shouted at Larsen,

"Pinkerton is here! I should know because I was there at Saxton House last night casing it out. His agents all over that place you idiot! Charlie will never get in let alone recover the packet!"

Hans was slowly losing consciousness. He cried out, desperate for life.

"Yes, he will. I've got it all figured out. They know Charlie. They'll let him in. Believe me, it will work!" Garrow snorted in Larsen's face.

"It won't work Larsen. Even if he did get it, he'd be too late and my time has run out. So has yours you stupid fool. Besides my dear Hans, the Feds are unto you and have been for some time. You've become a liability to the 'Cause'."

He dragged Larsen to a nearby window. Eddie remained transfixed in the far corner, his eyes popping out of his head. Garrow hissed into Larsen's ear.

"Goodbye Larsen. You've screwed up one too many times. Take a good last look at the world outside."

Hans saw a flash of lightening illuminate the rain streaked window pane in front of his face. There behind him was Horatio Garrow slowly squeezing the life out of Larsen's thrashing body. Hans Larsen died quickly. Garrow dropped the body onto the floor with a crash. He turned to Eddie Finch.

"Eddie, help me with useless piece of trash. Find a rope. Our incompetent friend here is about to commit suicide."

Eddie returned with a rope and gave it to him. Eddie was scared stiff, horrified upon witnessing a murder. Larsen stunk, for he had voided himself as Garrow was strangling him. Eddie was about to throw up but the vomit stuck in his craw. Garrow eyed him evilly while he quickly fashioned a slip knot. He reached for a nearby chair and put it directly under a metal gaslight that hung from the ceiling high above him. Standing on the chair, he reached up and tied the other end of the rope around the gaslight base plate then jumped down. He hissed.

"Now get on the chair. I'll lift him up high enough for you to put the noose around his neck. Once I've done that, he'll just hang there swaying in the breeze like a preacher caught with his pants down."

Garrow grabbed Larsen's dead weight under the armpits. He looked up at Eddie. "Ok? Ready, go!"

The body rose high enough for Eddie to put the noose around Larsen's neck. Eddie nearly fainted as Larsen dropped. There was a sharp crack. A spray of fine white ceiling plaster came down over both of them. Garrow carefully placed the chair on its side under the twisting body. He stood back dusting off his blue jacket. Satisfied, he said,

"You see how easy it is to kill someone. You'd be dead too if I didn't need you. So, my friend, make sure I'll always need you. I'll be right back. While I'm gone, ransack the office. Make it look like a robbery."

Eddie's fear trickled down his leg as he searched Larsen's swinging body. Shortly thereafter, Garrow returned wearing one of John Saxton's jackets he'd found in another room. He faced Eddie,

"Hopefully for your sake, you'll never see me again. Do I make myself clear?"

As he said this, he grabbed him by the throat. At that moment, the office telegraph started a calamitous clicking. Garrow released Eddie and looked down seemingly mesmerized at the telegraph. He said,

"Eddie, someone's asking for Larsen; should I answer it or not?" Eddie nodded no. Garrow agreed.

"You're probably right. I do have a distinctive fist. The Confederacy needs an inside man like you to keep an eye on what's going on at Saxton Shipping. An agent will contact you later. You will never be connected to what happened here. My train leaves at three. I have to be on it as my insatiable wife waits to take me to safety away from this choleric city. We might have lost this battle but we haven't lost the war."

Garrow looked deep into the eyes of a totally terrified Eddie Finch. He hissed again,

"Remember, as long as I need you, you'll stay alive and be very well paid for the privilege. You and your brother would love to be rich now wouldn't you?" He patted Eddie's cheek.

"So, my sweet Lad, you've seen nothing, you've heard nothing and you'll certainly say nothing. Besides, you wouldn't want anything to happen to your brother now, would you? Remember that Pinkerton is very smart but we're smarter, aren't we?"

Garrow patted Eddie's cheek again, knowing that the lad would be the only suspect in the killing. Garrow would be free and clear with no one on his trail. He had been careful to leave the blue coat behind, hidden in the waste basket. He also knew that Charlie Finch was in a hopeless situation for the simple reason that he was outgunned by the Pinkertons. He looked into the face of the young man again, saying,

"Now off you go to the gatehouse like a good boy."

Eddie flew out the door as if the devil himself was behind him. He was. The office telegraph chattered again as Garrow leaped down the stairs and out into the pouring rain.

Pinkerton and his agents arrived ten minutes later at the gatehouse. While trying desperately to remain calm, Eddie unlocked the gate. A train whistle blew two times in the distance. Pinkerton stopped and looked at his Hamilton fob watch. It was three o'clock. The sun had come out. For a moment he was indecisive then he turned about and ran for the warehouse. He rushed up the stairs to Larsen's office.

Pinkerton arrived too late. Larsen was already quite dead. He'd messed his pants as he died. The stench was nauseous. A puddle of urine was found directly under his body, while another pooled in the far corner of the room. Pinkerton made sure no one stepped in them or disturbed the fallen chair under the body. Turning his attention to the body, he climbed upon another chair and looked closely at Larsen's neck. He left the rope around it noting that the knot was a slip knot commonly used by sailors. There was nothing unusual about the rope itself. He asked agent Styles to lift the body upwards in order to slacken the noose. As Styles did so, Pinkerton moved the knotted rope over ever so slightly. Long narrow bruises lay beneath the ligature marks. Styles let the body go. Larsen had been strangled first then hanged.

Pinkerton climbed down and put the chair back exactly where he found it. He then produced a twelve foot cloth tape measure. He asked Styles to hold the twisting body still while he measured it. Larsen was five foot, six inches long. Pinkerton concluded that even if Larsen tried to hang himself, even on tip toes with his arms straight up, he was still short by about eight inches. Someone very tall and very strong murdered Hans Larsen. Perhaps the murderer was not alone. Perhaps he needed someone to put the noose around Larsen's skinny neck. The rope was far too short to hang him from the floor. Larsen had been lifted up onto the chair to hang. Pinkerton pondered.

Whoever it was ransacked the room because they were in a hurry. Either the murderer(s) worked there and had to be quick about it as to not be missed or it was a stranger under threat of imminent exposure. Or perhaps it was all staged to look like a robbery. Pinkerton became suspicious, very suspicious. The wall safe was open and empty. Either Larsen had the safe open as the murderer walked in on him unexpectedly, or he was forced to open it or the murderer knew how to pick it. This particular Chubb safe was very difficult to pick. Only Hale in New York could have done it in less than thirty minutes. Pinkerton looked closely at the key hole on the safe. There were no fresh jimmy marks. No, Hans Larsen may or may not have been forced to do it. He must have known his killer(s). Pinkerton noticed a waxed packet lying on the floor. It had been torn open violently, its contents scattered about the room. He picked it up. Shreds of old newspaper fell out of it as he read the label upon it. He remembered Virginia talking about a second package. The name 'Alfred Nobel' was written neatly across it. He looked about the office for any specimen of Larsen's handwriting. A letter lay on a counter. Pinkerton compared its writing to that of the packet. They matched.

The intrepid detective knew that whoever killed Larsen did it because the real packet had been taken. That much he was sure of. Whoever it was, discovered the fake packet and in a fit of rage showered the room with its contents. Pinkerton thought of Garrow but he'd heard that he'd been thrown, mortally wounded into the Hudson River. He must be dead and that was that. Pinkerton heard voices coming up the staircase. Police Chief Taylor and two of his constables entered the office. Chief Taylor approached Pinkerton. They conferred briefly. Taylor nodded, turned and left the room holding a handkerchief over his face, his two men right behind him. Pinkerton grinned, thinking,

'Christ almighty! What a stinking mess!'

He reached up and touched the body. It was still warm. Rigor mortis had not yet set in. He searched the body. Nothing! Larsen was stripped clean of whatever he had had on him. Agent Styles continued to search the office, and a nearby bathroom. Styles came back with a blue riding jacket. It had a small piece missing from its right sleeve.

"Where did you find it Styles?"

"It was hidden in a trash basket next door. Shall I keep it Sir? There's nothing in it, however there is some blood on it."

He handed the garment to Pinkerton who took out his silver loupe attached to a thin chain in his breast pocket. He held the jacket up, examining it minutely. Pinkerton murmured then threw the garment to Styles.

"Styles, stand on the chair, reach up and hold the jacket against the body."

He did so. It was several sizes too large. Pinkerton told him to keep it as evidence. Styles stood down and put the jacket in a cloth satchel. He marked a paper tag attached to it.

Presently, another agent brought in Eddie Finch. Finch was shocked as he looked up at the body. He gasped.

"My God! I don't believe it! What happened?"

Pinkerton studied his reactions closely. He wanted Finch to see the body, smell the body and touch the body. Finch looked up and saw the rope tied to the gaslight hanging from the ceiling then down to a wooden chair lying on its side underneath it. Larsen's body slowly turned in front of him. Pinkerton asked Eddie to assist him as he had the body cut down and laid out on the floor. Eddie refused point blank. Pinkerton looked closely at the body again then stood up and motioned Finch to follow him. Next door in another office, Eddie Finch sat down. Pinkerton strolled about the room chewing a spent cheroot. Styles took notes as Pinkerton droned on.

"Mr. Finch, I'm chief detective Allan Pinkerton, it's good of you to cooperate Sir. Now, I am speaking to Eddie Finch, not your brother Charlie am I not?" Finch nodded. Pinkerton continued.

He offered Finch a cheroot but Finch declined. Pinkerton lit a fresh one, stomped out the old one and continued strolling with his hands behind his back, black bowler firmly set down onto his smallish head. He turned and looked upon a very uncomfortable young man. He said evenly,

"I do hope so. You two are identical to be sure. Anyways, where were you and your brother one hour ago?"

Eddie looked up and wiped his long blonde hair away from his face.

"Why Mr. Pinkerton, I was at the gatehouse as always, playin' solitaire."

"I see, and where is your brother Charlie?"

Eddie became restless, his demeanor increasingly defensive. He squirmed in his chair.

"At home I guess. He'd just got off shift and headed there before I showed up." Pinkerton stopped walking.

"That's odd Eddie, leaving the gatehouse unattended. Does it happen often? Was anyone there when you arrived?" Eddie looked up at Pinkerton, his eyes riveted upon him.

"Mr. Larsen was there. Strange it was too as it never happened before."

"Never before you say? How odd indeed. Now tell me Eddie, how long have you and your famous twin been working for the Saxton Shipping Co., how long sir?" Eddie brightened up, eager to please.

"Ten years, Mr. Pinkerton, nearly ten years now. It seems like yesterday it does when old man Saxton saw us strollin' cross Scollay Square dressed identical like. He asked if we had a job. We didn't. He laughed about us lookin' identical. So, he hired us both on the spot he did. Bin here ever since drivin' the unsuspectin' public crazy we have. Mr. Saxton said we were the only employees he had that worked twenty-four hours a day, seven days a week. Came to be sort of a joke you know. He paid us well not because of what we did but because we drove his friends nuts tryin' to figure out which one of us was what, if you know what I mean."

Pinkerton smiled then went on.

"I'm quite sure you did. How did your own mother tell you apart?"

"She couldn't sir. She died as we was bein' born. Never knew her. My father has since died too. Seems the only difference is---I've got bigger ears." Pinkerton looked closely.

"Indeed you do son. So you think your brother is home right now?"

"Like I said before, he's probably at 1020 Canal Street, Room 112. We live together you know."

Pinkerton asked if he or his brother had ever crewed on any sailing ships, or steamers? "No."

Had he ever met or heard of a Major Horatio Garrow?

"No."

Pinkerton motioned to an agent. He came over. They whispered. The agent left to return with the blue jacket.

"Eddie, try on this jacket for me please."

Finch reluctantly complied. He put on the jacket. It was too large but not by much. Finch looked guilty as Pinkerton asked him to give it back. Eddie was very nervous. Pinkerton asked him to roll up his shirt sleeves. He did. There were no tattoos. In a burst of questioning, Pinkerton asked Finch if he'd ever seen the jacket before. He did not. Was it his brother's jacket? It was not. Did anyone who worked here own the jacket? "No". Again he was asked if he had ever seen the jacket before. "No", he lied.

This went on for a few more minutes. Eddie sank back into his chair. There was a knock at the door.

"Come in" replied Pinkerton. An agent came over and said,

"Charlie Finch is not home." Pinkerton turned to Eddie,

"Do you know where your brother might be?"

"How the hell do I know?"

Pinkerton went to the window and looked out at the cheerless rain as it streaked the square crown glass panes before him. Without turning around, he said loudly,

"Eddie, why did you and your brother kill Hans Larsen?"

Dead silence filled the room. It was as if all the air was instantly sucked out of it. There was an audible gasp behind him. Pinkerton turned just as Finch jumped up out of his chair screaming,

"I didn't kill anyone! I didn't kill him! Please believe me." Styles came over and forced Eddie back down.

Pinkerton motioned for Styles to back off. He did so, standing directly behind Eddie, arms crossed over his chest. He looked on as Pinkerton walked over to Eddie and peered down at him, his cheroot clamped between his teeth. Finch flinched as he took it out and pointed it at him.

"You're a goddamn liar son and I'll prove it." Pinkerton motioned to Styles saying,

"Do you have a comb?"

He did. Pinkerton took it then reached for a writing pad with a black paper cover. He went over to Finch.

"Don't move son. I'll just be a few seconds."

Pinkerton ran the comb through Finch's fine hair. Tiny bits of white plaster fell onto the black paper where they showed up like icebergs floating upon a black arctic sea. Pinkerton motioned to Styles to come over. Pinkerton whispered in his ear. Styles remained in the room as Pinkerton said,

"Please take off your shoes Eddie."

Eddie looked bewildered but did as he was told. Styles picked up the shoes and left. A few minutes later, he came back and Eddie was given his shoes. After he finished putting them on, Pinkerton looked at Styles and declared, "Cuff him."

Finch protested as the agent put a pair of Thompson cuffs on Eddie's wrists. He snapped them on tightly with Eddie's hands in front of him. Styles then locked them with a little brass key. Finch sat back down, head bowed. Pinkerton explained.

"First of all Eddie, bits of ceiling plaster came down upon your head as you and your brother lifted up Larsen's body to tie the rope to the gaslight stanchion. The weight of Larsen's body was too much for it. Pieces of ceiling plaster showered down upon you and your brother. It's all over the floor too. I didn't let you into the room because I wanted to see if you had any on your shoes. You do not; the puddles outside washed it away. But, I noticed it in Larsen's hair as I examined his body. I'm sure your brother will have it in his hair too when we catch up to him. You bachelors hardly ever wash your greasy hair, do you?"

Finch looked up defiantly. Pinkerton ignored him.

"Secondly, the ceiling plaster showered down upon you as you stood on the chair then when you got off the chair, you left an outline of a shoe that matches yours exactly." Pinkerton shouted down at him, one jarring question after another.

"Why did you do it Eddie?

Why did you and you brother kill Hans Larsen?

Was it for money Eddie? Were you going to sell the packet to the highest bidder? Larsen tried to stop you so you killed him didn't you? You and your brother strangled him then hung him up trying to make it look like a suicide."

Pinkerton reached down and pulled Eddie up by his lapels.

"Where is your brother? Tell me now before he gets hurt!

Where is he damn it?

Where is he?" Finch spit in Pinkerton's face.

"Well Sir. If you're so smart you find him. I've nothing more to say." Pinkerton released him, wiped his face with a handkerchief and said.

"By the way Eddie you've pissed your pants twice tonight. I made sure no one walked into the two little yellow oceans staining the floor of Larsen's office. Coincidentally, one of them was directly under Larsen's hanging body. And I know he didn't do it because he was already dead before you hung him. So something or someone scared you to death. If it wasn't your brother Charlie, who the hell was it?"

Eddie continued to remain obstinate knowing that Garrow or Blackstone would kill him if he betrayed them. Pinkerton nodded to Styles. Immediately Styles grabbed Eddie by his collar, roughly pulling him up from his chair. Pinkerton yelled,

"Get him out of here Styles. Take him up to the Fitchburg train station on Causeway. He's going to Washington tonight. Get that traitor out of my sight! Take Larsen's body to Rowland's. Tell them to bill Saxton Shipping."

Finch was led out of the room. The telegraph began to chatter in Larsen's office. Pinkerton ran to the other room. He listened intently. The key quit abruptly. Pinkerton whirled about grabbing his overcoat while yelling,

"Jesus Christ Styles, I'd know that woman's fist anywhere! Belle Brown has just told me that Charlie Finch has taken Virginia Saxton, hostage. He wants the Nobel packet in exchange for her life. Well, we'll just see about that!"

The Saxton House loomed up large and foreboding as the small group of Pinkerton agents thundered up Snowhill Street towards it. They reined in at the bottom of the gravel drive. Other agents came out of the nearby brush. Pinkerton gathered everyone around him. Just as he was about to speak, gunshots were heard inside the house. Pinkerton and his agents ran up the driveway like geese fleeing a fox. His agents fanned out around the house, guns drawn. Rodney met them at a side gate. He was holding onto the four Mastiffs for dear life. The dogs growled and bayed as the agents ran past them. As the beasts' excitement grew, Pinkerton pulled Rodney aside, saying tersely,

"Rodney, for Christ's sake, take those Goddamned dogs around to the front of the house. By the way, have you seen Charlie Finch?"

"No Sir."

"Step aside, Styles and I are going in through the mud-room."

Pinkerton ran up the back steps and opened the door. All was quiet. Through the mud-room and into the kitchen the men moved slowly. Pinkerton opened a nearby door and peered around the corner, nothing. Styles crept ahead down a dark carpeted hallway. Muffled voices could be heard coming from a room farther down. The two moved cautiously forward. They came to a junction at the foot of the grand staircase.

Jack came down the stairs with a red ball in his mouth. He saw Pinkerton. He liked Pinkerton. He dropped his red ball in front of Pinkerton. Pinkerton picked up the red ball and threw it through the open French doors of the Grand Salon. As he did so, he and Styles burst into the room. Charlie Finch was distracted by the barking dog. As he raised his pistol to fire, his hostage fainted. This threw him off balance exposing his upper torso. It was a fatal mistake.

Pinkerton's Colt put two bullets into Finch. He fell with a crash, lying in a widening pool of blood. Pinkerton kicked a Colt .44 away from him. Styles knelt down and searched Finch for more weapons. There was none other than a small Buck-knife. Finch was still alive but barely. Pinkerton looked at Charlie's hair. It was not speckled with chips of white ceiling plaster. He was stunned.

Packard and Belle ran over and laid Virginia's unconscious body on a couch. Millie was crying, still in deep shock. Packard grabbed her arm and led her out of the room. The rest of the household staff remained cowering in front of a blazing fireplace. More agents rushed into the room. One said,

"Has anyone else been shot? No one was. Pinkerton exclaimed.

"Well boys, I think he's done for. Styles stay here. The rest of you search the house for any others. He might have not been alone but I doubt it. When you've finished, put half the men on guard duty for two hours. As for the others, stable your horses and get something to eat. I think Finch here is trying to say something. Get everyone out of the room NOW!"

Moments later, Finch reached up to grab Pinkerton's overcoat lapel. Blood gushed out through his mouth. He tried to speak. Pinkerton put his ear to Charlie's mouth. His last word shocked Pinkerton as he heard him say, 'Garrow'. Slowly his body relaxed. Finch was dead.

Two hours earlier; BB, Horatio Garrow and Harley Blackstone boarded the Fitchburg train. Also stepping on board was the crew from the SS Night Hawk. They'd arrived in twos and threes while the train was waiting at the Causeway Station. All were in disguise, having changed their clothes at Larsen's house. Some posed as businessmen, others as Union soldiers on furlough or men of the cloth of various denominations. All were fully armed and ready to take over the train if need be. However, as planned, the whole troupe got off the train at Lunenburg, Massachusetts without incident.

There, waiting to take them south to Leominster were three Landau coaches. At Leominster, they were to board a succession of trains that would eventually take them to Washington DC. All along the way, the Night Hawk's crew would be on constant alert for any opposition as they sat surrounding BB and Horatio. This was the plan but as Robbie Burns once said, "The best laid schemes o' mice an' men, gang aft agley."

A Mrs. Anthony Crawford was not surprised that her errant husband had entrained just in time. She watched him as he sidled down the aisle towards her. Horatio put his leather luggage in the overhead rack above her. Their eyes locked in loquacious lust as he sat down heavily beside her. Her white gloved hand immediately stroked his groin. It rose to meet her attentions but he brushed her hand away instead.

"My dear BB, please control yourself, for someone might think we're on our honeymoon." She replied coyly,

"Well we are aren't we?" He laughed as she brazenly whispered in his ear what she was going to do to him later. After a few fruitless moments BB backed off reluctantly. She simpered,

"Well you're no fun my dear. I guess you want to tell me all about why you didn't bring the packet here." He turned to look at her, saying,

"BB, for Christ sake speak quietly." She giggled,

"Look around you Horatio. Every seat beside, behind and in front of us are filled with, shall we say loyal Southrons. Other than the conductor and passing strangers, we are as one would say 'au solitaire.'" Garrow rejoined adroitly,

"My Dear BB, perhaps you're right. Allan Pinkerton got the packet from the Saxton House before I could get there. There were too many agents around the Mansion; needless to say four giant Mastiffs, their armed handler and an armed household staff. I know, because I cased it out the night before. I tore my riding jacket trying to chase away some little dog playing with a red rubber ball. It spooked a horse in the stall I was hiding in. Christ! I just made it out of there in time. No BB, the house was a fortress." She tittered.

"Oh men, they are so imprisoned by their fears and impulses. Women like me are always cleaning up after them. Such is the case now. One of my agents is in Boston as we speak; to steal the packet, take it to Jeffries Point, board the Reliant and sail away to Canada where it will be safe for the time being. Do you really think that Sandy Keith had no idea what was aboard the Night Hawk? Spying is double jeopardy at the best of times. So my love, don't worry. Sit back and relax. Oh I forgot. Where were we?"

Garrow took her hand and put it back on his groin. His arousal she misinterpreted. Instead he was thinking of Hans Larsen as he slowly strangled him.

BOOK TWO: CHAPTER 12
DESPERADOS

Allan Pinkerton looked about Larsen's office carefully. Despite looking after all the details; lodged in the back of his mind there was one detail that he'd overlooked, but what? He recounted what had happened and mentally checked each item off. Eddie Finch was in custody waiting for the next train out of Boston. Charlie Finch was dead and resting comfortably beside Hans Larsen at Rowland's funeral parlor. The Saxton House was secure and sealed. Pinkerton had thoroughly searched the Night Hawk for more Confederate agents; questioned the crew and grilled Captain Sound. Larsen's apartment and the Finch Brothers garret had been completely gone over for any clues. Nothing. Whoever it was, was a professional. Pinkerton respected that and continued to ruminate.

He had Tyler 'Shell Man' Wicks, watching a fast steam cutter, the SS Reliant. Word had reached Pinkerton through his numerous underground contacts that the Reliant was docked at Jefferies Point. Sandy Keith, a well known smuggler was back in town. Apparently he'd offloaded a tall man and his mute brute. In the interim, Keith had been acting rather suspiciously.

Even the denizens of the Jefferies Point slums knew Keith was chary at the best of times. But one night shortly after arriving in Boston he'd gone to the Bell In Hand Tavern near Haymarket Square. While in his cups he bragged to one and all that he, Sandy Keith, would soon become famous indeed. However Keith remained silent over the details when questioned by one of his drinking buddies, a Pinkerton informant. Sandy Keith was immediately put under observation for Pinkerton surmised that the miscreants might try to escape out to sea. Wicks concluded after a few hours of fruitless surveillance that maybe Keith was aware of being watched and might be hiding the Confederates in a 'safe' house somewhere in the warrens of East Boston. If so, no one would ever find them in its twisting narrow alleys, especially those of Jeffries Point.

'Birds of a feather do flock together,' mused Pinkerton. As for escape by rail, there were six different railways coming in and out of Boston. They could have been on any one of them. He paced about Larsen's office morosely. The afternoon cleared up as the storm passed, however the day was getting warmer apparently in concert with Pinkerton's famous temper. He didn't like feeling helpless. Inaction and doubt in his mind were as lethal as poison to most men but Pinkerton was not like most men. As usual he was chewing on a cheroot, stroking his beard; his black bowler wedged firmly on his head. He stopped pacing around

Larsen's gallows still hanging from the office gaslight. Styles sitting nearby knew from long experience that a sea change was going to happen soon. It did.

Suddenly, the missing detail dawned on Pinkerton. He asked Styles,

"What time did that train whistle blow when we first came to the crime scene?" Styles started to speak. He was too late.

"God Styles, it was three." He looked at his fob watch. It was five o'clock.

Pinkerton rushed out of the office, down the warehouse stairs, through the Saxton gates and jumped into a waiting Hansom cab while clutching the precious packet under his arm. Three agents slid in beside him, guns drawn. Pinkerton paid the driver handsomely for getting them to the Fitchburg Station in record time. They did. Breathlessly, he sprinted to the Station's telegraph office. A startled Station Master confirmed it. A train had left for Fitchburg, Massachusetts at three o'clock. It was now five fifteen. Whoever was on it had more than a two hour head start. Pinkerton recited the following message to the telegrapher at the Fitchburg Station. The train would be arriving there in thirty minutes.

"MOST URGENT: To St. Master, Fitchburg
STOP Delay train #302 until Feds arrive
STOP Spies aboard STOP Possibly twelve
men, one woman STOP All armed STOP
A. Pinkerton standing by at Boston Stn.."

Pinkerton prayed that he wasn't too late. He was. The Army searched the train. Nothing was amiss. The murderers had escaped. All Pinkerton knew was that they must have gotten off earlier, but where?

He went back to the Saxton office where he began telegraphing stations all along the Fitchburg line. It was three hours later when he learned that a dozen men including a tall man accompanied by an ugly companion detrained at Lunenburg Station. Apparently, three Concord coaches were waiting for them. The Station Master at the time thought it was very odd indeed because these types of coaches were usually found on the post roads. The party in question had also been accompanied by a tall, beautiful young woman. The Station Master remembered her because like every other man there, married or otherwise, he couldn't take his eyes off her.

Pinkerton ran through his mental list of female Confederate spies. The only one that fit the bill was Betsy Bolton. Pinkerton wondered,

"What's BB doing so far north? She usually stays near her home in the Shenandoah Valley of West Virginia. The only question is; is she heading north or south?"

Pinkerton knew that once in Canada, Colonel Jacob Thompson, Commander of the Confederate secret operations in Toronto would protect her. He mused,

"With her penchant for danger, I'm sure she will get along with that other scoundrel, John Beall."

After further deliberation he'd decided that BB would probably head south. He said,

"I wonder if the Night Hawk crew is with her. A large group like that would need three coaches. They'll probably be disguised and will split up if they haven't already."

After a few minutes he put that notion aside reasoning that three large post-road coaches seen at the Lunenburg Station meant that the fugitives were all travelling together, namely Bolton and the crew of the Night Hawk.

Pinkerton was exasperated in extremis thinking,

"But who was the tall man and his burly companion? Besides, someone who knows this area has to be helping her escape."

To Pinkerton, there was only one anti-union group that could help anyone escape from him and the Federals. He cursed.

"Christ, it must be the Knights of the Golden Circle!"

Then, another detail emerged. The station master mentioned that the tall white man had a tattoo on his left wrist. He had seen him washing his hands in the station lavoratory. Pinkerton was shocked.

"How could it be? Charlie Finch was right. My God, Garrow is alive!" Pinkerton knew then that no one was safe, not even he.

Pinkerton and Styles put their heads together. They knew Bolton would never give up trying to get Nobel's packet. Pinkerton guessed that their coaches were heading for one of three post roads from Boston to New York City that linked up at New Haven, Connecticut.

The Upper Post was the most popular because it had the fewest and shortest river crossings. The Middle Post was the shortest and fastest route. Pinkerton also guessed that they would never travel on the B&O RR because the railway employed his detectives to rout out any skullduggery that might endanger the line. He concluded that the fugitives would take the middle route since it was also the less traveled. From Fitchburg they would probably meet the Upper Post road at Douglas then ride on to Hartford. After much discussion, Pinkerton made up his mind. Hartford, Connecticut, was where all roads met. It was there that he would set his trap. In the meantime, what to do with the packet?

Pinkerton, in order to get back into favor with Lincoln, had to take it personally to Washington DC, but how? Perhaps someone was watching him right now. About an hour after Pinkerton arrived, Tyler Wicks came into the Saxton Shipping office. He said he wasn't sure if anyone was on the Reliant or not. Pinkerton was becoming uneasy. He thought,

'What if the group on the train was a ruse? Just to be on the safe side, I'll send Wicks and Styles back to seize the Reliant no matter what as Garrow might be on it as we speak. Besides, Keith might know something as well.'

He motioned for Styles and Wicks to approach him. Pinkerton concluded saying,

"Major Horatio Garrow is alive; Charlie Finch said so before he died. Be very careful Wicks as he has proven in the past to be lethal at the best of times. His companion is probably Harley Blackstone. He's deadly too. Take Styles here with you back to the Reliant. Capture them alive including Sandy Keith if possible. I'll telegraph Commander Franklin at the Charlestown Navy Yards to assist you. Go there first. A Naval Patrol boat will be necessary in case the Reliant makes a run for it. Get going you two and good luck. The two agents beat a hasty retreat while Pinkerton walked over to the office telegraph. He pondered a moment then got down to business.

Pinkerton had to get the packet to Washington safely and speedily without any interference from Garrow or Bolton. A train was out of the question; too risky. Two lone pony express riders, each carrying half a packet, taking different routes was also out of the question. Half a packet was of gobbledygook was worthless. Maybe, a warship from the Charlestown naval yard was the right choice.

Pinkerton knew there was one docked across the harbor at Jefferies Point in East Boston. He had seen it from the Saxton wharf. Pinkerton telegraphed Commander Franklin explaining the gravity of the situation. Two patrol boats in fact was already there, about to depart. They would wait for Wicks and Styles. Pinkerton was grateful but he had another matter on his mind. Perhaps the Commander could do him another favor. He did. A few minutes later, Franklin conferred with the USS Niagara's Captain, Thomas T. Craven. As luck would have it, the Niagara was finished installing its new cannons and was departing in one hour.

Right on schedule, the USS Niagara, glided past Boston Harbor Light with the packet safely aboard. It was guarded by twenty marines and Allan Pinkerton himself. It arrived safely in the Washington Naval yard two days later. At that time, the USS Niagara left Washington returned immediately for Boston where it would continue the process of upgrading its guns. Apparently, Captain Craven found out that the new cannons were making his ship too top heavy. The cruise would be a success for both parties.

Alexander 'Sandy' Keith watched the USS Niagara slip its moorings and disappear on the morning flood tide. Pinkerton had the packet. That much he knew from Blackstone. The ship's steam was already up, engine running, its smoke escaping through a metal roof vent directly above it. The doors to Keith's warehouse opened wide. The Reliant slipped down two greased ways into the harbor. Within minutes it was headed through the inner harbor seawards to the Atlantic.

Sandy's cutter had been well hidden. In fact it had been sitting all along on a slipway inside a warehouse at Jeffries Point. When in port, Keith and his men lived upstairs in a well appointed loft. The rest of the large building was filled with contraband. Despite Pinkerton's best efforts to find Keith, the man and his boat simply vanished. The denizens of the Point protected their own.

Keith was happy. He'd been paid well for his efforts. As the Reliant steamed across the outer harbor towards President Roads, he didn't notice two Naval Patrol boats bearing down on him. Keith had survived for many years on his inner ear. This ear started ringing alarm bells. He turned about just as an explosion of seawater climbed high above him. He spun the helm and yelled into a brass voice pipe,

"Gimme more speed Freddie! Be quick about it man! The Feds are after us again!"

Within minutes, the steam cutter surged forward doing well over twenty knots. Another shell exploded next to him. Seconds later, a geyser of water off his starboard bow shot up into the air drenching the cabin. The Naval gunners were starting to get the range. Governors Island swam through tidal mists on his port side. Keith would make a run for the shallow channel between Shirley Point and Deer Island three miles away. Finally after many close encounters, the Reliant slipped away into the bosom of the vast Atlantic and headed north to Canada.

A diminutive black man stood on the deck of one of the patrol boats, his eyes glued to his Porro binoculars. There was no Garrow or Bolton on board his prey. He knew then that the devil and his minions had escaped by train, not by sea. The pungent smell of gunpowder blew back into his face as the vessel swung about into a freshening wind.

Allan Pinkerton was ushered into President Lincoln's office by William Johnson his aide and body guard. The 'Great Man' was flanked by Edwin M. Stanton, Secretary of War and Captain Lafayette C. Baker, newly appointed head of the Union Intelligence Service. Pinkerton had recently fallen out of favor with these men including Lincoln but now he hoped that this recent success concerning the Nobel papers would erase the past. He was to be sorely mistaken. Lincoln smiled as he turned to face the detective. Pinkerton offered his hand. Lincoln accepted, always the peacemaker,

"Well Allan, I must say you've pulled another rabbit out of the hat this time. I thank you and the nation is grateful for your splendid efforts. Besides, as I understand it, you knew about the Nobel papers even before the Rebels did. Why didn't you tell Lafayette here about them?" Pinkerton lit a cheroot. His moment of triumph had arrived. He was going to savor every moment.

"Well Mr. President, I waited for two reasons. One, I don't trust Baker here to keep any secret and secondly, why not have someone else steal Nobel's formula for us. Sweden is neutral. If the Union was caught with its hands in the till, all diplomatic hell would have broken out especially with England. It's bad enough that the Limey's buy goods from the Rebs let alone allow their sailors furlough to smuggle contraband. My agents in Boston knew Hans Larsen contacted a Rebel spy in England. It's just our good fortune to have been in the right place at the right time."

Stanton shook Pinkerton's hand but Baker snarled and turned away. He stood stolidly looking through the long windows that afforded a view of the Potomac. Lincoln was nonplussed.

"Yes Allan, a coup indeed. The war is still going badly for us right now. The only good thing about it is the effects of the blockade. The Emancipation Proclamation I delivered last

January has turned the war into a war of attrition. We, as a nation are being torn asunder. Martial law has paralyzed the freedom of law-abiding citizens. Lawless brigands run rampant from California to Maryland. Are we headed towards total ruin and damnation?"

Stanton left his perch by the fireplace and moved across the small room. A portrait of Andrew Jackson peered down on everyone from high above the mantle. Stanton lit a cigar. The smoke sailed upwards through shafts of light streaming through dirty tall windows behind him. He was optimistic,

"With all due respect Mr. President, please be patient, Grant will take Vicksburg soon. When that happens, our armies will literally squeeze the Confederates between the Mississippi River and the Atlantic coast. Lee will be outmanned, outgunned, and out supplied." Lincoln added,

"And hopefully outgeneraled with General Meade in the East and General Grant in the West. Lee ran 'Fightin' Joe Hooker ragged at Chancellorsville with fewer men. But Lee lost General Stonewall Jackson. Apparently, he was shot by his own men by accident. He was a great General and drove McDowell, Banks and Fremont crazy, going back and forth in front of but mostly behind their lines. Good God, he was once in sight of the Potomac itself! Now, I hear Jeb Stuart's cavalry is riding roughshod." Baker faced Pinkerton, his right arm pointing at the detective. With malice aforethought he said,

"Too bad he escaped Mr. President. I wonder how Mosby knew when Stuart would be near Briscoe Station,"

Pinkerton calmly walked to the window and grabbed Lafayette by the ear. Baker howled in pain as Pinkerton literally towed him towards the President. He released him in front of an astonished Lincoln. Stanton was aghast. In a rich Scottish brogue, the detective said,

"Ay doughface, it was on your watch in the State Department that the incident happened, not mine you paranoid son of a bitch! My lads pinched him and you let him get away. Perhaps John Mosby tapped your telegraph wires. I hear you're scheming to do likewise on everyone else in Washington these days including you Stanton!"

Pinkerton continued unabated. He began shouting.

"Perhaps your bad behavior as head of the San Francisco Vigilante's still persists. I'll bet your office in the Old Capital building is nothing more than a jail for those arbitrarily pulled out of their beds at two in the morning. Death to traitors...my ass!"

Lafayette Baker's red face matched his red ear. Stanton's bully boy fled the room, slamming the door behind him. Pinkerton turned to the President giving him a full written report of the Nobel affair. Lincoln handled it with aplomb, carefully putting it on top of a tall disorderly stack of correspondence. Pinkerton walked to the fireplace, turned and said,

"By the way, Mr. President, you can thank Belle Brown and Virginia Saxton for exposing the Nobel spy ring. My agents are laying in wait at Harford for the traitors. Perhaps you've heard of these fugitives Mr. President."

"Who are they Allan? Perhaps I have heard of them."

"Mr. President, I'm sure you have indeed heard of the infamous Major Horatio Garrow and the Rebel spy Betsy Bolton." He had. Lincoln exclaimed,

"Well Gentlemen, especially you Allan, make sure you get them. And you Stanton make sure he does. Am I clear on that? Both men answered,

"Yes, of course Mr. President." Lincoln smiled then asked Pinkerton where the criminals were. Pinkerton was sure of himself now.

"They're coming in by coach on the Middle Post Road." He paused,

"Mr. President, without the courage of those two ladies, General Lee would be shelling your office from twenty miles away as we speak."

He walked over to Stanton and waved his cheroot in front of the man's face not giving a damn who or what he was. Pinkerton had had enough of his backroom political shenanigans.

"As for you Stanton, be wary of Baker. You're both too eager to annihilate the South without taking into consideration the long term effects of their defeat." Pinkerton turned and addressed the President directly.

"I'm sure Mr. President, that the sooner this nation heals, the better. I should know. My Scotland fought for its independence from the British for centuries. Look where it got us. William Wallace, Rob Roy, Robbie Burns and Bonnie Prince Charlie are all the memories we have left."

Pinkerton reached for his bowler. As he shook Lincoln's hand he said,

"Mr. President, I beg of you, let them down easy. An 'Act of Forgiveness' would be the greatest peace treaty you could ever sign."

The door closed softly behind him leaving the President and Stanton alone.

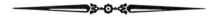

BB and her party boarded three Abbott Concord coaches waiting for them when they left the Fitchburg train. Their transport was provided by the local Castle of the Knights of the Golden Circle, a secret society that plotted against the Union. Once comfortably aboard, the fugitives traveled south to Leominster Station through intermittent snow storms. She knew that her party would have to split up sooner rather than later. It was at Leominster Station that one of the Night Hawk sailors dressed as a Union officer, came rushing back to the three coaches parked just outside of town concealed in a grove of sugar maple trees. He gasped,

"Miss BB, the Feds are waiting for us in Hartford, and there was no message from Boston."

"How do you know?"

"I heard it on the telegraph at the Station Masters Office. I was leaning against the ticket wicket waiting for the telegram when the key started pounding out the alarm. It said the 79th

Pennsylvania Volunteer Infantry there are scouring the countryside." He looked anxiously at BB. Garrow was furious. He railed about leaving Eddie and Charlie Finch alive. He swore,

"I should have shut both of them up permanently when I had a chance. Jesus Christ! Now Pinkerton is once again on my tail. Goddamn it all to hell!"

BB remained calm and said,

"Get everyone together. We'll have to make a decision. Pinkerton thinks that we would head to Washington DC if we didn't have the packet. I know now my agent in Boston failed to get it." Garrow looked at her in amazement,

"And just how do you know he, or might I add she failed?" She smiled and fondly caressed his cheek.

"Women have their ways my dear. There was to be a coded message waiting here but there was none, so Pinkerton has the packet and will most certainly take it by ship to Washington. I can only guess, but that ship is probably the USS Niagara. Keith said it was the only one in Boston ready to sail." Garrow laughed,

"You are really something, really something." BB purred,

"Of course my dear, everyone loyal to the cause knows that. But for now, we'll have to change our plans. We're not going to Washington because Pinkerton expects us to. Instead we'll go to New York City. We'll leave here in one coach then ride on horseback later after we split up."

Two teams of horses were unharnessed after their coaches were hidden behind some bushes. She and Garrow would be in the remaining coach driven by two of the Knights who knew the country well. Blackstone and another Knight would be scouting ahead of them on horseback. BB asked the two drivers what they thought was the best way to get around Hartford. After much deliberation an alternate escape plan was born. Simply put, they would use the Upper Post Road to Spencer then ride for Springfield. From there they would stay on that Post Road till they arrived at Windsor on the Connecticut River. Once there, they would hire a boat to take them past Hartford at night. They would get back on the road at Weatherford then steal a coach and four then proceed on to New York City. The others would be left to their own devices. They would hopefully all meet again in New York City at the Saint Nicholas Hotel. The Knights would reserve rooms there for all of them as the leader of the Knight's New York Castle conveniently owned the hotel.

A few hours of hard traveling ensued as incessant rains made the roads nearly impassable. It was late at night and everyone was trying to catch some sleep. They stopped at a nearby roadside inn for supper then moved on. Blackstone stole two fresh horses replete with English saddles at Ponakin Mill. Lancaster City and Clinton lay ahead of them. The country road passed through the rolling hills and valleys of central Massachusetts. Using circuitous country back roads and BB's interminable charm at Federal roadblocks, they managed to reach the town of Spencer late the next day. From there they travelled south-east through

Brookfield, and Palmer. They did so without incident. However, it was at North Wilbraham, that Belle got an inkling of Garrow's secret past. It all started with a valise.

Horatio Garrow had never taken his eyes off his leather valise since boarding the train in Boston. BB guessed correctly that it contained something rather important. It occurred to her that perhaps her beau was double-crossing her. Was the packet in his valise ready for sale to the highest bidder? She had to find out. It was at North Wilbraham where they stopped for breakfast at the Collins Inn. Garrow went in to reconnoiter the premises. He'd left the valise under the watchful eye of Harley Blackstone. BB didn't like Blackstone. She didn't trust him and had always listened to that wee inner voice telling her when to be extremely cautious. But what was in the valise? Harley was standing beside the coach eyeing her. BB sitting inside, reached over and lightly caressed his shoulder, saying,

"My dear Harley, do you mind if I move that valise over? It's in the way my dear."

Before Harley could react, she grabbed the handle of the valise. To her surprise it was extremely heavy. Harley Blackstone reached in, grabbed her wrist and snarled,

"Don't you ever do that agin' Missy or you'll rue the day we ever met."

His yellow teeth gleamed in the dim light. Garrow returned to take her into the roadhouse. She took his hand as she stepped from the coach. She smiled, knowing it was coinage, not the packet, in his valise.

Their journey commenced the next morning as their coach and four clattered through a covered bridge spanning the Chicopee River. From there they drove on to Springfield ten miles away. Only Garrow and Belle were in the coach. Harley sat high up on the drivers' seat with two lead reins in either hand. Two Knights were scouting ahead. Harley seethed every time he felt the Concord rock back and forth on the level stretches of roadway. He knew what BB and Garrow were up to as gales of laughter followed by moans of unbridled passion welled up from beneath him to bewitch his senses. Blackstone grew hard as he imagined what he would do to that bitch. He pleasured himself in the knowledge that his opportunity would come soon enough.

Fresh horses were waiting for them at Springfield. Their empty coach turned around and headed back the way it came. BB surprised the men by her excellent and daring horsemanship. Sitting astride a tall thoroughbred, she was easily the equal of any one man including Garrow. She laughed thinking,

"Oh how I wish I was astride Fleeter!"

The group decided at Windsor that the Connecticut River was probably being watched as well. After much discussion with their guides, a map was drawn out for them. They bid adieu to their two escorts as the three fugitives took another and more arduous route west of the Connecticut River to Bloomfield then due south to Meridian. They reached New Haven at night staying at the Tidewater Inn in the Village of Madison just outside the city. The next morning, they rode off in a snow storm that had swept ashore from Long Island Sound. The following night they stayed at the Old Drovers Inn near the town of Stamford. After a sound sleep, early the next morning, they crossed into New York State at the Village of Rye. The long tortuous journey had taken its toll not only physically but mentally on the group. Blackstone was as claustrophobic as ever, refusing to ride in the coach or sleep in the tiny bedrooms of every inn they came across. He welcomed riding even though he suffered from innumerable saddle sores. Sadly for BB, she learned that Garrow was not the white knight she'd longed for.

They had been in the Village of Rye having breakfast at the Square House Inn. One of the inhabitants sitting in a dark corner recognized Garrow and Blackstone from the Howard Grove Military Hospital in Richmond, Virginia. He was obviously very drunk. He got up and staggered towards them clutching his clay mug of ale in one hand and pointing the other at Garrow. A room filled with early risers watched as the man yelled,

"Well boys if it ain't Captain Garrow himself and his rucker side-kick, Private Harley Blackstone." The man swore,

"Hey, you bastards, murdered anyone lately? Sergeant Morgan was my brother Blackstone, and you killed him. I was a Union soldier on a prison work gang at Howard Grove before I got injured and was paroled out. I know all about you two bloody cowards!"

He limped towards them for a better look but Garrow walked up and grabbed him by his arms. The man spit in his face while taking a swing at him with his beer mug. He missed. Garrow threw him onto the saw-dust covered floor where he lay in a pool of vomit, beer and shards of clay. Through bleary eyes the figure of Garrow loomed large above him. The man looked up crying out,

"You deserted Garrow. You're a goddamned deserter! You helped Blackstone escape then you both took off. I hope you two rot in hell!"

Blackstone reached down and picked him up by the throat. His fist smashed into the man's jaw, cracking it with a laudable snap. Harley released him. With that, the man fell to the floor unmoving. BB looked on horrified as a tall, well muscled bystander ran over. He examined the man whose eyes had rolled back into his head. The stranger stood up and glared at the trio. He cried out to the other men sitting at tables around them,

"Jimmy Morgan is dead fer sure. Wadda ya say boys; let's give these Johnny Rebs a little taste of northern hospitality."

For the first and only time in her life, BB's world was filled with visceral fear. She backed up slowly trying desperately to be inconspicuous. BB grabbed her overcoat; her purse then gathered her skirts about her and ran from the men fighting around her. A back door was ajar. She fled to her horse, looked about, her panic rising. A road sign beckoned her. It read, NEW YORK CITY>. Shots rang out. In one fluid motion she swung onto the side saddle and rode away.

Many miles later she crossed over King's Bridge spanning Spuyten Duyvil Creek. She rode into the Bronx at a full gallop. Her only wish was to escape from Garrow and Blackstone. The very thought of him touching her became repellant when she found out that she had been in the arms of a deserter. Killing for the 'Cause' she could stomach but not a betrayal of it. BB had principles, apparently Garrow did not.

She galloped hard down the muddy post road. Her intuition told her to abandon any hope of escaping from him unless she could tell him that she was through with him without giving him a chance to kill her as she did so. She had to tell him but how? Then she remembered the Albany road sign. Desperately she rode back over the Kings Bridge. After a mile or so, she came upon a road sign. Painted on it in neat black letters was ALBANY>.

She pulled up, the reins tight in her grasp. She laughed as she untied her blue satin bonnet, reached down and tied it to the sign. Wheeling about, she fled up the Albany road, stopping at the top of a hill a half-mile from the junction. She swung her lathered horse under a chestnut tree beside the road. Within its shadows BB waited, having a clear view of the post road junction far below her. A few minutes later, a bloodied Garrow and Blackstone came upon the bonnet. Garrow leaned over and retrieved it. Suspecting that she was watching him from afar, he stood up in his stirrups and waved her bonnet. BB relaxed as the two rode away. It was over. The pinch of the game had arrived. There was no remorse; no second thoughts of going back to him. She swung her horse about and headed towards Albany. She was going home.

Garrow knew that BB was finished with him. He laughed as he put the bonnet in a saddlebag. There would always be another woman in his future; that much he was sure of. Moreover, Garrow had bigger fish to fry. Another fortune, smuggling war materiel out of New York City for Boss Tweed awaited him. Besides, he'd met William 'Boss' Marcy Tweed, the 'Sachem of Tammany Hall' a few years before. Perhaps Tweed might hire him to run his smuggling enterprise.

Garrow and Blackstone rode at a full gallop towards the Five Points area of the city. A few days later, both men would put on a spectacular display of their demonic talents in the draft riots of July, 1863. Within weeks, Garrow's own smuggling ring was in business for Garrow had been rejected by Tweed. Thereafter Garrow's credo was, "To hell with Boss Tweed."

BOOK TWO: CHAPTER 13
FIRST BLOOD

Months before, the Maasai Rangers regrouped, licked their wounds and sailed aboard the Nimsi for Fort Monroe five hundred nautical miles to the south. The Anaona stayed astern of her for the entire ten day voyage. Once there, the Nimsi was ordered to join the Union fleet. Commanded by Admiral Rodgers; this fleet constituted the Galena, Aroostook, Port Royal, Monitor and the Naugatuk. The Confederate defeat at Hampton Roads the week before left the Confederate capital of Richmond exposed once again. Only Fort Darling atop Drewry Bluffs, twelve miles down the James River from Richmond, stood in Rodger's way.

The Rangers refueled at Norfolk, Virginia. From there they sailed to Fort Monroe thirty miles further up the James River estuary. The Nimsi followed the fleet while the Anaona, under the interim command of First Mate, Duncan Toller stayed at Fort Monroe. Rodger's gunboats steamed up the James River towards Richmond. But first they had to get past Drewry Bluffs.

On the evening of May 13, 1862, Marcus with two mounted squads in tow went ashore a mile downstream from City Point. Once there, they torched the train depot building, killing anyone trying to flee on the Petersburg Railway to Richmond. Marcus rode his 'Warden' through dense smoke and fire, the reins in his teeth. Muzzle flashes winked at him from the windows of the departing train. His second squad brought in one of the Nimsi's Gatling guns in pieces on a pack mule. They mounted it on a captured gun carriage trailing an ammunition caisson. Pulled by two mules, the Ranger's Gatling raked the Rebels from locomotive to caboose. Return fire plinked off the gun's shield but no one was hurt. Shortly, thereafter white flags from nearby buildings appeared. The shooting ceased. The USS Galena wouldn't shell the City until five weeks later on June 27. On that day with General George McClellan on board, two boatloads of marines went ashore and destroyed the rebuilt depot buildings that the Maasai Rangers had already torched. The General was derided for not being ashore with his army. Lincoln relieved him of his duties four months later for being too cautious in battle.

Meanwhile, the Nimsi proceeded up river in the lowered position. The Confederate snipers never saw her as she slid by them in the dark, hugging the river's left bank. Ten Rangers disembarked to reconnoiter upriver for nearly ten miles. Pitched battles with Confederate patrols slowed their progress. Only their superb Ranger training saved them. On the morning of May 14th, from deep cover close in, they glassed Fort Darling sprawled out a hundred feet above the James River. What they saw was dramatic. The Rebels were sinking old steamboat hulks in the river opposite the fort thus forcing any Union ships closer to the fort's cannon. Earth and log redoubts were also being hurriedly constructed downriver from it. A masked battery, sunk into the river bank behind a thick log and earthen bulwark waited to ambush the unwary.

Squad leader, Corporal Smith sent back two Rangers to warn the fleet's flagship, the USS Galena of the rebel trap. By then the Galena was only a few miles downstream from the fort. The two Rangers successfully avoided all enemy patrols then shot a soldier guarding some rowboats. Taking one, they rowed over to the Galena under a white flag. A knotted rope was thrown down. While one Ranger secured the rowboat to it, Corporal Walker scrambled up the wooden steps that ran up the curved side of the armored flagship. After identifying himself, he reported to Commander Rogers. Rogers returned his salute.

"I'm Maasai Ranger Walker reporting Sir."

"Go ahead son, and make it brief."

"Yes of course Sir. I've just come back from glassing Fort Darling. The Rebels there are reinforcing it with heavy cannon and masked batteries. They've also sunk several old steamboat hulks out in the river in such a way that you'll be forced close in. As for snipers Commander, the river banks are crawlin' with them." He stood back.

"Thank you Ranger. I'll take this information under consideration." Rogers paused, leaned back in his leather chair, reached over and picked up a long clay pipe by its bowl. After tamping the tobacco within, he lit it. He exclaimed.

"Maasai Rangers you say? Are they all black? They are! I must say that it is very unusual to see buffalos hereabouts. They're usually fightin' west of old Muddy like Terry's Rebel Rangers out of Texas."

He leaned back in his chair sucking his pipe, watching the Ranger very carefully as the boy stammered.

"Sir, all I can tell you is that I'm part of a guerilla unit out of Boston. We trained at West Point. Here we live off the land or aboard the SS Nimsi. We're presently stationed at Fort Monroe."

Rogers sucked on his pipe. It died. Truculent, he put it down, leaned forward, eyeing the Ranger like an owl before it pounces. He queried,

"Never heard of you fellas, but the Nimsi I know about. Its Captain is John Saxton from Boston. I met his old man Thomas in China in 54' fighting rebels on the Canton River. Ok, son, you stay aboard for now, I might need you." Walker saluted and cried, "Yes Sir!"

The Galena cruised up river, leading the fleet right into the massive eight and ten inch Columbiad guns of Fort Darling. Roger's ordered pickets ashore to deal with snipers but they were soon recalled. The two Rangers on board returned accurate sniper fire as the battle intensified. The Galena's lead men were shot dead. Commander Rogers immediately ordered all the ships to fire on the shore batteries lining both sides of the river.

Two miles downriver from Fort Darling, a scouting party led by Marcus returned to their ship. Their mules were stowed aboard, brushed, watered and fed. An observer was sent aloft in the ship's balloon about one hundred feet up. There was very little wind as the observer glassed the surrounding area. In the clear light of dawn, he could see for ten miles in all directions. On the deck of the Nimsi, its Gatlings, and mortars were readied as well as an ordnance rifle. Two squads fanned out in a skirmish line a hundred yards from where she was tied up. The Galena was receiving semaphore signals from the Nimsi's balloonist high above them. She was warned to stay away from the Drewry's bluff but nevertheless pressed on with devastating results.

The Galena took a severe beating. Seventeen cannon shells went right through her new overlapping armor. Sixteen sailors were killed and over twenty were wounded. The Rangers were allowed to row back downstream where they boarded the Nimsi. One was wounded on the way but not seriously. The Nimsi's balloon came down under fire as the Gatlings and mortars opened up, beating back a concerted Rebel assault late in the afternoon. The Rangers ashore, fought fiercely in hand to hand combat with a Confederate force of considerable size. The balloon was stowed after which Marcus signaled for his Rangers to retreat. They did so in good order without casualties. The last man aboard was Marcus himself. As he jumped through the wheelhouse hatch, bullets began pinking all around him. In the woods nearby, three electrically initiated Rains mines exploded. Laid by the retreating Rangers, they killed and maimed all those unfortunate enough to be within fifty feet of them. With ordinance exploding all about, the Nimsi sank lower into a cove of slack water, her stacks protruding above the water. Within minutes, she was far out into the middle of the James River, her wake bubbling behind her as she turned upstream.

Minutes later, a very confused and bleeding Confederate Corporal emerged from the verge of cottonwoods bordering the river. In vain he searched for any signs of the Yankees until by chance he spotted what looked to be a sinking ship cruising upriver. He aimed his Tower Enfield carefully and fired, hitting a small metal stack that rose up atop the behemoth. His gunned jammed. Cursing he spun around as something began flapping in the breeze behind him. He looked up. A large piece of paper stuck to a tree branch caught his attention. He ran over and tore it down. On it was drawn an elliptical shield with two spears crossed behind it. Below the drawing were printed the words,

'We are the Maasai Rangers. Death to the Confederacy'

He looked around; the hair on his neck rising. Unsure of what to do next, he scuttled off through the bracken; the paper in his breast pocket. Harley Blackstone began to run and didn't quit until he ran through the main gate of Fort Darling. Once there he showed the note to his Commander, Ebenezer Farrand. Hard of hearing, Farrand replied gruffly, his right hand cupped to a rather large cauliflower ear.

"Speak up man. I'm nearly deaf with all the shellin' goin' on. You say you found this a few miles downstream from here." He looked at the paper again.

"I've never heard of 'em Corporal. They were what? All niggers? Remarkable! Could fight too eh? Listen well son; I want you to double the pickets downstream but move them closer to the fort, no more than a mile. Do it Corporal!" He paused, a hand over his right ear,

"What was that? You're trying to tell me that they were invisible." Blackstone nodded vigorously. Farrand sputtered, as the officers standing by guffawed loudly.

"Please Corporal; I do realize you've been through hell lately, but invisible! I don't think so. What was that? You say that they have an ironclad that can sink out of sight." Farrand looked about for support. It was ludicrous.

"Really Corporal! We'll certainly keep an eye out for it, won't we gentlemen." They all laughed. The Commander turned to face the other officers standing about. Blackstone still at attention was now only a footnote, ignored and ridiculed. Commander continued oblivious to Harley's embarrassment.

"Gentlemen, the Galena looks like it has smallpox but that damned Monitor is bullet proof. I swear I'll kill Jeff Davis for blowing up the Merrimack."

In one last desperate attempt to salvage something, Blackstone enquired about Major Garrow's health. Farrand replied,

"Sorry to hear about Major Garrow gettin' wounded Corporal. He's still in Howard Groves Hospital convalescing. I understand Beauregard promoted him just last week to Major. That'll be all Corporal."

Blackstone saluted, turned and left the bunker. All around him shot and shell exploded. He ran off towards his picket Captain deep in the forest. He found him slumped against a tree, dead. Blackstone lit a cheroot. A bullet flicked past him. He and his cheroot dropped to the ground as more shots were fired. He growled,

"Goddamn it all too hell, life was a lot safer on the Wanderlust. Christ, I'm the unluckiest son of a bitch alive! The bastards have Spencers. Christ, I'd give my balls for one right now!"

Bullets zipped by his head. He hunkered down, straining to see where the rifle fire was coming from. It stopped. He crawled over to a fellow picket. The young boy was lying on his back, shot through the left eye. Harley laid aside his musket and started digging with a trenching tool as were all the other pickets around him. Even though it was a sunny day, only meager shafts of light shot through the canopy above him. Occasionally a shadow shifted here and there. Another picket screamed to his right. Blackstone took no chances. He crawled on his belly towards the scream. Another picket lay dead, his throat slit from ear to ear, a note on his chest said, "Death to the Confederacy". Blackstone froze. A twig snapped right behind him. He whirled around. Nothing was there, nothing at all. Blackstone jumped up and ran blindly back through the forest.

Lieutenant Wright and his Rangers returned to the Nimsi, which was tied up even closer to Drewry Bluffs. On the way, they routed Rebel pickets a mile or so downriver from the fort. Later in the afternoon, after a series of raids and reconnoiters, the Nimsi slipped away downstream. After four hours of shelling Fort Darling, Roger's armada retreated in disarray for Newport News. Richmond was spared. The Nimsi tied up alongside the Anaona at Fort Monroe. Other than a bullet-hole through one of its air vents it was relatively unscathed.

A week after the siege of Fort Darling, a courier arrived with a message while the Rangers were being instructed by balloonist, Thaddeus Lowe. Both Saxton and Marcus were ordered aboard the Galena for lunch with Commander John Rodgers at 1200 hours the next day at the Norfolk shipyards. It seemed that Rogers needed their opinions about certain naval matters. Just what matters they didn't know. They complied, wary and alert.

At precisely 1200 hours, Marcus in his green Ranger uniform and Saxton in his Navy Whites stepped off a Navy cutter thirty miles downriver. Norfolk had just recently been recaptured by Union forces. The destruction left behind by the retreating Confederates was surprisingly minimal. Both officers were impressed by how quickly the yard had been restored considering that only a year had passed since the Union blew up nine ships there to prevent their capture by the Rebs. The yard was very busy repairing a fleet of damaged ships. Saxton and Marcus were also impressed by the thousand ton ironclad USS Galena as it lay berthed in the yard. The mutilation by the Rebel artillery inflicted upon it had been immense. Many men had died and many more had been wounded. Some of the minor damage had already been repaired making the vessel's living quarters suitable for the crew and its officers. Later on after months of picket duty along the James River, the 'Gallant' Galena would be stripped of its ineffective armor plating in Philadelphia in May of 1863. The vessel would remain a wooden ship for the remainder of its days.

The Commander's burgee flew from the masthead of the USS Galena. As Saxton and Marcus came aboard, Commander Rodgers was there to greet them. The Captains saluted. They followed him past a wooden lookout tower amidships on the aft deck to where a large white canvas had been erected over a long wooden table. A gentle breeze crept over the sloping iron sides of the Galena, cooling the air as Navy stewards attended to them. The new Commander of the USS Monitor, a Lieutenant Samuel D. Green, and Commander Rogers stood waiting for them as the men ducked their heads under the low canvas. After introductions, the four men sat down. Drinks were ordered and a light luncheon was served. The Commander expressed his condolences to Saxton upon hearing that his father had passed away. A short time later, Rodgers stood up saying,

"Gentlemen, a toast to the Union and God bless America." Admiral Rodgers turned to Marcus looking at him closely,

"I do believe you are Sir, a most unusual specimen I've ever seen. Where do you come from? The facial scars, your height, are most intriguing to say the least." Marcus looked at Saxton and winked.

"Gentlemen, I'm a savage from the darkest heart of Africa, a Maasai cannibal that loves to eat Johnny Rebs, day or night, it doesn't matter. In fact you won't see me eat much today, instead I'll mix Rebel blood with milk before I bunk up. As a child I was clawed by a lion before I killed him with my bare hands."

Saxton sat back as he and Marcus tried to keep a straight face. Lt. Green leaned forward to inspect Marcus more closely but backed off quickly as Marcus snarled at him. Rodgers sensing a prank drolly remarked.

"Well Green, what do you say? Better to have him on our side don't you think?"

Green agreed. Marcus asked Samuel if he was related to a Lieutenant Israel Green of West Point.

"No sir, not to my knowledge but I did hear some scuttlebutt that he was trainin' some niggers to play at soldierin', how preposterous indeed!"

Rodgers leaned over and whispered in Lt. Green's ear. The man stood up abruptly and faced Marcus.

"I'm damned sorry Captain. No offense."

"None taken," Commander Rodgers laughed,

"Well gentlemen let's get down to business and a well earned cigar, a bottle of bourbon and intelligent conversation. First of all Captain Brown, I should have listened to one of your Rangers. I do believe his name was Thomas Walker. Anyway, he and another came aboard and warned me about getting too close to Fort Darling. I didn't listen. I should have, for we suffered too many dead and wounded. It certainly proved that we are not shot proof."

He looked over at Green. The Commander's high forehead thrust forward, curious and introspective. After rolling a cigar in his rough hands, he casually bit off the end spitting it out over the side. He remarked,

"I understand Lieutenant, that you only got hit three times with no damage. It's amazing really, considering the Rebs were throwin' everything at us includin' the kitchen sink. I know now that interlocking armor is crap." He thundered,

"Now close to the waterline and eight inches of armor plate, that's the ticket!"

He looked around wildly, puffing like a steam engine. Marcus laughed. The Commander looked at Marcus. A note of displeasure passed over his face. He growled,

"Well Captain Brown, what is your opinion on modern warfare? Go on lad. Tell us."

Marcus, a thumb under each lapel of his uniform, began speaking very seriously,

"Modern warfare gentlemen, is upon us. New weapons, new ships, new fleet maneuvers and so on are now our purview. But the main weapon in any man's army or navy is pure common sense. The Generals and the Admirals can go to all the fancy military academies in the land but once in the field, they have to throw away the rules and rely on information gathered in the field. Knowledge is power, pure and simple. It wins wars gentlemen; it wins wars. That's my job as leader of the Maasai Rangers. The knowledge I and my men gather behind enemy lines, gives my superiors a winning edge in the field of battle. Secondly, we go behind the front lines to harass the enemy where and when we can to full advantage. That's all I'll tell you for now gentlemen. How we do it and where we do it is secret, very secret." Marcus sat down and calmly lit a cheroot.

Saxton rose. He addressed Lieutenant Green, looking down on him with a measure of admiration.

"The Monitor will be obsolete soon Lieutenant, even though it performed well. You are to be congratulated. I too live below the waterline. I'm sure we both suffer from the damp, claustrophobia and the stench of human sweat." Green nodded, as Saxton went on,

"And may I say John Ericsson did an admirable job of designing both our ships even down to the flush toilets. However one has to learn how and when to operate those damn levers, otherwise it becomes a disaster." Lieutenant Green responded,

"You're right Saxton. Sitting on one under fire is quite an experience. I still have the scars to prove it."

Rodgers interjected over the laughter,

"You don't say Saxton. Quite the ships they are too. That revolving copula on the Monitor is the first one I've seen. My, my, it certainly looks like the Navy is in for some big changes." Green asked,

"What do you mean Commander?" Rodgers stood up, straightened his blue uniform and began pacing about.

"The Monitor is the future and my ship, the Galena obviously represents the past in terms of naval design. Steam power, will I'm sure replace sail completely for it allows ships to go wherever they want. Ironclads will replace wooden ships. Rifled breech loading guns will replace smooth bore muzzle loaders. Yes my friends, the Navy and the Army are in for big changes and soon. It always seems that way when war erupts, with one side trying to out gun the other. I'm sorry to say it gentlemen but I now command a relic."

At that moment a Steward came forward and whispered in the Commander's ear. His eyes widened. The Steward stood back and waited at attention. Rodgers looked down at Saxton somewhat perplexed.

"It seems Captain Saxton that a certain gentleman named "Pinky" is waiting for you on board the Nimsi.

Alan Pinkerton strolled about the deck of the Nimsi puffing away on a large cigar; his hat was jammed tightly onto his small head. Behind his large black beard, his eyes literally jumped out of his head. A few hours later, a Navy steam cutter puttered through late evening sea haze towards him. Pinkerton sighed as he looked upon the oncoming vessel.

"Jesus Murphy, I'm getting too old for this nonsense! There must be a better way of earning a living!"

Allan Pinkerton had a very good reason for his frustration. With nearly five hundred Secret Service agents in the field, Pinkerton as head of the Service had aged considerably. Recently, 'The Eye' as all America knew him, had fallen out of favor with Lincoln over the premature release of a Confederate spy, Rose O'Neal Greenhow by the US War Department. Months before, three Union agents were spying in Richmond, Virginia. Rose fled to Richmond where she recognized them in a hotel lobby. Webster, Scully and Lewis were arrested and later hanged in April of 1862 on Webster's testimony. Thereafter, Pinkerton's paranoid rival, Lafayette C. Baker would garner favor with Secretary of War, Edwin Stanton by convincing him that Pinkerton's methods were unsubstantial and too lenient. General McClellan, Pinkerton's last ally would be relieved of command by Lincoln soon after on November 5th, 1862. From then on, Lincoln would defer to Stanton's judgment on the matter.

The naval cutter slid into the dock smoothly, its propeller thrashing the water in reversed. Two passengers jumped ashore. Pinkerton approached them. Saxton and Marcus were shocked at his appearance. Saxton cried,

"How good to see you again Allan, but you look dreadful. It appears to me that you've slept in your clothes for a month!" Marcus added,

"It must be true. Your company motto should be 'I Never Sleep'". Pinkerton took off his bowler and wiped his forehead with a handkerchief. He put on his hat and laughed. As he stuffed the damp cloth back into a trouser pocket, he said,

"You're both right. I don't look good and my sleeping habits are even worse. Blame Lafayette, Stanton and Lincoln in that order. I'd say Lincoln sleeps less than I do!"

He paused, looked around and said,

"Say now Gentlemen, let's get out of the wind and talk in your stateroom. Christ, do I ever need a decent drink."

Pinkerton put on a pair of canvas booties then clambered down the ladder into the Nimba's Wheelhouse. A few minutes later everyone was comfortably seated in Saxton's cramped living quarters. Makers Mark was poured all around. Saxton looked up at Pinkerton who resumed his 'habitual ritual' as Saxton called it, of endless pacing. It seemed the little man was eternally restless as if rigor mortis was a constant possibility if he stood still for any length of time. Pinkerton started to light a cigar, but was told in no uncertain terms that smoking was not allowed. He cried piteously,

"We should have gone aboard the Anaona. Sorry Captain, I plum forgot. But first of all news from home gentlemen as both your families are well and thriving, especially the dog. Jack is his name and red ball is his game."

They laughed. He continued as he reluctantly sat down.

"They all send their love. Everyone's doing fine."

He reached into a pocket and gave them both small studio photos of their wives. Saxton and Marcus looked at them greedily. Both men put them in their breast pockets. Pinkerton sat back satisfied. They would do as he asked, no questions asked even though he knew furlough was on their minds. He addressed it.

"They're lovely aren't they? I must say those two wives of yours have had a tough time of it, especially Belle. Despite her ordeal, I know one thing for certain; this war will last a few more years despite our blockade, and despite Lincoln's best generals. Our nation needs both of you, our President needs both of you and your wives need both of you to continue to take the fight to the enemy. I hope you understand gentlemen that you will lose everything if the Rebels win. You two especially will lose everything. You're in for the long haul now; you can't go home as yet." Both men knew he was right.

Saxton watched, fascinated as Pinkerton took a note out of a lower pocket. He thought, 'Jesus H. Christ! He's looks just like 'The Fakir of Ava' doling out cheap gifts.

Pinkerton gave the telegram to Marcus. As he was about to read it, Saxton stopped him, walked over then closed the door and two roof vents above him. Satisfied he sat down before Marcus said,

"To: Commanding Officer, Operation
Maasai Ranger STOP Capture JEB.
STOP Good luck STOP Redstone."

Pinkerton retrieved the telegram and put it in his breast pocket.

"May I remind you gentlemen, no telegrams to anyone, right?" They agreed, knowing that the secrecy of every mission was paramount. The detective continued.

"Now my friends, about the illustrious Jeb Stuart, where does one begin?"

Time passed quickly as Pinkerton outlined the amazing military career of James Ewell Brown Stuart. A Brigadier-General at only 29, Stuart was the leader of the Confederate Calvary that triumphed at Manassas, holding Munson's Hill within sight of Washington DC. He also brilliantly covered the retreat of the Confederate Army from Yorktown and opened the fighting at Williamsburg. He was literally, the eyes and ears of Generals Jackson and Johnston who were about to meet McClellan on his campaign to take the Rebel capital of Richmond, Virginia. Pinkerton told them that Stuart was in Richmond. Saxton was about to ask him how he knew but Pinkerton demurred, his finger on his nose, his black eyes twinkling mischievously.

In time a course of action was agreed upon. Simply put, the Maasai Rangers would sail up the James River in the Nimsi backed up by the Anaona. Once in position, the Rangers would go ashore, reconnoiter the area then sneak through enemy lines on foot or mule, capture Stuart and then take him back to Fort Monroe. It seemed impossible but both Marcus and Saxton agreed to it right away. The war would turn in favor of the Union. Besides, God was on their side. Pinkerton was relieved. He stood up and proposed a toast.

"To the success of the Maasai Rangers, may God bless them and protect them!"

They raised their whiskies together. The solemnity of the moment passed quickly as Pinkerton unexpectedly laughed. Something else was on his mind. Saxton and Marcus looked at each other bemused. Pinkerton took off his jacket and rolled up his sleeves. He spoke as if he had been given a direct order,

"Captain Saxton, I have a request from the President. He wants to know if that infernal toilet of yours really works. May I?" Saxton was equal to the occasion.

"But of course Allan. Follow me."

Saxton led the small man over to a closed door. He opened it. Inside the head sat a white porcelain toilet bowl. Arrayed on its right side were three brass levers. Saxton showed Pinkerton how to use them correctly, warning him of unpleasant results if he didn't follow directions. The door closed. Moments later the roar of the toilet could be heard. The door flew open and 'Stinky Pinky' stood there completely covered in crap.

BOOK TWO: CHAPTER 14
THE DIE GAME

The Anaona with one squad of Rangers aboard anchored across from the Shirley plantation on the north shore of Turkey Island after dark. Its mission was to guard a narrow river channel through which both ships could avoid being seen by the Rebels at City Point. A camouflaged mosquito net was thrown over the vessel as it lay in a large slough awaiting the Nimsi's return. It was mid June, 1862. Long and narrow fields of corn nearby were starting to sprout. The James River was high and running fast as all of its tributaries were in flood. Saxton and Marcus were on the hunt for General Jeb Stuart, the formidable eyes and ears of General Lee.

A Union spy, Elizabeth Van Lew or "Crazy Bet" as she was known, being very astute; noticed unusual cavalry movement around Richmond for two days, June 12-13th. Lee's Confederate army was facing off against McClellan's. For no apparent reason, twelve hundred cavalry high-tailed it towards the Winston Farm twenty-two miles north of Richmond. She suspected Stuart was going to ride around McClellan's right flank. She was right, for the very next day he swung southeast along the Pamunky River towards Tunstall's Landing. Why? Was it to cut off the York River Railway; the main supply route to McClellan? Apparently not, for other agents reported that Stuart moved on to Forge Bridge nine miles further south. Forewarned, Federal forces missed capturing him by mere minutes below Sycamore Springs just after the Rebels burned a makeshift bridge behind them. It now became apparent that Stuart's ride was one of reconnaissance only. General Lee had indeed sent Stuart to reconnoiter the right flank of McClellan's army of the Potomac. At one hundred thousand strong, it would be devastating if Lee's army attacked north of the Chickahominy River. To stop this from happening, Lincoln personally ordered the deployment of the Maasai Rangers to capture General Jeb Stuart.

Under a magnanimous full moon, the Nimsi slipped unseen up a long narrow river inlet called Four Mile Creek. Despite being narrow at times; because the creek was in flood, the Nimsi was able to maneuver to within two hundred yards of the New Market Road. The old road connected Malvern Hill to Richmond, fifteen miles away to the west. The ship lay there like an alligator, sunk low into a backwater slough, unnoticed. Two squads were ready to disembark with their mules. However, a scout came back and said that they were only a mile from the Turner Road Junction; therefore the mules were not necessary. Marcus agreed and the beasts remained aboard while twenty five Rangers disembarked into the dark and brooding woods.

To all concerned, the Rangers figured that Stuart would probably come along the New Market Road although two other roads paralleled it. This road was the shortest route to Richmond. The Rangers decided to fan out on either side waiting, silent and invisible where the road was pinched between the river and a low river bank on the Edgewood plantation. It was the perfect place for an ambush. They didn't have to wait long.

From their vantage point on the ground and in nearby water oak trees, the Rangers saw a lone rider coming 'hell bent for leather' towards them. It had to be important, for the rider carried CSA marked leather courier bags. A signal was given and as the rider came within range, one of the Rangers threw a knife into his chest. The rider cried out as he fell onto the muddy road. Two Rangers ran out, seized the horse then removed all tack, saddle and insignia. By slapping the animal hard on its rear end, the horse was gone in an instant towards Richmond.

A Ranger ransacked the courier's saddlebags, finding a note inside from Stuart telling Lee about the weak right flank of McClellan's army. The rider was still alive. He was propped up against a tree. Bloody bubbles poured out of his mouth. He was young, scared and dying. Marcus asked him,

"Son, what's your name? Tell me your name son and I'll see to it that your family knows what happened here."

The young man's blue eyes dimmed. He gurgled,

"I'm Corporal Turner Doswell of Beckley, West Virginia. You have kilt me fer sure." He died moments later in Marcus's arms.

They carried the body into the bushes off to the side of the road. General Stuart would be on the New Market Road and therefore his scouts would be along shortly, followed by his cavalry. Marcus knew he must capture Stuart but how?

Marcus reasoned that his troops were probably exhausted after riding many hard miles since they left Richmond. Marcus called his men together and issued his orders.

"Squad One, go down the road towards Charles City a pace and form a skirmish line on the right side about ten yards from the edge. Squad Two, take up sniping positions in those trees over there behind them. As Stuart comes abreast of you, Cornel and I'll throw flash bombs behind him and in front of him. Meanwhile the remainder will pose as slaves weeding that cornfield over there while the rest of you will be cover them from across the road. As soon as the action starts, you weeders retrieve your weapons then kill as many Rebs as you can. Retreat to a skirmish line near the Nimsi. Once in position, you'll cover our withdrawal."

He turned, looking through the brush down the road as a large staked wagon piled high with hay and pulled by two mules rumbled towards them. Thinking off the cuff, Marcus whispered to his Rangers.

"Bobby and Bill, strip to the waist then run towards that wagon as if you're slaves in a panic. Stop it and ascertain whether or not the driver has any news of Stuart's column. After which sap, bind, gag then hide him in the bushes. We're going to stuff Stuart under the hay after he's bound and gagged. Here's some twine and a hanky. Charlie, you and Emmett will drive the hay wagon in behind the bushes near this here tree. Get Stuart out and hightail it back. We'll fall back to cover you." He pointed to another Ranger.

"Tom, you go and tell Saxton to get keep a head of steam up. Bobby and Bill, off you go. The rest of you get ready as soon as we have the wagon. Now get under cover. Remember men, Stuart will stand out. He's famous for wearing a short gray jacket covered with buttons and braids. A gray cape over his shoulder is lined in scarlet, but most of all, he will conspicuous by his broad hat looped with a gold star and topped by a black ostrich plume. He'll also be wearing high jack boots, gold spurs, a tasseled yellow sash and long leather gauntlets. Behind him will be his own regimental Captains. You snipers, shoot them dead. I don't want any interference from them. The column will most certainly be strung out for over a mile. They're probably tired and their guard will be down as they're only a short distance from Richmond. They more than likely spent the night in Charles City a ways back, so they might be hung over as well. I hope so. Good luck everyone!"

Tom ran back towards the Nimsi. Bobby and Bill raced down the road yelling in a panic as a large hay wagon approached them. Marcus watched as the wagon stopped; the black driver pointed back down the road the way he had come. He was abruptly pulled down onto the road where he was knocked out, bound, gagged and dragged into the bushes. As one squad formed their skirmish line fifty feet down the road from the wagon, the others posing as slaves weeding a tobacco field took up their positions. Marcus and Cornel hid behind a black walnut tree. They retrieved four of eight lycopodiun powder bombs Marcus had in a black canvas knapsack.

It was none too soon as the first of Stuart's scouts came pounding up the road. A dawning sun was barely above the eastern horizon. Two scouts, guns drawn galloped by ignoring the hay wagon and its black teamsters. All was in place. The trap was set. Soon after, the 'slaves' talked to an itinerant black peddler hauling dry goods from Charles City to Richmond. From him, they learned that Stuart had been welcomed as a conquering hero and was just down the road having coffee at Rowland's Mill on the Edgewood plantation. It wouldn't be long now. After the peddler had disappeared, Marcus put his ear to the ground. A faint trembling spoke volumes. A large cavalry force was a mile away and moving towards them more rapidly than he expected.

Jeb, as Stuart was known to his friends, rode along confident that General Lee knew he was coming. His Adjutant Lt. Robins, a daring young man, was scouting the New Market road while Stuart's other scouts John Mosby and Bill Farley were to the column's right. Farley was over on the Darbytown Road and Mosby was on the Charles City Road. Both paralleled the New Market Road and both led to Richmond, a few miles ahead.

Stuart gathered his grey cape about his broad shoulders. His boyish face and large prominent nose were framed by a wide reddish brown beard. He grimaced as he looked up. One of Stuart's escorts, a Private Pierson rode close to him complaining because it was going to be another rainy day. Storm clouds were gathering in the west. The road ahead twisted and turned as it wound its muddy way between the Tulip poplars flanking the James River on his left and young tobacco fields on his right. He was enthusiastic. McClellan's right flank was weak, barely defended. Stuart had ridden nearly one hundred miles through enemy territory without encountering any real opposition. He looked ahead confident as heavy rain started to come down in earnest. A hay wagon driven by two black slaves was parked beside the road.

Marcus recognized Jeb Stuart immediately. The man was bracketed by a Corporal and two Privates. Luckily, a driving rain had washed away any footprints on the road. Stuart was fifty yards away and closing in on the hay wagon. His mud streaked troops and their mounts were tired but still trotting along at a fast gait. Marcus knew everything had to go perfectly or he and the others were dead. With two bombs in each hand, both men lit their fuses with a cheroot. Four bombs sailed through the rain bracketing Stuart.

Instantly, the snipers opened up and picked off the three men nearest General Stuart. The bombs exploded with a BANG! BANG! BANG! One was a dud. Stuart's black roan reared up throwing Stuart down onto the road. Two Rangers weeding beside the hay wagon sapped Stuart and picked him up, hiding him in the hay wagon which then rumbled away. Two Rangers ran after it down the road where it careened wildly around a bend a hundred yards further on then disappeared behind a thick grove of hazelnut trees. Meanwhile the snipers retreated under covering fire from Rangers hidden beside the road. Stuart's Calvary was pinned down for a hundred yards. Many brave men died as they tried to rescue their beloved General. Confusion and chaos were the order of the day as horses threw their riders onto the road blocking others from moving forward. A cloud of dense white smoke completely engulfed them for many yards in either direction. Marcus and Cornel threw four more bombs adding to a vast and impenetrable smoke screen that impeded the cavalry's ability to deal with their assailants.

Saxton heard the shooting and the bombs exploding. The Nimsi was ready to go as four Rangers carried a lifeless General Stuart back to the ship. Others came rushing back in twos and threes. More shots rang out. Marcus clambered aboard just as the ship began pulling out into the slough. Within seconds it vanished into a rain squall leaving only a thin bubbling wake as an inkling it had been there at all.

An hour later, Marcus boarded the Anaona. With the Nimsi astern of her, she sailed forth into the wide waters of the James River near Harrison's landing. Both cruised downstream on the south side of the six islands away from any prying eyes looking for them. Marcus knew that Rebel scouts would be racing for Charles City, fifteen miles away to the east without hesitation knowing full well that Stuart's abductors would be headed for the safety of Hampton Roads fifty miles away downstream.

Once out from behind the shelter of six islands, the two ships split up. One hugged the left bank of the James River while the other hugged its right. Saxton knew that any trouble would come from the left bank. The mortar crews on both vessels were ready. As Marcus passed the Winslow plantation, shots were fired. Instantly, the Anaona's mortars spewed their deadly canisters of grapeshot. The firing stopped. Her Gatlings cut down more Rebels following in rowboats and armed sloops. Marcus ran up the Stars and Stripes. It flapped in a wet breeze that came off the river. They had been discovered although the Nimsi had not. Bullets pinged off the iron shutters. Marcus peered through them as he steered for the middle of the river. Minie balls ricocheted off the armored wheelhouse.

The James River narrowed at the village of Blairs on their starboard side as it made a sharp 'S' curve beyond the Charles City estuary. Enemy rifle fire ceased as the Anaona fell in behind the Nimsi. Sporadic small arms fire zipped by as the towns of Brandon and Claremont came into view. Luckily, the Confederates had already abandoned their cannons behind the earthworks by an old brick church in Jamestown. The two ships slid by it an hour later headed for Fort Monroe or 'Freedom's Fortress' at Old Point Comfort on the tip of the Virginia peninsula.

Surrounded by a deep moat, the hexagonal fort was completed in 1834 and covered eighty acres. It was named in honor of President James Monroe. Since May, 1861, any slave reaching the fort was a free man. Once there, all such former slaves were put to work reinforcing its defenses. The Confederates were furious as General Butler, the Fort's commander, claimed that the ex-slaves were to be considered contraband in spite of the Fugitive Slave Act of 1850. Word spread amongst the nearby plantations. Soon after, hundreds of slaves mobbed the fort seeking freedom. As the number of refugees grew, Fort Monroe could not accommodate them all.

Outside the fort, a ramshackle village sprang up called the Grand Contraband Camp. It was however, nick-named 'Slab town' by its industrious black inhabitants. Here was the genesis of the first self contained African American community replete with many businesses, churches, schools and social orders; all created by former slaves. It was here the Maasai Rangers spent their shore leaves with much enthusiasm and sexual recklessness.

A year earlier, a military balloon camp under the direction of aeronaut John La Mountain was set up near the fort. However, Thaddeus Lowe who installed the balloons on the Anaona and the Nimsi fired La Mountain and assigned regular military balloons and crews to Fort Monroe. Thaddeus continued training the Rangers and the Nimsi's crew while stationed at the fort. Every Ranger and sailor became a qualified balloonist; even Saxton and Marcus.

As darkness settled over the James River estuary, two ships tied up on either side of a camouflaged canvas hangar within which a finger pier separated them. Marcus climbed aboard the Nimsi, embracing Saxton as he emerged out of the wheelhouse hatch. He looked down.

"My God Sax, we made it! What a show that was indeed!"

Within minutes, General Butler and his staff left the fort. They came down to the wharf to welcome the Rangers back. The Maasai Rangers lined up on the pier and snapped to attention. In the meantime Saxton had raised the Nimsi and opened its main deck hatch. Despite the large smoke vents, the canvas roof kept the light rain out. The mules were unloaded up the ramp in pairs and led away to their new corral within the fort. The Nimsi backed out of the shed, engines idling as its crew began cleaning the mule corral with steam hoses. Two deck cranes were erected. They clanked and hissed while lifting two clam-shell buckets over the side. Piles of mule manure floated away on the ebbing tide. Flocks of Laughing Gulls swooped down through the warm spring breeze squabbling over the scattering dung. After the noise and smell had been eliminated, the cranes tied down, the Nimsi glided back into its shelter. General Butler and his entourage climbed aboard and walked down the wide cleated ramp to the lower deck. Saxton and Marcus followed into the main galley.

Dr. 'Bones' Barstow was just leaving the infirmary. He laughed as he turned to face Saxton saying,

"Well Skipper, the Brigadier-General has woken up and wonders where he is, handcuffed to his bunk, headache n'all. Shall we gentlemen?"

He turned, opened the door and stepped aside as the visitors entered the room. Jeb Stuart was sitting up on a canvas cot, a bandage wrapped around his head, leg irons around his ankles. Surprisingly he was quite jovial even though two guards, guns drawn; eyed him with suspicion and a large measure of respect. Obviously, his reputation had preceded him. Stuart stood up and looked at the men before him who snapped to attention. He returned their salutes with élan then quipped,

"I must say gentlemen, you can release me, I give you my word that I shall not attempt to escape, however I will try to eat anything you might prepare for me."

He sat down on the edge of his cot looking somewhat puzzled for he muttered,

"By the way, why are you all wearing canvas slippers?"

After introducing himself, Marcus and General Butler, Saxton promptly offered General Stuart two cotton booties. They laughed as he put them over his bare feet. Stuart stood up and said,

"Who were you black fella's anyway and how did I get here? He looked around.

"I must be on some sort of ship. Am I?"

"You are Sir."

"All my friends call me Jeb, so please do so."

Marcus moved forward to shake his hand. Stuart refused. Marcus looked down at him.

"I'm Marcus, the Maasai Ranger's Captain. Welcome aboard General. I'm sorry for giving you a swelled head. It must come as a complete shock to be a prisoner of war." All eyes were on Stuart,

"I've heard of you Marcus. You're the 'Big Nigger'. A certain raffish Major Garrow speaks ill of you. He arrived in Richmond a little while ago. Says he wants to even the score or something to that effect. He was in rough shape. Seems he was knifed, thrown in the Hudson River and left to die by you Sir. Anyways, he managed to get medical attention, jump a train and head south. He and a companion were found by one of my scouts, Bill Farley. Major Garrow is convalescing in Howard Grove hospital as we speak."

Abruptly Marcus grabbed Stuart by the throat raising him off his feet, his ankle chains dancing on the deck below him. Marcus hissed in his face,

"That scum and his so called crew of criminals raped my wife. He also ran a gang of cutthroats in New Orleans called the Deacon gang. He killed my housekeeper there with a knife. I saw it happen. Horatio Garrow is no credit to the human race. The sooner he's dead, the better."

The General dropped to the deck with a thud. Stuart stood up, brushed himself off and declared,

"I deeply regret Sir, what happened to your wife. The Confederacy fights with honor Sir, with honor. Before I was captured, and may I say with skill and daring; along the way, we left many of your Blue Birds in a hospital unmolested. Garrow will be punished for his crimes. You have my word on it."

Marcus nodded as the General jovially cried out,

"Anyone here have a cigar? I'm dying for a smoke." Saxton responded,

"Sorry General but there's no smoking on board. Just on the main deck above us. Put your uniform on, we're going ashore."

Saxton nodded to a guard, who immediately took off the General's leg irons. They watched as the Stuart dressed. When finished, he asked for his hat. Saxton gave it to him. Stuart cried,

"Where's my black ostrich feather. It's my good luck charm Sir. Can I have it back?" Saxton grinned,

"No General. I'm keepin' it as a souvenir. In fact it will be kept in an honored place."

"Where's that?" Saxton produced his hat, the feather adorning it. He said,

"I need all the luck I can get General." Stuart replied, pointing to a button hole on his jacket.

"Bully for you, at least I still have my rose."

The General was handcuffed, hooded then led up the ramp out of the Nimsi and onto the dock. An armed escort was waiting for him. The hood was necessary for the general's keen eye and photographic memory was legendary. Saxton would not let him see any more of the ship than was necessary. Stuart knew it and was marched towards the fort. Once inside on the way to his cell, the jaunty Stuart smoked a large cigar courtesy of Commander Butler.

Ironically, Jeb Stuart was imprisoned in the same cell casement that Jefferson F. Davis, President of the Confederacy would be imprisoned in, later on in 1865. Stuart was incarcerated for twenty hours until a special Orange & Alexandria train arrived. Unfortunately for the Union, the train was derailed by Confederate Brigadier General John S. 'Grey Ghost' Mosby near Briscoe Station, Virginia. Stuart evaded capture, reached Richmond and immediately went to the newly constructed Howard's Grove Military Hospital. He was too late. Major Horatio Garrow had already escaped with a Private, Harley Blackstone. Two weeks later he was forced to retreat from Evelynton Heights only a few miles from where he was captured by the Maasai Rangers. However,

General Jeb Stuart continued his illustrious career until he was killed at the battle of Yellow Tavern, Virginia, May 11th, 1864. A true knight fighting for a doomed cause did not survive what he himself called 'The Die Game'.

BOOK TWO: CHAPTER 15
ORDERS

After many months conducting 'suicide' raids along the James River and its tributaries, three more Rangers perished. In the late spring of 1863, the seventeen remaining men were about to embark on their most dangerous journey yet; sailing to Port Hudson on the Mississippi River. Marcus's orders came from Admiral David Farragut, Commander of the West Gulf Blockading Squadron via Commodore, John Rodgers. The journey would take two weeks depending on the weather. Saxton's orders were cut by Brigadier-General of Volunteers; Benjamin H. Grierson in New Orleans. If Port Hudson and Vicksburg further up the Mississippi River fell, then the Union would win the war simply because Confederate supplies and other war materiel would dwindle down to nothing. The blockade of the South's sea ports as envisioned by General Winfield Scott were about to bear a terrible fruit.

The Anaona's mission was to carry war materiel across the sand bar at Pass au d'Outre at the mouth of the Mississippi River to the war upriver. It would along with hundreds of other shallow draft steamers sail up the Mississippi to supply General Grant's Federal forces besieging Vicksburg and General Nathaniel Banks who was besieging Port Hudson. The Anaona would also be carrying medical supplies from Fort Monroe to the Union ships blockading the last three major Confederate ports: Wilmington, North Carolina; Charleston, South Carolina; and Pensacola, Florida. Thereafter, it would report to Admiral David Farragut off the mouth of the Mississippi River. The Nimsi would carry on to New Orleans, the Federal's main base in the Southern theater.

Although reluctant to leave the pleasures of 'Slab town', the Rangers left Fort Monroe for Norfolk on May 20th, 1863 to refuel. However, five men had contracted syphilis and were shipped to Armory Square Hospital in Washington DC for treatment. Marcus was furious but eventually he resigned himself to the situation. He wondered if he had enough men to accomplish what they had set out to do. However, he kept his thoughts to himself. Besides Baker's Rangers had only eighteen men and he knew his men were far superior to them in every way. Ten mules were left behind, the 'Warden' not being one of them. Like men, some mules were found to be too difficult to work with while others were injured, maimed or sickened by sea travel.

After both ships were refueled, they slipped out into the James River estuary early in the morning of May 31st, 1863, entering the Gulf of Mexico two weeks later. At Fort Taylor in the

Keys, they received fresh food, water, and fuel while the mules were exercised ashore. Both crews parted as Commander David Farragut's blockade fleet hove into view off the bar at the Pass au d'Outre. First Mate, Duncan Toller took over the Anaona while Marcus came aboard the Nimsi. Marcus was about to have a far more pleasant passage past Fort Jackson and Fort St. Philip than he did before. At least he wasn't under threat of Rebel gunfire. Seventy miles further on past English Turn the Nimsi reached New Orleans, June18, 1863.

There, she tied up at the Saxton wharf to unload her cargo. Ten mules went ashore to be corralled in the newly rebuilt Saxton warehouse. Later that day, they would make a strange sight as the 'Warden' led them down the streets of the French Quarter. Chaperoned by three Rangers, the Appaloosa mules amazed passersby by their behavior. They didn't knicker or bray. Their hooves were shod with special leather boots so they swept along in total silence as they trotted over the brick streets. The mules returned silently a few hours later to their corral.

An Army courier had arrived earlier with a message for Saxton along with the most recent copy of Harper's weekly newspaper. Saxton received the message in his cabin. It read,

"Captains Saxton-Brown, are to report to
Gallier Hall, 545 Saint Charles Ave. at 1230
today for further orders. Brigadier-General
of Volunteers, B.H Grierson"

Saxton showed it to Marcus who read it, put it in his coat pocket then picked up the Harper's Weekly. After browsing through a few articles, he exclaimed,

"Look at this Sax; do you know who this man is? Why he's a hero!"

Saxton looked doubtful,

"I must confess, I've never heard of Grierson." Marcus laughed as he folded the paper.

"Oh, you will, believe me. Now get into your whites, shine your shoes, and grab your cover. I'll read it all to you on the way so you'll show proper reverence to a real guerilla fighter. From what I can gather from the article, what this man did two months ago is really astounding."

They caught a Hansom cab just outside the Saxton warehouse gates. Behind them, the Rangers and crew of stevedores were busy sweating under a hot summer sun loading aboard ammunition destined for Baton Rouge. The Nimsi's crew took a rotational twenty-four hour shore leave. Most of the single young men headed straight for the delights of Bourbon Street. Marcus watched them as they scrambled through the main gate and up Canal Street. He wondered how many more of them he would lose to the pox. Even though he had lectured them again, he was powerless to stop Mother Nature from claiming victory in the Elysian fields of passion.

The Captain's cab made its way towards Gallier Hall located next to La Fayette Square. Along the way, Marcus read with enthusiasm about Ben Grierson, a former school teacher.

Apparently, he'd been kicked in the head as a child by a horse and thereafter was deathly afraid of them. However, through sheer determination on April 17th, 1863, he led seventeen hundred US Cavalry six hundred miles through Rebel territory from La Grange, Tennessee to Baton Rouge, Louisiana in seventeen days. They'd fought practically every mile of the way without much food or rest. In the process, they ripped up fifty miles of railway track and telegraph lines; captured three thousand rifles, plus one thousand horses and mules. Their daring tied up two regiments of Rebel artillery and one third of General Pemberton's Cavalry that should have been at Vicksburg.

By the time the two Captains pulled up to Gallier Hall, Saxton was duly impressed. They ran up the white Tuckahoe marble steps. Saxton stopped. He looked about and thought the Annapolis Capital building was indeed impressive until he looked up at the two rows of fluted ionic columns floating three stories above him. He remarked,

"Rather grand, isn't it. I never did like the neoclassical style." Marcus looked at him and said,

"Neo-what style?"

They laughed then ran through the tall front doors into the expansive foyer.

An Aide looked at both men sharply especially Marcus. Stiffly he directed them to General Grierson's office. Saxton knocked twice. A commanding voice from within hollered,

"Come in and close the door behind you."

They did so, entering with their hats tucked under their left arms. A tall man with brown wavy hair, a full beard, blue eyes and broad straight shoulders rose to meet them. The Captains snapped to attention and saluted. After returning their salutes, the General said,

"Please be seated Gentlemen. Excuse the mess as I've been rather busy since I came here two weeks ago; June 3rd, I believe. However, it's far more relaxed here than what I've been used to lately, especially since Colonel John Logan's cavalry drove me plum crazy up at Port Hudson."

Marcus laid the newspaper on the General's desk saying,

"Seen the latest Harper's Weekly General?" The school teacher from Pennsylvania smiled like a Cheshire cat.

"Of course Captain; I sent it along with young Geoffrey my Adjutant, so you'd know what I have in mind for you two." Saxton leaned forward,

"Just what do you have in mind General, another raid?"

"Well something like that. By the way, congratulations on capturing Jeb Stuart; too bad he got away."

Shock registered on their faces.

"You mean you didn't know." He paused apologetic.

"I'm sorry to tell you he escaped when his train was derailed outside of Briscoe Station. Damned Mosby did it. Stuart got clean away; a fine man, that Stuart. I hear he's a real gentleman and a hell of a cavalry leader." Marcus agreed,

"But Sir; your little escapade made Stuart's look like a walk in the park; a walk in the park by a long shot. As far as I'm concerned you matched him and then some. I also want to say that it's too bad General Sheridan chastised you for treating colored troops like human beings. That's a poor way of rewarding someone. Why you showed what blacks can do in the field under fire."

General Grierson sighed then reached for some telegrams on his desk. After a few moments of reflection he countered,

"Well gentlemen, there's always someone more daring, more audacious, and more clever than I. I'm just getting reports in now about a Confederate raiding party ravishing our troops north of Tennessee as we speak. It's drawing tens of thousands of our soldiers away from our Tullahoma campaign. The raiders are led by a daring and resourceful Brigadier-General, John 'Thunderbolt' Morgan. I'll tell you more once General Banks arrives."

Just then there was a loud knock on the door which opened abruptly before the General could respond. In walked Major-General Nathaniel P. Banks, General of Volunteers. Of average height, well muscled, his short brown hair swept across his forehead like a tidal wave. General Banks strode into the room as if he was charging the enemy. He had returned to New Orleans to confer with Admiral David Farragut for a few days during a lull in the siege of Port Hudson a few miles upriver. He'd heard that the Rangers were in town to collaborate with General Grierson. He wondered if he'd make it in time to crash his own party. Everyone stood to attention. Crisp salutes flew around the room. Grierson offered everyone a chair. Sensing a favorable lapse in propriety, Banks replied,

"Thank you Ben. I'll also have one of your fine Cuban cigars." He directed his next comment to the two Captains. He laughed as he passed a cedar humidor around.

"Of course I gave them to Ben as a present for his courageous raid into Rebel territory. Wish I'd been there. Why it makes one mighty thirsty just thinkin' about it. Say how about some sippin' whiskey General? I'll ring for the orderly."

In moments the four men were drinking whiskeys and smoking. While the others sat, Banks stood like an owl perched above a picnic of mice. He stroked his well groomed mustache as he began pacing about the room, glass in hand.

"Goddamn it Ben, you really had 'em goin' didn't you?" He paused for effect, took a sip then said,

. "Looks like he wants my job gentlemen; will get it too I'm sure. Grant loves a man who would rather quote Byron than ride a horse."

After the laughter died down, Banks turned his attention to Saxton and Marcus by saying,

"I've heard good things about you two. I imagine Jeb Stuart is having nightmares with all that's gone on. Too bad he got away, although it's no fault of yours. Oddly enough, the papers on both sides of the Mason-Dixon Line have been mute on the whole escapade. Can't blame 'em really. Bad for morale I'd say. Captain Marcus, were you the 'Big Nigger' everyone was gunnin' for last year? I must say, that my predecessor 'Spoons' Butler has the highest regard for you. Now Saxton, that ship of yours is a real wonder I hear. Perhaps I can hitch a ride on it back to Rouge. On a more serious note, I heard that Ben here and his advisors have worked out a plan for your future here in the Western theater of war. But first, let's toast the Union. Vicksburg will fall then Port Hudson believe me and soon from what I hear. Grant will throw everything including the kitchen sink at Pemberton now that Ben here lured away most of his cavalry."

They stood and raised their glasses of sour mash as Banks declared,

"Here's to the Union gentlemen and total victory!"

Banks continued to hold forth. Occasionally he'd stop and point his fat cigar at Marcus and Saxton while looking at Grierson for support. It was as if he was two men. Saxton cleared his head of the idea as Banks wandered about declaring,

"The war so far here in the western theater, has been very fluid up to now, but Ben, I understand has put together a campaign that might make the best use of what I might say are your Ranger's 'special' qualifications. Perhaps General you can enlighten us." Grierson rose up. He began,

"Simply put, the Maasai Rangers will be engaged in three separate missions. I'll explain them and map them up and show you.

First of all, the SS Anaona, will stay where it is for now, offloading cargo at the Pass au d'Outre. In the meantime, the Nimsi was to have joined Rear Admiral D.D. Porter's fleet at Vicksburg but our priorities have changed. From here you report instead to Commodore Andrew Hull Foote in Baton Rouge. Poor Foote, He was injured last year and is now sailing a desk. Scuttlebutt has it that he's now well enough and will be leaving soon for Charleston to command the naval attack on that city." Cocking his head to one side, he looked closely at Saxton saying,

"I hear young man that you were on the last ship out of Fort Sumter. Chased all the way and shelled repeatedly. Were you really on your honeymoon?" He paused. Saxton grinned.

"Well I'll be damned! Your wife must be one hell of woman, manning two mortars under heavy fire like she did. Some honeymoon!" Saxton quickly retorted,

"Some woman!" They laughed. Grierson paused then said,

"Her name was, uh?"

"Virginia Sir," Saxton said quickly.

"Virginia. Yes, that's right. Strange though, never saw anything about it in Harper's. "

He looked at Banks pacing by a nearby window; impatient, dogmatic, chewing at the bit, puffing on his cigar like a locomotive working up a head of steam at grade. He continued pacing about completely absorbed by his thoughts and therefore at times, totally oblivious to his audience. Grierson as Brigadier General of Volunteers and Banks as Commander of the Department of the Gulf had discussed the Rangers campaign for the western theater a week before. The ex school teacher decided to let Banks have his say before the man exploded. He sat down, while waving him over to a mobile battle map rack set up for the occasion. Banks walked over to it, grabbed a wood pointer and pulled the map rack across the room. He began attacking a map as he spoke.

"Now where was I? Oh yes, the Nimsi's mission will be as a scouting ship and raider here up the Arkansas River in search of the William Quantrill gang. I'll get back to him later. It's nearly five hundred river miles from here to Fort Smith. The Rebels hold it right now but I'm sure you can sneak by it and get to Fort Gibson right here further up river then on up the Neosho towards Fort Scott here on the Little Osage. The Arkansas River is rising so you'll have plenty of room to maneuver. However it's another matter on the Mississippi. As you've probably seen, its river waters are low, making it very dangerous. Thus any ship on the river is susceptible to Rebel fire because they're all in mid-stream. Even though the Mississippi will soon be in Union hands, it doesn't mean the war is over, far from it. Oh, I nearly forgot. There has been a rash of explosions recently. It appears that the Rebels have been making coal and log bombs." Marcus looked up sharply at the General,

"What are those General? Log bombs? Why I've never heard of 'em." The General explained.

"The Rebs hollow out cordwood, fill 'em with gunpowder so when they're thrown into the boiler, the ship blows up. They also cast hollow iron lumps that look like coal. These coal torpedoes are filled with gunpowder then slipped into the coal bins of ships. Clever bastards, aren't they?" He lit yet another cigar then continued his enthusiasm unabated.

"The Nimsi as I've already said before will sail up nearly five hundred miles of river. Captain Saxton, your pilot will be Horace Bixby, one of the few pilots with three river licenses, the Mississippi, the Missouri and the Ohio. Besides, he served on a gunboat under Commodore Foote for ten months and is now at loose ends. He's a real character though, a living legend, so watch out. I suspect he'll be waiting for you aboard the Nimsi after our meeting here is over."

There was a knock on the door. Banks bellowed "Come in!"

Adjutant Corporal Geoffries saluted. He handed Grierson more decoded telegrams who read the telegrams with growing agitation. Finished, he thrust them at Banks who read them quickly then flipped another operations map over the first revealing the Union's Tullahoma campaign. He looked one particular telegram pensively, the pointer prodding it at several different points. He swore,

"God almighty, that son of a bitch Morgan has taken twenty-five hundred cavalry and a battery of light artillery, from Sparta, Tennessee northwards. He's up to something. Our troops are having one hell of a time chasing him in Kentucky. I think General Bragg sent him on a suicide mission to derail our Tullahoma campaign." Geoffries continued to bring more telegrams and reports. After a few moments, Grierson replied somewhat reluctantly, "I'm sorry General but that's old news for now."

Banks sat down totally exasperated, the pointer across his lap. Grierson leaned back in his chair sipping his second glass of whiskey. He calmly exclaimed,

"Well boys, Morgan's clever, bold and decisive. I should know."

Grierson took another swallow then put the empty glass down. He became emphatic.

"Well Nathaniel we better get Marcus here onto Morgan right away. Do you think you can handle it Captain?" Marcus queried,

"I thought I'd be going along with Saxton Sir, but if you want the Rangers to go after Morgan, I'll give my best shot General. Do you want him dead or alive?"

Banks, recovering his composure stood up, pointer in hand, puffing on his cigar. He walked over to the map rack and flipped over another battle map then proceeded to speak in a clipped Bostonian accent,

"Alive would be preferable Marcus. The Nimsi will go to Baton Rouge here; unload its balloon, its mules and one squad of Rangers. Then it'll proceed to Port Hudson here and transfer it's ammo to wagons waiting downriver at Ross landing right there. Bixby knows where it is. I've laid siege to those damn Rebs for over two months now. I'll need two squads of Rangers to go ashore and infiltrate the defenses there, especially the Citadel here and Fort Desperate there. Requisition the maps you need at the on your way out. He paused, took another drag on his cigar and continued.

"After that, Marcus and any Rangers still alive will come back to Rouge, refuel, load up and go to Memphis on the Nimsi. From there they'll go by rail to intercept Morgan." Marcus laughed.

"Well General, at least this time I'll be riding the Memphis & Charleston in comfort, not on the baggage car roof like last time." Banks grinned.

"I heard." He looked around expansively,

"Captain Saxton, you'll off load the mules in Rouge for R&R so to speak. You'll get them into fighting condition suitable for rolling, flat and unpredictable prairie terrain. They'll need it. Christ, I hear they've been on board ship for nearly a month now. Mule shore-leave is in order I'd say. How many mules do you have aboard anyways? I heard tell they've been specially trained to sing, dance and say grace!"

Marcus dead panned,

"General Banks, there's twenty mules and they do have special skills." Banks became somewhat jocular.

"By the way Captain Saxton, I'm hitchin' a ride with you tomorrow morning. My transport awaits me in Rouge. I'll answer any questions you might have on the way there. Besides, I've heard a lot about the Nimsi, especially its famous toilet." Saxton chuckled, saying,

"Sorry Sir but the toilet is rather difficult to operate. Lincoln wouldn't use it until Pinkerton tried it out first. He did. The results were less than satisfactory I must say." The General laughed, turned to Saxton and in a more serious tenor continued.

"Saxton, your mission is to scout for Major-General John M. Schofield, Commander of the Department of the Missouri in St. Louis. Your base of operations will probably be Fort

Scott which is equidistant between Fort Leavenworth and Fort Gibson. Your mission will be to assist Schofield and Governor Thomas Carney in Fort Leavenworth, Kansas. Your Rangers are to track down and kill the Confederate raider, William Quantrill." He paused as he watched for General Grierson's reaction.

"Yes folks, another school teacher is on the rampage."

Banks, as serious as before said to Saxton,

"You'll also be charged with the capture of Quantrill's first Lieutenant, 'Bloody Bill' Anderson. Watch out for him. He's real crazy. Seems our soldiers murdered his father and sister. He's a sadistic bastard too; tall, strong as an ox, and an excellent shot. Don't underestimate him. He kills and tortures just for the fun of it, taking scalps then hanging them on his stirrups. No one and I mean no one has ever been released alive after he has finished with them. Apparently, his mean little piggy eyes scare the hell out of everyone, including Quantrill. God help us if he ever forms his own gang. Saxton, you and your men will be given supplies, an armed escort and wagons to transport your balloon and its hot air generator. Quantrill's guerillas are wreaking havoc on our supply lines all over that territory. They number from three to five hundred men, all of whom are seasoned fighters who know the lay of the land on the Kansas-Missouri border very well. It's an area the size of Britain. I hope your Rangers are up to it. Welcome to "Bloody Kansas." He sipped more bourbon then continued.

"It will also be your job Saxton, to assist a Colonel C.W. Marsh in chasing and killing as many of these confederate brigands as you can. You're not under anyone's command except Stanton and President Lincoln. I believe they've signed orders to that effect." The Captains nodded. Banks continued.

"Good. Now, both of you and your men will get winter gear at Fort Gibson. It'll be there when and if you arrive safely. You'll be in service for the next year in both theaters. Hells bells, it gets so cold out there, one has to warm their bullets up in a frying pan just to fire them." He digressed.

"So there you have it gentlemen; Marcus's Rangers will go aboard the Nimsi, sail to Port Hudson while Saxton stays in Baton Rouge. Once reunited, you'll both proceed to Memphis where General Grant will advise you as to Morgan. Once that mission is complete, then it's off to capture Quantrill. From what I've heard about you two, it'll be all in a day's work." He laughed.

Banks stood as did everyone else. The meeting was over. Grierson concluded,

"The quartermaster will send what you need down to the Nimsi. Pick up a supply requisition form before you leave gentlemen. Good luck and thank you for your sterling service to the nation. I hear President Lincoln's watching your campaigns quite closely."

General Banks walked over to Marcus. He looked up at his face, stepped back, took another pull on a cold cigar and declared,

"Captain Brown, where in the hell did you get those scars on your face?"

Those scars leaped out as Marcus drawled,

"I killed a lion after he clawed me when I was a young man on the Mara Maasai."

Saxton noticed the General's skepticism saying,

"It's the gospel truth."

The General leaned forward for another look exclaiming,

"No wonder Lincoln wants you on our side!"

He stood back and laughed. After a few moments, General Grierson intervened.

"Gentlemen, I'll have your new orders cut right away. Give them to Foote when you get to Rouge." Marcus and Saxton snapped to attention.

"Yes Sir."

Both Generals returned their salutes. Next door, Corporal Geoffries quickly processed the new orders. Both Captains then headed for the nearby quartermaster's office. A half hour later they were free to go.

On the way back to the ship, Marcus pointed out La Fayette Square; where he, Belle and Cotton hid from the Deacon Gang. He showed Saxton the Ursuline Convent where he and Belle were married. Marcus recounted the tale of the Bishop and the Mother Superior. On impulse, he jumped out of their cab, ran down the stone walk then knocked on the door at the Convent. A small metal slot in the door opened. He asked a nun about the Bishop and the Mother Superior. She curtly told him that they were no longer there. The iron slot slammed shut.

They were driven to the ruins of La Belle Maison. It felt strange for Marcus to be on the same streets where he and his family had once been hunted like animals. The secret door behind which Marcus and his family hid fascinated Saxton. Farther on down Pirate Alley, they came to the iron grate from which Marcus emerged covered in sewage. Marcus got out of the cab and knelt down. The soft whump, whump of a paddle wheel still echoed in the sump far below his feet. Driving around the corner they came to a halt. La Belle Maison was still in ruins. Marcus managed to salvage a few precious articles for Belle.

A short time later they arrived at the Saxton warehouses brimming with Federal ordnance and other war supplies. SS Night Hawk under Captain Owen Sound had tied up while the two were sightseeing. Both men scrambled aboard to see him. Horace Bixby was aboard drinking in the ship's saloon, regaling the Captain with stories about his life on the Mississippi and Missouri Rivers.

Later that evening after Bixby was safely stowed aboard the Nimsi, Captain Sound told Saxton and Marcus the news from home. Both were shocked by the deaths and treachery of Hans Larsen and Charlie Finch. Apparently, Virginia and Belle were heroines whose sixth sense uncovered a Confederate plot to steal the formulas for a new, more powerful explosive. Captain Sound was equally shocked when he found out that half his crew hired by Larsen were in fact Confederate Agents.

He went on to recall that he'd been relaxing in his cabin when his door was thrown open with a crash. Two Pinkerton agents severely questioned him for the next two hours, while others were turning his ship inside out. The crew were searched and questioned as well. Nothing incriminating was found and they were eventually released. Captain Sound, smoked a long clay pipe. He bit the end off it. Becoming even more agitated, he swore,

"Good God, it was a bloody nightmare! Really, I had no idea whatsoever that these despicable men pilfered a packet of scientific importance. Apparently the traitors stole uniforms from a worker's closet and marched right into Nobel's office at his plant in Karlskoga. Then the crooks took the information at gunpoint and walked out to a waiting carriage. Meanwhile the Night Hawk was docked in Stockholm unloading cotton." Saxton interrupted.

"Well Captain, how did the Confederacy find out about the new explosive in the first place? It all seems a bit farfetched to me." Sound nodded,

"Yes, it is odd but according to Pinkerton, Larsen was 'turned' by Silas Wilkins who was in fact was 'turned' by Horatio Garrow. Captain Wilkins often sailed for Europe, especially to Liverpool, England."

He stopped, shook his head as if coming to some conclusion, sat down and tapped the pipe ashes into an ash tray beside him. A whiskey glass next to him was half empty. He finished it then jumped up. He exclaimed,

"Anyone want another? They did. The Captain, fully refreshed once more continued on with his story.

"Where was I gentlemen? Oh yes, I remember now. It was in Liverpool where Wilkins was contacted by Confederate spymaster, James. D. Bulloch. Apparently Bulloch had a working relationship with the shipping firm of Fraser and Trenholm. Larsen himself was from Sweden. Through contacts provided by him and Bulloch's business compatriots in the arms community, they learned that Nobel was working on a new explosive. The rest is history as they say." He paused, weary of it all.

"One never knows what side the chap sitting next to you or working along-side you, is on do you? Of course my crew and I were cleared but the culprits apparently escaped on the same train as Garrow and his so called wife. I do hope it never happens again. I'm too old for that kind of daring do!"

Captain Sound knew all this because in the interim he'd become an agent employed by Pinkerton although he still sailed for the Saxton Shipping Co. In that capacity he informed Saxton and Marcus that everyone at Saxton House was safe and well protected. They mustn't worry. Saxton remembered that he had told Allan Pinkerton before he left, to reinstate any level of protection that he saw fit on the same basis as their original contract.

Marcus and Saxton were shocked that Major Garrow and Harley Blackstone were still alive. Captain Sound went on to say that Garrow strangled Larsen then escaped by train that same day. Eddie Finch confessed to helping Garrow do it. He told Pinkerton that he had to or he would have been killed. Secretary of War, Edwin Stanton, on Pinkerton's behalf agreed to lift the charge of murder if Eddie would spy for the Union. The lad agreed to provide the Confederate spy ring in Boston, false and misleading information about war materiel cargos, troop transport figures and so on.

The next morning, Marcus, Saxton and the Rangers wrote letters to their families. Marcus especially wrote a heartfelt letter to Belle, renouncing his life at sea and then expounded about his dream. It said,

"Dear Belle, Cotton and Rufus, I love you.

Please forgive me, as for too long now I have been away in my mind somewhere over an ocean's horizon; where I do not know. However, those days and nights of wandering are behind me for I have finally reached the distant shore of my dreams. There to meet me were you and the boys. Hallelujah! Take my hand Belle my darling as I lead you all up Elder Mountain, near Chattanooga, Tennessee; to a realm of resurrection where a peaceful fastness awaits us after the war is over. Upon its summit, we will build a future not only for us but for all those unfortunates scarred by the war, former slaves or those cast out from their homes by carpetbaggers who will surely come to ravage the South.

The aftermath of the war will be a terrible time where I foresee the victor's foot on the throat of the defeated. Revenge seekers will sweep over Dixie in a firestorm of death and destruction. Regaining their honor at any cost will be their watchword.

I have a dream where all mankind will be my brother regardless of their race, religion or way of life. I have a dream that will free us from the agony of suffering the bigotry that surely awaits us no matter what sacrifice we make or what sufferings we endure for our country in this most uncivil war. My Darling Belle, hopefully the Saxton's will come with us, however I doubt that Virginia could ever persuade Sax to leave Boston and his shipping business. But one never knows.

I know what real freedom is. It awaits us on the mountain. There we'll be free to live as we please, free to love, free to live with dignity, free to live in peace. Oh my dearest, our children's children will have that precious gift, that wonderful blessing.

With all my Love,

Marcus."

Saxton gave the mail to Captain Sound who was departing for Boston in three days. The Nimsi was refueled, restocked and readied.

The Rangers were safely on board but somewhat the worse for wear after tasting the delights of Bourbon Street. Swinging out onto the broad shoulders of the 'Big Muddy', the ship bulled its way to Baton Rouge, one hundred and twenty-five river miles upstream. General Banks with everyone else sat on the hatch covers and gazed out at the Crescent City as it paraded before them. The wreck of the SS Saladin was still impaled upon the levee. It too disappeared out of sight as the river veered northwards. With the Nimsi hugging deep water running along the river's right bank, the sweaty smell of river water and the silver haze upon it in the morning light, brought back memories to Marcus, especially those of the little keelboat and Nate, his fast friend and companion. He reached Baton Rouge two days later.

Once there, twenty mules were off loaded, corralled, watered and fed. Their conditioning and training for plains warfare would start two days hence under Saxton's direction at Camp Moore forty-five miles due east. A former Confederate training camp, it was situated on four hundred and fifty acres just north of Tangipahoa. The balloon and its attendant equipment was also sent ashore and stowed aboard a large transport wagon. General Banks immediately boarded the SS Hartford, flagship of Admiral D.D. Porter and proceeded upriver towards Port Hudson. Saxton and Marcus were introduced to newly promoted Rear Admiral Andrew Foote.

Foote was quartered at the Samuel M. Hart House in Baton Rouge. He received both Captains graciously on the morning of June 21rd, 1863. After saluting, then presenting their new orders, an aide brought them coffee. The Captains sat down in wicker armchairs facing the General seated behind a desk piled high with correspondence. Foote stroked his full salt and pepper beard and declared,

"Sorry about the mess gentlemen; but I'm leaving for Charleston tomorrow. General Nathan A.M.Dudley will be here soon after I'm sure. I hear he's all Army spit and polish. Well us naval types aren't much for that especially on a filthy gunboat."

He tried to stand up but the right leg gave out and he sat down heavily. He continued scowling,

"Damn injury. Had to drop anchor and sail a desk. Christ almighty, I think Charleston will be my last post before I finally kick the bucket." Marcus grinned,

"You sure have a peculiar way with words Admiral."

Foote looked at Saxton's orders, grunted then handed them back. However, he did a double take as he perused the orders pertaining to Marcus.

"Says here that you are to pursue, capture or kill Brigadier-General John Morgan. Well son, I hope you bucks are up to it. Morgan has nearly three thousand men and artillery. How many buffalos you got Captain?"

"Buffalos, Sir?"

"Captain Marcus, soldiers of color are called that out here. They're damn good too I hear. Now Captain, how many men are you takin' to catch Morgan? Marcus looked him in the eye.

"Ten Sir." The Admiral's jaw dropped. He sputtered, and yelled,

"Only ten goddamned buffalos! Have you lost your mind? Why Blazer's Rangers has a hundred men mounted on prime horseflesh armed with the latest repeating Spencers."

He sat down, swept his brown hair aside with one hand while his other pointed at Marcus like a dagger.

"Are you plum loco boy? I know you bucks are good. I heard all about ya gettin' Jeb Stuart but he had only twelve hundred men. But this! This is ridiculous!"

Foote quit yelling. Instead he started to laugh. Marcus remained impassive as he watched the Admiral laugh, tears rolling down his cheeks.

"Just ten men, are you nuts? Well I'll be Goddamned!"

He stood up and walked over to Marcus. He looked up into his scarred face.

"Say, where are you from anyways; Africa? Jesus, those scars give me the willies. Where'd you get em'?"

Marcus explained. The Admiral laughed saying,

"Well they look just like Sergeant Stripes." He laughed again,

"That lion musta bin a buck private who hated the upper ranks." He handed Marcus back his orders while turning to Saxton.

"Look son, I suspect Rear-Admiral D.D. Porter and General Blunt are on the SS Hartford right now. Porter will be trying to get seven gunboats past the Citadel at Port Hudson. Hope he makes it. Anyway, I'm glad you avoided him for he would have sent you down to the Red River for sure. I hear he's taking every boat he can lay his hands on to attack Shreveport." He turned his attention back to Marcus.

"Once you get to Memphis Captain, report to General Ulysses S. Grant's HQ at the Phelan Mansion on Beale Street."

"I know where it is Sir." He saluted, turned smartly about and left.

Foote thought the whole idea was fraught with danger.

'At least Marcus and his squad are takin' the railway from Memphis to intercept Morgan. It will be a hell of a lot quicker than by boat. I still think those Rangers are crazy. Imagine that; ten men against thousands!'

He looked up at a banjo clock. It was noon. He yelled for his Adjutant,

"Campbell, get in here on the double. You'll never believe it."

After a short stay in Baton Rouge, Twenty Maasai Rangers sailed for Port Hudson twenty-five miles upstream on June 23rd, 1863. Saxton stayed behind to oversee the mules, conduct telegraphy practice and continue specialized balloon training at Camp Moore. However, he was also there to keep incoming Army Colonel Nathan Dudley from stealing his five Rangers. Saxton really wanted to be in the thick of it with Marcus, but he knew that his greatest challenge lay ahead of him in the trackless prairies west of the Mississippi. While in New Orleans, Generals Grierson and Blunt had given Saxton detailed maps and a complete update of the area known as 'bleeding Kansas'. Saxton's Rangers depended on accurate, up to date maps. Besides, not only the mules needed conditioning. Saxton was in good shape but nothing compared to the Rangers. While training at Camp Moore, Saxton would have to endure the arduous hikes, sniper school, night stalks, mortar practice, balloon exercises and his favorite; hand to hand combat. Even if Saxton led by exemplary example, Marcus was their true leader. Saxton knew it, the Rangers knew it and as he often joked, even the mules knew it. He hoped that the Rangers would eventually accept him. As it turned out, that acceptance wouldn't come until he faced certain death at a place called Goat Hill.

The Maasai Rangers relaxed as they cruised up the Mississippi. All along the wide river, dozens of Federal ships, small, large, sail and steam, plied the waters of the 'Father of all Rivers'. No longer was the Nimsi an oddity, for many ironclads on the river were low and nearly invisible at night. Powerful gunboats such as the Arizona, the Genesse, the Winona, steamed 'hell bent for leather' up the river. Heavily laden cargo steamers such as the Red Chief, the General Banks and the Anaona were more ponderous in their progress as the river pushed hard against them. It was a formidable flotilla of more than forty ships under Admiral Farragut's command.

Marcus, afloat on a living entity, experienced the power and mystique of the vast river once more. There was no horizon, no rogue waves, and no gales. The James River had been but a mere trickle running down the leg of eastern America. The Mississippi however, poured like an ocean down the middle of America, squeezed between the thighs of a mighty continent.

BOOK TWO: CHAPTER 16
THE KILLING GROUND

Strategically situated at a sharp bend in the Mississippi River, a line of low bluffs fronting Port Hudson completely dominated the passing of waters beneath them. There, for over two months, seventy-five hundred Rebels under the command of Major General Franklin Gardiner held at bay over forty thousand Union troops under the command of General Nathaniel Banks. Rebel entrenchments ran hither and yon a behind the city for nearly three miles. Its crenellated log and dirt embankments stretched in a great arc from its southern point called the 'Citadel' to its northern extremity aptly named 'Fort Desperate'.

For weeks, Porter's gunboats and Bank's inland artillery pounded the Rebel lines without much effect. Great swaths of trees mowed down by the relentless cannon fire penetrated the entire length of the Confederate defensive lines. Protected by deep ravines and ridges, it was nearly impossible for neither man nor beast to move forward without encountering withering rifle and shell fire. An elaborate series of earthworks begun a year earlier faced the Federal forces. As one Confederate officer put it succinctly,

"For three quarters of a mile from the river, the line crossed a broken series of ridges, plateaus and ravines, taking the advantage of high ground in some places and in others extending down a steep declivity; for the next mile and a quarter it traversed Gibbon's and Slaughter's fields where a wide level plain seemed formed on purpose for a battlefield; another quarter of a mile carried it through deep and irregular gullies, and for three quarters of a mile more, it led through fields and over hills to a deep gorge, in the bottom of which lay Sandy Creek."

Whilst the Union Army combined artillery fire with sharp-shooting riflemen, the Navy added their big guns to the bombardment. General Banks ordered a massive bombardment all along the line early Sunday morning, June 14th. Ten days later, the Nimsi raised itself a few miles downstream and tied up at Ross landing to unload its cargo of ammunition. Lookouts went ashore. While sweating black stevedores unloaded it onto heavy drays, Marcus decided to call a council of war in the ship's mess. Outside, the noise was deafening as Bank's bombardment continued. After the unloading was finished, and all hatches were closed and secured, steam pressure was kept at maximum levels in preparation for a rapid retreat if necessary. The lookouts clambered aboard. Once the cargo hatch closed, Marcus dealt with the first order of business which was where to land the Rangers. Bixby was called upon to give his opinion. It was to be the longest speech the taciturn pilot would ever give. He stuck an unlit cheroot in his mouth, chewing it as he spoke.

"I've bin a pilot on old Miss for many years now. Never seen so much hellfire and damnation before! Gettin' ashore will be easy gentlemen. It's the gittin' back part that'll rub you'all the wrong way, that's fer sure. The river levels hereabouts change so rapidly, that one day a slough is full, the next it's drier than a drunk's mouth on a Sunday. We could be stranded under enemy fire, or even worse, bitten by mosquitoes. I've heard tell they carry a disease of some kind. We call it swamp fever in these parts. You call it malaria. Sure glad 'Bones' has been given you boys lots of quinine. You're gonna need it. I figur that half the killin' round here will be done by swamp fever. Always has and always will."

With that said; Bixby retreated to the wheelhouse, opened the armored hatch and lit his cheroot. He took a long happy drag on it as he gazed out upon his beloved river. Meanwhile below him, Marcus laid out a Port Hudson battle map on a canvas table. Twenty Rangers gathered around as he charted their path of insertion through the enemy lines. It was very simple really but only if the maps were up to date.

"We'll advance only at night and hole up under camouflage nets during the day. After going ashore, we'll reconnoiter the Troth House located here about a mile north-east of the river landing there. Cornel's squad will proceed from the Troth House through no-mans land to a breach in the Confederate lines a quarter mile due North of 'Fort Desperate' right here." He looked at Lieutenant Wright.

"Once you're there, you'll contact Brigadier-General Curvier Grover. After breaching the Rebel line, you'll proceed to the steam mill located just behind the fort here. It's manned by the 15th Arkansas. From there you'll attack the rear of General Steedman's Confederate lines giving Generals Weitzel, Grover and Paine an opportunity to overrun it. Apparently the Federals have not been able to do for over a month of trying. Any questions men?"

There were none. Marcus smiled knowing that the Rangers were entering a very dangerous and fluid situation. Only their wits, patience and caution would save them. Marcus continued, stabbing at the map with a cold five inch cheroot.

"My squad will by-pass the Confederate's forward post at the Troth House here and contact Brig-General Dwight over here. I'll then proceed up a deep ravine that runs due north for half a mile then turn right towards the Rebel embrasures here. Once in place, six armed Rangers would sneak through a break in the walls disguised as slaves carrying discarded picks and shovels. Their camouflage clothes will be turned inside out to look like ordinary shirts and trousers. Stuffed Inside these will be mosquito netting. Using flash bombs, the last of us carrying the squad's supplies, will overpower the defenders in a coordinated attack as the Rangers already within the walls already will provide covering fire. Once outside the north embankments, you'll all lay low close to the river behind the Citadel over here. The Nimsi here will give us covering fire as it lays concealed a little ways upriver right under the noses of the Maxey's and Gregg's brigades commanded by a Lt. Colonel, W.N. Parish.

Under this barrage, we'll storm the Citadel from the rear, turn the guns about and shell the Confederate revetments all along the line to the north-east. This distraction should allow Brigadier-General W. Dwight's 2nd Division here to storm the 31st and 32nd Confederate divisions located a quarter mile north-east of the Citadel. Thus General Miles left flank would be exposed."

There was silence as if Marcus had put a death sentence on all of the men. To the Rangers, especially Marcus, nothing on paper would ever come close to the reality of the battlefield, especially one that had been in a constant state of flux since May 21st.

After mess, the men wrote letters, cleaned their weapons and stowed their gear, Marcus reflected on what was about to happen to them. He knew that the Rangers were ready physically but were they really ready for a concentration of human slaughter that certainly lay before them? Any wounded would most likely be left to die on the battlefield. No quarter would be given to any of them if they were captured alive. The tender mercies of the enemy would be unrestrained. He wrote another letter to Belle, expanding on his dream all the while wondering if Belle would receive it since Pinkerton was no where nearby to deliver it. He didn't blame him as Porter's gunboats fired shell after screaming shell over the Nimsi.

Marcus looked fondly on the young men as they dressed in their sniper paraphernalia. The men laughed and joked with each other easily yet underneath their levity was an underlying current of fear. Marcus felt it too. He was pleased, for fearful men were careful men.

Hours later, First Mate, William Baxter came up into the wheelhouse. The pilot looked at him as Baxter, an effeminate young man, crowded into the small circular room. Bixby intoned gravely,

"Well lad, it's time to weigh anchor I suppose. There's no other reason for it. Don't need a map son. I'll let you know where to off-load 'em."

Baxter wisely concurred. He issued crisp commands and the Nimsi slipped low and away into the twilight embrace of a moonless night. Bixby sat on the open wheelhouse hatch giving steering corrections as he stealthily approached the right bank a mile further upriver from Ross Landing, slipping unseen into a shallow lagoon. The Nimsi's exhausts fore and aft burbled quietly. Two squads of nine men each, exited four aft hatches and slid into black brackish water. As hard as Bixby tried, for the life of him he could not see them. Not even a white ripple of water betrayed their passage as they swam through the reeds to the distant shore.

High above, the night sky was torn apart by star shells and bursting canisters of grape shot. Gunboats of all shapes and sizes were instantly exposed by their cannon's muzzle flashes. The Rangers had only maps, stars and compasses to guide them through the ensuing barrage. Silent as ghosts, they moved forward, keeping low as to eliminate being outlined by cannon flash. Across a broad plain, completely cratered by shot and shell; dead and dying Union troops were everywhere identified only by the sweet smell of their rotting flesh.

371

After two hours of crawling across this tumultuous terrain, out of the gloom appeared a log and earthen breastworks over fifteen feet high. An abitis of fallen trees, their branches cut off and sharpened, lay in a row before them. Beyond it, a wide ditch filled with murky water and sharpened pine poles waited to impale them. According to their maps, there was no other way around these defenses. Distraction, speed and surprise would have to do. The Rangers lowered themselves carefully into the morass, trying to avoid being skewered. Once safely across the moat, they could hear Rebels talking high above them. When everyone was ready, Marcus gave the signal. Numerous flash bombs were thrown over the parapets, along with steel grappling hooks. The Rangers stormed the breastworks.

After what seemed an eternity of fierce hand to hand fighting, all of the Rangers except two slipped away towards Troth House a quarter mile further on. With cries of alarm, savage in their intensity sounding behind them; the Rangers fled into the night over broken ground towards the Troth house. Thereby it they lay concealed beneath their mosquito netting, arrayed in cells of two or three men; a spotter and two snipers. From their concealments, they fired scoped Spencer's and Henry rifles, cutting down their pursuers. They were effective at night because of a very early variant of Paul Vielle's smokeless powder called Poudre B, as well as a very crude Zeiss rifle scope. During the day, iron sights were used to avoid reflection.

The Rangers remained motionless for three more hours then Marcus gave the clicker signal to rise and move out. It was time for the two squads to separate. The Maasai gathered his men about him. Bobby and Tom from Marcus's squad were missing. He knew that there was no time for mourning. That would come later. Marcus wished Cornel good luck before the Lieutenant's squad vanished eastward towards the Union lines of General Dwight.

Marcus had to get his men into position fast as dawn would be breaking in four hours. His squad crawled past the Troth House rising on their left flank. The two story brick house lay in ruins but had been fortified with Parrot rifles or 'swamp angels' that spewed forth their eight inch shot and shell at the Union lines, one thousand yards due east of it. They turned left and entered a shallow ravine choked with fallen trees and infested with mosquitoes. Every man wore special netting over their slouch hats and slathered copious amounts of bear grease all over their bodies to quell the little monsters. Marcus grimaced as the flying hordes descended upon them. Their buzzing increased to a roar as the tiny insect's frustration mounted. However, the squad kept moving, slithering ever forward through a thick muck of human remains.

Eventually they reached their objective. Once there, they remained undetected in a deep moat as dawn broke above them. They were now at the mercy of the enemy as they lay directly under the sloping walls of the Confederate battlements called the Citadel. These earthen embankments were being hastily repaired as they had taken a beating the day before. As Marcus lay there under his netting, he could only hope that Cornel's squad had safely reached Brig-General Dwight's HQ. If not, they would soon be shelled.

Lieutenant Wright had indeed reached the Union lines of the 14ᵗʰ Maine Infantry com-manded by Colonel Thomas W. Porter. Before Porter's soldiers knew it, the Rangers were amongst their ranks. An astonished Colonel received Lieutenant Wright in his tent while the Rangers relaxed and ate their rations outside. The Colonel rose and saluted as Lt. Wright approached him.

"I see Lieutenant that you're not in army regs. What are you in? I've never seen this type of uniform before."

"Colonel, I'm one of the squad leaders for the Maasai Rangers out of West Point. Ever heard of us?"

"Can't say that I have Lieutenant, can't say that I have. Please present your orders Sir."

Wright did so and smiled as the Colonel read on in growing disbelief. Porter looked up sharply.

"But it's utterly ridiculous. Why, Colonel Clark was repulsed just yesterday. We lost near-ly eighteen hundred men. It's impossible that only eight men can infiltrate the Confederate lines. However, I'll try anything at this point. You have my full blessing. Just let me know where and when the other squad is located and I'll make sure that they're not shelled."

"Thank you Colonel. Here's a map I have. Please update me as to any changes in the lines. I have a pencil."

The Colonel did so. Cornel Wright was shocked. His map was useless. However, the Colonel laughed, saying,

"Don't fret none Lieutenant; the Rebs have useless maps as well, for by the time we get updated maps, this damnable war will be over. So don't worry. I have a pretty good idea from my forward observers were everyone is. Please continue.

"So, Colonel, once they're in, they'll send a green flare up. Then you can shell the hell out of them like you did last night." The Colonel laughed saying,

"I guess you heard it."

"Colonel, we heard it ten miles downriver."

On June 26ᵗʰ, 1863, at several points along the front lines at Port Hudson, a second informal truce was arranged by the troops of both sides. Thereafter, Confederate and Union troops constructed their defenses in full view of each other without any harassment. During the next week, there was sporadic firing along the entire front but nothing of consequence. This interlude was just what the Rangers needed. 'Cornel's Rangers' as his men called themselves, managed to remain concealed as they made their way along a deep gulley north-east to their next objective a mile further on. It was the Gibbons house. There, they came upon a mobile mortar battery commanded by a Captain Roy of the 1ˢᵗ Indiana Heavy Artillery. Six smooth bore muzzle loading Coehorn mortars were lined up in a ragged row every fifty feet. Their gun crews worked feverishly unlimbering them from their carriages unto prepared plank platforms. Each mortar was turned on its 'nose' before the carriage wheels were removed. The mortars were then lowered onto the platform and prepared for firing. Two men using tongs seized each ball by its 'ears' to lower the projectile into the mortar allowing the round to be centered properly. All six were fired in sequence, began laying down a continuous bombardment on the Rebel trenches a short distance away. The swampy ground quaked in anguish as the ten inch shells flew upwards at a forty-five degree angle. One reporter from the Harper's Weekly later described a similar barrage,

"And, now was heard a thundering roar, equal in volume to a whole park of artillery. This was followed by a rushing sound accompanied by a howling noise that beggars description. Again and again was the sound repeated till the vast expanse of the heavens rang with the awful minstrelsy."

Fizzling fuses of the hundred pound shells or 'wash kettles' betrayed their arching flight path. After a few salvos, the mortars put back onto their carriages and moved to new positions further down the line. This tactic inspired by Confederate Artillery Major John Pelham, created a 'Flying' battery which fooled the enemy into thinking their foes were more numerous than they really were. It was between these barrages that the Rangers crept towards some bomb-proofs built nearby. Dug into the sides of a ravine, these bunkers were constructed of heavy logs covered over by a thick layer of dirt. It was there that they came upon Captain Roy quite unexpectedly. After a few moments of sheer terror, the Captain calmed down. Cornel released his grip on the Roy's revolver. He saluted.

"I do apologize to you Captain for our unorthodox arrival. We're Maasai Rangers on our way to General Weitzel's lines. Here are my orders Sir. The rest of my men are in hiding all around you. We'll leave for General Auger's HQ if you can be kind enough to direct us there."

Captain Roy carefully put his revolver in his holster as a Private approached him with a dispatch. He read it under the light of a coal-oil lantern while Parrott shells screamed through the night airs in the background. Finished, he yelled at the mortar crews to cease fire. Suddenly, the night air was quiet. Captain Roy cried out, his voice unnaturally loud.

"Yessiree, you scared the hell out of me. Where you from anyways? Boston you say? Well I'll be damned."

Three hours of crawling across the wasteland of Slaughter's field, brought Cornel's Rangers to the Slaughter's House which they by-passed it by creeping around a low hill to their left. A narrow trace led them through a shallow gully. Thereafter they emerged from a dense tree line onto the Bayou Sara road. It was one of the main roads going west into Port Hudson. Again, the ravines ahead of them were choked with fallen trees, and steep declivities. Dead and dying Union soldiers lay hither and yon. They avoided these obstacles by running down both sides of a substantial plank road east towards the Plains Store.

Once there, they became invisible, staying within the shadows. Lt. Wright spied the HQ of the 1st Divisions commander Major-General Christopher C. Augur, a large canvas wedge tent situated off to the side of the encampment. He led his Rangers towards it, silent and unseen. Two sentries patrolled around the tent. A Ranger timed their routine. They had only sixty seconds to slit the rear canvas wall and get all the men inside. Cornel watched as the sentry disappeared. Instantly, all nine Rangers were inside the General's tent before he was aware of any intrusion.

Once the group was inside, two Rangers held the canvas wall together as a sentry passed by outside completely oblivious to what had just occurred inside. In fact the Rangers had caught General Augur asleep in his bunk. Scattered around the inside of the tent were wooden chairs, weapon racks, and two large canvas tables covered with maps, mapping instruments and other paraphernalia.

Lt. Wright parted the mosquito netting covering the General's cot. He bent down and clamped his black hand over the General's white mouth. Augur's eyes flew open in alarm.

"Easy does it General, you're lucky I'm not John Mosby! We're the Maasai Rangers from Boston under special orders from the President. You don't have any cause for alarm General. I'll take my hand away now. Easy does it Sir. I'm squad leader Lt. Wright and we're reporting for duty. Sorry about the interruption, Sir."

The General sat bolt upright. His long mutton chops quivered like a brown cat sneaking through summer grass. He roared,

"Christ all mighty man! You damn near gave me a heart attack. Where are my sentries? How did you get in here anyway?"

The General swung his pale legs over the edge of his canvas army cot, and quickly put on his blue field trousers followed by a white shirt. A sentry opened the tent's front flap, peering in with a lantern held high in one hand and a cocked Remington revolver in the other. The General motioned for the sentry to leave the lantern on a table.

"It's ok Pike. Tell the rest that I'll speak to them later. Leave us alone now. Off you go Sergeant?"

It was then that the General noticed two Rangers holding the tear in the rear wall together. Cornel nodded and they let go. The tear widened and as it did so the warm night air rushed in along with hordes of mosquitoes attracted by the lamp light. The General quickly blew out the lantern and cursed as the tiny insects bit him. He cried,

"This place is a stinking hell whole; full of bugs, bullets and bodies. War is hell and this is hell personified. You boys are good, very good at sneakin' up on innocent Generals in the dead of night." Cornel grinned.

"Sorry Sir but unless we do sneak up on people, they seem inclined to shoot at us."

The General shook his head as he looked at Lt. Wright who, along with his squad stood at attention and saluted. Auger returned their salutes. Cornel stepped forward.

"Here are my orders General."

"At ease son while I light another lantern. I can't see a damn thing without my glasses."

After a few minutes, the tent filled with flickering light. The General put on his reading glasses and looked more closely at the official documents. Finally he looked up at the Lieutenant.

"Says here you're to sneak in behind Fort Desperate and set up a snipers shop in the steam mill behind it. Christ, I don't believe it!"

He reached for a large mason jar filled with bear grease.

"I'll grease up then show you the latest maps."

Once finished, he walked over to a large canvas table, selected a large map and spread it out before them. He hung a lantern on a pole and said,

"Gather round boys and I'll show you how to get to hell. Comin' back is your problem. Here is Priest's Cap, a rebel strongpoint and over there across from it is what the Rebs call Fort Desperate. It's constructed of logs and earth built on top of a bluff in the half-moon shape of a lunette. The fort is manned by over two hundred men, mainly the 15th Arkansas, commanded by a Colonel Ben Johnson. Company B of the First Mississippi Artillery Regiment is up there right now. I have to admit that Lieutenant Edrington's two twelve pounders have been mighty effective. God almighty their grape shot has been deadly." He pointed at the fort.

"Here and here; my three divisions attacked them repeatedly and may I say unsuccessfully. Those buffalos under Weitzel's command damned near took it but were pushed back with heavy losses. General Paine's black sappers are diggin' a trench right now up to the Rebs. They're within forty feet of it now. It should be ready soon, God willin'. I have to tell you boys that the ravine there called Sandy Creek has bin a real killin' ground. Their snipers are good, real good. Not just there, but all along the line. In fact they've constructed some sort of sniper tower from which they're sniping at us through holes cut through heavy wooden barrels. Can you believe it? Why, the effect has been lethal.

The New York 160th under Lieutenant Colonel Van Patton was cut down awhile ago like summer wheat in a hailstorm. Well, I wish you well Rangers, and kill 'em all if you can. By the way, General Banks is a quarter mile due north of us right here. Just get to the Port Hudson-Clinton RR line here and follow it north. I hear he's waitin' for ya. By the way, what are those funny streaked rags you're all wearin'; I must say I've never seen uniforms like those before. What do they do Lieutenant?"

"They keep us alive, Sir."

The Rangers slipped out the way they had come in as a salvo of Whitworth shells whined eerily overhead. The General's light went out. They could hear him swear and slap at the tiny tormentors that swarmed into his tent. After hiking due east along some railway tracks, a rail yard appeared choked with freight cars loaded with ammo as well as locomotives and flatcars weighed down by heavy artillery. Dawn was breaking. Along with it came the sudden roar of an approaching shell. The Rangers dived into a hole as a Columbiad shell weighing two hundred and twenty-five pounds exploded in the woods nearby. It missed the freight cars by a mere fifty yards. Even then its shrapnel wounded many men and animals. It wrecked one of the ordinance wagons and shredded a waiting locomotive on a nearby siding instantly killing an engineer.

The Rangers sprinted one hundred yards further on to a red brick train Station House where General Banks was just sitting down to breakfast. It was five o'clock in the morning. Cornel's Rangers slipped by three posted sentries and brazenly walked right up to the General's front door. Lt. Wright knocked. A voice shouted,

"Come in quickly, and close the damned door even more quickly!"

An Aid-de-camp inside drew his revolver as the ragged men scrambled into the room. They stood at attention and saluted. General Banks laughed as he chastised his subordinate,

"Paisley, for Christ's sake man, if you're going to shoot anyone, shoots me! I can't take the goddamn heat or the bugs any longer. Now take these fine gentlemen to the mess, on the double!"

Paisley saluted and fled with the Rangers in pursuit. The General motioned for Cornel to stand at ease saying,

"I wondered when you'd show up. Surprised you're still alive. Where's Marcus and Saxton, Lieutenant?"

Banks was hard of hearing. He motioned him closer. After a few moments of listening to Lt. Wright, he grinned, saying

"Well I'll be damned! You're serious aren't you? Marcus and six men are going to get into the rear of the Citadel and you're going to set up shop behind Fort Desperate."

Thirty minutes later, Paisley returned with the Rangers from the mess. Cornel had eaten his breakfast of navy beans and corn bread with Banks presiding.

"Enjoy your last meal Lieutenant, because it will be, I can guarantee it." Paisley cleared their dishes, taking them back to the mess. The Rangers relaxed, standing about the room. The shelling stopped. After a while a stiff west wind picked up, bringing with it the stench of bodies littering the front lines only a short distance away. Wright and the General stood side by side looking out a broken window. Before them heavy railway cranes came in to clear wreckage from the side tracks. Locomotives huffed and puffed as a continuous string of freight was unloaded onto drays by gangs of black stevedores. A harried quartermaster and his assistants scurried about checking every crate against a master list. He cursed volubly as he was told by his clerk of smashed and broken crates, barrels of spoiled food, sundries that had been pilfered and ammunition calibers that had been mislabeled.

Long lines of soldiers paraded single file past the General's headquarters. Some of them were colored troops. All however, were very young and had never been in combat before. Many of them would never see another day.

General Banks was interrupted by Paisley. He handed the General a message from the front then left. Banks read it then exclaimed,

"Looks like the rank and file have sued for a truce. Hells bells, I was ready to launch another attack at four points along the line later today."

He turned about once more and looked out onto the railway yard. As an aside to Cornel, he said,

"Bin working on the siege fortifications for days now. I've got only three hundred volunteers. A thousand to build the four siege fortifications is what I really need. Perhaps the lower ranks know somethin' I don't. We'll wait and see. In the meantime we'll also keep a diggin' into the Citadel, Priest's Cap and Fort Desperate. Gonna blow 'em all to hell."

Banks turned from looking at the rail traffic. He continued,

"Come to think of it Lieutenant, I actually do need a truce right now. I've got Captain Joe Bailey of the 4th Wisconsin Engineers building a cotton-bale fortress so we can shell the Citadel. Should have it finished in a week. Looks like Marcus had better get his Rangers behind it pretty quick or they'll really gonna get it."

He went over to a nearby map table and called everyone around it. The General explained everything in detail as the Rangers committed it to memory. An hour later, Brigadier-General Godfrey Weitzel, Commander of the 2nd brigade, 1st Division walked in and saluted General Banks. Cornel yelled "Ten Hut". All the Rangers stood at attention and saluted.

General Weitzel, 2nd in his class at West Point was an engineer but also a humanitarian as evidenced later when his troops entered a burning Richmond, Virginia. He'd led black troops before and as Commander of the right flank here at Port Hudson, had seen the extraordinary bravery exhibited by his beloved 'Black Phalanx'. Immediately, upon seeing the Maasai Rangers, he exclaimed,

"Why General, how did you manage to cram a thousand soldiers into this room?" Banks roared his approbation. Weitzel drolled,

"I do hope these Rangers are mine Nathaniel? I've heard of them. I do believe they captured Jeb Stuart. Too bad he got away." Cornel winced. Weitzel noticed,

"Don't feel bad Lieutenant, I hear Stuart has slowed down a bit. He's probably lookin' over his shoulder right now. So, what are their orders General?" Banks stood up,

"They say that they can get to the steam mill and pick off the entire 15th Arkansas officer corps. Ain't that somethin' Godfrey?"

Banks looked for support. He got it as Weitzel exclaimed,

"Yessiree, I do believe they can do it. But they'll have to be quick about it because my boys are digging like gophers towards Fort Desperation as we speak. We're gonna blow it all to smithereens soon as this truce is over. I sure could use some help keepin' the Johnny Rebs from shootin' us as we advance. You boys got a heap of learnin' to do in short order. I hope you're invisible and can fly. Before you do, however, I want you boys to report to Colonel Justin Hodge, Commander of the 1st Regiment of Louisiana engineers. He'll be due west of here about a quarter mile away so be mighty careful boys, the Rebs have a peculiar fondness for buffalo meat.

Marcus's Rangers endured bugs heat and as one Ranger quipped later, "Early signs of rigor mortis" for nearly twelve hours. The enemy worked on their fortifications feverishly right next to where his Rangers lay as still as death. One man even peed on Marcus without knowing it. Many blacks worked on the embrasures along with white Union prisoners.

Darkness descended, thick and oppressive but work on the embankment kept on at a feverish pace under torch light. Work gangs were rotated every four hours, with what seemed to be only five minutes between rotations. It was during one of these rotations after midnight that the Rangers made their move.

As the last man staggered off, totally spent, three Rangers rose up, took off their clothes, pulled them inside out and redressed. They fell in behind him, armed only with a pocket pistol hidden in their trousers. Each man carried an ax, shovel or a pick that they had found discarded nearby. Once inside the embankment, they lay down amongst the other workers but as close to the perimeter guards as possible. There they pretended to go to sleep.

Four hours later three more Rangers showed up and lay down on the other side of the enclosure. Many armed guards patrolled the yard, their rifles slung over their shoulders. A bugle sounded the alarm after a series of explosions shattered the night air. Rebels raced to their defensive positions. Each of six rangers in the yard selected a guard and shot them dead. One Ranger ignited a green flare. It soared skyward with a loud swoosh.

Moments later, artillery shells began whistling overhead as General Dwight's first of many barrages bracketed the compound. Heavily laden, Marcus charged through a smoke-filled gap in the wall. More shells exploded. One of the Rangers screamed as a piece of shrapnel pierced his chest. Charlie Smith fell to the ground writhing in pain. Slowly he sat up, firing his bloody Spencer as the enemy ran headlong towards him. Within seconds the remaining Rangers vanished into a forested ravine within yards of the fortress.

Thirty minutes later, the surviving Rangers were less than a quarter mile south of a Lieutenant Colonel Paul F. de Gourney's four heavy artillery batteries. These batteries covered the river on General Miles's left wing from atop the low bluffs overlooking the river. Behind them was a deep and wide ravine through which a creek meandered. Marcus's Rangers stayed within this ravine as they headed back south-west towards the river. As a ragged dawn broke over their shoulders, the Rangers found hiding places amongst shattered trees that littered the muddy banks of the creek where they tended their wounds and slept.

Marcus wept for three of his own was not coming home. A storm of tears swept in from the west swelling the creek to within a few feet from where they lay sheltered under camouflaged rubber cloaks just north of the Citadel's rear escarpment. Far below the Rebel stronghold, black sappers were hard at work digging a tunnel. Captain Joseph Bailey would fill it with thirty barrels of high grade gunpowder. Marcus and his men were literally lying upon a gigantic bomb.

BOOK TWO: CHAPTER 17
RIVERS OF NO RETURN

At one thousand feet up, the earth curved slightly from one horizon to the other. A silver glint thrust itself far to the west betraying the presence of the Mississippi River. To the south lay the tourmaline waters of Lake Pontchartrain over which flew squadrons of white pelicans.

Saxton looked down entranced. Far below him lay Camp Moore. For Saxton it all brought back memories of the Silver Ghost as the wicker basket he stood within swayed gently beneath hydrogen filled silk balloon. Bathed by a desultory morning breeze, he tapped furiously on a brass Caton telegraph key, transmitting messages over an insulated wire to the ground. The telegraph's batteries were working perfectly.

As an emergency alternative, he had tried writing on pieces of paper, numbering them, putting them into weighted sacks before throwing them overboard. Fluttering like wounded birds ever downwards, they carried instructions for the five Rangers scrambling to find them far below. The balloon and its hydrogen generator had not been deployed since leaving Fort Monroe.

It was there that Thaddeus Lowe had given the Maasai Rangers their first lessons on how to mix iron filings with sulphuric acid. A correct mixture would inflate the small balloon with fifteen thousand cubic feet of hydrogen. Only sixteen feet in diameter, the balloon used less gas, could inflate faster and could be used on windy days. Lowe had insisted that all ballooning be done tethered to the ground. His nemesis, John La Mountain on the other hand, championed free flight as he successfully demonstrated at Fort Monroe later on. Both Marcus and Saxton agreed with Lowe. Thereafter, any balloon flights by the Rangers would be tethered no more than five hundred feet from the ground.

The Caton telegraph was said to be better used on the ground because it took up too much room in the balloon's small basket. However, Saxton was finding this to be untrue. The heavy Grove cells and miles of No#14 copper wire had to be packed on a wagon drawn by muscular Belgian mules. Although sometimes troublesome, these heavy battery cells provided General Grant and others with excellent performance in the field. A single telegraph wire running through glass insulators had to be raised up above the ground wherever possible. The lighter Caton pocket telegraph instrument used only one wire instead of three.

While at Camp Moore, the Grove cells performed flawlessly, but for how long? Simply put, Saxton did not know. The Nimsi's balloon could be towed or tethered by silk cordage to a heavily weighted buckboard. Both balloons on the Anaona and Nimba were made at

Lowe's factory in Philadelphia. However, their hydrogen gas generators had been built to his specifications at the Washington Navy Yard by master joiners.

Saxton realized early on that in order to kill Quantrill or at the very least immobilize him, the Rangers had to know the lay of the land intimately. Maps and charts had failed the US Cavalry. Speed, surprise and mobility were Quantrill's trademark upon terrain that he knew like the back of his hand. However, a mobile, low altitude camouflaged balloon that could rise up out of a ravine or river valley would be ideal, giving anyone pursuing the bandit, a tremendous advantage.

By using a modified Portuguese heliograph, together with a telescope and a Caton telegraph, messages could be sent by mirrors or tapped into a secure telegraph pole. On a clear day at five hundred feet, a radius of nearly forty miles could be glassed. Properly directed from on high, canisters of grapeshot shot would decimate any intruders hiding nearby. To get close enough would be very difficult but the Ranger's special skills might get the job done.

On July 5th, 1863, a telegram arrived at Camp Moore announcing the surrender of Vicksburg the day before. The camp was jubilant. All leave was cancelled. Saxton realized that Port Hudson was the last Confederate stronghold left on the Mississippi River. Ensuing reports indicated that forces under General Banks command had suffered mightily. Saxton could only pray that Marcus and his men were safe. Everyone knew that Port Hudson would have to surrender. Rumors abounded that its defenders were starving. If true, the Nimsi would arrive back at Baton Rouge very soon indeed.

Saxton while aloft used his hands to direct the Coehorn mortar crews onto their moving targets. The mortars, requisitioned from the Army, were mounted on a revolving turn table bolted to the bed of a heavy dray. The 'War Wagon' was pulled by two large Belgian mules who, surprisingly got used to the roaring thunder behind them. In fact the mortars could be fired as they pulled the dray at a dead run. Combined with the balloon above and the scouts ahead; Saxton felt this combination would prove successful. He could only hope.

The light blue of the balloon's silk bag matched the blue of the wide prairie skies. From the ground Saxton knew it would be nearly invisible. Long silk ropes with thin steel wire cores imbedded within them would tether the balloon. On one occasion while aloft over Fort Monroe, Lowe found out to his chagrin, that oil of vitriol had eaten through the old manila tethers, setting him adrift over enemy lines. He had to be rescued behind enemy lines by Marcus and a squad of Maasai Rangers.

Saxton's men practiced their sniper skills from various heights at both moving and stationary targets. Every Ranger drilled ceaselessly for nearly two weeks. The Rangers in return took their frustrations out on Saxton by teaching him hand to hand combat. Although covered in bruises, he suffered without complaint. Saxton was earning their respect albeit grudgingly for he had three strikes against him namely; he was white, rich and married to the most beautiful black woman in Boston.

A few days after the fall of Vicksburg came the news that Port Hudson surrendered on July 9th. And so, on a hot muggy afternoon just before lunch mess as 'Saxton's Folly' floated high above Camp Moore, the caton telegraph key in the balloon's wicker basket clattered again. It simply said,

"Rangers, two miles due west."

Saxton's men were lined up and waiting as Marcus's Rangers rode towards them. Lazy dust balls rose high into hot summer airs betraying their passage over the parade ground. After dismounting, the two squads turned and wheeled about.

Marcus yelled, "Ten Hut!" The squads snapped to attention. Saxton saluted, stepped forward and bear hugged Marcus. Saxton released him, wheeled about smartly and yelled,

"You are dismissed. Now clean up and mess up!"

Immediately the squads ran towards each other. Joking and laughing, they made their way to the stables with their mounts in tow. Within minutes a hideous braying was heard as the Rangers fussed over their mules. Saxton and Marcus followed them. Saxton noted that Marcus had lost a lot of weight. Saxton also noticed a gap in the ranks. He turned to Marcus.

"Who's missing Marcus, who's missing?

Marcus held his friend by both shoulders,

"Sax, we lost Charlie, Bobby and Tom. We couldn't recover their bodies at the time, we just couldn't. I'm sorry Saxton, Charlie was badly wounded. He stayed behind and covered our escape. I tried to call him back but he just kept firing. We heard him screaming behind us as we dived into a nearby ravine. After Port Hudson surrendered, we retrieved what was left of him. It was horrible beyond anyone's imagination. We kept all their remains in cold storage aboard the Nimbi. An ice wagon is bringing them here. It should arrive in a few hours. They'll have a proper military funeral tomorrow." Saxton wondered saying.

"I hear that there's a new medal being given out to soldiers displaying bravery beyond and above the call of duty. It's called the Medal of Honor. They all deserve it for sure."

Marcus agreed. After washing up, the Rangers walked over to the mess hall. Inside, Marcus and Saxton were waiting. A dozen or so of Colonel Dudley's soldiers were eating over in a corner of the vast mess hall. While Marcus began to address his men, the white soldiers moved closer. Marcus noticed them as did his young Rangers. He began by saying,

"I just want you all to know that we lost three of our own. But I know Charlie, Tom and Bobby were heroes. They fought for their country, bravely and honorably. Tomorrow we will bury Corporal Charles Smith, Private Tom Preble and Private Bobby Bourne right here at Camp Moore with the same respect and ceremony as any other soldiers who died for our nation."

He turned and pointed to a white Corporal.

"Corporal, go tell Colonel Dudley that I, Captain Brown of the Masan Rangers wants to see him after mess in his office at 0100 hours. Could you do so now Corporal? Thank you." Marcus continued gravely.

"As soldiers, we are expected to obey orders whatever the reason, without question. However, as Rangers, you have been trained to think for yourselves regardless of the situation. Charlie in particular, despite my entreaties to escape, refused. His delaying actions saved many of us, myself included. Tom and Bobby also gave their lives, fighting against insurmountable odds, ensuring our escape."

Marcus was pleasantly surprised as the white soldiers listened politely. He was even more surprised a short time later as the Corporal was followed a slightly inebriated Colonel Dudley into the mess hall. Immediately, everyone including the Rangers stood at attention. Both Captains saluted. The Colonel reciprocated in kind then yelled "At ease!" He stood looking about at his unusual audience then said,

"As the new Commander of the 30th Massachusetts Volunteers stationed here at Camp Moore, may I have a few words Captain Brown?"

"Yes of course Colonel." The Colonel nodded while swaying slightly.

"I've, just arrived back from Port Hudson as Commander of the Third Brigade under General Augur who I am told had a very interesting encounter with these Rangers especially those led by Lt. Cornel Wright. Wherever he is, please stand up young man."

Lt. Wright stood then sat down. Cornel's Rangers laughed as others joined in. The Colonel was just getting into his stride.

"From what I've heard, both squads acquitted themselves admirably and honorably." He paused significantly,

"And from what I've read of the dispatches, Cornel's Rangers captured the Steam Mill behind Fort Desperate in fierce hand to hand combat. From there, they laid down enough accurate fire to protect the sappers digging trenches towards the fort in question. They also picked off many of the enemy's officer corps."

He paused again, turned, nearly losing his balance.

"These brave Rangers also killed most of the 1st Mississippi Battery B gun crews, making it possible for General Weitzel to advance on their right flank. However, our offensive halted when the starving defenders surrendered." He faced Marcus unsteadily, saying

"The same story applies to Captain Marcus and his buffalo Rangers in their actions during the battle of Port Hudson. After sneaking through a gap in the Rebel defenses, they advanced to the rear of the Citadel, a Rebel strong point. Once in place, they too took out by sniper fire, most of the gun crews stationed there. Not only did they devastate the Rebel batteries but they did it at night while being hunted by the enemy. They were also aided by the mortars on board the Nimsi. It was that ship's extremely accurate grapeshot which kept their enemy at bay. Whoever the pilot was on that boat did an excellent job of keeping the enemy guessing. He's to be congratulated. It has come to my attention that three Rangers died at Port Hudson and that you wish for them to be buried here with full military honors. Normally, however, for whatever reason, this would not be allowed."

The Colonel braced himself as a chorus of jeers filled the hall then turned to cheers as the Colonel continued, his speech slurring noticeably.

"So it is with verrrry great pleasure that whatever burial they deserve, they will get tomor-rrrrow at Metaire cemetery."

With that said, the Colonel supported by his Adjutant grimly dragged himself towards the nearest exit.

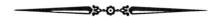

The Nimsi arrived at Memphis, Tennessee on July 21st, 1863. Marcus and Cornel's Rangers went ashore with all their mules, tack and other supplies. They proceeded to the Memphis-Charleston rail yards where they waited for their Commander, Captain Marcus and his Lieutenant, Cornel Wright to return from General Grant's HQ at the majestic Phelan House on Beale Street. Captain Marcus and Lt. Cornel Wright, dressed in their dark green Ranger uniforms, walked the six blocks from the waterfront docks to Phelan House, as throngs of Union troops gawked at them. The tall Maasai and his short sidekick realized they were making quite an impression. For the rest of the way, they swaggered up Union Avenue to Beale Street.

River traffic to Memphis had been severely congested. While the Nimsi steamed up the great river, Horace Bixby literally swore his way through a myriad of ships to the lower wharfs nestled beneath the Chickasaw bluffs. Ironclads, gunboats, transport steamers all vied for valuable river frontage. Across from Memphis, the wharves at Island No#10 were jammed with materiel piled up high upon them. Marcus remembered climbing the bluffs and hallooing his farewell to Nate far below him. Nothing had changed, just the ship. It too, looked like a bug in a puddle. Saxton would wait until Marcus returned with confirmation of his excursion east. War might be hell but it also was a bureaucratic nightmare of sudden assignment changes.

Earlier, as Marcus, his squad and their mules made their way along a familiar wharf to a hastily constructed mule corral; he remembered the Shell Man running for his life from an angry mob of black draymen. Upon leaving the mules, baggage and their keepers behind, all these memories evaporated as they neared the colonnaded Phelan House, its architecture reminiscent of the Federal style. With their green field hats wedged securely under their left arms, Marcus and Cornel ran up the steps and presented their credentials to a very suspicious pair of guards. They entered the cool confines of a paneled foyer. From there they were escorted to General Grant's office. The Adjutant held up a white gloved hand and with the other knocked softly. A gruff voice answered,

"Come in and close the door behind you."

Major-General Grant rose and returned their salutes, offering each of them a chair. Numerous packing boxes were stuffed to overflowing about the room. As he spoke, his Aide de Camp worked feverishly at filling more of them with books, maps and other items. Grant was built like a tall fireplug. Everything about him screamed 'Danger, do not touch'. He stood before them, a shorter version of the Colossus of Rhodes and said,

"I'm sorry for the disarray gentlemen, but 'Old Brains' Halleck has been promoted and will be stationed in Washington. I'm to take his place at Corinth, Mississippi as soon as possible. The train will be here soon. I hear you'll be on it. Perhaps we can chat then. Would that be ok Captain?"

"Of course General, and may I add our congratulations Sir."

Both men rose, saluted and left for the rail yards. Marcus sent a message to Saxton by courier to keep waiting aboard the Nimsi. Two hours later, Marcus's Rangers and their mules entrained. After the dust settled, eleven Rangers were crammed into the General's private coach. The previous conversation continued as an impatient Conductor waited for the General's permission to pull out. Marcus remarked,

"The last time I rode this train, I was on the roof. It was only a few miles ahead of here that I was knocked off the coal truck by a low bridge near Chattanooga." The General laughed,

"Yes, I heard about that from Lincoln himself. He said you should've bought a ticket."

Grant motioned for all of them to gather around a large map table. Thereon he pinpointed where Morgan's raiders had come from, where they had gone and where they were at the present time. The train's telegrapher was in an office next door. At each station on the way to Memphis earlier, he would receive telegrams for Grant or be hooked on to a nearby line to transmit them. In this way, Grant was constantly informed of the Union's efforts to capture John Morgan. The General pointed at a large map of Indiana, Tennessee, Kentucky, Ohio and West Virginia as he spoke.

"Gentlemen, I've just been informed that Morgan crossed into Ohio as of this morning. Colonels Hobson and Judah are in hot pursuit about here. General Burnside has sent a regiment from Marietta, Ohio here to hold the ford at Buffington Island on the Ohio River about here."

He stabbed the map with a stubby finger and continued unabated, his enthusiasm gathering strength as he did so.

"Two days ago at Buffington Island our gunboats patrolling all along the Ohio River captured seven hundred of Morgan's Raiders trying to escape into West Virginia. Morgan was not among them. Seems his raiders are down to eighteen hundred men. Perhaps we might not need your help after all."

He paused stroking his full black beard thoughtfully as he realized the Rangers were visibly shaken by the news. It was about to get worse.

"As for John Mosby's Partisan raiders, the Thurmond brothers, Turner Ashby, the Jesse's Scouts, the 'White Comanche's', Terry's Texas Raiders, the Thomas Legion and other confederate guerilla groups; Secretary of War Stanton has a cavalry unit called Loundon Rangers hot on Morgan's trail."

The General paused to light a fat cigar. He bit the end off then sucked at it until it glowed brightly. Satisfied, he continued,

"Regrettably however, I've been informed that the Loudoun Raiders have had no formal training. The loyalty of Captain Mean's, their commander, a Virginian is now in question, and his Rangers appetite for liquor is becoming legendary. So, by September, Captain Grubb of the Loundon Rangers along with the Blazers Rangers will assist Captain Means or more to the point make sure he doesn't betray the Union. All three are now being organized as one cavalry unit of a hundred men armed with the latest Spencer rifles commanded by a Colonel Carr B. White. They've been modeled on Terry's Rangers who have proven to be effective."

Once again Marcus's Rangers were disappointed. Grant decided to give them some very useful tactical information. The Conductor knocked on the open coach door but again Grant waved him away. He puffed on his cigar then flicked a long ash into a nearby metal ashtray saying at the same time,

"Before you go Gentlemen, I've studied how John Mosby goes about his business. First of all he operates in secret, telling no one but his guide what he's up to till the last minute. He plans everything carefully in advance. His men know every backwoods trail and turkey trot. He usually attacks at four in the morning when his prey is fast asleep or not alert. He uses stealth by riding over soft fields, snow and through heavy rain to mask any sound from his horse's hooves. No canteens or sabers are allowed. They make noise. He saves energy by moving slowly into a raid then retreating quickly, resting his men and horses no less than three days before another raid. He has penetrated the minds of our soldiers and uses fear as a weapon. Mosby's Raiders ride only thoroughbreds trained as jumpers. Rubber ponchos cover their weapons during rain storms and they wear woolen overcoats in the winter. He splits his forces into groups to attack our weak points simultaneously over a large area. If surrounded, his men scatter in all directions at once. It seems he knows what we're going to do next. Christ, he's tied up nearly thirty thousand of our troops. He's driving General Sheridan crazy with his continuous raiding forays. To give you an example, this March, he and twenty nine men pretending to be Union Scouts, entered Fairfax County, captured three high ranking officers including Brigadier General Stoughton and fifty-eight horses." Marcus laughed saying,

"Yes, I heard General that he went up to the Brigadier General's bedroom, pulled the sheets back and slapped his rear end. Apparently the General shouted,

"Do you know who I am?" and Mosby replied,

"Do you know Mosby, general?"

"Yes, have you got the rascal?"

"No but he has got you!"

After the laughter died down, General Grant went on to say,

"Yes indeed, for after that episode I told Sheridan to hang any of Mosby's men without a trial. The President himself said,

"Well I'm sorry for that. I can make new Brigadier Generals, but I can't make horses."

Grant concluded by stating that Mosby's Raiders were now as of June 10th, known as the 43rd Battalion of the North Virginian Cavalry.

"Maybe he'll fight fair now that he has a battalion, but I doubt it. I wonder if Baker's Raiders will ever corner him. I doubt it."

He noticed that the Rangers were still crestfallen. So, he offered them hope.

"General Banks has informed me that Captain Saxton will be going after William Quantrill. Gentlemen, perhaps you'll join him before he leaves Memphis. I'll counter-sign your orders to that effect right now."

After a few minutes, Grant handed Marcus his new orders. Marcus and his Rangers stood at attention and smartly saluted. As they were leaving, Grant said,

"I hope you learned something here today. I wish you all good luck."

The Rangers and their mules detrained and stood stoically as it disappeared into a maze of railcars spread out before them. An hour later the Rangers and their mules were stowed safely aboard the Nimsi. At noon, it slipped quietly down the 'Big Muddy' to another war.

Two days after leaving Memphis, the Nimsi reached the confluence of the Arkansas and Mississippi rivers. After lowering itself into the river, the Nimsi, for the first forty miles followed a broad water course of the Arkansas river as it meandered ever westward. Medina, Pendleton, and Kimbrough were passed unseen. The river was in full flood thus making the journey even more hazardous than the low water of the Mississippi. Deadheads, snags and sweepers all threatened the Nimsi as Horace Bixby, once again swore his way skillfully upstream. The ship arrived near Pine Bluff in the lee of a large island. A swollen sun put its golden hand gently down upon the rolling bosom of the western horizon as they tied up under a canopy of Cottonwood trees.

Sixty miles upriver was the Confederate 'stronghold' of Little Rock, the state capital. Saxton set the guards on their details and went to sleep but not before trying to decide whether or not to shell Little Rock's Old Arsenal on 9th Street or by-pass the city altogether. Bixby advised against shelling the Arsenal as many of its four thousand inhabitants were fleeing south to the Red River already. Helena was about to be overrun by Major-General Frederick Steele since Vicksburg had fallen July 4th. Little Rock's feeble defenses were rumored to consist of rifle pits and redoubts, nearly three miles downriver from the Capital on the north bank of the river. Bixby was aggressive,

"Shell the hell out of the rifle pits son. Give them Johnny Rebs somethin' to talk about. I was there a few years ago. Then it was supposed to be the up and comin' Mecca of commerce in the whole state. Why hells bells, their so called railway is still in the blueprint stage. The only decent cannon they have, is 'The Lady Baxter', a sixty-four pounder they got off the gunboat Ponchartrain and I hear tell it's still pointin' at City Hall. Yes son, give the Rebs somethin' to talk about. I know just where those rifle pits are too. With the river bein' this high, why we can get so close that you'll be able to reach over the side and give their Captain a decent shave!"

Dawn broke the next morning like a fresh egg in a skillet. Rangers prepared for battle. The mule corral was cleaned out, all loose gear was stowed, the mortars were primed and five lookouts were posted prone on the deck in camouflage gear. The Nimsi cast off. Bixby used the middle of the wide river to his advantage. About five hundred yards from the rifle pits, the armored hatch covers opened upwards with a hiss. After being chained down, the open hatch revealed a cross-cleated ramp descending at a steep angle into the bowels of the ship. At the foot of it six mules and their armed riders, waited patiently for the signal to go ashore. Meanwhile the Gatlings were dragged up the ramp and secured fore and aft. Two Rangers scoped the unfolding shoreline carefully as the Nimsi hugged the north side of the river. Bixby steered the ship into a sheltered slough just downriver from the rifle pits. A long pontoon gangplank was thrust out onto the river bank. Three Rangers led by Marcus went ashore to scout ahead. Corporal Bill Hagen led the muleteers ashore. They trotted out a mile inland towards the little village of Dixie.

Saxton waited. He was soon horrified, for by chance he'd come ashore only a hundred yards away from the Rebel rifle pits. Three Rangers burst through nearby brush. Shots rang out. Saxton screamed, "Fire at will!"

The mortars threw their deadly canisters of grapeshot vertically over black cottonwood trees right onto the advancing Rebels. Horrendous explosions shattered the morning air. Screams of the dead and dying lingered for many moments. Marcus's Rangers had thrown themselves to the ground, waiting. A line of men approached them through tendrils of river mist caught in the underbrush. Rifle fire crackled as Marcus and his snipers cut them down. The enemy retreated in disarray. All of the Rangers advanced, bayonets fixed towards the shattered cottonwood grove. Dense smoke from the mortar explosions drifted out over the river.

More shots were fired. Saxton could tell that they were meeting no resistance for only Spencer and Henry rifles could be heard. He blew the ship's whistle twice. The muleteers came galloping back ten minutes later, thundered up the gangplank then clattered down into the hold. Every Ranger returned to the ship on the double. Battened down once more, she eased into the river and struck out for the opposite shore. Once there, it burbled past the city of Little Rock using the river mist as an effective smoke screen. Thirty miles later, as darkness fell; they passed Lollie Village on the north bank and tied up five miles downstream from the Toad Suck ferry crossing. Saxton posted pickets ashore. Everyone aboard tried to sleep through a restless night as if death itself was in bed with them.

Fort Smith, a Confederate strongpoint, lay one hundred and fifty river miles ahead up the Arkansas River. After five days of tough sailing against a strong current, the Nimsi slipped by the fort in the early hours of a calm prairie morning. A month later, Fort Smith would be captured by Union forces without a shot being fired. The Nimsi arrived at Fort Gibson on the Grand or Neosho River three miles from its junction with the Arkansas and Verdigris Rivers on August 7th, 1863. They were supposed to stay there for the next two weeks.

Fort Gibson or Fort Blunt as some were forced to call it; looked out over gently rolling hills towards the west bank of the Neosho River a half mile away. Built originally in 1824 as a log and earthen fortification, Fort Gibson over the years progressed from a few log cabins to that of a substantial brick and stone fortress, to become the Union Army's key post in Indian Territory. During the Civil War, it became a haven for pro-union refugees.

Upon the Ranger's arrival, Fort Gibson was still being fortified. The Rebels had been run out of it April 12th, by a Colonel William Phillips. Confederate forces under Brigadier General Douglas H. Cooper tried to retake the Fort's supply depot at the Battle of Honey Springs, twenty miles south, a few weeks before. However, due to wet powder, Cooper's troopers were defeated by Major-General James G. Blunt. Soon after, the Confederates moved their forces to Fort Davis just downstream from Fort Gibson on a bluff across the Arkansas River overlooking the three river junction. There, they drilled behind a thirty foot high Indian mound lying in the center of their log fort. This allowed them a modicum of privacy from the hated Blue Bellies just across the river.

The Nimsi as it did at West Point; nestled snugly against the Fort's long wharf before anyone knew it was there. And, just like the incident at West Point, a sentry by the name of Private Blakney saw the 'river monster' rise up out of the clear waters of the river almost at his feet. He ran up a winding wagon road to the fort crying in alarm. Immediately, a squad of soldiers from the 1st Kansas Colored Infantry came running down towards the river. In the meantime, Saxton raised the Nimsi, rotated its internal gangplank and tied up. Ten mules walking in twos trotted out onto the dusty road led by the 'Warden' towards a hay field where they intended to graze.

Meanwhile the buffalo soldiers dropped to the ground and formed a skirmish line a hundred feet from the wharf. Behind them their commander, Colonel James M. Williams rode forward on a magnificent black stallion. He wondered at the time,

'Where had the mules come from?

He galloped past his troops lying prone on either side of the road. As he came closer, before him on the wharf stood ten Rangers in their dark green uniforms, Spencers by their sides, their chins up, standing stiffly at attention. The crew in their white ducks lined the length of their ship. Marcus and Saxton stood side by side. Horace Bixby sat on an air vent smoking a pipe as he savored the silliness that was about to take place.

The Colonel dismounted, pistol in hand and warily approached. Saxton saluted. The Colonel hesitated, put his pistol away and returned Saxton's salute saying truculently,

"I say Captain; your men could have been shot down like ducks in a barrel. It's rather silly of you to appear like this."

"Why Colonel you're mistaken, instead I do believe that you're the ducks in a barrel. Wouldn't you agree Sir?" He pointed back to the fort.

The Colonel swung about amazed, for there stood his men with their hands in the air, their muskets lying in the grass beside them. Slowly they began walking towards the Colonel. Behind each one was a camouflaged Ranger with a pistol jammed into a captive's backside. They came abreast of their Colonel, their faces flushed and downcast. Saxton walked forward to shake the Colonel's hand. He said,

"I'm Captain John Saxton of the SS Nimsi and beside me Colonel is Captain Marcus Brown and his Maasai Rangers from Boston. They are under the direct orders of President Lincoln and the Secretary of War Stanton."

Marcus stepped forward, saluted and also shook the Colonel's hand. He said,

"I'm sorry Colonel but we have to do this all the time or nobody will take us seriously." He turned to Lieutenant Wright.

"Squad leader, release your prisoners." He paused and winked at Saxton.

"If you please Colonel, keep your eyes on the hay field to the right of the road."

Wright grasped a metal clicker and pressed it twice. Immediately, five appaloosa mules miraculously stood up draped in their camouflage netting while the other five mules about them continued to graze. Saxton clicked three more times and these mules dropped to the ground completely immobile. He clicked it four times and the five camouflaged mules dropped like stones. Saxton turned,

"Well Colonel, what do you think of that?"

Major-General James G. Blunt, the area commander and his second in command, Colonel William A. Phillips, rode down the hill at a full gallop. They dismounted and ran onto the wharf. Blunt returned everyone's salute, walked up and blustered,

"Quite a show Captain, yes quite a show indeed! Present your orders please." The General perused them quickly and gave them back to Marcus saying,

"Well Captain, your Rangers are after Quantrill are they? You'll have to wait some. I need men like you right here and now. I could have used you at Honey Springs a few weeks ago. But we outflanked them. Thankfully, the whole territory north of the Arkansas is now under my control." Marcus disagreed.

"With all due respect General, I don't think so. Quantrill is raiding your supply wagons at will, tying up thousands of your troops in the process. Captain Saxton and our Rangers are here to catch him. We have special equipment and skills that you don't have Sir. Our orders come directly from President Lincoln, countersigned by Secretary of War Stanton and General Grant. I would advise you Sir to not interfere in the carrying out of our Federal assignment. However, with your indulgence, we might assist you in a local campaign as we intend to rest and train our men here for the next two weeks. We'll stay aboard our ship. Only our mules need graze ashore. What do you say General? Do I and Captain Saxton have your permission?"

The General quietly discussed his options with the other two officers. After a few minutes, he came forward.

"Sounds good to me, and might I say timely too."

The meeting was over. The General concluded by saying,

"Good, that does it then. Captain Saxton, may I tour your vessel? I've heard bits of gossip here and there about it. I also heard that someone shot the hell out of some Rebel redoubts below Little Rock a few days ago. That wouldn't have been you now would it?" Saxton pointed at Horace Bixby sitting on the wheelhouse hatch.

"Blame it on our pilot over there, Horace Bixby. He's the fightenest pilot I ever seen. He hates the Rebs more than our lead mule, the 'Warden'.

General Blunt, Colonel Phillips, and Colonel Williams toured the Nimsi including its famous toilet. 'Cookie' made sure the cold storage locker was locked and under guard. The local infantry would hear soon enough that his pantry was stuffed with all sorts of southern culinary delights as hard tack and chick peas were the usual diet out in the field. Both Captains accepted General Blunt's invitation to dine at the Officers mess. They would meet there at ten that evening.

Once the tour was over, Captains Saxton-Brown and their men were invited for a walking tour of Fort Gibson itself. Behind them, the ship's crew began unloading the war-wagon, the second balloon and its attendant apparatus.

The two Captains and their guide, a Sergeant Collins from the Kansas 1st, strolled through the fort's imposing stone walls, whereupon they gazed upon the an immense court yard encompassing nearly ten acres. An early morning river mist had evaporated, replaced by a shimmering veil of heat. There before them log and stone buildings were scattered about. Hovering over them, Shumard Oaks, Lacebark Elms and common Hackberry's provided welcoming pools of shade.

General Blunt's headquarters was a long one story log cabin sporting a field stone chimney at either end. Supported by six stone pillars; a long covered veranda ran down the front and back of the structure. Across from it were a small blacksmith-ferrier shop and a two story stone barracks backed by wide, full length verandas on each floor. An Adjutant's office, powder magazine, and married quarters completed the setting. Down a pace, a small hospital, a whitewashed bakery building complimented a large square stone well. Long lines of dray wagons from were parked in front of the Sutler's store and warehouse further on. The tour concluded back at the Nimbi in time for Lunch.

Nearly two thousand veteran soldiers, White, Black and Indian were stationed at Fort Gibson. Hundreds of Sibley tents were picketed in neat rows inside the fort. Wood smoke from numerous cooking fires wafted through the surrounding shade trees. Before the war, thousands of Creek, Cherokee and Seminoles Indians stopped at the fort for rations, supplies and equipment on the first leg of 'The Trail of Tears'. Now, hundreds of pro-union white refugees camped just outside the walls, having fled their farms and towns as the war came to them. For Marcus it was 'Slab town' and Fort Monroe all over again.

That evening in the officer's mess, General Blunt explained what he had in mind over a simple supper of roast buffalo calf with all the trimmings. The General rose and proposed a toast, saying

"To the Union gentlemen, and hopefully this intolerable war will end soon with our great nation still intact!" He continued.

"I arrived here May 14th of this year to find this fort in total disrepair, undermanned, poorly defended and the countryside around it infested with Rebels, brigands and renegade Indians. However, the situation has changed dramatically. Our recent victories at Vicksburg, Port Hudson and Gettysburg have all but crippled the South's will to fight. However, Fort Smith, sixty miles south-east of us is still being held by nearly three thousand Rebels commanded by a General W.L. Cabell. Further down the Arkansas River at Little Rock is another nest of vipers we'll have to get rid of. Gentlemen, this war is far from over especially here on the western frontier." He turned to Marcus.

"I'm sorry Captain but after further deliberation, your foray against Quantrill will have to wait."

Saxton and Marcus looked at each other, wondering if another shoe was about to drop. Marcus started to protest but Saxton pulled him down. The General smiled indulgently,

"You can train your men here and join in on our military excursions. My next objective is to secure the south bank of the Arkansas River. To that end, Fort Smith with your help will be taken soon."

He sat back, completely filling his chair.

After supper, the General's party left for his comfortable headquarters down the road for refreshments. As the party walked towards it, dozens of coal oil lanterns lit up the evening air like wandering fireflies. Hundreds of troops went about getting ready to bed down. A group of buffalo soldiers from the 1st Kansas had gathered around a crackling campfire. Someone played a violin as they sang a black battle hymn. Each man, his face shining in the firelight, would in turn sing a verse such as,

"Hark! Listen to the trumpeters,
They call for volunteers,
On Zion's bright and flow'ry mount
Behold the officers."
Then the rest would join in singing the refrain,

"They look like men,

They look like men,

They look like men of war.

All armed and dressed in uniform.

They look like men of war."

The General and his officer's hummed the tune as they passed by totally unaware that the song was a parody directed at them.

The recent battles at Honey Springs and the attack on a supply wagon train three weeks before at Cabin Creek made everyone edgy. It was readily apparent to both Marcus and Saxton that something was about to happen sooner than later. Once inside his HQ, the General passed around cigars and whiskey. As soon as they were settled and comfortable, Marcus took up the former train of thought by answering the General's previous question.

"Well General I just got back from Port Hudson and I can tell you that the Rebs are far from being licked. However, fighting here and fighting there is obviously going to be quite different. I'm sure you won't be digging trenches, earthworks of any size or deploying heavy artillery. It seems to me that like the battles I fought on the plains of the Masan Mara, the action here on the plains is more suited for guerilla warfare than traditional infantry deployment." Blunt interrupted,

"I agree Captain, but we are not a small army of a few hundred Mountain Rangers like the Missouri State Militia. I wish they were here but sadly they were disbanded this past March."

Blunt, in a moment of clarity, realized the two Captains sitting before him were never going to obey his orders. Thereafter he became somewhat conciliatory.

"Perhaps Gentlemen, your Rangers go on command for us between here and Fort Scott."

Marcus and Saxton brightened. The General continued knowing he'd made the right decision. He moved on.

"For now, Fort Scott is my actual HQ. After Fort Smith falls, I'll be moving there lock, stock and barrel. Quantrill usually plays his murderous games around here on his way to his winter headquarters in Texas. The prairies around here are perfect terrain for his cat and mouse tactics. The Rebels are losing the war but they employ renegades like Quantrill and others to harass us. Confederate Brigadier-Generals Cooper and Cabell no longer have the ability to wage war. Their efforts have become futile and are weakening as their troops desert, fall sick or die from infection." Colonel Phillips took up the conversation.

"Indeed, the whole thrust of the Confederate threat has certainly been blunted, no pun intended."

Blunt was not offended. Phillips continued.

"Gentlemen, the bigger battle will be fought on the Red River south of us, at Shreveport, Louisiana. After that, it'll only be a matter of time before the Rebs there with their backs to the wall."

Blunt relaxed as others took up the convivial mood of the evening, exchanging ideas back and forth like a capricious tennis match. Finally, after all was said and done, two squads of Rangers led by Captain Marcus Brown would escort the next supply train back to Fort Scott over one hundred and fifty miles to the north-east. Captained by Saxton, the Nimsi would scout the Neosho River one hundred and twenty miles upriver to Oswego, Kansas at the same time. Someone suggested that the river could be used as a possible supply route using coal barges pulled by steam tugs. Saxton even floated the idea of using a balloon to protect the barges as Thaddeus Lowe had successfully demonstrated on the George Washington Parke Curtis and John La Mountain on the 'Fanny' in 1861. His suggestion was met with ardent skepticism.

All of them however, agreed that they would meet back at Fort Gibson by the end of August for the attack on Fort Smith. Blunt rose and walked over to a long map table. His guests crowded about him as his Adjutant, Major Henry Curtis, produced a myriad of maps charting every possible known ravine, creek, river tributary and hillock for miles around. Saxton and Marcus were astounded as to how much detail was needed in the planning of even a simple excursion. Because of the vastness of the territory, the supply of men and equipment to a certain point and the coordination needed between many mobile units was staggering. The war machine was complex but the dying was still very simple.

The next morning, Saxton, his crew and five Rangers said goodbye as the Nimsi lowered itself into the Neosho River. Saxton and his crew were no longer upon the wide and mighty bosoms of the Arkansas and Mississippi rivers. Saxton preferred not to call the river, the Grand, but the Neosho or 'Clear Waters' as the local Osage Indians called it. The river was over four hundred miles in length but shallowed in August, meandering somewhat as it flowed through the rolling prairie swales skirting the western edge of the Ozark Plateau. It's heavily wooded banks provided some protection from the ceaseless prairie winds but was also was perfect cover for Rebel bushwhackers.

Horace Bixby had never navigated the Neosho River before. Many miles upstream where the water shallowed, a crewman was always throwing a lead line giving Bixby the river's depth. Calls of 'Mark Twain' rang out from time to time indicating a depth of 12 feet. The Neosho was not in flood whereas the Arkansas was. However, the Neosho River was well over two hundred feet wide right up to Oswego, the head of navigation. For a ship the size of the Nimsi with a draft of six feet, it was sufficient. Only a smaller vessel could navigate fifty miles further on past Oswego to Parsons. The observation balloon towed behind would hopefully go a long way to forestalling any sneak attacks. The Neosho's course roughly paralleled that of the supply wagon train's road called the Fort Gibson-Fort Scott road.

The Fort Gibson-Fort Scott road was surveyed in 1839 by W. Hood of the US Topographical Bureau. The narrow twisting dirt road was completed in 1845, and became known as the Fort Leavenworth-Fort Gibson Military Road. Fort Wayne was abandoned, having been replaced by Fort Scott at the Spring River crossing, eighty miles south of Fort Leavenworth. The Fort Gibson-Fort Scott road, known as the 'middle section' was well over one hundred and fifty miles in length. It crossed the Neosho River at Rogers Ferry near the little town of Miami, Kansas. From there it passed over a treeless prairie that rolled westward from the Ozark Plateau, two thousand miles east of the Rocky Mountain foothills. Known as 'Indian Territory', it was populated by a hundred thousand warriors from fifty different tribes, their loyalties to any combatant unknown.

As soon as Lewis and Clarke returned from their epic journey in 1804 overland to the Pacific, the American government built dozens of forts throughout the west. All of them were used to control, eliminate or deport the Indians from their traditional territories. It was into this potpourri of unrest that the Rangers found themselves. It became very clear that as neophytes to this vast land, only their superior weapons, equipment and training would give them any chance of survival.

For example, a compact Portuguese heliograph prototype acquired by Pinkerton, was mounted on a tubular metal track that encircled the balloon's basket. Thus Saxton could keep in constant touch with Marcus. On cloudy days, or at high noon, semaphore would be used. Saxton figured that every little advantage over Quantrill or any other Rebel was worth it. Even the wicker basket including the floor was lined with thin sheets of armor plate offered some protection against small caliber rifle and pistol fire. Winter would be a reality in two months. The last thing the Rangers wanted was to spend months on the wind blasted plains of Kansas. The sooner Quantrill was dead, the better.

Marcus stood on the Fort Gibson wharf as the Nimsi slipped away into the clear waters of the Neosho River. He turned and faced his men. All of them were tired and beat up by a war which to them had been nothing but civil. Although General Blunt had been obdurate at times, Marcus, Saxton and the General had more than war in common. All three had gone to sea on sailing ships. Blunt was only fifteen when he had become a sailor and twenty when he became a Captain.

Blunt's war record however was checkered, for he was defeated at the First Battle of Newtonia, won the Battle of Old Fort Wayne after which General Thomas C. Hindman forced him to a draw at the Battle of Prairie Grove. However, the Battle of Honey Springs near Fort Gibson in July of 1863 would be his crowning victory. The nadir of his career would happen on October 6th, 1863 when Quantrill would slaughter most of Blunts' armed escorts near Baxter Springs, Arkansas. At the time, General Blunt was moving his HQ from Fort Scott to Fort Smith on the Arkansas River. Only the General and a few of his men escaped back to Fort Scott alive. Perhaps if the Maasai Rangers had been there, the outcome would have been entirely different. The reason they were not, was of course General Blunt's undoing.

Two days after the Nimsi sailed for Oswego, a long wagon train of fifty heavy duty freight wagons trundled out of Fort Gibson for Fort Scott to the north-east. The sound of black mule skinners cracking their long braided bull whips over the backs of each six mule team shattered the early morning airs. Sharp sonic pops ricocheted off the fort's stone walls like gunshots. As the wagon train slowly paraded past them, scattered groups of buffalo soldiers and Indians watched from under tall shade trees. An escort of twenty cavalry soldiers flanked the wagons. Scouts had been sent ahead to warn of any danger. Trailing the column were two water wagons, a chuck wagon and wagons containing a balloon, its gas generator, and telegraph batteries. Three supply wagons and the war wagon brought up the rear of the long dusty column. Behind the war wagon were tethered a string of five spare mules.

Marcus and five Rangers rode out onto the rolling swells of prairie grass that stretched far out before them. To Marcus, the land looked like ocean waves crowned by windblown drifts of white pussy toes. An occasional hackberry tree spread its meager shade over a grassy watercourse, bordered by pink prairie rose bushes. Meadowlarks burst into song above his head while white tail deer hid deep within numerous red willow thickets. Bank swallows dipped and dived over shallow creeks undisturbed between the grass-covered hills. Slowly the sun rose high above a white haze trapped in cool hollows. Heat waves shimmered on the cresting swales above them, giving the land definition as it awakened.

Lt. Wright rode up, coming abreast of Marcus. The young man with the infectious smile tore off his wide brimmed hat and wiped his face with his sleeve.

"Sure is goin' to be a scorcher today Capt'n." Cornel swung a thin arm out over the horizon.

"It feels good though, to get away from the ship and especially Fort Blunt as the Gen'rl calls it. I sure as hell wouldn't want to be under his command, that's fer sure."

Marcus stirred in the stiff cavalry saddle.

"I agree Cornel; for some reason that man comes across peculiar like. I can't put my finger on it but I wouldn't want to have to rely on him to come to my aid if I was in real trouble. The man is a doughface for sure. Williams is a better man. Even Phillips would do in a pinch. All Blunt does is complain about him needing to do more work at getting the fort better fortified. Poor Phillips; who knows, he might 'galvanize' any day now."

Wright laughed, saluted and went back to join the rear guard. Hours passed as the wagons creaked stolidly onward. A pair of mules brayed as a rising road strained their muscles. Two days later the Rangers crossed Hudson Creek and stopped for a heliograph-telegraph test about four miles downriver from Miami, Kansas.

Feathery cirrus clouds began pulling at the four corners of a deep blue sky. A slight breeze caressed the sweltering plains. Later that day, a few hours before dusk, in a sheltered valley that meandered eastward to the Neosho a mile away, a balloon rose five hundred feet above Hudson Creek. Tall switch grass swayed by slight breezes lay far below the inflatable. Saxton looked up, thinking if his modifications would prove successful.

While he was at Camp Moore, Saxton modified the balloon dramatically. Its basket now hung forty feet below it preventing the gas bag from blocking the sun entering the heliograph device. More silk tethers stopped the wicker basket from severely oscillating back and forth. The Caton telegraph was also secured into the basket, its wire running down the main line to batteries in a wagon below it. The balloon crew had tethered its lines to a triangle formed by three wagons. The war wagon sat on a low hill a mile north of them under the shade of a red cedar tree. On two other low hilltops immediately to the south, ten Rangers and their mules lay under their camouflaged mosquito netting. From their vantage points, they scoped the surrounding plains. After thirty minutes, the balloonist tapped out a message to Marcus waiting at the key far below him.

"I can see the Nimsi's balloon and possibly Fort Scott."

Marcus wired back for the balloon to come down. There was no answer. He looked up alarmed. The telegraph key started to click again. The message said,

"A large force of unknowns is coming from the west. I've warned Nimsi's observer. Pull me down."

Marcus barked out orders to the crew. Within minutes, the pale blue balloon and its gas generator were safely stowed in its dray. Rangers galloped in from their flanking posts. To Marcus, the approaching unknowns could be hostile Indians, Confederate Army units or Quantrill's raiders. In either case, his men would be ready. Two Army scouts were sent north to warn the wagon train.

BOOK TWO: CHAPTER 18
DELUSIONS AND DREAMS

The Army's supply train formed a ragged semi-circle. It backed onto a low bluff beside the Neosho River a mile upriver from 'Mud Eater' bend. Marcus put four of his wagons inside the semi circle as a second line of defense. He sent Corporal Bill Hagen to make contact with the Nimsi. Just as darkness swept away any remaining light lingering amongst the sumac bushes, a full moon rose, bathing the prairie in its golden reflection. Marcus wasted no time. He yelled,

"Lieutenant Walker, how about a little surprise for whoever's out there. Get the war wagon ready and let's go hunting." Walker wheeled about to shout orders.

Marcus rode over to Lieutenant Wright. Both men knew that it might be for the last time.

"Well Cornel, good luck. I'll leave you in charge here. It's not the best defensive position I've ever seen but it'll have to do for now. I'll try to hold 'em off as long as I can and I'm sure your boys will too. Remember, the best defense is always a better offense."

They leaned over and shook hands. Nothing more was said. They wheeled about.

Within minutes, Lieutenant Walker aboard the war wagon lashed out. The team of four Belgians leaned into their collars. With Marcus were four other Rangers who had practiced at Camp Moore for just such an occasion. The whole procession with Marcus riding point, lumbered through a gap in the wagons towards the hostiles. Lieutenant Wright stood high in his stirrups and watched it disappear around a low hill into the gloom.

Aboard the Nimsi, 'Saxton's Folly' and its hydrogen generator were already stowed below decks for the night. Bixby maneuvered the ship under some overhanging branches of a grove of custard apple trees. These trees bordered a large slough on the eastern bank of the river across from the low bluffs looming low before them. Camouflaged mosquito netting was thrown over the whole ship. The fore and aft Gatlings and Coehorn mortars were readied. An ordnance rifle loaded with a high velocity shell was locked in position beside the two open freight doors. The gangplank had been thrown out onto the bank and tied down. Saxton sent ashore Corporal Hagen with four Rangers and their mules out on picket duty. Previously, Bill Hagen had swum across the river towed by his mule. After a hasty conference, Saxton and Hagen decided that they should stay put, for they didn't know if anyone from the village of Miami, three miles upstream had spotted them. They weren't about to take any chances on the Rebs attacking from the rear.

All lights aboard ship were doused including cigars, cheroots and pipes. The boilers were banked but steam pressure remained high enough for any sudden departure. Swarms of mosquitoes were once again frustrated by yards of fine netting thrown over the freight doors. Finally, only the mute murmurings of the sibilant river could be heard. Everyone waited. Nothing happened until about four the next morning.

It was then as Saxton paced the wheelhouse floor that he heard the war wagon's Gatling on the other side of the river blasting away. The sound of it was getting closer, much closer. Immediately, he threw open the wheelhouse hatch, and climbed out. As he stood on deck, he scoped the low bluffs opposite him over three hundred feet away. There was movement at the base of them. Saxton whispered to his gunners and deck snipers. He asked a crewman for six calcium light flares. On the count of three, Saxton and two Rangers fired all six directly at the bluff at three different points.

For seven seconds, the opposing shoreline lit up like a sunny day. The Nimsi's guns found dozens of targets, cutting a deadly swath through the attackers like a scythe. At that moment one of the Gatlings jammed. The other kept firing for the whole bluff for a hundred yards was covered by dozens of assailants, many of which started firing back at the flickering Gatling. Minie balls pinged off its steel shield. Six more flares were sent over revealing the bluffs littered with dead and dying. What Saxton didn't know was that some had managed to climb up onto the top of the bluff itself. Saxton screamed into the open wheel house cover,

"AHEAD FULL Bixby. We're gonna put the boat ashore over yonder, NOW!"

He wheeled about, grabbed an ax from its rack, and ran to the lee side of the ship where he proceeded to chop every mooring line in two. The ship shuddered beneath him as it began to pull away, ripping the camouflage netting asunder. Saxton ran over to the steel plates fronting the hatch. There his men fixed bayonets. The Nimsi picked up speed and now was only a hundred feet from the base of a twenty foot bluff looming darkly before them. Without warning the whole ship lurched violently as it slammed up and over a barely submerged sandstone spur. The ship's rear propeller thrashed in vain as it tried to force the ship ever closer to shore. Intense rifle fire from intruders still alive at the foot of the bluff assaulted the ship. Saxton ran from the shelter of the armored deck covers with half the ship's crew right behind him. Covering fire from the rest of the crew allowed Saxton and his men to wade ashore and engage the enemy in close quarter combat. Only one thing mattered to John Saxton and that was total victory over an enemy whose numbers were vastly superior.

The first wave of over one hundred raiders had been decimated by the war wagon's armament as they approached a mile away from the river bluffs. Marcus had taken the raiders completely by surprise as the war wagon swung out of a covering draw right into their midst. Beneath the bright light of a full moon, both mortars rotated left and right firing their deadly canisters. As the raiders were about to close in on it; the war wagon turned about and fled pell-mell for the river. A wall of hot lead savaged the raiders again. It apparently had a desired effect for the pursuers came to a grinding halt, their ranks bloodied, dead or shell shocked. Those foolhardy enough to follow died in their saddles. Within minutes the war wagon roared back through a gap in the ring of wagons waiting on the river bluffs. Not long after, hundreds of raiders screaming 'Osceola' unsuccessfully tried to breach the encircled wagon train. Rangers hidden up on two nearby hillocks managed to pick off many of them as they galloped through the tall lace grass. This action forestalled the main thrust of the raider's momentum. The survivors regrouped once more then rode forward. In a classic pincer movement, two large groups wheeled in front of the wagons on either side. This created a diversion while a third group hidden by the first two, smashed into the center of the ring, jumping over the wagon tongues.

Within minutes the defenses were breached in the front and in the rear. Shortly thereafter in fierce hand to hand combat, the combatants fought it out in the growing light of dawn. Cracking small arms fire, screams of the dying, the clash of metal on metal and the grunts and cursing of many men locked together in mortal combat, consumed the entire battleground. Marcus rallied the defenders behind the second line of wagons for the situation was getting much worse as waves of attackers climbed up and over the low bluffs behind him. His men fought desperately back to back at very close quarters. Marcus heard a Gatling chatter away from across the river. He knew Saxton would come, but when? The raiders were relentless as they stormed the Ranger's meager defenses. Someone screamed behind him.

Marcus whirled about. A tall, lithe, black bearded ruffian stood before him wearing a black felt hat fronted by a yellow star sewn upon it. Small piggish black eyes framed by high cheekbones looked down in disbelief as his long barreled Colt .44 misfired. As it did so, he swore drawing his saber. Viciously, he attacked Marcus, his point of death deflected by Marcus's Bowie-knife. The clashing of steel on steel rang out. Nothing was ever said between the two desperate men as they grappled for any advantage.

All around them, a maelstrom of men slashed at each other in an arena of growing fury. Mules brayed and horses whinnied as a terrible turmoil engulfed them. Tall prairie grasses underfoot were summarily beaten to a bloody pulp. Rifle fire poured forth from every quarter. Marcus screamed as he his assailant's sword sliced clean through his right arm just below his shoulder. He staggered backwards, his adversary pressing a deadly advantage. Marcus fell to his knees in agony but in one fluid motion he grabbed his severed arm, stood up and began to beat his assailant with it. He blacked out just as his opponent was about to turn and flee.

Meanwhile, Saxton and his crew had fought their way up either side of the low bluff. A dawning light trickled over bits and pieces of a terrible battle that engulfed him. Men were everywhere, thrusting their swords into human flesh or shooting at anything that moved in their direction. Saxton looked for Marcus but couldn't see him in the dusty confines of battle. He spun about as a bullet drilled through the fleshy part of his shoulder. Saxton's cry of anguish was lost in the wailing of injured men lying at his feet. Once again he was engaged in a violent struggle with deadly forces that threatened to destroy everything he stood for and everyone he loved. Saxton staggered forward, his energy spent. He leaned against a shattered wagon wheel, blood seeping through his uniform, his arm numb. A smoking Colt .44 dropped to the ground.

A horrific scene reminiscent of Hades itself surrounded him. Wagons were burning furiously. Many were turned over, their teams dead, dying or had run off onto the vast prairie. The mutilated bodies of soldiers, mule skinners, raiders, Indians and Rangers littered the battlefield inside and outside the circle of death. Saxton heard a deep moan. To his right was Marcus sitting up against the other wagon wheel, his eyes wide open, a yellow star upon his bloody chest.

At first Saxton didn't notice that Marcus was severely wounded until 'Bones' went to lift him up. As he did so, the severed right arm was revealed still within the Maasai's grasp. Marcus groaned. The Rangers were aghast. Saxton stood back and ordered the survivors to check on the dead and dying as quickly as possible and report back. Armed pickets ran up the surrounding hills, binoculars swinging from their necks. 'Bones' leaned over and released the severed arm from Marcus's right hand. The Doctor yore open his medical bag then proceeded to clean the bleeding stump. Finished, he bathed it in rubbing alcohol. 'Bones' applied a tourniquet above the stump to stop the bleeding. Using a bayonet heated in the ashes of a burning wagon nearby, he cauterized the wound. Marcus screamed. Convulsions racked his body. 'Bones' gave him laudanum to kill the pain then turned his attentions to Saxton. An hour later, makeshift canvas litters filled with the wounded wended their way to the Nimsi's infirmary below the bluffs.

During the assault, the guerillas killed many soldiers and mule skinners, most of whom were scalped. Ranger snipers had ran out of ammunition while they and their mules lay camouflaged amongst the winged Sumac trees crowning the nearby hillocks. None were discovered. After the second wave of raiders passed them by, the snipers rode their mules into the camp, picking weapons from the dead wherever they found them. The carnage they inflicted upon the enemy was immense. Although bloodied and worn out, they, along with the other survivors went to work cleaning up the butchery.

A group of prisoners were sitting under the watchful eye of Corporal Bill Hagen. One of the prisoners was a black man. Saxton was intrigued. He pointed him out. Hagen rousted him forward, dragging him by the scruff of the neck, saying,

"Captain, this back stabbin' nigger ain't no brother of mine."

Before Saxton, stood a well built black man of average height attired in a collage of clothing. Buckskin breeches held up with a wide leather belt were fronted by a buckle turned upside down. A ragged US Army field jacket turned inside out was complimented by a wide felt sombrero. A red neckerchief and Indian moccasins completed the man's ensemble. This splendid creature presented a vivid and lasting impression on anyone who'd ever meet him. Saxton asked him his name and why was he fighting for the Confederacy. The man, despite his appearance was forthcoming, his Missouri accent quite evident.

"Name's John Noland, chief scout for Quantrill. As to why I'm fightin' you Captain, my family was ambushed by Jay Hawkers. My father shot dead. Missouri's my home and no white bastards are gonna walk in and take it away from me. I'm a freed slave 'cause I'm willin' to die for my freedom. Don't be so naive Captain, for thousands of us are fightin' you Yankees. Hell, from Texas alone, the 8th and 35th Texas Cavalry and others are all loyal Southrons."

He laughed, turned about and sat down amongst his fellow prisoners. Saxton's moral foundation upon which sat his abhorrence of slavery had developed its first crack. It wouldn't be the last. That night, John Noland escaped into the bosom of an endless prairie.

The guerillas stole the Rangers' five wagons and twenty loose horses. Strangely, this was the only booty taken. The Army's mule skinners were lucky to be alive as well as the ten soldiers guarding them. As for the rest of the defenders, 'Bones' and his assistants spent the morning dressing wounds, setting broken bones and sawing off limbs.

After the war was over, it was learned that 'Bloody' Bill Anderson spared the life of just one man because of his bravery. That man was Marcus Brown. Lieutenant Wright and two other Rangers were found dead later that morning near the edge of the bluff. Around them were the bodies of over thirty raiders. The three Rangers would be given a military funeral in Fort Scott.

The Nimsi had broken its iron spine on a sandstone spur that jutted out from under the bluff above it. A falling Neosho left the ship high and dry but on an even keel. Saxton decided that he would salvage what he could and burn the ship. The remaining mules, food, medical supplies, ammunition, and assorted armament were laboriously hauled around the bluffs and stowed in twenty dray wagons. After this was done, Saxton lit a black powder fuse. The ship was torn in two as strategically placed barrels of gunpowder within it exploded. After the pall of destruction passed, Saxton saluted the gallant ship from the top of the bluff. Horace Bixby stood behind him, his hand on Saxton's shoulder, his voice soothing.

"Tis a fine thing you've done Laddie. She was a brave and noble vessel to be sure. I don't think I'll ever pilot another one quite like her again, that I can tell you. It's always sad to see a ship go down like that. Oh well, you can rest assured that her steel heart will always remind us all of what we are a fightin' for. Come on now my boy, no use frettin'. Let's be goin' now, there's always another ship waitin' for us to board."

To Saxton, Bixby's words of encouragement rang hollow for the entire expedition west of the Mississippi had been a disaster. The Nimsi was gone and Marcus his best friend was severely wounded and on death's door. Rangers Lieutenant Cornell Wright, John Hawkins and Emmitt Tercell were dead as well as many other good and decent human beings and for what? John Saxton was at an emotional and philosophical crossroads having suffered through a crisis never to be the same again. Those who espoused slavery had defeated him. There was only one thing to do, pick up the pieces, go forward, lick one's wounds, heal and live to fight another day. But, despite the sacrifices, Saxton had one thing to grasp onto that would eventually salve his mind and soul, namely a dream that lived deep within the heart of 'Marcus the Maasai'.

As the sorry group of Rangers left the battlefield, a dream that had been spawned in the mind of Marcus long before, began to take root in the shadow of defeat and grow into something real, possible and victorious. Saxton rode to where Marcus lay unconscious on a canvas litter stretched across the breadth of a lumbering freight wagon. A wide strip of shade canvas wavered in the wind over him like a flag of surrender. Marcus seemed at peace as his body bounced about as the wagon rode over every hill and dale. Saxton thought,

'Marcus might have lost an arm but I'm sure he'll embrace his dream as if he had two.'

Saxton watched his friend twist and turn on the litter. Doctor Barstow would periodically climb up on the wagon to change a bloody dressing wrapped around the stump protruding from the Maasai's right shoulder. Far behind, a line of freight wagons like beads on a string, wound their weary way around grassy hillocks, across shallow creeks and over endless stretches of flat prairie. Upon its rolling bosom, man and beast were blasted by a hot wind that desiccated the living and the dead in equal measure.

To the living, the war was raging elsewhere, consuming vast quantities of hopes and dreams. The South had lost the war but the Rebels didn't know it yet. Despite the Union's blockade, the Confederacy was proving to be too stubborn, too proud and too enraged to surrender. To Saxton, the Maasai Rangers remained a viable fighting force despite their misfortunes and now it was his responsibility to make sure they continued to be one.

For all intents and purposes, Marcus was out of the war as a fighting man. Man Rangers blamed Saxton's counterattack at 'Mud Eater' bend as too little too late.

Saxton heard and felt a growing undertow of dissent flowing amongst the men as they sat by the campfire each night or rode down the line each day. The mantle of leadership fell upon Saxton like a hammer. He wondered if he'd ever get their respect as his orders were grudgingly obeyed. This all changed however, for a few days into their journey to Fort Scott, Marcus woke up.

At that moment Saxton heard a joyous shout far ahead of him as he was at the rear of the column where he could watch everyone's backs. At least there, not unlike his years on the Silver Ghost, he didn't have to turn about in his saddle and look at the Ranger's scowling faces or hear their jibes. Saxton galloped up the line to investigate the commotion. He hung back as Rangers surged forward around him. To everyone's delight, Marcus was sitting upright with 'Bones' right beside him. Dr. Barstow looked around at the gawking crowd then exclaimed,

"He's alright men. Now go about your duties and let the poor man alone. He's bin through enough without you boys a yellin' at im. Now git, the lot of you! He needs rest and plenty of it."

'Bones" eyed Saxton like a piece of fresh meat. He was still querulous.

"Captain, come over here, Marcus wants to talk to you." Barstow stayed put as Saxton leaned over and looked down at his friend. Marcus raised his stubbled chin, eyed Saxton and whispered,

"Remember that day you came home and met your parents after years at sea?" Saxton remembered.

"I told you then that once you stepped through that door, you had to be a man. Well you have done so but now you have to go through another door my friend, a door that will lead to a world where the unexpected will be common place and the expected will never be unless you overcome any doubts deep within you. My days as Captain of the Rangers are over. You, my friend are in command now, for "Bones" told me that the Nimsi is no more."

Saxton sat up in the saddle abruptly. Marcus was tired. 'Bones' waved Saxton away as Marcus lay back in the litter and closed his eyes. His great black body relaxed. To Saxton, he didn't know if Marcus was sleeping, unconscious or dead. But one thing John Saxton did know was that the morale of the Rangers was dangerously low. In times like these, he knew most men, even strong men, could break like brittle twigs underfoot, snapping without warning, sharp and deadly.

Saxton was white. The Rangers were black. Other than their time after West Point, these young men had only known a black man as their leader. It shouldn't have mattered but it did. Saxton sensed it, for Marcus was more than a black man to his men; he was an inspirational leader, a superb fighter, and an icon of freedom. Saxton's greatest battle was about to begin, not one of bullets but one of words. But, to succeed, he had to be patient. The Rangers were fragile like old bones in an ossuary.

After a week on the trail, the dusty, torn and bleeding survivors of 'The Mud-Eater Massacre' arrived at Fort Scot on a hot afternoon, August 14th, 1863. A week later, John Noland rode ahead and scouted the town of Lawrence, Kansas. Hours later, Quantrill's Partisan raiders massacred 183 men and young boys in front of their families as the town burned down around them.

The Maasai Rangers might have failed to stop Quantrill but after the Lawrence raid, Union General Thomas Ewing Jr. issued Order No#11. This Order forced the evacuation of thousands of Kansas farmers from their farms whether they were Southern sympathizers or not. Later on in 1864, 'Bloody' Bill Anderson had a falling out with Quantrill. He formed his own gang, one of whom was a very young Jesse James. On October 26th, 1864, just south of Richmond, Missouri, Bill Anderson and his guerilla band were ambushed by Captain Samuel P. Cox and his Union troopers. As Bill and a friend fled, Anderson was shot dead, riddled with bullets. His body was shortly thereafter put on display. A few days later he was decapitated; his head placed on a nearby telegraph pole. The remains were dragged down Richmond's main street then buried in an unmarked grave in Richmond's Pioneer Cemetery. In 1908 'Bloody' Bill was given a proper funeral by another outlaw, a retired Frank James. Later in 1967, a veteran's tombstone was placed over his grave. Bloody Bill's murderous companion, William Quantrill at 27, during a raid in Taylorsville, Kentucky, was ambushed by Union forces May 10th. He died of a gunshot wound to the chest three weeks later on June 6th, 1865.

The survivors of the 'Mud eater Massacre' recuperated at Fort Scott. While there, Saxton had offered the Ranger's services to General Blunt but he refused saying that they had proven to be ineffective. Two days later, October 6th, 1863 while Blunt was moving his HQ from Fort Scott to Fort Smith, Quantrill's raiders ambushed his wagon train and nearly wiped it out. Blunt barely escaped. Later, he was demoted for failing to protect his column at Baxter Springs. The Ranger's surviving mules were left in Fort Scott, requisitioned by General Blunt upon his return from Baxter Springs. It was said thereafter that no man ever rode the 'Warden' again. As for the loose horses, five wagons including the war wagon, the balloon wagon, its gas regenerator, and other paraphernalia, stolen by Quantrill; it was rumored that all five wagons were lost crossing the flooded Canadian River as Quantrill made his way through the Texas panhandle to his winter headquarters in Brownsville.

While in the Fort Scott Hospital, Marcus's wounds became infected. Therefore Marcus amongst other wounded Rangers boarded the SS Red Rover, a hospital steamboat bound for the new Army hospital at Jefferson Barracks, a few miles south of St. Louis on the Mississippi River. It was mid October of 1863. The Rangers who were fit enough stayed at the St. Louis Hotel while Marcus and five others recuperated. By early November, all were well enough to be released. The party including Doctor Barstow boarded a Memphis-Charleston train bound for Nashville, Tennessee.

As they traveled along, Marcus told everyone of his vision of the future. With Saxton's encouragement, the Rangers decided to board another train to Bridgeport, Alabama, because they learned that General Grant was in Chattanooga, Tennessee.

Forty-five thousand Confederates under General Bragg surrounded Chattanooga. Facing them, were fifty-six thousand Union soldiers commanded by Grant. Under his command were Generals Sherman, Hooker, Breckenridge and Thomas. The citizens of Chattanooga were desperate for food and supplies. The Rangers decided that they would see what Marcus's dream was all about, then report for duty at Grant's HQ if and when that was possible. From Bridgeport, they rode 'requisitioned' horses north along the Tennessee River to Kelly's Ferry. Once across the river, they followed a narrow trace through Pan Gap to a fork in the road a quarter mile north-east of the village of Cummings. From there they rode nearly three miles to Brown's ferry. There, a tenuous pontoon bridge consisting of fifty-two flat boats had been strung out across the river by General 'Baldy' Smith. On the north side of the river, thousands of horse drawn wagons loaded with ammo, food and supplies snaked their way along Haley's Trace. Often coming under intense Rebel sniper fire, the survivors straggled over Poe's Road to another pontoon bridge a quarter mile downstream from Ross Island. On the other side of the river, the besieged populace of Chattanooga eagerly awaited them.

While the rest of their companions crossed over 'Baldy' Smith's makeshift pontoon bridge at Brown's Ferry, the Rangers slipped away two abreast up the slopes of Elder Mountain. Their horse's hooves dug deeply, getting purchase into the steep surface of an unfinished artillery road. The Rangers looked back through the leafless water oaks as the flooding river muscled its way out of sight through the 'Grand Canyon' of Tennessee. For now, the weary men would enjoy the peace and tranquility that surrounded them. The melodious twitter of a Mountain Skull Cap serenaded them as they plodded ever upwards over the craggy bosom of the mountain.

The surviving Rangers and those from the Nimsi's crew all wanted to go home but Marcus by sheer will power alone, persuaded them to follow him up the mountain of his dreams. He had spoken with passion and conviction many times in the past about starting a post-war colony of blacks and whites. There, everyone would live in equal harmony, away from a racist world of hate, prejudice and bigotry that the war would surely spawn. Fortunately, Saxton came to share that dream too as the unfolding scenarios of the mountain cast a spell upon him. Swaying in the saddle, lulled by the rustling canopies above him, Saxton began to weigh the possibilities. It was if he was back aboard the Silver Ghost's crow's nest listening to Marcus talk about freedom. Saxton suddenly had an epiphany moment. The thrill of it, the orgasmic soul wrenching importance of it changed him in an instant. He became excited, thinking about what he had to do or more to the point what he must do.

Living in Boston amongst the social gadflies had been a necessary drudgery he couldn't stomach anymore. He'd sell Saxton Shipping and come up on the mountain with Virginia and Felicity to live in blessed solitude. John Saxton had had a belly full of war. Perhaps his crew would join him. He needn't have worried as many of them were becoming more enthusiastic as they passed through serried ranks of chestnut, hickory and oak groves.

Marcus outlined the idea of buying the whole mountain from its aging owners, John and Hannah Morrison. To Marcus it was a natural fortress of sheer cliffs rising well over a thousand feet straight up over a bend in the Tennessee River called the Gorge. Water and game were plentiful. By his calculations, there were over five thousand acres of saleable hardwood timber on Elder Mountain, for Marcus had been here previously for months recovering and building up his strength. While convalescing, he scouted the whole mountain top. There were creeks everywhere that could be dammed for water power. There was at the very least two hundred fertile acres of rolling land on top of another steep set of cliffs that rose up vertically another five hundred feet. It would be in fact a fortress on top of a fortress. To Marcus, it was a fastness redoubt; a perfect place to survive the terrible times he knew would be coming after the war was over.

Sensing a sea change in Saxton, Marcus listened as Saxton outlined a simple plan to log the extensive stands of old growth trees. He knew from experience that there would be an insatiable need for dressed lumber after the war. Because of his political connections, he would be privy to any reconstruction plans that would certainly take place in the South. Marcus continued enthusiastic, driven on by hope.

"Fifty acres of pasture lay just below the west side of the mountain. Saxton, we would mill the wood around them, take it by wagon down the mountain road and sell it quickly in Chattanooga, Nashville and other cities along the Tennessee River. Besides, we're less than four miles from Brown's Ferry crossing. Saxton agreed. Marcus cried out in ecstasy, his cold breath rising vaporous in late autumn airs. The Rangers listened in rapt attention to Marcus as they rode up the mountain.

"Saxton and I have discussed this idea thoroughly whether he knew it or not." Saxton laughed, saying,

"Listen well Rangers. We can all have our own little piece of paradise right here on this mountain. We have the resources to make it happen. When the war is over, you'll know where we are. I guarantee that this will be a safe and prosperous refuge for all. Whether he knows it or not, Marcus will handle the loggers and the mill, while I will deal with the transportation of the lumber to market." He looked at Marcus as they both cried out together,

"......as long as we can convince our wives to come along!"

Pungent tendrils of wood smoke drifted down towards them. Marcus and Saxton were in full stride as they continued to expand on their vision of the future. The war had seemingly bypassed this little part of Tennessee or at least the top of Elder Mountain. Presently, a tidy clapboard cabin nestled within a grove of chestnut trees hove into view. An old red bone dog barked. Two colored boys ran out from behind a large barn scattering a flock of Barred Rock chickens rooting amongst fallen chestnut leaves. They yelled,

"Momma, momma, we's got company!"

A large black woman came out onto a wide porch. It was Sweet Daphne, the woman who nursed Marcus back to health years before. She wiped her hands on her apron, stopped then started crying. Sweet Daphne rushed down the steps and across the barnyard, her arms outstretched. Marcus dismounted; the reins loose in his left hand. He dropped them as the woman ran towards him. She cried,

"Welcome home Marcus. Welcome home!"

Marcus hugged her. Tears flowed down his scarred cheeks. She looked up into his face holding it between her wet hands. Gently she released him, touched the stump of his missing arm lightly then put her head upon his chest. He held her once more. She murmured like a lark in summer skies.

"You're home now Marcus. You're where you've always belonged. Your home is here, right here on Elder Mountain".

On November 17th, 1863, Marcus and five Rangers were paroled out, boarding a hospital train for Boston on special orders from Lincoln himself. Inside Marcus's satchel was a bundle of letters the Rangers wrote just before his departure. To Marcus and Saxton, Elder Mountain and especially their dream had to be guarded against carpetbaggers and land grabbers. Saxton tried to persuade Marcus to join him as he planned to see General Grant, but Marcus would have nothing to do with the idea. Seated on the front veranda of Sweet Daphne's cabin one morning after breakfast while the rest of the Rangers were working in the barn or patrolling on guard duty, Saxton waited, sipping his cup of chicory coffee. He knew his friend was stewing inside. He was right. Marcus put his cup on a side table, stood up and glared down at Saxton. He pointed his one arm like a sword, saying.

"Look Sax, a one armed nigger is as useless in a war as tits on a bull. Besides, Grant is a fighting man surrounded by fighting men. The last time he saw me, I was a fighting man too; a man, not half a man. Do you understand Sax?"

Saxton thought about Admiral Nelson's heroism at Trafalgar but kept quiet. No amount of reasoning on his part would change the Maasai's mind. Marcus was adamant. The next morning, Marcus and his retinue rode down the mountain to Brown's Ferry. Saxton was not with them.

After spending the next few days talking with the remaining men, all was settled. The ship's crew would stay behind to protect Daphne's family and their dream for the remainder of the war. Corporal Bill Hagen was promoted to Lieutenant and squad leader. Saxton assumed command of the Rangers and promised the men that he and Marcus would buy the mountain after the war was over, then return and build a dream. Everyone knew that his word was his bond. The men also knew then that the dream would survive if he or Marcus lived.

Saxton, and his eleven remaining Rangers, reported to General Ulysses S. Grant's field headquarters at Orchard Knob on November 23rd. Leaving them to guard their equipment, Saxton and Lt. Hagen were admitted into a small log cabin after their credentials were inspected by a guard. Although graciously received by the General, Saxton knew he had bigger fish to fry. The General returned their salutes, delighted to see them but his mood became somber as he lit a cigar.

"Captain Saxton, it's a damn shame Captain Brown and many of his Rangers are dead or wounded. It's a damn shame indeed. I can understand why he didn't come here to see me before he left. I know better than anyone what war can do to a man, especially when a proud man loses an arm or a leg or the will to fight. Some men withdraw into themselves, some commit suicide while others overcome their injuries and move on. Perhaps it's best for me to remember the Maasai as he was. You know Captain, the war will be over one day and I'm sure we'll meet again when Marcus and our nation have healed up." Saxton agreed but the words of John Noland bothered him. He stepped forward and said,

"May I be granted permission to speak freely General?" Grant nodded. Saxton spoke.

"Could you tell me if there's any colored troops fighting for the Confederates hereabouts other than those in Texas." Grant was stunned. He looked sharply at Saxton then laughed saying,

"Captain, where in the hell have you been son? Got your head buried in the sand? Why I've been fightin' blacks since the war started. To name a few; there's the 1st Louisiana Guard, the Jackson Battalion, the Palo Alto Confederates, and others. Tennessee, Alabama and Georgia have colored troops, especially Georgia. Hell, Laurens County alone has six, count 'em, six colored regiments alone. Stonewall Jackson at Frederick, Maryland, had three thousand black troops. The Richmond Howitzers, Battery #2 especially at Manassas were deadly. Mark my words Captain; Jeff Davis will change his mind about Cleburne's proposal giving blacks their freedom if they fight us. I know Cleburne's got some. The Rebs need fightin' men pure and simple and more so as the war turns against them. Too bad we didn't have more like you boys. Hell, I told Lincoln I'd resign, hand over my sword and fight for the Rebs if this damn war was ever goin' to be fought solely over slavery. Besides, Lincoln himself said he wouldn't interfere with any State's right to use slaves if their elections were conducted without fraud."

He paused as a wave of shock swept over Saxton and Hagen like a slap in the face. The General stood fast. He put down his cigar and glared, steely in his resolve and with just a touch of malice, said.

"Rangers, you and everyone else in this man's army are fightin' for one thing and one thing only and that is to preserve the Union, nothin' more and nothin' less. Anything else is political shenanigans. Do I make myself clear?" He swore, saying,

"For Christ's sake let's get down to business. I need snipers. Lt. Hagen, I heard your boys wiped out half the Rebel officer corps at Port Hudson. The question is Captain, can they do it again?"

The General marched over to a large table. Strewn upon it were layers of various maps of the immediate area. Grant pointed a fat cigar at one map in particular. Ashes fell upon it. Grant wiped them away, put a thick finger on a point of interest and said,

"Gentlemen, considering our position here as we face Pat Cleburne's control of Missionary Ridge; something daring has to be done to drive his left flank back to Tunnel Mountain over there and soon. Perhaps Bill Sherman can use you boys."

Grant wrote Saxton's orders out and signed it, saying,

"Here Captain take this and report to him immediately and good luck. You can't miss his HQ. It's a quarter mile due west of here surrounded by miles of mud, swearing mule-skinners and mountains of supplies. Just remember what you're really fightin' for."

Saxton saluted, orders in hand, turned about and left. The Maasai Rangers greeted Saxton as he exited Grant's headquarters. All pressed about him eager to hear what had happened. Saxton stood watched their faces closely, marveling at how young men including himself could age so quickly. A Ranger stepped forward, saluted then inquired.

"Capt'n what's happening? Are we still fightin' or goin' home?" Saxton pointed at a series of four low hills due east of him.

"Rangers, we're going to fight right over there on Missionary Ridge. He turned about and marched away. The Rangers fell in behind him two abreast, their rifles and duffel bags slung over their broad shoulders.

General William T. Sherman's round Sibley tent squatted in the middle of a vast muddy field, a quarter mile from Orchard Knob surrounded by thousands of smaller wedge tents. As Saxton and his Rangers picked their way through the morass, dodging drays loaded with supplies, an occasional Rebel shell tempered the atmosphere with shards of splintered steel. Saxton and his Rangers took no notice as no one around them did as well. However, as they approached General Sherman's Command tent, a Sergeant Bodkins did. His detail was guarding the General. Another shell exploded nearby. The Sergeant dropped like a stone. After picking himself up, he brushed himself off then noticed the Rangers staring at him. Embarrassed, the rail thin Sergeant waited until Saxton entered the General's tent. But Saxton paused for he heard him yelling behind him. The Sergeant's detail was arresting the Rangers. Saxton grinned and proceeded further as an aide drew aside the inner tent flap.

Outside, Lieutenant Hagen was livid but complied,

"Stand down Rangers. Our Captain won't be too long."

General Tecumseh Sherman had no time for niceties. After returning Captain Saxton's salute, the little dynamo gruffly enquired.

"Where's your orders Captain." Saxton handed them to the General. Sherman looked up and said,

"I've heard of you. Put on quite a show at Port Hudson. Seems that every Rebel officer there abouts was either shot dead by you boys or stayed underground for the duration. Quite a show indeed. Too bad about 'Mud Eater' though. Musta been one hell of a tight scratch."

Saxton appeared shocked that the General knew about Mud Eater. Sherman offered Saxton a cheroot, laughing as he lit it saying,

"Good news travels fast but bad news travel even faster son according to Lincoln and Grant. By the way I hear Captain Brown's bin paroled out. I'm glad he's goin' home to his family in Boston. I've also heard that both your wives are real corkers, especially yours. Why Captain I can't imagine a more exciting honeymoon than what you experienced at Sumter. Besides, after that Nobel fiasco, if I was Lincoln, I'd a made both women generals." His staccato laugher bounced around the circular tent rising upwards to its point above them.

Sherman motioned Saxton over to a chart table. The General asked,

"Any Rangers left Captain?"

"Eleven fit for duty Sir."

"That many? Hell I'da thought you'd be the only survivor. Are they here abouts?"

"Yes General. They're right outside under arrest."

"Under arrest? By whose orders?"

"Your Sergeant of the guard Sir." The General growled,

"Stay put Captain."

He strode over to the tent's entrance, waved aside his aide de camp holding the tent door open for him and disappeared. From outside, a loud series of exclamations and apologies ensued. The tent flap was flung back as fourteen Rangers scrambled into the round tent followed by the General and a red faced Sergeant Bodkins. Once they were inside, Saxton yelled "Ten Hut". The Rangers lined up facing Saxton and snapped to attention. Sherman said.

"At ease Rangers, but not you Sergeant." Bodkins remained at attention and was summarily dressed down by the General who concluded,

"And Sergeant, make sure a Sibley tent bigger than mine with all the appropriate trimmin's is set up right next to me. These men are my personal guests. I just wish I had a thousand more like 'em. That's all Sergeant." The General was grim.

"I'm sorry about that Capt'n. We don't see enough buffalos round these parts. It does make me wonder if Bodkins ever served under Sheridan."

Saxton and his men were ushered over to a map table by the General. After carefully scrutinizing the battle maps, Sherman summed up their operation. It was simplicity itself.

"Get yourselves fed and watered. Clean your guns and equipment. Write letters then disappear when I tell you. Ya hear?"

"Yes Sir, General!"

Despite the damp and cold, the Rangers were literally in the lap of luxury inside a brand new Sibley tent that the quartermaster brought them two hours earlier. At that time, a squad of black laborers began erecting it on a planked platform under orders from a jocular Quartermaster named Monty Meigs who couldn't get over the fact that a bunch of niggers were being treated like royalty. Neither could the enlisted men that surrounded them. Their amazement multiplied as three large drays pulled up. Ten black mule skinners began unloading three canvas bathtubs, a case of toiletries, fifteen cots, bedding, a cord of firewood, a cast iron stove, three barrels of fresh water, a portable latrine/shower, five sacks of vegetables, a slab of beef, a hind of salted pork and a complete kitchen fully equipped including a black cook and his helper.

A young soldier stepped forward, his blue uniform ragged, his black bootees covered in mud. He addressed Lt. Hagen.

"Who the hell are you nigger? I've never seen your kind before. It seems the General has taken a real shine to you boys." Another man crowed,

"What'd you do Buckwheat, wipe his ass and lick his boots?"

He stepped back as other soldiers around him hooted and hollered. Saxton stepped forward and grabbed the man by the collar while imitating his best version of a southern drawl.

"Now boy, you listen good, ya hear, cause I'm only gonna tell ya once."

Saxton pulled the stricken man about to face the Rangers who were helping to unload the drays. He shouted,

"Ten hut Rangers!" The men as one stopped what they were doing by dropping their loads or jumping down off the drays. They lined up in a row facing Saxton at attention. Saxton yelled, "At ease!" The soldier grimaced as Saxton hauled him before the Rangers.

"Now soldier, unless you've been deaf, dumb, blind or plain stupid; these here men are the Maasai Rangers!" He let go of the man who staggered away, disappearing into the growing mob of soldiers attracted by the commotion.

The unthinkable happened as one soldier after another stepped forward and saluted. Lieutenant Hagen yelled, "Ten Hut!" The Rangers snapped to attention again for Hagen had spotted General Grant astride his horse Fox. The General flanked by two Captains came riding their way. Saxton took his cue, spun about and saluted. Grant shouted,

"At ease Rangers! At ease! What seems to be the problem Captain Saxton?"

"The locals were curious as to who we were and what we were doing here."

"Is that so Captain? That's all well and good, for one never knows when one needs a guardian angel next to them in battle."

The General looked down on the scruffy crowd of soldiers gathered about. Suspecting their morale was shattered by their recent defeat at Chickamauga a few months earlier, he stood up in his stirrups and yelled,

"Gather round boys. These men are your guardian angels, the Maasai Rangers and their Captain John Saxton. Tomorrow on Missionary Ridge, we'll take that position and hold it." He turned and pointed down at the Rangers arrayed before him saying,

"These buffalos were at Port Hudson. Before that they captured Jeb Stuart." A soldier in the back yelled,

"But General, he got away!" Everyone laughed. The ice was broken. Grant grinned then continued.

"Yes that's true soldier but no one got away at Port Hudson." A Sergeant stepped up and said,

"That's right Gen'rl for I was there. These boys are real heroes and valiant warriors. How about it Gen'rl? Let's give 'em a right bully cheer." The soldier stepped back, saluted and yelled,

"Hip hip hurrah! Hip hip hurrah! Hip hip hurrah!"

412

John Saxton lay in a Rebel rifle pit, a sliver of shrapnel lodged deep in his left thigh. He was bleeding to death. Lieutenant Bill Hagen and two other Rangers lay near him. Where the other Rangers were, Saxton had no idea but he suspected that they were nearby. Hagen heard the Captain moan but could do nothing as the area was crawling with Cleburne's patrols. That morning General Sherman attacked what he thought was the northern end of Missionary Ridge but tragically he was mistaken. Instead the whole line was pinned down on a rocky spur completely separated from the main ridge itself. This area would be known thereafter as Billy Goat Hill.

After several hours, Saxton could still hear Rebel bullets splatter into the woods around him. He moaned again, for the pain, the thirst and the oppressive weight of the dead lying upon him were unbearable. Like a mirage, Hagen was beside him. Saxton felt the Lieutenant pull two Rebel bodies away that were partially lying upon him. Hagen looked at Saxton's bloody thigh and without saying a word bound the wound and applied a tourniquet using a broken branch and a bit of twine from his camouflage gear. Pulling a wooden canteen from his satchel, he whispered,

"Stay put skipper. Here's some water. Use it sparingly. In the meantime we'll cover you til it gets dark. Just don't move." Saxton groaned again saying,

"Don't call me skipper!"

Throughout that day, Rebel patrols wandered about but none of them spotted Saxton near death in the rifle pit. As he drifted in and out of consciousness, memories of the past twenty-four hours came back in ragged pieces, each one more horrific than the others.

Hours earlier, Saxton's Rangers advanced through thick brush and trees up a tenuous trace that petered out under a long limestone bluff. Camouflaged, they fanned out into their sniping cells. After awhile, Saxton lost track of them. Although totally alone he knew the Rangers were nearby. Above him Rebel artillery waited for the hated Blue Bellies to get even closer.

In vicious hand to hand combat, the Maasai Rangers overpowered a Rebel battery of James cannons, turned the guns about and shelled Cleburne's troops as they retreated to Tunnel Hill. However, a savage Rebel counterattack led by Terry's Texas Rangers later that day regained the lost ground but at a terrible cost. After spiking the guns, Saxton and his men retreated.

It didn't bother Saxton that Lieutenant Hagen assumed leadership of the remaining Maasai Rangers. Of all them; Hagen's temperament, physical size and leadership skills matched or nearly equaled that of the big Maasai. Saxton's reverie snapped like a twig. A voice rang out above him.

"Hey lookee here boys, it seems we've got ourselves a prison....." The man's voice exploded as a 50 caliber slug tore through his chest. He and four other Rebels on patrol nearby dropped to the ground. Three were already dead, but two were not. They jumped into the rifle pit. One crouched down beside Saxton. They other lay nearby curled up fetus-like. He screamed,

"Oh Momma, I'm dyin' sure as blazes. Oh sweet Jesus it hurts sooo bad! Sooo bad!"

He lay clutching his chest. His brown eyes looked over at Saxton pleading for help then closed for the man knew then that none was forthcoming.

His terrified companion, a feckless country boy barely into his teens, looked down on his Sergeant lying there at his feet. Blood oozed forth in black freshets from the Sergeant's mouth every time the big man took a breath. Within a few minutes the man was covered in blood, expiring of a lung shot. The boy sensed that his Sergeant didn't have much time. Saxton, delirious and disorientated reached out to the boy. The lad screamed, dropped his musket and ran up and out of the deep pit. Saxton heard a single shot then silence.

Shortly thereafter, a presence made itself known to Saxton as someone moved him into a sitting position. A trickle of cool water passed over his cracked lips then coursed down his throat. Other hands took off the tourniquet which had loosened as Saxton was too weak to keep it twisted tight. Dirty bandages came away soaked in fresh blood. A voice whispered,

"We'd better get him out of here or he'll bleed to death." Another disagreed,

"I don't think we can Bill. The Rebs are east of us and Cleburne's next counterattack is gonna hit us right here. Christ we've already lost Winston and possibly Ticky and Pete. Lieutenant what are we gonna do? We're out of ammo and surrounded." Lieutenant Hagan was blunt.

"Destroy our rifles and hide until they move on. That's an order Corporal!"

There was a long pause. Musket fire close by accompanied by men screaming like animals assaulted Saxton. A clod of dirt hit his face, awakening him from his lethargy. Saxton struggled to see, wiping his face with the tattered sleeve of his green uniform. Above the ragged rim of the log and earth rifle pit, Saxton saw two men in a deathly dance, struggling to kill the other. One was a black man dressed in a tattered butternut uniform, the other in Maasai Ranger camouflage. Both were fighting desperately to stay alive. Their violent struggle carried them headlong into the rifle pit.

For Saxton, the end had come. All the pain, the hurting and the misery of defeat had finally driven any sense of righteous purpose out of him. He closed his eyes. A warm flood of delirium swept over his broken spirit, therein a woman's voice called out to him, sensuous and familiar. His blue eyes flew open. There above him on the edge of the rifle pit stood Virginia, a white gown flowing about her black body. In her arms was Felicity. Saxton reached out crying,

"I love you, my arms will always be around you!"

A gruff voice above him laughed. Rough hands pulled him upwards. John Saxton was a prisoner of war.

END OF BOOK TWO

'RESURRECTION'

"FORGIVENESS IS THE FRAGRANCE THE
VIOLET SHEDS ON THE HEEL THAT CRUSHES IT"
Samuel Clemons, 1885

BOOK THREE: CHAPTER 1
LETTERS

"Dear Virginia and Felicity:December, 24th, 1863

"A very merry Christmas to everyone and I love you both very much. My arms are around you. Every waking moment I have, is consumed by an all encompassing love for you. I know that you're all praying for my safe return, but only God knows when I'll be home again. My fervent hope is that you are safe and well. This is my first letter to you since Chattanooga and perhaps my orderly Lucas, will get it to you by post soon enough. I'm hoping and praying that Marcus and his Rangers have safely returned home and have told you about our common dream. Oh how I ache to be with you and Felicity upon the mountain; away from war, away from the fear and the hate I see every day all around me. Both Marcus and I will go to the mountain, and like Moses with the Ten Commandments …lead the dispossessed, the victims of racism, of war to the 'promised land', a better place, a better life, a better world.

I'm now a prisoner of war, but do not burden yourself with worry for I'm being very well looked after at the General hospital here in Danville, considering the circumstances. My wounds are not serious enough to mention but it will take a while for them to mend. Lucas says that I'll probably be sent to Salisbury prison in North Carolina. At least it won't be Andersonville, that hell-hole on earth. I still have my lucky brass buckle that saved me on our honeymoon.

The doctors really have their hands full here as it is overflowing with many wounded, sick and dying young men from both sides. My friend Lucas, an orderly, tells me that he was wounded a few months ago at the battle of Chickamauga as a drummer boy for General Longstreet. Barely 15 years old, he's the only friend I have here for making friends with anyone else is temporary to say the least. You make a friend here and the next day they're dead or transferred out. As such, my one friend Lucas confided that his wounds prevented him from becoming a full-fledged soldier; however, whatever job they give him will suffice. The lad says that he's trying to find his father who's a Captain. I do hope he's successful although at times depression overcomes him as of late.

Lucas is a good looking lad; tall, with a finely chiseled tanned face and wide shoulders. The older Confederate soldiers like him although his fellow orderlies tease him unmercifully. Of course none of them have 'seen the elephant' and are useless scum, stealing from the dead, dying and even the wounded soldiers here. In many ways everyone including myself will be glad to get out of here. Lucas says there's a rumor going around the wards that we'll all be shipped out tomorrow. So my loves, parting is such sweet sorrow. Bye for now.

Lucas has arrived to change my bandages and feed me the gruel they have the nerve to call food.

Make no mistake dearest, I will survive this cruelty called war and come home safe but perhaps a little less sound after it's all over. In the meantime it is my hope that Marcus will assist you in running the Saxton Shipping Co.

Hugs and kisses...Sax.

PS: Spoil Jack for me."

Saxton folded the letter and put it in a plain brown envelop, his Boston address scrawled upon it. He licked the rim, sealing it tight. Lucas came around the corner pushing a metal meal cart before him. With a measure of some difficulty, Saxton raised himself up on his canvas cot, the envelope in his hand.

"Say Lucas, could you post this for me before they load me like a wounded cow onto the train?"

Lucas reached down, took the letter, looked at the address then tucked the envelope into his stained white tunic.

"Sure Saxton, I'll see to it. It might take some time to reach Boston though."

Saxton put the precious pencil stub under his pillow. With some measure of conviction he looked up at a tall grimy window,

"Lucas, I sincerely hope that we both survive long enough to go home to our loved ones."

The boy stood mute as a cloud passed over his face. Beside him was meal cart. Upon it squatted a round metal soup caldron. Under it on were stacks of tin bowls, cups and cutlery. Swirling about in the depths of the pot was a watery gruel flecked with yellow fat. A sour aroma assaulted the boy as he spooned a large portion of it into a battered tin bowl. Saxton took it and drank it greedily. The boy watched him then said,

"I'm worried about you Saxton. You've lost a lot of weight, too much in fact. I mean you're becoming like the rest of them."

It was true. Long rows of Union soldiers lay stretched out on either side of Saxton. Lucas once again remained silent until he was satisfied that Saxton would not throw up as he had done so earlier that morning. He took the bowl, putting it under the meal cart. Without saying a word, he turned about and finished his mealtime rounds. After a few minutes, Saxton watched him from his cot as Lucas pushed the empty meal cart down the hallway, turned a corner and disappeared.

After he left the kitchen, Lucas took Saxton's letter to the post master on the second floor. From there, any mail that made it past the censors would be taken by mail coach to an exchange area south east of Danville at Greensboro, South Carolina. It was a neutral area amongst many, where both sides exchanged prisoners and mail. Saxton's letter passed inspection after some of it had been blacked out by the censors.

The next morning was born cold and wet. After another bowl of chick-pea soup for breakfast, approximately five hundred Union soldiers deemed fit to travel, were herded to a nearby railway station. Beside it a long procession of rickety wooden cattle cars were waiting on a siding. The Piedmont Railway prison train was about to leave for Salisbury Prison, ninety miles to the south-west.

Saxton grimaced with pain as he was hoisted into a boxcar by another prisoner. Since he was one of the first to board, he spied a dark vacant corner of the boxcar. There within the shadows, a crushed, lice infested pallet of filthy grey straw was to be his bed. He was lucky. Large fly-blown honey buckets sat in every corner. His shoulder ached where a bullet wound healed, leaving a ragged scar; but a fragment of shrapnel lodged in his left thigh, throbbed painfully especially when it was cold. He hobbled over to the car's open door. A familiar voice called out to him. It was Lucas.

Saxton hung on grimly to an iron door stanchion as he looked down at the lanky young man who barely filled his dirty butternut uniform. He grimaced again in pain as the train lurched forward into a light drizzle. Lucas started to limp along side it, yelling out above the noise of the rattling boxcar.

"Hey there Saxton, I've got something for you. You might say a little goin' away present."

He shouted down at Lucas,

"And what's that my good friend? Is it a full course Christmas dinner with all the trimmings?"

"No, not at all Saxton, but I've been transferred to the Junior Reserve at Salisbury Prison. I'm catching this train too."

The locomotive wheezed then started to move slowly through a light drizzle. Saxton remained where he was. Lucas shouted over the locomotive's laborings as the train wobbled over wet twisted rails. Lucas shouted again. The old train began to pick up speed.

"By the way Saxton, I never got your last name."

"It's John Saxton of Boston, what's yours?"

"Lucas Garrow of New Orleans!"

The boxcar's slatted door slammed shut. A guard slid a heavy metal bar through an iron slot and locked it into place. A whistle blew twice. Saxton was on his way to prison.

John Saxton was crammed into a North Carolina RR cattle car along with dozens of other prisoners. After they changed trains in Greensboro, all they had to eat was one dried codfish each. The salted fish however, created a terrible thirst that was rarely slacked. It was only the beginning of Saxton's suffering. Over five hundred men were on their way to Salisbury prison. Anyone unfortunate to be near the tracks could smell the prison train if it approached them from downwind. After two days, a perfidious odor clung to Saxton's tattered green uniform. The stench seemed to resemble the dank, moldy, and somewhat sweet smell that exuded from the battleground after the dead laid there for awhile. Another prisoner, described his arrival in Salisbury by train a year later as such,

"About four o'clock we arrived in Salisbury, N.C., and we were marched through the town to the prison yard, through a cold drizzling rain which made us wet outside as we had been dry the day before. We had been two days and nights on flatcars and had had nothing to eat but the codfish. When we arrived in the yard, we were marched to a part of it where there were no tents, nothing but mud, three or four inches deep. The officer told us that it would be impossible to get us any tents or food until morning, so we would have to 'make ourselves as comfortable as possible'. What a mockery there was in that sentence! Only one in our circumstances could realize it."

Despite everything, Saxton was still in shock as the revelation that his new friend Lucas was a Garrow. The name stung like the bite of a poisonous adder. Saxton remembered that Lucas mentioned his father often. Apparently he was a Captain in the Confederate Army. The boy obviously adored his father and as such probably didn't have any inkling that his father was a vicious killer. Saxton decided to keep his thoughts to himself until he learned more. To survive the prison camp, he had to have Lucas as a friend. Besides, with Lucas as a Junior Reservist, this would certainly increase Saxton's chances of survival.

For nearly three long days, a series of standard and narrow gauge rails carried Saxton and the others towards an open grave. Because most Confederate steam engines were old, ill repaired and worn out; the prison train progressed slowly over broken, splintered and rotting railway ties at no more than eight to twelve miles an hour. These 'wheezy old engines' used double the fuel and thus frequent stops were made at wood and water stations every four or five miles. At each stop, Saxton expected Lucas to greet him but he did not. A fellow prisoner sitting next to Saxton, later wrote a diary, describing the prison train journey on the Richmond-Danville RR as such.

"During this ride we suffered for water, for the day was intensely hot, and we had nothing to get it in, but had to drink it from our hands or from holes found by the side of the track. The stations along this route are not villages such as you find on our Northern roads but consist of five or six houses dignified with a high sounding name, grand enough for a corporation. The depots are small unpainted buildings with but a few conveniences and much dilapidation."

Two days later, the foul smelling prison train crawled across the long, low Yadkin River Bridge towards the town of Salisbury, North Carolina. John Saxton peed between the slats of his cattle car into the river as the old train labored forwards. The air inside Saxton's boxcar was warmed by dozens of bodies stacked like vertical cord wood. The constant swaying of the train long ago made any sense of propriety a distant dream. Body lice infected the entire entourage. A constant scratching of head and groin only added to the torture.

The train came to a wheezing conclusion as if it had expired. Presently, loud voices were heard outside, coming ever closer. Steel on steel rang out as door after door of the long line of cattle cars was slid violently aside. A cold December breeze rushed into Saxton's squalid world expelling the humid air. Instantly, a fetid fog rose from within, clinging to the ragged men as they jumped down onto a wide wooden landing. Intense cold claimed Saxton's body as if he was wearing no clothing whatsoever.

He watched as hundreds of men stood on this platform stamping their feet, trying to get their circulation going. A clean shaven Dr. Nesbit came by. His bearded assistant began taking the names of the sick, injured or dying. These poor frozen wretches were then summarily carried by litter over a long bridge through a high wooden front gate. Others, less wounded, were given forked branches in lieu of crutches. Once these bedraggled apparitions stumbled through the prison's gate, they were led to one of three brick multi-storied hospital buildings. They squatted just to the left of the main road that ran through the middle of the encampment.

A steam whistle blew in the distance. A guard near Saxton laughed, saying,

"You lucky men have arrived just in time for lunch."

As part of the last group to leave, Saxton gathering his few possessions in a burlap sack, then he and his shivering compatriots marched double file through the tall wooden palisade towards a large four story brick building once known as the Maxwell Chambers Factory. A former cotton textile factory, it had been vacant for over twenty years. Nearly eighteen hundred prisoners; made up of turncoats, deserters, criminals of the worst kind and civilians accused of crimes against the Confederacy were crammed inside it.

A burly guard was surprisingly civil as he led Saxton's small group ever upwards to the top floor of the building. Therein, straw pallets lay upon long rows of wooden bunks set low to the floor against opposite walls. A row of dirty windows lined both sides of the narrow room which to Saxton seemed to go on forever. A large multi-paned window was set into a tall red brick wall that formed an arch at either end. Ragged pieces of laundry hung about the windows on thin ropes.

Saxton was shown his pallet. His name, rank and unit were taken by a pencil-necked junior clerk. The young man shook his head in bewilderment as Saxton told him he was a Maasai Ranger Captain.

"What do you mean, a Maasai Ranger?" Saxton laughed as a few men gathered around him.

"Well let's put it this way sir. I fought for the Union as John Mosby fought for you."

The clerk was nonplussed. He persisted, somewhat irritated, as the husky guard standing next to him called for quiet. The clerk continued aggressively, looking up at Saxton. He hissed.

"Were you a spy or a sharpshooter sir? If so, I must tell you Blue Belly that your life here will be precarious to say the least." Saxton threw his gunny sack on his pallet.

The clerk backed away sharply as Saxton turned, grabbed him by the lapels with both hands and growled.

"Don't threaten me sir. I served my country in battle and my wounds are provenance of it."

Saxton looked down disdainfully upon the weasel-faced clerk. He pushed him backwards onto a nearby pallet. The clerk lay there ashen faced. Saxton growled,

"You Sir, have probably have never heard of Mosby's Raiders, have you?"

The callow clerk stood, brushed off his frock suit and shook his head while the guard behind him laughed. Saxton continued; his anger barely suppressed.

"Now sir, finish your duties and leave us be."

With that said, Saxton winked at the guard who smiled as the clerk quickly took the names of all the new men. Within minutes he finished and as he left, Saxton knew that he had shamed the man. His sense of foreboding evaporated as his fellow prisoners eagerly crowded around him. They'd found their leader.

That very first evening at the prison, one of Saxton's roommates, a much older man, introduced himself. He offered Saxton a cheroot stub. He was John L. Ham of the 32nd and 31st Maine. In a clipped New England accent, he whispered,

"I imagine Captain that you may want to know the layout of the place seein' how you're holed up in it. They all do the virgins I mean, how about you?" Ham offered Saxton a match.

Saxton lit his cheroot and agreed. After a few moments of sizing Saxton up, John Ham warmed to his task. Both he and Saxton sat at a rough table next to a small window. Saxton knew that if he listened carefully, any information Ham gave him could be very important in an uncertain future. John Ham commenced to draw a map with a forefinger on a frosted window pane. From time to time he would stab at it to emphasize a point.

"This large brick building here is flanked on the Northeast and North sides by six small brick boarding houses right here; these are about thirty by sixty feet, and one and a half story. In this square thus formed is a natural grove of white oak trees. The grove comprises about one acre in extent… Immediately east and about thirty feet distant right here is a large wooden building used as a prison for political prisoners from the vicinity."

He paused, lit a cheroot stub then continued remarking all the information he'd already talked about. Saxton watched. Ham continued drawing, stabbing the drawing with a gloved forefinger from time to time. The room's temperature was barely above freezing. Ham's breath hung in the still airs like that of a dying man.

"Between these buildings here, is a very deep well used formerly to supply water for steam for the factory engine. The water in this well is very nasty and wholly unfit for use. It's bricked up-that is, its sides are laid in brick. The cook house is at the south end of the armory here and adjoining the same. The stockade runs along beside this building here, but only about thirty or fifty feet distant."

After Ham finished, he wiped off the window with his sleeve. Saxton sat back on his chair very sure that Ham was planning an escape. Saxton told him to count him in. John Ham laughed,

"Look Captain, escapes are a dime a dozen round here. Very few prisoners succeed and if they do, the locals shoot 'em all. No Sir, the war will be over soon enough. Besides you limp like a wounded duck. How far do ya think you'll get? No Captain, others say conditions here are pretty good compared to other prisons. My advice; stay put and wait."

A few days later, Saxton was assigned to the prison workshop where he repaired furniture, made harnesses, shoes, gunstocks and whiskey barrels of all types and sizes. The winter of 1863-64 was harsh but tolerable. The routine of imprisonment beset but his quarters were bearable and his room mates even more so. One of them, a George Gillingham, wryly remarked that Salisbury prison,

"was more endurable than any other part of Rebeldom."

Every one kept to themselves although as a group they played baseball, performed in the prison theatrical troupe and generally looked out for each others welfare.

Located in Rowan County, Salisbury Prison itself covered sixteen rolling acres surrounded by an eight foot high wooden stockade. The guards were mostly men of the Senior Reserve; being forty-five years or older, conscripted from various regiments; mainly the Gibbs and the Howard's. They were quartered in the Garrison House on East Bank St. near the prison along with the Junior Reserve guards. The latter were just young boys like Lucas Garrow, some of whom were barely able to hold a musket. At eleven dollars a month and a bounty of one hundred dollars for every prisoner they shot trying to escape; guard duty was not a popular occupation. But to many like Lucas, it was better than facing a wall of hot lead in some cornfield far from home.

In an interminable ritual, the prison guards walked along a wide catwalk between the thirteen sentry posts overlooking the prison yard. Two cannons guarded the front gate, while a third looked over the prison yard. A bridge forty yards long connected it to the prison's train station. Just inside the prison's thick plank walls was a trench, three feet wide and two feet deep called the 'deadline'. Anyone caught between it and the wall was shot. Dispersed amongst the numerous tall red brick buildings were groves of great oaks providing welcome shade in the summer and copious amounts of acorns in the fall.

Three dilapidated cookhouses along the north wall produced enough food for everyone although at times the quality was suspect and as time went by, seemed to be getting more meager by the day. Fresh meat was scarce. The usual meal was Indian cornbread and a weak cowpea soup. A garden of over two acres lay just outside the prison walls. It grew a wide variety of crops; namely corn, potatoes, turnips, beans and yams. However, the yield was low due to theft by those few prisoners lucky enough to be assigned to its care.

Salisbury Prison was one of two dozen large Confederate prisoner of war camps. Each one was different in terms of location, types of prisoners and capacity, but all of them were by late 1863, becoming more like concentration camps as thousands of new prisoners were crammed into them. A year later, Dante's inferno would pale in comparison beside these hell holes of human degradation and infinite misery. In the fall of 1864, the deadly trio of diarrhea, pellagra, dysentery and malnutrition became rampant at Salisbury. Groups of men carrying enameled chamber pots were constantly scurrying towards a long row of stinking latrines set back against the long south-west wall. A yellow fecal soup ran into a wide ditch that eventually through gravity alone, found its way into a nearby slow moving creek.

One day in early April of 1864, shortly after supper, Saxton was painfully making his way up the outside staircase towards his pallet in the attic far above him. As he approached the third floor landing, he paused to rub his thigh. Out of the blue, a muffled voice just above him cried out,

"Help me, someone please help me, I'm being robbed." A scream pierced the darkness.

A door above Saxton burst open. Two men rushed down the stairs. One of them tried to brush Saxton aside then cursed as Saxton moved to block his way. The man growled.

"Get out of our way man or I'll shank ya sure!"

Saxton reacted instantly. His training as a Ranger in hand to hand combat was instinctive. In a flash, the assailant's knife clattered down the steps behind him. Saxton struck the smaller man's arm with the side of his hand. With the other, he gripped the man by his collar and threw him over his shoulder. The man screamed as his body flew over the railing. His anguish continued for what seemed an eternity before he smashed into the muddy ground three floors below. Saxton had no time to react before the other man recovered enough to attack him. Both men struggled violently. Within seconds, the ruckus was being watched by dozens of men above and below them. Unknowingly, Saxton had come across two guards who were busily robbing the weak and the newly dead, while the rest of the able-bodied were away at dinner or at work.

The two combatants danced down the stairs, to the second floor landing. The larger man was built like a bull and his strength born of desperation was immense. As much as Saxton tried, he could not overcome his opponent. Shrapnel in his left thigh was proving to be an impediment. Finally he collapsed onto the landing with the other man upon him. Saxton's last vestiges of strength within him expired as if a dam had burst. A dark veil settled upon him. He lost consciousness. The voices of those about him faded into the distance. Once more he was spiraling ever downwards, this time surrounded by white slaves, their mouths wide open, silently screaming for help as their iron chains carried them ever deeper into a world of total blackness.

BOOK THREE: CHAPTER 2
THE DEVIL'S SPAWN

Saxton woke up delirious with pain. A bloody bandage covered his face so that only his eyes and mouth were visible if at all. He seemed to be floating above his body looking down upon himself lying prostrate on a straw pallet. His eyes opened. Someone quite close to him remarked,

"Hey boys, the Captain's awake; I think he's come to. Took a nasty blow on the head he did. Bloody guard never gave him a chance. Thank God he killed the other one! That Tom Stone was a brutal bastard to be sure. Good riddance I'd say. Whadda ya say boys! Let's get some water into him right quick or we'll lose 'im fer sure."

Saxton coughed as many hands lifted him up putting his back to the wall. To Saxton, It felt awfully good to be sitting up as the freezing brick wall worked as a count point to the hot fever that burned within him. Someone carefully pulled the dirty bandages away from his mouth to funnel some tepid water down his parched throat. Cool liquid flowed into him like a river flowing over a desert wasteland, cracked and hardened by an insufferable sun. Saxton's mind began to awaken his senses. The realization of where he was and what he had done startled him. Through swollen lips he whispered,

"Hi boys, seems I've been away for a while. It is nice to be back amongst the living."

Some men laughed as more water came flowing into him. He sputtered, gasping for air saying,

"Take it easy boys, I don't want to drown, just starve to death. Christ I'm hungry enough to eat a horse and chase the rider. Is there anything edible round here?"

Someone held a spoon to his mouth. Saxton involuntarily swallowed warm and thick, cowpea gruel. Another joked,

"Take it easy Curry or you'll choke him to death right quick. Remember, he's a northern boy, so no cornbread or he'll get diarrhea for sure. Christ almighty, he's been out for nearly a week, layin' there like he was dead. Lucky thing George here was laid up or the bastards woulda thought the Captain was dead then they woulda buried him fer sure; right Krugler?"

More soup went into Saxton until finally he waved the ever present tin spoon away. Saxton looked about and realized he was on his bunk up in the attic. He said,

"Looks like I'm in big trouble boys. I think I killed a guard. Did I really or have I been dreamin'? What about it?" Bill Richards, a big broad faced Irishman bent over him.

"Yes Capt'n, you kilt Tom Stone. Threw him down over the staircase railin' you did. The other guard beat you until you were unconscious. They killed Johnny. We were just comin' back from supper, heard the rumpus, rushed up the stairs and pulled him off ya right quick we did. The prison scuttlebutt says that Major Gilmore won't be puttin' you into solitary confinement down by the latrines just yet, until you're well enough to really suffer some."

The men laughed again as if the irony of the situation was too much. He continued,

"Yep, those two guards robbed and kilt one of the men on the third floor. You just happened to be at the wrong place at the wrong time. But the guard who injured you Capt'n was one of the Salisbury Ranger gang. Saxton looked up,

"Who are they?"

Bill Richards leaned over and patted Saxton's hand.

"Now don't you worry none Capt'n. We'll take care of the bastard ourselves if Commander Turner doesn't. Besides, he'll probably hang Stone's accomplice anyways as Turner doesn't take too kindly to muggers and killers here. Who's to say what the next Commander will do with you, especially if your still alive n' all!" He looked around then back at Saxton.

"Gilly here says, youse bin talkin' in your sleep ever since you got here; somethin' about startin' a village for black and white folks on the top of some mountain top in Tennessee. Why, if I might say so Captain, the idea seems real interestin' to all of us. Sorta got our curiosity roused you might say. Never heard of such an idea before especially durin' the war n' all. When you git better, tell us all about it Capt'n. It's not enough that we survive this place but if we do, it would be kinda nice to dream about somethin' other than food, don't ya think so men?"

The eight men standing and sitting nearby all agreed. The next day, Saxton, somewhat refreshed, spent the better part of an hour telling the men about the dream. After he was finished, he invited them all to join him on Elder Mountain after the war was over. One thanked him saying,

"Yeah Captain, it'll be real nice to have somethin' to think about other than food for once." He paused,

"By the way Capt'n, some young pip-squeak of a guard's bin askin' about ya in the yard. Seems he's a friend of yours named Lucas Garrow. He wants to see ya real bad; somethin' about you and his father. He wouldn't say any more. I think he'll come up here tomorrow or tonight sometime. Perhaps, after I tell him, you can talk some, if it's ok with you."

Saxton became uneasy. The man continued as he stood up holding an empty tin bowl and spoon in his big hands.

"Seems strange though, a white Creole kid here in a southern prison pullin' down guard duty. Doesn't seem natural does it but come to think of it there are a few coloreds workin' here?" Saxton's eyes widened then he fell fast asleep.

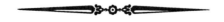

Horatio Armstrong Garrow or Edward Dawkins, as those other than his immediate circle knew him, sat in a booth behind its thick privacy curtains. The gloomy confines of McSorley's Old Ale House in the East Village of New York City had become a favorite haunt for him and his gangsters. It was St. Patrick's Day, 1864. Boss Tweed, the 'Sachem of Tammany Hall', was holding court in another, larger private booth directly across from Garrow. Tweed's cronies were drunk; singing a rousing and bawdy version of "When Johnny comes marching home again". However the lyrics had been altered to 'When Jenny comes to my bed again.' Gales of laughter swept across the darkened interior of the Old Ale House as newer verses, crude yet humorous regaled the denizen's within its cheery confines.

Long strands of green crepe paper bunting decorated every booth while large green banners emblazoned with various Gaelic greetings and salutations hung here and there from the tavern's low oak rafters. A buxom raven haired harpist strummed Irish folk tunes in one corner. Across from her, three young and brawny bartenders in green shirts and trousers poured a river of green beer in to rows of pewter mugs lined up on an immense mahogany bar. While the merriment in the pub was in full voice, the opposite was true in the street outside.

The perennial St. Patrick's Day parade down 5th Avenue had been cancelled once again; the last one being in 1862. The Civil War by early 1864 had claimed too many Irish Americans such as those enlisted in the Irish Brigade. The 'Fighting Irish' or 69th New York Infantry was one of five regiments in the Brigade. Casualties had been high. At the battle of Fredericksburg in December of 1862, the casualty rate was nearly ninety percent. From September, 1861 to March of 1864, the 'Fighting Irish' fought in ten major campaigns from Bull Run to Gettysburg. It was from the survivors of the Irish Brigade that Garrow recruited his gang based in the Five Points area of New York City. It was a paradox indeed that Garrow chose to ignore the fact that many of his acolytes were deserters.

The previous June, Garrow and Blackstone arrived in New York City from Boston just in time for the draft riots of July. Despite his initial rejection by Boss Tweed, Garrow's smuggling ring quickly became a success and more importantly, it became feared for its ability to kill anyone or anything that stood in its way. After awhile, even Tweed gave up trying to reign in his newest competitor. The immense port proved to be a profitable location for Garrow. Within months, he bullied, beat or murdered many of his rivals. Horatio not Tweed had become the undisputed king of the city's war time smugglers; controlling over eighteen hundred miles of waterfront docks and warehouses. His fast fleet of steam cutters ran copious loads of medical supplies, ammunition and guns down the Atlantic seaboard to various Confederate ports from North Carolina to Florida. He also acquired numerous 'safe houses' to hide himself, his gang and newly enlisted deserters whether they were 'galvanized' or not.

Pinkerton agents and others had tried unsuccessfully to infiltrate the gang. When found out, no mercy was shown to those who betrayed, informed or double-crossed Garrow. It seemed that every other day, another mutilated body was pulled from the East River by the Harbor Patrol. Although a deserter himself, Horatio was still dedicated to the Confederacy for a price of course. As the Union's blockade tightened its grip on the throat of Rebeldom, Garrow found new and innovative ways to thwart any attempts to stop him. He did so by bribing politicians, Customs Officers, Station Masters, Conductors, toll road patrols, Policemen, Judges, riverboat Captains, sea Captains and locomotive Engineers. His new gang was much bigger than the Deacon gang of old. Garrow knew that when the war was over, the smuggling had to be replaced with something. Therefore he began to diversify his various business interests. Prostitution, loan sharking, kidnapping, bank robbery, counterfeiting and blackmailing became his stock in trade. Despite being at the top of his game, he was lacking two things; namely the whereabouts of his son Lucas and Belle Brown.

Thus, while he was carousing with three nubile prostitutes from St. Nick's, his heart burned with revenge and lust at the same time. It had been two years since he last wrote a letter to Lucas whom he'd learned was a drummer boy for General James Longstreet. After escaping from the Howard Groves Hospital in Richmond, Virginia, with Harley Blackstone; his son's trail had gone cold. Lately though by using his extensive criminal connections, he learned that Lucas had been severely wounded at the Battle of Chickamauga in September of 1863. From there on, he didn't have a clue as to where Lucas had been transferred or buried for that matter.

Thus Horatio sat in the dimly lit private booth at McSorley's Old Ale House, with one hand grasping a large jug of beer and the other caressing an even larger one. The conversation turned from the ludicrous to the sensational. One of the working girls sitting next to him; a busty redhead, blurted out that she and five other girls were running a very lucrative escort service out of the St. Nicholas Hotel. Their pimp was the concierge, a diminutive Frenchman by the name of Piree Lafite. The redhead was obviously inebriated enough to keep talking. She had Horatio's undivided attention as she whispered in his ear.

"Eddie, if I may call you that my Dearrr. LIfe had been wonderful ever since myself and the other girrrls were nearly burned alive two years ago in New Orleans, Our Madam. Belle Brown, her husband, their two sons and their Irish Nanny barely made it to the levee."

She paused, removed his hand from her ample breast and sat back seemingly quite serious about the whole affair. Another flagon of strong ale passed her rouged lips as she contemplated what she was about to say next. Throwing caution to the wind, the tattler simpered,

"My girrrl friend Rebecca was shot dead. Only God knows how our ship ever escaped past the Rebel forts and river patrols guardin' the Big Muddy. Never did find out who tried to burn down Laaa Belle Maison either. However after maaanny weeks at sea, we arrived here safe and sound. Our Madam bought us all new outfits and us set up at St. Nick's where we've bin ever since. I still get letters from her ya know, tellin' us all the latest news. The letters come in regular like on the Saxton ships especially foooor us. We girls and Belle go back a loooong way you know. That nice nigger lady always treated us like family she did considerin' what we were really doin' there.

Garrow pulled her close. He poured the trollop another mug of ale. The woman was enjoying his steadfast attentions, now quite oblivious to her inner warnings about him. She said,

"It's verrry sad you know that Marcus Brown lost an arm in battle and that his best friend John Saxton is in Salisbury prison. Why we just got one letter from him laaaast week. Apparently he's aaall healed up after bein' in Daaanville General Hospital for awhile. Seems he met a new friend there who was wounded too. It is interesting how the two got together even though he's just a boooy and a Rebel too."

Horatio's interest by now was severely piqued. He held the strumpet even closer, while saying solicitously,

"My dear girl, I must say you've been most entertaining indeed. Did your Madam ever tell you that Lucas, her son, was from an affair she had years ago?"

The redhead put down her drink and looked at him sharply saying,

"My deaarr Eddie, how did you know that she had a son working at Salisbury prison?"

He looked deeply into her blood shot eyes and said evenly,

"I know because you told me so. I'm the boy's father."

The redhead recoiled from him as if he was the devil incarnate. She cried out, "Oh my God, you're Horatio Garrrow. You're the one that raped Belle and burned down Laaa Belle Maison!"

She struggled to get away but he held her fast sensing that she knew even more than she was letting on. Garrow pulled back the curtains and signaled Harley sitting in a far corner by the tavern's large buckshot front windows. He rose up, a brute of a man and shuffled across the saloon's sawdust covered floor towards Garrow. The harlot saw him and screamed as Harley grabbed her by the hair and dragged her kicking and yelling across the room. Blackstone let go. He then slapped her hard with one hand then stifled her screams with the other. Garrow paid for the drinks and hurried after the duo followed by his associates. The remaining harlots in Garrow's booth looked on in horror at the commotion. One in particular, sitting with Tweed was incensed. Upon pulling back the privacy drapes, a frightful scene was revealed to her. She was a black girl named Beulah Montgomery and she swore she'd kill Garrow one day. Boss Tweed upon seeing 'Blackie' dragging the redhead towards the front door, laughed out loud,

"Hey Blackstone, treat her like a lady!"

Garrow tipped his black derby and disappeared through the swinging front doors.

Another corpse was found in the East River the next day. It was that of a redheaded prostitute. Her alias was Naomi Devine, a well known escort who worked out of the St.

Nicholas Hotel on Broadway. After the cadaver had been pulled out of the river, one reporter described it as such.

"The body looked as white, as full, as polished as the purest marble, The perfect figure, the exquisite limbs, fine face, the full arms, the beautiful bust, all surpassed, in every respect, the Venus de Medici....For a few moments I was lost in admiration of the extraordinary sight...I was recalled to her horrid destiny by seeing the dreadful bloody gashes on the right temple."

Everyone living in the Five Points slums heard soon enough that Boss Tweed was not pleased with Major Garrow. Naomi Devine had been one of Tweed's favorite escorts. Thereafter any truce between Tweed and Garrow started to cool noticeably. No longer were the two seen together at social functions where the city's elite gathered to curry favors from and pay homage to the Sachem of Tammany Hall. The absence of Garrow at these functions was a sure sign to everyone else that the 'unfortunate one' had to be shunned in every way. Garrow's rage was finely honed like a surgeon's scalpel. Former threats were resumed and soon many of Tweed's inner circle were found floating face down in the Haarlem River. Tweed himself began to fear the tall psychopath who ruled the docks with an iron fist and had a penchant for killing without remorse.

Eventually, the two warlords came to a mutual understanding. Through intermediaries, they agreed to another truce for the simple reason that both of them were losing money, a lot of money. Garrow agreed to split the profits from his activities within the city limits equally with Tweed. In return William Marcy Tweed agreed to facilitate any expansion of Garrow's smuggling enterprise after the war ended. The Major also agreed to never oppose or interfere with Tweed's political aspirations then or ever. In return, Horatio was reintroduced into the social good graces of the city's elite as Tweed's equal. With that settled, the Major decided to bring Lucas to New York City as sole heir to his vast empire. To that end, he had to avoid detection.

His failure to obtain Alfred Nobel's new explosive formulae made him a wanted man by none other than his nemesis Allan Pinkerton, America's most famous detective. Coupled with that burden, a very persistent New Orleans police Sergeant, Milford Raines was still after him for multiple murders, rape and robbery. Desertion and murder were just a few of the crimes that the Confederacy wanted him for as well. Because of the incessant need to avoid capture, Garrow and his acolyte Blackstone never spent more than a few days in any of the 'safe' houses. Garrow, through sheer necessity became a master of disguise and deception. Despite being tall and Blackstone being a brute, both men became adept at changing their appearance. A hunch backed banker, an itinerant preacher, a priest, a sea Captain and even an undertaker were but a few of Garrow's personas. With every disguise other than being clean shaven; he sported a fake beard, a wig, mutton-chop sideburns or a clipped moustache. Blackstone was less able to disguise himself but often portrayed himself as a deaf mute, stable hand or carriage driver. A priest in a billowing black cassock was his favorite guise. These skills so necessary for his devious deceptions were learned under the expert auspices of one of Garrow's many mistresses, Lois Turner of the Wallach Theater.

In time as the empire of evil grew, Blackstone ran the criminal empire while Garrow concentrated on smuggling contraband to the Confederacy. To rescue Lucas from Salisbury prison and kill Saxton-Brown became an obsession. This obsession had to be requited soon, before Lucas died of disease in prison or more importantly, before Saxton revealed Garrow's true criminal past to him. The ultimate accusation of desertion however, continued to hang over Horatio like the sword of Damocles, although strangely enough his gang was comprised solely of deserters. Horatio, always a practical man, had to act fast. To retrieve his son from prison, it had to be someone totally dedicated to the 'cause'; someone who could pull it off without a hitch. After thinking for a few moments, Garrow knew of only one person who could do it and that person was BB. But upon reading a local paper the next day, he found out that she was currently imprisoned in Fort Monroe, Virginia. No, he sadly concluded, he would have to get Lucas out prison himself and take his chances doing it.

A few months later, Saxton was reading a copy of the Salisbury Post dated May 17th, 1863. As he sat beside a crude pine table on a hickory chair, he angled the torn paper under the light of a coal-oil lantern hanging from the ceiling. The newspaper was filled with stories about the war and how the Confederacy won the battle of Chancellorsville the week before. General Lee would certainly reach Philadelphia for sure as one article after another gushed about the genius of Lee and his repertoire of victorious Generals. Stonewall Jackson, Jeb Stuart, Mosby's Rangers and others were all described as true stalwarts of the Southern Cross. Nothing was said about the effects of the Union blockade. However, little things caught his attention.

Wedding banns were announced. Church services were scheduled and local news and events portrayed a busy social calendar for the inhabitants of North Carolina's fourth largest city of approximately two thousand souls. It seemed as if the unreality of war claimed the paper's front pages while the commonplace realities of life inhabited the rear of it. Saxton preferred the mundane.

He roused himself, easing over on his good leg to relieve the pressure on his injured one. Shrapnel imbedded deep within him, had a bad habit of grating against his thigh bone. Dr. Nesbit told him that one day it might eventually work itself free and drop down his pant leg like a coin through a hole in his trousers. How interesting indeed. Saxton spent the rest of the evening watching his fellow room-mates go about their daily routines. Some played cards on their straw pallets while others argued about whether or not to desert and become 'Galvanized' Yankees. Rumors abounded that nearly two thousand Union prisoners had already done; some even twice. Others in Saxton's group had been sharpshooters and were deathly afraid they would be found out and summarily executed. As one prisoner sitting next to him put it,

"Sharpshooters are not likely often to be taken prisoner, as death is considered their just penalty; for as they very seldom are in a position to show mercy, so, in like manner, is mercy rarely shown to them."

Saxton listened politely but kept his mouth shut, for at the battle of Goat Hill, his snipers held off a Rebel counterattack until they ran out of ammunition. He'd heard Hagan tell the other Maasai Rangers to destroy their rifles before being captured or shot dead. Later Saxton learned that General Patrick Cleburne, commander of the Confederate forces opposing them,

"Was very mad at them for not surrendering, instead holding out to the last against such odds."

Saxton was pleased indeed but haunted by the deaths of his fellow Rangers. He learned later from another survivor of that battle, that their bodies were never found. Saxton shuddered as he could only guess what the enemy did to them. Saxton painfully rose to go to his straw pallet for he still faced the odious task of using the bedpan and looking for lice in Gillingham's long hair. Just as Saxton grabbed his hickory cane, a voice behind him caught his immediate attention. In a thick southern drawl, it spit out a venomous indictment. "I'm goin' to kill you John Saxton. I'm goin' to kill you!"

The attic garret went deathly quiet as a boy's voice screamed again, "I'm gonna kill you John Saxton!"

Saxton turned to face his accuser. There before him stood Lucas Garrow, a Colt .44 in one hand and a letter in the other. The boy and the man stood a few feet apart. The boy's black eyes pleaded for Saxton to say something, anything that would make the pain go away. His gun wavered like a willow in the wind while the letter was thrust forward like a declaration of war. Before the boy knew it, Saxton's walking cane came up in a blur knocking the boy's gun to the floor. Gillingham sprang forward and pinned the boy to the wall as the other inmates recovered from their shock. Lucas struggled mightily but could do nothing. Two men raised him up facing Saxton who bent down and picked up the letter. After reading it, he said,

"I do believe Lucas that your father, Major Horatio Garrow has found you. I can't say I'm happy for you because he's a deserter, rapist and a murderer." Lucas screamed,

"That's not true, you lyin' bastard. It's because of you that he was thrown wounded and dying into the Hudson River."

Saxton smiled which enraged Lucas even more. He spit at Saxton as the two men holding him had their hands full. Saxton wiped the spittle from his face, turned about and said,

"George, go get some clothesline, tie him up and gag him. This might take all night but the truth will out."

Lucas was tied up. A cotton gag was stuffed into his mouth. Lucas was sat down by a table while Saxton sat down directly across from him. Hatred and fear played a duet across the boy's butternut face. He watched as his father's letter passed around the room. Each man there read it nodding occasionally before they in turn passed it on. As they did so, Lucas seemed to deflate as if the odium inside him that struggled mightily to get out was finally released in one mighty gasp. Lucas slumped over, his head between his knees. Saxton reached over and lifted the boy's head up to witness his father's indictment.

"Lucas, the letter is full of lies and George Krugler here will confirm it. Go ahead George, tell him what you know; you were there, you saw it all. Besides, the boy needs the truth from someone other than me."

A stolid man, George Krugler took a chair and sat down next to the stricken youth. His Bavarian accent thickened his speech in a guttural sort of way that made a mockery of the English language. However, as he spoke, his sincerity and honesty were unmistakable. The story he told shocked everyone to the core, and for a long time thereafter. His words, simple in their delivery, accurately conveyed the horrific series of events that occurred aboard the SS Anaona above and below its decks after he and others boarded it. His revelation concluded with the words,

"Gott in Himmel! The major was a devil. I and the others threw him into the Hudson River. I'm glad we did Lucas."

Another inmate came forward, then another and another until the evidence of Horatio's evil career became too much to bear. It seemed he'd cut quite a swath of destruction before and during the war, some of which even Saxton had been quite ignorant of. The whole exorcism appalled him. Finally, he took off the gag and untied Lucas. However, Bill Richards kept the Colt leveled at the young boy. Lucas looked away ashamed at what had been revealed. All the hope and expectations of a grand reunion with his father vanished as each word of evidence was like another nail being driven into a fresh coffin. Lucas was literally shriven in two. On one side was the truth and on the other were lies disguised to look like the truth. It was not over for Lucas. He reasoned that he must face his father, if not he would never be free of his father's past. Saxton gave the lad a cup of water. As the boy drank it, Saxton looked down saying,

"Gilly, light the lamps will you. It's getting dark. Christ it's nearly curfew." He turned back to the boy.

"Lucas, where did you get the letter?" No response.

Who gave it to you?" Again there was no response.

Where's the envelope?" Silence.

Was there a city of origin postmark on it?"

The boy put the empty tin cup upon the table then looked up at the gaunt men standing around him. Lucas wiped his mouth with the soiled sleeve of his field jacket.

"I got it from my Sergeant down at the guard shack. There was no envelope. I think he said that it had been given to him by a Captain Ben Wallace." He paused, took another sip of water and continued his spirit refreshed.

"Yes, I remember now, it's the Chief Clerk. My Sarge said he had a letter for me from my father."

The boy looked about him, trying to come to grips with his emotions. He cried,

"Why, I haven't seen or heard from him for nearly two years. The last time was a letter I got when he was lying in Howard Groves hospital in Richmond. Said he'd bin knifed by a seven foot nigger aboard a ship called the Anaona. He went on to say that another man, John Saxton led a boarding party killing his men. My father also stated that, after being terribly wounded, he was thrown into the Hudson River to drown."

Lucas looked at Saxton, his eyes narrowing in hate. The words spit out of his mouth like bullets,

"When I saw your name in my father's letter I couldn't believe it." He glared at Saxton then stammered, the words spilling out like water through a broken dam.

"Why didn't you stop them from throwing my father overboard?

Why didn't you take him as a prisoner of war?

Why did you leave to die in the river?"

George Krugler walked over, pushed Saxton aside, reached down and grabbed the boy roughly by the shoulders.

"Look here Jungling, Captain Saxton had nuttink to do vith it. Jawol mien Herr, we cadets threw him into the river, not Marcus or Saxton. Gottdammerung kinder, don't you understand? Your father was a terrible man, a teufel. Gott en himmel!"

George let the boy go then backed away, completely frustrated by the boy's obstinacy. The letter lay upon the table beside him like a poison pen letter. Saxton wasn't going to tell the boy at that moment that his father murdered Mary McPherson, Belle's nanny at La Belle Maison, or that he strangled Hans Larsen in Boston. No, he would wait for a better time and place to reveal the evil incarnate of Horatio the devil. Saxton he hoped the thoughts inside the boy's head would tumble forth revealing his true feelings. His silence was unnerving but Saxton continued, leaning across the table towards him, his voice insistent.

"Lucas, let me know if you get any other letters from your father. If he finds out that Krugler and I are here, he will kill us for sure." Saxton grabbed the boy's shoulders and shook him.

"Do you understand me Lucas? He must NEVER find out we're here or he'll have it arranged that everyone here in this group will die! I must tell you now Lucas that your father ran a smuggling gang in New Orleans called the Deacon boys. They murdered, raped and tortured many innocent people all over the South before the war started. God only knows if some of his gang survived. Maybe some of them work here, God forbid! You have to understand that all these men, if they survive the war are going back to their families who love them. What about your family Lucas? Do you have any brothers, sisters, grandparents, aunts or uncles to go back to? Is your mother still alive? Lucas recoiled, breaking away from Saxton. Krugler pushed him back down. Wrapped in the coils of total despair, Lucas cried.

"My father told me that no one's left alive, no one; only him!"

The boy put his head in his hands and began to sob uncontrollably. His thin body shuddered violently as if the spasms within were caused by his conscious mind struggling with the realization that he was utterly and irrevocably alone. Finally, he calmed down and asked for more water. Instead, George Johnson standing behind Saxton looked at Gillingham and said,

"Say Gilly, still got some of that moonshine left? I dare say the lad needs a nip before he's tucked into bed."

The men rocked with laughter as Gillingham retrieved a small brown jug from under his straw pallet. He sauntered back to Lucas, uncorked it and poured a few ounces into a tin cup. Lucas choked on the fiery brew. Johnson patted him on the back saying jovially,

"That's it Lucas. The hair of the dog is what ye need let alone the hair of a willin' woman."

Again laughter rocked the garret. Lucas grinned and took another swallow. This time he didn't choke. Saxton took the cup and Gillingham filled it up and so everyone had a nip from the little brown jug until it was empty. The shrill sounds of a curfew bugle ineptly played, shattered their revelry. Lucas was given back an empty Colt .44 and his father's letter. Saxton heard the boy's boots stomping down the wooden staircase as the lamps were extinguished. He grimaced, for his straw pallet awaited. To Saxton and the other prisoners, it seemed that their living hell was evenly balanced between night and day. Fiery stings of insatiable bedbugs started to inflame his groin. He cursed, remembering that he'd forgotten to pick lice from Gilly's hair. In an instant thereafter, John Saxton began dreaming about past Christmas dinners in the mansion on Snow Hill.

Lucas woke up the next morning, his head throbbing from the rot-gut whiskey of the night before. He groaned as the Irish Sergeant of the guard prodded his prostrate body with the square toe of his boot. It was still quite dark outside.

"Come on laddie. Up you get now. No time for dreamin' bout some sweet colleen back home son. We've got to eat and start guard duty quick enough. You'll be patrollin' the 'deadline' again today. Remember boy, shoot first then ask questions later."

The barrel-chested older man laughed as a near naked Lucas limped to a row of crude log latrines squatting just outside his barracks. Once that odious chore was finished, Lucas dressed quickly, grabbed his Enfield musketoon and made his way to the cookhouse. 'Dickie' Brackston, the scrawny cook's helper was from Kentucky and he was in his usual foul mood. He grabbed a tin plate from Lucas.

"God all mighty boy it's gittin' worse every day. How's we gonna feed everyone? Why more Blue Bellies are acomin' in by the train load every month. There's less food for us and our boys. The damn Yankees are tryin' to starve us out. We've got to whip 'em good while we still can. The war's goin' agin' us boy, agin us fer sure. Better eat all you can Luke, cause it's gonna get worse before it git's any better."

After Lucas hurriedly ate his plate of grits and corn bread, he hobbled over the prison bridge, through the main gate then across the wide expanse of the prison yard. Once through an expansive grove of white oaks, his post high up on the stockade wall awaited. A long row of open latrines had been erected close by. Lucas limped painfully up the plank stairs to the catwalk above. He gagged as a slight breeze wafted the latrine's offensive odors towards him. This post was always given to the Junior Reserve. The older guards of the Senior Reserve detested it, refusing to patrol anywhere near it. Lucas looked down upon the 'deadline' hour after hour while his thoughts about his father's letter and what it meant festered within him. Occasionally he would take it out of his breast pocket to read it, trying to make sense of it. Every word was burned into his brain, for they lay heavy upon him like molten lead in a bullet mold.

"Dear Lucas: I do hope this letter gets to you safely. It has been sometime since we last talked to each other. I've was promoted to Major shortly after the capture of Fort Sumter. I understand you've been wounded at Chickamauga and are convalescing in Danville Hospital. My prayers are for your full recovery. After which, I might suggest you join the Junior Reserve guards. They're all young lads like you who are too young to fight or have been sorely wounded. I know that the righteousness of our common cause still burns within you as it does me. Our whole lives thus far have been dedicated to one mission, the salvation of the Confederacy. I am well and trying to get desperately needed supplies to our brave soldiers fighting the damn Yankees. It is secretive work and therefore very dangerous for me and my loyal companions. Therefore I cannot tell you where I am but if all else fails, remember this; I do love you and no matter what anyone might say to the contrary, I am serving my country well.

The food you eat; the clothes you wear and the weapons you fight with have more than likely slipped through the Yankee blockade because of me and thousands of other brave men who risk death upon the high seas. Make no mistake Lucas there are those such as John Saxton of Boston who would try to take the food out of the mouths of our courageous soldiers.

This man has tried to kill me many times, especially his partner in crime, Marcus Brown, the Maasai, who stabbed me then threw me into the Hudson River leaving me to drown.

They've also spread lies about me in regards to my supposed desertion from the Army. It is not true. It's just a cover for the real work I'm doing for the 'cause'. As for any rumors that might surface about me being a murderer, or rapist are all lies, every one of them. I have only eliminated those traitors that threatened our holy work. We're at war not peace and as such no mercy or quarter shall be given to an enemy that tries to destroy our God-given way of life.

So son, it is my fervent hope that after the war is over, we shall be together again, just like we were in our old home in New Orleans. Life will be good for us there as it was before. No matter what happens; our love and respect for each other will last forever. I'm so proud of you son and I love you so very much.

Your Father.....Major Horatio Armstrong Garrow, CSA"

Every time Lucas read the letter, his heart soared only to be dashed by the words of those who had suffered at the hands of his father. The situation was intolerable. No, he was determined to meet his father face to face, the sooner the better for the torture of doubt was worse than being wounded in battle. In due course, Lucas began to plan his 'escape' from Salisbury as he walked high above a sulfurous sewer that slowly meandered past the stockade below him. He thought,

'I'm going to find my father, if it's the last thing I ever do!'

Hours later, he decided he would never desert. Instead, he'd ask for a leave of absence on compassionate grounds to visit his father. But where was he? There must have been a post mark on the envelope and perhaps in the past two days, the envelope was still in the office clerk's trash basket. He had to find out. Determination overwhelmed the young man. After mess was over, he'd go to the prison headquarters and ask Captain Ben Wallace, the prison's Chief Clerk for permission. No sooner were the thoughts in the young lad's head when a bugle blew for mess. While there, he'd get a gate pass from his patrol Sergeant, Shamus O'Reilly.

Lucas finished his lunch, a gate pass tucked carefully into his breast pocket. He headed for the main gate. The prison headquarters were just outside the stockade to the north. A large L shaped brick building fronted by a wide veranda; the two storied brick headquarters faced a two acre prison garden bordered by flowers. The fenced garden was delineated by neat rows of vegetables that had just been planted. Tall White oaks newly leafed, shaded the area making it a different world from that within the prison stockade.

On the veranda of the clerk's building, a dozen officers sat on chairs, benches and stools, enjoying a day that promised to be pleasantly warm and somewhat humid even though summer was still two months away. These men smoked cheroots and long clay pipes while eyeing the young private as he shuffled towards the building, his musket over his shoulder. Lucas pulled the Sergeant's pass out of his breast pocket. He showed it to the two guards standing on either side of the main door of the building. One remarked,

"Want to see the Captain do ya Boy? Good luck, ye'll have to wait some though, for all the others here are awaitin' on his highness too."

The soldiers laughed. Everyone but Lucas knew that the real power in the prison was not the Commander but the Chief Clerk, Captain Ben Wallace who had been there from the very beginning. Since September, 1861, the prison housed only Union spies, deserters, those waiting to be court martial and a few prisoners of war. However, six prison commanders would pass through Salisbury during his tenure. Wallace indeed had power over everyone, because his knowledge of what was going on before and behind the walls made him indispensable and definitely omnipotent.

Born and raised in England under the control of a sadistic father, Ben Wallace like Harley Blackstone was given no chance whatsoever to experience love, affection or respect. To both men, life's rewards came by their own hand and survival by any means was paramount.

Thus the rotund little man with the mutton chop sideburns and wispy beard had no compunction about rewarding his faithful servants and severely punishing those who opposed him. Equipped with a photographic memory and a penchant for taking copious notes on everyone working at the prison, it allowed him to use bureaucratic subterfuge to his advantage. Wallace therefore could embezzle funds, have disloyal guards sent to the front, make unruly prisoners disappear and control the supply of food and medicinal supplies intended for the hospital and the commissary. But most importantly, he could read, censure and control the mail, dispatches, telegrams and memos coming into and out of his office. Even Commanders feared him. Ben Wallace was totally opposite in nature to his Scots namesake. Unbeknownst to young Lucas, Ben Wallace was a senior member of his father's criminal organization, an organization that controlled the graft that was endemic in nearly half of the Confederate's two dozen major prison camps.

After waiting two hours, Lucas Garrow was ushered in before the Chief Clerk. As soon as Lucas appeared, Wallace rose up in a florid rage, chastising his Adjutant, Corporal Nevis, for letting the poor lad wait at all. Summarily dismissed, his Adjutant fled, quite perplexed, closing the door quietly behind him.

Wallace returned the boy's awkward salute then indicated where a very nervous young man was to be seated. Lucas sat down, his butternut hat in his lap. He leaned his musket against a thick chair rail behind him. His mind went blank when Wallace asked him about the nature of his business for he was very aware of who Lucas was and guessed correctly why the young lad was seated in front of him. The only fly in the ointment was that Wallace had no idea what plans his father had for him. So, he would be very careful, for Horatio Garrow suffered idiots poorly and disloyal ones even more so. The Chief Clerk began to sweat. He didn't like feeling somewhat helpless. He didn't like it at all. The boy stammered,

"Captain Wallace, my name is….is… Private Lucas Garrow and I have here a letter from my father. Sergeant O'Reilly gave it to me yesterday. Captain Sir, I've not heard from my father for nearly two years and I need to know where he is. I'm requesting compassionate leave to find him. Can you help me?"

The Captain's jowls shook much to the boy's surprise as Wallace replied.

"I'm sorry son but if every boy in this man's army requested leave to see their mommas or poppas, the Yankees would walk right through our front door laughin' and singin' Yankee Doodle Dandy at the same time. No son, you're gonna stay right here and serve your country just like every other soldier boy."

Lucas hung his head as if he had expected no less an answer of rejection. However, his young face brightened with hope as he said, letter in hand.

"Do you Captain, perhaps have the envelope this letter came in? There must be a postmark on it somewhere."

Wallace lied with authority that the office trash had been thrown out just that morning. As he watched the boy's growing despair, he leaned forward from behind his cluttered desk.

"I'm sorry son, but take heart for all is not lost. Perhaps I'll make some enquiries into where your father is stationed. I see you have the letter Private Lucas?"

The lad nodded eagerly, rising to put it squarely in front of Wallace. He sat back down, waiting nervously as the Chief Clerk adjusted his pince-nez reading glasses and pretended to read the letter for the very first time. After a few moments he finished and handed it back.

"You keep it Private Garrow, it might get lost here. It does seem to me that your father is very fond of you and has been looking for you for a long time. I do hope I can somehow arrange a reunion soon. However, to do that, we must make sure that prisoner John Saxton, the guard killer, never finds out. Do you understand me private? Whatever prisoner Saxton or anyone else has told you; don't believe anything they say. Trust your father. I'm sure he's serving his country well albeit secretively to be sure."

The Chief Clerk rose up, lit a cheroot for Wallace regained his confidence and thus reassured, began to strut back and forth like a bantam cock rooster. He continued; his face red and diffused with swarms of broken veins. The boy looked up in growing admiration hoping that all would be put right very soon. Wallace sensing a sea change, said.

"Son, the Confederacy needs your father and others like him to break through the damnable Yankee blockade so that our brave lads can defeat them. It's only right that that son of a bitch, John Saxton is punished for trying to kill your father. The Commander wants to give him three months in the 'tin can' for murdering a guard just recently. With the coming summer heat and all, why son he'll fry like a worm on a fence post in no time. I'm sure your father will be very pleased indeed to hear of it."

The boy laughed, his enthusiasm rising. Wallace paused as if hit by a bullet of an idea so profound that he wasn't sure if he should approach the lad about it or not. The boy looked up at him expectantly. Wallace stopped pacing and sat behind his desk. He motioned for the boy to bring his chair closer, much closer. Lucas did. The Chief Clerk shuffled some papers looking for something. He found it and began waving a paper flimsy in front of the lad then put it down pretending to read it. Finished, he looked at the boy for any hint of weakness. There was none; just a resolute young man bound and determined to serve the cause and find his father. Satisfied, Wallace leaned ever closer. He whispered,

"Private Garrow, how would you like to serve your country secretly just like your father?" He smiled as the boy remarked, "How so sir, what do you mean?"

Wallace was cautious for the boy's loyalty had yet to be carefully crafted. He needn't have worried, because it soon became very evident that the boy's father had done that already after many years of constant indoctrination. Wallace surmised as such before he said,

"Son, there have been some attempts by the prisoners to escape from this here prison and believe you me son I can't say that I blame them. In wartime, it is every man's duty to try and escape to fight again. However, if thousands of able bodied prisoners did escape, the Confederacy would be in dire straits. Don't you agree?"

The boy nodded vigorously while waiting for the Chief Clerk to continue.

"To serve one's country in a more discreet capacity is a sacred trust, an honor given to few men who have the courage like your father to do it and do it well. Now listen carefully son, because I'm going to say this only once, for nothing will ever be written down on paper. Simply put Private, how would you like to become 'Galvanized'?"

The boy looked up at the clerk, his face a blank canvas upon which the clerk was about to paint a picture of daring do and valor for the cause. In short order, the boy was convinced to spy on behalf of Captain Wallace. Lucas was going to cozy up to Saxton's attic fraternity as a sympathetic ally, give them extra rations and find out who was trying to escape by tunnel or any other means. Wallace was sure that Saxton was a born leader, looked up to by many for killing Tom Stone.

Stone and a few other guards for years had preyed on the weak and dying, pawning their stolen valuables to Wallace who paid them a pittance in return. Ben Wallace was going to be even richer as the number of incoming prisoners had become a torrent. Every three months, Garrow demanded his cut and received it by a trusted courier after Wallace secretly skimmed off twenty percent of it. It was a dangerous game but a very profitable one to both men. The boy would do as he was told. He might be too young and unfit to fight but he could be of service in other ways. Wallace would cheat Garrow on one hand and on the other be congratulated for giving his son a real chance of becoming a hero. The Captain concluded by saying,

"Private, report to me as soon as you hear of anything going on that seems suspicious. Hold your musket in your left hand if you have some information for me. I'll see to it that we meet in complete privacy. Don't write anything down. I guarantee that the prisoners will never know from whence the information came from. Your life depends on total secrecy. Remember son, if you are caught, they will kill you. Do I make myself clear? Other men have been trusted with this task and have died performing it. The few that have survived, you will never meet. Now supposing I do contact your father, do you want me to tell him that you're 'Galvanized' but still serving the cause?" Lucas agreed. The Chief Clerk continued succinctly,

"So remember Lucas, keep your friendship with Saxton and his fellow rats ongoing and maybe extra rations will loosen their tongues. Keep that in mind Private."

Wallace stubbed his spent cheroot out into a crystal ashtray. The meeting was over.

The boy stood up. Wallace nonchalantly returned his salute in kind. The lad put on his cover, grabbed his musket and opened the door, closing it with a soft thud behind him. No sooner was the lad gone when Wallace yelled,

"Nevis, get in here on the double!"

The door flew open as Adjutant Nevis ran into the room. Wallace glared at him.

"Nevis, I want prisoner John Saxton from A barracks, top floor, to be put in solitary first thing tomorrow morning after roll call. No food or water for twenty-four hours. Do I make myself clear?"

After Nevis left, Wallace sat down and commenced writing a letter to Edward Dawkins in New York City. It was short, in code and stamped URGENT. The Captain would deliver it personally to the Station Master in town that evening. From there, other Station Masters whose palms had been greased would send the sealed missive along the NCRR railway line, the Piedmont line and lastly the Richmond-Danville line to Richmond, Virginia. Once there, it would be put aboard one of Garrow's blockade runners until it reached New York City, ten days later.

Horatio Garrow while wearing a Priest's cassock, sat in a warming room opposite an even smaller kitchen. Therein a sheet iron cook stove was being vigorously stoked by Harley Blackstone. Three body guards were on duty outside; one in the hallway, another at the foot of the stairs and one outside across the street that fronted the decrepit tenement building. The meager heat from the stove was futile in its attempts to take the chill off the air. It was four o'clock in the morning. The fetid and frigid atmosphere that permeated the teeming Five Points slums around them was punctuated by an occasional scream, gunshot or wretched moaning. Garrow was somewhat garrulous. A coded note from Wallace arrived only minutes before. He read it again.

"Hey Blackie, imagine my boy being a spy like his old man! It's a dangerous game as you well know but, at least we had somewhere to run and hide. In that prison my boy will have nowhere to hide if they ever find out. On the one hand I'm damn proud of the kid, but on the other, I'm scared to death he'll get caught." Some pans rattled in the kitchen behind him as Blackstone cursed,

"Jesus H. Christ, I've burnt the eggs again. Always was a lousy cook. How long are we goin' to be holed up here anyways? Goddamn that Tweed! He's a double crossin' bastard if I ever saw one. Imagine a man like that with no scruples whatsoever putting Pinkie on our trail again." Garrow ruefully agreed.

"Now he's put the boots to our local operation, taking it over from the Bronx to the Point here and beyond. My God Harley is there no end to the prick's chicanery! Well I've arranged for a coach to take us to Poppy's. We've been holed up here too long. Let's eat and go!"

Garrow leaned back in his chair, watching Blackstone put the greasy contents of what had been perfectly good pork rinds and eggs onto two cracked china plates. Both men wolfed their food down, chased by a flagon of ale. Once finished, Blackstone threw the dirty dishes and cutlery into a small slate sink.

The two men left the dingy apartment for Poppy's Tavern that overlooked the east river. Both men were disguised as priests wearing long woolen overcoats over black cassocks. A hired coach waited for them outside, its driver a young muscular black man, sat high upon a padded leather seat. His tall top hat, matching black driver's jacket replete with a long cape gave the man a regal air. Unknown to Garrow, he'd been recruited by Pinkerton himself. His name was Donal E. Markle.

Minutes later five heavily armed men settled in as the coach rumbled down Anthony Street. The driver's horse whip popped occasionally as the team of four trotted briskly forward. Unbeknownst to the passengers, the Brougham had been specially fitted with a brass listening tube ingeniously hidden in its padded ceiling. Markle was able to hear every word and since Pinkerton had been impressed with his agent's remarkable memory, the inveterate Chicago detective was hoping for a coup of major proportions.

Pinkerton was at the time 1864, out of favor with Lincoln, Stanton and others in Washington DC. General McClellan, his guardian had been relieved of his duties over a year before. Lafayette Baker was currently in charge of the Union's secret service. A secretive paranoid, Baker was fast becoming a liability to Lincoln in that Baker was conducting unauthorized surveillance of all telegraph messages coming into and out of the White House. Pinkerton warned Lincoln and Stanton, but both men dismissed these accusations as an attempt by Pinkerton to curry their favor. He'd come very close to returning to their good graces when he successfully brought Nobel's new explosive formula to Washington aboard the USS Niagara from Boston. However his failure to capture BB and Garrow vexed him. Recently however, Pinkerton had been informed by none other than an associate of Boss Marcy Tweed as to where Garrow was holed up. Pinkerton, in no rush to arrest him just yet, wanted to capture the whole nest of vipers in one fell swoop.

As the Brougham rolled along, a large lug nut holding the rear wheel to its axle came off as Markle tried desperately to avoid a drunken sailor. The man had stumbled out from the shadows directly in front of the coach as it rounded a corner. The rear wheel of the coach came off as the nut holding it on dropped with a loud ping onto the street. Markle was thrown off his seat, landing in some bushes lining the narrow street. Therein he remained unconscious. The rogue wagon wheel hurtled down the street straight towards a large picture window fronting a bakery. Meanwhile, the unfortunate sailor was stomped to death by the panicked horses as they tried desperately to regain their footing. His bloody body rolled into a gutter. Fathers Garrow and Blackstone and their body guards hung on for dear life as the heavy coach slewed back and forth over the wet cobblestones. A fiery comet of sparks spewed forth from beneath it as the rear axle was dragged along. The runaway coach crashed against a large iron stanchion imbedded beside the granite curb then flipped over onto its side, its wheels spinning. It lay there under a gas light like some grotesque creature from Dante's underworld.

One of the bodyguards inside it pushed aside a door. All three crawled out onto the street, guns drawn. Nearby windows flung open all around them. Angry onlookers began to rain curses down upon them. Dogs barked. Garrow emerged, his fake mustache askew and his bowler lost somewhere within the dark recesses of the coach. Blackstone crawled out behind him. The gang was faced with a dilemma, stay or run. They did neither. Leaving Blackstone behind, nursing a bleeding head, Garrow somewhat gallantly, climbed back into the coach. Therein he retrieved his bowler and disappeared into a nearby alley followed by his body guards. Blackstone watched somewhat uneasily as his boss appeared to have abandoned him. Not to be outdone for boldness, Blackstone walked back to Markel's body. He knelt beside it, his ornate gold cross on a matching necklace resting upon the man's chest. There, Blackstone pretended to administer the last rites while discreetly searching the body for any valuables or identification. There were none. To the nearby residents, Blackstone's behavior was normal, for they all assumed he was probably one of the local clergy doing exactly what any man of the cloth would have done in the Bowery. Blackstone knew this. He also knew that Garrow was headed for Queens.

Within minutes, the coach was lugged off by a group of industrious young men. The matched team of prime horseflesh also vanished in the blink of an eye. All that was left was the lifeless Markle, who soon recovered enough to crawl into an oncoming Hansom cab hired by none other than Allan Pinkerton himself. An angry baker further down the street stood amongst the remains of his prized front window wiping his thick fingers on a floured apron. He swore volubly, shaking his fists as they passed by. A large wagon wheel lay behind him precariously perched upon an equally large tray of freshly baked bread.

A few miles away, Garrow and Blackstone were seated across from each other in Poppy's Tavern just across the street from the East River Ferry Co. dock at Hunters Point, Manhattan. Two former Deacon Boys lounged outside on either side of the Tavern's wide front door while another covered the back door. Both Garrow and Blackstone had been badly shaken by the accident. They had hailed a Hansom cab, and by using circuitous routes, made sure they weren't followed.

Once inside, Garrow chose a darkened corner booth despite Blackstone's virulent pro-tests. They draped their long overcoats on pegs driven into the plank walls behind them. Garrow's bowler rested on the hardwood seat beside him. It was now six in the morning. The Tavern was packed as workers began arriving at the Long Island train station just across the street. Shortly thereafter, a loud whistle blew signaling the arrival of a ferry boat, the SS Suffolk. A brass bell rang loudly directly above Harley's head. Blackstone cursed as his head throbbed. It was still bleeding slightly. The Tavern emptied quickly as most of the patrons worked on Long Island. Fifteen minutes later, another flood of workers invaded the Tavern determined to have a mug-up before walking to the many shipyards that lined this part of the waterfront known as Queens. During this lull, Garrow laid out his plans to Blackstone.

He'd been thinking about leaving New York City altogether ever since he had killed the harlot, Naomi Devine. Grabbing another mug of ale, Blackstone became maudlin as he leaned closer.

"I say, it's been three years now since you shoved that Colt .44 into my ugly mug at Fort Sumter; scared me half to death you bastard. However, I've bin happy ever since we hooked up despite everything we've bin through together. Ya know Horatio, youse the only mate I's ever had that's bin good to me." Before he could continue further, Garrow growled,

"Jesus Blackie, don't tear up on me or I'll box your bloody ears off."

He then leaned closer and whispered,

"Same goes for me mate. Let's drink to it and then get on with the business at hand."

They raised their clay mugs as one. Both laughed. Garrow said piously,

"Father Blackstone, how would ye like to go to prison?" Blackstone sat back in his seat, leaned forward, a handkerchief pressed to his forehead. He whispered nervously,

"Now Horatio me lad, that's not funny at all. Not funny at all. My head hurts like hell, and I'm bleedin' like a stuck pig……. youse only kiddin' me right?"

Blackstone started to sweat as his partner in crime didn't give any hint one way or the other. Garrow's eyes narrowed into slits, strikingly similar to those of a deadly serpent about to strike. Blackstone was always unnerved by the transformation. He thought,

'God almighty, he's at it again. Another hair-brained scheme is about to hatch in that cesspool he has for a brain. Whatever it is, it's probably dangerous as hell itself. Christ, what's next?' He sat and said brusquely,

"Well Garrow, what's eatin' you this time?"

Garrow pulled out two cheroots from beneath his cassock, ordered more ale and began to lay out his plans for Lucas as both men smoked and drank. After ten minutes, Garrow was pleased, Blackstone was not. He hissed,

"Christ almighty, are you completely insane. It'll never work. We're both wanted by nearly everyone I can think of. We've bin runnin' for nearly two years now from Pinkie, the Feds, the Rebs, and that bloody Sergeant Raines in Orleans. Christ man! How the hell are we, or may I say hopefully, YOU going to pull it off? I know you're crazy about the lad but he's just fine where he is. Leave him be man. At least he's servin' the cause, get's three squares a day, has a roof over his head and no cannon balls are whizzin' by his ears!"

Blackstone took another swallow of ale and waited for Garrow to agree with him. He didn't. What he said next shook him to the core.

"Look Blackie, I can understand your concern, but Lucas has to be groomed, and care-fully trained to take over my many business interests."

Garrow missed the shock of that registered in Blackstone's brain. Harley felt betrayed thinking,

'Jesus Christ, I've run the gang for nearly a year and now he's gonna give it all to his son. Is this the thanks I get for sayin' how good he's bin to me?'

However, Blackstone's composure remained unblemished by his inner feelings as Garrow continued to blather on oblivious to his partner's chagrin, saying,

"What else can he do Blackie? He's been badly wounded, therefore he's unfit for battle, but he has a good brain. Why, he got top marks at Pineville Military Academy in Louisiana.

General Sheridan told me personally. The boy has guts and brains too, what more does he need?" Blackstone countered,

"You haven't seen him for over two years. How do you know what he's like now mate? For all you know he's become a bible thumper of the first order or even worse, he's found out about your less than illustrious past and will shoot you on sight given half a chance."

Garrow pointed his cheroot at Blackstone.

"Don't ever question my boy's loyalty again Blackie. I raised him to believe in and fight to the death for one thing only, the cause. Now that the war is lost, there must be another cause in the boy's life to strive for and that my friend will be revenge. Yes, my friend, we're goin' to Salisbury disguised as a Doctor and his orderly. I've got everything arranged on the other side, on Long Island. Remember the Reliant? Well it's waitin' there to take us to Richmond. Don't worry Blackie, it can do twenty-two knots. She's outrun every ship who's ever chased her."

Blackstone agreed. He remembered Sandy Keith very well. Garrow continued unperturbed by Blackstone's momentary lack of attention.

"We'll be in Richmond, Virginia within a week. From there we'll take a train to Salisbury. Besides, I've cashed out. The war is lost; the contraband smuggling will be over in a year. Tweed has my other enterprises by the balls. After the war is over, we'll start fresh, as far away from here as possible. The Confederacy will be bought at a penny an acre, you mark my words. Blackie, we'll be there to pick up the pieces. I do believe my friend, that tremendous opportunities await us there after the war."

He was interrupted by the proprietor ringing a small brass bell. A wild scramble ensued. Meanwhile, Blackstone was relieved that Horatio was leaving New York. Perhaps he was right. Blackstone began to feel somewhat guilty over doubting his intentions concerning his son. Harley laughed, "Well Father, let's get the hell out of here too!"

Rising as one, their long black cassocks flowing about them, they put on their overcoats then proceeded to shoulder their way through the turbulent crowd. Behind them their parishioners hurriedly drank up and followed. One of them did not move. Another ferry boat docked. Fathers Garrow, Blackstone and their three cohorts disappeared into the mob that boarded her. As the overcrowded ferry boat pulled away, it began listing markedly to starboard. A Hansom cab pulled up to the Tavern with a flourish seconds later.

Allan Pinkerton and Donal Markle jumped out and rushed into Poppy's Tavern. It appeared empty. The proprietor was busy cleaning up. As he did so, Pinkerton noticed a very large bowler hat lying on a bench in a secluded corner. He walked over and picked it up. He took off his own bowler. Markle stood totally fascinated as Pinkerton put it on. It was three sizes too big. The proprietor, John Smith, looked over at Pinkerton. The big man stopped sweeping the floor. He leaned on the corn broom, saying.

"That bowler was left behind by a very tall man and his brute of a companion. Gave me the creeps they did. Tipped well though, I must say." He paused,

"They left for Long Island just a few minutes ago. Never did hear what they were talkin' about. Seemed important enough it did. Come to think of it, the tall one sported a waxed handle-bar moustache. Both he and his burly partner were dressed as priests."

He backed off as Pinkerton brushed by him followed by Markle. They ran for the front door. Pinkerton stopped, turned about and looked down at a young man slumped over in a booth by a front window. Blood oozed out of the man's left ear. Gently, Pinkerton lifted his head up from the table. Markle blanched. It was Pickett. Pinkerton swore,

"God damn it Donal! I told Pickett not to follow too closely."

Markle reached down and hefted Pickett's body over his broad shoulders then followed Pinkerton out through the front door. Pinkerton carried the over-sized bowler as if it was a brimming chamber pot. The Tavern's owner looked out a grimy window pane at them as they climbed into a waiting cab. He shook his head and started to sweep up piles stained saw-dust. In the distance behind him, a sharp clap of thunder heralded a squall line approaching up the East River from the north. Chain lightening flashed brightly over a sullen horizon. Just as Smith finished, another mob burst through the Tavern's battered front doors. Outside, a light rain began falling on the street outside. As it did so, tiny drops of fresh blood ran down between the granite cobble stones.

BOOK THREE: CHAPTER 3
SALISBURY

A merciless sun beat down upon the 'tin can'. Within its narrow confines, John Saxton lay prostrate completely withered by the repressive heat. A day later, its thick metal door was unlocked and Saxton was summarily released into the custody of a Mrs. Sarah Johnston. It was August 15th, 1864, Saxton's twenty-fourth birthday.

Mrs. Johnston, a widow, lived just outside the prison gates. With the permission of the prison's Chief Surgeon, Dr. Josephus Hall and its new Commander, Major Martin Burke, Saxton was sent to her house on a litter. For the next two months he convalesced there, very lucky indeed as Mrs. Johnston took in only those in dire need of attention, Confederate, Union or otherwise. No one doubted her loyalty as her own son was fighting for the Confederacy. In mid October, 1864, Saxton was released into the general prison population. What he came back, the scenario that lay before him was indeed horrific.

Recent Confederate defeats in the western and eastern theaters of war flooded many Confederate hospitals to overflowing. As more trains brought wounded Rebel soldiers to Salisbury, room had to be made for them. General Grant, commander of all the Union forces declared that no more prisoner exchanges would be taking place as long as black prisoners of war were not being paroled. Thus as the war progressed, Confederate prisons burst at the seams with thousands upon thousands of Union soldiers. Salisbury prison could only accommodate twenty-five hundred men, but by the time Saxton left Mrs. Johnston's care, the prison population at Salisbury had swelled to over ten thousand.

Food and water supplies literally dried up. The Union blockade was not only starving the military and civilian populations of the South but also those poor souls who were unfortunate enough to be incarcerated by the Rebels. To make an awful situation even worse, the winter of 1864 was the coldest in living memory. The stage was now set for a level of human misery not seen since bubonic plague ravaged Europe five hundred years previously.

In the early fall of 1864, all prison barracks at Salisbury were converted to hospital use. Saxton and his fellow prisoners were forced to live in a tattered Sibley tent. Those who came later were forced to burrow into the yard's hard red clay, constructing their underground hovels as best they could. These holes often became their graves as bodies would lay undiscovered for days, decomposing in the late Indian summer heat. Sewer rats feasted on the newly dead or dying. The prison quartermaster, Captain Goodman, tried to build new barracks for the men but General Winder, Commander of all Confederate prisons, proclaimed the buildings unfit for human habitation. Saxton was dismayed when the General ordered them destroyed for firewood. Clean bedding straw was also in short supply. Saxton laid the blame for the rising level of misery not on the General but squarely upon the Union and Ben Wallace who took advantage of the deplorable conditions the men had to live in..

By November of 1864, prison food was rationed most severely. A local newspaper noted,

"Mills were impressed and forced to grind wheat and corn, and agents to secure provisions were also sent."

The energetic Commissary, Major Myers, found it almost impossible to procure meat. As another prisoner, a T. J Libby, of the 12th Maine succinctly described it.

"We received meat thirteen times in six months. We only got the refuse pieces that the Rebels would not eat, the amount given at one time about one-quarter pound. Nothing occupied the minds of men more than the question of how to get more to eat. Men who under other circumstances would have shrunk from such deeds, would, when opportunity offered, lie and steal to get their comrade's food to appease their own hunger. The knowing pangs of hunger were so strong that they could not resist the temptation to take a comrade's rations if they got the chance. I saw a comrade shed tears as he confessed to a sick soldier that he had stolen his bread and begged him not to leave it again in sight, as he was so hungry that he could not help taking it. I saw a man receive his rations of thin soup—which was given us a few times, in his shoe rather than lose any of it. Rats and mice were caught and cooked. A dog that came to the prison with one of the soldiers furnished a meal for four men; what they could not eat they sold for twenty dollars, Confederate money. A bone as long as your hand was bought for a dollar; by breaking it into small pieces and boiling it in some water it would be better than nothing. Perhaps a spoonful of fat would help keep body and soul together."

Prison staffs, especially the older guards were increasingly frustrated by the heinous conditions but were helpless to alleviate the situation. Many of the townspeople of Salisbury like Mrs. Johnson did their level best to help the prisoners but the general population felt that their soldiers were more In need of food than any rabid Yankee prisoner. In fact, as Saxton shared a crust of stale bread with another prisoner, he was told that,

"A group of well dressed women came unto the guard's platform and looked down on our suffering and misery as if we were some kind of beasts. I saw them point out some poor wretch who was almost naked and laugh at his condition. Our men are here in this God forsaken wasteland, suffering everything they can suffer, dying by the thousands within a mile of the women's homes in the Village of Salisbury." Saxton was appalled.

Despite Drs. Hall and Nesbit's best efforts to improve conditions in the original, poorly placed hospital just outside the walls; rampant disease flourished within its dimly lit hallways and wards. Eleven new hospitals including the textile factory and the six former barracks were set up within the prison walls in the fall of 1864. By December, they too had become overcrowded, pestilent and virulent.

Malnutrition, rheumatic fever, smallpox, pellagra, dysentery, malaria, typhus, typhoid and cholera fed like vultures on human carrion. After November, 1864, the prison death rate soared from two to twenty-eight percent. Prisoners died at an alarming rate of nearly twenty per day by early December, 1864. Therefore, the emaciated and diseased dead were collected twice daily at the 'dead house', a small brick blacksmith shop. Grim prisoners stacked simple pine coffins five at a time onto a rough stone wagon pulled by four mules called the 'dead wagon'. From there the dead were taken to an 'Old cornfield' a quarter mile away and buried in mass graves; each four feet wide, six feet deep and two hundred and forty feet long. By the end of the war, eighteen such trenches had been dug.

Many of the nearly twelve thousand dead were buried "hatless, shoeless and coatless." Another prisoner reminded Saxton to be wary of the 'Salisbury Rangers' who banded together to steal or murder to get what they needed to survive. A vigilante committee led by Saxton was formed after their complaints to Major Burke proved ineffective. The committee captured, tried and condemned one of the Salisbury Rangers but his execution was never carried out. Saxton suspected Captain Wallace of complicity in the whole affair. There were also certain areas in the prison yard that were not safe such as the grove of white oaks, the latrines and the far southern corner of the yard. Saxton was warned by Bill Curry, who implied from bitter experience that,

"Such things as loose shoes, haversacks, or pails had to be securely tied to his person or else they would be stolen while he slept."

After a few months, other acts of chicanery came to Saxton's attention. He and other prisoners who made coffins in the prison workshop suspected that something was awry. Many looked like they had been used time and again, so much so, the Rebel claim that all dead soldiers would be buried with military honors was becoming suspect. Saxton suggested they put secret marks on all the coffins. Sure enough, after a few days, they realized that the Rebels were using the same coffins over and over again.

Thereafter, once exposed as liars, the Rebels dispensed with the coffin charade and threw the diseased directly upon the 'dead wagon' like cordwood, thereby saving all the coffins for their own. For Saxton, the Rebels were forced to be honest about their degradation of the Union prisoners. This event in its singularity convinced him that the Confederates were carrying out a systematic plan of killing as many prisoners as they could in order to save food and medical supplies for their own desperate troops. Those that persisted in living would work as slaves until they died. Saxton's life became very similar to that of a slave from Africa, no different and no less demeaning. As one newspaper reporter saw it,

"Once strong, able bodied, happy men were now changed to gaunt and ghostly forms, slowly perishing from hunger, exposure and ill treatment." Another newspaperman reported,

"I saw men wandering back and forth, their heads bowed, their eyes searching the ground for a stray bone or morsel of food dropped from a weaker hand. I saw men with clasped fingers and streaming eyes praying for their dear ones at home, into whose loving eyes they would never look again. I saw men in delirium beat themselves and curse God. And I saw shuddering as I looked, the dead cart and in it Gods images tiered up like sticks of wood. Death or desertion was the only sure chances of release for our men."

Some twenty-one hundred Union prisoners deserted as 'galvanized' Yankees to escape the prison's terrible conditions. Saxton and his cell mates were tempted but resisted as the topic was often discussed. Another prisoner from a tent next to them came over one day and said,

"Shall we all go out and join the Rebels? They will take us and at least we'll have enough to eat." Saxton waited as the man continued.

"To be loyal, must we stay here and die like dogs?"

It was a powerful incentive but Saxton and his men decided not to desert. However, he learned later, that the man returned to his men where they argued the pros and cons for several days. The man returned again and told Saxton,

"When we put it to vote, three of our seven wanted to go; four to stay and die, if need be." Some time thereafter, the same man came around for the last time, saying to Saxton,

"The three who voted to go lie buried now in the trenches outside the prison yard and I'm the only one of the four who voted to stay that is still alive."

Saxton's tent mates, the 'Attic Rats' as they now called themselves, decided upon hearing this bit of news, that they'd all stick together as long as they could. Thereafter, they all lived together near the old cotton factory they had recently been evicted from. The compound around them had become a quagmire of red clay mud with the consistency of mortar. The incessant autumn rains combined with the trampling of thousands of feet created it. Many prisoners simply died of exhaustion trying to slog through it.

After weeks of fighting the sticky red gumbo, Saxton became too weak to work in the prison workshop. Consequently, he was thrown into solitary confinement. Upon his release, he became an orderly in one of the prison hospitals mainly through the influence of Captain Wallace and the new Commander; a doctor by the name of Major John Henry Gee.

Major Gee, forty-seven years old, was of average height, though a bit slight. His brown hair, grey moustache and goatee were highlighted by piercing blue eyes and an aquiline nose. However, he shared one thing in common with his predecessors; he too was afflicted with an anxious expression.

Saxton was grateful until he saw what faced him. He knew then Wallace was probably trying to keep him alive, but why? He put this worry behind him as the full magnitude of the human disaster within the hospital unfolded before him. Saxton's fellow orderly, Henry Talbot, a tall gangly young man from Connecticut was also appalled. He showed Saxton part of a diary he was writing. It said,

"This place was the most complete slough of despondency that ever existed on this side of the infernal regions. The suffering and dying patients lay with their heads to the wall in a row around the room, and with no covering save their clothes. A little straw and an abundance of vermin served for a bed. There was no fire for two months, and when fire was finally obtained there was about enough sufficient to warm one-twentieth of the interior."

The month of December was even worse as Talbot again recounted,

"During the early part of December (1864) there was a continual amputating of feet, toes, legs etc., the victims in a few days going off in the dead wagon. Some were crawling around with their flesh almost dropping from the bone. Others were afflicted with dry rot, and led a fearful existence until death relieved them. Some were insane, crying and cursing, and nearly all were dying. It was one continual scene of human woe, heartrending agony, groans, curses, dismay and death."

To Saxton, the human carnage was, by the coming of winter, insufferable. As conditions worsened, he was hard pressed to find anything to eat. Having lost nearly seventy pounds, his once strong muscular body wasted away so much so that his skeleton was held together by a sack of skin the color of old tallow. The three prison cookhouses were putting out only thirteen thousand rations a day instead of the required forty thousand. By December, food was so scarce, that the prisoners were eating raw acorns that fell in their millions below the great white oaks. To make matters worse, potable water was being taken from the creek upstream from the latrines in the mistaken belief it was germ free. It wasn't. It was at this time that Saxton decided to escape.

Every prisoner in Salisbury or any other prison for that matter thought of only three things; food, freedom and family in that order. A reporter, an A. D Richardson of the New York Tribune and another reporter Junius Browne escaped from Salisbury prison the previous December. Richardson recalled the conditions, his liberation spared him.

"...the heavy crushing weight of captivity. It is not hunger or cold, sickness of death which makes prison life so hard to bear. But it is the utter idleness, emptiness, aimlessness of such a life. It is being through all the long hours of each day and night for weeks, months and years if one lives so long. Absolutely without employment, mental or physical, with nothing to fill the vacant mind, which always becomes morbid and turns inward to prey upon itself."

For John Saxton, the agony around him and upon him was becoming too much to bear. He knew the loves of his life, Virginia and his baby daughter Felicity were pining for his return. He'd not seen them for near on two years. However, a burning ember of hope was fanned one evening when a fellow prisoner in a tent next to him called out.

"Saxton, come here man."

Though very weak, Saxton crawled on his hands and knees over hard scrabble snow towards a tattered wedge tent whose roof sagged precipitously to one side weighed down by a thick sheet of ice. As he struggled the last few feet, he stopped, stood up shaking in the piercing cold. His frozen breath steamed round his sallow bearded face. Saxton pulled Gilly's woolen blanket tightly around him. He knew Gilly wouldn't mind for he'd died a few days earlier. The frozen prison yard about Saxton, reminded him of the prairie gopher towns straddling the Military road in Arkansas between Forts Gibson and Scott. Before him thousands of men lived in frozen hovels dug into the hard clay. Their heads would occasionally pop up from within their burrows from which wisps of smoke rose straight up through the still and frozen air. Saxton thought, his friend Thomas described the scene well.

"There we sat, night after night in the thick darkness, inhaling the foul vapor and acrid smoke, longing for the morning when we could again catch a glimpse of the blue beaming sky."

Saxton pulled aside the ragged tent flap. The miasma fouling the cramped tent did not deter him. Within its dreary confines, four ragged ruffians huddled together trying to keep warm. Their scraggly beards served two purposes, one of warmth and one of disguise. To Saxton they all looked alike; debilitated, dissolute and desperate. One of the apparitions was bent over a small fire that glowed weakly in the dimming wintry light. The man croaked,

"Saxton my good man, does this here look like smallpox to you? I've bin stickin' myself all over with this hot needle. You're an orderly, you've seen the pox. Does it look real enough to fool Doc Hall and get us into a hospital?"

Saxton was incredulous. The man's waxy arms, hands, face and neck were covered with what looked like supporous red sores. He stared vacantly up at Saxton, his mouth a black cavern bordered by two yellow stalactites imitating teeth. The living dead man tried valiantly to smile but could not as the terrible circumstances into which he had been thrust for so long, prevented his brain from remembering how to do it. Saxton replied, his words shooting out of his mouth as clouds of steam.

"My God Dickie, what the hell are you doin' to yourself? It sure looks like the pox because it's infected, that's why. How long you been doing this?" Dickie whispered,

"Two days now, two days." One of the other apparitions disagreed.

"Come on Dickie, youse bin doin' this for a week now!"

"Really?"

"Yes, we've all bin doin' it together since the pox strikes in groups, right Saxton?" He nodded off as Saxton sat down between two of them.

"Look everyone, you're really going to get hell if Dr. Hall finds out the truth." Dickie snorted,

"We're in hell right now Saxton, what's the difference? At least we won't freeeeeze to death in the hospital. Food's better too I hear, isn't it?"

Saxton's heart went out to the men sitting around him. As he rose to go, Dickie pulled at his sleeve, wretched but resolute. He pleaded.

"Please Saxton, get us into the hospital. I'll make it worth your while. We hear that you and two others need passes for an escape soon, very soon. I know a Junior guard workin' in the Chief Clerk's office; a young kid, a Creole boy from Orleans. Says he has passes for sale; twenty dollars each. I can get three of them for you. No use bein' shot like all those poor bastards were last month on the twenty-fifth. I hear over two hundred died rushin' the front gate. Wadda ya say Saxton, a deal or not?"

Astonishment must have flashed across Saxton' face for two of the men laughed out loud. One cried,

"Christ almighty Saxton, there's tunnels bein' dug left, right and center. Why, a ladder was found just last night leanin' all alone against the wall." The man rubbed his hands nervously. Another said,

"And, just last week a squad of prisoners sent out under guard as a burial detail, escaped." Saxton queried,

"How's that Quint?"

"Well it seems that the stiff was a ventriloquist unused to bein' buried alive." The men laughed except Dickie. Quinton continued,

"When the first shovelful of earth hit the corpse, it began to protest in rather strong language. The two guards were so unnerved, they ran away and the burial detail took off." Saxton said,

"Come on Quint, you're funnin' me for sure." Quint was somewhat indignant,

"As God is my witness, it's true, ain't it boys?"

One of the men sat up dislodging a thick sheet of ice on the roof. Condensation dripped down on the men huddled together. Saxton prepared to leave, wrapping his wool blanket around him as the bitter cold bit into the back of his legs. As he did so a shadow thrust itself into his conscious mind. A deep and abiding sense of foreboding washed over him.

"Just one question Dickie, why aren't you guys buying the passes to escape. You've been talking about it ever since I've known you. Come to think of it, why aren't you and Quinton, not buying the hospital passes?"

He looked at them sternly. Lester Baxter in the back put his hand on Dickie's shoulder to restrain him. With great effort, his face twisted with pain, Baxter's sunken rheumy eyes looked up at Saxton. He wheezed,

"These two idiots tried scapin' from Andersonville last year but the dogs got 'em just outside the wall. Near tore em' to bits. While here, we've all tried diggin' tunnels under the stockade nearest the railway tracks. On one occasion, we woulda got clean away too but the roof caved in. Too bad a fat Sergeant stuck his boot clean through it. Dickie was right underneath him. Another time, one of our tunnels was discovered and the Captain of the Guard sent a nigger down the hole. He came back a few minutes later with the wooden box I'd used to carry out dirt to throw down an unused well. The Captain said,

"That's the third time I've arrested this box. You boys better find another spot to dig." He paused.

"It seemed after a while, to be a game between us and them." Saxton countered,

"I hear that there's at least sixteen tunnels bein' dug here right now so why aren't you guys in there digging again?"

Baxter looked up surprised. Gaunt and tired, he wheezed,

"We're plumb wore out Saxton. Mostly new guys are diggin' cause they're still fresh and strong. But they won't last though. They'll work like dogs, escape then die of exposure or bullets. They all do ya know in the end."

Saxton made up his mind.

"Dickie, get me five passes to visit the old hospital. I've got the money. I'll be here at ten tomorrow night."

Early the same evening, Captain Ben Wallace watched Private Lucas Garrow standing before him at attention. Lucas, his musket still gripped tightly in his left hand was very nervous as he was about to issue his first report. Wallace leaned back, eyeing the boy like a bug in a bottle. The boy so far had been of limited value. The extra rations he'd given to Saxton's men and Saxton while he was in solitary, kept them all barely alive. Thankfully, Mrs. Johnson fattened him up. Garrow also wanted him alive for Wallace received a coded letter from him instructing him as such. Garrow was also very pleased much to the Captain's relief that Lucas was spying on the prisoners, especially Saxton. Wallace knew that while solitary often broke most men, he was not surprised when Saxton crawled out of the Tin Can, his will to live still unbroken. The Chief Clerk's musings were abruptly interrupted.

"Beggin' you pardon Captain, but you did want my report; Sir?"

Wallace sat up, leaned forward, the insincerity on his face quite oblivious to the eager lad in front of him.

"Yes of course Private, do proceed at once."

The lad began giving more detailed information on three tunnels that were currently being dug under the east wall to the garden. Wallace had already named them Grant, Sheridan and McClellan after Union generals. He would wait until they were just about finished then expose them. His attention became more acute as the lad started his report on John Saxton.

"As to Captain Saxton Sir, I have been informed by a prisoner Dickie Shaw that Saxton will be by his tent at ten tonight to pick up five hospital passes signed by Dr. Hall. What should I do Captain?"

"Well son, we cannot let Saxton escape. Do you know the names of the other two men involved in the plot?"

"No sir I do not. But I feel that I'm getting close. Perhaps, Saxton won't be alone tonight. If I follow him, he might lead me to the others. What do you say Captain?" Wallace was not about to take any chances.

"No Private Garrow, if you go by yourself, it's too risky. Report back here tonight at 9.30 sharp. We'll go together. Ok?"

The lad's heart leaped for the Captain was going too. Saxton would never escape, never. His black eyes gleamed with fervid anticipation as he saluted, his musket resting on his right shoulder. The Chief Clerk casually saluted and let him out a side door. Thick snow was falling. Ben Wallace smiled. The trap was set. All that was needed were three blind mice.

Saxton slogged towards Dickie's tent. The weather had changed for the worst as a gale became a full blown blizzard. Within minutes, the prison yard was covered with a deep white blanket that buried all the tents and underground hovels until they magically disappeared. To Saxton, the prison yard was cleansed of its filth and degradation wherein men slept peacefully or died peacefully under the white shroud that fell upon them. Saxton tore aside Dickie's frozen tent flap and stepped into hell itself. Out of the shadows, a strangled voice commented brusquely, "You're early." Saxton was careful, replying evenly,

"I thought I'd get here while I still could."

Without further ado he paid Dickie the money in gold double eagles he'd sewn into his clothes. After inspecting the hospital passes carefully, Saxton turned and fled out into the night. The whole world had changed. He couldn't see his hand at arm's length. Luckily, Saxton prepared well, knowing instinctively that the weather would be changing for the worst. After being at sea all those years he knew the tell tale signs. He was meeting Thomas Wolfe and Bill Davis at the south-west corner of the old textile mill where the Attic Rats first met. He struggled mightily, following a white string in the snow that he painfully wound it up as he struggled through the drifts. Slowly, with each agonizing step, he plodded to where he had tied it to the steps of the barracks near his tent.

It had all been a ruse. Richardson and Browne had known Thomas Saxton, back in New York. Because of his considerable influence, both reporters working for the New York Tribune were given plum assignments by Horace Greeley its owner and chief editor. Currently prisoners at Salisbury, both men were shocked at seeing his son imprisoned there as well. After carefully explaining his plans, they readily agreed to help John Saxton escape. In return he would acquire hospital passes through another orderly, his close friend Henry Talbot.

After warning them about Wallace and Garrow, Saxton passed Lucas false information about who would be involved in his escape attempt. As a result, Lester Baxter and Quinton Fowles were closely watched by Lucas, while Browne, Richardson, Wolfe and Davis were not. It needn't had mattered, as Saxton looked back, his tracks had disappeared so completely that only the thin white string in his hand kept him from total disorientation. It was nine thirty. Wallace and Lucas had arrived too late at Baxter's tent. Saxton had gone mere minutes before. Any footprints had been wiped out by the blizzard. Defeated, they spent the night freezing in Baxter's foul tent, trapped by the storm.

To Saxton mere yards away, the white twine he was raveling into a ball had become his life line, a thread of hope in a landscape of despair. Ahead of him, blackness loomed out of the whiteness. After a few more tortuous steps, Davis and Wolfe appeared, waiting, hidden under wooden steps that sprang down the side of the tall building in a series of leaps and bounds. The young men stamped their feet as they crawled out from beneath the staircase. Both men stood very close together for the blizzard reached ultimate white-out conditions. They shook hands. Saxton gave them four passes. Saxton bent down and entered a dark recess under the staircase. Once there, he quickly changed into new clothes that he and his friends pilfered earlier. Minutes later, he emerged as Dr. Hall. He found the end of another piece of white twine in the snow. Saxton was exhausted, freezing and hungry. Ironically, capture was the least of his worries. Bill Davis hugged him saying,

"Saxton, may God hold you in the palm of his hand tonight and forever more. God speed and good luck my friend."

With that Saxton turned and walked into the jaws of death. Davis and Wolfe stood there stamping their feet, watching Saxton disappear in the blink of an eye into nothing.

The blizzard raged all about John Saxton, its bitter breath beat snowflakes through every crack and crevice of his clothes. His body shook as the wind buffeted it about like a feather in a chimney. Head down, Saxton willed himself to move forward. It was not a long way to the main gate, perhaps just over two hundred and fifty feet, but it might as well have been as many miles to Saxton. He became weaker and weaker for his thick woolen overcoat and woolen gloves became covered in a rime of frozen snow.

His outer garments had been liberated for him by his roommates. A black woolen over-coat lay over a white physician's smock pilfered from Dr. Hall's office closet along with a grey bowler. Saxton's only fear was that young Henry Talbot would be blamed not only for that but for the theft of the good Doctor's medical valise.

After what seemed an eternity, Saxton literally bumped into a guard standing in a dark corner by the main gate trying to stay warm by standing out of the bitter wind. His feckless, clean face looked down at Saxton's small black leather bag intently. Saxton presented his pass. The white string lay in the snow at his feet. The guard looked at the shivering specter closely, ignoring the pass altogether. Moments later the guard waved Saxton on, giving him back the precious pass as he did so. Saxton started to trudge away, but the guard yelled behind him. Saxton stopped; turned about, convinced he'd been discovered. Expecting the worse, he smiled trying not to look too guilty. The young boy simply waved and said,

"Have a nice evening Dr. Hall."

Saxton waved back and disappeared into the white void. Some distance away he stopped and raised the leather valise close to his frozen face and scraped the snow from it. On it in was the name...Dr. J. Hall MD. The golden letters seemed to burn through his clothing every time it bumped against his right leg. He shuffled forward, beyond exhaustion over the bridge to the railway station. Saxton staggered up to its front door. Unfortunately, the station was locked and empty. However, a North Carolina Railway mail train sat beside it, its feeble engine occasionally spitting steam into a strong and bitter wind. Saxton brushed deep snow from a bench, sat down wearily and wondered what to do next. He didn't have long to wait. Two railway guards fought their way through the gale towards him. As they came closer, they appeared to be arguing over something. Saxton rose, shaking snow off of his black overcoat. He folded the yellow cardboard pass in half so that the only words CSA PASS PERMIT in large bold letters were visible. The guards stopped. One, a tall thin man approached. In a loud authoritative voice, Saxton said,

"Gentlemen, good evening, I've been here freezing my ass off waiting for someone to open the Station House. Do you know who has a key? I'll be Goddamned if I'm going to stay here another minute waiting for a train."

The thin guard eyed the leather valise then waved away the pass.

"Doctor Hall, I'll see to it right away. By the way, where are you going?"

He looked at Saxton, his sallow face full of expectation. Saxton replied in a burst of inspiration,

"Why young man I'm headed for Howard Groves Lazaret in Richmond. I'm a specialist in contagious diseases."

He paused to scratch his groin while moving closer to them. The two guards edged away from him as if he had the plague for Saxton certainly looked like he was infected already. He pressed his advantage, sensing their discomfort.

"You know, cholera, bubonic plague and other equally horrid diseases that have been prevalent here at Salisbury Prison. Why I..."

It was too much for the guards. They backed up again.

"Doctor, you're fortunate indeed. Follow us, we know the conductor, a Mr. Dixon. We'll see to it that you get aboard right away. I do believe this mail train is going to Greensboro where we exchange mail and prisoners with the Yankees. From there you'll have to transfer to the Richmond & Danville line."

The older guard disappeared while the younger one stamped his boots and beat his gloves together. His musketoon leaned against the Station House, where an odd snow flake disappeared down its wide muzzle. He grabbed his weapon, put it on his shoulder and as he left, with Saxton close behind him, he said,

"It should take a few days, but considering the weather hereabouts, probably longer though. God it's so cold Doctor!"

Saxton was put aboard. The wizened Conductor, a Mr. Dixon, showed him a seat at the rear of a coach. It was the mail train and as luck would have it, it was waiting for another train to turn onto a siding a short distance away. Dixon was eager to have a long conversation with the Doctor but quickly changed his mind, for the Doctor was fast asleep. Beside him, a black leather valise inscribed with the letters, DR. J. Hall MD, glared back at Dixon. The conductor scratched his salt and pepper chin stubble, thinking,

'Where have I seen those initials before?'

Saxton woke abruptly as the train moved away from the station in short bursts of energy. The coach was dark and cold. He pulled his overcoat around his thin legs to cut the draft then ate a crust of bread. Clouds of steam swept by his frosted window like the breath of old men. A whistle blew loudly from the 4-4-0 Danforth & Cook locomotive in front of him. The mail coach began rocking back and forth as the train picked up speed. An iron snow plow fitted to the locomotive's cowcatcher, swept wayward snow drifts aside then stilled as it rumbled over the Yadkin River Bridge. A passenger train waited on a spur line a short distance further on for the mail train to pass it. Dr. Horatio Dawkins and his burly assistant sat looking out its frosted windows as the mail train flew by it in a flurry of steam and blinding snow.

BOOK THREE: CHAPTER 4
HELL'S ANGEL

The great blizzard of December 10-12th, 1864, paralyzed much of the Piedmont area of the Southern states. From Atlanta in the southwest, to Richmond in the northeast; telegraph lines, railways, roads and river traffic were in a complete state of chaos thereafter for many days. Unfortunately, for a very thin and dissolute character by the name of Dr. Josephus Hall, the storm did delay his escape from Salisbury Prison. It was in Greensboro, North Carolina, where he tried to board a train to Danville that a suspicious conductor, a Mr. Dixon, realized where he had seen the name Dr. J. Hall MD before. Dixon knew the bearded, sour smelling character asleep in his mail coach was not the real Doctor Hall in question. Saxton was rudely awakened as the business end of a Colt .44 was jabbed into his scrawny neck. He was promptly arrested and sent to Danville Prison #3, in irons on the Piedmont RR, since the tracks back to Salisbury had been wiped out by the storm.

To Saxton, Danville No#3 prison had the same smell, same food or lack of it, and the same disease and despair as Salisbury. While there, a fellow prisoner, Major Abner Small of the 16th Maine Volunteer Regiment complained,

"Our quarters were so crowded that none of us had more space to himself than he actually occupied, really a strip of the bare hard floor, about six feet by two. We lay in long rows, two rows of men with their heads to the side walls and two with their heads together along the center of the room, leaving narrow aisles between the rows of feet…I remember three officers, one a Yankee from Vermont, one an Irishman from New York, and a Dutchman from Ohio, who messed together by the wall opposite me. When they came to Danville they were distinct in feature and personality. They became homesick and disheartened. They lost all interest in everything, and would sit in the same attitude hour after hour and day after day…It grew upon me that they were gradually being merged into one man with three bodies. They looked just alike; truly I couldn't tell them apart. And they were dying of nostalgia."

The scenes of horrible crowding at Danville reminded Saxton of what Marcus said once about a slave ship he'd seen, captured off the coast of Georgia long ago. Within that horrid hulk, slaves laid side by side chained together, immobile, unable to perform even the basic rudiments necessary for their cleanliness and comfort. Saxton mused ruefully that slavery was indeed color blind because it picked its hapless victims by circumstance rather than by race. Luckily for Saxton and hundreds of other unfortunates around him, he was there only three weeks before Danville prison was scheduled to be closed down. Apparently, the irate citizens of Danville had been petitioning the Confederate Secretary of War, James A. Seddon since February, 1864, to close the prison because,

"The sick prisoners who were located in the middle of the town were infecting the entire population with smallpox and fever."

The city's enraged citizenry succeeded just before Seddon was relieved of his duties in January of 1865. Thereafter, Saxton, because of his past, was considered a spy amongst hundreds of others who were likewise considered too dangerous for normal prisons. These 'treacheries' were put on a heavily guarded train courtesy of the Danville & Richmond RR. They were summarily unloaded from their freezing boxcars into the belly of the infamous Castle Thunder Prison, located in the eastern regions of Richmond, Virginia. It was February 3rd, 1865 when Saxton first set foot inside it.

Castle Thunder, a 'high risk' institution, consisted of three former tobacco factories. They were large, separate red brick buildings crowned by rusting tin roofs. There were Palmer's holding up to four hundred prisoners, Whitlock's with up to three hundred and fifty prisoners and the largest, William Gleanor's with up to nearly seven hundred prisoners.

Saxton was imprisoned in Gleanor's, a large three story former tobacco warehouse on Carey St., between 18 and 19th Avenues. Palmer and Whitlock's located on either side of it were connected together by a long brick wall which encircled a small square yard. Numerous guard posts looked down onto the yard from atop nearby buildings. A common area behind these buildings was used for an exercise yard and for the prison's latrines.

Castle Thunder, converted in August of 1862, was mainly for those convicted of the worst acts of human depravity, the worst of which were called 'Pug-uglies' from Baltimore and the 'Wharf rats' of New Orleans'. Also included in this dissolute population were numerous union spies, traitors and northern sympathizers. It was said that conditions here were miserable at best. Not only that, one newspaper said,

"Even Southerners fear this loathsome place." And when death struck,

"One simply stretched out the man's limbs, put a piece of wood under his head, and notified the guard with the jocose remark, 'There's a fellow here got his discharge and wants to get out'".

Many prisoners delighted in their fearsome reputation as the prison's brutal guards were led by a Commander George Alexander, referred to by some, as the 'Anti-Christ'.

By the time Saxton arrived, Alexander had been relieved of his duties and conditions thereafter improved somewhat. The prison's former hospital was reinstated on the third floor replete with a promenade upon the roof of an adjoining wing. The prison's surgeon, a Dr. W.W. Coggin ordered lime to be spread upon the floors as a preventative measure against smallpox. The dormitory walls were whitewashed. It was into these conditions that Saxton, led by a black guard dragged himself down a long hallway. As he moved along, white whorls of lime dust rose about his leg-irons. The guard took him to the soldier's section. Within the confines of that dreary space, dimly outlined in the shadows, lay a familiar straw pallet with its attendant bugs waiting to feast upon his wasted body. Some wag near him commented that the lice were more loyal than any soldier, never leaving and always ready for duty, uncomplaining and reliable. On either side of Saxton were many rows of men tormented by body lice. These cadavers squirmed and twisted under thin woolen blankets. Saxton, luckily, had picked the lice off of his shirt while on the train.

His overcoat was somewhere in Danville prison, stolen from him as he lay asleep in a state of complete collapse. The room was very cold as the weather was unusually inclement. Frosted whirly gigs encrusted squares of dirty window panes above his head. Wood was scare. No heat permeated the stark premises. Steamy clouds of spiraling exhalations expunged from hundreds of suffering men, drifted towards the high wooden ceiling like souls wafting upwards towards a distant heaven. These unsavories coughed, passed wind, wheezed, defecated and groaned all about him. Some cursed, or cried out thrashing about on their pallets in a final paroxysm. As they died, they'd seen the 'elephant'.

Saxton in some ways became inured to the terrible tragedies he had witnessed. His conscience was numbed by it all, unable to understand the why of it. He lay on his right side, the shrapnel imbedded in his left thigh. His last waking thoughts that first night were of his family. He wondered why he'd received no mail from them for nearly two years as everyone else had. He murmured,

"Virginia, my arms are around you." John Saxton fell into an abidingly warm and strangely comforting deep sleep.

In early 1865, Castle Thunder became the principal prison in Richmond. Gleanor's first floor housed store rooms, an armory, a large kitchen and the 'halls for confiscation', while prisoners were incarcerated on the second floor. There they were divided up into soldiers and civilians. A series of copper bells communicated with every part of the building, forming a sort of tintinnabulation telegraph, greatly facilitating operations for the gaolers. It was these bells that woke Saxton the next morning. He roused himself, weak from exhaustion, to find 'Crazy Bet' Van Lew kneeling down beside him. Her soft southern voice whispered,

"You've just arrived haven't you?" He nodded weakly, his features gaunt, vacant. She continued,

"I'm Elizabeth Van Lew." As she wiped yellow drool from his beard, she enquired,

"And who are you Sir?"

Saxton's mouth was tinder dry. He struggled to speak. Recognizing his dilemma, the woman produced a metal flask of fresh water. Saxton drank it greedily until she released it from his grasping fingers.

"Sir, that's enough for now. As I was saying, what is your name?"

Saxton sat up; his exposed skeleton flush against a cold brick wall. He shivered while he drew a thread bare woolen blanket about his bony shoulders. Van Lew waited patiently, having been with such men many times before. Saxton relished the very presence of her.

Tiny, blondish, with high cheekbones and a sharp nose, Elizabeth in her forties was a spinster, prim, angular and nervous in movement. Saxton's attention was drawn to her brilliant blue eyes. They commanded him to speak.

"My name is John Saxton of Boston. Do you work here?" She tilted her head as her laughter tinkled like cat's feet walking over broken glass.

"Yes, John Saxton, you might say I do if they'll let me in. Here is some soup."

From under her cloak she produced a large clay thermos of warm leek soup. The smell of it was intoxicating. To Saxton it was the most delicious odor he had ever experienced. She wiped his scraggly beard with a clean rag then poured the heavenly brew straight down his throat. Warm and spicy, soupy tendrils found their way into his shrunken stomach. A wave of nausea overcame him. He sputtered, coughed and nearly threw up. Van Lew wiped his beard again and poured more soup into him. After a few mouthfuls, Saxton was full and could take no more. Grateful, he thanked her as she rose to administer her benedictions on others worse off than he.

A weak light straggled about the large room. After his eyes grew accustomed to the gloom, Saxton was amazed at just how many men were crammed into the space. It was Danville prison No#3 all over again. Literally, rows and rows of what were once robust young men were now pale imitations of what even the most imaginative mind would conceive to be human beings. A total degradation of the human species spread out before him.

Over the next few weeks, Saxton learned that Elizabeth Van Lew had grown up in Richmond, Virginia; the only child of a prosperous hardware merchant. And, like Saxton, Elizabeth inhabited a similar mansion on the highest of Richmond's seven hills called Church hill. In the past, both homes were often filled with important and talented figures of the day. The Van Lew mansion had accommodated such luminaries as Chief Justice John Marshall, Edgar Allan Poe and the Swedish soprano of note, Jenny Lind. But most importantly, both Saxton and Elizabeth were ardent abolitionists who detested slavery to their very core. Before the war, Saxton learned that Elizabeth persuaded her widowed mother to illegally free nine slaves, some of whom stayed on Church Hill as the war approached.

During the war, Van Lew's views on slavery were considered appalling, even treasonous to the good citizens of Richmond, the capital of the Confederacy. In her diary she wrote,

"Slave power is arrogant, is jealous and intrusive, is cruel, is despotic, not only over the slave but over the community, the state."

Although loathed by the citizenry of Richmond, she'd become known as 'Crazy Bet'. Unknown to Saxton and the city's irate citizens, Van Lew had amassed a spy ring of over a dozen operatives who had nearly three hundred farmers, trades people, school teachers, prostitutes, laundresses, business owners, church leaders and former slaves feeding her vital information on the whereabouts and intentions of any Confederate army within three hundred miles of Richmond. Among them was a clerk in the Adjutant-General's Department who had access to returns showing the strength of the Rebel forces and their whereabouts.

Another was a man in the Engineer Department who made accurate plans of the Rebel defenses around Richmond and Petersburg. Letters, maps, plans were regularly delivered to General Grant at City Point in the soles of heavy brogans worn by two trusted slaves. Hollow eggs, double walled warming plates or letters that were ripped into many pieces, then balled up to be palmed off when a propitious moment presented itself were other methods used.

It was this intelligence network that warned Van Lew of a certain Dr. Dawkins, his burly man servant and a young orderly registered at the Spotswood Hotel on Main St. They had gone to the Provost Marshall, Is H. Carrington enquiring about the whereabouts of a prisoner by the name of Captain John Saxton. To Crazy Bet, the presence of this unholy trinity ensconced in a local hotel roused her suspicions. She had to be careful for her daily activities were being closely watched by Confederate operatives. Her house and grounds on Church Hill were searched by them many times but to no avail. She later said,

"I turned to speak to a friend and found a detective at my elbow. Strange faces could be seen peeping around the column and pillars of the back portico."

Crazy Bet and her quiet mother were suspected of helping many prisoners to escape; the breakout of February 9th, 1864 being her most successful. At that time, over a hundred Union officers escaped through a tunnel, all of whom were later hidden by her organization.

A few days later after Saxton's arrival at Castle Thunder, Elizabeth Van Lew convinced Provost Marshall Winder into moving more sick prisoners to the hospital upstairs. Saxton was amongst them. At that time more information came in to her. It was made known through her intermediaries that a certain Dr. Dawkins was enquiring about Saxton's whereabouts at Castle Thunder. Unfortunately, Saxton's health deteriorated despite Elizabeth's best efforts to improve it. She would have to get him out of prison immediately to her private doctor. Because of Allan Pinkerton's interest in Saxton, Van Lew soon realized how important this John Saxton was. She had to get him safely out of prison immediately, but how?

Being a woman of means, she simply bribed the head of the prison's burial detail. After she'd given Saxton a powerful sleeping potion, his appearance became deathlike indeed. A yellowish pallor settled upon his visage with even more effect. To the prisoners lying near him, his head seemed carved out of a block of spoiled tallow. That evening, Elizabeth watched as an orderly stripped him naked then put his skeletal remains upon a canvas litter. Saxton was carried downstairs and laid out amongst the newly dead on the prison's 'dead wagon'. Van Lew followed it to a secluded area just outside the prison walls. Once there, one of her black servants took Saxton out of the 'dead wagon' and wrapped his emaciated body in a woolen blanket. The cadaver was put in a simple pine coffin then hoisted into a buckboard pulled by an old mule. A canvas tarp was tied down over it.

Changing into shabby clothes, Elizabeth Van Lew climbed into a nearby democrat, whipped her Tennessee Walker into a fast trot and headed home to Church Hill. While she wended her way through the darkened streets of Richmond, she bobbed her head, muttering to herself, occasionally flinging her dark unruly locks back and forth across her pinched vacant face. She'd become the target of what she described as

"The threats, the scowls, the frowns of an infuriated community……."

Meanwhile, deep within a warren of side streets near the financial district of Richmond, another identical buck board replete with an identical mule burst out of an alley as Saxton's buck board pulled into it. Screened by a high hedgerow, the driver jumped out unnoticed. He untied the black tarp then pried off the coffin lid, rousing an awakening corpse. He easily lifted Saxton out of the coffin and into a closed Portland carriage waiting nearby. Immediately, he jumped back onto the buck board containing an empty coffin covered by a black tarp and drove back to the prison posthaste.

Saxton lay supine on a wide leather seat in a closed carriage. His wounded left thigh throbbed from the beating it took inside the coffin. A distinguished looking Doctor Winslow administered another potion, covered him up then monitored his breathing closely as the carriage sped away in the opposite direction. Saxton was headed to a farm Van Lew owned just outside the city limits.

BOOK THREE: CHAPTER 5
NATION OF GRIEF

It was early morning on Valentine's Day, 1864. Virginia Saxton walked naked across her spacious bedroom to a large fieldstone fireplace at the far end of it. She reached up and carefully took down a framed Valentine card. Thomas Saxton had given it to his wife Muriel on Valentine's Day exactly two years earlier. Both of them were dead, but for Virginia, an undying duet of love lived in the words of a poem written on the card. Whenever Virginia needed hope and reassurance, its words comforted her.

To Virginia, the poem seemed to rekindle a hope that her husband John Saxton was still alive. Once more like years before he would come home and make his loved ones whole again. There was a sharp knock on the door. She dried her tears, set the framed card back upon its honored place and put on a red silk night gown. A reedy male voice behind the door said,

"Mrs. Saxton, I've a letter for you. It's from the War Department."

Virginia rushed to the door and swung it open, her eyes wide with expectation. Packard her black butler proffered a silver salver. On it was a cream envelope and a silver bone-handled letter opener. The butler backed away, waiting; his coal black eyes looking down upon her.

She grasped the envelope like a bible thrown to a drowning soul. She thought,

'Oh God, please let him still be alive. Please God have mercy upon him.'

Virginia deftly slit open the envelope then carefully took out a single sheet of cream colored stationary.

She looked at it for a few moments as if she could not, would not open it, because in doing so it might release any pain contained within it. She stood there immobilized and mute; Packard gently reached down and took the letter from her. He read it silently, nodded encouragement then handed it back to her on the silver salver. By this time Millie, her maid, and Nancy, her nanny arrived curious to see what all the fuss was about. The trio stood transfixed while Virginia began to read the letter. A few moments later, her shoulders sagged. The missive fluttered to the floor. Packard grabbed her. Millie and Nancy led her back into the bedroom. Other household staff arrived for Jack's persistent barking had aroused their curiosity. Packard's voice was hushed as the assemblage listened with to him in rapt attention.

"To Mrs. John Saxton, 102 White Road, Boston, Mass

From the Office of E.M. Stanton, Secretary of War.

It has come to my attention that your husband, Captain John Manly Saxton, of the Maasai Rangers, is missing in action. It is now presumed that he has been captured by the enemy during the assault by General Sherman's troops on Goat Hill near Chattanooga, Tennessee, November 25th, 1863.

I hereby apologize on behalf of the War Department for taking so long to notify you of the circumstances. However, it is my pleasure to tell you that your husband has won the Congressional Medal of Honor along with another Maasai Ranger, namely Lt. Charles Smith, who perished in the Battle of Port Hudson. The President himself has followed the actions of the Rangers very closely and considers his friendship with all of them as very special. As for your husband, Captain Saxton, I'll quote the citation for you now.

"On the afternoon of November 25th, 1863, General Howard's brigade on orders from General Sherman attacked the entrenched Confederate forces of General Cleburne along the northern flanks of Missionary Ridge known as Goat Hill. Captain Saxton leading a squad of Maasai Rangers successfully scaled the steep ridge under severe and accurate musket fire from enemy pickets. After intense hand to hand combat, they captured the enemy's cannons and while still under fire managed to turn them about inflicting heavy casualties on the Rebels. Although being wounded in the thigh by shrapnel, Captain Saxton and his Rangers maintained a steady fire upon the enemy. After a massed counter attack by the enemy, Captain Saxton was captured but only after he and his men spiked the enemy's cannons. His Rangers were helpless to prevent your husband's capture for they too were either severely wounded, dead or in retreat. Due to Captain Saxton's bravery and that of his Rangers, General Sherman was able to finally take the ridge, forcing Confederate General Bragg to abandon his left flank and retreat to Chickamauga Station.

It is with profound regret that I, the President and General Grant, have to give you this news. However, I'm hopeful that Captain Saxton will be found alive and well soon. Captain Saxton before, during and I'm sure after the war is over, has been and will be a credit to a grateful nation.

Edwin M. Stanton, Secretary of War
Washington, DC January 14, 1864."

Millie and Nancy returned from the bedroom and carefully closed the door. Packard gave the letter to Nancy. Millie looked up at him, his eyes question marks.

"I've given her a strong sedative Stylus. She's asleep now. I'll check in on her every hour for the rest of this morning. As for you Nancy, keep her daughter away from her until our mistress recovers from the shock of it all." Nancy gave the note to Millie. Packard, head of the Mansion's household staff spoke up.

"All I can say is that Master Saxton's life is in God's hands and may he bless and comfort the families of those brave Rangers who are not coming home. I'll get Rodney to notify Belle, Marcus and Virginia's parents right away. It seems the office telegraph is not working again. In the meantime, all of you attend to your duties."

Packard took the circuitous note from Millie, bent down and picked up Jack who'd returned with his red rubber ball. Nancy came forward, saying in her rich Irish lilt,

"Ay Packard, give me the wee rascal. I'm sure he'll be a comfort to his mistress. I'll put him on the bed beside her. It does seem remarkable that our new Jack has taken a real shine to his new mistress. Remarkable indeed it is!"

The telegraph connecting Saxton House to the Saxton Shipping Co. office on the waterfront was for some reason not working. Packard asked Rodney, the family chauffer to deliver the good news.

After breakfast, Rodney Tubman drove a democrat down the Snowhill Street towards Boston's inner harbor. As he rode along down the hill, the once brawny boxer was but a shadow of his former self. At fifty-five, withered and arthritic, he wheezed every time any physical effort was required of him. No longer master of the mastiffs, Virginia kept him on as a chauffeur and messenger boy. After riding down Snow Hill, the Saxton Warehouses rose to meet him. They were literally brimming over with war materiel destined for New Orleans. Rodney was excited that his master was still alive. He'd heard that Saxton had won the Medal of Honor. Rodney's only hope was that Saxton would be alive to receive it. His buggy came to a halt in front of the massive iron gates fronting the Saxton's waterfront property.

Rodney was let in through the locked gates by young Eddie Finch. He heard the young man close the tall iron gates behind him with a clang. Rodney dismounted, taking the thin reins in a boney hand. He looked at Eddy as the redheaded bit of a man ignored him. The gatehouse door shut with crash behind him. Rodney knew that Eddy was probably playing another game of solitaire. 'Fitting' he thought.

Rodney tethered his horse and walked into a vast maw of darkness called warehouse No#3. The Saxton Company office was perched high on the peak of the warehouse's pitched roof in such a way that one could glass all the ships that entered the inner harbor below long before they tied up. A rickety spiral of wooden stairs ascended ever upwards before him. Rodney grasped a thin iron railing and sighed. He knew Belle and Marcus would be up in the office. A Saxton Co. Captain in dress whites ran lightly down the steps towards him. He stopped abruptly saying,

"Do you have good news Rodney, for Belle's on the warpath? I was lucky to get out of there alive. The Katanga's been lost at sea. Poor Captain Carter, he was a good man and a dear friend." He clapped Rodney on the back saying,

"Cheerio my friend for I'm shipping out tomorrow for New Orleans." Rodney rejoined,

"Always did like New Orleans."

The Captain paused, telling Rodney that recently he'd been given power of attorney to complete the sale of Belle's properties there. With that said he made his way through a maze of stacked wooden crates. Rodney climbed a few more steps then stopped as the Captain's garbled voice ricocheted about below him.

Strangely enough, his final words were clear, ringing out like a cry from a coffin.

"See you later Rodney. Good luck and batten down the hatches."

Rodney grimaced. He watched the lithe Captain slip through a small door set into the tall sliding doors of the warehouse. The old man continued on his way ever upwards, his arthritic black hands grasping both railings for support. He paused once again breathing hard, thinking,

'I'm gettin' too damn old for this nonsense. Maybe I should go back to New York City and drive the Company coach like I did on Saxton's honeymoon. God almighty, lookin' after horses, then drivin' everyone hither and yon is takin' its toll on me. I need to settle down with a good woman like Connie Woods, the house cook. Maybe I'll try sparkin' her sometime; she seems nice enough.'

He resumed plodding upwards but stopped as Belle's voice bellowed above him. He thought ruefully,

'All I need right now is to have Belle mad at me. Hell, I'm just another poor innocent nigger doin' his duty. At least I've got good news.'

Children's voices rang out within the dark confines of the vast warehouse. Rodney paused on another landing amused by the antics of seven year old Cotton and his two year old brother Rufus as they played hide and seek amidst the mountains of wooden crates stacked in long rows below him. Their squeals of laughter and shrieks of discovery, defined their imaginary world. However, their merriment ceased abruptly. The warehouse became as silent as a tomb, as a wavering light far above them appeared, spectral and ominous. The boys hid behind a crate. Belle Brown emerged from her lair ready to administer justice. She didn't notice Rodney resting just below her. Belle leaned over the iron railing, an 'Inspector' lantern in her hand. She peered through the gloom then pointed the narrow beam of light at where she thought the miscreants were hiding. They remained out of sight as their mother screamed,

"Cotton Brown, I've told you a million times not to play in the warehouse. It's far too dangerous. Now get back to the ship. Look after your little brother until I get there. I won't be long. Now skedaddle both of you or your metakas's will see your father's hand for sure!"

Both boys ran off through the warehouse. Before Belle turned to go, Rodney felt the urge to speak. He knew it was a mistake as soon as he opened his mouth but it was too late. He wheezed,

"I say Belle Brown, you still have a way with the men in your life don't you girl!"

Rodney shrank into the gloom as Belle's lantern focused on her next victim. She hollered,

"Rodney Tubman, you come up here right this moment, you uppity New York City nigger. You hear me boy?"

She held the harsh lamplight high above her, looking exactly like a lighthouse. The black Val Kyrie thundered again.

"Come here right now Rodney! I want to talk to you in the office. It's important."

She turned about and disappeared from sight. Rodney thought woefully,

'The fat's in the fire now, you uppity New York City nigger. I wonder what she wants.'

Rodney continued to climb the last few steps as if he was a condemned man approaching a gallows. All he needed was a priest chanting the last rites beside him. The very thought of it made him giggle. He couldn't help himself. By the time he reached the office door his laughter rang throughout the bowels of the warehouse below him. Belle and Marcus Brown stood transfixed as a rollicking Rodney entered the office.

Tubman came to an abrupt halt. He took off his black bowler, wiped the sweat off his brow with a neckerchief then stood stiffly at attention. His black jowls swayed below his sparkling black eyes as he continued laughing, powerless to stop. Belle tried to stare him into submission but her will succumbed to his mirth. Slowly her full lips parted and soon she too was beside herself, totally caught up in the hilarity of the moment. Marcus, grim and unsmiling, walked around both of them and closed the office door.

After a few moments, the two sat down and silence regained the upper hand. Marcus remained standing. He offered his wife a clean linen handkerchief. Belle wiped the tears away and handed it back. Marcus retrieved the damp square of cloth and stuffed it into his trousers pocket. At over seven feet tall, he looked down at the two of them like a stern school master who just caught them smoking behind some outhouses. He said rather evenly,

"Well you two, are you all finished? I suppose a good belly laugh is a balm for a body's constitution occasionally, especially today, yes, especially today. My Lord, the telegraph here is down again and we've lost Captain Carter and his crew on the Katanga. As the company's interim manager, I'll have write distressing condolence letters after the required ninety days before its official with Lloyds of London. What a tragic loss." Marcus sat down beside her on a settee. Belle caressed the scars on his face.

"Yes my dearest, the Captain was very special. Everyone loved that dapper young man. My! My! Imagine losing two Captains in one year. First, it was Captain Wainwright in the South China Sea and now Captain Carter off Mombasa."

She let go of the tall Maasai. Her eyes however, continued to float upon his face like a soft cloud caught on a jagged mountain top. He smiled at her then upon Rodney who had taken a letter out from within the left breast pocket of his black riding suit. Rodney stood up and motioned for the couple to remain sitting. He hovered above them like a homing pigeon returning with a message. Nothing was said as he handed the letter to Belle. She opened it carefully and after a few moments, she held her hand to her face in utter despair but in the next instant the wave of depression passed like a black cloud over still waters. The letter, held high like a torch in the deepest part of some remote cave, waved about as Belle cried,

"Oh Marcus, Marcus, our Saxton is alive! He's alive!"

The Saxton house like millions of others in the nation of grief as some called the 'Disunited States' was held hostage by two opposites; despair and hope. Both of these volatile emotions rose and fell with every scrap of news, factual or otherwise. In a sense, each family directly affected by the Civil War was as such, incarcerated in mind and body as surely any prisoner of war. A third element of human nature that often forced its way into the equation was hatred; a total unconditional loathing of the enemy.

To Virginia Saxton, it seemed that the longer the war went on, the more she detested the Confederates. Man, woman or child, it did not matter, for Virginia was now utterly consumed by a deep and abiding hatred of them all. Perhaps the letter from Saxton with the news that he was alive yet a prisoner of war, unsettled her mind. The letter became a mantra of hatred, pure and simple. The enemy had taken her Saxton away from her. The letter was framed and put on the bedroom mantle beside Thomas Saxton's Valentine card. The two perched there like birds of a different feather, ready to fly through the eyes of those who gazed upon them directly to their heart of hearts.

Belle came to pay Virginia a visit early one morning in late April of 1864. Virginia had not come out of her room. It was ten o'clock already and Packard was very worried about her. After he let Belle into the foyer, he told her that Virginia was indisposed again. Packard's memory was long and accurate. Stylus was all too familiar with the depression that beset his former mistress Muriel Saxton when Saxton Junior had been at sea. The lad had been away for nearly three years on the clipper ship, the Silver Ghost. With this in mind, he took Belle's overcoat saying,

"Oh Belle, I'm so glad that you could come today. I'm really quite worried about Mistress Virginia. It seems that the letter from Saxton has unsettled her mind. For one so young, the consequences could be tragic indeed. Why I remember Muriel..." Belle took his hand to calm the distraught man.

"Hush up some. Stop frettin' and get us a tray of Freans and coffee. I'll be upstairs with her shortly." She looked directly into his eyes.

"You're a good man Stylus Packard. Don't let anyone tell you otherwise. Forty years under this roof has done little to curb your eaves-droppin' ways though."

She laughed as Packard made his way to the kitchen. Belle ascended the grand staircase. She laughed again as Packard far below her said something about 'women'. Millie met her at the top of the stairs, a load of dirty linen lay piled in a large wicker basket beside her.

"Oh Belle, thank God you're here. Everyone is worried about Mistress Virginia. She's still abed and it's after ten already. We're all at our wits end about her. Her parents, the

Reverend Clover and the rest of her friends are shocked by her state of mind. Stylus says she might even start walking on the widow's walk like her late mother-in-law Muriel did years ago, spyglass in hand. The very thought of it makes me ill. Oh Belle, I know you've tried to assure her before but please try again for her sake and ours. It seems like we're all being imprisoned by her grief, rage and hatred."

Millie picked up her basket and hurried down the grand staircase. Belle steeled herself. She padded down the long hallway towards Virginia's suite of rooms. Belle had been through this before when she ran 'La Belle Maison' in New Orleans. Many of her 'soiled doves' were young girls far from home, unschooled thus totally dependent upon their bodies to survive. Belle had been one herself for many years but through luck and circumstance prospered. Feelings of hate, love and fear ran like a trio of rivers throughout everyone. The trick was to keep them away from each other. If one overflowed its banks into the other two, the resulting pollution would forever make them indistinguishable from one another. Thereafter, the luck-less human heart would forever more be broken, unable to function, unable to live. Death by suicide was according to Belle, the usual solution. Her musings ceased as she continued to pad ghostlike down a long carpeted hallway.

Upon knocking on the door of Virginia's bedroom, there was no answer. She knocked again but louder. Silence. She tried the door but it was locked. Someone came up behind her. It was Packard with the Peek Freans and coffee. Belle took the tray while Packard took out a brass master key and unlocked the door. It swung wide open. A flood of morning light streamed through tall windows guarding either side of a large four poster bed. Temporarily blinded, the couple entered the large room. Packard took the tray from Belle and put it on an ornamental sideboard. Virginia was nowhere to be seen. Instantly, Belle knew where she was.

Without a word being said, she dashed out of the bedroom with Packard close behind her. Down the hallway they ran until they reached a door that led to the roof. It was wide open. Gasping for air, both Belle and Packard ascended a narrow staircase. The door leading to the observation deck was also wide open. Belle's heart was beating like a trip hammer as she and an exhausted Packard burst onto the roof's deck. To their relief, Virginia was sitting in Muriel's rocking chair, wrapped in a wool blanket, Jack Two on her lap, looking far out to sea.

Soon after, Belle and Marcus decided that Belle and the boys would move into the Saxton House where Belle could keep an eye on Virginia. Although the separation was difficult, Marcus was kept very busy in the Saxton Shipping office. They hired someone, a Theo Baxter, to replace Belle as bookkeeper. Belle by then realized that her two boys were too often being caught running around warehouses. Besides, the sale of her properties had gone well and she was financially independent. The boys needed a full time mother and for that matter a full time aunt for Felicity. They were just what Virginia and Felicity needed.

Over the next few months, Virginia put the hatred behind her and emerged fully healed by a river of hope into which Belle baptized her.

Strangely though, or perhaps inevitably, both women gravitated to the 'widows walk' perched like a fortress on the top of a mountain. The warming weather, blue skies and scudding cumulus; delighted everyone who sat there looking out upon the harbor activity going on below them. Both Belle and Virginia had known abject fear, intolerable violence and most of all, encompassing despair. For them there were real villains in the world, as well as really nice wholesome individuals. Some said that the natural world ran smoothly when in balance and some intellectuals even argued that the unnatural world of mankind needed villains to keep everyone else on their toes. These and other topics were discussed upon the roof top that became a haven for deep thought and even deeper emotions. It was here that Virginia and Belle decided that bigoted Boston must be put behind them. One sunny afternoon after church, Belle said to Virginia,

"Even though blacks here in Boston are free, they are estranged from the very society that freed them. My dear Virginia, it's not going to be too long before I'll have to move away, far away."

It was true enough, for Felicity and the two boys, Cotton and Rufus, were growing up fast, perhaps too fast as Cotton one day out of the blue said to Belle,

"Momma, some old man in town swore at me. He called me a nigger. What's a nigger momma? Is it bad? If I'm one, are you and daddy niggers too? Rufus and Felicity aren't niggers momma, cause they're both babies, right momma?"

Belle was not surprised. She dreaded the day when her children realized that color in America made a difference; that color mattered. To Belle, one's color was like paint; you couldn't scrub it off but you learned to live with it. She picked up her angry son and let him settle into her lap. His brother Rufus and Felicity were asleep upstairs having their afternoon nap. Packard and Millie sat nearby, completely silent as Belle began to tell her story.

"Yes Cotton, long ago in a place far away lived many people like us. I guess the hot sun over the years caused all the people there to turn black. In fact, I'd say from what I've read, that wherever there's a lot of sun, people living there bouts eventually go black. I'd say it's God's way of protectin' those folks from dryin' up and blowin' away so to speak." Cotton looked up, his large brown eyes full of wonder.

"I guess your right momma cause the sun is not so hot here; that's why I see a lot of white folks, right? Will we go white too if we stay here long enough? I don't ever wanna look white momma!"

Belle held him closer, kissing the top of his head.

"Cotton my son, folks like us will never ever go white no matter how cold or dark it gets around here. God made us black and black we shall stay forever. Besides, more people around the world are black than white. Be proud of who you are Cotton. It's the inside of you that counts; not the color of your skin. We're all red blooded inside son; white, black, yellow or brown, it doesn't matter. We're all God's children, equal in every way. No one is better than anyone else according to our Lord."

Cotton jumped off his mother's lap and stamped his feet on the floor in a fit of rage. He cried as his fists beat upon the top of the kitchen table.

"I'm goin' up on the roof and I'm never comin' down again."

Packard reached over, picked the little boy up and put him on his bony lap.

"Why's that Cotton? Why's that son?"

The boy squirmed away from him, leaping to the floor like a cat. He turned upon all of them. He cried,

"When Momma and Aunt Virginy go up there, they laugh. They're happy up there close to the sun. Besides, if I'm a nigger, at least up there I'll be a happy one."

With that, the boy ran from the kitchen before his mother, Millie or Packard could catch him.

BOOK THREE: CHAPTER 6
THE BOYDEN HOUSE BASTARDS

Salisbury's main train station loomed through drifting snow like a white monolith. Garrow and Blackstone detrained. They retrieved their luggage and stood in the cold airs, stamping their boots under a central square column resembling the bell tower of Lourdes cathedral. The aperture was flanked for some distance on either side by two appendages covered in thick white plaster. They looked remarkably similar to the merchant houses of Bruges, Belgium. They in turn were separated from the central tower by low three arched porticos. The entire structure was roofed in red tile.

The great blizzard had transformed the whole edifice into something that resembled a grotesque lopsided wedding cake. However, Horatio Garrow and his cohort Harley Blackstone were not there for a wedding but rather a funeral, Saxton's.

It was near midnight. A long line of Portland sleighs waited in the snow. A black porter signaled for the lead one to approach. It did. He loaded their luggage aboard it, as Garrow and Blackstone climbed in making themselves comfortable under a buffalo robe. Immediately, the black driver cracked his whip and the two horse team trotted off through the falling snow. The wind had died down but the snow was still very deep as the two horse team bulled their way towards Boyden House.

This opulent hotel opened in 1859. It was a handsome three story brick building topped by two massive copulas, a fine example of Beaux-Arts commercial architecture. Highly ornamented, and fronted by a six columned portico, it was luxurious by the standards of the day. When not in use, the 'Sample Room' was often used by traveling salesmen. From time to time, it was converted into a roller-skating rink measuring thirty by eighty feet. Boyden House too, was layered in freshly fallen snow. An old night watchman swept snow off the wide granite steps fronting the whole width of the portico. A black hand tipped a cloth hat as Garrow's sleigh glided to a stop in front of him.

Black leather-bound baggage was carried up the wide slippery steps by another black porter. The sleigh's matched team of Tennessee Walkers pawed the frozen driveway; their breath freezing instantly to their black muzzles. Garrow and Blackstone disembarked, followed the porter through the hotel's massive doors to the main desk and signed in. The porter was given a large brass key by a sleepy night clerk. On it was stamped Room #203. Before they departed, Garrow wrote a note. He handed it to the black night clerk along with two silver dollars then said curtly,

"Boy, make sure this note is delivered to the Sergeant of the Guard at Salisbury Prison by nine o'clock tomorrow morning, weather permitting."

Captain Ben Wallace read the note two days later. It said,

"Go to Room 203-Boyden House by noon.

Bring money and Lucas. Have John Saxton

held in irons ready for transfer into my

custody. Dr. Dawkins, MD"

Wallace was nervous, very nervous. The time had finally come when he had to pay the piper. He unlocked a small drawer in his desk and drew out a tin box. Within it were over two hundred gold double eagles. He pocketed twenty of them, hoping the remainder would be enough to satisfy his boss knowing full well that Garrow didn't trust currency notes issued by railroads, roads, utilities, manufacturers, associations and banks. As the war dragged on, metal coinage was being rapidly replaced with paper money, nearly half of which was counterfeit. Wallace as of late was forced to exchange paper money stolen from prisoners or given to him by the local pawn shops into gold double eagles at the local banks. There were many reasons to be very nervous.

For one, when John Saxton escaped, Wallace panicked but two days later a telegram arrived saying that a Captain John Saxton had been caught and transferred to Danville Prison No#3. He was presently awaiting transport to Castle Thunder to Richmond, Virginia. Saxton, reclassified as a spy, would never be sent back to Salisbury. Wallace, much relieved had another worry. By skimming the take from his criminal activities inside Salisbury prison by as much as twenty percent over the past year he played a dangerous game. If Garrow ever found out, Wallace was a dead man. The only problem was that he didn't realize he was dead already.

Lucas, while working in a nearby room as Wallace's new assistant overheard him and Les Baxter, the new leader of the 'Salisbury Rangers' talk about it. For some strange reason, the idea of amassing an illegal fortune during a war appealed to the young lad. Wallace needn't have worried because Lucas didn't know at that time that the ill-gotten loot belonged to his father. Therefore, to Lucas, the enemy had to be exterminated at all costs. If not by killing them, then most certainly by ruining them financially even if they were helpless prisoners. For Lucas, the lines of battle became drawn in a much smaller world; his mind. The boy was barely sixteen.

The Great Blizzard of December, 1864, was over. Railways, city streets and roads were once again busy as the war machine that gripped this part of the world began to function. Lucas had been told to get ready for a transfer the day before. He was excited for by then the prison had become an object of total abhorrence to the young lad. Lucas couldn't pack fast enough. The Chief Clerk implied that someone important was waiting at Boyden House for the lad. It was top secret. Therefore Lucas thought that possibly he was going to be promoted as a fully fledged spy, ready to take on Allan Pinkerton's minions himself. Wallace didn't discourage him from such naive ideas.

At precisely ten, armed with two gate passes; Wallace and Lucas climbed into a green cigar-box cutter and sped through the prison gates, over the prison bridge, past the prison train station and towards the town of Salisbury itself. Another trainload of misery passed them by as their cutter whistled over an icy trace. Presently, Boyden House rose up before them. They slid to a whispering halt. A black porter ran down the steps and took Lucas's heavy cloth carpetbag. He was waved off by Wallace who had good reason to do so, for he was carrying a small leather valise, heavy with gold coins. Despite his physical impediment, Lucas took the steps two at a time as the older man struggled along behind him.

Horatio was nervous too. He'd been waiting nearly two days for the snow storm to abate. Luckily he arrived just as it renewed its original fury. The hotel restaurant was severely hampered as to what it could offer. After two days of milquetoast and eggs cooked a dozen different ways, both men were ready to surrender. However, on the bright side, copious amounts of cheroots, corn whiskey and two local prostitutes kept them very busy and quite drunk.

Blackstone for the most part was laid out cold in a claw foot bathtub. One of the girls checked up on him from time to time to make sure he hadn't drowned. Finally, she pulled the plug leaving the brute laying there with a dirty water mark running along his back-side. The women were paid well and left the next morning. A black house maid accompanied by the hotel manager cleaned up the mess. Garrow apologized for the broken furniture, bathroom fixtures and the two holes in the bedroom ceiling. Apparently, his Colt .44 went off accidentally as the two women were servicing him. To make amends, the Major paid Nate Boyden, the hotel's owner, fifty dollars to repair the damages.

Someone knocked on the door of Room 203. Blackstone, dressed and sober, opened it. In stepped Lucas and Wallace followed by a black bellboy who promptly fled at the first opportunity. The door closed tightly behind him after sucking all the warm air out of the room. Lucas stood stock still then saluted his father. Both moved forward to formally shake hands. Captain Wallace and Blackstone stood side by side watching the formalities. Finally, Blackstone said jovially,

"For Christ's sake Horatio, give him a big hug. He's your son ya know."

Without a word being said, both stepped forward as if cast in stone. Horatio moved first, putting his arms around Lucas. His son stiffened then he too complied. Both father and son hung onto each other as if years of separated were being paid for in tears. Lucas wept as his father embraced him. The boy, now as tall as his father broke away and held him at arm's length, saying

"I'm proud of you father for what you've been doing for the cause."

Garrow smiled, secretly pleased that his years of training Lucas paid off. He thought,

'He's going to be all right, perhaps even more than all right. We'll see soon enough what he's made of.'

Horatio clapped his son on the back, saying,

"Well everyone, let's celebrate with a drink.

Blackie, pour us all some Beam; cheroots anyone?"

Wallace put his valise on a nearby table as Garrow looked at Lucas,

"Christ, look at him! He's a man now. Thank God you haven't seen the 'elephant'!"

Lucas didn't smile. He took a glass of Beam and in one fluid motion threw it back. He motioned Blackstone for another.

"Yes father I've seen the 'elephant' but it died of fright before I had a chance to kill the son of a bitch."

The boy's father was stunned by the sudden change. Lucas laughed in his face, realizing what had just occurred. Blackstone laughed too.

"Well Major, I can see that the nut didn't fall very far from the tree did it? The lad has grit in spades."

His remarks fell on barren ground. Lucas stood there, facing Ben Wallace. Everyone watched as Lucas walked over to the prison clerk. An unnerving coldness emanated from every pore from the boy's body. It began filling the room in an embrace that chilled Wallace to the bone. Looking down at the him; Lucas was transformed,

"I've learned a lot about death and destruction in the past four years, perhaps more so than most. My first allegiance has always been to the Confederacy. There is no room for mercy when facing traitors, isn't that so Captain Wallace."

Lucas moved before the befuddled Captain could react. With one powerful blow, Lucas smacked the smaller man across the face, knocking him down. His grey slouch hat lay crumpled beside him. He tried to get up but Lucas kicked him in the ribs. Wallace screamed and rolled over trying to get away. Lucas went after him, grabbed him so that his head bent back towards him. He hissed.

"Gotta knife father, I'm goin' to slit the bastard's throat right now."

Garrow didn't move. He was watching himself as a young man doing the same thing to a whore who tried to cheat him back in New Orleans. Lucas asked again,

"For Christ's sake, will someone get me a goddamn knife?"

Wallace tried to speak, as Horatio restrained his son. Wallace stood up gasping. Lucas looked down on him in total disgust.

"You're lucky, you little bastard for I woulda killed you. Done it before you know. All traitors die. Brave men die once, cowards die a thousand times, right father?"

Blackstone knowingly grabbed the Captain's valise from a table near him. He opened it. His large hand pulled out a torrent of gold coins.

"Look at this will ya! The man's honest to say the least. Came through right proper he did." Wallace stood up, patted down his uniform, then moved forward, his confidence restored; saying,

"Major it's all here. Two hundred double Eagles."

But before he could say another word, Lucas grabbed him by the lapels of his uniform and threw him onto a settee. He snarled in his face,

"You thievin' bastard. I counted them last night and there were two hundred and twenty of them. Major, I think he's bin takin' more than his fair share. I never realized that these were meant for you."

Wallace went white as a sheet. Lucas's next words chilled him to the core.

"And that's not all, John Saxton escaped on a mail train two days ago headed for Greensboro I'm told. I bet our Ben knows all about it don't ya Captain?"

Wallace groped for his whiskey on a coffee table fronting the settee. His shaking hands grasped the glass, causing the amber liquid to spill over. Acting like a wild animal trapped in a snare, he drank greedily then wiped his whiskers with the soiled sleeve of his field jacket. He teared up as he protested,

"Yeah I did for I and some others were settin' him up to catch his two accomplices. But Saxton took off early all by himself with a stolen hospital pass. He got through the gate and caught the evening mail train impersonating Doctor Hall. I still can't figure out how he ever made it through the white-out. Christ, you couldn't see your hand in front of one's face. You saw it. You know how bad it was. God almighty man, it took two days for your note to get to me! Worst storm hereabouts I ever saw. But I've got good news. They caught him in Greensboro. A telegram to that effect came in a few hours ago. Says he's not comin' back. Instead he's goin' to Castle Thunder in Richmond, Virginia."

Garrow lit a cheroot. He calmly poured another Beam and held it up saying,

"I salute you Captain John Saxton for bravery in the line of duty." He laughed at Blackstone.

"Hey Blackie, the bastard passed us while we were cooling our heels on the siding down by the Yadkin Bridge. We'll get him though. I've a score to settle with that man."

Blackstone agreed,

"He's a slippery one that Saxton. I've fought him twice now and lost. It seems I always end up rowin' away from him."

Wallace and Lucas looked at Blackstone blankly as if he was totally insane. Horatio stared at the clerk, his reptilian eyes paralyzing the man. The terrified Chief Clerk knew what was coming. He cringed, waiting for the Major to say something, anything at all. With the last reserves of courage, he pleaded.

"Goddamn it Major, your kid here took the money and is trying to frame me. Goddamn it all to hell! I caught him a few times with his hand in the cookie jar. What kind of whelp have you got here anyways?"

Horatio looked at his son who smiled back maliciously. He spoke evenly, as his reptilian stare refocused on Wallace. As he did so, Garrow became aroused.

"You're probably right as rain Captain. But he stole from you not me, and you stole from me. He reached down, grasped Wallace's collar and pulled him to his feet. Then with one fluid motion, he drove a Buck-knife into his victim's neck. The man dropped back onto the settee like a stone down an empty well. Lucas looked down on the Captain, rolled the body onto the floor and kicked his head viciously with the steel toe of his high boot. The man's skull cracked like an egg. Lucas stepped back in a rage. He turned on his father, screaming,

"Don't you ever do that again father!"

Horatio backed up, completely taken off guard. It was if he was looking into a mirror.

"Don't ever do what son?"

Lucas was now eye to eye with his father. He snarled,

"Don't ever stop me from killing someone ever again!"

Blackstone ran to the bathroom. He came back with a towel and a pitcher of water. He rolled the body away from a widening pool of blood. The big man was not happy.

"Give me a hand Lucas. We'll put him in that chair over there. I'll clean this mess up and pack our luggage cause we ain't stayin' here any longer. Jesus H. Christ Horatio! Why the hell did you kill him here! Why not kill him in the alley behind the hotel at night? I'll say it once; anywhere but here and anytime but now!" Horatio was pacific.

"You always worry Blackie, mostly over nothing."

Horatio reached for a half empty bottle of Beam.

"Here, pour some Beam on him. We'll walk him out the front door before he stiffens up, like we're carryin' out a drunk. From there we'll hire a covered sleigh, throw him into it and skedaddle. After we're well away from here, we'll dump the driver too. The railway telegraph will warn everyone once we're gone but we're not going to use the railway." Lucas looked at his father in mounting admiration.

"What are we going to do father?" Garrow held his son by his thin shoulders and said,

"Son, we're going to think our way out. To the north are the Yankees. To the south-east is Rebel held Wilmington, on the coast. I have a map. We'll take the Pee Dee River road or a boat to Old Hundred then catch the WCR to Wilmington. From there we can ride to Richmond on the Wilmington & Weldon. If that's not possible, I've many contacts in Wilmington. One of them is an old friend of mine, "Dickie" Wilson, who runs a cotton smuggling operation out of Wilmington to the Bermudas. It's called the Crenshaw Shipping Company. Either way, we'll be in Richmond in a few weeks. Saxton won't be going anywhere soon. But, we'll have to hurry some for if he's in Castle Thunder too long he might just die on us. I've heard the place is even worse than Salisbury. What a pity, I'd be denied the pleasure of killing him."

Blackstone finished mopping up. Two bloody towels were thrown under the bed. Harley grabbed their luggage and the valise containing the gold. Horatio gave him a ten minute head start; more than enough time to hire a sleigh. It was noon. Lucas was expected back shortly to start his shift. After that Sergeant O'Reilly would come looking for him. The unholy

479

trinity didn't have much time, so to have more time Horatio splashed the remains of a bottle of Beam all over the Captain's body. Lucas reached down and put the clerk's slouch hat on his head at a rakish angle. He laughed, saying,

"Well Major I suspect our dear Ben Wallace is three sheets to the wind."

Father and son with the lifeless clerk being held up between them, dragged him downstairs pretending as if the man was dead drunk. Blackstone proceeded ahead of them, paying for their room under the name of Dr. Theo Walker and party. He was impatiently waiting for them outside at the bottom of the hotel steps beside a covered Portland sleigh.

The weather in the meantime had cleared and the day promised to be sunny and cold. The clerk's body was lifted onto the front seat. Garrow and Blackstone climbed in on either side to prevent it from falling over. Lucas sat across from them, their luggage at his feet, including Wallace's leather valise. Everyone wrapped buffalo robes around themselves. The Chief Clerk was beginning to stiffen up and his face had become a pasty white. A black bushy mustache fortunately hid his blue lips. The black driver turned about and asked,

"Where to Sir?" Horatio replied urgently,

"Take us to the train depot boy."

After a short distance while traveling through a secluded copse of trees, Lucas stabbed the driver in the back killing him instantly. As the driver slumped over, Lucas jumped forward on the seat and grabbed the reins saying,

"I'm sorry Major, but we can't have any witnesses, not even a nigger."

After they finished disposing of two bodies behind a snow drift, Lucas whipped the two horses into a fast trot. Blackstone sat back and thought,

'Maybe the kid will be alright after all. Besides, I'm getting too old for this crap. I've heard there are lots of fancy villas in Mexico with hot and cold runnin' maids.'

The sleigh passed the prison then headed north to the Pee Dee River Road. The unholy trinity was on its way to Castle Thunder.

BOOK THREE: CHAPTER 7
JUSTICE FOR ALL

Virginia Saxton had not heard from her husband for nearly two years. She expected an occasional letter from him as both sides of the conflict exchanged mail and prisoners at various points along the front lines. It seemed that it would be only a matter of time in the early winter of 1864 that Salisbury would be liberated, however that was not to be the case, as the front lines were at that moment over four hundred miles to the north-west, near Knoxville, Tennessee.

Virginia Saxton lay in her bed reading the New York Tribune's front page. Splashed across it was the glaring headline,

'DARING DUOS DASH FOR FREEDOM'

Apparently, two of its reporters, Richardson and Browne, successfully escaped from Salisbury prison on December 18th, 1864 with two other men, Wolfe and Davis. Other northern newspapers were also enamored of their exploits. The clever escapees used stolen hospital passes to get by guards at the front gate. Once outside, they remained hidden in a nearby barn for twenty-four hours then walked through enemy territory to Knoxville, Tennessee, over four hundred miles away. Upon reading further, Virginia saw the name of her husband buried deep within one of the articles. It read,

"It is with eternal thanks to Captain John Saxton that we are even able to breathe the sweet airs of freedom that we do at this moment. Without his determination and bravery, the four of us would still be prisoners within the belly of the beast called Salisbury prison. It is my pleasure to announce to his family that he escaped a week before we did and as I write this column I do believe despite his poor physical condition that he boarded a mail train to Greensboro during a blinding snowstorm. May God protect him and may his escape into the waiting arms of his loved ones be successful."

Virginia leapt out of bed screaming for joy as the hapless newspaper was crushed by the hysteria of her emotions. Jack scampered off the bed, barking as the excitement of his mistress echoed down the long hallway. The grand staircase was no more an obstacle to Virginia than a bit of sand stepped over by an elephant. She literally flew into the kitchen, the stricken newspaper waving about her like a flag of victory. Packard and Millie heard her cries and were about to attend to her but before they could, Virginia was amongst them like a whirlwind, the little dog close upon her heels.

She cried out, "Praise the Lord, Saxton's escaped."

Packard was overjoyed but quickly rose as one of ten little numbered copper bells above his head tinkled loudly. Someone was at the front door. Packard, like a ship of state, sailed through the kitchen's swinging double doors headed for the foyer. Moments later he returned with a buff envelope resting upon a silver salver. He intoned sonorously, as he approached Virginia,

"It's for you Madam."

Virginia put down the tattered newspaper and took the envelope. It was from the War Department. She disemboweled the envelope, tearing out the missive in one fluid movement. Her eyes flew open in alarm. She sank on to a chair in total despair. Just like before, the second letter from the War Department once again fluttered to the floor like a wounded bird. Millie picked it up and read it as Packard hovered over her. It stated that,

"General John H. Winder, head of the Confederate Bureau of Prison Camps for the eastern region of Richmond, Virginia, has informed the War Department in Washington DC, that your husband, a Captain John Saxton, was captured in Greensboro after escaping from Salisbury Prison. He was then incarcerated in Danville Prison No#3 for three weeks but on February 3rd, 1865, was moved to Castle Thunder Prison in Richmond, Virginia, where he currently resides in the prison hospital. He is considered to be a spy for the Union and will not be paroled under any circumstance. It is with regret that the War Department has been unable to secure his release as he is physically unfit for any active duty. President Lincoln has expedited a request to Confederate President Jefferson Davis, for the timely release of your husband. If there are anymore developments, the War Department will telegraph directly to your office in Boston.

Best Regards:
E. Stanton, Secretary of War. February, 07, 1865."

For the next two weeks everyone jumped, especially Belle if any of their telegraphs chattered. Everyone knew that Castle Thunder was a criminal prison, housing Union spies, traitors, deserters and hardened civilian criminals. All prisons in the area were by mid February, 1865 were closed down and their populations sent to Salisbury, and other prisons. Many prisoners were paroled. The smallpox hospital at Howard Groves and other institutions of incarceration had taken in the rest. Intense stress caused by waiting for word of Saxton's present whereabouts took its toll. Virginia once again took to her bed under heavy sedation.

One day in early March of 1865, there was a knock on the front door of the Saxton House. Packard opened it to find Allan Pinkerton standing there as bright as a new Indian penny. His bearded face beamed as Packard took his famous bowler and woolen overcoat. Shortly thereafter he was shown into the drawing room where he made himself comfortable, namely by helping himself to a handful of cheroots Virginia had set aside for him for such occasions and a decanter of Ben Rinnes. He poured the expensive whiskey into an old fashioned crystal glass. The smoky peat essence within the twenty-eight year old scotch reminded him of heath and hearth back in the home of his childhood. As he savored the whiskey, he lit a cigar, sat down in an easy chair and muttered,

"I hope the Bonny Lass likes good news because I know I do!"

As he thought about drawing another wee dram, the door burst open. Virginia and Belle swept into the room followed by Marcus. All of them came to a sudden halt then embraced the diminutive detective as he moved to greet them. He sputtered in his rich brogue,

"Ay, you make me blush three shades of red heather you do. Please sit down because you will anyway after what I have to tell you."

The two women sat down together holding hands on the settee while Marcus chose a chair under a window. Pinkerton turned to the closed door and cried out,

"Packard and Millie quit eavesdropping, Get in here!"

The door opened. Both of them stood beside it. The tension in the air was palpable. Pinkerton, always the one for theatrics, pulled out a small piece of paper and passed it around. On it were written a series of numbers. He explained.

2 4 5 3 6 4 5 2 6 3 5 35 1 3 3 5 51 1 3 3 6 31 3 4 6 1 1 5 3 6 1 1 1

My agency, in cooperation with the War Department made contact with a Union spy stationed in Richmond, Virginia, week ago. Our cryptographers in Washington have deciphered this message as such. 'Saxton alive in my care.'

It took a few moments to register then Virginia hugged Belle as Pinkerton continued,

"Simply put Virginia, your husband is in a 'safe house' run by a skillful and courageous agent. From what we can ascertain, your husband is very sick but not near death's door…." Virginia jumped up crying,

"My God Allan he's alive! He's escaped from Castle Thunder prison and this agent is looking after him." Packard cried, "Oh praise the Lord!"

Pinkerton drew out another small piece of paper and as he did so his face clouded over. Virginia saw the warning signs. She sat down and grasped Belle's hands as if anticipating a coming storm. He passed the note to Virginia. On it were more numbers like the first. Her eyes told him, begged him to relieve her of the burden she dreaded for so long.

"Allan, when did this message arrive?" He nodded soberly. "Two days ago."

Belle sensed that Virginia was on the edge of hysteria. She snapped,

"For God's sake Allan, tell me what it means, NOW!"

Pinkerton gave the note to Marcus, who quickly scanned it and gave it back saying,

"You better do as she says Allan." Pinkerton looked at it. The second note read,

1 4 5 3 6 15 2 3 4 5 15 2 5 2 2 13 3 6 31 4 4 5 5 2 6 16 2 3 3 1 3

"Garow looking for him"

Virginia gasped as Belle shuddered at the very mention her rapist's name. Marcus leaped up and thundered,

"The son of a bitch will never find Saxton. I make this sacred vow that he will die by my hand and as such be sent straight to what you Christians call hell. By all three gods of the Maasai, I curse his name, the spawn of the devil." Pinkerton walked over to Marcus, his eyes playing across the Maasai's scars.

"Marcus my friend, I'm quite sure you want to kill him, one arm and all laddie, but I have a plan. I'm donning my old disguise. I'll once again be Major E. Allan of the CSA. Five of my operatives and I will go to where Saxton is hiding and make damn sure he is protected. If he's as ill as I suspect he is, it would kill him to move him. Apparently, the Union spy in question has a wide circle of contacts, 'safe houses' and other resources at her disposal. At least Garrow is in the area. That's to our advantage. Perhaps we'll get him this time. Lincoln has instructed me personally to rescue Saxton or at least protect him until General Grant takes Richmond, possibly by April. Before then, the Rebels will be interested in more important matters than looking for Saxton. No, I want Garrow alive." Belle stood up her voice rising, full of malice,

"I pray that he's preferably dead Allan, preferably dead indeed! By the way, you said the spy was a woman. Who is she?" Pinkerton remained silent.

Marcus pleaded with Pinkerton to take him but after much discussion realized that he was needed more at Saxton House alive than somewhere else dead. It would be a double tragedy if he too, was never to be seen again.

An unholy trinity acquired a large suite of rooms on the second floor of the Spotswood Inn in Richmond, Virginia. Main Street stretched out below, affording an excellent view of the goings on around them. Ever cautious, especially since their escape from Howard Groves Hospital a few years before, Major Garrow disguised himself as a rich country gentlemen. Lucas was similarly attired and mannered. Blackstone however, remained dressed as the proverbial man servant. He complained bitterly,

"God almighty Horatio, do I have to wear this monkey suit all the time? And this beard is the worse for wear. Besides, it itches too."

Horatio looked at Blackstone dressed in a pair of black trousers, an ill fitting black double breasted linen jacket, a white cummerbund, a red silk vest, a stiff celluloid white collar and a pair of white cotton gloves. His black patent shoes were one size too small. As a result, Blackstone's walk was more like that of a very large pigeon-toed penguin crossing a slippery ice floe. On any other man, the effect would have been quite handsome but on Blackstone the effect was totally ludicrous. Garrow laughed,

"Harley, nothing on earth will cover up the fact that you're pug-ugly. You'll always have a nose that's three sheets to port and your size is equivalent to that of a gorilla."

Blackstone growled as Horatio walked over and put his arm around the man's broad shoulders.

"But my dear friend, polite society demands propriety as they say. So bear it well Harley and I'm sure your wicked mind will be rewarded."

Exasperated, Harley sat down. His face vacant, for he didn't have a clue as to what Garrow was talking about. He began again, his deep voice petulant tinged with desperation.

"For Christ's sake Horatio enough of this palaver. Let's get something in train. We'll steal a carriage, go to Castle Thunder, present the Provost-Marshall's request for a prisoner transfer, get Saxton, kill him and get the hell out of here!" Horatio laughed,

"My! My! You always were impatient. Patience they say is a virtue, so let's become very virtuous indeed. There's no need to be too hasty my friend. One never knows what dangers lurk in the shadows waiting to jump out at you. No my friend, I've missed the boat too many times trying to kill Saxton however I must say you have succeeded on occasion."

This old joke did not sit well with Blackstone. He stood up, stubbed out his cheroot then drained a nearby whiskey glass.

"I've had enough. Those Boyden House whores have given me the pock. Christ man, I'm peeing fire night and day. How about you mate?" Garrow shook his head. Blackstone swore.

"You're a lucky bastard. God almighty, the three weeks we spent gettin' here nearly killed us! Nothin' seemed to go according to plan. First the damned sleigh broke a runner. We barely made it into Old Hundred. The Reb's train was a day late cause the tracks were blown up. Then the trip itself was less than satisfactory. Jesus Christ, the smell of those wretches in the prison cars upwind of us was worse than the hold of the Wanderlust. Why I stay with you Horatio is beyond belief. I'm goin' to get us a buckboard and a spare horse at Head's Livery right away. I think it's right proper transportation for a pompous country gentleman, his bratty son and his, may I say, his proper manservant. Give me some money. I'll be back in an hour. Be ready."

Harley stuck out a massive paw. The Major, taken aback by Harley's attempt at a tirade, meekly gave him three double eagles. The gold coins looked like three peas on a coal shovel. Harley strode to the door, slamming it behind him. Garrow looked at Lucas.

"Well Luke, you heard the man, let's be ready in one hour. I'd say there's more than enough time to figure out where and how we're going to enjoy ourselves with that nigger pokin' dog, Mr. John Saxton."

The Garrow party arrived at Castle Thunder only to be told that a Captain John Saxton had died two days earlier and was buried at Oakwood cemetery. Horatio was livid that in life and now in death, Saxton slipped through his fingers. When informed that a certain Elizabeth Van Lew attended to Saxton's body, he became uneasy. While he was in Groves Hospital, Horatio saw 'Crazy Bet' making her rounds. Her reputation as a Union sympathizer was well known even early on in the war. No, something unnatural and devious was going on.

The trio left the prison posthaste for the Office of the Prevost-Marshall, a Mr. Samuel McCubbin. The Prevost-Marshall was out for lunch but his assistant Mr. Thomas Doswell was more than willing to aid a southern gentleman. Garrow explained that although he was shocked to find out his cousin was a spy for the Union, his cousin was dead and as such deserved a proper burial in the family plot in the City Point cemetery. After a short desultory conversation, the trinity left for Oakwood Cemetery with a disinterment order for John Redford, the groundskeeper. To Garrow, it somehow had all been too easy. Why?

Again, Horatio felt a spasm of trepidation as he approached Oakwood cemetery. Horatio reined in his horse at the crest of a hill overlooking the cemetery. He lit a cheroot. Blackstone drove the buckboard under a grove of pines. He leaned over, tying the reins to its brake handle. Both he and Lucas jumped down. Blackstone went for a pee. A few moments later, Lucas heard Blackstone curse. He laughed at Blackstone's dilemma as he walked over and held the reins of his father's mount. Meanwhile Horatio looked down upon a flat desolate plain. Strewn amongst scrawny pine trees were long rows of wooden grave markers that leaned this way and that as if planted in haste then left to fend for themselves. Horatio lit a cheroot.

"Luke, you stay behind right here under these trees." He leaned over.

"Here's a pair of binoculars. While Harley and I are down there, watch us carefully. We could be walking into a trap—I don't know, but I just have to find out if Saxton is still alive, I just have to. One day you'll understand why."

He paused. The Major pointed at a small house barely visible through trees dotting the cemetery. Lucas turned slightly, scanning the cemetery even more closely. After a few moments, Horatio reached down and took the binoculars away from Lucas. He adjusted them then focused in on a group of black grave diggers far off to his right. To his surprise, over forty coffins were laid out in neat rows. Some had been there too long as the bodies within them had bloated, bursting the pine coffins wide open. The wind changed and within minutes a sweet sickly stench wafted its way towards them. The two mules pulling the buckboard heehawed. Blackstone walked back, buttoning his fly, cursing as he did so. He grabbed the halters, calming the mules. Garrow's mount stamped its hooves nervously while Horatio continued to scan the cemetery. He stopped as he came upon the area where Union soldiers were interred according to Doswell.

There, more coffins were laid side by side. The weather was warming although the day was somewhat overcast. The Major dismounted and gave Lucas the binoculars. Lucas mounted his father's horse in one fluid motion. As his son scanned the cemetery, his father came to a decision. He walked around to look up at his son perched high above him. Garrow stubbed out his cheroot on the sole of his son's riding boot. He looked up.

"Luke, if anything goes awry, I'll take off my hat. If that happens, get out of here fast. Do not hesitate and for Christ's sake do not go back to our hotel. I have a friend, John McCrutcheon at the Rebel House. It's located in the basement of the Exchange Hotel right across the street from the Ballard. He'll have a package waiting for you. Follow his instructions to the letter. Promise me now." Lucas did so, but reluctantly, saying,

"You're my father who I love dearly. Please let me go instead. I'm still just a boy. Whoever is down there will never suspect me if they're looking for you. Besides, I've seen Saxton as a prisoner, you have not. Men change dramatically if the conditions in prison are bad enough, and believe you me father, Salisbury was terrible. Saxton will be shrunken, bearded, and totally different from what he was. Can you be absolutely sure that anybody down there will be that of John Saxton?"

His father watched a play of emotions cross his son's face. Garrow was firm, saying,

"I'm sure I can recognize him even in death." Lucas wasn't so sure, saying,

"How's that Major?"

Garrow laughed as he looked across at Blackstone taking another pee under one of the tall pines.

"You see son, Saxton has scars on his neck when Blackie had him by the throat at Fort Sumter." He called out,

"Blackie, you poxy bastard, come here and tell Lucas about the scar on Saxton's neck."

Blackstone walked over and as he did so flexed his long fingers. Each one ended in a long, pointed and very sharp fingernail. He thrust them forward like a row of freshly sharpened knives. Lucas shrank back. Harley laughed.

"Cut him on the neck with these I did."

"Right here it was, about two inches long on the left side. Too bad I was in too much of a hurry at the time. If I hadn't been, we wouldn't be here layin' our balls on the line. Major, 'Let sleepin' dogs lay, says I." Horatio ignored him.

"Well Luke, Blackie and I are off to see if that dog is really sleepin' or not. Let's go."

He shook his son's hand, stood back and saluted sternly, his eyes strangely soft and moist. The Major regained his composure.

"The cause Luke, remember the cause if it's the last thing you ever do."

Lucas tried to speak about something deeper, more important but before he could, his father jumped onto the buckboard. Blackstone slapped the leather reins against the boney withers of the two mules. Two shovels under a canvas tarp behind them began to rattle like loose teeth in an old skull. Horatio turned about and waved at his son one more time. After a few minutes, he disappeared around a bend in the road. Lucas dropped the reins. He adjusted the binoculars carefully. A few minutes later, the buckboard came into view. He saw his father jump down then walk up a narrow path towards a small log house set back in the trees. A skinny man, presumably John Redford came out to greet him. The Major gave Redford the disinterment order. Lucas continued to fixate on his father's hat. Nothing seemed suspicious as the two men were led by a black gravedigger to a section of newly dug graves. Blackstone followed driving the buckboard.

Once there, Redford pointed out a marked grave near a copse of pine trees. Lucas watched closely as the grave was dug up. The young gravedigger jumped into the hole and with one mighty effort lifted one end of the coffin up, resting it against the foot of the grave. Just as the gravedigger climbed out, Garrow took a shovel and smashed open the coffin. The thin pine boards splintered, revealing a coffin partially filled with rocks. The gravedigger fled into the trees. The Keeper tried to restrain Garrow but he was knocked down. As Lucas watched, his father reached into the coffin and retrieved what looked like a piece of paper. Lucas was sweating. He wiped his eyes and face with a cloth then looked once more through the binoculars. A group of men armed with rifles emerged from the tree line. Lucas watched in horror as Blackstone began firing at them. His father turned and waved his top hat. Lucas put the binoculars into the saddle bag, grabbed the reins and rode away at a gallop. He didn't look back.

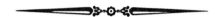

John Saxton was not enjoying himself at all, even though a Major Allan showed up unexpectedly with five suspicious looking subalterns trailing behind him. A Doctor McGovern nursed Saxton back to health by feeding him copious quantities of pea soup. Saxton was grateful that the good Doctor didn't have Freans on the menu. Although weak and disheveled, he tried to rise up in his bed as his old friend was ushered through the door by the gruff curmudgeon, who declared,

"Mr. Pinkerton, he's weak and tires easily. You've got five minutes sir; five minutes then I'll have to ask you to leave."

Pinkerton nodded and took out a cheroot. The good Doctor admonished him by saying gruffly,

"And no smoking; he'll cough his lungs out."

With that said, he closed the door. Saxton tried to laugh but gave up saying,

"Stuffy old bugger isn't he?" Saxton eyed his friend saying,

"Well now, are you not the very same Major who missed all those guns and ammo hidden on the Folkstone back in '61? A very sloppy inspection indeed Major." Pinkerton as he chewed the end of a hapless cheroot.

"I guess you're right Captain. I must reprimand whoever was in charge at the first opportunity I get."

As usual Pinkerton paced the floor, his small hands clasped behind his back. He looked worried. Finally he took a chair prisoner and sat upon it with a thump. His butternut field hat was expertly thrown upon a nearby card table. The savaged cheroot was carefully replaced in a tin humidor tucked away in a breast pocket. Pinkerton brushed bits of tobacco off of his double breasted tunic, leaned forward and said evenly,

"Garrow's in town looking for you. The lady that sprang you from Castle Thunder has taken preventative measures to stop him from finding you." Saxton grinned,

"Are you one of those preventative measures Pinkie?"

"Yep, you might say I am."

"And, if I may ask, what are the other measures?"

Pinkerton rose and started pacing again. He went to a window, pulled its green drapes back slightly and looked out across long fields of cotton, newly leafed and pregnant with soft white wonder. The window, through which he peered, overlooked a large barnyard over-run with bantam chickens. A flock of white Peking ducks wandered over from a small pond. A narrow gravel road ran between two outbuildings, crossed a small stream, bolted through a gate then wandered back and forth, skirting a series of rolling hills until it disappeared miles away to the north. A wisp of dust on that road rose above the distant hills. Pinkerton turned abruptly,

"Company's coming Saxton, so stay put. I'll send Agent Thomas up to guard you. Gotta gun?" Saxton nodded.

Pinkerton left. A few minutes later, Thomas appeared. A small man like his boss, he sported a well fitting grey overcoat that covered a butternut uniform. His epaulettes indicated the rank of First Lieutenant. However his broad field hat was two sizes too large for it sank below his brow. He tried to compensate by pushing it back over his forehead. The effect was comical. However, he was all business as he moved quickly to the window. Thomas looked out to the road, thinking whoever it was out there a mile away, was making no attempt whatsoever to hide their presence. Down and to his left four other agents in Confederate uniforms were hiding in strategic locations around the farm house. It was then that the dogs began barking.

Saxton lay there wondering what all the commotion was about until he heard what seemed to be a buggy coming to a stop in the yard just below him. Thomas didn't say a word but kept looking out the window at the horizon. Saxton stiffened. He reached for a pepperbox pistol hidden under his pillow. Soft footfalls on the landing outside the door stopped. Someone knocked three times. Thomas looked at Saxton without alarm. The door opened and Elizabeth Van Lew stepped into the small room.

Like a small bird, she alighted on a chair, carefully preened herself, took off her yellow leather riding gloves and laid them across her blue dress. Pinkerton came into the room a few moments later. Thomas left and closed the door behind him. Saxton cradled the pepperbox pistol on his chest. Elizabeth's tinkling laughter floated across to him like a zephyr on glass wings. Her brilliant blue eyes sparkled as she exclaimed.

"Oh Saxton, I've just heard the most hilarious news. Garrow and his brute of a butler were told by Assistant Provost-Marshall Doswell that you died in Castle Thunder hospital two days ago. Apparently, the Major was not convinced of your untimely demise, so he got a disinterment order to exhume your coffin. Guess what gentlemen? There was nothing in the coffin but rocks and a note, of which I have a copy right here."

Saxton tried to laugh but couldn't. Pinkerton was given the note. After a few moments he handed it to Saxton saying,

"Well I'll be damned!" As Saxton read it, he finally with great effort, laughed and laughed saying,

"How could you Elizabeth?" The note, in neat copperplate script simply said,

"Dear Mr. Garrow and your rucker butler, a Mr. Harley Blackstone. Welcome to the cemetery at Oakwood. You are under arrest for murder, desertion, and other crimes against the Confederacy too numerous to mention. Don't move a muscle as the Provost-Marshall, Mr. Samuel Maccubin and his assistants will disarm you and take you both to spend your first night of many in the inhospitable confines of Castle Thunder. Goodbye and might I say, good riddance." It was signed, John Saxton.

Saxton looked at the homely woman across from him as if she was the most beautiful person in the world. He could scarcely believe what she had done. He croaked,

"They don't call you 'Crazy Bet' for nothing!" She replied demurely,

"Why John Saxton, how could you possibly imagine that I, Elizabeth Van Lew of Church Hill, could be remotely accused of an unsettled mind and a tawdry demeanor."

Saxton was grateful. "I still think you're crazy, but I don't care, I'll love you always my dear". Elizabeth blushed slightly. She chirped.

"The Doctor says that you're well enough to travel a short distance but no longer, however the war is rapidly coming this way. I must get you into Richmond before a general panic erupts. I'm quite sure there'll be curfews and food shortages. I've prepared for it in the last place they'd ever look for you. The Ballard House Hotel on the corner of Franklin and 14th streets is the perfect hiding place for an unsavory person such as yourself." She laughed.

"I've already made arrangements for you to stay in suites that take up the whole top floor of the hotel. You'll be safe enough there, as all its employees in are in my organization including John Ballard the owner. We'll go tonight. You'll be let into the hotel from a back alley. I've brought some new clothes for you Saxton as I burned your lice infested old ones long ago. As for you Allan Pinkerton, I thank you and your brave men for coming here, risking your lives every mile of the way. By the way Allan, you and your men will be staying there as well." Pinkerton nodded in agreement. Saxton rose up, his body still stiff and sore.

"How long do you think we'll be there Elizabeth? Every day away from my family is an agony, the pain of which I can hardly bear anymore."

Saxton started to weep then lay back completely spent.

The next day, March 22, 1865, Saxton and company were safely ensconced within the luxurious confines of Ballard House. The affable owner, John Ballard, saw to it that their every need was looked after with punctilious perfection. Of course his dedication was encouraged by the fact that Pinkerton brought with him a generous supply of double eagles for just such an occasion. Saxton had his own small bedroom from which if he sat up in bed, could view the city of Richmond spread out before him. A few mornings later, to his utter amazement he saw a platoon of black Confederates drilling in the street below his window. Saxton watched as they marched away cheered by white crowds lining the avenue on both sides. He asked himself why then crawled back into bed exhausted by delusions harbored so carefully over the years. The answer eluded him until he remembered John Noland.

Pinkerton arrived with Saxton's coffee and that day's copy of the Richmond Whig newspaper. Saxton lay back on his double bed and scanned through the paper for a local perspective of the war. An intriguing notice buried on page twenty-one, caught his attention. Its bold header said,

'MILITARY TRIBUNAL HANGS TWO SOLDIERS'

His interest aroused, he read the article. It was a revelation. It said,

"According to reliable sources, a Military Tribunal consisting of Provost-Marshall Is H. Carrington and two Judges convened at the Lewis F. Powell Jr. Court House on Main St. yesterday at noon. Evidence against the accused, a Major Horatio Garrow and a Private Harley Blackstone, was conclusive enough for the Tribunal to find both Confederate soldiers guilty of murder and desertion. The accused were hung last night behind the courthouse. Their bodies will be interred this morning at Oakwood cemetery. They'd been incarcerated at Castle Thunder since their capture strangely enough in the aforementioned cemetery.

At that time they were caught trying to exhume a body. Sources close to this reporter, say that the coffin oddly enough, was with rocks upon which lay a letter. The missive in question was supposedly from a dead prisoner, a Union spy, Captain John Saxton. Military records pertaining to this case have been destroyed. When asked why, Assistant Provost-Marshal, Mr. Thomas W. Doswell refused to comment. This reporter will keep our readers posted on any further developments in this bizarre case."

Saxton looked up at Pinkerton. "Those who live by the sword shall die by the sword." Pinkerton nodded in agreement.

"I hope his son Lucas doesn't blame you for his father's death. Apparently he deserted Salisbury Prison to be with him. A young man was also seen fleeing Oakwood cemetery on a black horse at the time of his father's capture. Beware Laddie for sometimes chickens do come home to roost." There was no response. Piqued, Pinkerton became truculent, saying.

"Saxton are you paying attention to me?" He looked down. Saxton had fallen asleep.

Pinkerton reached over, took the paper off Saxton's chest, folded it, put it under his arm and quietly left the room.

Richmond, Virginia, was founded in 1737. The original streets were laid out by a William Mayo. Located at the head of navigation on the James River, it later became the Confederate's Civil War capital replete with a White House only one hundred and ten miles from its larger counterpart in Washington, DC. Both capitals were much sought after by either side as a psychological objective. If either was captured, it would have been a crippling blow to the other's will to fight. While Washington, DC was more of a bureaucratic nexus, Richmond was not. Its extensive Tredegar Iron works, vast naval yards, multiple medical centers and many warehouse supply depots, made Richmond a prime military target.

Seven major Union campaigns assaulted the city during the Civil War. Two came within sight of it but were beaten back in 1862 and early 1864. Throughout the late summer and fall of 1864, General Grant continued to threaten Richmond and its smaller satellite city, Petersburg. Nearby Fort Harrison was captured in September of 1864. However, the savage winter of that year brought military operations by both sides to a close. In the interim, massive and extensive trenches were constructed by the Rebels around Richmond. During the memorably bitter winter of 1864, just staying warm and finding enough to eat for its defenders was very difficult. With the coming of spring, Grant's offensive started again against an enemy whose soldiers were deserting en masse. General, Robert E. Lee was forced to retreat from Richmond on April, 02, 1865. Oddly enough, General Grant never set foot in Richmond but went directly to Appomattox Court House, Virginia, instead. Both Lincoln and General Grant agreed that the honor of being the first Union troops to enter the city would go to a regiment of the USCT (US Colored Troops) under the command of General Weitzel. To the stricken white residents of Richmond, their nightmare had come full circle.

Upon evacuation of the city, the Confederate government of Jefferson Davis ordered the burning of all government warehouses and the supplies within them. This reckless act resulted in considerable collateral damage to factories and houses in the city's business district, nearly two thirds of which, burned to the ground. More of the city would have succumbed if it hadn't been for the Union troops commanded by General Weitzel. Without their help, undermanned Richmond firemen would have been severely tested indeed. As it was, Union troops also restored order and prevented further looting. General Weitzel opened up the remaining warehouses, allowing a starving population to be fed and clothed. A Sallie Putnam, who lived in Richmond throughout the war, witnessed the fall of her beloved city. She later wrote,

"As the sun rose on Richmond, such a spectacle was presented as can never be forgotten by those who witnessed it...All the horrors of the conflagration, when the earth shall be wrapped in 'flames and melt with fervent heat, were, it seemed to us, prefigured in our capital. The roaring, the hissing of the flames, the bursting of shells at the Confederate Arsenal, the sounds of the instruments of martial music, the neighing of the horses, the shouting of the multitudes...gave an idea of all the horrors of Pandemonium. Above all this scene of terror, hung a black shroud of smoke through which the sun shone with a lurid angry glare like an immense ball of blood that emitted sullen rays of light, as if loath to shine over a scene so appalling...[Then] a cry was raised: 'The Yankees are coming! The Yankees are coming!"

From his hotel suite, Saxton sat in a chair close to a front window. From there he looked down on the conflagration as it spread all about him. The Ballard Hotel was surrounded by flames. John Ballard was frantic. The Exchange Hotel directly across from him was on fire, its roof and east side burning with furious abandon. Pinkerton remained with Saxton while his men went up onto the roof of Ballard House with wet blankets and buckets of water. Sparks and burning embers swirled through the dense smoke all about them as they beat out any fiery comets that landed near them. Hour after hour the men wet their blankets and stood vigilant against a growing holocaust that was to consume most of the city. Saxton and Pinkerton looked down upon the chaos below them. Gangs of Rebel soldiers drunk from stolen liquor prowled the main thoroughfares followed by a drunken mob bent on looting any and all stores unlucky enough to attract their wanton attention. The Richmond Whig newspaper reported that,

"The streets were crowded with furniture, and every description of wares, dashed down to be trampled in the mud or burned up, where it lay. All the government store houses were thrown open, and what could not be gotten off by the government, was left to the people, who everywhere ahead of the flames, rushed in, and secured immense amounts of bacon, clothing, boots, &c."

Coincidentally, Ballard House where Saxton hid out, and the Lewis F. Powell Jr. Court House where Garrow and Blackstone had been hung, survived the firestorm. The Union's occupation of the city was complete by noon the next day and order was restored. By four that afternoon the worst was over. The fire had simply run out of material to burn.

The day before up on Church Hill at her mansion, Elizabeth Van Lew retrieved a large Union flag she had hidden during the war. A few days before, she had also hidden a pro- hibited skinny buckskin horse in a padded bedroom. Hours before the arrival of the first Union troops, she raised the Stars and Stripes over the stricken city; the very first to do so. An angry mob of citizens threatened to lynch her and burn her house to the ground but the courageous spinster faced them down. As the Richmond Daily Dispatch reported later, the defiant Van Lew cried out to the mob from her front steps,

"I can tell you, too that Mr. Grant will be in this city within twenty-four hours, and if you harm me or burn a single stick of my property you will suffer. Your house, Mr. Dabney—yours, Mr. Johnson, will have to go. And so she went on calling the names of individuals and defy- ing them until the mob dispersed without carrying out any of their threats."

President Abraham Lincoln came to Richmond the next day. The brave heart that beat within him was dismayed by the carnage. The great man and his son Tad walked the streets of Richmond totally at the mercy of the crowds. One group of newly freed slaves knelt down before their messiah crying "Glory Hallelujah". Lincoln chided them gently urging them to rise up, saying,

"Don't kneel to me. You must kneel only to God, and thank him for your freedom. Liberty is your birthright. God gave it to you as he gave it to others, and it is a sin that you have been deprived of it at all."

A week later, the Great Emancipator' would be assassinated by John Wilkes Booth in Ford's Theater in Washington DC. The Civil War for all intents and purposes was over. General Lee sued for peace and at the McLean house a few miles away on April 9, 1865; General Ulysses S. Grant received Lee's unconditional surrender. Strangely enough, the surrender document was originally drafted by a Seminole Indian. A month later at Palmito Ranch near Brownsville Texas, the Union's 62nd infantry fought the last battle of the war. They were routed by CSA Colonel John 'Rip' Ford. To many, the Civil War was at an end, but to John Saxton another war was about to begin.

After Lucas had fled the Oakwood Cemetery, John McCrutcheon, proprietor of the 'Rebel House' handed a large brown wax paper cardboard box to Lucas saying,

"Lucas me lad, I've known the Major for many years ever since we worked together in New Orleans. He trusted me and I'm honored by it. Now take this box and walk over to Locust Alley just around the corner between Main and Franklin Streets. Knock three times on a large red door. Belle Jones, the landlady will be waiting for you. She'll put you up until it's safe to leave Richmond if you wish to, besides, the war's still raging and Grant's about to start his spring campaign. I'd stay put if I were you son. I hear they're even trainin' niggers to fight. Anyone over twelve years old will be conscripted to defend the city. Thank God I've got a wooden leg." He laughed,

"And that might not be enough. Now Lucas, you listen good ya hear? Stay outta sight for another month or two. There's no tellin' what's gonna happen, besides you're a good lookin' boy. The girls will like you."

Lucas blushed.

"Don't get the clap son and stay out of trouble with the law hereabouts, for I hear Provo McCubbin would throw his own mother into Castle Thunder for singin' Dixie out of tune. Now if you positively have to get laid, Mary Ann Godfrey and Kate Mills are, I believe still relatively clean but rarely sober. Besides, they're the prettiest." He laughed at the boy's discomfort saying,

"A youngling are you? They'll soon take care of that."

He clapped the boy on the back.

"Don't you worry none boy, I'll take your horse back to Head's down the street and retrieve the buckboard later. I'm really sorry 'bout the Major and Blackie bein' captured. They'll probably put 'em in Castle Thunder for only spies, deserters and criminals go there.

Don't try to visit them kid. Stay away or you'll end up there too, a deserter from Salisbury I've heard."

Lucas started to protest but on second thought decided to keep his mouth shut. The big man noticed.

"Don't blame ya boy. I hear it's a hell hole, worse than Salisbury I've heard. Good luck Lucas, I mean it. Any trouble, just say big John's lookin' after you. It's the least I can do. Your old man was like a brother to me. I'll let him know where you are. One of my girls will try to see him. Now stay put, and stay out of trouble."

He offered his hand. Lucas shook it then lifted the heavy box off the bar. McCrutcheon ushered him out the rear door, up some stairs and into a back alley. Lucas heard the iron door close with a loud clang behind him. It was getting dark. Eventually he found Locust Alley. Upon arriving there, long shadows groped at him as he made his way to the infamous red door. He knocked three times, his heart pounding. Slowly the door opened, its rusty hinges squealing as it did so. A black hand reached out, grabbed him firmly by the collar, and pulled him into a dark, narrow foyer. The door slammed shut behind him.

The War for Lucas ended as suddenly as it had started. His stay at the house of soiled doves had been interesting but short lived as the whole area burned to the ground the day before Federal troops entered the city. Like so many others, Lucas fled on foot carrying all his worldly possessions. However, before he did so, he fell totally in love with one of the establishment's comely slatterns, a Laura Belle Roan. She had taken his virginity and his heart, all in one fell swoop. Although the experience was delightful, it was bittersweet in that before Lucas left the city, two of the most heart wrenching events occurred; namely the news that his father had been hanged and the other that his father had lied to him.

It was an older prostitute, Madame Dubois, who told Lucas that his beloved father lied about his mother. The Madam was a black Creole from New Orleans's Nigger Town. It was in Nigger Town at the 'House of the Rising Sun' that Madame Dubois first met the shy, hardworking girl, Bellefonte La Fontaine. And it was there, a few years later that Belle at seventeen had become so beautiful that men came in their pants just looking at her. It was also there that she was raped by Horatio Garrow, giving birth to a white Creole boy nine months later.

Lucas tried to stop Madame Dubois's story from going any further by holding a cocked Colt .44 against her temple but was quickly disarmed by one of her customers, a William Caruthers who had heard the commotion. Lucas was inconsolable. However, after meeting a few more Jimmy Beams, he became a drunken maudlin as Madame Dubois told the young man sitting across from her more about his obnoxious father.

"Trying to console him as best she could, she continued, saying sweetly,

"I'm terribly sorry Luke that you had to find this out in this manner. I'm sure your father had his own reasons to hide it from you. But the truth remains son, that Belle Lafontaine or Belle Brown as she later became, is your mother. You had to be taken you away because she was too young at the time, and penniless. Your father, I'm sure loved you because believe you me he was incapable of loving anyone else. I've still got the scars to prove it."

She stood up turned her back to Lucas, raised her shift and exposed a series of long ugly welts that crisscrossed her broad back. Lucas was aghast. He refused to believe it.

"You worthless excuse for a human being, I don't believe a word of it. The Major was good to me, respected me and would have died for me! No, I'm taking Laura Belle and we're heading to Tennessee. My father's wish was to settle as far away from the war as possible. I'm going there and raise a family."

Madame Dubois, her demeanor suddenly volcanic, taunted the boy.

"No you won't Luke! I just realized that you're too much like your father. You're going to be a lying, cheating, and more than likely, a murdering son of a bitch to boot. I'm glad they hanged him. Now get out of my sight! I don't ever want to see you again. May God help Laura Belle whose middle name will always haunt you, you bastard! Now get out before Billy next door lays a good one on ya!"

Lucas limped out of the Madam's sitting room. As he climbed the stairs to his room, he screamed,

"I'll kill all of those responsible for my father's death if it's the last thing I ever do!"

BOOK THREE: CHAPTER 8
A DREAM CALLED HOME

On April 20th, 1865, the Fitchburg Hospital train arrived on time at its Boston terminus on Causeway Avenue. Waiting along with hundreds of others was Virginia Saxton, her daughter, the Browns, the Rowlands and the Clovers. White coated medical staff began unloading hundreds of canvas litters upon which lay wounded soldiers home from hell itself. A large name-tag was pinned to each man's tunic. Amputees on crutches or sitting in wicker wheelchairs left the train to be greeted by their loved ones. The scene was heart-wrenching and joyous at the same time.

For Virginia, it was the culmination of hope and despair that had settled over her like a mantra for nearly two years. Her heart leaped as each car was unloaded only to realize that her beloved was not amongst them. Sensing her rising anticipation, her friends gathered around the stricken woman trying to protect her from the vicissitudes of a possible disappointment. The Good Reverend Clover tried to comfort her but the more he spouted biblical platitudes, the more she wanted him to go away. Finally the station platform lay deserted. No more men came off the train. Virginia became distraught, screaming,

"Where is Saxton? Oh where is my Saxton?"

A whistle from another train was heard in the distance coming slowly towards them. The Station Master, a grizzled old man, ran out onto the platform. A cracked green celluloid visor perched upon his bald head like a crown of thorns. He handed a telegram to Virginia but Belle intercepted it as Virginia was by then incapable of reading it. The telegram simply said,

"To Virginia Saxton STOP Special train, Fitchburg RR arriving
Boston, April 20, 1300 hours STOP Captain John Saxton is
Aboard STOP Congressional Medal of Honor STOP From a
Grateful nation STOP By order of President Andrew Johnson"

Belle handed the telegram to Marcus. Their eyes met as he put his arm around her and whispered,

"I am honored to be his friend with or without any medal Belle."

"Me too." She said, "Me too."

Both of them hung onto their sons Cotton and Rufus. Belle bent down and whispered,

"Your Uncle John is comin' home boys. Praise be to God; his victory train is rollin' in."

Marcus laughed to himself, thinking,

'And may God have mercy on us all."

Saxton lay in bed. Jack Two, the terrier whined. Saxton threw Jack's favorite red ball out the doorway. The small dog jumped like a rocket towards his quarry. Virginia snuggled closer to Saxton being careful not to awaken the metal in his thigh. She realized that her husband like so many others that came back from the war would never be the same. Emotionally and physically crippled, these men came home to find their world changed forever. They could never go back. For some men suicide solved their problems like Edmund Ruffin the famous orator and resolute exponent of the Confederate cause. Others joined various hate groups bent on revenge for what they considered a just cause, while for others like Saxton, a distant dream was their only solace and salvation.

It had been four years since the war ended. The Saxton Shipping Co. became enormously profitable, for the period of reconstruction in the South required copious amounts of all types of dry goods. These goods were shipped by a growing network of railways and shipping companies in ever increasing amounts as the ravaged lands of Dixie rose from the ashes of the war like a phoenix. In the spring of 1872, the Saxton- Browns decided it was a good time to sell the company including the SS Anaona. There were a number of bidders, but the Clyde Line owned by Thomas Clyde was successful. Saxton was happy that an old and dear friend of his father was buying the company. Besides, New York would be the company's new headquarters taking over the offices, warehouses and fueling facilities of the Saxton Shipping Co. that were there already in place.

With the company was about to be sold, Saxton and Marcus were free to pursue their dream of building a utopia on top of a mountain in Tennessee. A few weeks later, the two men went to No#19 at the Merchants Exchange building in Boston to see Saxton's solicitor of many years, a Mr. Abiel Abbot of Watertown. At their request, Abbot went to Chattanooga and exercised the option on their behalf that they acquired on the mountain property in 1864. Because of the war, Hannah Morrison, now a war widow, was more than eager to sell at the previously agreed to price. As a result, all of Elder Mountain from just above Brown's Ferry landing all along the river gorge around to Massengale Point belonged to Saxton and Marcus on an equal basis. There, on the mountain, five thousand acres of old growth hardwood forests waited for them to do with it as they pleased. The market for hardwood products lay in nearby Chattanooga. By 1872, the city had once again become a major railway hub and a growing industrial city. The Saxton- Browns felt the time was propitious. They wondered if anyone would remember the dream so eagerly talked about nearly ten years earlier. All they could do was wait and see.

No one in Boston knew what they had been up to until one day in January of 1872, a small notice in large type simultaneously appeared in the Boston Post, the New York Herald and the New Orleans Picayune newspapers. It simply said,

ATTENTION
"As of July 1ˢᵗ, 1873, and not before,
The Saxton-Brown families will begin
the dream. Those in the know will go."

Saxton and Marcus sat in the parlor at the Saxton House. Both men read the notice with anticipation. Marcus repeated the password, 'harmony' the exclaimed,

"Yeah, those in the know will go hopefully by January 1ˢᵗ of 1873 instead of July. Only those who we really trust will be there early to help us set the operation up. I'm glad that those few we really trusted were told about the notice years ago. Perhaps they too will come by July 1st."

Saxton wasn't listening for he was reading something else in the New York Herald.

"Saxton, did you not hear a word I said?"

"Here Marcus have a look at this."

Saxton handed him a recent copy of the Herald. There buried in the classified section was,

FOR SALE
SAWMILL/PLANNING MILL
"Brand new, steam powered.
Contact Mr. B.L. Goodman,
Located 6 miles east of Ellijay
due north of Atlanta, Georgia.
$5,000 cash. Serious buyers
only. There are no liens."

After much discussion back and forth, Saxton and Marcus decided to buy it. Despite being able to saw logs up to thirty-eight feet in length and six feet in diameter, the capabilities of the Taylor 'Up and Down' water powered sawmill in Derry, New Hampshire, were limited. Steam powered sawmills had come into being in the 1860's and by the late 1870's were more reliable and productive as they ran all year.

Goodman's sawmill would have to be dismantled and shipped to Chattanooga by rail. From there it would be loaded on barges then floated downriver to Brown's Ferry landing. The owner, a B.L. Goodman was delighted. He even offered to dismantle it and reassemble it himself for another $500 by November of 1872. His offer was accepted. Once it was unloaded at Brown's Ferry Landing, the steam engine, its boilers and other large components would be taken on heavy sledges pulled by teams of oxen up the steep mountain trace. Once there, it would be reassembled beside a dammed pond for its water supply. After it was up and running, the mill would produce all the lumber, posts, beams, and planks necessary for constructing every building on the mountain. The wood would come initially from the mill site, dam site and the planned farming sites. The lumber would be kiln dried in time for any initial construction. After everything was ready, the rest of their families would come to the mountain right after the Saxton House was sold.

During those post-war years, after many heated discussions back and forth, the two families made some concrete decisions. It was decided that Marcus would boss the saw mill and horse logging operations while Saxton would market the lumber and be responsible for shipping it down the mountain. Virginia in those post-war years had become a trained nurse and mid-wife. She would look after the infirmary, and nursery. A Dr. Lapsley Y. Green, a former Confederate surgeon from Chattanooga was put on retainer to visit Harmony Farm once a month. Nancy the nanny had recently finished her training as a teacher and would be in charge of the school. Meanwhile Belle would manage the Company office and, to everyone's amazement, a large church cum meeting hall with rectory attached. Its bell tower would serve as a watch tower as well. Belle said,

"And I know just the man who will jump at the chance to be our minister and that man is Otis Tillman who I believe was an itinerant preacher but is now living in Knoxville. Believe me, he is a man of God of the first caliber." The Saxton-Brown's would also try to find a Catholic priest for the settlement.

Rodney Tubman, the chauffer, wanted to be in charge of all farming operations, specifically; the dairy. Apparently he grew up as a slave on the Archibald Smith plantation in Georgia. As a free slave who spent many years in New York City driving for the Saxton Shipping Company, he was ready to be a country boy at the age of sixty-five all over again. This time however, he would be the boss. Belle exclaimed,

"My dear Rodney, no matter what kind of a hayseed you become, you'll always be an uppity uptown nigger to me."

The rest of the staff at the Saxton House was offered employment at the new colony but all of them declined as their families lived close by in Boston. Packard agreed to follow his masters. He would be head of all housekeeping staff that serviced the owner's residences. Millie agreed to be his assistant. Security, the armory, the three defensive bunkers, two watchtowers, and bloodhound kennels would be left to the surviving Maasai Rangers commanded by Lieutenant Corby Cutler.

Marcus and Saxton left for Harmony Farm as it was called, in May of 1872 along with five of the original Maasai Rangers. Six of the 'Attic Rats' from Salisbury Prison were going to meet them there as well. They would widen and grade the old Rebel artillery road from the river to the mill site, then clear the mill site itself. Saxton would be busy setting up lumber contracts, making shipping schedules for the colony's lumber and supervising the

Company's maintenance crews. Sweet Daphne and her two boys Hudson and Little Willie, who were still living on the mountain, could stay put or join the colony. Sweet Daphne was elated that everyone would sleep and eat at her place while Harmony Farm was being built. Later she agreed stay and be the bunkhouse cook.

A former Union Army engineer, Brigadier-General 'Baldy Smith' was hired earlier on to survey the mill site and build the dam. In July of 1872, he started construction of a large log and stone dam near the headwaters of a creek that tumbled down the steep mountainside to the 'The Skillet'. The mill pond would be four hundred feet long and one hundred and fifty feet wide with a depth of twenty feet. Baldy would also dig three deep rainwater collection ponds lined with impervious clay two feet thick for fresh water and fire suppression. One pond was dug out in the lower pasture, another next to the village and another past the bunk-house. The ponds became a necessity because test holes revealed that porous limestone rock underlying the mountain's sandstone cap was too porous and any water found there was also fouled by minerals.

The mill site itself would cover two acres; more than enough for a sorting shed, drying kiln, planning mill, three large curing sheds, loading areas, log storage area, finishing mill, sawyers and parts supply shed, and a large Tennessee walk-through barn for the work animals and some other outbuildings. Loggers, teamsters, millwrights, sawyers, and survey-ors were all hired by December to assist Goodman in getting the saw-mill up and running properly. An early and persistent frost made the ground hard enough to take heavy loads of equipment and materials up the artillery road from Brown's Ferry.

The Saxton-Browns looked at the detailed plans Saxton commissioned a few months earlier from a survey firm in Chattanooga. They all agreed that with nearly two hundred acres of farmland available on the mountain, this limited how many people could live there. The soil, as Sweet Daphne told Marcus, was suitable for herbs, some broad leafed vegetables, potatoes, silage corn, burley tobacco and hay but not for grain. An eighty acre lower bench lying just above 'The Skillet' was good grazing land, easily irrigated but very difficult to get to without a road down to it. The only route possible was to start a road at the junction near the top of the mountain, go down a draw, then around a steep cliff to the bench land. Saxton hired an explosives firm to blast away tons of rock to make the road. There were three other large rolling benches on the south side of the mountain totaling another fifty acres that were possible grazing pastures that could be connected by the same road. It was concluded that no more than twenty-five families and fifty single men totaling three hundred colonists could live on the mountain. But what type of accommodation would entice anyone to live there?

Again, after much discussion it was decided that each family would have their own rent free two story 'Company' house, big enough to accommodate a family of eight. A company maintenance crew would look after all the buildings, grounds and out buildings. Built of field stone, twenty of these large identical craftsman style houses would face each other across a ditched road broad enough for a team of four horses and a wagon to turn around in. Each house would be heated by steam. Exterior walls two feet thick were pierced by large windows protected by black iron shutters with rifle ports. The roofs would be covered with fire proof slate tiles. Between each house would be a row of rainwater barrels for drinking water and fire suppression. Behind each house was a private garden sufficiently large enough to feed a family of eight. Indoor plumbing, an indoor bathroom and a root cellar completed each abode. The farm's piggery would take any other kitchen or garden scraps. Most importantly to Belle,

"There wouldn't be any damned fences."

Plans that were meticulously drawn on paper, in effect became reality, with surprisingly few alterations. The flow of ideas and counter ideas continued. It was decided that any access crops would become common property to be sold or stored as the situation dictated. A fortified 'Saxton Village' located on a flat thirty acre knoll along the main road, guarded the farm's only entrance. A large rectangular one-story bunkhouse for up to fifty single men enclosing a fortified courtyard combined with a common dining hall would be located near the mill a mile north of the village. Near this location would be the Brown's house situated on a knoll overlooking the mill and a large baseball-soccer field. The Saxton House would be exactly the same design and size as the Brown House. It would be on top of another knoll overlooking the village connected to it by a sloping gravel driveway bordered by chestnut trees.

Marcus and Saxton were very aware of social differences being portrayed by the size, style and location of their houses. Beacon Hill in Boston, Knob Hill in San Francisco and Church Hill in Richmond all signaled to those unwashed masses living beneath them, that those on the hills were important, and rich. The Saxton-Brown's decided that their houses would be modeled on the Mellen house in Natchez, Mississippi. Marcus had sent away for the plans of the Folk Victorian house that he'd seen near a river bluff as he poled up river with Nate years before.

The two story house with a steep pyramidal roof bisected by a large upright gabled dormer was fronted by a wide porch. This porch was backed by two long windows on either side of a wide Palladian doorway and ran across the front of the building. Supported by six turned spindles, the porch was centered by wide board steps that ran down to a red brick walkway. A small rectangular lawn in front of the structure was bordered by clipped box-wood shrubs and surrounded by a low black wrought iron picket fence. Built on high knolls for security reasons, the two houses would provide a last line of defense and be large enough to accommodate invited guests of importance. A colony such as this would certainly attract attention, perhaps positive but most certainly negative if the morals, working conditions and buildings were below the accepted standards of the day. Once everyone had a good idea what the colony would look like, the question was, who would live there let alone in harmony.

Despite their frequent differences of opinion, the Saxton-Browns somehow drew all of their final ideas from an amalgam of many inspirations, namely; the advocacy of respect for his employees demonstrated over many years by Thomas Saxton; the communal capitalistic spirit of 'Slab Town' beside Fort Monroe, the utopian socialism experiments of Robert Owen in New Lanark, Scotland and New Harmony in Indiana, and the ten commandments. Harmony Farm might have been perceived as a 'Company Town' but in effect it was not. Previous communal experiments elsewhere failed because some the inhabitants didn't measure up. Social rot set in and the whole chain broke at the weakest link. Thus all those selected for Harmony Farm would first and foremost be veterans of the civil war; Union, Rebel, black and white. There would be no segregation, no sectarianism and certainly no sexism.

The Civil War was over but lingered on in the conscience of America like an endless nightmare. Out of the ashes of the great conflict was spawned another horror. It was simply called the Ku Klux Klan or KKK. The resentment and hatred many white Southrons felt in the aftermath of their defeat resulted in a tidal wave of widespread race based terror. This secret society, thundered across the war-torn South, sabotaging local reconstruction governments with a reign of oppression that lasted five years. In response, Northerners, as one onlooker mused,

"Saw in the Klan an attempt by unrepentant Confederates to win by terrorism what they couldn't win on the battlefield."

In the first few months after their defeat, Southrons had to contend with abject poverty, physical and mental disease, homelessness, an occupying army, ruined farms, cities and transportation systems. Re-constructionists in Louisiana tried to replace white ruling authority with appointed former black Union veterans. This occurrence, the loss of loved ones and most importantly, the loss of southern honor was too much to bear. Thus the timing of the emergence of the KKK to ride off into the night spreading terror and tribulation was preordained by such circumstances.

Ironically, it all began when six bored Confederate veterans on Christmas Eve of 1865, formed a secretive social club called the KKK. Its birthplace was Pulaski, in Giles County, Tennessee. A year later, the Klan had swelled by many hundreds, most of them veterans. Lucas Garrow was one of them. It was into this circle of hate-mongers that he found a sanctuary of kindred spirits. Therein, he could serve the 'cause' as his father had wished. Lucas like most young men was fascinated by the unusual names given to its hierarchy, the white sheets, night rides and the name itself. The protection of poor white sharecroppers, secrecy, elaborate rituals, initiation ceremonies, comradeship and the aim of regaining lost southern honor were the early stimuli that kept the Ku Klux Klan from becoming a footnote in history.

Much to the consternation of its six founders, the KKK turned violent. Its true purpose became deadly serious----take back from the re-constructionists what whites lost in the war, by fear and violence if needs be. For many aristocratic whites elected to bankrupt southern state legislatures, a series of Black Codes were enacted as a compromise, amounting to a virtual re-enslavement of blacks. President Andrew Johnson, Lincoln's successor, did nothing to prevent these odious Codes from being enforced.

Wide spread violence erupted against blacks and Union supporters in the South. To protest the Black Codes, southern senators and representatives were refused admission to Congress. President Johnson's veto was over-ridden by an enraged Congress which soon after passed the Re-construction Acts whose sole purpose was to abolish ex-Confederate State governments. All former Rebel states and territories except Tennessee, became five military districts charged with the registration of black voters, the holding of free elections and the subsequent reconstruction of an infrastructure lying in ruins.

The KKK responded violently. However, in the ensuing chaos, many of its members were appalled at the ability of the night riders to go out with total immunity to rob, assault, rape, murder and commit innumerable acts of arson. Sadly, it was too late to stop the Klan as it spread like a malignancy from Tennessee to North and South Carolina. Federal spies planted within the KKK were usually caught, stripped, mutilated then lynched. Initially jeered by some as a joke, by the late 1860's, the KKK had become the de-facto law in many southern counties against which many state officials were unable to oppose.

Out of the many editors, ministers, political leaders and former Confederate officers, emerged a leader from behind the white sheets---General Nathan Bedford Forrest. The only man to ever rise from a Private to a General in the Civil War, he was the Klan's first Imperial Wizard, and its chief emissary. Highly respected, he travelled all over the South establishing new Klan chapters. A wave of shootings, lynching and floggings spread across Dixie in 1868. Incredibly, various KKK groups began fighting each other. The Black KKK, a gang of outlaws from Nashville, Tennessee, waged guerilla warfare against the original Tennessee Klan.

Radical legislatures in order to deal with the rising bloodshed; began to pass harsher laws. President Johnson imposed martial law in some counties. However, hundreds of Klansmen found guilty of night riding, were rarely put behind bars. The terror continued unabated till the mid-1870's when laws passed by white southern legislatures instigated what is known as segregation. Many whites called the new system, 'separate but equal.' To others, especially the disenfranchised blacks, it was 'separate but rarely equal.'

President Grant made membership in the 'Invisible Empire' illegal in 1870, by passing the Force Act of 1870 and later the Ku Klux Act of 1871. Even Nathan Bedford Forrest, the first Grand Wizard of the Klan had by 1869 called for the KKK to disband because of the wanton violence its members espoused, stating that it,

"Was, being perverted from its original, honorable and patriotic purposes, becoming injurious instead of being subservient to the public peace."

There were other violent groups who espoused white supremacy such as the Knights of the White Camellia from Louisiana. It was modeled on the Klan and was even more extensive. The White Brotherhood, the White League, Union Guards, Black Cavalry, White

Rose, the '76 Association and dozens of other smaller societies sprang up after the Civil War. Their common goal was to protect poor southern whites from northern carpetbaggers, scalawags, armed black militias and the hated federal re-constructionists. It was into this volatile atmosphere in western Tennessee that the dream embodied by Harmony Farm first took root in what seemed to be stony soil.

The Saxton-Browns reasoned that the safety of the farm was paramount. Thus the first colonists would all be former soldiers ready, willing and able to defend their families. All colonists would be skilled tradesmen, able to work in one or more of the farm's many industries. Belle insisted that all of them be chosen from those who'd lost everything in the war. Harmony Farm would give them a second chance where no one else would; because of their race, lack of social status, their poverty or their physical disabilities.

The last qualification was that of moral fiber. Harmony Farm had to be a place where peace reigned supreme. Liquor and morphine would be banned and any infraction would result in instant banishment from the farm. A small jail would be built to hold those suspected or blatantly responsible for any crimes until the authorities in Chattanooga could come for them. If convicted, they were banned from the farm. Only Baptists and Catholics would be accepted at first, as these formed the common religious backbone of the South. Sunday morning services would be set aside for the Baptists and the afternoon services would be Catholic. A minister and a priest would live together in the rectory. This idea at the time was novel in extremis.

So far everything had gone according to plan. By the beginning of November 1872, the dam, the mills, and all the company buildings were complete. Only the village and Saxton's house were unfinished. Marcus, his men and a crew of nearly one hundred tradesmen hired in Chattanooga stayed behind to finish the work. Sweet Daphne and her two boys moved to a 'new' home near the bunkhouse. Some might have said otherwise, for her old house was moved lock stock and barrel to its final resting place. A large sledge pulled by twenty oxen did the deed one sunny afternoon. The little cabin was whitewashed; a new roof, windows and a new porch completed the restoration. Marcus made sure that everything in the old house survived the trip. Sweet Daphne once saved his life and it was the least he could do to make her happy. He knew the loss of her husband Big Willie would have been too much to bear if all the memories of him were burned to the ground. Sweet Daphne was content. Her staff of ten, cooked for the single men living in the company bunkhouse by the mill site. Saxton went home to Boston to complete the sale of the Saxton Shipping Co. He arrived on November 8th, 1872. The next day, Boston experienced the Great Fire.

1872 was a catastrophic year for the Saxtons. The Great Boston fire swept through the city from the Commons to the waterfront. Seventeen hundred firemen from twenty-seven counties fought the conflagration. A virulent form of equine flu epizootic had disabled half of the city's horse-drawn fire wagons. Five hundred men were enlisted to pull the heavy wagons by hand. Old water mains were either broken or unable to keep the fire hoses going. Finally, Boston's embattled Fire Chief John Damrell was forced by the Mayor William Gaston and US Postmaster General John Creswell to use explosives. Blocks of buildings were blown up to starve the fire. The Old North Church was saved as well as the Commons. Ships all over the inner harbor were ablaze as the wind carried burning debris far out into the bay. However, the raging inferno spared the Saxton Shipping waterfront facilities along with five of its new steam ships including the SS Anaona.

All the Saxtons could do was sit on the widow's walk and watch the destruction taking place south-east of them. Virginia began to panic as the wind turned, sweeping long fingers of flame towards them. They barely had enough time to load three large dray wagons with their most precious and necessary possessions including Jack Two. They and their household staff fled away over the Warren Bridge to Charlestown. As Saxton looked back, tall cumulus columns of black smoke obscured an orange sun. To him it was Richmond burning all over again.

The pain of it was too much to bear. Physically weakened by the war and the intolerable stress of recent weeks, Saxton collapsed, unable to move. Virginia held him in her arms as Rodney lashed at the horses. The Saxton House, out buildings and everything therein went up in flames as embers carried afar from the fire itself landed on the tinder dry mansard roof. Hours later, only a smoldering pile of memories remained. Nothing of any value was left as looters ransacked the stately old house. Any firemen or police that arrived to extinguish the fire were stoned by the mobs.

After fifteen hours with a heat so intense it created its own wind, the fire abated. In the aftermath, over one thousand businesses and numerous homes were smoking piles of charred rubble. A month later, the Saxton Shipping Co. was sold to the Clyde Shipping Company at a handsome profit. However, in New Orleans, the mighty Mississippi River dropped to record levels, practically isolating the Crescent City from the sea. Five Saxton ships docked in New Orleans were trapped. For how long, no one knew. Months passed. They too were sold at auction for ten cents on the dollar as they lay rotting in the mud by the levee.

Thankfully the Saxton's and what remained of their staff arrived at Harmony Farm on Valentine's Day, 1873. Marcus, Belle, Tyler Wicks and the others rejoiced at their safe arrival. Saxton, fortunately, had paid all his bills before the fire and Marcus had brought his remaining double eagles with him to pay the wages of the workers. The farm was complete in every detail. The village was a model of simplistic design and function. Every house, fully furnished, lay in wait for the laughter of children to spill out from every doorway. The Brown and Saxton houses were of the Folk Victorian style popular at the time. The Mellen house in Natchez, Mississippi was copied down to the last detail from plans Saxton had procured from William P. Mellen while there on business. Both houses looked down upon dreams born of hope that came to fruition. All Harmony Farm needed was a warm wet spring for the crops and a flock of new colonists to get things up and running. But, another catastrophe, the Great Panic of 1873 was about to smite them.

In September of 1873, Jay Cooke and Company, a major component of the country's banking establishment, found that it was unable to market several million dollars in Northern Pacific Railroad bonds. President Grant's monetary policy restricting the nation's money supply only made matters worse. The failure of the Jay Cooke Bank set off a chain reaction of bank failures and the New York stock market was temporarily closed. Factories began to lay off workers and unemployment quickly reached fourteen percent. America slipped into what became known as the 'Long Depression'. After it was all over, the Saxton-Brown's would be nearly penniless as their other investments became worthless. Although the Saxton's were not poor by any means, their vast wealth had evaporated.

For the next five years, Harmony Farm teetered on the edge of extinction, unable to sell its lumber. Therefore, lumber continued to be sawn but was left to cure. Everyone agreed that the depression would never last and when it did end, the demand for cured close grained hardwood lumber would be immense. The only saving grace was that the farm was self-sufficient and as the national crisis grew worse, many destitute soldiers and newly freed slaves found a peaceful sanctuary high up on a mountain top in Tennessee.

One autumn afternoon, Belle sat in her favorite high back wicker rocking chair on the porch of her house. White strands, the color of Spanish silver, flecked her long obsidian tresses. Still a stunning Creole beauty at forty-four, Belle was enjoying the warmth of the afternoon sun upon her aquiline face. She closed her eyes as the sound of an autumn wind in nearby chestnut trees soothed her and carried her away to another time and another place. Golden leaves fell upon the grounds in clusters after every freshet of wind. The plopping sounds of chestnuts coming down upon the brittle slate shingles roused her. She remembered with wonder, the beauty of Elder Mountain the very first time she'd ever laid eyes on it.

It was in the winter of 1873. Browns ferry broke through a thick palette of river ice to take her party to the mountain road at the foot of the mountain. Belle, Virginia, Saxton and their three children Rufus, Cotton and Felicity were nestled under thick buffalo robes within two Portland sleighs. Their teams of Percherons and Belgium mules waited patiently, their breath wafting in white clouds about them. Millie, Rodney, Nancy and Packard sat in a cigar-box cutter. A stiff, cold breeze off the river befell them as they boarded the ferry. The river's liquid muscles gripped the scow's flat bottomed hull in an embrace as it was pulled forward. Slowly the squat cable ferry crawled crablike across the ice strewn facade of the river until it came to a stop alongside a decrepit snow bound wooden wharf. Two husky black ferrymen tied the ferry scow to it then hand cranked its heavy bow ramp down onto the frozen river bank. Astride their horses, waiting for them, were Marcus and Tyler Wicks. Unknown to Belle, three former Maasai Rangers stood on guard concealed under nearby cottonwood trees.

The party crossed a flat riverine terrace traversed by Ferry Road that rose onto O'Grady Road as they wended their way alongside limestone ledges lying beside them. A narrow trace gave way to a wide snow bound track that disappeared into a dense hardwood forest. Their procession swung left past a neatly painted sign.

'HARMONY FARM
ALL WELCOME'

Elder Mountain, Brown's mountain or as some called it Raccoon Mountain, towered over eighteen hundred feet above them like a colossus as the road began to wind its way ever upward. Ancient groves of hardwoods and white pines crowned ledges high above them, their bare canopies covering the road ahead with crenellated shadows. The horses labored mightily past snow covered layers of ancient rock flowing alongside them. It was totally fascinating to Belle. After a few miles, yellowish lower Mississippian limestone and grey flinty shale cliffs above gave way to striated layers of hard Pennsylvanian sandstone. These layers were laid down three hundred and fifty million years ago in the Cambrian to Devonian ages by an ancient sea. This part of the Cumberland Plateau rose sixteen hundred feet straight up in a series of narrow ledges above the river as it flowed around the mountain knob of hard sandstone rock that capped it. The startling effect of such striations upon the mind was most apparent if one saw it from a distance.

Belle smiled as she thought about it. The inherent significance of the river was not lost on her because the wide rivers and oceans of Marcus's life had left an open wound deep within her. Serendipity, through another river full of fury and determination had brought them all together again as one. She'd come full circle. For her, the destination was not important but the journey. At last she understood why Marcus loved the sea and by staying up on the mountain to make her happy, she knew what total love it must have taken to make that sacrifice a reality. A quotation from Pope Innocent the Third rang in her ears. "The sea will grant each man new hope, his sleep brings dreams of home."

Belle opened her eyes. The air had cooled as the blue sky that trickled through the canopy above her was retreating. As she gathered her woolen shawl around her, she began singing the hymn, 'When we gather at the River'. After a few verses, she felt a presence behind her. Marcus put his hand to her neck caressing it gently. It was as if he knew what she had been dreaming about for he said as she rose to meet him,

"I love you Belle as I loved the sea. There's no going back my dear. There's no going back."

Harmony Farm prospered after the 'Long Depression' worked its way out of the national body like the small piece of shrapnel that eventually found its way out of Saxton's thigh. To both, there was a sense of relief followed by the sudden realization that a second chance at a full life lay before them. America was back stronger than ever from under a dark cloud of financial ruin as was Harmony Farm. The oak-pine woods on Elder Mountain rang with the sounds of crosscut saws and double-bitted axes. Besides white pine, loblolly pine, Virginia pine and shortleaf pine; old growth American chestnut, white oak, and hickory were the most valuable species logged, followed by yellow poplar, hard and soft maples.

Even intense sunlight barely penetrated the vast groves of hard and soft woods that crowned the mountain plateau. To Belle and Virginia, all trees were beautiful, to be admired, treasured and respected.

The American chestnut trees were Belle's favorite. Some of them were over ten feet in diameter, reaching skyward nearly two hundred feet. Their narrow spiky green leaves that provided cooling shade, turned a spectacular honey-yellow in the fall. Its fruit developed during the hot summers into a spiny green burr that expelled three nuts after the first frost of autumn feeding a multitude of wildlife. The children of the farm gathered the nuts and roasted them.

To Virginia, the hickory tree with its small yellow-green catkins produced in the spring was her favorite. With its pinnately compound leaves and large nuts, the hickory was ideal wood for use in curing meat. Their husbands had other ideas in that the trees were only a means to an end. To Marcus, the wood of the Chestnut tree was straight and close-grained, easy to saw and split. Being rich in tannins it was resistant to rot making it ideal for furniture, split-rail fencing, shingles, and flooring. Saxton in turn thought of Hickory wood as extremely tough, yet flexible. Tool handles, wheel spokes, gunstocks, cannon carriages and carts were some of the uses Hickory wood was put to. The tannin within both species was used for tanning leather in the farm's new tannery. Over time, Belle and Virginia prevailed, as sections of the mountain were set aside as natural conservatories. After four years living on the mountain, the colony's families enjoyed the rich natural diversity of their mountain world had to offer.

By 1877, the Saxton-Brown children were quite precocious and a constant challenge to their parents. Rufus and Felicity were fifteen years old. Cotton was twenty. Although Rufus was a mischievous and extroverted being, he loved to curl up with a book by Charles Dickens, Jules Verne or Samuel Clemens. Cotton was being groomed to run the mill. Felicity had a natural affinity for animals and spent most of her time after school with the draft horses stabled in the barn. Rufus was Rufus. No one, especially Belle, knew what to do with him.

One day Rodney wheezed up the lane to her house crying,

"Belle come out here now. I've got to show you somethin'."

The screen door opened and clattered shut as Belle emerged wiping her hands on a small white dish cloth. Her arms were covered in flour dust. She instinctively queried,

"What is it Rodney? Is Rufus in trouble again?"

Rodney, carrying a small gunnysack came up and sat down wearily in one of the wicker rockers that adorned the wide veranda. Belle looked down on him.

"Can I get you anything to drink? Maybe some iced tea, or iced lemonade perhaps?" The stocky black man winked at her.

"Dear Belle, I think iced lemonade would do nicely. God knows I could use a stiff Beam right now. I need it!"

Belle laughed, turned about throwing her towel over a broad shoulder. She gathered her red gingham dress about her, opened the screen door and disappeared only to return moments later with two iced lemonades. She sat down beside him. They remained there for a few moments, enjoying each other's company. Rodney put down his glass and opened the gunnysack. Belle gasped as the man withdrew what looked like two bloody bull-whips. Belle exclaimed,

"Where on God's earth did you get two cows tails tied together?"

Rodney smiled, revealing two missing front teeth. The air whistled through the gap between them as he spoke.

"Well now Belle, I was down on the lower pasture when all of a sudden two cows, Bessy and Linda started bawlin' somethin' awful. I thought maybe a coyote or a wolf was nearby or they'd tried to run through that newfangled barbed-wire that Saxton bought last year. I ran over and as I did so, I saw Rufus and Teddy Smith runnin' up the trace to the upper pastures. Anyways, I got there and found this lyin' in the grass with the two cows standin' there, their boney tails stickin' out of their rear ends. I couldn't get near em' for a closer look. I guess their milkin' days are over for a little while until we can get Doc Webster to look at em'. What a mess Belle; what a god awful mess!"

He put the tails back in the gunnysack. Belle stood up and took it away from him. She had fire in her eyes. Rodney thanked her for the lemonade and fled down the hill. Behind him he heard Belle bellow,

"Rufus Brown, you come home RIGHT NOW!"

Her voice pierced the air like a sword. The hair on the back of Rodney's neck stiffened. He thought,

'As God is my witness, that boy is in real trouble. Thank the Lord she's not mad at me. You'd better git boy wherever you are 'cause your mamma's gonna wail you good and proper.'

The only trouble with that scenario was that Rufus Brown and Teddy Smith were lost. They'd seen Rodney and fled into the forest. Once there, the guilty boys hid in a small cleft in the sandstone cliffs that capped the mountain. Fearing imminent capture, the young scalawags crawled further down into a widening fissure. Rufus had some matches with him. Both boys had come upon the cave months earlier and planned on exploring it further. To this end they stashed some oil soaked rags wound onto sticks. These provided a flaring light as they made their way ever downward. A steady breeze of cooling air bathed their faces as it rushed past them towards the surface behind and above them. After walking in another hundred feet, any remaining light from above was swallowed up.

As they wound their way down into the belly of the mountain, their torches continued to flare even more so as freshets of air welled up from somewhere deep below them. Exhausted, they sat down on a wide ledge that led horizontally away from them. It seemed that small passages, piles of rubble, sinkholes and slabs of gritty rock greeted them at every turn as they tried to define a path through the twisting maze before them. After many false starts, they decided that they couldn't go back but only forward and deeper into the colossus of that had consumed them. No longer were the walls of the cave mineralized sandstone but a yellowish, crenellated limestone karst that presented a miasma of unknown potential for harm. Calcite columns, opalescent in the torchlight hung down from the ceilings like icicles strung along the bottom of an eaves trough. Others rose up underneath them, growing ever closer together as over the millennia, the patter of water pregnant with calcite built them up one drop at a time. However the truants had no time to admire the wondrous handiwork of Mother Nature.

Panic stricken, the two lost boys followed a river of fresh air ever forward and ever downward. After squeezing through innumerable narrow tunnels, sliding down smooth curtains of limestone and wading through shallow rivulets of water; they came to a debris field of shattered rock that lay under the collapsed roof of an immense cavern. High above them, clouds of bats swirled overhead disturbed by the sobbing cries of the twosome far below. As the boys waded through pools of guano dust, a shimmering light of increasing intensity appeared directly ahead of them.

Unknowingly, they'd found another entrance to the infamous Pitch Fork Cave. The cave's lower mouth overlooked the Tennessee River flowing a hundred feet below it. A favorite haunt of river pirates, refugees and other riffraff; the cave's thick deposits of bat guano had been mined in the recent war to manufacture saltpeter for making Confederate gunpowder. Round wooden vats, metal strainers and other mining paraphernalia were still there, untouched and abandoned. The boys wandered amongst this debris then out into daylight where the Tennessee River roaring past below them. The noise of it reverberated back and forth inside the cave's cavernous stone jaws sounding like a monster about to devour them. Spooked by their vivid imaginations and also the possibility that Cotton's mother was hot on their trail, they fled. At least it sounded like her.

Hours later, a weary pair of boys having walked three miles along a narrow trace to Brown's Ferry, staggered up the mountain road back to Harmony Farm. Their parents and most of the settlers had been looking for them for hours. Both boys were sobbing as their anxious parents swept them up into their arms and took them home. After being washed, fed and put to bed, their parents began pondering the boy's crime and punishment. In the end, Rufus and Terry his partner, enjoyed a full breakfast the next morning. After they'd eaten their fill, their fathers brought them out behind the walk-through barn by the mill. Felicity and her best friend Amy Smith watched from the hay loft above as the two boys were given the worst whipping of their young lives.

In a way, the discovery of the secret upper cave entrance proved fortuitous for Harmony Farm. No longer would anyone have to travel down the mountain to Brown's Ferry then hike another three miles along a narrow shoreline trace to the cave. After much discussion it was decided to enlarge the upper entrance, install lanterns along tortuous passages, build steps with railings where the path was precipitous and widen narrow openings. All these alterations would make the caverns safe places of refuge just in case the colony was ever threatened. Paranoia was to prove a blessing in disguise.

A gatehouse was built at the bottom of the mountain, just above Brown's Ferry. It was able to comfortably accommodate four armed guards for a week although only two at a time stayed there on four day shifts. A newly installed telegraph line connected it to both the Saxton and the Brown residences. Over the next six months at the farm, Marcus supervised the construction of ten wooden drift boats. These boats had been pre-assembled on the farm above then taken apart and carried piece by piece through the bowels of the cave to its lower entrance. Once there, they were reassembled and put on iron wheeled wooden cradles then stowed behind two six inch thick iron double doors with no outside lock or hinges.

These two massive doors manufactured by Robert Craven's Chattanooga Pipe and Iron Foundry, were rafted downstream to Brown's Ferry. The smaller door was taken by ox sledge to the farm and the larger double door was taken by a log raft complete with six oxen to a narrow beach that lay below the entrance of Pitchfork Cave. Once there, the three ton door was pulled up into place along a greased ramp using a system of pulleys. The work was difficult and tedious after which the oxen were taken back along the shoreline trace to the foot of the mountain. To the Saxton-Brown's, the last pieces of securing the mountain against uninvited guests were in place.

Since the area was remote and the river gorge not really suited to commercial traffic since after the war, the rapid growth of railways marked the end of the river's steamboat era. Therefore, this hive of activity went largely unnoticed by the river men riding the rafts of bundled logs downriver. Only the local populace or the rare steamboat that successfully navigated treacherous waters on an upstream journey to Chattanooga noticed anything un-usual. By December of 1877, ten, twenty foot drift boats were ready to launch at a moment's notice into the Tennessee River. Packed with weapons, preserved food and supplies; each was capable of holding fifteen people.

BOOK THREE: CHAPTER 9
A LADY IN QUESTION

A hooded Lucas Garrow yelled, "There's no going back Billy, there's no going back!"

He wheeled his horse about, worried that an act of mass murder had gone too far. The screams of black militiamen locked inside a clapboard church could be heard just down the road. Moments before, a dozen 'Ghouls' of the Klan had torched it after they galloped yelling and screaming into the town of Hamburg, South Carolina. Flying the 'Southern Cross' battle flag; they'd ridden in after midnight on the orders of their Grand Magi, Mathew C. Butler. He and many of its white citizens were furious with the re-constructionists who had arbitrarily appointed blacks to positions of power in the town's local government. Especially galling to the KKK, was a black Constable who sat in his office chair one hot afternoon, "Fanning himself very offensively,"

This was reason enough to put an end to black rule in Hamburg. The Baptist Revival Church continued to burn throughout the night and into the next morning. By then the Grand Cyclops and his minions had escaped back into Tennessee pursued by Federal troops.

Lucas Garrow became an early follower of the KKK after he and Laura Belle Roan had a falling out shortly after fleeing Richmond. Her body was found beside a country road, beaten, raped and shot. Eventually, he teamed up with another vagabond, Billy Dee Trelean. Billy, a prodigal son was headed for Pulaski, Tennessee where his parents still lived. Lucas tagged along. Once there, he became part and parcel of the Trelean clan, a family he could trust, be part of, be respected, be loved and serve the sacred 'Cause' all at the same time. Ten years later at the age of twenty-seven, Lucas was a veteran member of the Klan.

Newly appointed as a Grand Cyclops, Lucas was in charge of a Den that included the town of Hamburg in Aiken County, South Carolina. Much to his joy and elation, President Rutherford B. Hayes rescinded the Reconstruction Act in 1877. At one stroke of the pen, Oliver O. Howard's efforts as head of the Freedmen Bureau set up to assist newly freed blacks after the Civil War, was undone. The KKK's reign of terror had succeeded in creating a segregated southern society that would last for over eighty years. After years of lynching, burning, whipping, torture, and intimidation; Lucas became a devoted disciple of violence. But after 1877, their mission accomplished, the once feared KKK became dormant, not to be resurrected again till 1916.

In 1877, Lucas was at loose ends ready to further his father's sacred 'Cause.' He would accomplish something his beloved father failed to do; find then kill John Saxton and Marcus

S.A. Carter

Brown. He'd heard rumors that his father's smuggling business in New York City had made very lucrative. Although his father never discussed his finances, his companion Harley Blackstone had. But any salient information was lost or so it seemed, for Blackstone had been short on details and long on enthusiasm. Lucas was in a quandary. He could certainly use the money his father must have left him to finance his plans of revenge. The only problem was that he didn't know where the money was hidden.

Any clues in the cardboard box John McCrutcheon gave him years ago were long gone. Only his father's Army slouch hat remained. Lucas faithfully kept it as a lasting reminder of his father. Other items in the box had been stolen, lost or left behind. The Major's slouch hat however, was back in Pulaski at the home of Billy Dee's parents. Lucas reasoned that it just might give him a clue to the smuggling fortune Blackstone bragged about from time to time. It seemed to Lucas that his father was unusually possessive of that particular hat. No One else could touch it let alone wear it.

As the 'unholy trinity' fled to Richmond near the end of the war, his father alluded to that the hat held a secret and that in time, at the right moment, he would reveal it to Lucas. However, his father was hung before he'd had a chance to tell Lucas the hat's significance, or where his ill gotten gains were stashed. It did seem strange upon reflection that his father went to the Oakwood cemetery wearing another hat. Why? His father also used the other hat to signal danger. Lucas concluded that his father was sending him a message, but what? Why didn't he simply take him aside and reveal all before going to the cemetery. Lucas knew his father was very wary of the situation. Was his lack of communication devised to protect his son from harm? Lucas remained mystified. Again, he suspected that his father must have buried the loot and left a map somewhere because he didn't trust banks or their paper currency. Reckoning that the loot was too bulky to always be at hand, Lucas guessed that it was buried, perhaps on the outskirts of New York City. Blackstone was dead and while he was alive never mentioned anything about it. Lucas made up his mind. He had to get that hat!

After the Hamburg raid, Lucas and Billy Dee rode like the wind straight for Pulaski with Federal forces in hot pursuit. Once there, Lucas barely had enough time to gather his effects including the grey slouch hat and ride away. Billy however, died in a gun fight with the Federals while covering Lucas Garrow's escape. Thirty miles later, after riding all night, Lucas entered Fayetteville, Tennessee. An old Klan friend of his, Farron Smart served in General James Longstreet's army beside Lucas. Smart lived in a boarding house on Elk St.

Lucas arrived there early the next morning totally exhausted. His friend let him in through the back door. Lucas slept most of the next day. On the second day, while alone in his room, he tore his father's hat apart. He found nothing. All he had left was a braided leather hat cord with large silver acorns attached as a souvenir. He stayed on two more days then moved on disguised as traveling salesman selling business insurance.

It was an effective cover, for business insurance had become extremely popular since the great Chicago fire of 1871 and the Boston fire of 1872. The Long Depression was over and America was booming again. After three days traveling by secondary roads, Lucas reached the city of Winchester, Tennessee. Riding on, he spent the next night at a red brick Inn, located at Tim's Ford Lake just outside the town. It was there that it happened.

While sitting on a bed in his small room, Lucas was utterly frustrated, trying to understand the enormity of what his father had done to him. Tantalizing his greed were bits and pieces of forgotten conversations with Blackstone about smuggling and what he and his father did with the proceeds. His father always said,

"Look son, don't ever trust a bank unless you're on the board of directors or own it. Don't ever trust anyone unless it's close family. And most of all son, the best place to hide anything of value is in the arms of Mother Nature cause she ain't talkin'."

In a fit of anger, Lucas whipped the hat cord against a nearby table. As he did so, he heard something pop as one of the large silver acorns broke apart. Lucas jumped up as the bottom half of one of them skittered across pine floorboards. From then on, every movement was in slow motion. The stress upon his mind was intolerable. I was as if his eyes were looking through a glass darkly, totally focused on a small ball of paper that rolled in the other direction across the room. He retrieved it, sat down, and carefully unrolled it. In the light of an Aladdin lantern flickering above his shoulder, he saw that the note was in his father's neat English round hand. It said,

"DEAR SON. IF U READ THIS, I'M DEAD. BEWARE H.B. GO 1.5 MI N KING'S BRIDGE ON BOSTON POST RD TO ALBANY RD SIGN. DIG 20 FT. N. OF IT.

Lucas memorized the note then burned it in a large ashtray. He watched as the last living link with his father slowly curled at the edges, glowed brightly, flared up and then was totally consumed. The torch of revenge had now passed on from father to son. He picked up the two halves of the silver acorn. Upon closer inspection they did seem somewhat larger than others he was familiar with. The two halves could be screwed together as one. Lucas looked at the other acorn. It too could be unscrewed. This he did but it was empty. He wondered, "Why?"

Later that afternoon, Lucas, posing as an insurance salesman, stopped by a small Catholic church. He sauntered in, murdered the priest and stole his cross on a necklace, celluloid collar, black cassock, bible and other sundries. Within minutes, he'd become a servant of God rather than that of the devil, namely an itinerant priest wearing a homespun black cassock. The large baggy garment was perfect for hiding a virtual armory beneath it. A waterproof poncho protected his sleeping blankets. His black business suit was tied up in a saddle bag behind him on an English saddle. A Winchester rifle thrust into a leather scabbard lay under his right thigh. Ten days later by using back roads and byways he rode into

New York City. Along the way he narrowly avoided preaching two sermons by claiming he was ill. He arrived at King's Bridge early in the morning after riding all night. He proceeded to double back many times, making sure he wasn't followed.

King's bridge, a two lane wooden structure, straddled a narrow river. The frail looking wooden railings that bordered it continued on as the road swung to the right due north. Lucas proceeded to ride slowly for one mile, two miles then five miles further on as he searched in vain for the post sign that said ALBANY>. Nothing even remotely similar was to be found. He was beginning to worry.

In the past twelve years the area had certainly changed dramatically. New buildings, roads, wagon yards, and many businesses had all been built in there. The road to Albany from the Boston Post Road apparently, according to the locals, had been realigned to allow for a railway right of way. Lucas became frustrated and increasingly bitter. Why hadn't his father told him before he was hung? Why?

It was dark when he rode on to Yonkers. He signed in at the Getty House on Main St. and Nepperham Avenue as a Father J. C. Johnson from New York City. The hotel was a large wooden structure formerly known as the Indian Queen Inn, the Eagle Hotel, the Nappeckamack House and the Stage House. A black boy stabled Garrow's horse in the Livery across the street from the hotel. Lucas was given directions and a brass key to Room 10 on the second floor. As he was about to go upstairs to his room, the waspish desk clerk inquired,

"Ah, Father Johnson, how long do you plan on staying here?" Lucas intoned piously, careful to keep his voice sacramental,

"The Lord's work is waiting for me. It shall be done soon my son. Amen."

Lucas picked up his saddle bags and limped up the stairs to his room, closing the door behind him. An hour later he'd washed, shaved off his beard. Only a neatly clipped chevron mustache remained. Within minutes, he appeared as a businessman for dinner at a small tavern located downstairs. After a simple supper of chicken and dumplings, a flagon of ale and a chcroot; he retired for the night. He'd spoken to no one, yet early in the morning as he lay fast asleep, the door to his small suite was forced open.

A tall lithe figure crept towards the bed and in an instant sapped Lucas where he lay. The assailant then closed the door locking it. Moments later the small room was bathed in yellow light from an Aladdin lamp sitting upon a night table. The intruder strode to a solitary window and drew its heavy curtains shut. His military bearing exaggerated his height and well muscled body. A middle aged man, sporting a neatly trimmed goatee on his full lower lip, returned to the bedside. A priest's black cassock caught his attention. After looking through its many hidden pockets, he put it back exactly where he found it draped over a chair.

The stranger's clothing was quite the opposite of a country priest for he was impeccably dressed. A black swallow tail coat, a low cut red silk vest worn over a white shirt was crowned by a black cravat. White kid gloves were set off by gold cufflinks, the initials HB being engraved upon them. After half an hour of fruitless searching, the man gave up and left the room, quietly closing the door behind him.

Lucas remained unconscious until late morning. He was awakened not by the sounds of his attacker but that of the hotel's desk clerk knocking on his door. Momentarily stunned by reality, Lucas swung his bare legs over the edge of the bed. His head throbbed. Quickly, he rose and gathered a long cotton robe about him. He padded towards the door irritated by the unexpected interruption, saying, "I'll be right there in a minute." An anxious voice on the other side said.

"I've a note here for you Father. I'll slip it under the door."

Lucas bent over and watched as a long white envelope slid towards him. He took it back to the bed wondering what was in it since there was some weight to it. While sitting on the bed rubbing his sore head, he realized that someone had gone through his effects. There was no evidence as such but it was the little things that gave the charade substance. Lucas threw the unopened envelope on the tousled bed sheets, shuffled over to the narrow window and drew back the damask drapes. He remembered that he'd left them open. Sunbeams shot through with dust motes rising, pushed the shadows back into the deeper recesses of the room. Quickly Lucas checked his leather saddle bags, his suit of clothes, wallet, and his personal effects. Nothing seemed amiss but everything was amiss. Perhaps the letter would explain the mystery?

The envelope lay there on the bed sealed with a blob of red wax; innocuous, innocent, yet potentially full of danger. Lucas opened it. He shook out the letter and as he did so, a silver dollar fell onto the bed. Lucas picked it up and was ready to put it aside when a glint of light caught his eye. There upon the coin was scratched an X. Puzzled; he looked at both sides, turning the coin over and over in his long fingers. He put it in his robe's right pocket. It too like the letter began taunting him. Its paper was of a very high quality, and written upon it in a distinctly feminine hand were the words,

"Dear Father Garrow. I apologize for my colleague hitting a man of the cloth on the head last night. However, I make no apologies for surmising that you are in New York and in disguise to recover your father's ill gotten gains. Twelve years after your father hung in Richmond is a long time to wait for many of us who were unfortunate to have known him and that lout Harley Blackstone. Obviously last night we did not find what we were looking for, however it is highly likely that your father's memories of me might have inspired him to hide his wealth in this area. If so, we might be able to help each other in this regard. The marked coin will identify you once I've found you. If you are interested, meet me tonight dressed as a priest at Bashford's Tavern at ten. It's near the sloop wharf on the Hudson at the mouth of the Nepperham (Saw Mill) River. BB"

Lucas read the letter again and again as he fingered the silver coin in his pocket. It was very obvious to him that his father and BB or whoever her was, had had some sort of liaison that later soured. His father never mentioned a BB or for that matter much else. In fact Lucas in retrospect did all the talking and his father very little. Why? His mind returned to the matter at hand; where was that damned money? Obviously, it was worthwhile enough to wait twelve years for. His father's rivals were many and it was also true they had long memories. An unpleasant sensation within him emerged fully formed and dangerous. His father's enemies were now his. He laughed bitterly,

"What an inheritance this is turning out to be! They know I'm here looking for my father's money, yet why haven't they taken me some place and tortured me?"

It all made no sense whatsoever. Lucas looked at his Hamilton pocket watch. It was noon. Perhaps he might try again to find the spot but he quickly decided that caution would be his watch word. No, he would have a rest and think things out. His father's words came back to warn him,

"Son, we're going to think our way out." and "Let's not be too hasty. One never knows what dangers are lurking in the shadows just waiting to jump out at you."

Lucas took his father's advice to heart. Disrobing, he quickly dressed in a black frock suit. He was attired once more as a simple business man. After locking his door, he ran down another flight of stairs and exited by a rear door into an alley behind the Getty House.

.

The livery stables were across the street from the hotel. Lucas decided to ride into Yonkers that afternoon to seek out a gunsmith. Two hours later, after entering the hotel the same way he'd come in, he entered his room. After locking the door, he threw a waxed paper packet on the bed then sat down to unwrap it. Within minutes, a Richardson .36 caliber single shot boot pistol slid down his right riding boot. Next, a small bowie knife in its scabbard was nestled against his spine while a five round .31 Caliber Pocket Colt in a shoulder holster found a home under his right armpit. A priest's cassock lay on the bed. After he had put it over his suit, he looked at himself in a full length floor mirror then pirouetted about. He laughed,

"Christ almighty, I'm probably the only priest hereabouts that will shoot first and then say the last rites over the dead moments later."

Lucas would play the game but on his terms, however what he didn't expect was to fall in love all over again.

Lucas left by the back door of the Getty House for the livery stables across the street. Dusk was falling. The stable boy, Simon Crest, eyed him as Lucas came into the gloomy confines of the building. Crest continued to shovel horse apples into a wooden wheelbarrow. Lucas limped carefully down the aisle. Horses nickered softly, while others stamped their hooves. Some stood stoically with one hind foot suspended above their straw bedding. The boy heard errant footfalls coming closer. He looked up to see a priest, his long black cassock flowing around his feet as the air in barn lifted the lower edges of it. Simon stood his shovel against a support beam and moved swiftly away to a horse stall further down the row.

A tall black warm blood was already saddled as instructed. The boy patted the horse's warm muzzle, reached over, grabbed the halter and swung the animal around and out of its stall. The priest took the reins from the lad and swung up easily onto an English saddle. The boy stood back as the rider shifted his weight and arranged his cassock. Simon followed him as the rider's horse clopped its way slowly towards a pooling of light at the far end of the long building. Once there, the boy called out. The priest swung around to look down upon him. Crest looked up at Lucas, scratched his head and drawled.

"Ah, Father Johnson, I might be too bold but weren't you in a frock suit yesterday and you're now clean shaven and dressed as a priest once again?"

The lad shook his head as Lucas reached down and gave him a twenty-five cent paper shinplaster.

"Now my son, that'll be our secret we'll both have to share with God, won't it?" The boy nodded.

"What's your name boy?"

"Simon Crest."

"Ok Simon, I want you hide a casket for me." The boy's eyes widened.

"You mean a coffin don't you Father?"

"Yes my son, a special coffin. When it's delivered here, hide it under the hay mow over there in the corner until you can find someone to help you put it in a buckboard under a tarp. Is there anyone here a bouts you can trust boy?"

"Why yes Father, my boss Jacob Swartz."

"Good. You tell him I want a heavy buckboard and a two mule team in a Brichen pulling harness. If he buys it for less than fifty bucks, tell him to keep the change. As for who wants to buy the team, you don't know who."

The boy laughed. "Don't know Father, why's that?"

"Just say that the good Lord told you what to do and nothin' more."

Lucas handed him a leather sack of coins. He reached into a pocket and took out a silver dollar saying, "And here's some more silver for your tro…"

The boy reached up and snatched the dollar before Lucas could finish.

"Can I trust you Simon?"

"Yes sir, I mean Father.

Garrow looked at the boy fondly, patting him on his nappy head as he did so.

"Remember Simon, mum's the word. Don't tell anyone other than Jacob. Don't forget the bill of sale, I'll need it." He winked at the boy.

The boy stood to the side as Lucas rode off into the gathering dusk. It began to rain.

Lucas arrived at Bashford's Tavern an hour later. On the way there, he doubled back and forth, making sure he wasn't followed. Satisfied, he found a muddy toll road that led to the Hudson River. Once there, a heavily rutted side road led south to the sloop wharf where the Nepperham River meandered sluggishly into the wide Hudson. At their confluence was a motley collection of ship chandleries, shipyards, net lofts, small fishing shacks, warehouses and Bashford's Tavern.

Surrounded by a wide court yard, the three story brick building was a hive of activity. Lanterns glowed on either side of its massive front entrance, while others winked salaciously from every upper window. He tied his horse to an iron ring that pierced a wooden post, just one of many that surrounded the building. Carriages, stage coaches, and buggies of all sorts waited in the pouring rain. Drum rolls of thunder pounded the eastern horizon like a military barrage. An occasional flash of rocket lightning between dark and brooding clouds far off down river only deepened a sense of foreboding Lucas felt as he entered the busy Inn.

John Bashford, the Tavern's ebullient owner came over as Lucas was taking off his oiled rain slicker. The corpulent little man was all red; in fact he was blushing red in every dimension. His red hair and red mutton-chop side burns were overshadowed by a large red nose that was completely swathed in bursting red veins. These were all combined with a reddish hue that bathed his huge head, making him look like a talking tomato. Yet, the whole bizarre effect went completely unnoticed as soon as he spoke. Like the sound of thunder that rolled through the heavens outside the Inn, his deep and resonant voice commanded attention. Garrow was mesmerized by it. It was exactly like the voice of Moses or even God for that matter. Bashford held out a red beefy hand and said,

"Welcome aboard Father. I'm John Bashford, the owner of this den of inequity." Undulating red waves of fat rolled up and down under his red chin, as he laughed heartily.

"We're all angels in these parts so we don't see too many men of the cloth hereabouts. What's your pleasure Father?"

Without waiting for an answer the red man turned towards the bar and roared,

"Duncan my lad, take the good Father here to a private booth in the back and be quick about it before he changes his habits." He laughed at his own witticism.

A young snaggle-toothed man sprinted out from behind a long mahogany bar. He wiped his hands on a dirty apron. Bashford clapped Lucas on the back.

"Follow Duncan Father. I'm sure you'll be alright. Have a pleasant evening."

With that, he turned and went back to the bar and began pulling more red ale into red ware mugs for the thirsty throng that milled about before him.

Lucas chose a booth in a secluded corner with an eye to a nearby exit. From there he could see the front door. He hung up his overcoat and hat on a peg rammed into a post then ordered a pint of cream ale and waited. It was still early. Whoever BB was, he was ready. The game was afoot and danger lurked in every shadow. Lucas scanned the room for any sign of what he imagined her to look like however none of the ladies present seemed to fit. He knew his father eyed every tall, comely wench that crossed his path on the Pee Dee road to Richmond and at all the hotel parlors in between. After thirty minutes, none of the tavern's female patrons fitted his mental image.

The crowd became more raucous as more patrons came bustling through the swinging oak doors of the tavern's inner foyer. Their dripping coats were taken by a buxom wench who hung them on high oak wall pegs in a warming room off by the kitchen. Soon the tavern's sawdust floor was awash in spilled spirits. Cigar, pipe and cheroot smoke hung heavy under an ornate tinplate ceiling, bisected by hand hewn black oak beams. A gilt plate glass mirror spanned the rear wall behind the bar making the room appear to be filled with even more tipsy people. Heavy wooden benches and their attendant tables were weighed down with numerous jugs of grog and platters of sausages and sweet meats. Loaves of bread, pots of butter, jars of pickled eggs, and cheap cutlery lay scattered about. Clay salters and pepper pots huddled amidst them. Without warning, someone swung the tavern's double doors open with a loud crash.

The room's male clientele turned as one and stopped breathing. To a man, all eyes gazed upon a tall, young woman who walked in. She paused for dramatic effect, surveying the unwashed masses until her sapphire eyes alighted on a humble priest barely visible in a dark corner by the rear exit. She doffed a blue satin cape; her impeccably dressed escort took it from her with a flourish. John Bashford appeared as if by magic beside her. He kissed her proffered kid gloved hand. She smiled coyly, her perfect white teeth dazzling in the soft light. Lucas watched as Bashford gallantly indicated a small private booth by the front door. However, his chivalry was ignored as the lady indicated otherwise.

Taking her escort's arm, the woman proceeded to mince through the unruly mob like Marie Antoinette parading through the hall of a thousand mirrors at Versailles. Her long dark black ringlets spilled out from beneath a blue satin bonnet trimmed in white feathers. Wide, bare shoulders moved erotically back and forth as she strutted towards Lucas. A perfectly formed longish face was centered by an aquiline nose that separated her arresting blue eyes. Rouged lips, full and pouting, parted slightly, revealing the tip of a wet pink tongue. All these elements conspired to draw one's eye helplessly towards her. A long, fully flounced evening dress of dark blue silk completely failed to hide her hourglass figure. Every man's imagination devoured her as she sauntered towards Lucas unrestrained by any shred of modesty or decorum. Lucas pretended to ignore her as she and her consort approached.

He leisurely drank his ale and leafed through a small bible he'd stolen from his hotel room. He waited; she waited. Finally, her escort reached down and swatted the bible out of Lucas's hands. Before the man attempted to push his advantage, Garrow's right fist smashed into the man's genitals. The man howled while Lucas eased himself out of the booth. He took the man by his collar, pried the rear door of the Tavern open with his boot and pushed the lothario into the dark alley beyond. As the stricken gallant floundered about in a substantial mud puddle, Garrow closed the door and barred it. He turned about and stopped. The lady was pointing a deadly looking .41 double barreled pocket derringer directly at him. Lucas whispered,

"Madam please, it is quite unseemly for a young lady such as yourself to be seen in public with a priest in a place such as this let alone pointing a gun at him. You certainly have me at a disadvantage. Do I have time to say the last rites?"

Lucas looked down on her quite amused. The gun disappeared into her handbag as John Bashford came rushing up behind them, his face even redder than before. She turned to meet the red man. He blustered,

"My God Lady Ashton, what is going on here? I don't mean to be uncivil Father, but while my establishment does have a certain reputation for frivolity, it certainly has up until now been devoid of murder. Please Lady Ashton, keep your theatrics to Niblo's Garden and not here, I beg of you."

His red eyes pleaded with her. Lady Ashton kissed the man on his red forehead. He bowed and retreated as hastily as he had arrived. Lucas turned and took her arm in his. He led her back to the booth. Once seated across from each other, Lucas ordered more red ale then drew two red velvet curtains to a close. A pair of gaslights above them sputtered as he waited for the Lady to begin. Before she did so, he took a marked silver dollar out of his pocket and placed it X up on the oak table between them. He smiled saying,

"I think this will pay for our drinks. Don't you agree Lady Ashton or is it BB?"

He waited patiently, his heart racing as her gloved hands slid across the table grasping his hands firmly. She pulled him to her. Their faces were mere inches apart. Her ruby lips parted slightly making way for a long tongue that slowly baptized them. Her eyes roamed back and forth across his face until they found what they wanted. What they wanted was his total attention to what she was about to say. She smiled knowingly then let him go, sat back and leisurely lit a cheroot. Tilting her head upwards, she inhaled deeply then casually blew smoke out through her nostrils. As she did so, she reached over, patted his hands and said coyly,

"You are indeed your father's son Lucas. I hope that our relationship will be short, sweet and unblemished by chicanery of any kind. Perhaps we'll even become lovers, who knows? However, your father used me terribly after he stole my heart. For that I can forgive him as a man, but his desertion of the cause was unforgivable."

She recoiled as Lucas slapped her face. BB wiped a bloody lip with one hand, the cheroot still clutched firmly in the other. Lucas spat out the words,

"The Major was never a deserter Madam but was working undercover, exposing traitors to the Confederacy and killing those who dared oppose him. He died a hero trying to save it. No madam, the war might be over, but the cause will never die. To that end, I intend to rid myself of a loathsome burden by killing John Saxton and Marcus Brown. They are the antithesis of everything the cause stands for. Besides, both men killed my grandfather Josiah and my father. I have to finish what my family started. To do that, I need money, lots of money to find them and punish them for what they did to my family and the Confederacy.

Madam, the war might be over for you but it will never be over for me until Southron honor has been restored."

He reached over with both hands and grabbed her by her shoulders. Without warning she was upon him, her tongue deep within him. Her lips fell away upon his, her eyes daring him to release her. He tried to back away but she held him tight, her long arms wrapped around him pulling him across the narrow table towards her. Her tongue continued to probe him then she released him, sat back, smiling salaciously. BB continued to smoke her cheroot as if nothing had happened.

Lucas sank back on the padded bench fully aroused, his celluloid collar askew, his hair tousled, and his mind ablaze with passion. Without a word being said, he stood up, took her cape from a wooden peg behind her and offered it to her. While he straightened his collar, she combed her hair. He recovered his overcoat and broad hat, leaving the marked coin on the table. They rose as one and left by the rear door. Her former escort had vanished into the night. Lucas was wary, very wary as the lady exclaimed,

"That bastard Hargrove took my Phaeton." She flicked her spent cheroot into a large and growing mud puddle.

Lucas eyed her, imploring him to rescue her. He responded as she knew he would.

"Why, Lady Ashton, there are plenty more Phaetons where that came from. Here, stay in the shadows. I'll be right back."

She didn't have long to wait as the priest returned with a pilfered drop front Phaeton behind which was tethered a magnificent black horse. Off they went into the rain swept night as the horses trotted over the water filled ruts of a muddy road. The Lady sat close; her hand reached down, unbuttoned his fly and began caressing his aroused manhood. As the carriage jiggled this way and that, he came in her mouth while barely able to hold onto the reins. Again and again as they drove through the night, he came until he could bear it no more. A mile from the tavern, they stopped, hidden within a secluded copse of trees.

As the storm raged above them, the Phaeton rocked back and forth, its inhabitants completely oblivious to the elegant man who painfully followed them from Bashford's Tavern. The man grinned. His scheme was unfolding exactly as planned. It wouldn't be long before he, Hargrove Black would be fabulously rich. Black watched as the Phaeton pulled away, heading for the Getty House two miles from the river. His mentor, Boss Tweed would be pleased, perhaps even advancing Black's political aspirations, for he too had been swindled by Horatio Garrow. Hargrove Black and Boss Tweed would exact revenge in a most terrible way imaginable. They would find the gold and kill the spawn of the devil and his wanton paramour at the same time.

Lucas let BB off just down the street from the Getty House giving her his key to Room ten. He told her to register at the hotel as a Miss Smith, a school teacher new to the area. As soon as she registered, she was to go to Room Ten and let herself in. He told her to lock the door. He'd knock softly four times. Lucas assured her that he wouldn't be long. And so,

BB did as she was told knowing Hargrove Black was not far behind her. She laughed at the thought of him watching the Phaeton jumping up and down amongst the trees. Somehow the experience unnerved her as she remembered Horatio and her making love in the Landau. She remembered fleeing down the Post road with that deviant driver Harley Blackstone just inches above her head. But BB lived for many years on the edge of disaster as a spy for the Confederacy and became inured to danger, imminent or otherwise. A figure hiding in the shadows hissed,

"I've tied the Phaeton behind the hotel in the alley Lady Ashton. From what I've witnessed tonight, our plans are unfolding beautifully indeed."

She stopped, startled by the intrusion. She pretended to look at her pendant watch. Hargrove became impatient, rubbing his sore groin as he did so.

"What room is he in Lady Ashton? What room?"

It was midnight. BB faced him enjoying his discomfort.

"Oh my dearest, it's room ten. I'll leave the door slightly ajar. Garrow will be there shortly. He's in the livery across the road. I'll sign in as a Miss Smith. Give me a few minutes my dear Hargrove. Black rejoined,

"Be careful. The bastard is dangerous. Christ my nuts hurt! When this escapade is all over, I'll take great pleasure in killing him."

As Black disappeared, BB remembered that she had no luggage. The realization of it made her stop. She had an idea. Before she entered the Getty House, she mussed up her hair and dress then unfastened the bone buttons of her wet blouse exposing an ample cleavage. She adjusted her cape then ran through the front door of the Getty House into the lobby crying piteously. The sudden entrance of a distraught maiden standing there drenched and desolate startled the waspish desk clerk severely. He stood there mesmerized. The lady wailed,

"Oh my, oh my, I've been robbed. He took everything and stole my buggy. Please sir is there a constable hereabouts? I'm such a mess, why look at me."

The clerk did look at her, quite closely, in fact too closely, as she backed away from him. The man came around the corner of the front desk, his bony hands reaching towards her in lustful sympathy. BB staggered away from him to a nearby chair as if she was having the vapors. The clerk recovered his wits, ran back and rang the desk bell. A bellboy appeared. By now BB saw that the coast was clear. She rose to her feet and declared,

"Gentlemen, you are so kind. I do think I need a room to recover from this horrid incident. It's very late and I'm afraid of going back to my room at Bashford's."

The desk clerk bristled at the name of his competitor. She continued coquettishly.

"Perhaps you'd be so kind as to assign me to a room? Luckily, I managed to hang on to a small wallet hidden upon my person. Do you mind if I asked you both to turn around? You see my wallet is hidden, in what you might say is a most delicate location."

Minutes later, she was in room ten, the door partly open. Black tapped lightly on the door. BB opened it wide. They kissed passionately then she slipped him her key to Room 11. She waited for him to enter the room next door. He did, closing the door behind him.

BB sat waiting for Lucas. It was then that she realized Hargrove was a cad, totally selfish and untrustworthy. She also knew he was a well paid bully boy for Boss Tweed. Black often went to Niblo's theatre where Lady Ashton was a part of Lydia Thompson's bawdy burlesque troupe. They were performing a risqué play called the 'Ixion'. It was there that she first learned two bits of news. Firstly, Lucas Garrow had arrived in New York. Secondly, BB, an inveterate reader of the Times classifieds, had found John Saxton's article quite by chance. The cryptic message, 'Those in the know will go' intrigued her. Perhaps Lucas had seen it too and knew more. She would find out in her own way when the time was right. Both Lucas and BB hated Saxton and Marcus. Perhaps, she even more so, for it was their wives as she later on found out from Horatio that foiled the Nobel plot. She took off her cape and hat, sat down on the bed and fumed,

"Goddamn it! Those two bitches will pay dearly. No one who was involved will survive my revenge... no one!"

Her reverie was shattered by four imperceptible knocks on the door. She leapt off the bed and opened the door, the brass room key in her hand. Garrow stepped into the room and brushed her open arms aside, closing the door with a bang behind him. He wrenched the room key out of her hand and locked the door. BB was stunned. He grabbed her by the throat then picked her up bodily and threw her down spread-eagled on the double bed crushing her hat. Drawing his pocket Colt from under his armpit at the same time, he straddled her, pinning her to the mattress. Her eyes widened in horror as he caressed her face with cold steel. She struggled but he slapped her. He thrust the gun's muzzle into her mouth and snarled,

"Suck on this bitch! Who was in the room with you a few minutes ago? I can smell his aftershave. In fact it smells just like that dandy I threw out into the alley at Bashford's. I told you to lock the door but it was not locked."

"He smacked her again. She started to cry.

"By the way, what's his full name?"

He withdrew the gun barrel from between her lips. BB gasped,

"Hargrove Black, the stage manager at Niblo's Burlesque Theater where I'm performing. Why are you doing this to me Lucas? Why?"

He looked down at her, determined to expose her chicanery.

"Yes my lovely, my father told me to watch out for a man with the initials HB. I thought he meant Harley Blackstone but he's dead now. What's going on between you two? Are you planning to kill me after we find the money? Is that it? Are you Mrs. Black? Is that it you slut?"

She struggled, crying,

"Get off me, you're hurting me. Please get off me, I can't take it anymore!"

Lucas caressed her face one more time with the pocket Colt. He looked at her, his eyes reptilian.

"Don't make any sudden moves or scream out because I will kill you. I'll kill anyone who gets between me, my father's money and the cause. Do you understand me?"

Lucas realized that the young woman was terrified or at least pretended to be. She'd just admitted she was a burlesque actress. To Lucas that meant she was a loose woman and a convincing liar. So far she was both. The latter would come out sooner or later, preferably sooner for he was running out of time. He eased off the bed, the pocket Colt leveled at her heart. Her rouge had run down onto her blouse and her hair was wet with sweat. Two red welts on her cheeks were beginning to swell. She sat up on the bed, her feet over the edge planted on a floor rug below. BB reached for the remains of her hat then started to sob.

Unknown to Lucas, Hargrove was on the other side of a thin wall separating the two suites. To hear their conversation, he'd taken a water glass and by pressing its open end against the wall, his right ear to its bottom; all he heard were snatches of what was going on. What he did hear, he didn't like. Black put down the glass and scribbled more notes in a small red leather diary. He put the diary and its pencil in a pocket. From another, he took out a S&W pistol. He carefully opened the door to his suite and looked both ways down the narrow hallway. No one was around. He slipped out, pistol at the ready and tried to open the door to room ten. It was locked. What next? Should he burst in or continue to listen? He crept away noting that discretion was the better part of valor. He thought,

'Maybe Falstaff was right after all.'

He backed away slowly and entered his room, locking the door behind him. Once more he picked up the water glass and continued his eavesdropping.

Lucas tossed BB a handkerchief. She dabbed at her eyes. The linen cloth came away black with wet makeup. Lucas caught the balled-up hanky. She spit back at him.

"You bloody bastard! You're even worse than your old man. At least he never beat me or put a gun in my mouth." Lucas laughed making her even angrier. She managed to restore her hat to a reasonable facsimile of the original. She threw it across the room at him. He deftly caught it and laughed. Furious, she hissed as she buttoned her blouse,

"You ruined my hat you son of a bitch! I'll see you in hell first BOY! Did you hear me BOY?"

She was taunting him now, expecting him to rise to the bait, but he just stood there, the lethal looking pocket Colt pointed at her heart. He grinned as he calmly sat down across from her, put his boots up on the bed and lit a cheroot with his free hand. It was an impressive performance not lost on the actress sitting across from him. Not even his old man was this cool. At that precise moment BB knew that she'd finally met her match. Lucas was going to kill her. Hargrove Black was going to kill her. And, if they both failed, Boss Tweed's thugs would surely kill her. She thought ruefully,

'I have no money. I cannot go back to my flat in the Bronx because one of Tweed's thugs will probably be watching it. If Horatio didn't trust Black then I won't either. What am I to do? Goddamn it all! Lucas needs me as much as I need him'

The realization that Black was now a lethal liability caused her to laugh. In fact she laughed so heartily that Lucas hissed at her,

"Shut up BB! I'd just shut up if I were you."

He cocked the pistol. The sound of it was dramatic, final and therefore quite effective. She stopped abruptly. Lucas released the weapon's hammer carefully, saying,

"That's much better. Now once more, who is Hargrove Black? Tell me now or I will kill you."

He rose up, reached behind his back, lifted up his cassock and retrieved a Bowie- knife. She cringed; her face white as a sheet, her eyes large and dilated. Lucas bent down and pressed the knife against her long neck just under her perfect chin. A thin trickle of perfect blood wound its way down her perfect neck and disappeared between her perfect bosoms. BB whimpered,

"He works for Boss Tweed. Your father cheated Tweed out of millions. Tweed wants it all back, all of it; so he hired me and Hargrove to get it." Lucas was stunned, "Hmmm millions eh?"

He smiled at her, the knife still pressed against her. While doing so, Lucas entertained a few moments of reflection. He remembered vividly Chief Clerk Ben Wallace's iron grip on the inner workings of Salisbury prison. Knowledge was power and Wallace's power was achieved through informants. Probably the weasel in the hotel lobby below was one of Tweed's spies. Lucas was right. The desk clerk and hundreds of others like him were the eyes and ears that made Tweed so feared and powerful even while incarcerated behind the bars of Ludlow Street prison.

The moment passed as BB continued, confident now that she would live.

"Your father passed around a picture of you when you were a cadet at Pineville Academy. The similarities between you and your father are very striking. I nearly choked the first time I saw you Lucas, Christ, you look just like your old man. Tis eerie indeed."

Lucas took the bloody blade away from her throat. He cleaned it with her hair and put it back in a worn scabbard. BB remained on the bed, holding her arms across her chest. Lucas stood beside her, thought about the situation, and became more conciliatory.

"Look BB, I have to find my father's swag and I can't do it without your help. You know it and I know it."

He holstered the pocket Colt under his left armpit. As he did so, he took off the gold plated crucifix from around his neck throwing it on the bed. It lay there ablaze in soft lamplight. His black cassock came off in one fluid movement followed by a celluloid collar. BB watched him closely, licking her swollen lips as she did so. One of her eyes was closing shut and starting to blacken. Lucas took off the heavy shoulder gun holster, throwing it on the bed. It broke the cheap metal crucifix in two. A linen shirt, trousers and other vestments followed until only his underwear remained. He sat down on the bed beside her and laughed.

"Christ almighty girl, you look awful. Go and see if you can fix yourself up. I have to think, but before you do, I have a question for you."

He paused as she rose off the bed and walked over to a mirrored wash-board. There, she poured cold water from a porcelain pitcher into a matching wash bowl. Her nerves were on edge, exposed, raw, and tender. A swollen face peered back at her in the mirror. BB waited for Lucas to speak. He did not for she knew he was watching her closely. She swore under her breath. There she rubbed an amber bar of Pears soap on a wet face cloth and cleaned the blood off her throat. The bleeding stopped. Lucas got up off the bed and come up behind her. She flinched as he held her shoulders in both hands. They looked at each other in the mirror. He whispered in her ear,

"Did you ever screw Hargrove Black?" She watched his reflection.

"Maybe I did, maybe I didn't. What do you care?"

She continued to watch for any sign of jealousy, any sign of pain. There was none.

'Christ', she thought, 'He's even more heartless than his father. How can I control him if he doesn't get jealous?'

Lucas took the soapy cloth away from her and started to bathe her face tenderly while standing behind her. She didn't move. He rinsed the cloth free of its soap and finished washing her face. Grabbing a nearby fresh towel, he gently dried her cheeks, forehead and neck. All the while his groin was pressed into her from behind. He put the towel back on its bar and resumed holding her shoulders but more firmly. She could feel his hardness growing. He whispered once more into her ear, his breath hotter than before, his earnestness more evident.

"Did you ever screw him BB?"

She reached up, each of her hands grasping his. She pulled them down onto her large high breasts. His hands instinctively cupped them from underneath. His pleasure was not impeded by a corset. She shuddered, her head turning slightly. Leaning back, her face rested against his cheek.

"No Lucas, I've never mixed business with pleasure. Besides, the man was loathsome, vainglorious and boring."

Lucas turned her around, her back to the mirror. The effect was startling for she appeared in his mind's eye unblemished and even more beautiful than before.

"Where is Black now my dear? Where is he? He's nothing to you now. Now is the time to tell me truthfully before he kills us both." She blanched as she remembered.

"Oh Lucas, he's right next door in room eleven. Oh my! The walls here are probably as thin as newspaper." She gasped,

"My God, he's heard every word, every word."

Lucas put his fingers to her lips, whispering as he backed away from her,

"Still got that toy gun in your hand bag?" She nodded.

"Get it out and lock the door after I'm gone. I might be awhile. Stay put no matter what happens. If I'm not back by morning, pack up everything here and leave by the back door down the hall. Got any money?" She nodded. Lucas gave her twenty gold coins anyway. He continued.

"Go to the livery across the street and see the nigger, Simon Crest. He'll get the Phaeton ready for you. Drive out to Bashford's. Rent a room. I'll meet you there. I'll knock four times either here or there. Any less, don't open the door."

He kissed her on the forehead. Lucas opened the door quietly then looked both ways down the hallway. She watched as the door clicked shut behind him. BB ran over and locked it. She walked over to a table and retrieved her purse. She sat down heavily then took out the double-barreled derringer. She broke the tiny gun open. It was loaded. She snapped it shut. A bottle of Jim Beam on a side board nearby winked at her in the lamplight. BB walked over, found a glass, poured herself a drink and sat down at the table. An Aladdin lantern beside her sputtered as if it was about to run out of coal oil. Moments later, a last bit of wick within it glowed weakly, casting a feeble orange halo around her until it slowly burned out. She sat there like a sphinx in the darkness; a Beam in one hand and a derringer in the other.

Black had heard quite enough, thinking, 'The bitch is going to betray me!' That much he was sure of. He raged inwardly as he heard BB talk badly of him. Hargrove considered himself to be quite the ladies man. His record on this regard was impressive. At fifty-five he could still charm the knickers off any woman. He counted on doing so to the most beautiful woman he'd ever meet. As stage manager at Niblo's, he'd watched from behind the curtains as grown men fawned over Lady Ashton before, during and after every show. Her burlesque was so erotic that every man in the theatre hardened up as soon as she pranced onto the stage. The other girls were dross compared to her. Her every move teased the male imagination until the torture became unbearable. Night after night, Black watched as patrons ran from the theater unable to restrain their groins from exploding in ecstasy.

BOOK THREE: CHAPTER 10
DEAL WITH THE DEVIL

Black left the hotel through a rear exit. He had to see William Marcy Tweed, the 'Tiger of Tammany Hall'. Even though the 'Tiger' was imprisoned in the Ludlow Street Jail at the time, he still ran his criminal empire from within it. Yes indeed, no ten foot cell for the Boss. Tweed had influence. He occupied the Warden's luxurious and spacious parlor for seventy-five dollars a week. Hargrove had to seek Tweed's advice. He'd heard Garrow slap Lady Ashton hard, perhaps hard enough to make her talk about their plot. Black couldn't take a chance and he was too much of a coward to confront the younger man, no matter what opportunity presented itself. He did however know one thing; Tweed's carefully crafted plan of seduction had gone awry.

He had counted on Lady Ashton to use her considerable charms to get the deed done, but Lucas Garrow was too good, too smart and too cool. They had failed and the very thought of facing Boss Marcy Tweed made Black's blood run cold. He knew that if he stayed, Garrow would kill him for certain. However, if he was quick enough, Boss Tweed's thugs would have time to ride to Getty House and force the secret from Garrow, slowly, or quickly but most definitely.

Black ran down the muddy back alley to his Phaeton. Twenty minutes later, he was miles away, literally flying through a rising storm. Black lashed his horse as if his life depended on it. It did, as he drove recklessly towards the Bowery. If he was really lucky, he and Tweed's thugs would be back at Garrow's hotel in less than one hour. After awhile, Black was drenched and his horse was slowed by the muddy road. The beast veered sharply at a turn in the post road just after a bolt of lightning struck a nearby tree. As the Phaeton careened over on two wheels, Hargrove Black was thrown into a low stone wall, breaking his neck instantly.

BB had fallen asleep in an armchair. Her glass lay empty on the floor beside her bare feet. The derringer lay heavy on her lap. Lucas picked up the gun and the glass, putting them beside her on the dresser. After getting undressed, he spread the cassock over her then went to bed, his Colt tucked under his pillow. Moments later he was dead to the world.

When BB awoke, Lucas had gone. She threw off the priest's cassock; stood up, went to the window and parted the drapes. A large family coach pulled by a matched set of grays was parked below her in front of the Getty House. The rain had stopped. BB remembered what Lucas said. She turned away as it was late morning and her face was still tender. A note lay on the dresser. To her relief, it said that Lucas would be back at noon and that she mustn't leave the room. Another item caught her attention. It was a large silver warming tray. The savory scent of food had found its target.

BB lifted a domed metal cover. There before her was a large plate upon which lay a breakfast of fried bacon, a large fluffy egg omelet, two toasted scones, and pots of butter and plum jam. A mug of coffee sat beside it clothed in a quilted warmer. A bowl of sugar and a glass of cream rested nearby. Silver flatware was arrayed with precision beside them. Within moments, the meal was being consumed with relish. BB savored the expensive coffee.

Once satiated, she sat down in front of the large walnut dressing mirror and tried to repair the facial damage she'd acquired the night before. Her reticule contained rouge, face powder, lipstick, tweezers, cotton swabs, cosmetic pads, a silver handled tortoise comb and a matching hair brush. A skilled actress, BB was used to applying cosmetics and within an hour she was as beautiful as ever. Her gold pendant watch lay open on the dresser. It was past noon. She thought, 'Where is Lucas?' She needn't have worried. Four light taps on the front door sounded like cannon fire. She ran to the door and asked,

"Who is it?" A familiar voice responded, "Its Lucas."

Boss Tweed was not happy at all. Hargrove Black had been found lying dead on the side of 230th St. in the Bronx earlier that morning. Something had gone horribly awry as noted in a diary found on the body. All the sordid details, descriptions of Garrow and the scraps of eavesdropped information were hastily written. Tweed lifted his stout body off a padded wing chair and pulled a braided silk cord. Moments later a prison guard knocked on the door of the Warden's parlor, waited, then entered. Tweed gave the man a sealed note. Words were exchanged and the door closed. William Marcy Tweed returned to a large red leather wing chair and continued to read what the local papers were saying about him. He lit a cigar, poured himself a drink and remained unhappy for the rest of the morning.

Tweed had been imprisoned for graft, for he'd apparently embezzled over one hundred million dollars of taxpayer's money while running Tammany Hall. City Sheriff, James O'Brien, once a loyal supporter became incensed when Tweed refused to allow the Orangemen's parade in order to avoid another riot between the Irish Catholics and Protestants. O'Brien went public.

The New York Times was offered five million dollars not to publish evidence of Tweed's crimes. It didn't work, however Tweed's real anger was directed towards the famous Harper's Weekly cartoonist Thomas Nast, the man who first put Santa Claus at the North Pole. But Tweed was no Santa Claus for over the years Nast had drawn many satirical caricatures of Tweed and his gang of thieves. Tweed was alleged to have said,

"Stop them damned pictures. I don't care so much what the papers say about me. My constituents don't know how to read, but they can't help seeing them damned pictures."

After being arraigned on charges of graft, corruption, and political skullduggery, Boss Tweed jumped his eight million dollar bail and fled to Spain where he was later arrested.

He arrived back in New York City, on November 23rd, 1876. The 'Tiger of Tammany Hall' had been supposedly defanged. Now he waited for news that Garrow's treasure had been found.

Tweed needed the money badly to bribe his way out of jail for his bank accounts and other sources above and below ground had dried up. He'd been behind bars for over a year, ill and desperate. Major Garrow and Harley Blackstone had been hung in Richmond as the war was about to end. Tweed remembered it well, thinking,

'Goddamn it all to hell! That bastard stole my money. I know it, but where the hell would he hide it? The horde has to be near here but probably no where's near his safe houses, but one can never be absolutely sure.'

Tweed also remembered Horatio talking about a certain 'BB', a confederate spy. From what Tweed had, heard, the two were intimate. Perhaps she became his confidant as well and therefore might know some likely places where that scum would hide something. By sheer coincidence Tweed learned from Hargrove Black, that the very same trollop had fallen on hard times and was currently a chorus girl at Niblo's Theater. Her stage name was Lady Ashton.

Within hours, the devil's contract was sealed between Black, BB and Tweed. There would be a handsome return for everyone. The only problem for Black and BB according to Tweed was that they would never live to collect it. Tweed knew that Lucas Garrow was in town looking about. That meant his father hadn't told him where his treasure trove was. The Major's money he reasoned would save him. Tweed became apoplectic just thinking about it. He called in his criminal favors quickly. An hour later, a well armed posse of well mounted and well paid killers was thundering down the old Post Road, north, towards the Getty House.

Lucas limped into Room 10, brushing BB aside as if she was an insect. She backed away. Any warm feelings she felt for Lucas instantly evaporated. Lucas had changed his appearance. He now looked very much like a country squire. His attire was comprised of a grey woolen tweed riding jacket over a pleated white shirt. A black bowler hat, black riding breeches and long black leather riding boots completed the mélange. She wondered how he acquired the disguise so quickly. Lucas wasn't about to tell her that another body similar to his lay in the bushes just down the road. The victim had been a tall, well dressed gent at the hotel. Lucas chatted him up as they rode out of the livery stables towards the Bronx. While resting their horses in a secluded grove of trees, Garrow stabbed him to death. He stripped the body, redressed then rode on to the Bronx; the victim's horse tethered and trotting along docilely behind him. After selling the horse and its saddle, he commenced shopping along a row of stores, one of which was a dry goods store and another, a casket manufacturer. Two hours later, Lucas returned, slipping into the hotel via a rear door.

Under Lucas's arm was a large waxed paper package tied by a piece of twine. He threw the package on the bed and said tersely,

"Get dressed, we're in big trouble. Black has gone most certainly to see Tweed. I've read the papers. Tweed might be in Ludlow jail but he still can kill us. We have to leave soon. Christ it's late! I'm surprised his thugs aren't here already. Get moving woman!"

She obeyed as Lucas began to pace about the room. He lit a cheroot and poured himself a whiskey. The metal breakfast platter lay before him, its contents devoured completely. He laughed saying,

"I see you've eaten a proper breakfast. It might be your last. I hope you enjoyed it."

BB was half dressed. Lucas grabbed her hard by the shoulders. She stiffened.

"I don't trust you and I have no reason to even like you. You use men wantonly and have for many years now. You're incredibly vain, a chronic liar and totally irresponsible to boot. One false move and I will kill you, treasure or no treasure!"

BB started to protest but he shook her so violently that her hairpiece came undone. She looked up at him as if he was mad. He saw her distress and let go of her. She fell backwards onto the bed beside the waxed package. She remained still, hardly breathing. He snapped.

"Get up and get dressed. We're going to find the damned money and split it after I find Saxton and Marcus, but not before." Now totally oblivious to BB's presence, Lucas possessed by hate and rage, mumbled to himself,

"I think they're in Tennessee near Chattanooga. I heard Saxton tell the 'Attic Rats' in Salisbury prison that he and Marcus were moving there after the war. The rest I couldn't get out of any of them. They just suddenly clammed up. Goddamn it!"

BB got up, wary and somewhat apprehensive. She thought,

'My God, his mood changes from one minute to the next just like his father!'

She finished dressing not comprehending what Lucas was babbling about. Shortly thereafter, she too was dressed in riding clothes. The waxed wrapper lay wrinkled and ripped upon the bed. BB began to preen and primp but stopped as Lucas said,

"There's no time for that. We're leaving by the back door. I've got more supplies in a buckboard. The stable boy will drive it towards the Albany Post Rd. junction. He'll be waiting for us hidden in some nearby woods. A small strip of red cloth tied high in a tree will mark his location. Let's get a move on. Our Phaeton is tied up behind the hotel in the alley. Oh by the way, we're now Mr. and Mrs. Lucas Darwin of Westchester County, New York. Get used to it."

He reached into a breast pocket. BB looked at the cheap wedding band made of pot metal lying in the palm of his gloved hand. She slipped it onto her ring finger, saying,

"Oh, how generous of you my dearest, I'm going to treasure this ring forever." Lucas ignored her sarcasm. He remained serious.

"We're looking for the lost grave of my dear departed father, Silas Darwin. Remember, only talk when asked and let me do the rest. He reached into a larger pocket and retrieved a black mourning veil.

"Wear this Mrs. Darwin, for you're in mourning, besides right now your memory is more important than your looks."

He retrieved her evening dress, matching cape and bonnet. She wrenched them away. Lucas was nonchalant.

"BB my dearest, do put your evening dress over your riding clothes and cover up with the cape. Wear that ridiculous hat as well. Don't forget your loaded handbag."

Lucas turned and threw the cassock over his riding clothes belting it at the waist. He walked over and took at himself in the mirror over the dresser. After checking his appearance for any flaws, he took a small bible from the dresser and gave it to her.

"I hope you've made your peace with God. If not, start reading the Psalms 23.4." She threw it on the bed.

Lucas laughed at her discomfort. An idea came to him quite out of the blue. The wax paper from the clothing packet lay on the bed. He picked it up and flattened it out on the table. After he rooted around in a night table beside the bed, he found a pencil.

"BB, we have to have more time. Tweed's gang will be here any minute. Here's a pencil; start printing what I say in large letters. Remember the bastards probably can't read so they'll take it downstairs to the weasel. Now let's get started."

She sat down at the table. As he spoke over her shoulder as she printed a short message. Lucas watched carefully. She finished. He said, "Now sign it."

She did. Lucas bent over her shoulder and read it.

"Garrow's money is buried in the basement of 105 Mulberry St. We are

going there now. For God's sake help me. He's going to kill me. BB"

Lucas grinned. "Good girl! That should give us more time. Did Tweed know about our meeting last night?" She nodded. He scowled,

"God almighty, the clerk will show them which way we've gone too. We'll have to double back and forth. Tweed probably has spies everywhere. I remember my father saying that the two biggest things in a small town are eyes and ears. Now, you do as I told you and I'll pay the bill as if nothing has happened. Now let's get out of here."

He balled up the wax paper and threw it on the bed where it lay next to the bible, and a broken cross; the other half of which lay on the floor. He looked at the broken cross thinking, 'The crucifixion of my enemies is about to begin.'

BB left for the Livery stables while Father Johnson paid his bill with a golden Double Eagle. The desk clerk wondered,

'What was going on? First Father Johnson was an itinerant salesman wearing worn out shoes and now he's a priest once more wearing expensive riding boots.'

A few minutes later, one of Tweed's goons burst into the lobby followed by five others. The biggest one growled at the stricken clerk.

"What Room Wilbur? What room is the priest in?"

Wilbur Post tried to explain but was grabbed roughly by the throat.

"What Room?" The clerk squeaked, "Room ten-- but, but..."

The leader let him go. The man fell down behind the front desk. The head thug began began issuing orders to his motley crew.

"Charlie, cover the alley out back. Puggy and Dix see if that nigger in the livery cross the street knows anything. Don't be gentle. You two follow me and be quiet about it, remember Tweed wants 'em alive."

Seconds later, the door to Room 10 was torn off its hinges despite the fact it was unlocked. The room was empty, the bed tousled. Upon it was a large ball of waxed paper, a bible and a broken metal cross. It was a curious combination. Sensing an opportunity, the leader picked up the ball of paper and unrolled it. A message appeared. The leader said,

"Can any of you mugs read?" Nobody moved.

"Well ain't that a shame. Let's get the weasel to read it then." He ripped the note out of the larger piece of wrapping. With that they all ran out of the suite and down the stairs to the lobby just as Wilbur Post was putting on his toupee. He didn't quite finish as the leader shoved the note in front of him growling,

"Read this message Wilbur and I don't have all day. Now read it!"

Wilbur, his toupee askew, primly adjusted his pince-nez reading glasses and read it aloud. The leader smiled and said,

"I wonder if this is a ruse or not. A lot's at stake here. We can't afford to take any chances. Smith, go get Puggy. Ride to the Five Points and search the basement of 105 Mulberry St. Dig the floor up if you have to. If you find anything, stay put. The rest of you mugs follow me to the livery, we'll need fresh horses." He bent down, picked up the broken cross, hefting it in his hand.

"The stupid bastard forgot his cross. Two of you go north and the rest of us will go everywhere else. Look for a priest and a harlot. They should be easy to spot. They'll stick out like Wilbur's toupee."

The thugs laughed as they headed through the hotel foyer to the livery across the street.

Simon Crest waited nervously in a grove of hackberry bushes some distance from the main Post Road. He was wondering what kind of trouble he'd gotten himself into. He'd heard Tweed's thugs yelling for him in the livery as the boy drove away only seconds before. However, he trusted Lucas which was rare for the boy. Orphaned by the war, Simon fled from Benton, Georgia, by train riding the rods. Old man Swartz caught him one night sleeping in his stable. Instead of sending him on his way, Jacob put him to work. Simon was relieved of his memories as Lucas and BB drove their Phaeton into the thicket. From his perch on the buckboard's seat, Simon looked down upon them. Lucas and BB got out of the buggy. Lucas limped over to the buckboard. Simon continued, trusting his instincts. Nothing seemed amiss.

"You two sure look peculiar. I hope nobody foller'd you. Yessiree Mr. Salesman, Priest or whatever you are, I doubled back and took the old Wilson trace to git here. Lots of strange white boys bin ridin' slowly by here lately but I hid real good, didn't I?"

"Yes, you did Simon, yes you did indeed."

Before the boy said another word, Lucas grabbed him by his collar, pulled him off the wagon and slit his throat. BB remained impassive to the horror confronting her. Calmly, she reached into the Phaeton for her handbag. She withdrew a cheroot and lit it.

"I told you to kill that nigger. We don't need any witnesses." She pointed,

"There Lucas, drag him over there behind those bushes." BB tied the buggy's team to a bush. Finished, she watched Lucas as he searched the body. There was nothing on the boy, nothing at all. He dragged Simon behind the bushes. There, he found a shallow depression and laid the boy into it. Lucas covered the body with dead branches. Finished, he hobbled over, climbed onto the buckboard's plank seat to untie a red strip of cloth tied to a tree. Meanwhile, the buckboard's mule team stood in their tracks stoically. The air, cooled by recent rainsqualls, swept in from the Hudson River. Wood thrushes twittered here and there above them. Lucas and BB went over to the buckboard, removed a black canvas tarp then rolled it up, leaving it on the wet grass beside the wagon. Numerous brass grommets along the tarp's edges had been hooked into nail heads all around the outer sides of the wagon box making the wagon box water proof. Inside the wagon's long box lay a long pine crate. Taking a crow-bar from the Phaeton, Lucas pried off the crate's lid and threw it aside. Inside it the polished mahogany surface of a large casket gleamed brightly. Two thick brass lifting bars ran down either side of it. Shafts of sunlight coursed along them like lightning bolts.

Lucas opened the casket. The interior was lined with quilted black cotton pads three inches thick. The coffin had been specially constructed with a reinforced false floor six inches deep hidden by the padding. Lucas commissioned the specialty casket a week earlier for a handsome price. Since it was a rush job, it had been paid for in gold. In the wagon box beside it were two shovels, a long iron pry bar, two long probing rods, two coal-oil all weather lamps, filled to capacity, ten large bags of oats and two feed bags for the mules. A boxed supper of cold meats, bread and beer lay under the front seat. BB's arm slid around Lucas's narrow waist. She cooed,

"I'm impressed Luke. You've seemed to have thought of everything. I'm going to have to look around while it's still light out. Let's take off these outer garments and go for a country stroll. The lay of the land is coming back to me." Saxton laughed,

"I certainly hope so!" She pretended to ignore him, turned about and whispered in his ear,

"If anyone asks, just say we're looking for our Phaeton. What do you say, my horny husband?"

The day was getting long in the tooth so Lucas agreed. Warily, they exited the grove and started walking, directed by BB's somewhat erratic memory. A posse of horsemen rode by them at a full gallop. Clods of wet mud sprayed the pair as the men swept by. Lucas suspected who they were as did BB. After the horsemen disappeared, she turned to Lucas, pulling him away behind some bushes. She was excited.

"Guess what dear? You'd never know it but I think we might be standing on top of the money." Lucas grabbed her roughly,

"Don't play games with me BB! Your memory's not that good, besides there's no sign post hereabouts. It's probably rotted and thrown away ever since the railway was built here years ago."

At that very moment a steam locomotive from the New Haven & Hartford RR roared past them. The wet earth under their feet shook violently and as it did, a piece of half-buried white wood caught Garrow's eye. The train rumbled on as did another lathered group of thuggish looking riders returning from somewhere to the north. Both disappeared around a bend. The train's whistle blew three times at a distant railway crossing. Seven loutish men waited there for the long train to pass them by. The horsemen began arguing with each other and soon came to blows. The train had long gone but the group had dismounted. The brawl continued unabated as one side squared off against the other. A shot rang out and one man staggered and fell down. A mounted gunman pointed a pistol at the others. The rest of the group suitably subdued, remounted and rode south into Yonkers.

Lucas prodded a patch of wet grass with the toe of his riding boot. He reached down and pulled a broken white signboard from beneath it. The square stub of a rotting sign post was still in the ground beside it where it was put years before. The duo looked upon its faded black lettering which said, ALB... BB laughed hysterically and hugged Lucas. Lucas shrugged her off.

"Stay here. Are you armed?" She nodded.

"Good, I'll be back shortly. I'm going to get the buckboard. If needs be we'll retrieve the Phaeton later. Stay out of sight and be quiet."

Lucas sauntered out of the bushes, looked both ways and hobbled back to the grove where the horses and the buckboard were hidden. It was getting dark. He thought,

'Perfect. It's getting dark and another storm is rolling in. Who knows, we just might get lucky.'

He climbed aboard the buckboard, saluted Simon's shallow grave then drove out onto the deserted road. The mules trotted away with it to the south. It wasn't very far. Within moments the buckboard was once again well hidden. Lucas carefully stepped down from the buckboard .Moving to the wagon box he reached in and retrieved two long iron probing rods. BB rushed over. He gave one of the probes to her, saying.

"My dear BB, stay near to me and probe deeply. God knows how far down the chest will be. I hope it's an iron box, for a wooden would have rotted by now and as such we'll never find it."

He put his left boot next to the rotted post. Taking a long cloth tape measure and a small compass from his pocket, he determined the direction, due north. Before him lay a flat wooded glade covered in long weeds. He motioned BB over, saying,

"Hold the end of the tape on the center of this post stub." She did. Lucas measured out twenty feet exactly.

It didn't take long for their iron rods to hit something solid. Just as Lucas hoped, something was buried exactly twenty feet north of where the sign post was unearthed. After digging for what seemed an eternity, all was revealed. They both sweated trying to lift a large iron chest out of the ground. It wouldn't budge. They sat down exhausted, looking at a two rusty padlocks that secured the iron lid. Finally, Lucas took out his pocket Colt and pointed it at a solid looking Yale. He wrapped his cassock around the gun to muffle it. BB peered out of their hiding place to see if any post road traffic was about to pass them by. As she did so, a loud crash of thunder exploded over the Hudson escarpment to the north.

The mules remained calm but the two horses harnessed to the Phaeton broke away from their picket lines. The pair, dragging the Phaeton behind them, galloped away in a panic. Five miles further south, alongside a side road, two of Tweed's goons found the Phaeton. It had overturned and its team was mired in a deep ditch thrashing about entangled in their harness. Both horses were shot dead. One goon rode off for the bowery, the other stayed to guard the Phaeton. An hour later, another hue and cry erupted as a triumphant posse began following the team's hoof prints back to the Post Road. One of the horse's pulling the Phaeton had thrown a shoe marking its passage as it fled from the thicket to the north. As luck would have it, a sudden rain squall obliterated the tell-tale tracks just as the gang emerged onto the Road. An argument ensued. North or south, that was the question. Their leader issued an order. The gang wheeled about, riding at full gallop to the north.

Garrow waited long enough. His gun went off with a muffled thud--nothing. The thick iron padlock was still intact, insolent and dented slightly. After four more rounds, the padlock was mangled but still obstinate. Lucas took a stout iron pry-bar from the wagon, knelt down and slipped the pointed end of it through the hasp. After much effort, the lock snapped open. He did the same to the other lock. Finally, at last, Lucas lifted the heavy iron lid revealing a golden horde. BB screamed in delight. Lucas stood there dumbfounded. He closed the lid. A hard rain began pelting the ground. Lucas limped over and unrolled the tarp. Using a ball of twine from his saddle bag, he and BB constructed a shelter that covered the iron box and the casket. Time passed by as well as a posse of desperate men searching for them.

Flashes of ribbon lightning speckled numerous gold bars, coins, ingots, gold dust, and many large gold nuggets with fire. All of it was rapidly stored in the casket along with numerous canvas bags of cut and uncut diamonds, sapphires, and emeralds. Both Union and Confederate greenbacks of various denominations and strings of large black pearls were likewise stowed away inside it above and below its false bottom. Lucas searched the iron box for a message from his father. Inside one of the larger canvas bags he found a short note. It read....."Live for the Cause, love HG." The exhausted twosome shoveled wet earth back over the box, leaving it exactly where they'd found it.

After further camouflaging the site, they headed north along highways and byways, finally reaching a New York Central Railway spur line near Somers, Westchester County, New York. It took ten days of hard traveling to reach their destination as it rained nearly every day. They bivouacked in woods, under bridges, in abandoned barns and once in a hay mow near a country road. Every night they slept under the wagon, taking turns at guard duty. If their two mules sensed any danger, they stamped their flinty hooves. Twice the animals saved them from capture by the Tweed gang who realized BB's note was a mere ruse and that their quarry was probably headed north.

Along the way, the hardships Lucas and BB endured together brought them together even though both thought of killing the other. But their greed was overwhelmed by their common hatred of Saxton and Marcus. The 'Holy Cause' became a mantra for once separated by distrust, they both found in each other a kindred spirit. Lucas was the planner, a soldier immersed in minutia while the flamboyant BB was less so. Her acting skills, her erotic beauty; provided fresh opportunities for food gathering, the acquisition of new disguises and assorted sundries that they sorely required. In short, they needed each other to survive in a hostile world, half of which it seemed intent on killing them.

After arriving in the little village of Somers, New York, they stayed at the Elephant Hotel, Therein, they enjoyed catered cuisine, a deep claw foot bathtub and a huge four poster king sized feather bed replete with a silk canopy. A few days earlier, Lucas concluded that they needed legitimate protection to get the treasure to Chattanooga. For all intents and purposes, Tweed would never give up trying to kill them. BB laughed at the very idea of retaining the services of three Pinkerton agents to assist them in an audacious ruse. Lucas wired ahead to the Pinkerton office in Somers. He would meet them there at the elegant Elephant Hotel. The heavy wagon loaded with a padlocked pinewood crate was parked inside the hotel's livery out back. Lucas guarded it until the guards showed up. He told them that he and his wife were taking the embalmed remains of a very obese father back to his home town, Chattanooga, Tennessee.

The three story red brick, colonial styled hotel, was built by a Hachaliah Bailey in 1830 in memory of his pet elephant 'Old Bet', who died three years earlier. Before that unhappy event came to pass, Bailey had years earlier purchased the pachyderm to do heavy farm work. But the incessant curiosity of the locals caused him to take the animal on tour. Proving to be a very lucrative option, Bailey started his famous circus. BB laughed as she pulled Lucas to their suite's narrow front window. Dusk was falling. She pointed,

"Look Luke at the statue of 'Old Bet' atop that granite plinth. I bet the old girl is buried beneath it." Lucas retorted,

"It would make a great location to bury our trove."

B.B. giggled, turned and ran naked back to the bed. Lucas sat down on a settee to read the classified section of the New York Times he'd bought in the hotel's lobby. There on page six was an advertisement, 'Funeral Home for Sale, Chattanooga's finest'. Lucas put the 'gray lady' down and innocently said,

"My dear BB, how would you like to own a funeral home?"

"What a brilliant idea my dear, our casket would feel right at home with no one the wiser for it."

The next day, they and their treasure were escorted to Purdy Station. There, they boarded their own private coach complete with a chef, a maid and a butler while the two Pinkerton agents slept in the baggage car beside the locked casket. The 'Dawson' party arrived safely in Chattanooga, Tennessee via Cincinnati three days later. The casket and its immense load of treasure were taken immediately to the Chapman Funeral Home where it was given a decent burial in a Diebold 'Cannonball safe' weighing nearly two tons.

BOOK THREE: CHAPTER 11
BECAUSE OF A MADMAN

In the early summer of 1878, Boss Marcy Tweed of New York City died of pneumonia in the Ludlow Street Jail. Newspapers across America heralded the happy event. A relieved Mr. and Mrs. Lucas Darwin of Chattanooga, Tennessee, no longer looked constantly over their shoulders while living incognito above the Chapman Funeral Home at 114 Pine Street in downtown Chattanooga.

Their elegant three story building replete with a chapel was located downtown. It had been bought earlier in Somers through a local lawyer. Upon their arrival in Chattanooga, they were discreetly married. A justice of the peace, a recently retired Judge John C. Gaut tied the knot. There were no banns, no church wedding and no honeymoon. However, Lucas bought BB a two carat flawless emerald mounted on a wide twenty-four carat gold band. The purchase impressed the jeweler so much so, that the two were immediately ushered into the good graces of the upper crust of local society. In fact most of the social busybodies in town were already talking about the young rich couple living in luxury above a funeral home of all places! Over time, the home's employees were let go only to be replaced with an equally discreet and knowledgeable staff, all of whom were former officers of the KKK. Garrow's funeral business thereafter continued to serve the unsuspecting citizenry of the city.

In October of 1878, a yellow fever epidemic killed nearly four hundred people in Chattanooga and over five thousand statewide. The disease was keeping everyone away from Chattanooga to the nearby mountains. All rail service into the city stopped as outlying towns quarantined the city for fear of being infected. Only eighteen hundred souls remained out of a population of twelve thousand. The Chapman Funeral Home on Pine Street meanwhile enjoyed a very lucrative business during the epidemic. While Lucas and BB stayed inside the large building, safely sequestered upstairs in their suite of nine rooms, their every need was attended to. Downstairs, their trained staff dealt with the newly dead with practiced aplomb.

A portion of the treasure trove the couple dug up was deposited in the vaults of the local banks; namely the Bank of Chattanooga, the Bank of Tennessee and the State Union Branch. By the end of 1878, over three million dollars was sitting in three separate bank vaults. Of course Lucas was shortly thereafter invited to be on the board of directors of all three banks.

Two things happened because of this financial activity; namely a Mr. Lucas Darwin became a leading citizen of Chattanooga and secondly; he accumulated enough political influence through his largess to the old line Democratic Party to finally challenge Saxton-Brown, no questions asked. Besides, many of Chattanooga's leading citizens were former officers in the Confederate Army who chafed under the Federal reconstruction programs and sympathized with any attempt to thwart them. They viewed any northern politician with his hand out as nothing more than a carpetbagger. Lucas was among loyal friends ready and willing to implement his grandiose plans for what he called, The New Confederacy. Once ensconced on Elder Mountain, his dream of a mountain top fiefdom replete with a docile and obedient population would be the nucleus for a rebirth of the sacred 'Cause'. Lucas fully intended to be avenged in full and in control of an empire that would bring the body politic of the defeated Confederacy back to life.

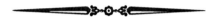

Harmony Farm prospered mightily in 1879, for Chattanooga experienced a renaissance of sorts in the late 1870's. With its central location amongst vast coal fields and mountains of iron ore, capitalists by the droves came in and built foundries, factories and many other businesses. Chattanooga, 'The Dynamo of Dixie' was soon one of the most active, commercial centers in America. Hundreds of new industries, half a dozen major banks, three new railway lines, five major newspapers, and others of note took root there. A new court house, school system and many pieces of municipal, state and federal underpinnings centered in Chattanooga so much so that the city swelled from two thousand before the war to over eleven thousand souls a short time ten years later.

In the late 1870's Lucas too flourished by investing in many profitable ventures and within two years his father's ill gotten gains disappeared into the financial heart and soul of the city. None of his father's stolen loot could thereafter be traced back to him.

Lucas, unlike many others of means within the elite of the City, didn't join a secret society but rather he started one. It was simply known as 'The Cause'. It had only one goal, resurrect the Confederacy through the financial manipulation of the American economy. By inserting its members into key local, state and federal political positions of influence, the Cause would run the New Confederacy from the boardroom of Garrow's financial empire. It was not unlike the so-called corridors of power already present in the White House. Lucas did not want a utopian Union but a dystopian Confederacy ruled by one man; himself. Its fruition would come simply by paralyzing the economy of America through economic blackmail. If Lucas was not allowed to resurrect the Confederacy, with him as its President then he would destroy the United States.

Simply put, while planning to take over Elder Mountain, Lucas Garrow, in the spring of 1879, installed the largest and most comprehensive counterfeiting operation ever built. Its lair was deep within the limestone caves below Harmony Farm. It was fortunate for Lucas that one of his funeral home employees had worked in the very foundry that had built and installed the doors that sealed off the entrances to Pitchfork cave. With both entrances closed off, the need for an air vent of sufficient size into the lower cavern was necessary. Apparently, thick deposits of bat guano within the murky recesses of the cave's many passages were giving off toxic vapors. To gain entry to the underground fortress, the vent had been penetrated. A man skilled in lock picking was lowered down and the doors to the lower cave were opened wide.

With the Farm's sterling reputation as a front, no one would ever suspect that a criminal undertaking of such magnitude was in place directly underneath it. Although his counterfeiting operation was up and running successfully by late spring, Lucas would try to take over the farm through legal means first. In this way litigation would direct any attention away from his underground operation. It was very much like a Plover dragging a broken wing away from an arctic Fox. However, if all else failed, his private army would over-run the farm quickly and permanently, leaving no witnesses.

Garrow's private army was born In August of 1879, when nearly one hundred men, all members of the KKK, boarded drift boats and barges loaded with supplies. This armada sailed down the Tennessee River from Chattanooga to Williams Island. Lucas had purchased the uninhabited, somewhat swampy island of nearly seven hundred acres just after his arrival in the city the year before. The owner, a Sam Williams was only too glad to rid himself of a bug infested piece of real estate. Upon arrival, any mosquitoes were eliminated by spraying oil upon their swampy habitats. Once that task was accomplished, the men set to work clearing six acres of vegetation and digging drainage ditches to make way for their camp. Rows of wedge tents were set up, as well as a cookhouse, a corral, stables, a blacksmith-ferrier shop, an armory, parade square, mess hall, an infirmary, a large garden, an abattoir and a smokehouse. A line of latrines completed the site. Armed guards patrolled around the compound, rotating every four hours.

Within days, young men began drilling, riding, waging mock battles and conducting weapons training at a firing range. Local authorities were given what seemed to be perfectly good reasons for their presence there as well as perfectly good forged documentation explaining what they were going to do when finished. Supposedly, a privately funded group had been commissioned by the US Government to train soldiers specializing in Indian warfare out on the western frontier. Their mission: capture Geronimo, leader of the rebellious Chiricahua Apaches in New Mexico. Commanded by a Captain Goddard, an ex-confederate who fought under General P.T.G. Beauregard at Memphis, this innocuous group continued training through November of 1879. In early December, they vanished over night, whereabouts unknown; leaving their camp intact and deserted.

Garrow's grandiose schemes were ready to begin without interference from the locals or the Federals for that matter. Thus if attacked by Union forces at his mountain fortress, Garrow would defend it while immediately flooding the world with billions of counterfeit American currency. By the summer of 1880, these dollars would be in hundreds of locations all over America, ready to be released like a virulent disease. Financial chaos would be a certainty as America's gold reserves would not be large enough to back up its supply of paper money. America would eventually collapse, unable to pay its debts or buy goods necessary for its survival. Hyperinflation would devastate the American economy. To Lucas, the timing was perfect for such a nefarious plan to succeed, for by 1878, most of the world had adapted the gold standard. Gold had become a transportable, universal and stable unit of valuation. The United Kingdom, America's dominant trading partner, had a long standing commitment to the gold standard. By 1879, Garrow's megalomania was assuming major proportions. As Lucas often said to his cohorts in crime,

"Every journey begins with the first step and my first step will crush my nemeses, Saxton-Brown. I need that mountain for the Cause. My father's revenge requires an ultimate ecstasy."

Lucas could have ignored the Saxton-Browns and let them live out their lives in peace and seclusion upon Elder Mountain a few scant miles away. However, the very idea that someone other than he could create a flourishing world out of the ashes of the Civil War was taken as an affront. It was also a threat to his megalomaniac schemes. Harmony Farm was to be eliminated legally before Lucas could proceed without public scrutiny any further. To do this required patience and cunning then total and overpowering action. Lucas calculated that in another two years, his secret society contacts coupled with his four step program to obliterate Harmony Farm would be ready. 1881 would be the beginning of the end for the hated Saxton-Browns.

Lucas quietly proceeded to buy Brown's Ferry including the land around it as well as the land across the river from it where the ferry docked. No longer would the Farm be able to send their wood products across the Tennessee River to the railhead in Chattanooga. Without a source of income, Harmony Farm would suffer financial ruin. The farm's settlers would leave for better paying jobs existed in Chattanooga and elsewhere, especially in an America that was enjoying an unprecedented period of prosperity. Lucas would further isolate Harmony Farm through an intensive propaganda campaign based on half truths, outright lies and innuendos. The Farm would also be infiltrated by a trusted spy whose sole purpose was to spread dissent and give Lucas knowledge of where the weaker points were in the settlement's security system.

Lucas's lawyers would also delve deeply in order to find fault with the pre-emption agreement between Saxton and the original owners. Quite possibly the land deed itself if was defective in some way. The legal battle would be death by a thousand cuts, becoming so expensive that the Saxton-Browns would eventually surrender. Garrow would buy the whole mountain for next to nothing with counterfeit money. The irony of it delighted him. The conquest of Elder Mountain would be done legally, albeit barely within the precepts of law but legal none the less. Penniless, Saxton and Marcus would also be helpless. An unfortunate accident here, a mysterious disappearance there and soon the whole nest of undesirables would be dead. The Cause would prevail. What nobody knew, was that after the whole sordid operation had been completed, the financial destruction of America would commence.

It was June 27ᵗʰ, 1879, that the Saxton-Browns first heard about the mysterious arrival of a very rich couple to Chattanooga. In that time, the Saxton-Browns had been far too busy to take notice of whom or what entered the city. The arrival of a new undertaker and his wife was hardly something to fret over. Besides, the Saxton-Browns stayed away from the same gossip mills in Chattanooga that bedeviled them in Boston. But, as time passed the Saxton-Browns began to hear snippets of polite conversation from bank tellers, post masters and other gossips that something strange, mysterious and certainly unique had arrived in their fair city. Apparently, a Mr. and Mrs. Lucas Darwin arrived from New York City to take over the renowned Chapman Funeral Home. The whole town was atwitter over this strange occurrence for two reasons. The couple arrived with a large casket in tow and secondly, Mrs. Darwin was hands down, the most exotic creature the male population of the city had ever laid eyes on. To Saxton, this event meant only one thing, trouble. He had to find out for sure if it was Lucas Garrow. He needn't have bothered.

A week later as the Farm and all of America was celebrating July 4ᵗʰ, a Mr. and Mrs. Darwin showed up at Harmony Farm's gatehouse at the foot of the mountain. It was a time when the colony was bursting at the seams with new settlers and their families. Every house was full of children, lots of children. Nearly three hundred souls lived at Brown's Mill and in Saxton Village. An itinerant black preacher Otis Tillman lived in the church rectory with a middle-aged Catholic Priest, a Father Max Manilow.

Tillman, the preacher in question was grateful to be alive. He had known Belle La Fontaine years before in New Orleans where they'd met at Dixie's Gambling Den in Nigger town. Years later, the preacher's bad habits finally caught up with him in Nashville. Not unlike Tyler Wicks who was beaten; poor Otis was strung up by an irate crowd whom he cheated at cards over the previous three months. The fact that most of the mob before him wore white hoods over their faces and dressed in white robes didn't seem to faze the tall, skinny preacher at all. Moments before he was about to swing from a cottonwood tree while astride a horse, he began to exhort the crowd to forgive him. It was his finest hour as he preached what he later called his 'Sermon on the Mount'.

John Saxton had been in town arranging lumber contracts when he'd heard that a 'Nigger was gonna hang down by the river'. Saxton's inner voice said, 'Stay away.' But he went anyway to try and stop it. He did so simply by buying the condemned man's life for he just could not walk away from the poor soul. Saxton's conscience cost him two thousand dollars. Ever since, Otis stayed at Harmony Farm, faithfully preaching the gospel as only he knew it. Every Sunday a happy throng enjoyed his entertaining and enlightening sermons.

Tillman's counterpart, Max Manilow, a former faro dealer on a Mississippi river boat, fought for the Confederacy. While fighting at the first battle of Bull Run, he was severely wounded. He converted to Catholicism while convalescing at Saint Francis De Sales hospital in Richmond, Virginia. Ordained in 1872 by pro-slaver Bishop Verot in the diocese of St. Augustine, Manilow was sent to Chattanooga in 1875 to work amongst the poor and dispossessed. It was only a matter of time before he was drawn to the mountain after having a vision in the sacristy of Our Lady of Perpetual Help.

It was Otis who ran up to Saxton with a message from the gatehouse at the foot of the mountain. Marcus had installed a telegraph system that connected the mill, the village and the guardhouse to each other a year earlier. It saved a lot of time and money to be in continuous touch with each other. The Saxton-Brown houses were connected to it as well.

Saxton read the message aloud. It said,

"A Mr. and Mrs. Lucas Darwin wish to see you immediately. They and their driver are unarmed, and riding in a coach. Mr. Darwin says that he wants to meet his mother. Shall I let them pass unescorted?"

Saxton was shocked by the revelation. It was extremely unsettling to him. He tried to remain calm as he looked at Marcus sitting across from him. They were all sitting at a festive picnic table, one among many set up under numerous shady chestnut trees that lined the baseball field. He handed Marcus the missive. After a moment Marcus handed it to Belle, who after reading it got up and ran up the hill towards her house. Marcus ran after her. Saxton picked the flimsy off the grass and handed it to Virginia. After reading it, she exclaimed,

"My God Saxton, Belle should be upset. Could it be that Lucas is her son? She's never said anything about it, never." She pressed him saying,

"Did you know about this Saxton; did you?"

"Yes Virginia, I had my suspicions. I'm the only one of us who's seen Lucas in the flesh. His skin is tanned slightly but he could easily pass off for a white man. If Belle, a black Creole is his mother and Horatio is his father, then Lucas is a white Creole. Besides, Belle and Horatio had a long history together even before Marcus met her. We know she was a working girl in New Orleans servicing the social elite of that city. Captain Garrow as Chief Customs Officer was probably allowed into that social circle. I suspect that he most certainly took bribes and did favors for them."

On the veranda, Belle waited for Marcus to catch up to her. She was sobbing as he gently wrapped her in his embrace. He kissed the nape of her neck below where her hair had been piled up into a bun. Belle moaned as Marcus continued to caress her. They separated searching each other for secrets. Finally Belle's sobs subsided, only a trace of tears remained on her cheeks. Marcus offered her a handkerchief. She accepted, blowing her nose and dabbing her eyes. Her eyes cleared. In a small voice she said,

"Oh Marcus, I've kept the secret too long, too long. All those years ago after the Anaona incident, I guess I was torn up inside unable to come to grips with it. It was if a poison attacked my conscience, my heart, my soul. Luke is my child. That I'm sure of but do I love him as a child? Possibly."

She shuddered again as Marcus embraced her. Her tears flowed like a river. Marcus smelled the essence of rosewater as he had done innumerable times before. That scent always reminded him of her looking down upon him as he emerged filthy and stinking to high heaven from out of a man hole in New Orleans. He started to laugh at the thought of it. Belle pulled away from him, confused by his response. Marcus looked down upon her, smiling through the scars that crawled across his face.

"Belle darling, I'll always love you no matter what. Luke might be your son but he's not mine and could never be after what he's done; after what his father did to you. No I'm sorry, but the spawn of the devil is not ours to claim and never will be. You were raped, savaged and left alone. Garrow is dead and his son is insane, the living dead."

He grabbed her, his black eyes upon her like two iron bolts riveted into hot metal. "Who else knew that you had a son with that swine Horatio?" Belle recoiled at the sound of the fury in his voice. She was scared, for now the other man in her life was in grave danger. Belle, despite her misgivings spoke, unable to quell another secret. She whispered,

"Saxton." Marcus was stunned. "How Belle and when?"

She held onto Marcus who tried vainly to break away from her. He swore in Swahili.

"Mavi, mavi."

Weakened by the struggle, she surrendered, her will broken. She stood facing her husband unable to speak. Marcus shook her until Belle cried out, her voice, a plea for mercy.

"Saxton found out while in prison that Lucas was Garrow's son. Lucas tried to kill him twice but failed. You were terribly wounded and recuperating on the mountain. Even after you were paroled to Boston, I kept the secret from you, Virginia and anyone else that could tell you. I knew that it would tear you apart as it is now. I begged Saxton not to tell you. He followed my wishes because he loved you too. I believe he's been sorely tormented by it as secrets have never come between you and him." Marcus wavered, his anger banked like hot coals in a stove. Sensing a change of heart, Belle shocked her husband by saying,

"Oh Marcus, the torment of the grave is known only by the corpse." The Massai was stunned by the Swahili proverb. He cried out,

"Adhabu kovu hajaona jeraha." As he spoke the words, Belle fell into his arms forever.

Saxton's attention was caught as Belle and Marcus walked hand in hand back down the hill towards them. Virginia ran to meet them taking Belle into her arms. Marcus continued on as Saxton rose to meet him. Marcus came close and looked down at Saxton.

"You knew about Lucas didn't you Sax. Tell me now."

Saxton nodded wearily, as Marcus continued. The two women returned and stood by watching quietly.

Marcus stood there waiting as everyone else did. Saxton sat down on the picnic bench, his head in his hands, silent as a grave. Otis Tillman came forward and put a thin black hand upon Saxton's shoulder saying,

547

"My children please don't be angry for I know why Saxton was silent for the simple reason that Belle has suffered enough. We all have our secrets but I know about hers better than most. I've known her since she started workin' the 'House of the Rising Sun' in Nigger town. May I say here and now that our relationship was strictly bubonic as they say. Why we..." The tension broke as Belle said,

"Otis my dear friend, I think you mean plutonic. And I'm sure Saxton shouldn't be blamed. I should be as I was scared of losing Marcus, of not trusting him. However it's all settled between us. Lucas is my son and I'm sorry that I've caused you all to feel distressed because of it." She became quiet as Otis continued.

"From what I've heard as an itinerant preacher traveling throughout the south, he married after Lucas was born but his wife mistreated Lucas terribly. They say her body was thrown into one of the bayous near New Orleans. She'd been shot. Garrow was never charged with her murder and he never married again. Lucas was only a few months old when she disappeared. One of my friends, a Madam Dubois told me later that Garrow thereafter told Lucas that his mother died in childbirth."

Belle started to weep. Everyone gathered around her in a laying on of hands. Otis Tillman started to pray in a strong and vibrant manner.

"Oh Lord forgive those that trespass against us for they know not what they do. May sweet Jesus himself lay his healing hands upon her heart and give her eternal peace. For those of you who are without sin, here is a stone to cast upon the sinner standing before us. Yes, sweet Lord, sanctify and refresh anew the holy vows between Belle and Marcus now that the wayward prodigal son has returned to her. Amen."

Belle wiped away her tears as Marcus took her under his arm. At that moment, Cotton came running over from the ball field yelling,

"Ma I'm tired of baseball. Felicity tagged me out on second when I knew I was safe. I quit. Where's the food Ma? I'm starved." Belle pointed.

The young man was totally ensnared by youth. He turned and ran over to the large tent that had been set up to steal some food. His little brother Rufus was already there. Soon their parents heard the two squabbling over who had what and how much. Otis laughed,

"May they be fruitful and multiply." Marcus was prompted to say, "Two's enough Reverend, two's enough."

After waiting an hour for their armed escorts to arrive, the Darwins were given permission to proceed. Two Maasai Rangers followed the heavy coach as it wound its way up the mountain road. Slowly the majesty of the mountain unfolded before them. Sunlight dappled the grassy glens on either side as shafts of light broke through a vast canopy of leaves high above them. There was no evidence of any logging for four hundred feet on either side of the 'Grand Staircase' as Belle called it. The lower part of the road just above the guardhouse was known as the 'Foyer'. Further up, the road wound its way through a narrow gorge emerging in the middle of a large grassy glade known as the 'Grand Salon' and so on until the road found its way past the dairy, the piggery, the tannery, the smithy, the apiary, the bakery and into Saxton's Village as everyone called it.

Large groups of happy parents sat on the wide verandas of every freshly painted house. A wide gravel avenue ran between them. Festive red, white and blue paper bunting festooned the little village from one end to the other. An American flag high up on a robust flagpole fluttered over the one room school house. Children of various races played together with hoops, balls and other toys along the verge of the village. A motley pack of mongrel dogs ran barking back and forth excited by the arrival of a large black Landau coach and four.

It stopped in the middle of the village, its matched team of four Grays breathing hard. A polished door opened. Lucas got out of the coach dressed in a black double breasted frock suit, and a black patterned Chinese silk vest. A black bow-tie topped his white pleated shirt. His black trousers, polished black patent shoes and a broad brimmed low crowned black felt hat completed the picture. A gold watch chain and large solid gold cuff links added just the right touch of elegance. Standing well over six feet, with wide shoulders, a narrow waist and long legs, Lucas was indeed a spectacular specimen of the male species. However, his appearance paled with that of his new wife BB.

The first sign of her was a long slim arm covered in yellow satin sleeves ending in a white cotton glove. As more of her emerged from the coach, interest amongst the male spectators started to take on a new measure of adulation. Here was someone entirely beyond the realm of their earthly experience. Mrs. Darwin timed her entrance perfectly as she daintily took Lucas's kid gloved hand and stepped lightly from the coach. There she stood with a yellow parasol in hand. Nearly six feet tall, she stood in black patent shoes each adorned with a large silver buckle. Her long black locks fell in rivulets down to a hooped, fully crenellated yellow silk gown. It was flocked in black satin trim then gathered at her tiny waist by a red silken sash. Large full breasts peaked out over a tight corset. Fully rouged and painted, her ruby lips and deep blue eyes centered her perfect face upon which rested a yellow satin hat trimmed in black silk. It was fashionably offset by a short spray of red feathers. She paused then looked around disdainfully as if she was Marie Antoinette watching a mob crying for bread. The couple stood there for a few moments glaring at the crowd gathering about them. Lucas looked up at his driver. He sneered,

"Ligo, find out from the old nigger over there where we might find Saxton-Brown."

The driver, a rough hewn white man, glared down at an old black man sitting nearby on a veranda. He motioned him to come over. The man got up from his shaker rocking chair and ambled over slowly, taking his time in an easy southern manner. As he drew closer, the coach driver looked down upon him and said loudly,

"You heard him nigger, where's Saxton- Brown? Tell me quick or I'll horsewhip ya right now."

Tom Peeks stared back up at him without malice. The coachman snarled.

The long whip in his hand moved like lightning, cutting Peeks across the face. Unbelievably, he never moved a muscle. Again the whip struck, this time around his man's legs. A shot rang out. The whip went flying as the coachman screamed. A Maasai Ranger stepped out of the forest nearly two hundred yards away further down the road. Lucas was stunned thinking,

'My God, how could he see the whip let alone hit it at that range.'

Before he could continue, the old man looked up at the coachman holding his bleeding hand against his chest. With a voice tinged with mercy, he said.

"You're hurt sir. Please get down from there and my missus will fix you up good and proper."

The coachman looked down at Lucas. Lucas agreed for he knew that he'd been bested already even before he had met Saxton and Brown. He smiled wickedly at his wife. She knew that look. Her husband had something more dreadful, more catastrophic in mind for the peasants that surrounded them. She smiled back. The burly coachman climbed down and dutifully followed the little old black man into his house. A trail of bloody spots on the road's pea gravel marked his sorry passage. A crowd of villagers gathered round. One of them, a stocky white man picked up the driver's bull whip and lashed out expertly decapitating a tall tuft of wheat grass unfortunate enough to be growing nearby. The man looked at Lucas and said roughly,

"If I was you mister, I'd skedaddle before youse git hurt some. Old Tom didn't deserve what you gave 'Im. He's a better man than you'll ever be. Forty years ago he coulda whipped ya good mister."

The man recoiled as Lucas who seemingly bent down to adjust his boot rose up, with a Richardson boot pistol in his right hand. Lucas smiled as BB laughed, pointing her closed yellow parasol at the man. She hissed,

"Well mister, can you out whip a little biddy gun like that?"

Lucas moved forward and took away the man's whip by its thick braided handle. The man's head snapped back as Lucas brought the whip handle up hard under the man's chin. Everyone watched the stocky man's legs slowly crumple underneath him. A few women screamed. A few children cried. A few men stood stock still, swearing loudly. And a few men acted accordingly. A Maasai Ranger quickly disarmed Lucas from behind, keeping him in a choke hold while another Ranger waved a rifle at an enraged BB whose demeanor only worsened as Belle and Virginia emerged through the crowd before her.

Even in her plain gingham dress, Belle's natural beauty outshone BB's facade as the moon is backlit by the sun. Virginia ran over to Saxton and held onto his arm. Jack Two, the terrier ran after her, a little red ball in his mouth. Virginia ignored the dog. She tried to gather her last resources of courage within her. Virginia Saxton knew that Lucas was going to attempt killing her husband and Marcus sooner or later. Saxton nodded and the Ranger let go of Lucas. Garrow clutched his throat, his eyes glazing over into a reptilian stare exactly like that of his father Horatio. Belle recognized the danger signs. She moved like lightning and slapped his face. Lucas moved back stunned by the suddenness and ferocity of her attack.

Belle spoke with a mother's rage, her arms on her hips ready to deal another blow if need be.

"I'm your mother Lucas and don't you ever dare to behave badly in mine or anyone's presence ever again. I might not have had time to love you son, for you were taken away from me before I had a chance to. But now that you are here, you will act like a man with manners and not a boy with none. Do I make myself clear?"

Lucas started to speak out but BB grabbed him and held on to him, saying to Belle,

"We'll be back niggers! We'll be back, and next time we'll walk in here and throw you and you and you…" She started pointing at all the settlers around them screaming,

"Out on your ear, do I make myself clear?"

Marcus moved forward to stand beside his wife, his one arm around her slim waist. Saxton spoke to Lucas and BB. He was straight forward, calm, yet his words struck home like spikes driven deep into a cross.

"Lucas, you were once my friend but are no longer. Your father's death was by his own kind not mine or that of Marcus. Your time as a guard at Salisbury amongst the horror of it, changed you into a cold, self-serving young man driven by hate towards those who suffered your father's cruelty. The war and a desperate desire to please your father have driven you completely mad. I hope and pray that you'll leave us be but I know you are controlled from your father's grave like some obscene marionette. Leave us now in peace and don't come back. Any attempt to attack Harmony Farm legally, physically or mentally will be repulsed in short order."

He moved even closer to Lucas, his voice becoming somewhat jovial. He motioned for Tyler to step forward, saying loudly so everyone could hear his voice,

"Tyler Wicks, please relieve them of their shoes and socks."

He did. They didn't dare resist as more than a few weapons were pointed at them. The unhappy couple was barefoot. Saxton continued issuing orders, his voice sharp and dangerous like cold steel on a grinding wheel.

"Bobby, you and Gardner drive their coach down to Brown's ferry. Take extra mounts." He turned back to Lucas saying,

"Lucas, our Dr. Green will care for your coachman until he's well enough to be taken to Chattanooga hospital." Saxton continued ignoring the Darwin's plight.

"You two start walking! It's only two miles to Brown's ferry. These Rangers will escort you. When you arrive at the gatehouse, your footwear will be returned to you."

They began walking, followed by the coach and their escorts. Everyone cheered. Saxton went over to a thin young man and said,

"Magnus, telegraph ahead and tell them to let us know when the 'Duke and Duchess of Death' have arrived."

The unpleasant episode with the Garrow's soured Harmony Farm's Independence Day celebrations. The settlers spent the rest of the day in a lethargic trance. Many of them were dispossessed sharecroppers who'd been driven off their land by men such as Lucas Garrow. No respite had been given to newly freed slaves either as many sought the 'Promised Land' envisioned long before by the 'Great Emancipator'. In many respects the northern climes were more divisive in separating blacks from whites. Northern cities by the 1870's were ghettoized as their original inhabitants; the Irish, Chinese, Italian, Jewish and other groups competed for work with a flood of desperate blacks from the South.

Racial tensions in southern cities boiled over between the two solitudes many times since the Civil War ended. From 1866 to 1880, fourteen major race riots spread death and destruction in Louisiana, Tennessee, South Carolina and Mississippi. Over thirteen hundred lynchings were attributed to the KKK during these years as well as other heinous atrocities. Those longing for honest work, those dispossessed from their land and those deprived of their civil rights, came to Harmony Farm. Once there, they thrived as equal shareholders in the farm's many successful businesses.

By 1880, the farm had diversified into value-added products. Instead of shipping out raw lumber at a lower value, the farm's wood products manufactured on the mountain ranged from making barrels and wagon wheels in their own cooperage to furniture. A long term Federal contract was signed for making office furniture for government buildings all over America. Marcus and Saxton had put all these enterprises into one company called Harmony Hardwood Products. The logging industry had changed dramatically after the war.

John Dolbeer, a friend of the Saxton family, was living in Eureka, California. A founding partner of the Dolbeer and Carson Lumber Company, he had been working on a new invention called the logging engine. Instead of using teams of oxen to pull the logs to a collection point, a 'steam donkey' as he called it would do it faster and cheaper. After months of conversing by telegram, Saxton had convinced Dolbeer to ship out a prototype. In return, Saxton would invest in his invention.

The logging engine arrived in the summer of 1880 accompanied by John Dolbeer himself. Ironically oxen skidded the contraption up the mountain. Within weeks, under Dolbeer's expert instruction, the 'steam donkey' was in business. Comprised of a powered winch, a boiler and sitting upon skids; a 'line' horse would carry a steel cable out to a log. The cable would be attached to it, and, on a signal from the 'whistle punk' operating the engine, it would drag or 'skid' the log towards a collection area where oxen would drag it away to the mill. By attaching a cable to a strong tree hundreds of feet away, it could drag itself overland to the next 'yarding' location. Luckily no one was killed as Dolbeer finally worked out the 'kinks'.

It was a large federal furniture contract that saved the farm from financial disaster. However, the first inking of trouble happened rather suddenly.

A load of government office furniture from the farm was about to be taken aboard the ferry at Brown's landing one day in the fall of 1880. Lucas himself was there to stop it.

Dressed in blue riding breeches astride a magnificent black thoroughbred, he spoke to the farm's wagon master, Dorkin Dease.

"Tell Saxton-Brown that they'll have to find another way to get to Chattanooga 'cause they ain't usin' Brown's Ferry ever again. I own it lock stock and barrel and I've made damn sure that no one else can build another one anywhere's near here. So, you go tell them good and proper."

Lucas laughed heartily as he rode his ferry back to the other side. The high cliffs of Elder Mountain across the river echoed eerily with his laughter. The sound of it was very similar to that of a tortured scream ricocheting off the brick walls of a solitary cell deep within an insane asylum.

The news about the ferry ban struck the farm's populace like a thunderbolt. The Saxton-Browns gathered together at the Brown's house above the mill. While seated on the wide veranda in white wicker chairs, a cool autumn air at the end of a very long day did nothing to dampen the hot fires of determination deep within them. Saxton stood up, lit a cheroot and started pacing. To Belle, it seemed that all the men in her life started pacing when deep in thought. She laughed to herself,

'Perhaps I was wrong; their brains are in their feet.'

She continued to watch Saxton closely as he became more exasperated.

"How the hell are we going to get our products to market if we cannot use Brown's Ferry? You know and I know that without it, we'll lose those government contracts. If we do, the farm will suffer. What about our people. My God there are over forty families here trusting us to look after them! Goddamn that Lucas! You mark my words, this is just the beginning."

Saxton sat down. He looked at Marcus for an answer. There was none forthcoming. They all knew that the very reason Brown's Ferry was at that exact spot on the river, was that there was a gap in Stringer's Ridge that led right into Chattanooga. A very busy Manufacturers Road and the Chattanooga Traction Line ran through it and had done so for many years. The desolate group was stymied or so they thought until Belle came up with a possible solution. She sipped her lemonade, lit a cheroot and turned to Saxton. She said sweetly, "Please Sax, sit down. It's my turn to pace about." Belle looked down, put a hand on his slumping shoulders and purred,

"Saxton, why don't you contact Montgomery Meigs the federal Quartermaster-General in Washington DC? Perhaps he can force Lucas to let us use the ferry. I'm sure the Government won't brook any interruption of our services to them. Besides, I understand you met him when you were here during the war with General Grant. Perhaps he can help us too. I believe an ex-president will still have some political clout?" Marcus chimed in,

"Besides, he's a Republican. Grant will vouch for you Saxton, especially a friend who's also a Medal of Honor winner. In fact I read that the Republican Congressional Convention will be here in Chattanooga next year. Republicans Sheriff Springfield, Trustee Gahagan and Representative Wiltse, have all been newly elected. They'll back us for sure. Remember all the refugees we took in last year during that yellow fever epidemic? Well Saxton, the city fathers were very grateful." Marcus was right.

Harmony Farm, through the efforts of Belle and Virginia, was a major contributor to the Chattanooga Orphan's Home founded in 1878 two years before. This institution directed by a Dr. Mary E. Walker, was one of many institutions in the city that the farm had continued to support financially. Harmony Farm would certainly get their support. Marcus looked at both women expectantly. Belle for one knew what was coming. Marcus became enthused.

"Virginia and Belle, could one of you please draft a letter for Meigs, explaining the problem? In the meantime Saxton could disguise himself as a land agent looking for Garrow. That way he'll get across the river to garner letters of support from everyone we've talked about. He should be back in a week. What do you say Sax? Besides, you'd be less conspicuous than a seven foot tall, one armed nigger now wouldn't you?"

They all laughed and agreed just as the steam whistle at the mill blew, signaling the end of another day's work.

With the task in hand, although onerous, it was completed within three weeks. A courier delivered a registered telegram to the Covenant Funeral Home, a copy of which was sent to all the local, state and federal bureaucrats having any powers remotely connected to the shipping of, collection of, or the distribution of, any and all products manufactured by Harmony Harwood Products Ltd. Lucas read it with growing unease and molten rage. It simply said,

"To: Mr. Lucas Darwin, Prop: Chapman Funeral Home,
114 Pine Street.Chattanooga, Tennessee. Nov. 01, 1880.

"You or your agents are hereby ordered to cease and desist immediately from impeding in any way the lawful trade, transport or distribution of any and all goods and services of Harmony Hardwood Products Ltd., via Brown's Ferry or any other form of transport in the these United States. You cannot charge their businesses any Ferry rates deemed to be usury by the Quartermaster General of the United States. Failure to abide with these conditions stated above will result in the immediate confiscation or repair of the ferry service in question by the US Corps of Army Engineers in order to guarantee the reliable delivery of said goods. Any such costs will be borne by you. Failure to do so within thirty days will result in the immediate confiscation by the Government of the United States of said ferry, landings, easements to and from or any other lands pertaining to its use.

By order of the Quartermaster General of the United States of America,
Montgomery C. Meigs,
Washington DC."

Lucas knew that every other agency in the state of Tennessee and the city council of Chattanooga would have a copy of it. He reasoned that he might have lost one battle but not the war; not by a long shot. As for Lucas's smear campaign against Harmony Farm, that scheme was proceeding at a faster pace than he had ever imagined. Some local newspapers were patrons of the Democratic Party led by a Mr. G.G. Dibrell who had garnered the lion's share of the County vote in the elections of 1878. The majority of Hamilton County's white population hadn't voted in protest, allowing the black vote to sweep Dibrell into power for a four year term. Thus the County was basically divided along racial lines meaning blacks voted Democrat while whites voted Republican. Therefore, wealthy Democrats who owned these newspapers, printed scurrilous headlines that screamed,

'Harmony Farm run by former Harlot'
'Elder Mountain spawns Secret Cult'
'Harmony Farm source of Yellow Fever'
'Harmony Farm trains cannons on City'
'Slaves of Harmony Farm flee Torture'

The blatant smear campaign went on for over a year. Finally, the Mayor of Chattanooga, J.T. Hill, a personal friend of President Rutherford B. Hayes, put a stop to it by refusing to renew the business licenses of any city paper that continued to print lies about the farm. He had to, as Harmony Farm threatened to sue him, his Council and the City of Chattanooga in general for not dealing with the libelous rags that were allowed to print such trash. Since the farm was outside the city limits, no local legislation pertaining to its operation could be enforced. Letters to the editor from Harmony Farm's diverse supporters flooded in. The newspapers began to lose advertising revenue as Saxton's Republican business friends came to his aid. Thus, as quickly as the smear campaign had started, it ended with a whimper in the spring of 1881.

Lucas however, had from the beginning sought legal retribution. He hired the firm of Clift and Frazier to investigate the title, deed and pre-emption papers filed by the City Clerk, R.H. Guthrie in 1864. By coincidence the surveyor, a James W. Clift hired by Saxton to determine the exact property lines of Elder Mountain was none other than a close relative of one of the lawyers, a Mr. M.H. Clift. The Harmony Farm's legal response was that there was a definite conflict of interest and that the potential for collusion between the surveyor and the legal firm could be proven in a Court of Law. After months of expensive litigation, Lucas was informed by his lawyers that nothing amiss had been found in the deed and title documents pertaining to the purchase of the mountain. And, after careful consideration, they were not going to pursue the matter any further. Moreover, a legal bill of over ten thousand dollars was to be paid by Covenant Funeral Home within ninety days, or the matter would be taken to County Judge McRee.

The infiltration of Harmony Farm by a spy had been more successful. After being severely wounded by a well placed Ranger bullet to his hand, Ligo Watts was cared for by Dr. Lapsley Green or 'Lousy Lapsley' as he was affectionately nicknamed. After having 'seen the light', Watts lived in the village with his new wife, the recently widowed Marie McCarthy and her three children right next door to the very man Ligo horsewhipped just a short time before.

However, by 1881, Lucas's KKK friends found out that he was not as pure as they were. Any hint of black blood in any member, especially a Grand Magi, was considered a stain on the 'Brotherhood'. The army of soldiers Lucas spent a fortune training were in effect, no longer dedicated to him. The businesses that Garrow put them into fell on hard times as his KKK employees found jobs somewhere else. Lucas was to be considered a white nigger, a reality that repulsed his wife.

For BB, it was too much to bear. Horatio Garrow, a deserter from the Army and now his son was a paranoid, megalomaniac nigger in a white skin. She'd married him for his money, all of his money. She thought,

'Perhaps now is the time to shoot the bastard and claim it was an accident. No, it would be too obvious and messy. However, I did read once that some poisons are undetectable." BB's interest in poisons took her to the library on Broad St. where she became interested in strychnine. She grew more animated as she plotted and waited for the right time and place to rid herself of her husband. The 'why' of it she knew; the how of it eluded her.

One evening a few weeks before Christmas while the maid was out, the Darwins were wondering where to go for dinner that evening. A naked BB leaned over her naked husband as he sat reading in a walnut throne arm chair in their expansive master bedroom. Her black locks fell over his face as her long arms embraced him. Her tongue wound its way up the back of his neck and into his right ear. The newspaper flew across the room. He reached up and pulled her around the chair to sit naked on his lap, her back to him. His groin hardened as she deliberately ground herself into him. He clasped her narrow waist and lifted her body upwards then slowly down upon him as she guided him into her. Her hands then pushed down against the hard arms of the chair as he began rhythmically thrusting himself up inside her. His hands grasped her large hard breasts, pushing up from beneath them. She moaned as one orgasm after another came between them. Lucas remained hard for a long time until he too could bear the ecstasy no longer. With a cry like a wounded animal, he thrust himself deep within her one last time. She arched her back as he came, trying to draw every last bit of him into her. She turned slightly, her face burning against his. She said breathlessly,

"Oh my Darling, I have an absolutely poisonous idea!"

BOOK THREE: CHAPTER 12
A POISONOUS IDEA

Brynhild Paulsdatter Stoerset arrived at the Chattanooga Train station on 9th Street in the summer of 1881. She had changed her name to Belle Gunness in order to fit into American society more comfortably. She was twenty-two years old and had grown up in dire poverty in the little Norwegian village of Selbu. At five feet, eight inches tall and nearly two hundred pounds, Belle Gunness was larger than life. She'd been hired by the Darwin's as a maid and cook through a New York City agency. Apparently, as it was learned later, Belle in 1877 attended a county dance while pregnant. There, she'd been kicked in the stomach by a deranged stranger. As a result, she lost her baby. After that horrific episode, her once sweet personality changed for the worst. The man who attacked her died shortly thereafter from what was supposedly stomach cancer. The next year, while still in Norway, she was hired to work as a nanny on a wealthy estate for the next three years. During this time she saved enough money to come to America.

BB liked the plain looking outspoken woman who, as she was about to find out, was just as crazy for money as she was and was willing to do anything to get her greedy hands upon it. It took no time at all for the astute Gunness to realize that BB's marriage was a façade and that Mrs. Darwin was going to kill Lucas Darwin in order to inherit his fortune. That fortune was currently worth nearly twenty million dollars. With this in mind, Belle made her move and soon the two became conspirators in plotting the demise of one, Lucas Garrow.

Because of her maid's previous success with poison, an unwitting BB was persuaded by Gunness that she alone would provide the means and BB would provide the opportunity. The means would be strychnine poison administered orally and the opportunity would be at a lavish Christmas Charity Ball at the elegant Read House Hotel on Broad Street. Belle agreed to a princely sum of one thousand dollars to devise a means of administering the poison. So, a few months before the Christmas Party, both women began working in earnest on 'the poisonous idea'.

It is said that strychnine can be fatally introduced into the human body by inhalation, swallowing or absorption through the eyes and mouth. Depending on the dosage, ten to twenty minutes after exposure, the muscles of the afflicted begin to contract, starting at the head and neck. Soon these spasms spread to every muscle in the body followed by continuous convulsions. These convulsions increase in frequency and intensity until the backbone of the victim arches. Two to three hours later after enduring indescribable agonies, death by asphyxiation occurs because the neural pathways that control the victim's breathing are paralyzed. Total exhaustion caused by the body's convulsions can also suffocate the unfortunate soul.

While Lucas was away on business in Nashville, the two women got together in the upstairs kitchen to decide how to do away with him. Belle looked at BB sitting across from her dressed in a cotton housecoat. She reached for a square bottle of Johnny Walker whiskey and poured some into two shot glasses. With a wide pine-board table between them, BB eyed Belle and raised a glass of whiskey saying,

"My dear Belle, may I propose a toast to our success and may the devils spawn die as horribly as his father did."

The two women put their glasses together then got down to business. Gunness asked BB,

"My dear, you've got the tickets to the Read House Christmas Charity Ball, correct?"

"Yes Belle and I'm sure that you have an alibi as to where you'll be the exact moment he dies?"

Gunness finished her drink looking exactly like an owl swallowing a mouse.

"Ya, I've got an alibi. I'll be at my sister Nellie's place in Ohio for Christmas a few days before. After my holiday, I'll return to find that Mr. Darwin died unexpectedly and it will be such a loss for both of us, right?"

They laughed hilariously as they continued to plot. Gunness asked BB what her husband liked to drink at dinner parties. Belle laughed.

"Funny you should ask, but a new drink called the Martinez from California could be our drink of choice especially since an olive's put into it. Seems the pitted olive soaks up the Old Tom Gin and aromatic bitters that make it up. Come to think of it, the Martinez reflects his personality, which has been aromatic but quite bitter as of late."

Again both women found the comparison hilarious. Gunness became quiet. She was thinking.

Suddenly, she exclaimed, "Ya! Ya! BB, I think I've found a vay of putting poison in his drink. Yoooo cannot wear a poison ring my dear. It would be too obvious to Lucas and others around you. Noooo, a better vay would be to slip two olives filled with the poison into his Martinez. Within minutes his drink, the olives in it and his life will be consumed forever. Vat do you think my dear?"

BB was inspired. She gulped her drink down with a flourish and reached for the bottle for a refill. With an air of bravado, so characteristic of her when she was flushed with excitement, she cried,

"It's perfect Belle. Perfect indeed! No one would ever suspect an olive. Besides it would have been chewed up, swallowed and gone." Gunness cautioned her by saying,

"Don't get toooo enthusiastic or Lucas vill become suspicious. You know how paranoid he is already. Is he addicted to morphine like so many other veterans? He must be. My

God BB, in the short time I've been here, his personality has become dark, moody and hallucinatory at times. He seems to have an aversion to bright light as well. I've also noticed how possessive he is. How do you stand it being under such scrutiny?" Her husky voiced lowered becoming more intimate, more possessive.

"Why, even the employees downstairs vatch your every move BB. They follow you around town and make notes on whoever you see and talk to. It must be sooo distressing my dear."

She reached across the table and took BB's hand in hers. Her voice became aroused,

"Vell my love, he doesn't know that the fox is already in the hen house does he now?"

BB rose and beckoned Belle to come with her. They held hands as they made their way to Gunness's suite. The door closed. A few moments passed then laughter rang out followed by moans and cries of ecstasy. An hour later, Belle Gunness changed into her going out clothes. She went downstairs to the parlor, left the building, hailed a Hansom cab and bought the poison at the Funeral Supply Company a few blocks away. She told the clerk about an infestation of rats under the funeral home, and that there was one big one in particular that needed attending too.

Long lines of Landau carriages, Rockaway coaches, Phaeton buggies and others were arranged on either side of Broad Street that flanked the palatial Read House Hotel. Opened on New Year's Eve 1872, by John T. Read, it replaced the Old Crutchfield Hotel that burned down in 1867. The new hotel with over one hundred rooms within its three stories was elegant and provincial in style. The Read House Hotel quickly became the social center of Chattanooga. It was here that the well heeled elite of the city gathered for the annual Christmas Charity Ball, Saturday, December 22th, 1881.

Liveried black servants doted over two hundred guests who wined and dined throughout the evening. A spruce Christmas tree rose over twenty feet towards a painted plaster ceiling. Colorful tinsel, bright foil baubles and other incredible decorations were festooned upon it amidst lighted candles set into metal holders. The entire hotel, from its immense lobby, to its 'Silver Ballroom' was awash in anything to do with Christmas. Cedar boughs woven into wreaths, decorated with baubles and foil, graced every door. Mistletoe hung over every doorway, corridor and vestibule. The effect was amazing as dozens of gaslights therein, caste a golden glow upon all of the guests and their opulent surroundings.

Within the vast gas lit 'Silver Ballroom', sitting upon a large stage depicting the North Pole, was an orchestra. Green elves conducted by a rotund Santa Claus played Strauss waltzes, the Mazurka, Quadrilles, the Virginia reel, the Schottische and the Spanish Dance amongst others. The ballroom's parquet oak dance floor constructed without nails was sprung with two inches of densely packed horsehair. Around its perimeter were phalanxes of large round banquet tables seating ten guests apiece. On every linen shrouded table was a central bouquet of fresh flowers drowning in a crystal vase surrounded by battalions of sparkling sterling silverware and fine porcelain dinnerware.

At eight, the diners were promptly served by long lines of black servants each bearing a large silver salver upon which lay a portion of the Christmas feast. Suckling roast pig, wild turkey, duck, geese, and chicken were stuffed with breadcrumbs, walnuts, wild rice and exotic spices. Mince-meat pies, tarts, tureens of soups and innumerable other delicacies adorned the tables. Five bars were set up around the room. Harried black bar-tenders mixed and poured all kinds of drinks non-stop for their thirsty white patrons.

The Darwin's arrived at the hotel about six. The suave concierge, Maxim Roy knew the routine perfectly from many years of experience. As soon as the doorman spotted their Barouche, he tipped his grey top hat as a signal for everyone to be ready. After the Darwin's alighted from their carriage, they stopped to adjust their matching black sable coats. The lustrous fur shimmered in the soft gaslight pouring down upon them from innumerable wall sconces lining the front portico. BB's diamond tiara set into her long black hair, was piled high and held in place by a diamond-studded silver pin. A matching diamond necklace of incredible beauty, size and workmanship wrapped itself about her long neck. Mere inches above a swelling cleavage was suspended a stupendous fifty carat blue sapphire. One's eye was drawn to either depending on whether or not the admirer was still breathing. Mrs. Darwin was a perfect specimen in all respects; a heavenly beatitude wrapped up in a gossamer red silk evening gown. Her husband, not to be outdone, was attired in a matching deep blue silk double breasted suit to complement his wife and the frivolity of the occasion. He wore a five carat diamond mounted on a heavy gold stickpin that centered his black silk cravat.

The Concierge scraped and bowed as the pair swept up the marble stairs to the grand foyer. Once there they doffed their fur coats. Two bellboys took the couple's luggage, their coats then led the couple to the hotel's brass Otis steam elevator. Once on the top floor, the entourage made its way down a wide carpeted corridor to the infamous Room 311. The bellboys left the luggage at the door and fled. BB laughed at the sight of them scampering away.

Lucas opened the door. His wife stepped into yellow gaslight that flooded the large room. There they would try to spend the night undisturbed by the fact that the suite was an exact replica of another Room 311 that had existed in the old Crutchfield Hotel. Apparently during the Civil War, a Union soldier strangled a prostitute in room 311 for whatever reason. He was never charged and the woman's ghost ever since was known to roam room 311 screaming for justice from whoever was sleeping within it. It was titillating to both the Darwin's especially BB. She thought,

'The evening so far is going very well. Lucas is relaxed and unwary.'

She looked about and flung herself and her tiara backwards on an immense four poster bed,

"Lucas my dear, we're going to have a wonderful evening tonight and a better one right here after the party is over."

Lucas lit a cheroot. He poured both of them a whiskey from the room's large mahogany bar. BB sat up on the bed as she was handed her drink. Lucas looked down upon the most beautiful creature he'd ever laid eyes on. Her tongue licked the rim of the glass as he raised his to her saying lustily,

"To us my dear; yes to us and the ghost of Room 311! Wherever that harlot is hiding tonight, I'm sure a man such as I will find her."

After freshening up, the Darwins left for the Silver Ballroom. They arrived just as the orchestra was playing a lively polka. Pierpont, the Maitre' D, took their tickets and showed them to their table. Of course everyone who was anyone in Chattanooga had their own little clique at their own table. The Darwin's were no different. Their circles of friends were few for the Harmony Farm scandal had turned against them. Now they were social pariahs with too much money to be ignored. Another burden, the Darwin's had to bear was that the society that welcomed them as both being white were now rejecting them because Lucas was considered to be colored. Perhaps deep down, the conquest of Harmony Farm meant that he could be immune to the shunning and at the same time exact a terrible revenge on a white America that looked the other way. The other four couples unfortunate enough to be at their table were recompensed by BB's stunning beauty and Lucas's unsavory reputation. The combination of the two would keep the local titillates busy all night. In fact, as BB got up to go to the powder room, one could see her being followed by every male eye in the room, all two hundred eyes for that matter.

Once inside the 'Ladies' opulent powder room, BB entered a cubicle, closed the richly paneled door and sat down facing a gilt mirror. She didn't freshen up but instead opened her jeweled reticule and took out a small sealed glass tube. She held it up to a sputtering gaslight set into a wall sconce above her. Inside the slim glass tube, two large Black Ripe olives full of the bitter nemesis were immersed in a pallid liquid. BB smiled and put the tube back into its nest. Soon it would be over. She stood up, turned about, unlocked the door and exited the powder room unnoticed. Later that evening, her golden opportunity came as she requested that Lucas bring them a new drink called a Martinez cocktail. She gushed,

"Luke darling, it's all the rage in San Francisco. Let's order two. I believe it's delicious from what I've heard." Everyone agreed.

The evening went well; the dinner was sumptuous, the conversation salacious and the ambience frivolous. Everyone at the table, despite their original misgivings about the Darwin's, were having the best time of their lives, especially BB. Many of the single squires about the room were delighted as she accepted their unsolicited invitations to dance. Lucas, unable to dance, was definitely into his cups as he cavalierly waved BB's legions of suitors towards the dance floor. He was alone. Everyone was dancing. As he contemplated his situation, he idly looked at all the drinks scattered about the large dining table.

Lucas thought, 'The Martinez is a different drink indeed.'

His fellow diners liked the smoky juniper aromatic taste of the bitters within it. He reached over and held up his glass by its long stem. He peered into its amber liquid where two black olives were impaled on a silver skewer. The olives, he'd been told, complimented the exotic flavor of the Old Tom's gin that embalmed them. He put his cocktail glass down and reached for one next to his. It was nearly empty, with only one olive showing itself. He decided to try it. He put the black olive in his mouth and chewed. He grimaced as the bitterness of the fruit assaulted the back of his mouth. However, he swallowed it before he could spit it out. Lucas definitely did not like the sharpness of the bitters or the olive. He thought,

'The Martinez or whatever the hell it's called is not for me. BB seems to like it though. I might as well give her mine. She's had two already, she'll probably want another one.'

Lucas switched the identical glasses just before BB arrived, flushed and breathless with delight on the arms of another gallant. Without thinking, in a fit of bravado, she picked up the glass and drank the Martinez, then chewed the olives with relish. She swallowed them. BB put the glass down and turned to thank her suitor but she never finished. She brusquely pushed him away as she turned back to face Lucas. Her eyes looked down at the glass resting in front of him. The glass was empty. Her eyes snapped back to his. Lucas smiled up at her not comprehending the black cloud of horror that began to permeate his wife's conscious mind.

Seconds passed. She continued to stand there immobilized by the dread that consumed her. Everyone at the table was still out on the dance floor as the tempo of a Quadrille found groups of four couples interweaving through the intricate squares. By now Lucas was aware that something was terribly wrong with BB. He rose to assist her but she backed away from him, her face a mask of hate and fury. She screamed,

"YOU, YOU BASTARD!"

The double dose of poison was taking effect even faster than usual. She tried to steady herself by clinging to the table. She faltered, grabbing the edge of the tablecloth instead. She staggered backwards, her hand gripping the damask tablecloth for support. Lucas watched in horror as the table's entire assortment of cutlery, dishes, glasses, food and floral arrangements came crashing down upon his wife. The energetic Quadrille continued as passing dancers laughed at the beautiful woman lying on the parquet floor amidst the debris. Lucas yelled at them to assist him. They laughed and merrily danced away. Swearing, he knelt down to cradle his wife's head in his arms. BB's face had gone a deathly shade of pale. She tried to speak but could only whisper "Bastard" as the muscles in her head and neck started to twitch violently. By now a sizable crowd gathered around Lucas as the Quadrille stopped. Someone shouted for a doctor. A few minutes a women with an aura of authority arrived on the scene.

It was Dr. Mary Walker, a petite, mannish looking woman, and a former Union army surgeon. Walker pushed her way through the throng and knelt down beside BB. By now violent convulsions were wracking BB's body. Dr. Walker identified herself and instructed Lucas to back away. BB's eyes followed him as he stood to one side, her face pale and sweating.

Walker looked at a woman who was spasmodic from head to toe. The doctor removed BB's tiara and necklace, giving them to Lucas, saying evenly,

"Sir, are you her husband?"

"Yes, I am doctor. I'm Lucas Darwin."

Lucas was beyond himself.

"My God, what's happening to her Doctor? Please tell me!"

The City Sherriff, Colin Springfield; the Mayor, John A. Hart; Robert Cravens and John Read, owner of the hotel pushed through the crowd. Read looked on horrified as BB continued to convulse like a demented dancing puppet. Her back arched unnaturally, the bones in her spine cracking like a horse whip. The doctor stood up, faced Read, and said sharply,

"John, go get a litter with strapping and a buckboard with a fast team of horses right away. Read turned and vanished into the crowd. Walker stood up to face Lucas. Calmly, she said,

"Mr. Darwin, can you take her somewhere private? Can you take her home?"

"Yes of course doctor. I'm going to take her to back home to our apartment. Can you come with me madam? I'll pay you well for any services you might render." Dr. Walker replied evenly,

"There's no need for that Mr. Darwin. But I do believe that she's been poisoned, probably strychnine. I know the symptoms well enough."

Lucas and the others were taken aback by the doctor's comments. Immediately, wagging tongues spread the news like wildfire throughout the ballroom. Women fainted, and men cursed as they threw their drinks away. The long awaited Christmas party instantly broke up as everyone including Santa Claus and his green elves, fled the ballroom in a panic. By now, a canvas litter had arrived. Four young men lifted BB's violently convulsive body onto it then strapped her down. Lucas followed the entourage through the lobby. The Concierge however intercepted Lucas, while apologizing profusely for the disaster and enquiring about the contents of Room 311. Lucas ignored him as he ran after his dying wife. Curtains of snow started to fall as a Phaeton with Lucas and the Doctor aboard, led a wagon containing his dying wife back to the funeral parlor.

Betsy Bolton or BB as she preferred to be known as, died an hour later at 12.01 AM. The following afternoon, her remains were cremated in the new crematorium that Lucas bought in Nashville earlier that year. Only Lucas and a few of his assistants were present. There was no service, no prayers, no minister and certainly no sympathetic goodbyes. The Sherriff visited Lucas at the Funeral Home later that morning saying that BB's drink contained traces of strychnine. He also said rather forcefully that Lucas was not to leave town for any reason until her killer had been found. Lucas realized then that BB meant to kill him and the police suspected him of her murder. He also realized with clarity of hindsight that their house maid Belle Gunness was probably involved in the plot. Whoever Belle was, she most certainly had to pay for her attempt on his life. For days, two of Lucas's thugs waited patiently for her to arrive at Chattanooga's Union station after her holiday was over in Ohio. During this time he thought, 'The look on her face will be priceless when I stuff her bound and gagged into the crematorium alive.'

However, Lucas never got the chance to kill Gunness, for on her return the next day to the city, she happen-stanced upon a fresh newspaper. Someone had left it lying on a bench within the confines of the cavernous train station. There splashed across the front page of the Chattanooga Gazette was a headline in big, bold, black letters,

'THE DUCHESS OF DEATH IS DEAD'

BOOK THREE: CHAPTER 13
A CLASH OF WILLS

Allan Pinkerton arrived at Harmony Farm on the morning of New Year's Eve, 1881. The visit was totally unexpected. Belle and Virginia literally assaulted the little man as he got out of his Phaeton in front of Saxton's house. Virginia screamed in delight at seeing him standing there, bowler askew, the perennial cheroot driven into his face like a railway spike. She cried as she hugged him,

"My God Allan what a wonderful surprise. It's been too long, far too long between visits. You're just in time for the New Year's Eve festivities we're having tonight down at the church hall."

Pinkerton blushed as his Scots brogue hammered the air around him into submission.

"Ay, lassie tis been too long indeed."

He turned to face Virginia, a look of wonder coming over him. He declared as he held her hands, stepping back to admire her.

"Faith of our sainted fathers, look at you lassie, what a fine one you've turned out to be indeed."

He puffed on his cheroot as he spied Felicity. At nineteen years of age, the young woman stood nearly as tall as her mother. Allan released Virginia slowly as if the years between them had widened more than he dared to realize. Saxton's bear-hug seemed to be lost on the little man. It had been over eight years since he'd seen them last upon the hill at the Saxton house. Pinkerton followed their paths through his agency from Boston to Chattanooga, from Salisbury Prison to Castle Thunder. His immense pride at their ability to overcome adversity fueled his desire to see them again. It was a visit of reminiscing as the man in the bowler toured Harmony Farm with astute circumspection.

Treated to a lavish lunch at the Saxton's, Pinkerton became the center of everyone's attention and adulation. The Saxton-Brown's shared many outrageous stories of their escapades together before and during the Civil War. The jovial nature of the evening turned more somber as the diners moved to the grand salon for refreshments. Once Packard and Millie made sure everyone was seated comfortably, they discreetly retired closing the French doors behind them. The conversation continued unrestrained.

Felicity, a well-read young lady, grew increasing alarmed as Pinkerton vented his spleen on all labor Unions. His agency had been hired as strike-breakers to protect big business interests in America. The detective started to pace the room, a new cigar firmly clenched between his teeth. He railed at the slothfulness, waste and corruption of the labor unions who, in his vaunted opinion were nothing more than organized criminals holding large companies hostage through illegal strikes. Of course his anger was probably fueled by the fact he couldn't find any hard liquor no matter how hard he searched the pantry on his way back and forth to the toilet.

After one of his forays, Felicity had the temerity to remind him of the robber barons such as George Jay Gould who drove America into the 'long depression' or Jim Fisk, Andrew Carnegie, John D. Rockefeller, Cornelius Vanderbilt and others who conspired together to control every aspect of the working class in America. Alarmed, Virginia tried to change the topic as the two of them remained at loggerheads. Little did she realize that she should have suggested topics such as croquet, rose gardening or even sports, but sadly she did not do so. Virginia began lightly, saying with some enthusiasm, her eyes riveted on her friend.

"Please Allan, do tell us all about your latest book. I believe it's called 'Criminal Reminiscences and Detective Sketches'. Taken by surprise, Pinkerton was pleased with her prescient awareness of his literary talents.

"You're correct my dear. It came out last year. But I'm not here to talk about me but rather to talk about you and what you're all doing here on Elder Mountain. From what I've read and heard, you've had quite a time getting it going and functioning properly. What is it exactly are you trying to accomplish here that can't be done elsewhere in a more, might I say civilized setting?"

Pinkerton sat back in his chair, his tiny black eyes deep within him waiting for anyone to come forward. Saxton was the first to rise to the bait thrown out onto the murky waters of serious thought and timely dissertation. He intoned wearily,

"I've seen New York City, Boston and other large cities Allan, and may I say that the word 'civilized' doesn't come to mind. I grant you this that tough times are part of the package when one is a pioneer. People have fled racist cities, stolen farms and remote villages since time began. Here on Harmony Farm, those who want peace, productivity and parenthood in a setting filled with loved ones are welcome." Pinkerton snorted.

"Sounds a bit altruistic I'd say, for nobody can run away from the real world around them to some remote mountain top and try to fashion a nirvana with the very tools that caused their problems in the first place." Belle intervened,

"I'm quite certain Allan, that with all your experiences you could certainly be excused for having a more pessimistic, myopic view of the world very few people have lived through. The baser nature of man they say is skin deep, barely tamed by will and certainly infinite in its ability to control our emotions. But for me and I'm not talking for anyone but me; I too having seen the baser side of human nature, and have been a willing participant in the more erotic aspects of it. Over the intervening years, I've come to the conclusion that most people are willing to reach a compromise somewhere in their lives on how to live with it." Marcus continued the premise saying,

"Mankind is inherently good but also inherently greedy. Greed, contrary to popular opinion is good because it is the capitalistic engine that makes our lives better. People invent labor saving devices because the monetary rewards for doing so are great. Railways, toll roads, and shipping companies are created by risk takers who are greedy. Fortunately my dear friends, I'm a free man today because I was rescued by a Saxton Shipping Company clipper anchored off the east coast of Africa. Marcus laughed as he murmured,

"As we all know, Thomas Saxton was a greedy capitalistic shipping magnate. All I can say is, thank God he was." He continued, refreshed by their response.

"The rest of us cowards just go along for the ride, feeding off the scraps that risk takers such as Carnegie and his ilk throw away. Here at Harmony Farm however, there are no scraps. Everyone here has an equal place at the table. We all share the fruits of our collective greed." Pinkerton laughed,

"I basically said the same thing in a book I published three years ago called, 'Strikers, Communists and Tramps'. The working poor are working for the simple reason they didn't have the guts to risk everything whereas someone else did, and was well rewarded for their efforts. Unions however, are against anyone being successful. They want to control the economy rather than have the forces of greed inherent in the market control the economy. Nothing is more effective than greed. Unions want a dystopia where twenty percent of the labor force do enough work to look after the eighty percent who stand around leaning on their shovels. Indeed, especially today, it seems that protective Union agreements reward those who are lazy and persecute those who are not. There are no democratic procedures at union meetings. The Union bosses hire bully boys to keep everyone in line. Dissention within the ranks is snuffed out violently. There is no secret ballot. As long as the Union gets its dues, it has the means to intimidate those who oppose it."

By now Felicity had had enough. She jumped up and shouted at Pinkerton,

"Allan Pinkerton, you're a traitor to the honest, hardworking people of America. I know because the papers have been full of how your so called bully boys broke up railway strikes and labor unions who only wanted a fair working wage for its members. Pinkie Pinkerton you have a lot to answer for."

She got up to leave but Virginia, shocked by her daughter's outburst, restrained her.

"Felicity my dear, we've known Allan for many years. He's saved our lives more than once, and has been our constant protector and friend. You might not agree with what he believes in, but you have to share our respect for what he has done for the family."

Virginia looked at Allan and smiled, willing the man to defend himself but he remained silent. So she decided to act on his behalf, her voice firm and incisive.

"Mr. Pinkerton here, and correct me if I error in thought or judgment Allan, has done more for America than any other person I know of other than Abe Lincoln of course." She watched Felicity stiffen. Her mother continued.

"As you well know he organized the first detective agency in America and has brought many crooks to justice. Before the war, his cooperage was a station in the slave underground railway. In 1861 he foiled a plot to kill Lincoln. During the war he spied on the Confederacy, risking his life disguised as a Major E.J. Allan. In fact he saved our lives in Charleston just before the war started. His agency infiltrated the Molly Maguire's, a group responsible for terrorism in the coalfields. Ten of the Maguire's were hung for their atrocities. Dear daughter, my friend here is just that, a friend; a good and gracious friend."

She waited for Felicity to respond. She did, but not the way her parents expected her to. Her daughter stood up and faced the detective, her voice even yet barely able to control the emotions running wild within her.

"Mr. Pinkerton, it might be true what my mother has just said, but to me you are a hypocrite of the first magnitude."

Pinkerton puffed on his cheroot as Virginia rose to scold her. He motioned Virginia to sit down. He looked up at the young woman standing arms akimbo, defiant before him and said calmly,

"And my dear Felicity, why am I a hypocrite?"

She glowered down at him piqued, her words pithy.

"Mr. Pinkerton, the past exploitation of the slaves in the South is really no different than the exploitation of the workers in the North today. How can you justify the fact that before and during the war, you risked your life as an abolitionist yet six years ago you were hired by the Spanish government to help suppress a peasant revolution in Cuba? You used to be a pro-labor Chartist, now you are considered to be the anti-Christ of unionism. Why? The Cuban rebellion would have freed the slaves there and given them the right to vote. How Sir, do you explain that!"

She stood there defying anyone to attack her. Pinkerton rose up, walked to the fireplace and threw the stub of his cigar into the blazing fire pit. He turned and bowed towards her saying politely,

"My dear Felicity, you are correct in every detail. It is true that I've tasted the political waters from many wells and found them unable to slack my thirst for the truth. It is also true that anyone regardless of race, sex or religion should be free as long as their freedom is guaranteed to last once it is accomplished."

He paused to light another cigar then took up his familiar habit of pacing back and forth. Pinkerton relished an audience. He went on saying,

"In Cuba, the unions would simply have replaced the Spanish dictatorship with another more insidious one. It would have been less educated and certainly less able to retain the basic levels of service so necessary for good government. No Felicity, the campensinos's slavery would have continued none the less, whereas in America it was a completely different story. Here in America, many blacks were already well educated as were Belle's parents in New Orleans."

He paused again, looking at Belle for support. She smiled, urging him on.

"As I was saying, education was there for many blacks in the north before, during and more so after the war, whereas in Cuba, blacks remained uneducated. I mean, for example in Louisiana under the reconstruction program, despite the best efforts of the KKK to wipe it out, many blacks assumed public office, and were a credit to America. As for opportunities in education, the first black Colleges and Universities were started by black churches and other … may I say white investors. It began in 1837 with Cheney University in Philadelphia followed by Wilberforce University in Ohio in the 1850's. The Morril Act of 1862 extended post-secondary education to everyone black or white. In 1872, the Freedman Bureau was set up by the Federal government to assist blacks to integrate into white society after the war."

He paused, took another puff on his cheroot, looked at Felicity standing there with her thin arms crossed over her chest and said firmly,

"Cuba's unions did not have any resources at that time to duplicate what was happening in America. Simply put, they were anarchists bound and determined to destroy Cuba. In other words, the jealous husband kills his wife saying,

"If I can't have her, nobody can!"

Felicity was still not convinced but agreed there were two sides to every coin and that the man standing before her was more than a match for anyone. At that moment Cotton ran downstairs and called out,

"Look everyone, it's snowing, really snowing. It's a blizzard!"

Everyone got up and went out onto the veranda to see what the fuss was all about. Mother Nature had indeed taken a turn for the worst. What had started out as a cool but pleasant day was now consumed by a cold and tumultuous torrent of falling snow. The group moved back into the house, finding their places once again in the grand salon. Once there, Saxton turned to Marcus and whispered,

"You had better get down to the village immediately and make sure everyone has enough firewood. While you're at it, take your family home before the weather gets any worse. I'll wire the mill and call in the logging crews. I guess we'd better cancel the New Year's Eve party at the hall as well. We'll have it after the weather breaks. You never know if the steam pipes will freeze up like they did two years ago. Take some men from the bunkhouse with you. I'll also wire the gatehouse and tell them that you're coming for them. I'm sure no one will be coming up the mountain in these conditions. Wire me here at the house when you're ready to leave. Drop the guards off at my place to stay the night. I'll send them back down the hill after the storm is over. Take a sleigh, get your family home then pick up the guards. Take some firewood with you. You'd better hurry Marcus; I'm afraid we're in for a big blow. Collect Tyler Wicks while you're at it. I've been in one blizzard before and it will kill you if you're alone and not careful."

Marcus left for the stables. Belle and her boys dressed warmly then headed out through the front door into a world of white death. Saxton looked at Virginia and Felicity. He knew they were worried so he decided to put them to work. He motioned them over trying to remain calm. Meanwhile, Marcus brought a Portland sleigh around to the front of the house. Belle,

Cotton and Rufus ran out on to the veranda, down the steps to the sleigh. In seconds they'd disappeared into a white swirling mass of trillions of snowflakes. Saxton was worried.

"Look Virginia and Felicity, I don't mean to alarm you but do you remember where the emergency black twine is?" Felicity replied,

"It's in the stables by the tack room, why?"

Saxton remembered the white twine at Salisbury prison that saved him from dying in a blizzard many years before. He said calmly,

"I want both of you to string out the twine. You know the one with the red ribbons tied to it every ten feet. Anyways, string it out between all the buildings here using those hooks I screwed into the buildings that I showed you the last time we had a blow. Remember?" Virginia nodded.

"Good. Now listen carefully both of you. Always stay together. Now get going and dress warm, it's freezing out there."

As the two women left for the mudroom, Saxton turned to Pinkerton and said,

I'll wire the boys in the gatehouse and the mill right away." A few minutes later he returned.

"Allan, our guards Malcolm and Marcellus are fine but the gatehouse is freezing. They've run out of firewood believe it or not. However, they'll stay put until Marcus and Tyler get to them."

Three long steam whistle blasts rent the air calling the loggers in from the woods. Saxton began to speak but was interrupted as Felicity and Virginia came back into the house, wiping snow off their parkas. The urgency in Felicity's voice was disturbing.

"My God the weather is getting really ugly father."

Meanwhile, Marcus had taken his family back to their house above the mill. Shortly thereafter he wired back that everyone was safe and sound and that Cotton and his brother were connecting every building there with marked twine. On the way back from his house, Marcus picked up Tyler Wicks at the bunkhouse. Their sleigh proceeded swiftly through the forest. Finally the village loomed through the blizzard. Already over a foot of snow had fallen. Where mere minutes ago the sun was visible, now there was no sun, no light; only a diffused white gloom that cast no shadows. Ligo Watts ran out from his house onto the village road. A few men stood there stamping their boots as the sleigh approached. Ligo sounded worried.

"Mr. Brown, is there anything you want us to do?"

"Yes there is. Have everyone top off their wood bins in all the houses in case the steam pipes freeze again." A man said,

"We're doin' that now Mr. Brown. Do you want us to lay out twine from here to the Saxton house too?"

"Yes, get a few more men and lay it out now, but dress warm and wear snowshoes. Tell all the others to stay put. Run a line from the Rectory to here as well. Check in on Otis and Max. Tell them you'll send up some firewood in a sled. Make sure they stay put. Besides, the

Father is a better card player than Otis. The two of them will probably play poker all night. I wonder what kind of stakes they're playing for?" Bill Curry laughed.

"I can just imagine. Perhaps their sermons are up for grabs. Who knows?" Marcus started the sleigh forward saying,

"Anyways men, Tyler and I are going to get some wood for the gatehouse then we're off to pick up Marcellus and Malcolm."

Ligo watched as they vanished into the blizzard.

Saxton, Virginia, Felicity and their guest Allan Pinkerton, settled down before a roaring fire in the grand salon as Virginia called it. It was a replica of the grand salon at her former residence in Boston. Pinkerton remarked,

"Really Virginia, I can't see any differences other than the size. It's truly amazing how much it looks like the old place in every detail."

He walked over to the wooden mantle. Above it was a painting by Chester Harding from Boston. It portrayed Thomas Saxton standing behind Muriel seated in front of him. Thomas had one hand placed upon his wife's right shoulder. Both were looking serenely straight ahead. Behind them was the 'keel-mantle' over the fireplace of the grand salon, a Maasai shield and spear crossed above it. In her lap was Jack, a red ball between his paws. Below the large oil painting was the framed Medal of Honor that Saxton won in the Civil War. Pinkerton laughed,

"You and your old man were always full of surprises." Saxton was silent, for a Frean was just going down his throat.

Millie had arrived earlier with some Freans and tea. Packard stood by the entrance to the room watching her every move. Virginia caught him looking at her. She smiled as she remembered that the two were now engaged to be married. Millie was forty-five years old while Stylus was a very young looking sixty years of age. The two had worked together for many years in the former Saxton mansion. Both knew each other's habits, bad and good, to the letter.

One day Packard surprised Millie in the upstairs hallway so much so that she dropped a tea tray, spilling everything all over the hall runner. Instead of chastising her, Packard helped her clean up the mess. From that day forward, Packard was actually civil to her. Millie now saw a softer more vulnerable side to the tall skinny house butler. Stylus Packard was sensitive yet shy, therefore restrained, not uppity at all. Before long the two were in love, totally and unconditionally.

Subsequently, Virginia agreed to be Millie's bridesmaid and Saxton would walk her down the aisle. Felicity would be her flower girl and Rufus her ring bearer. His brother Cotton would be in charge of seating everyone. Marcus would be the groom's best man. The wedding was planned for June 24th in the village church. Since Packard was Catholic and Millie Baptist, both Father Manilow and Reverend Tillman would take turns presiding. It promised to be a celebration of major proportions. Saxton and Virginia were sending them to Bermuda for their honeymoon. Virginia laughed when they announced their wedding gift to the pair, saying,

"I hope you two finish what we started on our honeymoon. We never made it but I know you will for us. Just don't go near Fort Sumter. We don't want another war now do we?"

The storm continued unrestrained. Drifting snow piled up like waves crashing down upon a distant shore. Saxton become uneasy; it was as if he was still in Salisbury prison. While there, he like all the other survivors of that hellish place developed a sixth sense. It was the ability to trust ones' instincts sharpened to a razor's edge by sensory deprivation, imminent starvation and total incarceration. Saxton moved to a nearby window and pulled apart the heavy curtains, his breath glazing the glass with a cloudy patina of frost. He looked closer as a dark form burst out of the white world before him. It was Marcus and Tyler Wicks. Their black cigar-box cutter was bulling its way through the drifts that blocked the lane. Their horse began lunging forward, its nose covered in flakes of frozen ice. It stopped a few feet away steaming in the cold air. A few dogs in the village barked. Tyler jumped out and removed a blanket from the rear seat. Saxton couldn't believe what he was looking at. There seemed to be two bodies in the rear seat. Saxton turned and sprinted towards the foyer.

Marcus burst through the front door covered in snow. He stamped his feet and beat his hands together. His face was deathly pale; the scars upon it ran down like streaks of congealed blood. Virginia and Pinkerton came up behind Saxton. Pinkerton moved Saxton aside saying,

"What's happened Marcus? My God, what's happened laddie?"

Saxton ran out onto the veranda and down the snow covered front steps. He waded through deep snow to the cutter. Tyler was crying, his tears freezing white on his black face. Saxton grabbed a frozen tarp from his hand and flung it back. Snowflakes swirled down upon the bodies of Malcolm and Marcellus. Pinkerton pushed up behind him and he too looked down at them. He brushed away the snow that lay thickly upon them. Frozen blood covered their chests. Pinkerton turned to Saxton, his arm upon his shoulder.

"They've been shot laddie. I have a feeling that I'm going to be here a while longer."

The bodies of Malcolm and Marcellus were laid out on a temporary trestle in the stable behind the Saxton house. Both men were unmarried. Their families lived in other parts of the State. Signs that rigor mortis had set were evident as their bodies began thawing out. Only Saxton, Marcus, Tyler Wicks and Pinkerton were there. Before coming up the hill, Tyler Wicks put Ligo Watts and the rest of the security team on high alert. Saxton felt that whoever killed the guards might still be on the mountain although it was highly unlikely. Saxton turned to the others.

"God help anyone who might have been foolish enough to remain on the mountain. It's ten below and the snow is still coming down."

Pinkerton finished examining the bodies. He turned to Marcus, while putting his silver loupe back into his breast pocket.

"Did you see any tracks or shell casings about the shack?"

Marcus said he had not seen anything as it was snowing so hard their tracks had taken mere seconds to disappear. Pinkerton continued, his breath rising in puffs like a train leaving a station in a hurry.

"Well Lads, it seems that whoever killed them was probably known to the guards because the wounds have bits of gunpowder residue in them. That means they were shot at very close range. You said one body was found outside the shack and the other inside sitting in a chair by the wood stove. Is that correct Tyler?" The little man looked up at the detective,

"Yes, that's correct. If it was a total stranger, both men would have stood up, gone out and protected each other, guns ready. As a matter of fact, look here Allan."

Tyler walked over. The pistols of both men were still holstered. Tyler put the tarp back over the bodies. Marcus said,

"That's right come to think of it. We never checked their guns. So they must have known their killer or killers."

Pinkerton stood back and thought for a few moments, his bowler tilted to the side of his smallish head. He lit up a cigar. Saxton was firm.

"Sorry Allan but you can't smoke in here?"

Pinkerton chewed the cigar stub instead saying petulantly,

"Christ almighty you two; first it was booties and no smokin' on the Nimsi and now I can wear my boots but no smokin' or drinkin' around here. What kind of utopia is this anyways? It's, it's not civilized!" he sputtered.

Tyler Wicks was the first to regain his composure,

"The telegraph wires at the gatehouse were cut. That's why we couldn't tell anyone about the murders. However, I did leave a note for Tom and Terry down at the Guardhouse."

Saxton walked over to the two bodies lying under the tarp. He put his hands upon them and wept. After a short time he turned around to Marcus saying,

"Marcus, those boys were like my own flesh and blood. I loved their laughter, their love of life, their faith in the goodness of man. We have to stop whoever is stalking us. It can be only one man and that man is Lucas Garrow and his thugs. Cowards always hunt in packs. Yes, if he's on the mountain in this weather, I hope Mother Nature kills him for us before we have to do it ourselves."

Pinkerton threw the chewed rag of a cigar out the barn door into a snow drift. He pulled the door shut as Marcus lit a lantern and hung it up on a beam. Pinkerton began to pace. Saxton looked at Marcus. They knew the signs. The man was about to say something deep and startling. Both men were not prepared at all for what Pinkerton told them. They listened in stunned silence.

"Gentlemen, I might be retired but my two sons Robert and William are not. They've been running the Agency for a few years now. As you both know, my early expertise, in fact my very first case was exposing counterfeiters over thirty-five years ago. It has come to our attention that a major counterfeiting ring is operating somewhere in the State of Tennessee, most likely right here in Chattanooga. Local rumors have it that the ring might be operating nearby. Please correct me if I am wrong, but are there any secluded or hidden areas on the mountain that could conceal such an operation?" Saxton watched as Pinkerton pulled out another cigar and started to chew it.

"Yes Allan there is! The locals call it Pitchfork cave. It's part of our property."

Pinkerton began pacing about the cavernous stable. Horses snickered as he walked past them. Finally Saxton stopped him, exasperated.

"For God's sake Pinkerton, light the damn thing! I hate to see a man suffer." Pinkerton obliged.

"Thank you son and perhaps I can see that cave before I leave. Maybe the weather will break. Christ I do hope so. Now let's get back to the house, I'm freezin' to death."

Marcus snuffed out the lantern and followed the rest through the snow back into the house. As they did, thirty men wearing white winter clothing and snow-shoes were deep within the surrounding forest, heading for Harmony Farm. An hour later they split up into three groups. An hour after that, one of those groups emerged from the shadows behind Saxton's house. They waited patiently for a few minutes then snow-shoed furtively across the deserted barn yard towards the rear of the stable. Behind them their tracks evaporated within seconds. An hour later, the blizzard abated. The temperature rose and the dark clouds that smothered the mountain scudded eastward. A full moon bathed the undulating drifts around the Saxton house with pale light. Oil lamps lit up Saxton's house as dusk descended upon the mountain.

Allan Pinkerton strode back and forth across the floor of the grand salon. His audience seated about the room was mesmerized by what he'd already said and were about to be horrified by what he was to tell them. Indeed, he'd come to the mountain to see them for New Years Eve and he reveled in renewing his friendship with them once again. But, as they found out, the real purpose of his visit was more troubling, more profound and certainly more dangerous than they ever imagined.

In short, he informed them, that Lucas Garrow was suspected of housing a vast counterfeiting ring somewhere in the immediate area. He continued gravely,

"You might also be interested to know that since the war ended, at times nearly half the paper currency in America was counterfeit. In fact the Secret Service I helped set up in 1865, originated with the sole purpose of stopping the counterfeiters. The campaign started nearly twenty years ago has been very successful until now. However, over the past twelve months, millions of near perfect counterfeit twenties and fifties have flooded Tennessee and North Carolina. But my friends, it must stop or America could suffer another depression so devastating that our way of life as we know it will vanish, to be replaced by tyranny."

Saxton interrupted by saying,

"How's that Allan? Is it because the new gold standard is set up in such a way that for every dollar the government issues, one dollar of gold must be stored to back it up?"

"Yes Saxton, that's it pure and simple."

He reached into his coat pocket and withdrew a small brown envelope. He opened it and took out two ten dollar bills. At first glance they looked identical. He said,

"Here's a fake ten and a real one."

With that said, he laid them flat out on a coffee table, offering his jeweler's loupe to Virginia nearby. She took the loupe then carefully scrutinized the two identical looking bills with it. Exclaiming with vigor, she opined,

"Very interesting; I cannot for the life of me tell the difference. Where do they get the paper? I hear that it's very special. How do they do it?"

She reached over and gave the silver loupe to Tyler Wicks who moments later was also baffled. And so it went around the room from one to the other. Pinkerton waited until they had all finished then retrieved the small loupe, putting it back in his breast pocket. They remained seated as Pinkerton once again paced back and forth puffing on his cigar like a locomotive. He stopped.

"They buy up one dollar bills and bleach out the ink. Ever since the Feds started printing them in 1877, there's been quite an abundance of them."

He continued to puff furiously.

"There's one more item I should discuss. My two sons, William and Robert are here in Chattanooga. As you all know I'm trying in vain to remain retired but after thirty-five years I'm still wont to keep a 'bone in my teeth' so to speak. From what I've been told, you own all of Elder Mountain which presumably includes Pitchfork Cave. I ask you now, when was the last time you inspected your cave and secondly are you sure there are no passages that could unbeknownst to you be connected to it?" Saxton leaned back.

"I'll answer that one Allan. We inspect the caverns once every year and check the two entrances every month to make sure both are locked. We don't use the caves for storage or anything else for that matter. However, there are drift boats inside the lower entrance ready to launch in case we have to evacuate the farm in a real hurry. So far all the inspections have shown nothing amiss." Pinkerton replied,

"Who does the inspection Saxton and how long does it take?"

"Why, Marcellus and Malcolm have done it for years. However, Ligo Watts joined the team a few months ago. As a matter of fact, those three did the annual inspection today. They started early, right after breakfast and were back in one hour at the very most. It does seem strange though come to think of it." Pinkerton pressed him,

"Why's that?"

"Well Allan, I say strange for the simple reason that Ligo Watts took both men immediately thereafter in a buckboard down to the gate house for their four days on duty. Come to think of it, those two boys in particular usually wash up first then ride down themselves on horseback."

Pinkerton looked at all of them. He said calmly,

"Who is Ligo Watts and where is he from?" Virginia jumped up saying,

"Oh my God, Ligo Watts was Lucas Garrow's coachman who horsewhipped old Tom Peeks last summer. Bobby shot the whip out of his hand injuring Ligo severely. Peeks took him in. Watts said he's seen the error of his ways so we let him stay. In fact he married a widow living here." Pinkerton's tone was icy as he looked at Saxton.

"Where is he Saxton?"

"Why he and a few men started laying out marked twine a few hours ago. He should be home with his family." Tyler Wicks came forward.

"I'll put on some snowshoes and see if he's home; it shouldn't take more than ten minutes. I'll be back as soon as I can."

Pinkerton moved forward. Virginia had never seen him move so fast. He grabbed Wicks, startling the little man as he spun him about.

"Tyler, I suspect that Watts killed the two boys in the cave, not at the gatehouse. Malcolm and Marcellus discovered something they were not supposed to. But the big question remains, why didn't he just leave them in the cave and claim that they slipped off a cliff?"

Saxton intervened as Pinkerton continued to pace about the room.

"Maybe he just panicked and shot them, figuring that he had to show everyone here that the three of them exited the cave together. He probably knew full well that if he didn't, a search would have commenced in the cave and the counterfeiting ring would have been discovered. But what I can't understand is how he got the two boys down to the gatehouse?" Pinkerton smiled and said succinctly,

"Why, Watts got a wagon and put them on the driver's seat. This was done by keeping them upright. He tied their bodies to posts jammed through the floorboards at the back of the seat. Once out of sight in the forest, he put the bodies in the buckboard, threw away the posts, covered the bodies with a tarp, brought them down the mountain then hid them near the gatehouse." Saxton continued.

"Allan you're probably right. Come to think of it, Ligo knew the other guards at the gatehouse had to see a dentist. It was an emergency. Watts probably told them to leave as he would wait for the Malcolm and Marcellus to show up. After Tom and Terry left, he arranged the bodies in the gatehouse then high tailed it up the mountain before anyone noticed him missing. Even upon a closer examination, one would think they'd been robbed or that the farm was being attacked. Perhaps the counterfeiters are preparing to escape as we speak and the killing of the two would divert our attention elsewhere."

Pinkerton was interrupted by Virginia who had risen. She held onto her husband, her face pale, not yet comprehended the full portent of Pinkerton's deductions.

"That's impossible Allan, for Saxton telegraphed the boys that Marcus and Tyler were comin' down by sleigh to get them so they'd be back for the New Years Eve party at the hall. They answered." Pinkerton said,

"Did Watts know Morse Code?" No one knew.

"He could have. Ok then, Watts arranged the bodies, replied and took off up the hill. It's only two miles and it was starting to snow heavily, thus any tracks would have been covered quickly." Marcus had also risen. He interjected,

"No. Tyler and I were coming down to get them and bring them back up so we woulda run into him for sure." Pinkerton queried,

"Is there any place that Watts could have hidden a team away from the road, waiting for you to drive by?"

Virginia spoke up.

"Yes Allan, he could have hidden on the road to the grand salon." Pinkerton looked blankly at her saying,

"Grand Salon? Why we're in it now my dear. What do you mean?" They all tittered.

"I meant a large open glade on the right side, half way up the hill."

"Oh, alright then, he could have hid there, am I correct?" Tyler replied,

"Yes Allan, it could have happened as you say. As for the two boys, they always took their horses down the hill. In fact they were still tied up at the shack. We brought them back with us. That means Watts tied them to the wagon and brought them down. They sometimes used them to go into town on errands for the farm. I guess everyone who saw the three of them in the wagon figured they enjoyed each other's company and that Watts was going into town or pick up supplies left at Brown's landing. It happens all the time." Pinkerton wasn't finished.

"I noticed when I arrived here that this gatehouse you talk about is far more substantial than a shack. The damned thing is a house really. I've forgotten. How long do the guards stay there?" Marcus answered,

"Four days usually as all the guards are single men, well armed, well trained in combat, and all of them are conversant in Morse Code." Pinkerton pressed on.

"Are there only two at a time?"

"Yes"

"Where are the two guards that were there on duty before Watts and his victims showed up?

Saxton began to get an uneasy feeling deep within him. He turned to Marcus saying,

"I remember now. Two guards, Terry and Tom were going into town to see Doctor Boyd before their four days was up. Both men had abscessed molars. They were to come back and relieve Malcolm and Marcellus who filled in for them." Pinkerton looked at him vacantly,

"Boyd? Who's he or she for that matter?"

"He's the dentist who moved recently from Knoxville who we've retained for the farm. Both Tom and Terry needed fillings and molar extractions. Both were unable to enjoy the New Year's festivities anyway. I guess they had to leave for the ferry. In fact I forgot."

He reached into his trouser pocket and brought out a note. Pinkerton nodded and gave it back saying,

"It's a good thing they left early or we'd have four dead boys on our hands. I always hated going to the dentist but now it seems rather inviting considering what's happened here." With that said, he paused and lit another cigar.

"I did tell my sons to meet me here today at noon. If they see that there are no guards at the gatehouse, they'll know something isn't right and raise the alarm."

Tyler, looked at Pinkerton and said evenly,

"Well Sir, I left a note detailing what we found there. Tom and Terry will find it. I told them to stay there, and let no one past the gate whatsoever."

Pinkerton nodded, pleased with Tyler's presence of mind. He looked at him and said,

"Tyler, are they armed?"

"Yes, Allan. I am too."

"Good. Now go down quietly, stay out of sight and round up a posse right quick. Any trouble, ring the school bell. I don't know what it is but the hair on the back of my neck is starting to tingle." At that very moment, every dog in the village below them started to howl. Virginia cringed,

"Something's not right. The dogs are howling, not barking. That Lucas Garrow is up to something and a night like this would be perfect cover for an attack." Pinkerton looked at her then dismissed her reaction. He continued, oblivious.

"By the way, I heard that his wife BB died of strychnine poisoning at the Read House Charity Ball. William and Robert have Lucas under investigation already for reasons I told you about earlier." Saxton replied,

"Yes Allan, I was in town the day after on business and read it in the papers. Seems Lucas is a prime suspect. From all accounts the marriage was a sham. The money Garrow came into town with; apparently was the loot his father Horatio stole from Boss Tweed in New York City and the Funeral Home was just a front for his other nefarious enterprises. Persistent rumors have also surfaced that Lucas is planning to resurrect the Confederacy with him as its President. It's sort of a second coming of a southern Messiah, God forbid."

Saxton was becoming increasingly upset about Garrow's cockamamie plans as the conversation unfolded, saying,

"I, more than anyone, knew how Horatio's mind worked and I can tell you all right now that the nut did not fall far from the tree in this case. You all saw Watts whip a man. Why? Ask yourself why? The reason is simple. While in Salisbury prison I told Lucas all about the Maasai Rangers especially how accurate they were at nearly three hundred yards especially with a Henry rifle. Lucas had to get a spy into the farm but how?"

Marcus was stunned. He was just starting to understand where Saxton was going with his theory. He gasped,

"Oh my, what a smart bastard that Lucas is, just like his old man. You mean to tell me that Lucas ordered Ligo to get shot?" Saxton nodded.

"Yes, I wouldn't put it past him. The few men still loyal to him are all fanatics. Lucas knew that only a Ranger could shoot the whip out of Ligo's hand at well over two hundred yards." Pinkerton exclaimed.

"Amazing! So, as I understand it, Lucas knew that Ligo would be looked after on the farm and immediately thereafter Ligo 'saw the light', stayed on, got married to widow McCarthy then betrayed you." Marcus yelled in frustration,

"I'll shoot the bastard myself if I ever have the chance." Saxton walked over and held his friend back knowing that betrayal of any kind was a death sentence in the Maasai culture.

"No Marcus, Lucas is the one we really have to be afraid of. When he was here on Independence Day, you saw his eyes, heard his wicked laughter, felt the hate deep within him. If he's anything like his father we're all going to die slowly, painfully and soon if we don't prepare for his revenge. As far as Lucas is concerned, we're all guilty of killing his father and may I say, the Confederacy as well. To Lucas, Belle's a whore who happened to be in the room when he was conceived." Virginia took her husband's hand.

"No Saxton, Belle's not a whore, for she's his mother and I know she loves him as a mother. Perhaps he'll find that out before it's too late." Saxton had other ideas on his mind. He said,

"Times are a wasting Tyler. Get going now. Remember to send some men to arrest Watts and check out the upper cave entrance. Make sure it's locked. Report back here as soon as you can. Good luck."

With that the 'shell man' disappeared out the front door. The village dogs were in an uproar. Saxton followed Wicks out the door, clutching his frock coat tightly to him in the freezing cold air. He looked on from the darkened veranda as the little man snow-shoed down the hill towards the village. A row of bare chestnut trees came between them. He was gone. Saxton was about to turn back but his attention was caught be a shadow slipping through the trees to his right towards the stables. Saxton moved further into the shadows of the veranda. A figure carried a rifle. It was Ligo Watts.

Slowly, Saxton eased himself back into the house, his hand keeping the screen door from slamming shut. He quietly closed and barred the heavy front door. The group was standing in the foyer facing him. Virginia saw his face darken. She rushed forward.

"What's wrong Sax?"

Saxton took her into his arms and put his forefinger to her mouth. He whispered above her shoulder.

"We have armed visitors and Watts is one of them. Virginia, go get Millie, and Packard."

He was about to say something else when muffled gun shots erupted far away to the north. Saxton looked at Marcus.

"My God Marcus that sounds like rifle fire over by your place!"

Marcus moved like lightning towards the mudroom at the rear of the house. Once there, he put on his woolen coat, snow boots and felt hat before anyone noticed. Grabbing a Spencer rifle from an overhead gun rack he started for the rear door as Saxton ran up to him.

"I'm goin' to the stables Saxton and kill that bastard Watts. Then I'll hook up a sleigh. I've got to get back home to Belle and the kids. I'll rustle up a posse on the way then I'll wire you when I get home."

As Marcus disappeared, a telegraph started to chatter. Saxton rushed into the office. It was a wire from Belle. He stood transfixed as machine said,

"UNDER FIRE BY UNKNOWNS. LOW ON ...."

Pinkerton came up behind him. He scowled, "Christ, they've cut the telegraph line."

Ten minutes earlier, Watts was sure he'd not been seen snow-shoeing towards the stables behind the Saxton house. He'd told Marie that it was his turn to do his security checks. She kissed her husband goodbye knowing he'd join three others and would be back in a few hours, probably cold, wet and hungry. Her husband knew she'd probably warm up some pea soup. Watts stopped near the side door at the back of the stables. He rapped three times. The door opened. He stepped into total blackness. Momentarily blind, Watts was pulled down a dusty corridor into a small tack room.

An oil lamp was lit. As his eyes adjusted to the weak light, Watts saw Lucas and seven armed men dressed in white seal skin winter gear. They were all seated around the room under thick horse blankets with their backs to the board walls. Some were asleep, while others looked up and nodded in recognition. Above them all, hung leather harnesses, hame straps, halters, bits and saddles. The room smelled strongly of horse liniment. A horse blanket was hung over the tack room's one window from two nails.

Lucas moved forward. Ligo took off his snow-shoes and leaned them against the wall behind him. Watts saw Morley Sparks, the stable boy sitting with his back against the wall. His throat had been slit. Blood trickled down his blue shirt and black overalls. Lucas said,

"Get some sleep Ligo. You've deserved it. I hope you can use another five hundred dollars for your efforts today." He laughed,

"Don't worry. It's real money."

Watts began brushing off the snow from his white parka as he eyed the dead boy. Lucas continued to issue orders.

"Boys, we're moving out in a few minutes. More of us have come through the cave up from the river. Right now they've surrounding the village, the mill, the singles barracks and the Brown's residence. All hell will break loose once they've set up their firing positions. Congratulations Ligo, you unlocked the upper cave door just in time. It was nice of

Saxton- Brown to leave all those weapons and supplies for us down below. It is a miracle that five men have lived off them for nearly two years now undetected." He laughed,

"Well, we're finished here for now. I do believe the Pinkerton's are on to us. Tonight, we'll take over the farm and kill everyone who lives here. If that fails, we'll escape down the river to Bridgeport, Alabama where we'll set up all over again. Either way, it's all arranged. My trip to Bridgeport a few weeks ago was very productive indeed. I've got five new presses stashed away in a warehouse there. We'll be in business again and soon. Imagine that! Too bad everyone thought someone disguised as me was in Nashville buying a crematorium. Well done indeed Ligo." Lucas looked at his fob watch.

"Our boat crews are all well trained and ready down at the river. They're guarding both cave entrances now as the drift boats are loaded up. We'll leave the horses behind here cause we can't take 'em in the boats." He was interrupted as Ligo swore,

"Damn those two, Malcolm and Marcellus. We inspected the cave this morning and they saw the presses. I tried to bribe 'em but they wouldn't hear of it. So I had to kill 'em Lucas."

The men in the barn rose as one. Lucas came towards Watts who stood up to face him. Lucas growled,

"What do you mean? Just what do you mean?"

Watts sputtered, but failed to find his voice as Lucas pressed a knife against his throat. He snarled,

"Where did you leave the bodies?" Watts tried to back away. He squealed,

"At the gatehouse Lucas, I left them down at the damned gatehouse." By now Lucas was apoplectic.

"You stupid bastard! You shouda left 'em in the cave. Now the whole goddamn mountain is on the alert."

Watts tried to scream but Garrow's knife sliced through his carotid artery. A fountain of blood gushed from the wound as Watts dropped to the floor beside Morley's body. Lucas wiped his bloody knife on a horse blanket covering the window. As he did, a sliver of yellow light slipped out into the night. Lucas sheathed his knife and acted as if nothing had happened.

"Well boys, like I said before, we have to move anyway. Hopefully I lost that posse back in the city. My aide, poor Hadley, is probably being interrogated right now. No matter, he knows nothing. I had no problem getting on the ferry. Besides I made my ferrymen an offer they couldn't refuse."

He laughed out loud at the genius of it all. He went on to say,

"Thank God there's a full moon tonight, we'll really need it when our attack begins. They won't know what hit 'em! Boys we're gonna have a real good New Year's Eve party right here on the mountain. We're gonna kill those bastards real slo…"

He never finished his sentence as muffled gunfire erupted far to the east near the mill.

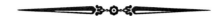

Earlier that day, William Pinkerton and his older brother Robert were lying in wait just around the corner from the Chapman Funeral Emporium. The telegram they sent Lucas via courier to flush him out said.

"Want 50 million US in 50/20/10's
By 12/01/82 Nash to 10.45
Usual terms. Proofs in 3 weeks."

Pinkerton's agents intercepted various wires from Garrow's funeral home in Chattanooga. Always three lines in length, each line started with the letters WBU representing the initials of a very reliable foreign client Garrow had dealt with before. The safe-houses that he used were always in code. Therefore, 1045 was a street address. Since there were not that many addresses in Nashville with such a number, it was only a short time before the safe-house was found and put under surveillance. Faced with an order of tens, twenties and fifty counterfeit dollar bills, Garrow would have to personally supervise a run of this magnitude, ergo he would leave the funeral home for his printing operation as soon as he could to supervise it. The Pinkertons surmised that New Years Eve would appeal to his immense vanity and ego. It was a pattern that Garrow had used for two years either to start a new enterprise or end one. Besides it would take at least six months to get the order ready for shipment. He would have to bleach millions of one dollar bills to do it. They figured that he would be accumulating millions more over the next year from banks all over America then shipping them 'underground' to Chattanooga. Garrow would make a move soon, but when? The Pinkertons had kept the Covenant Funeral Home under surveillance for over a week since Garrow received their note. Time was running out.

It was ten o'clock on a New Years Eve morning. A light dusting of snow that night covered a narrow alley behind the funeral home. Around a corner out of sight, were twenty mounted federal Marshalls led by big John. J. Lowry and Ned W. Wilbur of Chattanooga. One of them, a newly minted Marshall, was a former Sergeant, Milford Raines of the New Orleans Police Department. All the men were armed and anxious to capture Garrow but only after he led them to his counterfeiting lair. Their horses were shod in specially fitted hoof pads that muffled any sound completely. To the Pinkertons, it was paramount that Lucas be totally unaware that he was being followed. William and Robert Pinkerton sat on their horses behind the posse, hoping that the operation wouldn't fall apart. But, both men like their father were meticulous. Nothing would be left to chance.

Without warning, two identical black Phaeton buggies shot out of two carriage entrances behind the funeral home. One went one way and the other buggy went another. Each carried two men dressed identically in white parkas. Even the horses pulling the Phaetons were identical Tennessee Walkers. The Pinkerton brothers expected such a ruse might be tried. They too split up, each with ten Marshalls apiece riding pell-mell behind them. They'd agreed earlier that they would split up into even smaller groups until Lucas reached his destination. A central telegraph dispatch set up at Union station connected five other buildings in Chattanooga to each other. Any posse of Marshalls could check in and get the latest news of Garrow's whereabouts and continue the chase. Within minutes it became apparent that one of the Phaetons was heading for the newly built Tennbridge, just north of the city.

A Phaeton stopped at the east end of the railway bridge. Lucas got out. From a hidden vantage point, William Pinkerton watched as over three dozen horsemen emerged from an alley. They joined Garrow as he mounted a black stallion. William retrieved a Hamilton watch out of his vest pocket. He looked at it then turned to Ned Wilbur,

"Ned, send one of your men back to Railway Avenue. My brother's around there somewhere. He'll be checking in at Farley's freight office in fifteen minutes. Tell him to meet me at Brown's Ferry. Garrow owns the ferry and might have his operation on the other side of the river. Hurry, Ned." Wilbur turned about and gave the order to Sergeant Raines. In an instant the man galloped back into the city.

William muttered as he glassed Garrow's cohorts.

"They're all wearing white winter parkas and snowshoes are strapped to their rifle scabbards. Why?"

He kept his binoculars on the group as they rode over the railway bridge. He could hear their hooves pounding over the bridge's wide plank sidewalk. Pinkerton's posse charged after them just as their quarry disappeared through the gap in Springer's Ridge. William smiled as he headed straight for Brown's Ferry.

It began to snow very hard. William Pinkerton and his men made a mad dash through the gap and on to Brown's ferry landing. They were five minutes too late as the cable ferry had already cast off, with over thirty riders and their mounts safely aboard. In moments, it was far out into the river, lost in a vast whiteout unleashed from a dark and pregnant sky. Pinkerton tried to scope them but couldn't penetrate through the falling snow. Thirty minutes later in a billowing cloud of snow, Robert's posse came to a sudden stop beside him. William's brother cried,

"Sorry William, I guess I was wrong. I thought for sure that the counterfeiting was being done in the city somewhere on Railway Avenue in the waterfront area. But I never would have guessed the ring was operating on the other side of the river. Their press must be large and heavy and would have been transported by water or rail. The railway line to Cincinnati is too far away past Moccasin Point upriver from here. No, I'm sure now that Garrow's hideout is somewhere on Elder Mountain or nearby Raccoon Mountain."

William Pinkerton turned to Ned Wilbur.

"Say Ned; are there any large caves along the gorge on the other side of the river?" The wizened old man, pulled back on the reins. His horse nickered as snow fell upon it, tickling its muzzle.

"Why yes, there's only one that I know of. It's called Pitchfork Cave. Its mouth is about one hundred feet above the Tenny at the top of a steep slope. But Harmony Farm owns it and has since sealed the entrance with a double steel door made in town and floated down the river." William asked Ned,

"How much did it weigh Ned?"

"Three tons thereabouts."

Ned paused to stroke his white beard. He looked closely as the man smiled. William had seen the light.

"Why Ned, I'd say that if they could float a door of three tons, they could float a press too and get it up there. How'd they get the door up to the cave?"

Wilbur replied, telling him about the ramp and why it was built.

"Is it still there?" He nodded.

"It is! Why they could skid a large press up it too! Anything else we should know?" Wilbur scratched his chin.

"Folks round these here parts say there's somethin' fishy goin' on in that cave but the Farm is legit and well respected round these parts. But, who knows?"

"Why's that?" Both Pinkerton's were getting uneasy as Ned continued.

"Well if the rumors are true, it seems that a passage was found a few years ago that led from the lower cave right up to the top." Robert looked at Ned in alarm.

"Is there a trail from the ferry landing here to the cave?" Ned began to realize the gravity of Robert's question.

"Yeah, there's a path to it bordering the river, but it's hardly ever used especially in the winter as snow slides block it all the time. Seems the Rebs used it to get to sniper pits from which they fired on any Union troops usin' Harley's trace 'cross the river durin' the war. I also heard tell that the Rebs mined saltpeter there too. But still, if the path is clear, horses could cover the three miles of it in no time 'cause down by the river the snow's not too deep. Is that's where you think they've headed?" Robert brushed snow off his face. He nodded as his horse stamped its hooves, its withers shivering in the cold.

"I figure so. They probably cleared the road well enough to pack out the money by wagon to Brown's ferry then into the city to a safe house." William interrupted,

"I see. The printing press would probably be one of those new Victory Rotary presses. All they would need is a boiler, fuel and water to get it up and running. With those doors closed tight, nobody would hear it. There's probably an air vent through the cave's roof already. They could have camouflaged it quite easily. It would have been a perfect site for their operation." He turned once again to Ned Wilbur.

"Ned, have you ever been in the cave?"

"I have."

"How big is it inside?" Ned pondered a moment then exclaimed,

"It's big, really big William. I'd say fifty by a hundred feet and maybe sixty feet high with passages behind it runnin' every which way. Hell, I used to play inside it when I was a youngin'."

William Pinkerton stood up in the stirrups and called the men to gather around him and his brother. As they did, more snow fell in earnest.

"Gentlemen, we have to go back the way we came and get boats to cross over the river. Does anyone know where we can get some?" Big John Lowry rode over.

"I bet Braswell Shipyard has some. I don't know if the yard would be open today on New Year's Eve but it's a Monday, so they might be. Besides I know old man Braswell; he'll help us for sure." Robert stood up in his stirrups. He said,

"Men we're headed for Braswell's in town to get boats. We'll need more men too so we can block that river trail as well as the road to Harmony Farm. I also believe the farm is in grave danger. From what I've heard from my father and from what you've just told me, there's a blood feud going on between Garrow and the Saxton-Browns." Big John Lowry said,

"Yeah, it got downright ugly a while back. Garrow tried to take away the mountain every which way but the Saxton-Browns stopped him cold. Garrow is crazy for revenge. Why, we don't know. I believe he poisoned his wife a few days ago at the charity ball in the Read Hotel. Apparently it was somethin' terrible. Never saw a woman who could excite a crowd of men so. Maybe Garrow's resurrected that Klan army he was trainin' on Williams Island? Pay a man enough money and he'll do anything." He laughed at the Pinkertons.

"Hey that goes for us too, don't it boys!"

Robert Pinkerton was not amused. The Marshalls stopped laughing and they too listened as he explained.

"Garrow believes he has a large order for more counterfeit bills, in fact fifty million dollars worth. He needs extra men to protect that run and keep Harmony Farm from finding out about it over the next six months. Most certainly, the farm is in danger."

William cried out,

"My God, Robert, our father is up there right now for New Years Eve. Garrow's totally mad. He'll kill them all to protect his operation. That's why they were in white winter gear."

He turned in his saddle, his voice urgent. He pointed back they way they had come.

"Come on men, we've work to do. It's noon already. Let's go back before we're trapped here. God almighty, this snow is really getting worse. Damned the weather! I can only imagine what it's like on the mountain. We'd better get up there fast or there'll be a massacre for sure. It looks like we're going to need snowshoes and winter gear too." Big John yelled out,

"Follow me men. There's an Army Quartermaster depot in town. Perhaps they can help us. If not we're all going to look like the Klan as we ride past Fountain Square in white bed sheets courtesy my old friend John Read."

The posse wheeled about and headed back for Springer's Ridge. The storm swallowed them up within seconds.

BOOK THREE: CHAPTER 14
COURAGE UNDER FIRE

The storm had abated revealing a landscape not unlike that of the Saharan desert. Vast and endless hummocks of sand had been replaced by an equal measure of snow. Olapa, the moon Goddess shone down, bathing the mountain in her singular light. Marcus Brown stood in the darkened mudroom at the rear of Saxton's house. He leaned the Spencer rifle against a wall. As he peered out between the curtains towards the stables, he hefted a heavy .45 Colt Buntline Special in his left hand. With its flat top straps, folding sights and sixteen inch barrel, it was a good substitute for a rifle considering that Marcus had only one arm. His memory went back to 1878 when he had bought the gun in Cincinnati, Ohio from the B. Kittredge Co. In fact, out of the five the Company received from Colt's Graham factory, he bought two; serial No's #28807 and #28808. After three years of practice, he could easily hit a six inch bull's eye at fifty yards, ninety percent of the time.

Marcus refocused on what he had to do. Belle and his boys were in trouble. He quickly donned winter gear, strapped on his snow-shoes and opened the rear door of the mud room. Jack Two peered out, growled and backed up. The terrier looked up at Marcus then retreated into the house leaving his red ball behind.

Moonlight flooded the carriage yard. A tree line off to Marcus's left lay deep in soft muted shadows. Rounded pillows of fresh snow banked up against the west side of the large walk-through stables. A wide swath of deep snow fronting a high and wide sliding barn door petered out on either side of it. Marcus was wary, for Pinkerton's analysis of the situation probably was accurate and if not, was even more deadly than he imagined. He continued to scan the area immediately around the barn, remaining invisible in a dark corner of the mud room. His eyes became focused, in tune with a baleful moonlight bathing the northern side of the mountain. A momentary flicker caught his eye as a sliver of lamplight lay for only a fraction of a heartbeat upon a snow drift. It appeared from behind a window curtain that fluttered slightly. He thought,

'Ligo's in the stables. Why is he there and armed? It's not Morley because that window would be uncovered. Besides, Morely would be down at his parents place for New Years, not in the stables freezing his skinny black butt off.'

Marcus backed up, took off his bear-paw snow-shoes and crept back into the house. Pinkerton's 'Prisoners' were still talking with animation as Marcus reappeared. Jack Two was sitting in Virginia's lap. He growled. Marcus whispered,

"Watts is armed and in the stables. He probably has company. Morley might have gone home for the festivities. What do you suggest we do Sax?" Saxton looked at Pinkerton.

"Allan, go with Virginia and get plenty of artillery up here from the basement and be quick about it. If Ligo's here, then Lucas is here as well. Packard, go shutter all the windows, bar all the doors. Then and only then, extinguish all the lanterns. Remember folks don't let anyone in except us. Break some glass if you have to. All the shutters have rifle ports in them. When you're finished, Packard, and Millie cover the front; Virginia and Allan take the back. Don't shoot unless you're absolutely sure of a kill. If there are any white bed sheets and scissors in the house Millie, go get them now. Marcus and I need camouflage. We're going to slip out and see who else has paid us an unwelcome visit."

Millie promptly returned with two large cotton bed sheets and scissors. Within minutes, Marcus and Saxton were covered in white bed sheets, each man belted with a strip of white sheet at the waist. Large eye holes were cut out but not at the mouth as to avoid their breath giving them away. Both men had wrapped their weapons in white cloth, tying them with white twine. Packard suavely remarked,

"I was wondering if the Klan were here on the mountain. Now that I've seen it, my mind cannot believe it."

Pinkerton and Virginia came back from the armory. Jack Two was locked within it. His howls of protest were silenced as Virginia closed the basement door behind her. Shortly thereafter, everyone was armed, ready and waiting for Marcus and Saxton to leave. Marcus retrieved his snow-shoes from the mudroom, barred the door and closed its black iron shutters. Both he and Saxton left by the front door and stood in deep shadows on the long, wide veranda. All along the front of the house, shutters started to close and be barred from the inside. The front door behind them vibrated as a heavy metal bar dropped into place. Lucas Garrow had waited too long. His chance of a surprise attack was spent.

Appearing as diaphanous vapors, two men slowly made their way obliquely to the stables keeping an occasional tree between it and them. Their training started to take over as they swept towards their objective. Marcus went around to the rear as Saxton glided towards the front, squatting down beside a thick tree stump fifty feet from the stable's sliding front door. Fine snow clung to him like coffin-dust. The freezing temperature was beyond endurance, but both men put on special fur lined shooting gloves connected by a string running over their shoulders and through their jacket sleeves. The tips of their gloves were cut off to facilitate firing a weapon. Saxton didn't have to wait long. Two figures emerged from the shadows of the tree line, snow-shoeing towards him. They were armed. Saxton calmly shot both of them. The sound of his Spencer boomed like a cannon as if its sound waves were caught by Zeus and thrown back to earth as a thunderbolts. Immediately, more firing erupted from all over the farm. Saxton could tell from the barrage that the village, the mill and the bunkhouse were under intense attack.

The stable's front door was thrust aside. A red delivery sled mounted on wide yellow runners and pulled by two massive horses charged out of the stable. Winking muzzle flashes erupted from each side of it as two frantic Percherons bulled their way through deepening snow drifts ribbing the barnyard. Screams were heard as the double blast of a Colt .45 found its mark. Inhuman cries of agony and unspeakable anguish came from within the stables. Two men ran out of the barn through the snow chasing the fast moving work sled. A sinuous blood trail spattered the snow behind them. Saxton shot them both. By now the sled had fled out of sight around the side of the Saxton house. Packard and Millie began firing, killing two more intruders. More shooting erupted, as the sled flew down the hill swerving back and forth wildly over the wide driveway. Skeletal chestnut trees on either side screened the intruders from the first few houses nearest them. The village church bell began ringing an alarm. Dogs howled, barked and whined as the noise of a savage battle engulfed the village.

The main road through Saxton's Village became a death trap for the sled's occupants as it careened forward. The Percherons were nearing exhaustion but the beasts continued to plow valiantly through waist deep snow. Rifle-fire poured forth from the men still alive within the heavy sled. A few wooden porches were already ablaze as an initial attack by the intruders consisted of throwing flaming torches upon the roofs of the houses, but the slate tiles thereon foiled the flames.

Once past the village, the sled paused long enough to take on more intruders. Three bodies were thrown from the sled into the snow. A horse whip popped in the moonlight as the sled surged forward once more to vanish into the forest. There, the snow was not as deep allowing it to pick up speed. Minutes later, it stopped a few yards away from the mill site. A dozen men leaped out and formed a skirmish line along either side of the village road. Anyone pursuing them would enter their trap but never leave it alive. Bullets zipped past Lucas as he ran towards the mill. Parker and Simpson yelled at him from behind a lumber wagon.

"Garrow, come over here! Over here!" Lucas limped across the road, bullets zinging past his ears. He slid to a stop. Other men crowded close to him waiting for orders. Lucas rallied his men around him. After a few moments, they charged through the falling snow towards the curing sheds. There, a hail of lead from within it and the planning mill across from it drove them behind stacks of fresh lumber. Dozens of torches had already been thrown onto the roof of the mill and curing sheds, but the slate tiles upon them repelled any efforts to burn them. A fusillade of rifle fire continued to pour down on Garrow who realized that any frontal attack on the mill was futile. He ordered his forces to split into two and encircle the mill but it soon became apparent that their efforts were doomed to failure. Harmony Farm was a fortress, its defenders resolute and well prepared.

Meanwhile, the black and tan Percherons had bolted for the open doors of a nearby barn, dragging the heavy sled behind them. It slewed back and forth over the slick surface of the barnyard, its wide runners unable to come to grips with patches of black ice. A solid stone well blocked its path. As the team tried desperately to avoid it, the sled caromed into it, upsetting onto its side. The horses became tangled up in their traces. One had broken its rear leg against the tongue shaft and was screaming piteously. The other, wild with terror began rearing up beside it. Two rifle shots rang out from within the barn. Both animals dropped, one falling on top of the other. A large and growing pool of blood stained the snow near them as one animal in its death throes, thrashed the other's rib cage into a bloody pulp with its iron-shod hooves. Another shot killed it instantly. As its last breath wafted skyward, the beast quivered then expired.

Amidst the death and destruction, furtive figures swarmed out of the barn and from behind the mill. They struggled up the hill towards the Brown house; fanning out in a wide pincer-like movement. Inside the house, Belle, Cotton and Rufus were trapped. Belle thought she had prepared well for this moment. But now she had her doubts as Marcus was not with her. She'd heard shots being fired down at the village. The sounds were somewhat muted by the falling snow. Her telegraph message to Saxton's house remained unanswered as well as her attempts to contact the other buildings. She knew then that the telegraph wires had been cut. Belle was really worried. She and everyone else on the farm knew that someday, Lucas, being totally insane; would be out of control when he realized that his attempts at legalized revenge were for naught.

For Belle, it was as if the archangel Lucifer had descended onto the farm. Despite all the precautions, Harmony Farm was under a well organized and disciplined attack. Belle realized that someone must have betrayed them. A growing realization that it might be Ligo Watts shook her to the core, for he was the only person on the farm that was connected to Garrow in any way whatsoever. The thought of it made her ill as an image of a Trojan horse appeared in her mind. She stood tall, her eyes looking through the iron shutters of the Grand Salon. In the dining room next to her, Rufus was busy loading five Spencers with ammunition. His brother, Cotton was upstairs in the master bedroom. Belle watched as over a dozen apparitions carrying blazing torches snow-shoed up the hill towards her. She waited until they were too close to miss. She screamed,

"They're here boys. Fire! Fire!" She turned slightly and looked up at a painting of Christ on the cross.

Belle began praying, "Hail Mary full of grace…."

Bullets whined through a gun port next to her, shattering a gilt wall mirror. She heard the veranda in front of her go up in a fiery explosion for the intruders already knew that the roofs were impervious to fire. Rufus yelled,

"I got one mommy, I got one!" The boy continued to fire at anything that moved. More firing erupted upstairs, where Cotton laid down a withering barrage on anyone that snow-shoed towards the house. He noticed that his ammunition was running low. He screamed,

"Rufus, I'm out of ammo. Get up here with more now. Hurr..!" Cotton spun about, wounded in the shoulder. He'd been shot.

Downstairs in the dining room, Belle continued to fire five Spencer rifles. Methodically, she aimed, held her breath and fired, time and time again. Within minutes, the veranda in front of Belle was fully ablaze, limiting her ability to see her targets clearly. The bunkhouse below her spit rifle fire from its many gun ports for the men within it were well armed and shot the intruders as they attacked the one story fortress. It was well constructed of field stone, built in a square around an inner courtyard, lined by narrow windows and a wide veranda. All exterior walls were two feet thick with no windows. Its roof tiles were slate. Two wide iron gates barred either end of the compound. It was proving to be formidable. However, that was not to be the case where Belle and her two boys were desperately trying to stay alive.

Belle shouted over her shoulder. "I need more ammo Rufus! Do you have any left?"

Her son careened down the staircase then screamed as a bullet found its mark. Rufus fell down. Strangely silent, he crawled towards Belle skirting a pile of empty ammo boxes. A thin trail of blood stained the carpet behind him. Belle looked down, pulled him close, and examined his bloody leg. He cried,

"No Momma, I don't have any more, just what's in these rifles." She grimaced.

"Rufus, you're shot in your right leg. Go get a tablecloth from the dining room and rip it up. Put a tourniquet above it and tie it tight before you bleed to death. Can you do that?" He nodded. A round of bullets splattered against the shutters at the rear of the house.

Rufus turned about and painfully crawled to the dining room a few feet away as his mother returned to her duties. He could hear her curse behind him. Rufus pulled the linen tablecloth off the long table. A large floral bouquet upon it crashed down beside him. He ripped off a long narrow piece of damask table cloth and wrapped it tightly around his left thigh then tied it off by holding one in his teeth. The tourniquet was immediately soaked through with fresh blood. Rufus grabbed a Spencer, and stood up, using it as a cane. He hobbled back to his mother. From down the hallway behind them, came the sound of slate tiles crashing onto the floor. Rufus screamed,

"Oh momma, they're comin' through the kitchen roof. They'll get past the back door that way. I've got to stop them."

Belle watched him limp away. She turned about and continued to fire through the shutters. Cotton came bounding down the stairs, sliding to a stop beside her. She whirled around ready to shoot but at the last second recognized him.

"I'm outta ammo mother. Got any left?" Belle yelled over the roar of the raging fire outside and bullets plinking off the iron shutters next to her.

"Your brother needs you. Here's a 45. Get to the mudroom fast. Now git Cotton!"

He did so as if he was running for his life but he was too late. The back door was wide open. Three men stood over his brother's lifeless body. Cotton, in a rage, fired, killing two of them. A man fired back. Cotton fell down over his brother's body. A tall man stepped over the bodies then crabbed his way down the hallway towards the grand salon. Belle heard the shot. She knew that sound was not from one of their guns. Before Belle could turn around, she felt the hot muzzle of a gun pressing hard against the back of her head. Behind her a deep voice with a distinct southern drawl growled,

"Drop the rifle bitch and git up real slow like. Don't do anything stupid or I will kill you."

Belle rose slowly and turned around. There before her stood Lucas. Flames from outside the house flickered through a gun port behind her, painting her son's face with splotches of reds, yellows and pinks. Lucas backed away from her as if she was a leper. He screamed at her, his face twisted by hate.

"How dare you call me your son!"

He pistol-whipped Belle, but she stood her ground. Blood streamed down her right cheek. Her eyes bore into his, unrelenting in their pursuit of a conscience. They found none. At that moment, Belle knew her son was mad and that she was going to die. Her right hand flew out in a blur and clawed his face savagely, while the other raked his neck leaving a deep bloody gash across it. Lucas tried to shoot her point blank but his .44 S&W misfired. Belle brushed it aside and started fighting for her life. Her son was younger, bigger and definitely stronger but in the early moments of the struggle Belle prevailed until she was overpowered from behind. Lucas stepped back, glaring at her. He hissed,

"Harry, strip Nichols; get her into his boots and parka then tie her up. She'll be a hostage along with any others we can take along. We've just enough time to get down to the boats. From what I've seen and heard, our attack on the farm has failed. We'll have to get down-river to Bridgeport fast. Saxton and Marcus are still alive, maybe wounded, but they won't dare attack us if they know we've got Belle." He laughed.

"I'll leave a note to that effect right now." Lucas ran down the hall searching for an office.

A dozen men crowded into the grand salon. Dressed, and bound, Belle was pushed down the hallway. She nearly tripped over two bodies lying in the wreckage of her kitchen. Cotton and Rufus lay lifeless amongst broken roofing tiles strewn about on the bloody floor, Belle screamed,

"You killed them; you killed my boys, YOU BASTARD!" Harry dragged her kicking and screaming through the mudroom door to a cutter waiting outside. Moments later Lucas climbed in beside her.

"Well bitch we're on our way. Too bad your nigger babies are dead. I could have used them too."

Belle's eyes moistened as flames consumed her home. She started to struggle but Lucas slapped her hard. He reached into a pocket, withdrew a rag, balled it up and shoved it into her mouth. She sat there moaning, tears running over the welts rising on her face. Beneath the mask of despair however, was an iron will. Another man leaped into the cutter saying,

"We didn't find a safe or any valuables at all Lucas. We ripped up all the mattresses, clothes and smashed every possible hiding place in the house. We tried to find a safe but we had to get out 'cause the place was comin' down round our ears. C'mon Garrow, let's get the hell out of here."

As he said it, Belle smiled. She'd remembered to put on her "Gettin' out of town real quick dress' as the shooting started. The men on either side of her were unaware of three million dollars in jewels sitting between them.

Saxton's villagers ran out into the snow as Marcus and Saxton came towards them in a long piano-box cutter. A few minutes earlier, Marcus found Morley and Ligo. He put their bodies in the cutter. Four intruders that died near the stables and by the front of the house were also in the cutter. All were covered by a black tarp. The intruders were stripped of their white winter gear, snow-shoes and firearms. Marcus's cutter flew off down the hill towards the village. Upon arrival in the village, the bodies were unloaded and put beside other dead arrayed down the middle of the main street. While there, Marcus and Saxton put on the intruder's white winter gear for if they'd done so earlier, they would have been shot. Saxton began issuing orders as Marcus sped away in the cutter accompanied by two Rangers. Marcus was headed home. He lashed out at the team as gunshots continued to boom out far ahead of him. Saxton watched the cutter vanish into the forest.

Meanwhile, he was pleased to find out that the villagers had prevailed. Sadly, Tyler Wicks and one of the Rangers were dead, shot in the back while trying to save Ligo's family from being burned alive. Marie Watts was consumed by grief and fury. She'd no idea what-soever, that her husband was a spy. For that she hated him; her rage beyond comprehension as she cursed in Gaelic over her husband. She then walked over to the bodies of the twenty villagers including nine children. Once there, she wailed over them. A Gaelic dirge, the Caoine, rose up and around her. The effect was unearthly as if the dead had become a chorus of mourners singing behind her.

Saxton continued to assess the situation. He never imagined he would suffer so. Prison made him immune to suffering or so he'd thought. He wept over the bodies, especially those of Bobby, a Ranger and the 'Shell Man' himself, Tyler Wicks. Reverend Tillman came over to comfort him.

"Saxton, you cannot blame yourself for what happened. You did everything you could to protect them, giving them something to strive for; an ideal, a dream. They did not die in vain, for the dispossessed and desperate never do if someone loved them. You allowed them to live in dignity; respected and loved by their families and friends. No, do not tear yourself apart but give thanks to God for allowing those that survived to feel God's love by joining as one to build a better world for them and all of their children forever more. Today can be and will be a New Year and a new beginning."

Saxton agreed. He climbed into another cutter then stood tall on the driver's bench telling everyone to gather around. He spoke with a sense of hope, invigorated by their courage and determination.

"Ladies and gentlemen, the worst may be over here but I can still hear gunfire off by the mill site. Rangers are roaming the woods around us looking for enemy stragglers. Those of you who are armed, I want half of you to patrol the village. Your wives and children must stay armed and vigilant behind barred doors and windows until the church bell rings again. The rest of you men, dress warmly, bring your weapons, and assemble back here in five minutes. Oh, and don't forget lanterns. We might be going into the cave."

While Saxton waited, Reverend Tillman and Father Manilow came forward. Olapa baptized them in her soft light. There was an awkward silence as the two pious men stood before him. They looked at each other then Father Manilow nodded. He coughed nervously.

"John Saxton, I have a confession to make. I think the Virgin Mary killed an intruder at the church."

"How so Father?"

"She fell on him, all five hundred pounds of her." Saxton came closer to the priest, his hand resting on the man's shoulder. He looked into the priest's blue eyes. They locked.

"Was she pushed?"

Father Manilow bowed his head and declined to comment. Reverend Tillman stepped forward.

"Well Saxton, I do believe I shot a man in the rectory."

They both waited, heads bowed. Saxton grinned.

"My, my Otis, in the rectory you say; how painful it must have been!"

He stood back, facing both of them.

"Were both of you men of the cloth defending yourselves?" They answered in sync.

"Yes"

Saxton managed to retain his solemn composure, but barely. He murmured.

"Well then Father, return to the church with the Reverend and two armed men. See to it that those unfortunate souls are as dead as you say they are. If not, see to their wounds then bring them both to the jail. Are you two finished here?" Tillman replied,

"No we are not. We have yet to say prayers for the dead and administer the last rites to the dying. We'll announce a midnight mass and a prayer meeting of thanks for our survival and mourn those who died here tonight. In the meantime while more bodies are being laid out in the street, we'll ask God for strength and guidance in this terrible time. Won't we Father?"

Saxton watched as armed villagers returned under the flickering light of many torches. He climbed back up onto the cutter's seat. Saxton looked down upon them, steadfast and ready. As he looked down upon them, his hat in his hand, he cried,

"Men, I want to thank you for defending your families so courageously tonight. I know that some of you lost loved ones tonight. This war is not over yet. You men standing before me have faced death before on many battlefields only a short time ago. You now have to drive out the invaders who might still be on the mountain, after which I promise you we will rebuild Harmony Farm and carry on for our children's future. As for the dead who died defending our dream, we will always cherish their supreme sacrifice and will forevermore honor them. Now let's go and do our duty as God intended. Amen."

Thirty armed men, snow-shoed towards the distant mill behind Saxton as he sped slowly forward in his cutter. He looked back. Otis Tillman was praying loudly over the dead. He cried out over those who knelt down on either side of the deceased as they lay there embraced by Olapa. He raised his arms and cried out,

"Oh thank you almighty God for delivering us from evil here tonight. Hallelujah! Hallelujah! May the living be comforted with the knowledge that their dearly departed are now blessed with eternal peace. Amen!"

Father Manilow stepped forward, making the Signum Crusis as he did so. His voice like a spring freshet passing over loose stones began with the words.

"Our Father who art in Heaven, hallowed be thy name." He paused.

"Pater Noster, qui es in cael is, sanctificetun nomen tuum. Adveniaet regnum tuum. Fiat voluntas tua, sicut in caelo et in terra. Panem nostrum quotidianum da nobis hodie, et dimitte nobis debitanostra sicut et nos dimittimus debitonribus nostris. Et ne nos inducas in tentationem sed libera nos a malo. Amen." He continued.

"In the name of the Father and of the Son and of the Holy Ghost, Amen"

"In nomine Patris, et Filii, et Spiritus Sancti. Amen."

The holy men remained with their heads bowed as both Baptists and Catholics rose and went about their duties. The dead were put into a large sled to be taken to the Church followed by the Priest and the Reverend. The bodies were laid out in the snow and guarded throughout the night. When that sorry deed was done, the 'Dead Sled' made its way back up the hill to the Saxton stables. It would return to collect even more bodies in the morning.

BOOK THREE: CHAPTER 15
RIVER OF RESURRECTION

The Pinkerton brothers commandeered seven wooden drift boats from Braswell's Shipyards. In fact, Sam Braswell and his two sons, Peter and Gabriel volunteered to go with them, but the Marshalls insisted that they would rather have them call out the city's militia instead. William Pinkerton cried out to Samuel Braswell as he pushed off into the Tennessee River,

"Now Sam, don't forget to have them bring our mounts round to Brown's Ferry."

They agreed and waved goodbye as the drift boats were swept away upon the snowy bosom of the water. Their surly helmsmen, just minutes before, were carousing in a local waterfront bar getting a head start on the New Year's Eve festivities. They'd all been pressed into service at gun point. They were not happy.

The flotilla passed under a railway bridge, rounded Moccasin Point by the Craven yards then swung over to Brown's Ferry landing, tying up beside a long scow. It was four o'clock in the afternoon. A solitary drift boat continued downriver. It beached itself on the other side of Williams Island past Burris Bar across the river from Pitchfork Cave. Two US Marshalls scrambled ashore, armed with Sharp's sniping rifles. Through dense brush, they snowshoed across the island to where they thought was a safe hiding place.

That afternoon, another more powerful blizzard hit Elder Mountain in gale force for five hours and there was no sign whatsoever of it abating. In fact it intensified as it moved onwards to the east. The Pinkerton brothers clambered out of their drift boat onto the ferry scow. It was deserted and covered with two feet of snow. The scow rocked at its moorings as strong river currents played with it. Big John Lowry swore,

"Christ almighty I can't find that Struther Jones nowhere. I swear I'll shoot the son of bitch. How are we goin' to get the ferry back across the river?"

The answer came from behind some bushes. Two men left their hiding place, holding their hands high as they approached the posse. One of them, a taller black man said,

"Marshall, my name is Elwood Dix and I'm a deckhand for Struther Jones here. We run the ferry for Mr. Darwin. He threatened to kill us and our families if we didn't do as we was told to." Struther Jones, his white feral face pale yet alert, chimed in.

"In fact we was ahidin' from Mr. Darwin, not you boys. So I hope you understand cause we'll need some protectin' sure enough."

The two ferrymen remained where they were, stamping their frozen boots in the snow. The posse turned as one and looked across the river. There had been a sudden break in the storm. Big John Lowery stood up in his stirrups. He laughed,

"Well boys, I'll be damned if the whole Chattanooga Militia ain't waitin' over yonder!"

As everyone looked, the opposite bank of the river was swarming with militia, guns, wagons, sleighs, sleds, mounted cavalry and a Gatling gun bolted to a sled. Seconds later, the blizzard closed in as if white curtains were drawn across a stage. William Pinkerton spoke to the ferrymen standing forlornly before him.

"Now look you two, a Marshall will accompany you back across the river. Once you've finished here, you go back and wait. By the way, where did Darwin go anyway?"

They pointed to Elder Mountain.

"Good. Now boys, if we need you, we'll fire three shots. Do you understand?" They nodded then ran to the ferry. William could hear them arguing amongst themselves.

:Struther Jones, you lyin' son of a bitch. You damn near got us both kilt." Pinkerton smiled then addressed the posse.

"Before you go anywhere men, we'll have to shovel the snow off the ferry." He yelled,

"Hey Struther, are there any shovels, wide boards or rakes here abouts." Jones ran back to a small shed hidden in the trees. Half an hour later, the ferry deck was clear. William Pinkerton said,

"Better get going Jones. Big John will go with you two and see to it that you both earn your pardon?"

Lowry grinned and climbed aboard. Within moments the ferry was scudding back across the Tennessee River. After watching it leave, a Marshall walked up and asked Robert Pinkerton,

"Are we gonna wait for the Militia or go on?"

"No Nigel, we'll stay here and rest. It won't be more than an hour before we'll be on our way. They're bringing our horses for us and two doctors, Dr. Lapsey Green and Dr. Mary Edwards Walker from the orphanage in town. The farm will need her as nearly seventy children live there I've been told by Lapsley. Some might be orphaned by now, God forbid." One of the older Marshalls swore saying,

"I don't want no goddamned woman doctorin' me, no siree! Women are suppos'd to stay home, cook and raise kids. Why the hell is a woman doctoring anyways?" They all laughed until William Pinkerton said,

"Any of you boys fought for the Union?" Most of the men nodded.

"Anybody won any medals?"

Two raised their hands. One of them was the bigot. Pinkerton asked him,

"Stand up here and tell them what medal you won."

The man paused, looked around and said proudly,

"I'm George McFee and I won a campaign medal for survivin' Gettysburg. That I did."

Pinkerton smiled and said,

"Well George, Dr. Mary E. Walker, was a prisoner of war, a Union spy and an Army Surgeon who won the Congressional Medal of Honor. From now on, I don't want anyone talking badly of Dr. Walker. Have I made myself clear?" To a man they yelled,

"Yes Sir!"

An hour later the ferry returned with their mounts, two doctors and a Captain Hagen of the local Chattanooga Militia. The Marshalls swarmed aboard to retrieve their mounts. Moments later the ferry was going back for more men and supplies. The Captain of the militia walked up to the Pinkertons leading his horse. He declared grandly,

"I'm Captain Bill Hagen and who might be in charge of this here posse?" William looked down from his mount.

"We are. My name's William and my brother here is Robert Pinkerton. Glad to meet you Captain. What's on your mind sir?" The Captain laughed, his black face swelling up as he did so.

"Yesiree, it must be true that you boys never sleep. Where's your old man? Is he still writin' bout his adventures? Why I've read all his books. Where is he? Last time I saw him, I was a buck private in Boston?" Robert pointed into the blizzard,

"He is up on Elder Mountain and is in grave danger. Have you been briefed yet?" Captain Hagen laughed,

"Why hell's bell's, I was told to hightail it to the ferry on the double. Old man Braswell tried to come with us but in the stampede to git here, I seen 'im get bucked off his horse into a snow drift. My Sergeant went back to see if he was ok and he was. I guess he was madder than a wet hen."

They all laughed and talked as they waited for the ferry to come back again. Soon after, it appeared out of the blinding snow preparing to dock. William said,

"Captain Hagen I'll tell you all about it after the rest of your company arrives in a few minutes. I'm glad you're wearing winter gear because this emergency is two-fold. First of all, we'll have to survive the blizzard and secondly, we'll have to fight over thirty well armed and determined zealots. A lot is at stake. We suspect that there just might be a very large and sophisticated counterfeiting ring operating inside Pitchfork Cave downstream from us. Secondly, the criminal in charge of it is none other than Lucas Darwin; formerly known as Lucas Garrow." The Captain swore,

"Jesus H. Christ! Why, I've heard that name before. I do believe a confederate Major named Garrow was hung by the Rebs in Richmond for murder, desertion and a number of other horrid crimes. If his son is anythin' like his bastard father, we're in for a real scrap." Robert Pinkerton was very worried; his face dark and foreboding.

"My father's on the mountain Captain, visiting John Saxton and Marcus Brown and their families. Apparently they're old friends from before the war. Do you know them and if so, what kind of men are they?" Captain Hagen was surprised, saying,

"In that respect Robert, I'm glad Saxton and Brown are on the mountain 'cause they were my commanders during the war." Robert Pinkerton hesitated then exclaimed,

"You were a Maasai Ranger weren't you?" Captain Hagen stood in his stirrups. He replied to the assembled group in general,

"Yesiree boys, we were the best there was and no two finer men walk on God's green earth today than John Saxton and Marcus Brown. They'll keep 'em busy til we get there, don't you worry none." His voice changed, becoming hard, cold and deadly,

"You just tell us boys what to do Gen'rl and by God it will be done! But first I want you to know that I'm comin' with whoever is goin' to the cave. Lieutenant Wilson behind me here will take the rest of the militia to Massengale Point." Robert Pinkerton agreed.

Sherriff Springfield moved over towards Hagen. His deeply weathered face had seen many storms before. He spit out a stream of chewing tobacco into the snow and drawled,

"If I was you Capt'n, you'd better skedaddle right quick before it gits real dark! That Lucas Garrow's got a good head start on us and he's plum crazy to boot." He swung his horse about and yelled,

"Hey, you Pinkerton's, tell us what to do before we freeze to death a sittin' here jawin'. Besides, I hear that old man Craven and John Read are goin' to have a fireworks competition at midnight tonight at Fountain Square and I'll be damned if I'm gonna miss that pissin' contest!"

Another stream of brown liquid hit a nearby snow drift as the ferry unloaded its last cargo of men then pulled away into the blizzard as Marshall 'Big' John Lowry jumped ashore. Spare horses, sleighs, sleds piled high with ammo, snow shoes, pup tents, portable stoves, horse feed, rations, sacks of coal, medical supplies and a Gatling gun on a sled were hustled off the dock towards them. Robert Pinkerton stood up in his stirrups and spoke to Captain Hagen, his militia, the two Doctors and the Marshalls, saying brusquely.

"Everyone here today is to be commended for rallying to our support. We have a madman and over thirty of his henchmen who my brother and I think are about to attack the farm on the mountain above us. In these conditions the attack will be unexpected, swift and deadly. Their leader is Lucas Garrow who's suspected of killing his wife a few days ago. Not only that, he's purported to be the head of the largest counterfeiting ring in American history. From papers and notes found in a secret drawer in his desk in Nashville, we now know he intends to flood the country with millions of counterfeit bills and has started doing so already. I don't have to alarm your astute imaginations any further as to the consequences. My brother and I want him dead or alive, it doesn't matter."

He paused as the group started talking amongst themselves. Big John Lowry spoke up.

"Men, there are roughly three hundred men, women and children up there on the farm. For the most part all are former enlisted men, well trained and well armed. The farm as you know has been under all forms of attack by Garrow but has so far the Saxton-Browns have successfully resisted his attempts to overthrow it. They must have prepared well for such a day as this, as they knew Garrow would eventually exhaust every option except brute force. So, as planned, here are red arm bands for all of you so that they don't shoot you. The password is Harmony; so don't forget it."

Captain Bill Hagen conferred with the Pinkerton's before giving orders.

"Now men, as to our assault, Lieutenant Wilson will take the militia and Doctor Walker over Pan Gap to Massengale Point across from Kelly's Ferry, just in case Garrow tries to escape downriver through the rapids. They'll shoot a red flare if the gang goes downriver, a green one if they go back upriver. I hope we can see them. The rest of you split into two groups. One will go downriver to a point just upstream from the cave entrance. Big John here and four Marshalls will scout ahead on the shoreline trace in case there are any bushwhackers. If any of the gang tries to escape, move in, arrest them or shoot them if they resist."William Pinkerton concluded.

"The rest of you, my brother and I and the doctors here, will head for the road to Harmony Farm. Are there any questions?" He waited. No one moved.

"Good, then let's out of here. God bless you all and good luck. I hope we're not too late. From what I've heard lately, If Lucas takes the mountain redoubt, an army will have trouble recapturing it. Let's go!"

With that, the men scrambled through the snow, mounting their horses or trudging off towards their appointed drift boats. Six drift boats, each steered by a seasoned river pilot from Braswell's and rowed by conscripts splashed out onto the river. Silence, entombed by falling snow fell upon the ferry landing as the boats drifted away on the river.

An hour later the Pinkertons, Doctor Lapsley, Sheriff Springfield and five Marshalls arrived at the lower gatehouse. Tom and Terry were there to greet them. Tom, a big strapping white boy ran forward, his rifle pointed at them.

He shouted, "Stop, whoever you are. The farm is closed to all visitors."

Dr. Green got out of the sleigh. Tom recognized him instantly. Green calmed him down as Terry, a black boy, came out from behind a tree, a cocked rifle in his gloved hands. Both men were shivering as they led the group into the warmth within the gatehouse. Tom and Terry had returned early that morning because Dr. Boyd their dentist was closed for the holiday. This happened just before Garrow and his men crossed the river. The Marshalls examined the gatehouse thoroughly. The stove was hot, it's iron cheeks orange from the heat within it. Tom gave William a note he'd found lying on the kitchen table. William read it. His breath stopped. He turned to Robert,

"I have a bad feeling about this brother. This note says that two guards were found here shot to death. The note also goes on to say that, Tom and Terry are to stay here after coming back from the dentist. He turned to Ned Wilbur,

"Ned, you and Sheriff Springfield stay here with Tom and Terry and keep the stove going. Stay alert. You never know if Lucas will come this way. My brother and I will take the rest in sleighs up the road. No one but me and my party is to go up the mountain. The rest

of you Marshalls will bull a path through the snow ahead of us. But first I'll try the telegraph."
Terry said,

"Mr. Pinkerton, the line's been cut. I tried to fix it but I couldn't climb the pole. William replied,

"It's Ok Terry; we'll try to get up to the farm as quick as we can."

He turned to Mary and Lapsley.

"Are you two ready? They nodded. With that, their sleighs began following a twisting trampling in deep snow as they ascended the mountain. Dusk set in compounding the danger as the blizzard continued unrestrained. Even on a sunny day, the twisting mountain road was entombed by deep shadows. A Marshall was called back, to guide the two sleighs ever upwards through a perilous white-out. A mile further up, the storm subsided; revealing a bright full moon. Its pearlescent beams streamed through the woody fingers of a leafless forest, magnifying their presence as black streaks crisscrossing the road ahead. This beaten path became visible as it gradually unfolded around every bend. However this beautiful rapture was shattered as the resonance of distant gunfire and booming explosions ricocheted off the limestone cliffs about them.

The Maasai leapt out of the sled as he and his men came under fire from the intruder's skirmish line. Bill Curry scrambled over to him behind the sled, its team neighing in fear of the gunfire erupting about them.

"What's next Marcus?" The Maasai could see a red glow through a veil of falling snow. It was his house and his family was in it. He had to save them. He had to. He yelled,

"Curry, take the men, fan out and keep 'em pinned down. I'm gonna skirt around them, try to kill as many as I can, then go home before my family burns alive. Curry was about to say something but Marcus was gone. The woods resonated with the crackle of rifle fire as men struggled to stay alive and kill. Screams and cries for mercy rang out nearby as Curry knew exactly where Marcus had gone. The intruder's withering fire died down until only a whimper was left. With nothing more to worry about, Bill Curry and his men moved on, using the woods as cover on their way to the mill site.

Marcus snow-shoed up the hill as his mind began moving three steps ahead of his body. The heavy Buntline swung like a metronome, grasped in his left hand. Bodies littered the slopes around him. Some cried out just before Marcus shot them. A manic rage overcame the giant man as he flayed about in the deep snow. Ahead of him a muted fiery glow accompanied by a muffled roaring spilled forth through the body of the storm and into his mind. Only one thing mattered...Belle and his boys. In his haste to rescue his family, he didn't see a small note impaled on a stick in a snow bank.

As Marcus struggled ever closer, the heat from the Brown's burning veranda became oppressively intense but the fire so far had failed to burn down the rest of the house. Shuttered windows along the front of the house began to shatter. Marcus backed away, his hand over his face, the buntline pointed straight up like a sword. Three men ran up to him. Scotty Watkins yelled,

"Marcus, let's go round the back!"

All four ran around to the mudroom door. The fire had not reached there yet. They tried to force the door open but something or someone was blocking it. The iron shutters near it were closed and locked. Frustrated, Marcus raced back around to the front of the house. There, the fire raged like a wild beast before him. It was if the Tvaso lion was once again roaring and pawing the snow, daring him to attack. Flaming beams and boards from the veranda crashed down, littering the snow with charred debris and broken roofing tiles. A molten heat singed the white wolf hair that trimmed his parka. Marcus raged within as he knew his sons were probably in the basement hidey-hole unable to escape. The rest of his men came running up the hill towards him. Bill Curry grabbed Marcus and pulled him away.

"Christ almighty Marcus, don't you even think about it. You'll burn to death if you try."

Some say that facing one's fears defines who they are. Others say fear is like a mirage. Run towards it and it will retreat, just out of reach but still visible.

The Maasai took off his snow-shoes then screamed, "Samahani—forgive me!"

He threw Curry down onto the snow, turned about and ran straight towards the flames. His men watched in horror as Marcus's parka flared up in a ring of flames as he bounded up the front steps. Fire wrapped its red arms around him. The gaping doorway swallowed him whole. Instantly the entire façade behind him collapsed with a roar, making it impossible for his stricken companions to attempt any rescue. They fell back in disarray, paralyzed by fear.

Marcus rolled headfirst through the door like a rubber ball. He bounced to his feet, his Buntline clutched in his left hand. Marcus bounded down the stairs to the basement. The hidey hole was empty. He barely made it back upstairs in time, for the conflagration had spread into the grand salon. Heavy smoke, dense and dark was being sucked into the foyer of the house through the open front door and numerous gun ports. Long velveteen curtains in the grand salon caught fire, flared up, to be consumed within seconds. Marcus regained his equilibrium and raced for the rear of the house. There, in the mudroom he found Cotton lying across his brother's body. Both were jammed against the back door. He reached down and pulled Cotton away from Rufus. They'd been shot. Marcus unbarred the door, opened it, reached down and dragged Rufus out onto the snow. Immediately Marcus turned back for Cotton. Bill Curry raced by him. Seconds later he emerged carrying Cotton's lifeless body. The boy groaned; he was barely alive. His father stumbled down the backstairs, falling face down on the snow as the whole house seemed to implode upon itself behind him. Curry dropped Cotton onto a snow bank then ran over to Marcus.

The Maasai was horribly burned about his face, neck and hand. His heavy parka and thick woolen trousers however saved his body from the full fury of the flames. Everyone moved away from the towering pyre towards the stables. Marcus struggled to stand up. He stood mute, pointing to his boys. His men understood instantly. Cotton and Rufus were immediately taken to the stables, loaded onto a Portland sleigh and rushed to the infirmary in the village. As the sleigh's team thrashed its way down the drive, Marcus gathered his men together. One of them ran up with a ragged piece of paper clenched in his gloved fist. He thrust it at Marcus saying,

"They've got Belle and they've gone into the cave. If we follow them, Lucas says that she's gonna die"

Marcus gasped, the buntline dropped beside him as he toppled onto a drift of snow. A terrible wailing issued from him...

"Belle, Belle, I must, mus, mu......"

Moments later, Saxton saw a Portland sleigh come towards him as his group made their way towards the mill. A sleigh containing Cotton and Rufus whispered to a halt nearby. Cotton was wounded but not as seriously as he looked. However Rufus was dead. Cotton was crying, his brother's head in his lap. Saxton ran towards him. Cotton insisted on going with him but Saxton could not allow it. Just then another sleigh with Marcus aboard swept silently towards them. It stopped briefly. Saxton's mind was stupefied. The terrible burns his friend suffered; transfixed him. He cried as the sleighs then sped away into the open jaws of the forest. He screamed, "Follow me!"

A battered Saxton and his army stopped before the mill site. It was littered with the dead and dying but still its steam was up. Saxton assigned some men to keep its boilers going, guard the nearby curing and sorting sheds and take the wounded by sled back to the infirmary. The rest of the men ran towards the bunkhouse. Upon their arrival, its tall iron gates opened and all those within ran out.

Two had been shot dead; one was Hudson, Sweet Daphne's oldest boy. She stood there in the snow sobbing as her other son, Little Willie pleaded with Saxton to let him avenge his brother's death. However, Sweet Daphne held him fast saying,

"The Lord's will be done. I've lost two and I won't lose my only reason for living. No, son stay here and live for vengeance is mine saith the Lord."

Saxton drove his sleigh up the hill to the Brown's burning house. Bill Curry stopped him halfway there and showed him the note. Saxton had to make a decision and fast. Should he go and risk everyone's life or should he try to save Belle's? He knew that a few well armed men within the confines of the cave could hold off an army indefinitely. Besides, Lucas would know immediately if he was being followed and would kill Belle, that much was certain. Saxton sent two men to the upper cave entrance anyway. Even if he got into the cave, Lucas was smart enough to lay out a whole series of booby traps that would shoot, stab, impale or bite its unwary victims. No, there had to be a better way. Bill Curry and his men climbed aboard the sleigh. Saxton lashed the horses as he sped back to the bunkhouse. Once there, he explained the situation to the men and asked if anyone had a solution. The mill foreman did. His name was Eldin Crease.

Belle was no longer gagged but was still tightly bound and prodded with the business end of a rifle as a dozen men wound their way down through the belly of Elder Mountain. The air about them was surprisingly warm, acrid and humid; totally alien to what she had experienced the first and only time she'd been in the cave a few years before. Why? Behind them, the iron door which opened inwards was blocked by heavy stones keeping it shut. Lucas was certain that no one could break through it let alone in time. His laughter echoed throughout the chamber as he pulled Belle by a short rope behind him. He'd turn around occasionally and say,

"Mother, you must keep up with me now or I will hurt you my dear. I'm sure your nigger blood has over many generations made you immune to such violence."

Occasionally, Lucas would cut her face with a small whip. Belle never cried out when he did. This act of defiance infuriated him. After a few such incidents, even his loyal followers became sickened by his deprivations. One had the temerity to ask Lucas if Belle really was his mother. Garrow slit the man's throat then casually pushed the body into a deep declivity nearby used as a latrine. Once again his insane laughter echoed about the caverns that swallowed them.

To Belle, it seemed that an eternity passed until their lamps revealed a vast underground factory busily printing millions of dollars of counterfeit money. Her ears hurt for the persistent throbbing of two steam engines was deafening, its reverberations amplified by the rock walls of the cavity into which it had been thrust. Five Victory presses connected in tandem by leather belts, clattered and clanked, adding to the din. She looked about, shocked by the scene below her. Any smoke and steam had been cleverly and efficiently vented through pipes drilled from beneath through the roof of the cavern. Large metal drums filled with kerosene served as lanterns. Ringing the walls on every side; their wavering wicks cast tenuous fans of radiant light above them.

Four colliers were shovelling coal into two boilers. A duo of broad flywheels grasped by wide leather belts operated two massive leather bellows. As they wheezed through their contractions, they sucked in fresh air from the original air vent in the roof making the heat in the edifice barely tolerable. Belle's eyes and throat were sorely vexed by the pungent fumes of guano dust intermingled with vapors rising from vats of acid and smoking kerosene lanterns. She continued to suffer although those around her seemed immune.

Below her, millions of dollars in counterfeit money were stowed in waterproof rubber bladders. These in turn were being loaded into five long drift boats by a gang of sweating men. A swarthy pressman came forward and showed Lucas two metal plates for the 1874 version of the US fifty dollar bill. One had a picture of Benjamin Franklin on the left while the other had an allegorical figure of Lady Liberty on the obverse. He also handed Garrow two plates for the slightly revised 1878 silver certificate. Lucas was pleased, very pleased. He handed them back and said gleefully,

"Take them aboard along with the other plates. Are the boats loaded up now?" They were.

"Good! Everything else we'll leave behind. Shut her down right after the boats have been launched Clayton." The man ran away to do his bidding looking over his shoulder at Belle.

Lucas pulled her towards him. She fell into his arms. The scent of rosewater drifted upwards into his face. Mother and son looked deeply into each other's eyes. For an instant Lucas felt her heart beat against his chest as his hands slowly massaged her buttocks. His groin began to harden. She felt it and struggled, trying to get away from him. He released her.

"Once a whore, always a whore aren't you mother! I'm quite sure by now that you know what I'm capable of, don't you?"

He pulled out a long bloody knife and reached for her long hair, but as he did so, her boot lashed out, putting him off balance. Garrow staggered backwards, the knife falling from his hand. Only the quick reflexes of the animal within saved him from falling into a vat of acid directly beneath him. Upon regaining his balance, Lucas pulled Belle roughly to her feet. His whip sent a spatter of blood droplets against the limestone wall behind her. Belle spit in his face. Garrow wiped it off, his reptilian eyes glittering in the lamplight. He backed away, gagged her once more then pulled her along as the troupe continued down some wooden stairs towards the cave entrance.

Once there, Lucas dragged Belle to a drift boat. He pushed her into it and tied her to a wide board seat. It was the first in a long row of dories resting on iron cradles. Each boat was about twenty feet long, six feet wide, with high sloping sides, with a slightly curved bottom pointed at both ends. They weighed over a ton each and were packed with two tons of counterfeit money, food, weapons and munitions. A long steering sweep at the narrow stern sat between two wooden pegs. Two rows of rowing pegs or tholes lined both sides of the craft, each pair set forward from three plank seats. Three metal bailing scoops tied to the boat by twine, were spaced along its length. Two sets of long oars and a spare were stowed under the seats ready for a crew of seven. There were no lifejackets. The boats were painted a matte black.

The drift boats were ready to go. Years ago, the others had been used for boiler fuel until a secret supply of coal had been secured and shipped to the cave. Two colossal double doors groaned as they were pushed open by three men on either side. Moonlight flooded the cavern. Long iron rails revealed themselves. They'd been spiked into a heavy wooden ramp sloping down to the Tennessee River. The rails gleamed in the moonlight for any snow or ice on them had been removed. Another crew waited below on a narrow beach at the bottom of the steep incline. Pulled up beside them was a drift boat wherein a Gatling gun was mounted low amidships behind an iron shield. Its six long barrels were ready to spit a torrent of .50 caliber bullets at two hundred rounds per minute at anyone foolish enough to come within a hundred yards of it. The gang's horses had been tethered further down the trace at the old Rebel rifle pits, and left under guard.

Lucas gave the signal. A thick steel cable had been attached to the stern of his boat. The heavy drift boat was quickly lowered down towards the river. As the craft passed the halfway mark, a steersman reached down and pulled a release pin. The cable went slack as the vessel shot down the iron rails into the river with a splash. A line was thrown out to it and the craft was hauled ashore then tied to a tree before the river could claim it. Its four wheeled trolley was carried away by the raging current. Immediately, the steel cable was quickly winched in by the steam engine, attached to another craft and within minutes the process was completed until all five were massed at the river's edge.

High above them, the thumping sound of the steam engine sputtered then died. Clayton Thomas ran through the open doors, a black knapsack strapped to his body. He descended the icy wooden ramp then slipped and fell. Picking himself up, he limped to the bottom. Thomas dragged himself across a narrow sandy beach. He scrambled painfully into the nearest drift boat. Just then, two US Marshalls stationed across from them on Williams Island opened fire with their long range Sharps rifles. An oarsman fell dead, dropping onto a black bale of money. Another man hung like a wet rag over the high gunnel of Lucas's boat. He screamed as Lucas threw his body into the swift moving river. He bobbed about then sank into a whirlpool further downstream. Lucas yelled, "Fire, fire"!

Within seconds the canyon was filled with thunder as the Gatling opened up, cutting one Marshall to pieces. All the boats rowed out into the middle of a wide but rapidly narrowing river.

Saxton's scouts returned with the news that the upper cave door would not open even though there was no padlock on it. Saxton thought that it was very strange indeed. He asked Crease to draw a map in the snow. To the untrained eye, Elder Mountain was a formidable obstacle ringed by insurmountable vertical cliffs. But to Crease this was a fallacy. He knew that right above Pitchfork Cave, gently sloping benches ran down to the river where it swept by Suck Creek on the opposite shore. There was only one problem. They had to somehow get down Thomnson Creek first.

The narrow creek bed before them was steep, icy, dark and dangerous. However, some- one had the idea of tying a rope to a tree whereby all the men would hang onto it as they lowered themselves down through the darkened gorge far below them. Saxton knew that the idea was crazy but it might work if they were really lucky. After some discussion, a few married villagers went home to their families but the others, mostly single men, enthusiasti- cally volunteered.

Saxton would split his forces. Thirty armed men would go with Crease to the sloping bench then on to the old Rebel rifle pits down river. Once there they would fire on any drift boats that were trying to escape downriver. Saxton realized the boats in the cave were probably Lucas's only means of escape. Meanwhile he and two Rangers would continue down the creek bed to a point just above the cave entrance.

Shortly thereafter, a long rope, and a box of work gloves were brought back from the men's bunkhouse. The thick manila rope was tied to a pine tree growing by the edge of Thomnson Creek. Thirty minutes later, all the men, with Saxton leading the way, made it to the lower bench. The rope was barely long enough. In the perilous descent, two men suffered minor scrapes and bruises. Both agreed to stay behind and guard the creek bed to prevent an ambush. Another rope had been brought down as well. It was tied to another tree. Saxton and his two Rangers slid down a sheer cliff to a point just above Pitchfork cave where they sat concealed in some brush. They didn't have to wait very long.

A short time passed then the two doors below them began to open wide. To their amazement, one after another, boats filled with black rubber sacks and crews of seven appeared. They were lowered down the steep incline on wheeled dollies into the river. In one of them, Belle was sitting bound in front of Garrow, a Colt .45 pointed at her head. A thick woolen blanket was wrapped around her white parka. After the last boat was launched, Saxton heard what sounded like a steam engine, grind to a halt. A blast of hot air, twenty feet away from him, shot skyward into the moonlight. The trio watched as a man slipped and fell on his way down to the water. He picked himself up and hobbled through the snow to a drift boat. Saxton moved further down the creek bed to a ledge that ran horizontally to the cave entrance. Just as he and his escorts reached it, shots rang out from across the river. A boatman fell dead upon a black bag. Saxton watched as Lucas in another boat, threw a wounded boatman into the rapids. A Gatling gun opened up, raking the opposite shore with a hail of lead. All three observers ducked for cover until Garrow's fleet disappeared. They then scrambled down the slippery slope to the top of the launch ramp, turned and ran into the cave past the open doors. What they saw was the impossible being revealed as possible. Saxton stood mute, unable to fathom the depths of Garrow's deception.

All the boats inside the cave were gone. A circle of five gallon kerosene lamps hung from iron spikes driven deep into the limestone walls around them. They flickered brightly, their soft yellow light revealing mountains of coal, barrels of printer's ink, bushels of bleached dollar bills and other detritus littering the vast cavern. One of the men ran over to a printing press. He put his hand on it. It was still warm. Everywhere, black rubber bags filled with counterfeit money were stacked like cordwood. Garrow must have been in a hurry. One of the Rangers, a former printer, flipped open a steel flange on top of a press. There were no plates in the machine. Meanwhile, another Ranger ran up through the cave to the upper entrance. He came back thirty minutes later telling Saxton that the iron door was blocked by large stones. With one final look around then cave, he ran out and down the ramp to the river.

His two companions ran up behind him just as a fleet of drift boats filled with Marshalls came around the bend. The trio dived for cover. However, much to their relief, Captain

Hagen was aboard one of the drift boats. He waved and hallooed Saxton's name, his voice booming across the river. Saxton stood up and waved back. The fleet continued downriver as one boat broke away, turned and steered towards them. It ran ashore near them. Two Marshalls jumped out and headed across the narrow beach to the ramp. A tall black man stood up in one of the boats. He yelled at Saxton, it was Hagen.

"Come aboard Captain. It's been a long time Sir."

Saxton climbed aboard and shook hands with his former squad leader. They watched two men climb the launch ramp to the cave. Hagen turned to Saxton.

"I've sent Marshalls Thompson and Laird ashore to guard the cave. More men are riding down the shoreline trace to join them. They'll be here in a few minutes. Your two friends look the worse for wear. Perhaps they'd better stay too. Goddamn it Captain, It seems the bastard got away."

His words were barely out of his mouth when rifle fire and the chattering of a Gatling gun shattered the canyon walls further downstream. Saxton yelled at the boat crews to hang torn white sheets from their bows or they'd be shot as intruders. They did so, and pushed off onto 'The River of Death', rowing mightily in the grip of a terrible turbulence towards a defile only two hundred feet across. Through this narrow gap roared waters that had flowed down mountains covering over five states. Hagen and Saxton sat down and hung on for dear life as the river carried them away.

The intruder's horses were tied up further downstream from the cave. They whinnied nervously as the posse's drift boats passed by. The guard there had already been captured by Crease and his band of men. The pursuing oarsmen began pulling their boats ever faster down the river. Being much lighter, their vessels floated higher on the water with less resistance. A baleful moon bathed the canyon in aqueous light. The fleet, festooned with white flags, passed Crease and his sharpshooters without incident. These men emerged from their rifle pits, waving and yelling as the Marshalls swept by them. Eldin Crease leaped upon a large flat rock. He cupped his hands over his mouth.

"We killed five of them bastards and captured two guards. Two of their boats smashed into that pointy rock over there on the other side of the river. Mrs. Brown is still alive but she's bound hand and foot. Good luck. We're goin' back to the farm with the horses."

The men ashore cheered then disappeared into the forest. A red rocket blossomed skyward from the other side of the mountain. Saxton watched it climb high above then arch over disintegrating as it fell back down through the moonlight into the river. A Marshall seated nearby shouted over the roar of the river that such a signal meant that Garrow was making a run for it through the rapids further on around the bend. The river swung hard against the right bank of the canyon as it passed Suck Creek. Anyone careless enough at this point would be hurtled against a sheer wall of yellow limestone.

Garrow was enraged when he realized he'd been flimflammed. The note about the fifty million dollars had been correct in every detail. Someone had lured him to his lair. The years of planning, and accumulating a trusted crew were now for naught. Whoever was behind his betrayal would die. He knew the Pinkerton brothers were after him and that Sherriff Springfield wanted him for murder but who was it that betrayed him? Lucas looked behind him in horror as his pursuers rounded the river bend past Suck Creek. Lucas had never been on this part of the river before. He couldn't swim; he never had too. It didn't matter, for his meticulous preparations would surely pay off.

His boat bounced through the river's first tribulations as it passed over the Tumbling Shoals. Only two vessels were left, for the boat containing the Gatling had smashed into a large rock that snapped its steering oar like a twig. The undertow created by the force of the river sliding beneath an underwater ledge, sucked the boat and its crew under in a matter of seconds. No one survived as their bodies were dragged down by a swirling vortex created by a perfect marriage of moving water against smooth immutable stone. But, the money within the watertight rubber bags was more fortunate. Minutes later, far down river, twenty million dollars were thrust high above the river's surface. They began to bob merrily along downstream.

Lucas screamed in frustration as dozens of black money bags floated down the moonlit river behind him. All this time, Belle watched her son closely. Waves of emotions swept over his chiseled face, closely imitating the mood of the river beneath him. She'd been thrown into the boat, her hands and feet tied in front of her and her body tied to a board seat. Ever since then, Belle prayed that her family was safe. She knew her husband, Saxton and all the others were trying to save her but her son had planned well. She wanted to do something, anything to even the odds however she was powerless to prevent her manic son from escaping. Garrow's one remaining drift boat managed to catch up. Both vessels slowed in a part of the river called Dead Man Eddy but not for long as their oarsmen strained to propel themselves out of the slack waters around them.

Belle looked up as a sharp line of separation was drawn quite dramatically across the face of the raging river. Deep shadow suddenly engulfed her for the full moon was no longer high above but on the other side of the mountain from whence she'd come. The black drift boat following behind her vanished. Belle looked but could not see it anymore. Garrow turned about. He laughed, ghostlike, barely muted by the cloak of darkness that had just been thrust upon him. He shouted over the river's rage.

"Yes my dear, anyone waiting for us at Massengale Point will not see us until it's too late."

He tore off his seal skin parka, oblivious to the cold for it seemed that an inner fire, hot and growing ever stronger was burning deep within his body. He screamed, throwing the parka into the river.

"Blackness will protect me, for black has made me invisible. How fortunate it is for us mother."

His tone changed abruptly, becoming more primal, more manic. He screamed again as another dose of morphine began blossoming within his brain.

"Don't you understand?' Black is the absence of all color, just like you bitch!"

He came near to her, his eyes black pools of hate. The face before Belle assumed an abnormal hue of yellow as their craft passed close to moonfaced cliffs towering over them. Lucas reached for her, gripping her wide shoulders, his breath foul upon her face. He snarled,

"My dear, everyone knows that black is the absence of all color, yet you niggers call yourselves colored. How ignorant you are indeed!"

He released her then touched her cheeks; the fresh blood upon them coming away on his finger tips. He tried to capture any light in order to see the blood upon them more clearly. In a rage, he reached out; dragging a boney fingertip across her forehead making three large six's upon it. Satisfied, Lucas sat back on a black bale of money and vanished. Out of the stygian darkness his voice became funereal, hollow, a voice spoken through a human skull. It was forced to rise up over the roar of the rapids that surrounded them. He shouted at her, mocking her.

"The three six's I have put upon you is the mark of Lucifer that lies within you. Your soul is as black as the blood that came down to earth from that fallen Archangel. Therefore you and your kind must die to save my world from your contamination. I will create a world where any black will be seen as an abomination. No my dear, my world might not be a perfect world but it will be a white world, MY WORLD!"

A hand reached out once again from the blackness and held her jaw firmly within its grasp. As it did so, their craft leaped into the air as that part of the river known as the 'Boiling Pot', flung the drift boat about like a cat toying with a mouse. Cries of alarm rose up behind Belle. She fell hard against the tall sides of the drift boat while Lucas and his crew were literally lifted off their seats and thrown into the boiling river. Their screams pierced her soul as they and her son were swept away.

A black wave towered over her then smashed down upon her, throwing her boat completely onto its side. Belle's head struck the craft's gunnel knocking her out. Somehow the money sacks about her remained in place. Still heavily laden, the drift boat teetered precariously then slammed back down with a splash. Belle lay prostrate, unmoving against the money sacks. She remained unconscious, her body still tightly bound as the drift boat was thrown hither and yon in the 'Skillet'.

A grappling hook sailed through the air; its steel talons digging into her boat's sternum. At the other end of the line was John Saxton pulling for dear life against a river mad with power. Hand over hand he pulled until his quarry slewed about and banged up against his boat. Captain Hagen hung onto it while another crewman tied the grappling rope to an iron bow ring. Seven oarsmen immediately began rowing hard for Massengale Point where the Chattanooga militia awaited them.

Saxton leaped forward landing near Belle as the two craft came together. He made his way unsteadily towards her. She looked more dead than alive. He tore out the cloth gag then untied her. John Saxton gathered Belle in his arms and as he did she awoke as if from a deep sleep. She looked up, her face streaked with blood and screamed,

"Oh Saxton, Lucas is gone. My babies are all gone; drowned in a river of tears."

She began to sob. He held her close, her head upon his chest as high above them dozens of fiery bouquets heralded a new year and the resurrection of an old dream.

EPILOGUE

A golden eagle soared high above the depths of an ancient river gorge that embraced the stone shoulders of Elder Mountain. The great bird was thrust upward by thermals of hot air rising from layers of heated sandstone lying far below it. This gray capstone lay prostrate in the grip of a hot summer's sun. Still, silent and entombed by the crowning forests of hardwood that grew upon it, the immutable serenity of the mountain would soon be gone forever as a rising road, its feet wet from the passing of deep waters below it, climbed towards the crest of the precipice. Slab-like sinews of rock cut away by men of determination and imagination would overcome that colossus of stone and make it submit to their will.

Such were the men and women that colonized Elder Mountain. For many of them, the shores of Africa were but a distant memory enshrined in the ancient tales of their ancestors. To others, the broad rivers of America carried their hopes and dreams to the mountain where the sanctuary of that formidable fastness became the protector of those yearning to be free and bear fruit. The promise of its forests, fields and flowing waters found there, and its isolation from those who wanted to destroy it, gave form and substance to their lives. The scars of their ordeals from taming the mountain and those who later tried to wrest it from their grasp, were healing. The victors forgave those who trespassed against them but they did not forget why they fought them.

The Civil War that tore America asunder, acted as a catalyst bringing forth the renewal of a nation that had suffered through a fury. However, for many years thereafter, the scars of that struggle remained unhealed, fresh, and raw upon the imperfect face of a society that emerged into an uncertain future. Racism, bigotry and prejudice had indeed replaced the slavery that so many young men had died trying to abolish. But, in the fullness of time, the dream of a perfect world was kept alive at Harmony Farm. The idea that all men were created equal and could live together in peace, still beat within the minds and hearts of those who survived the 'troubles' on the dark side of the mountain.

THE END

ACKNOWLEDGEMENTS:

Ralph Purchase, Lt. Colonel, US Army Reserves Ret.; who edited the entire trilogy with judicious care and impeccable common sense.

My Step-daughter Katherine Woods; whose considerable computer skills rearranged my story into a more palatable concoction.

Larry Leitzell, 2nd Class Gunner's Mate, US Navy Ret.; whose travels to Fort Sumter were invaluable.

Adolf 'Blackie' Blackburn, Captain RCN Ret.; who made sure that all nautical terms were correct.

Barbara Howe; whose constructive critique kept me on the straight and narrow as to character development and story structure.

Shirley M. Gehring and the Suni-Sands Writing Club of Yuma AZ; for their sage advice and encouragement.

John Coultas, Yuma City Librarian Ret., Roberta Sve and the rest of the Rio Colorado Writing Club of Yuma AZ; for their encouragement and timely crititiques.

Published authors; Bill Russell, Dr. Jean Hounshell and M. Kay Howell of the Foothills AZ Writing Club; for their generous professional advice and support.

My friends and family who put up with my ramblings over the years.

The dozens of Literary Agents who rejected my queries by letter or e-mail thus making me more determined than ever to do better.

But most of all, I wish to acknowledge my wife, Daphne and my mother, Pearl Edmonds (now diseased), for encouraging me to keep on writing and believing in a dream.

Literary works by the author:
Novels:
The Dark Side of the Mountain
The Kingdom of Fear

Stage plays:
The Ramblers
The Tie-up Place
Clifford House
The Dark Side of the Mountain

Screen plays:
The Tie-up Pace
The Dark Side of the Mountain

A SHORT NOTE FROM THE AUTHOR:

While researching the novel, I discovered many interesting characters, fascinating events and unique locations that made the Civil War era of American history so intriguing. The fields of battle, ports of call, weaponry, buildings, city landscapes, prisons, railways, ships, cemeteries, fauna and flora, forts and geographical features mentioned, were very real. For example, the Elephant Hotel in Somers, New York State still exists today, delighting its guests as it did nearly two hundred years ago.

For some of the historical figures mentioned, their real names have been altered to prevent any aspersions on their character. However, Presidents, the Pinkertons and a host of military men, spies, river boat pilots, men of the cloth, guerilla fighters, and other characters were real people who fought on both sides in the Civil War. And aspersions on or distortions of their character were entirely fictional. For the most part, where they were, and what they were doing at the time, is historical fact. Any interaction between them in the novel is also pure fiction, yet their actions follow a well documented sequence of historical events.

Despite having all the resources of the internet at my disposal; dry facts, figures or quotes, do not bring characters to life. The depictions of the novel's characters, their emotions, heart-felt feelings of triumph and despair and their outpourings of love and hatred have I hope, been portrayed as plausible and real. To that end, I leave the rest to your imaginations. Enjoy.

S.A. Carter, author.

'KINGDOMS OF FEAR'

BOOK ONE: THE APOSTLE

BOOK ONE: CHAPTER 1
SHOCK AND AWE

Lucas Garrow was swept away by a river mad with power and full of fury. He could hear a woman screaming behind him as the icy waters of the Tennessee River tore at his body, tumbling him about like a rag doll caught in the teeth of a mad dog. Desperate to live, his mind battled with the sedating effects of the morphine blossoming within him.

Moments before, he'd taunted his black mother, Belle Brown, as they were carried along in a drift boat filled with large rubber bags of counterfeit money. Down through total blackness they were swept into the heart of the Tennessee River Gorge. Indeed, the very thought of his mother drove Lucas mad with despair and loathing. Surely his blood couldn't be tainted with the blood of a Creole whore. Gripped by the sudden and chilling possibility that she was indeed his mother, he took off his white seal skin parka and threw it into the river. Ripping his under shirt asunder, he revealed his upper torso. A once muscular body shone honey brown in the moonlight. Once again his addiction battled a stark reality that had thrown him out of favor with those dedicated to resurrect the Confederacy. Lucas still believed that he was white through and through, chosen by God to lead the South back into a good and gracious time when every black knew their place, their destiny and every white had dominion over man or beast.

An inner rage fuelled by the megalomaniac fantasy blooming within his mind was flung aside as the Tennessee River's tumultuous rapids known as 'the skillet' grasped his heavily laden drift boat and threw it high into the air. Every soul therein was thrown out except his mother who remained tied to a seat, bound hand and foot. Lucas fell head over heels down into the boiling waters of the gorge. The shock of its icy grip on his body was overpowering yet somehow his mind befuddled by the drug, prevented him from realizing the dire portent that lay before him. Down he sank into the belly of the beast until he was rejected as being too poisonous to consume. Thrust above the bosom of the river, the roaring waters carried him away past Massengale Point where a watchful militia awaited to capture him.

Notwithstanding the fact that Lucas Garrow was wanted for murder, conspiracy, fraud and larceny; he was most wanted for conspiring to bankrupt the United States of America. He had operated the largest counterfeiting ring the Pinkerton National Detective Agency had ever come across. It was discovered under Elder Mountain, in Pitchfork cave. Atop this mountain was a veritable fortress called Harmony Farm where over three hundred colonists farmed and logged. Far below it, the Tennessee River swept through a narrow defile that nearly encircled the mountain.

Lucas Garrow, a psychotic dilusional, needed the Farm as a strategic point from which to blackmail the Union into restoring the defeated Confederacy. If the Union did not submit to his will, he would flood the world with worthless Yankee dollars. Without enough gold reserves to back its currency, America would be ruined. After various schemes to take over the mountain failed, Garrow trained a small army and attacked under cover of a severe blizzard on New Year's Eve. However, his forces were thoroughly routed by the armed villagers led by John Saxton and a giant Maasai, Marcus Brown. These two former Army Rangers forced the invaders to retreat to Pitchfork Cave.

For two years a sophisticated counterfeiting operation deep within its cavernous confines had spewed forth billions of US dollars in various denominations. Now forced to abandon it, Lucas, with his mother Belle Brown as hostage, boarded one of five drift boats which were then literally catapulted into the jaws of the Gorge. An armada of drift boats filled with US Marshalls and the famous Pinkerton brothers; pursued the counterfeiters through the treacherous defile. Weighed down, all five of Lucas's vessels succumbed to the river's many rapids, hidden rocks, massive whirlpools and vicious undertows found within the canyon. Belle Brown was supposedly the only survivor of what many old timers called 'The River of Death'.

At midnight precisely, a hallucinating Lucas Garrow looked up as fireworks exploded over the city of Chattanooga a few miles to the north. It was New Year's Eve 1881. John Read and Robert Craven, two of the city's richest men were having a fireworks contest. During a lull in a massive snowstorm, dozens of fiery fans of light and fizzling rockets burst into glorious rainbows high in the glow of a full moon. At that moment, the last dregs of morphine spiked Lucas's frontal lobes with just enough power to last a few minutes more. After that he was not only at the mercy of reality but gripped by the sudden realization that he was about to die; if not by drowning, most certainly by freezing to death.

As luck would have it, out of nowhere, a large rubber bag the size of a double mattress bumped up against him. Instinctively he reached out and grasped one of its rubber handles. After many futile attempts he managed to slither aboard, hanging on for dear life as the river once again became truculent. A drowning man appeared. It was Clayton Thomas, his former head pressman. Thomas screamed,

"For God's sake Garrow, I'll drown if you don't help me get aboard."

The rapids continued to spank the man as he lunged for a handle. The bag sank under the man's weight as he tried to gain purchase. Garrow screamed at him for what seemed an eternity. The man hung on grimly as Garrow kicked at him. Finally the man let go and disappeared under the river. Exhausted, Lucas lay on the bag as it bounced merrily away downstream. Within its belly was three million dollars in newly minted American ten dollar bills. Further upstream a flotilla of similar rubber bags floated down the river into the moonlight. As they swept by Massengale Point, a sharp eyed Corporal sighted one of them. He shouted,

"Lieutenant Wilson Sir, look out yonder on the river. There's something floating by. It's too large for a body and it's not a boat. What the hell is it?"

Before Lieutenant Wilson could answer, a drift boat careened ashore. Besides its crew, were a white man, a tall colored woman and Captain Bill Hagen. Both men leapt out of the boat and lifted the black woman bodily out of the craft. She was moaning. The Captain spotted a campfire. They carried the woman through the snow towards it. Hagen began to issue orders. Dr. Mary Walker rushed over to Belle to administer first aid to her bloody face where her son had whipped her. Militiamen rushed hither and yon gathering blankets. Another canvas wedge tent was hastily erected. Inside it a canvas cot was set up. Someone lit a hurricane lamp and hung it on the tent pole. Captain Hagen carried Belle inside and covered her with blankets. She was still fully clothed. Saxton, standing outside, heard her screaming over the din of the fireworks booming away in the distance. Belle was delirious with anger and sorrow. She threw off her blankets, sat bolt upright and screamed,

"He killed my babies! The bastard killed my baby boys! Oh Rufus, oh Cotton you're gone, gone, gone...! May God curse the name Lucas Garrow, the spawn of the devil!"

She stopped as Walker soothed her face with a cold cloth. Suddenly Belle flung herself back and wailed in abject agony. She moaned as if her heart would break in two. The petite doctor opened her small battered medical bag. She quickly rummaged around and took out a bottle of Laudanum. Belle continued to sob, her hands pulling at her long black hair.

"Marcus, my precious Marcus, how will we ever survive the torment? How will we ever survive an everlasting grief that will burden us to our dying day? Oh merciful God, help us, please I beg of you!"

She thrust aside the blankets, raised herself up once more and swung her long legs off the cot. The doctor was thrown to the floor by the sudden violence of it. Belle had to be restrained by Captain Hagen. After recovering her composure, Doctor Walker administered a strong dose of Laudanum. Within seconds Belle was fast asleep. The Doctor nodded and Hagen left the tent, closing the flap behind him. Flickering lamplight revealed Walker about to strip Belle of her thick wet clothing. She never noticed the zippered pockets lining the inside of Belle's cotton shift. Outside, Hagen stepped forward, barring John Saxton from entering. Saxton understood. He beckoned Hagen to stand with him by the fire and offered the black man a cheroot. Hagen offered him a blanket. Saxton wrapped himself in it. After lighting up, he said,

"Captain, it's good to see you again. I thank you for helping out so promptly. The woman is Mrs. Belle Brown. She was kidnapped by Lucas Garrow her bastard son who tried to escape through the Gorge. He and his gang are all dead or captured; every one of them. Those who weren't killed on Elder Mountain tonight were most certainly drowned in the river. Lucas Garrow according to his mother, drowned. It looked like he couldn't swim. She saw it happen. No one could have survived the cold water, let alone the rapids. Only the devil himself could do so. As we speak, bags full of counterfeit money are floating down the river. We'll have to wait for the US Marshalls to get here before we can do anything about it. Thankfully your militia had a few fires going or we would have missed Massengale altogether. Both of us, especially Belle have been through hell itself. My God it's cold! However, Captain, once we've recovered, Belle and I must get back to the Farm upon the mountain. By the way I have an idea."

Hagen's face lit up as Saxton told him that he was posting a one thousand dollar reward for every bag of money they found unopened. The Captain agreed then remembered the tall, beautiful black women asleep in the tent. He wondered where he'd seen her before then realized she was the wife of his old comrade in arms, Marcus the Maasai. Oddly, the woman was dressed in a raggedy cotton gown covered by a white seal-skin parka. It was a strange combination. Adding to the bizarre effect was the fact that she was wearing matching seal-skin winter boots. The tall white man beside him was similarly attired. The only difference being that John Saxton was wearing seal-skin trousers. Lieutenant Wilson stepped out of the shadows and saluted Saxton. In respect, he took off his Hardee hat and said,

"Sorry to hear about your troubles Mr. Saxton. I'm Lieutenant Clifford Wilson of the Chattanooga Militia. Your exploits with the Maasai Rangers are legendary. Why I remember when your boys captured General JEB Stuart." Saxton interrupted the man saying,

"Yes indeed Lieutenant. Too bad he escaped." Wilson laughed, put on his hat and said, "Yessiree, you just took the words right out of my mouth."

As Saxton spoke, more drift boats began coming ashore below him at the ferry dock. The Lieutenant ran forward through the snow and grabbed a painter thrown ashore by one of the crew. He pulled hard. The long boat slowed about in the current before it ground through the shore ice and up against a low wooden pier. A US Marshall jumped out. He looked up at Hagen and yelled over the constant din of rockets exploding high over Chattanooga.

"Did we get the bastard Capt'n?" Hagen indicated otherwise.

The lawman was not pleased. The Pinkerton brothers; William and Robert climbed out of another drift boat. They were the spitting image of their famous father Allan Pinkerton, the detective. Both were short, dapper, clean cut and sporting neatly trimmed black beards. They strode forward and introduced themselves to Saxton. The tall black Captain stepped forward. He looked down at the Pinkertons and growled,

"It looks like you two boys have got your work cut out for you. I suggest you skedaddle Inspectors. It seems to me that we had better find all that tempting money before folks hereabouts are tempted too. Well fellas, you'd have to agree that I'm the highest rank round here, so you'd all better listen up."

The Militia Captain from Chattanooga mounted a horse and stood up in the stirrups as the booming sounds of the fireworks barrage suddenly quit. He waited for dozens of soldiers and US Marshalls to gather round him. Satisfied he had their attention, he began to issue orders. He drawled, "Lt. Wilson, I want you to assign someone to go back across the river in one of the Marshall's boats to Kelly's Ferry. Tell the ferryman to come right over and shoot him if he refuses. Once you're mounted and on the Mullin's Cove Road, beat the bushes south to Shake Rag. The other half of your posse can follow the Kelly Ferry Road up river to Suck Creek. Any resistance; shoot first and ask questions later. See what you can flush out. Keep pace with the drift boats searching your side. Make sure you keep in touch. The rest of my men will split up too. Half will leave here for Blue Hole along the north trace. The rest will come with me down the north shore trace to a point opposite Shake Rag. The river down-river from here is low and slow. We're probably looking for thirty or so large bags the size of a double mattress. The Marshalls will man the drift boats and search every eddy, slough and cove for bags and bodies up and down the river from this point. For youse goin' upriver, take it mighty easy. We don't want any more casualties. Christ we lost three boats just gettin' here. We'll leave the camp as is. Never know what the weather will do next. Doctor Walker, you stay here and tend to Belle and Saxton and any others who might straggle in."

He stood high in the stirrups once again and told the gathering about John Saxton's generous reward. The men took off their hats and whooped; their breath white like phosphorous floating on still water. The Pinkertons as one, said, "Well I'll be damned!" Captain Hagen looked down on John Saxton and said, "Capt'n, it was an honor serving with you in the war. Sorry we couldn't rescue you off Billy Goat Hill. I see you've healed up some. Lord knows we tried to save you but the Rebs were all over us. I understand they threw you into Salisbury Prison camp. What a hell-hole that was. I'm sure glad General Stoneman burned the place down. I also heard that you got the Congressional Medal of Honor. Congratulations. You and Ranger Charlie Smith deserved it. As Sherman said, 'War is all Hell'. Well I'd better be goin' now Sir." He saluted then continued,

"As for you and Belle; when **the** good doctor agrees and the weather permits; two Marshalls will escort you'all back up the mountain. Tell Mr. Pinkerton that his two boys are ok."

Two hours later, Belle and Saxton were bundled up in a cutter. She snuggled up against him. Their eyes met. Belle whispered, "Thank you Saxton for saving me. Marcus and I owe you so much."

After she spoke, she began to laugh. She had realized that she was wearing her cotton dress once again. Saxton wondered what was going on. One minute she sobbed uncontrollably and the next she was hysterical with laughter. Little did he know that hundreds of jewels were secreted away in zippered pockets under the lining of Belle's 'Gettin' out of town real quick' dress. Saxton kissed her forehead thinking of his young black wife Virginia waiting for him on the mountain. He looked back through the falling snow as their sleigh sped upwards to Pan Gap. Below him a flotilla of drift boats began rowing down river. A paling light revealed a widening river speckled with boats and bags. The roaring of the rapids faded away as Saxton was carried up the winding road. In retrospect, his troubled journey was ending while another was just beginning.

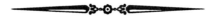

The Tennessee River, upon exiting the Gorge, returned to a more sedentary state as it carried Lucas into an eddy a mile below Massengale Point. Lucas limped ashore through pan ice and snow. With the last vestige of strength born of desperation, he painfully dragged the 'money mattress' up onto the snow-bound verge. Through crackling frozen river reeds, he pulled the heavy bag into a thicket of Snakeroot. He nearly blacked out as the leg wound inflicted upon him years early in the Battle of Chickamauga came back with a painful vengeance. Unknown to Lucas, his last glass vial of morphine lay crushed in one of his trouser pockets. His bare hands and upper body shivered violently. His teeth chattered as he retrieved a small Barlow knife from out of his wet seal-skin trousers. With a mighty effort, he cut a long stick from a nearby bush, then slit the rubber bag open just enough so that he could crawl into it. As he nestled in amongst the warm bales of newly minted money, the last image he would see was falling snow. In the coming hours, Lucas would begin to experience as agonizing withdrawal as his body yearned for another dose of liquid morphine. He was no different than thousands of severely wounded veterans during the Civil War who had become addicted to morphine. So for the next twelve hours, Lucas writhed and moaned within his rubber tomb. Above him a titanic storm cell lay prostrate over the Cumberland Plateau. It began to punish those below it in earnest. Within minutes, the black rubber bag with Lucas inside was buried. Occasionally, Lucas would try to remain lucid enough to thrust the stick through the slit to keep from suffocating. His attempts became less frequent and more feeble as the long hours dragged on.

Meanwhile out along the ice strewn river banks on either side of the river, two posses of US Marshalls along with their conscripted crews were busy. Bags of money found here and there were loaded aboard their drift boats. One such party passed within twenty feet of where Lucas was hiding. Aboard that particular drift boat, William Pinkerton wondered if he'd ever be warm again as the snow began to fall in earnest once more. He prayed that his father, Allan Pinkerton and the rest of the colonists were still alive atop the mountain.

A tenuous trickle of light had found its way into the tomb that Lucas Garrow lay buried in. After many hours, his body was nearing a state of hibernation. After many hours, the icy grip of the inclement weather outside began to permeate his entire being. Although dressed in white seal skin boots and matching trousers, he was basically naked from the waist up. As he was about to succumb to the dire circumstances that surrounded him, a gun shot rang out nearby. Startled out of his comatose state, he lay mute and immobile within the money womb. More shots exploded all around him. Muffled cries of anguish and triumph began to rent the frigid airs outside his sanctuary. Something heavy fell upon him then crawled away. Lucas sweated wondered what was happening. What was happening would have shocked him.

River scavengers from the small hamlet of Shake Rag seven miles downstream had come upon evidence of Lucas's struggle through the reeds and brush. Shattered shore ice, trampled snow, crumpled river reeds, broken branches and other signs pointed out where someone had dragged something heavy ashore. They suspected someone was hiding a money bag as they had found four of them already. Before all these signs were buried, a dozen or so armed ruffians scrambled onto the narrow beach. Behind them, five small drift boats lined up side by side. However the scavenger's search was interrupted by a party of US Marshalls returning upriver. Because of the intense snow fall, they literally bumped into each other. Upon seeing their competition, both groups opened fire at very close range. Men began dying on the beach and in the willow thickets as the battle raged back and forth. Fortunately, Captain Hagen and a platoon of Militia had ridden south down a narrow corduroy road that bordered the same side of the river. Hearing gunshots nearby, they charged through the Ash and Sweet Gum forest towards the sounds of battle. Once fully engaged and outnumbered, the surviving Shake Rag scavengers retreated back to their boats, casting off in haste to get away. Their retreat was successful as a thickening blanket of ice fog swept ashore, completely obscuring them in seconds.

Lucas needed fresh air. He was suffocating. Dazed and gasping for breath, he thrust the stick once more through a thin crust of snow. Fresh air, sweet and cold flowed into his lungs. He lay still trying to rationalize what was happening around him. Nothing but silence entered his tomb. He could wait no longer. Grasping his Barlow knife, he thrust himself through the slit and pushed upwards through two feet of soft snow. Startled Chickadees and Purple Finches flew off, chattering and twittering in alarm in the thickets as a bearded apparition burst forth into their avian world. He stood up, his arms hugging his shivering body. The sweat upon it began to freeze. The storm had passed on to the east. There, in a large clearing all about him were signs of a bloody struggle. After a few moments, he heard men shouting below him. Parting some bushes on the verge of the river bank, he looked down upon a ragged group of lawmen hastily stowing bodies and bags aboard a steamboat they had flagged down. Once their grisly task was completed, the boat's narrow gangplank was hoisted aboard and stowed. The little paddle wheeler backed out into a thinning layer of ice fog then slowly gained headway. Its tall twin stacks belched clouds of black smoke into a pewter sky as it puffed its way upstream. Lucas watched until it disappeared around a bend. Cottonwoods behind him clattered then became silent as the wind died down. A murmuring river filled with broken slabs of pan ice eased by him in the paling light of dawn.

Lucas had a problem or for that matter many problems. His first instinct was not to survive but to mark where he had put the bag full of money. Even though the snow had stopped falling, it might return and his loot would vanish forever. He grasped his torn undershirt and ripped off a thin strip of it. Within moments a red rag was tied high in a blueberry bush. It began fluttering in a cold wind as Lucas followed a thin tenuous blood trail through the woods. It ended a quarter mile, away down river. There, high up on the shore was a small white drift boat completely turned turtle and covered by a bank of snow. The blood trail disappeared underneath it. Tensing, ready to fight or flee, Lucas stopped and listened for any sounds emanating from beneath the craft. None was forthcoming. All he could hear was his teeth chattering. Pocketing his Barlow knife, he grasped the boat's gunwale and tipped it over. There beneath it, a young man's frozen body lay exposed in the grey light.

Garrow stripped the body of its woolen jacket, gloves, fur hat and scarf. He then searched the craft and found a black canvas haversack. He emptied it out on a patch of packed snow. Within the sack was a loaded .32 Pocket Colt pistol, a box of ammo, a Bowie knife, and a tin of safety matches. A pair of bear-paw snowshoes and a canvas bag full of frozen jerky lat stowed in a bulkhead. A Spencer rifle and a box of ammo were found stashed inside two white tarpaulins. Garrow cut two forked branches and propped the drift boat up on its side, its hull facing the river. He dragged the body out into the bush and covered it with snow. Returning to the boat, he threw a white tarp over it and used a snowshoe as a shovel to cover everything with snow. He needn't had bothered. Once more it began to snow. Lucas strapped on the snow shoes and plodded back to the money bag. From within it he pulled out stacks of bills and filled the haversack. He swept the snow off the money bag then covered it with the other white tarp. The blizzard intensified. His withdrawal symptoms intensified. Using his Bowie-knife, he marked all of the trees on his way back to the drift boat. He barely made it before everything around him disappeared into a white void. Within minutes he had a small fire burning under the overturned drift boat. He sat there on a bed of pine branches, hugging his knees as waves of nausea swept over him.

William Pinkerton sat beside his brother Robert in the tiny galley of the SS Chattanooga. The lithe paddle wheeler swung into the Tennessee River with a string of empty drift boats tied upon either side of it. They merrily bobbed about, occasionally smashing through slabs of river ice turned aside by the steamboat's stubby bow. The double-decker boat was heavily laden with canvas mail sacks destined for Chattanooga and Knoxville further upriver. High above the river, its silver haired Captain stroked his long white goatee and drawled,

"Well boys, I guess we're headed for Kelly's Ferry landing at Massengale Point upriver. Can't see nothin' through the fog. Seems this blasted storm has cut all telegraph lines and railways between Knoxville to the east, Nashville to the west and Huntsville to the south west of us. Goddamn it all, I've never seen a blow like this. The river bein' low and all, my pilot had a devil of a time comin' up from Bridgeport. Seems the river here 'bouts grows new rocks every spring like my daddy's fields back in Kentucky."

He leaned out the galley door then took a clay pipe out of his black double-breasted jacket. While tamping a fresh wad of tobacco into the bowl, he looked out over the railing. White wisps of hair blew about the fringe of his black sea cap. After lighting the pipe, he turned to William Pinkerton and the others and declared, "What the hell you boys got in them black bags anyways?"

On the boiler deck directly below him were twenty black rubber money bags taped and sealed, lying lashed to the foredeck. A flood of ice fog blowing up and over the steamboat's bow was dancing upon them. As the boat thrashed its way upriver, Robert Pinkerton laughed, saying,

"Skipper, you'd never believe me if I told you." The grizzled Captain spit a chaw of tobacco over the side. He turned and said, "Don't call me skipper!"

It had been a long and dangerous day for the Marshalls. One, a George McFee had died in the firefight with the river scavenger's. Both Pinkertons were tired and nearly asleep until a Marshall burst into the galley and cried, "Hey boys, one of the bodies we picked out of the river is alive; says he's the head printer for Lucas Garrow."

Everyone ran downstairs to the main deck where dozens of bodies were stacked like cordwood. Beside one of them, a US Marshall was trying to understand what a dying man was saying. He waved the Pinkertons away, nodded his head then stood up facing them. He said,

"Well gentlemen, this man said he's Clayton Thomas, Garrow's head pressman. Also says that Garrow is still alive and is headed for Bridgeport, Alabama. Apparently from what he said, five presses are hidden in a warehouse on Bleaker Street." Robert Pinkerton exclaimed, "I know it. It's two blocks away from the railway station." The Marshall continued, "Clayton also saw Garrow crawl aboard a money bag and hang on for dear life. He tried to climb aboard too but Lucas kicked him back into the river to die." William Pinkerton was skeptical.

"How do we know he's telling the truth? These men will do anything to throw us off their leader's trail. Believe you me, I've seen fanatics like this before. The Molly Maguire's and many other deranged and misguided groups come to mind."

The Marshall bent down once more over the man. Again he listened as the man whispered in his ear. Suddenly a death rattle broke the silence. Clayton Thomas was dead. One of the Marshalls, a Nigel Beauponte stood up and laughed.

"I think he heard you. Says he has something in his knapsack you might be interested in. He also said you could all go to hell in it!"

Robert Pinkerton stepped forward and rifled through the man's sodden knapsack. Deep inside it he felt something thin and hard. He withdrew a waxed paper packet. Upon ripping it open, he gasped. Inside, wrapped in oil cloth were the press plates for a US 1874 ten dollar bill and an 1878 US Silver Certificate. He looked at his brother then down at the body. He put his arm around his brother and said, "Well William, are you still ready to take a chance on whether or not Garrow is dead? What would our father do?" Beauponte didn't hesitate, saying, "I've known your father nigh on thirty years boys and I know for a fact he's track Garrow down until hell itself froze over."

It was decided then and there. A wire would be sent to the Sheriff in Bridgeport from Chattanooga, to be on the lookout for Lucas Garrow. Because of Belle, they had a very good idea what he looked like because in his hay day, Lucas was constantly in the news and photographed at every opportunity. Perhaps he would show up at the warehouse. In any event, the Pinkertons planned to take the next Nashville, Chattanooga &St. Louis train to Bridgeport, only thirty five miles away. Hopefully the tracks were repaired. But one of the Pinkerton's had an idea. After much discussion and copious rounds of Jim Beam, the steamboat Captain was persuaded to off load the mail at Massengale Point where the militia would take it to the main post office in Chattanooga the next day. As soon as that was done, the Captain would be one thousand dollars richer. After refueling, he would take the lawmen straight back to Bridgeport that day. As for Lucas Garrow, everyone prayed that their quarry would still be there. If he wasn't, they'd have a devil of a time tracking him down.

The snow storm passed. Lucas woke up. It was midnight. He was freezing once again for the fire had gone out. Only a slit of moonlight peeped through under the drift boat. He rolled over and poked a stick in the ashes of the fire. It flared wherever the bank notes were still pressed together. Encouraged, he blew into the fiery sparkles until they flared up. He reached over and put more fresh banknotes upon the tiny blaze. It suddenly burned brightly. Satisfied, he drew himself closer to the flames. He soon learned that money burned longer if it was packed tightly into rolls. Over the next five hours, he fed one thick roll after another into the fire. As he did so, he ate jerky from a canvas bag and washed it down with melted snow.

Sunlight released by the lifting veil of ice fog, flooded his frozen world. The day promised to be cold yet clear. But upriver, the ice fog persisted, hanging low over the passing waters of a troubled river. One hour later, Lucas broke camp and rowed upstream to where the red flag fluttered in the blueberry bush. After another exhausting effort, he managed to get the money bag into the dead scavenger's white drift boat. Pushing away from shore through the pan ice, Lucas rowed down river using the wispy remnants of the ice fog to shield him from anyone on the other shore. He knew travelling in daylight was risky but he figured he would freeze to death if he travelled at night. Besides, he was still hallucinating from time to time and at such times darkness only increased his inability to reason. Ten miles further down the river he drifted sight unseen past the village of Guild. It was there he decided to avoid rowing to Bridgeport all together. The only problem was he had to go through Bridgeport to get to Memphis. What he didn't know was that the Pinkertons and twenty agents on special assignment were waiting for him. They had staked out the rented warehouse on Bleeker Street, the train station, the bridge over the river and the waterfront. There would be no escape.

LaVergne, TN USA
09 September 2009
157245LV00001B/19/P